Aperture

Re-Imagine What Is

AC2492

"…You're aware of a deeper existence, maybe a temporary reassurance that indeed, there is no beginning, no end…and all at once the outward appearance of meaning is transcended, and you find yourself struggling to comprehend a deep and formidable mystery…"

David Bowie

(Visionary Musician)

"In the last analysis, we ourselves

are part of the mystery we are trying to solve."

Max Planck

(Visionary Originator of Quantum Theory, Nobel Prize in Physics 1918)

For All Inspired to Imagine

1

What is it with music and daydreaming? The things that come out of your head can be mind-blowing. As we all know, it happens a lot more often than we hope others will recognize. It can happen during quiet moments, maybe when boredom creeps in, or when you catch yourself daydreaming down a rabbit hole or two. It can be most evident after a major event while your mind is still reeling. Words, images and sensations converge to take shape in the form of scenarios, perspectives, and persistent scrutiny. And when something significant actually does happen, it is undeniably intriguing to contemplate how our brains navigate the response. That usually happens after the proverbial dust has settled, but can sometimes begin taking shape shortly after the event has occurred. For Emma Collier, the dust was just beginning to settle.

Recovering from an accident can take time. Physical therapy can be grueling and take weeks, months, and even years. Mental recovery can be even more challenging. Some have found that they were able to rise above difficult challenges and even find greater clarity to life and being afterward, but many sink into existential circumstance. The accident changed Emma's life. It was certainly altering her perspective. It wasn't the first major event to prompt a revaluation of everything, as she put it, but it certainly was the one that set her on a different track. There had been a few challenges in the past. Some had really tested her fortitude. This one came at a time when changes were probably warranted anyway. Emma always considered herself pragmatic and typically did whatever was required to endure. This one was a game-changer, but she handled it with predictable resilience. It wasn't until recently that Emma felt like the dust was settling. Until now, she had been taking it all one day at a time, one step ahead of the next. As she continued to persevere through recovery though, she meditated on a future that would conform to the new reality, the new 'what is' as she saw it.

That was why Emma was returning to this reality, or more specifically, to this place. Of course, circumstances were different. Although she had now lived in Canada most of her life and adopted it as home, she occasionally enjoyed returning to the Southland where she grew up. It was hot and dry here, very different from the northern climate where seasons could be extreme. Both felt like home to her, but this was where Emma wanted and needed to be right now. It wasn't family or friends she hoped to see on this visit. There were no cultural events she hoped to attend. This trip was about renewal and rediscovery, perhaps reinvention. Whatever the eventual outcome, Emma considered it a turning of the page, moving forward.

The accident and its aftermath still seemed a little hazy. Despite having spent some time in hospital, there was little point dwelling on setbacks. Life went on. "The arrow of time only goes in one direction," her father would have said. "We can't make progress by standing still." Looking forward now was a little different than it might have been when Emma was younger. It wasn't about considering career or even family, at least in the sense of planning for such things. Looking forward now seemed to be more about taking inventory, assessing and evaluating. It was about seeking new insight, determining what views, practices, beliefs and attitudes were worth continuing. Some were. Some were not. She wanted to reassess where she was going and how she would get there.

Emma had spent a lifetime working. She was successful, upwardly mobile, and enjoyed numerous personal interests. She was well-read, enjoyed stimulating conversation, and appreciated varying activities with friends. She was married and had raised a child who was now well into his twenties. Emma had experienced the passing of her parents, and was noticing more friends and acquaintances falling prey to various ailments, disorders and syndromes. Much of her life was now in the rearview mirror, yet she preferred to look ahead. She had come to within a few years of retirement before the accident and had already been thinking of possible redirections. Life wasn't only about work, was it? Sometimes it takes an event to give you a nudge and get moving. Even a good life can become routinized existence. For the first time in her life, Emma began to wonder what it was really all about.

Like many accidents, there was little warning of impending disaster. It was possible that Emma was daydreaming away to music at the time, but she often rode the waves of distraction to favourite tunes. Driving along the open road with good music playing was a medium for traveling the spirit roads in one's mind too. All the considerations, plans, responsibilities and errands one has to run on any given day need to be tempered by dreams, aspirations and simple appreciation for a beautiful day. Driving was the temporary respite, the time-out from bustling activities navigated at work, in a grocery store, or back at home. It was a momentary recapturing of one's personal space from the world at large. Whatever it was, the collision was an unexpected and abrupt surprise. From her peripheral vision, she noticed something suddenly approaching, almost upon her, but as soon as it registered, Emma's car was struck. She was forcefully shaken for what seemed like several long, scary moments. Everything suddenly became both very slow and very fast. She was aware of both vehicles running side by side off the road onto bumpy ground.

Everything shook violently until it didn't. Then everything went dark. All stood still. Time became irrelevant. Her memory failed her. There was no recollection. There had been the sudden, impending danger, but then quiet, an awakening, soft beeps and other noises, and confusion. What happened after that remained a blur. Images flickered in and out. Consciousness wavered, then was lost.

All of that was now behind her, Emma assured herself. Despite immediate complications at the time, she now felt like she had to ask the question. How serious was the accident after all? Today she felt as good as she ever had. Her life, as she perceived it at this moment, had not been diminished. If anything, it felt like she was on the road to something she intuited but couldn't quite put her finger on. Maybe that's what hope is, she thought. Maybe she was just happy to be alive and back in long-familiar territory.

People will often block out memories of events too painful or horrible to deal with. Given what seemed like a positive outcome, Emma struggled to understand why memories of her hospital stay were almost nonexistent. There were flashes of moments here and there, but when she really tried to nail down any recollection, it was elusive. Fair enough, she thought resolutely. Keep moving forward. Emma decided to consider it all a bump in the road, something that provided the impetus to be a more conscientious driver in life overall. She was shifting gears. The rest of her life wasn't going to be an enduring joy ride. It could be compared to climbing a mountain, she thought. One expects to see all when the summit is reached, but the climb itself is part of the reward. Happiness is in the journey. For Emma, switching gears meant stepping away from the day to day of her existence. It was important to find a retreat, a sanctuary, a place to withdraw. It meant going to a place that was new, but could feel familiar.

Despite the media-centered insanity associated with Los Angeles, it was once home. It wasn't the escapist hustle and bustle that Emma sought, but the beautiful, serene, remoteness of the outlying desert barely beyond its urban expanse. She didn't leave one hub just to come to another. Solitude could be found by forest and lake just outside most Canadian communities, but Toronto's sprawl now rivalled the Southland's and took a while to escape. Cottages were nestled so abundantly on picturesque real estate that escape now meant traveling north for hours. In contrast, L.A's northeast boundary gave way to the great expanse of the Mohave Desert. Solitude could be found even a short walk from most places along the road. Solitude in the desert is a place to clear one's head like no other. The desert is itself an oasis hidden in plain sight. It appears a

7

barren expanse, but the mind's eye becomes transparent like the waters of the oasis. It can see clearly there.

Emma was quite pleased with an accidental discovery online that caught her attention just days before. Airbnbs were popular in many communities, but this one advertised itself as a ranchbnb in the middle of nowhere, an oasis in the desert just opening for business. Situated only a little over an hour from downtown made it surprising there was even a vacancy. Emma booked a whole week. The place only offered a few guest rooms, but the write-up boasted semi-private reading nooks, a modest library, a small theater room, a headphones-only music lounge, and trails into the surrounding desert. It might just be perfect, she thought, a good starting point from which to sort things out.

Emma's Monday morning flight had landed a little over an hour ago. Customs was endured on the Canadian side before boarding, so leaving LAX with a rental car was quick and easy. The radio was already tuned in to KNX, L.A's go to station for traffic and news. She wasn't sure what difference it made knowing about slowdowns ahead of time. Alternate routes weren't usually feasible anyway. She would catch up on a round of the news cycle, then put on some tunes when the highway opened up. Then she could begin to disengage. Then she could loosen-up.

"Here are the headlines for February 17th, 2020," began the report. Emma usually caught up on the news watching CBC's *The National* back in Toronto most evenings, but she had no intention of turning any television on today. She was only half paying attention to the news now. Driving with spider eyes through L.A. traffic was the name of the game. Story descriptions weaved in and out as she kept her eye on the road. "Thirty-one people, including children, have been killed in Yemen airstrikes," the report announced. Emma was aware of the conflict but had tuned out reports for the most part. Insensitive or not, she often felt she couldn't contemplate ongoing situations she was powerless to do anything about. She consciously blocked out selective reports. "Over 1,100 former Justice Department officials are calling for Attorney General William Barr to step down, after he…" Emma wasn't particularly interested in the ongoing psychodrama of the current administration either. "The number of coronavirus infections continues to mount, with 71,000 confirmed cases globally and nearly 1,800 deaths. A Chinese man who was visiting France has died from the disease, marking the first fatality in Europe and outside of Asia." Another story that sounds like it could dominate news cycles for a while, she thought, and turned the radio off. Time for some tunes.

Stopped at the light on Century Boulevard just before the on-ramp to the 405 North, Emma reached over to the side pocket of her purse. She pulled out a USB stick she had brought for use this week. It was something she had updated regularly for years now and kept in the car at home. A love of music was something she, her husband Jean-Marc, and son Anthony enthusiastically shared. It had been a dominant topic of conversation between them at home for years. She speculated it might even be the glue that keeps the family together. Although each had their favourites, they enjoyed hearing about one another's interests. Jean-Marc loved experimental jazz, while Anthony tended to explore alternative music. Emma appreciated much of what she heard from both of those genres, but maintained a lengthy compilation of diverse tunes that tapped into all kinds of music, a virtual daydream factory. Once the traffic lightened up a little, this was going to set her free.

Emma still had lingering thoughts about a parting conversation she had with her son before leaving Toronto... "Humans need to start looking at the big picture. We get so focused on our everyday reality that we don't really see reality at all," Anthony had stated emphatically, or at least it was a close approximation of what he had said. Anthony often kept to himself. Much of the time he was listening to music, but at other times he indulged his enthusiasm for reading more than the average bookworm. He was actually an insatiable reader. The rare occasions when he did emerge from his apartment, he would walk over to his parents' place. Having few, if any other outlets, he would go on about whatever had caught his interest. Sometimes he went on about books, especially science and philosophy. At other times, he would ramble on about music. This time it was philosophy. Emma would politely continue to listen, but often didn't retain all that much.

How did he ever become so infatuated with this stuff? Emma realized that she hadn't really been paying attention to Anthony's sprawling details again, but that particular phrase had evolved into an earworm repeating in her head. "Humans need to start looking at the big picture. We get so focused on our everyday reality that we don't really see reality at all." It wheedled its way into her brain while on the flight from Toronto. Anthony would often barrage her with sudden explanations of things he had been reading. Emma wasn't sure if it was an OCD tendency, an exhibiting feature of his schizophrenic disorder, or just a basic need for intermittent companionship. For her own peace of mind right now though, she just needed to step back, catch her breath, and take everything in, or perhaps let it all go. It probably didn't matter which, she reminded herself again. This trip is about realignment. It's about refocusing.

9

Emma's roots were in Los Angeles. Home was up in the north end where Interstate 5 met the Antelope Valley Freeway at Santa Clarita. It was a great place to grow up in a niche distinctive from the rest of the great metropolis. As the home of many blue-uniformed Angelenos, the crime rate was low, wilderness areas were close by, and the desert expanse just up the freeway. As she drove past Newhall, Emma saw whole new swathes of suburbia planted on ground once occupied only by dry grasses, a few scattered oaks, cactus, tumbleweed, and reptiles.

There had been a lot of good times growing up in the Santa Clarita Valley. Emma had loved working her first job at Magic Mountain theme park back when it was still relatively new. She started working there in '76 just after the Great American Revolution roller coaster made her employer the first theme park to have one that looped 360-degrees. At that time they still used Trolls as mascots before being abandoned in favour of Warner Brothers' characters. She even had to get into full costume for several weeks before being allowed to transfer to the El Bumpo boats ride. The heat was unbearable inside that orange fur ball and although it wasn't funny at the time, she has since had many laughs about having to walk around waving hands and hugging children as Bloop the troll.

Emma had grown up going to the ocean – first out at Zuma with her family, and later at Venice Beach with friends. For a few years in the late '60's and early '70's, her family went to Zuma most weekends between May and September. Her father later used to joke that they should have continued. Maybe he would catch a glimpse of Neil Young, a favourite artist of his who named an album after the place.

As she got a little older, Emma discovered that if you were into musicians or just about anything else, Venice Beach in Santa Monica was an interesting place to go. Although she was far too late to have had a chance to meet Jim Morrison and Ray Manzarek there, the well-known busker Harry Perry, the guitar-playing roller blader was already a standard fixture on the boardwalk. She hadn't returned there for several years now, but it wouldn't surprise her if Harry was still there roller-blading back and forth.

Emma was not so enamored by L.A's much renowned film culture as she was with its equally-renowned music scene. Maybe her father never did see Neil on the beach, but there were many opportunities to see Young and just about everybody else on a stage somewhere, sometime in the City of Angels. Emma began to recall some of her own concert adventures. She remembered a particularly good period when she and an old high school friend were going out with a couple of guys. The boys considered themselves audiophiles and had clearly built a friendship around a mutual love of music. Although she agreed with her friend Karen that Enrique was the brightest of the two, the other was a musician who naturally captured Emma's attention.

Roger was also British and a couple years older. When Emma was still a teen back in the '70s, it just didn't get any cooler than that. He had come to California on a student visa and was attending UCLA. Emma remembered that she and Karen met him and Enrique at a concert. Roger didn't seem too interested in going to school, but he was clearly interested in being in the States. He was staying with American cousins who lived next door to Enrique's family, which is how they met and became friends. Emma, Karen and the boys only managed to hang out for a few weeks before it all fell apart. When Roger suddenly decided to drop out and join a band, his father back home discontinued financial support. Roger's uncle didn't have the heart to ask him to leave, but Roger chose not to complicate family matters and left anyway. Emma never saw him again after that. He left her reality as spontaneously as he had entered it. Enrique and Karen continued together for a short while, but predictably at the time, neither her family, nor Enrique's, were too keen on the relationship. It eventually dissolved. When Emma and Karen went off to different colleges soon afterward, they quickly drifted apart too. It's how life happens, she lamented. While some people might be fixtures, others emerge from, and recede back into, the sea of humanity, weaving their way into and out of others' lives as well.

As she continued past Santa Clarita up the Antelope Valley Freeway, Emma wondered about her friends from long ago. Did Roger ever make it well enough in some band to make a living, or did he end up having to go back to school after all? Maybe he's a lawyer somewhere, she contemplated wickedly. Enrique had planned to take a year off before going to university, she remembered, but who knows if things went as planned? Life can be strange. It takes on a course of its own. Random experiences can easily develop into significant life adventures. Each are like several different lives nested into one another like Russian dolls, enfolded life experience. Just then, Lennon's old single *Imagine* came up on the flash drive. She thought of the Beatle's famous dictum: "Life is what happens to you while you're busy making other plans." Isn't that the truth, she thought, cliché or not.

Emma had family and friends spread around the five counties that made up the great metropolis. Her mother died a year and a half earlier. It was the last time she visited the Southland before the accident. Emma felt she had a large enough dose of family on that last trip. She felt no guilt about skipping a visit this time around. Funerals and weddings, she thought. Complications often seem to arise. This funeral was no different. Who showed up, who didn't, who said what, and who didn't all mattered. Typical family pandemonium. Emma again reminded herself that this trip wasn't about anyone or anything else. Driving along the highway and listening to tunes began helping her slip into a more carefree mode. Even the earworm Anthony had deposited into her head was dissolving. It isn't just funerals and weddings, she considered amusingly. Parents and children have means of generating chaos and anxiety throughout life, even if that chaos and anxiety are actually coalescing inside my own head.

Then Emma's mood lightened up. She felt a genuine appreciation for the many little things in life, the things that are easily overlooked during life's march forward. Maybe she was right about this. It really was time to slow it down, to refocus or find a different direction. Life is about change, but that's different than direction, she told herself. Maybe her secret desire, or inclination, was to break out of the cocoon she had woven throughout life and take flight. Most people realize they could have taken many different paths in life, but few take more than one. Perhaps there was still opportunity to seek growth, illumination, enlightenment of some kind – just something she had never experienced before. Maybe her son Anthony was trying to tell her something she simply had not been listening to also. After all, Anthony may have his own issues, but he did appear to have come into a period of stability over the past year or so. Maybe he had found a way to transcend the more overt aspects of his own life situation. Maybe he had found a way to rise above it. Who knows, she thought? Emma smiled even more contentedly as she continued past familiar hills and canyons.

Family, friends, responsibilities and typical concerns all needed to be placed on the back shelf. In her head, Emma had planned for only a week, but even that was not set in stone. The plan was to keep her schedule flexible. It was all about cleaning the slate. Speeding past the Placerita Canyon cut off, it looked like there had been a recent brush fire along a good stretch of slope just behind the newest residential implants. Fires are a common recurrence here as she and everyone else familiar with Southern California knew well. Still, the advance of the great metropolis was likely to banish chaparral fires to places further up the highway and beyond. Brush fires in the concrete jungle? Everything in flux she mused. As she careened up the Antelope Valley Freeway from lane to lane, Emma marveled at the extent of local growth. Suburbs with myriad shopping plazas, services and business firms now occupied former brushland in Santa Clarita's Canyon

Country. Both the northern slopes of the San Gabriel Mountains to the right, and the slopes of the Sierra Pelona transverse range to the left, were giving way to cityscape.

The Southwest was where Emma grew up, but she enjoyed living in Toronto. It had now been home for many years, but much like the proverbial phrase stating one could take a man away from the sea but not the sea from the man, so too was there an element of that in Emma's return to the dry landscape of Southern California. Emma's appreciation of the nearby mountains and desert was ingrained, and the reason she wanted to return now. Climbing in elevation along the Antelope Valley Freeway, she glanced at the rocks protruding from the desert floor to her left. How many times in her life had she been to Vasquez? Many have scoured the main sedimentary uplift formations in the County Park, and virtually everyone who has ever been exposed to media knows the landmark, whether they have actually been there before or not. The rocks were in numerous car and truck commercials, probably as far back as television has been around to advertise. Vasquez had also been in several notable western movies. Films like the Flintstones have featured it as prehistoric, but it is portrayed futuristically in several Star Trek episodes. Amusingly, as Emma's father liked to point out from time to time, Vasquez was the setting of a different planet every time. The most notable was a first-year episode called 'Arena.' Emma, along with her dad, had watched Captain Kirk forced into unarmed combat against a lizard-like enemy starship captain enough times to remember it was known as a Gorn. The place is iconic. Vasquez was even the archetype for The Lion King's Pride Rock, a movie her son Anthony must have watched a hundred or more times. Other parts of Vasquez were less-known, even though the Pacific Crest Trail, spanning from Mexico to British Columbia, passed right through the park grounds in full view of the famous landmark.

Emma continued past Agua Dulce and on up the freeway to the edge of the Antelope Valley. A turn-off onto the Pearblossom Highway afforded a bypass of the last vestiges of urban sprawl. As she drove past the city of Palmdale, north L.A. County gave way to the vast Mohave Desert. Emma took in the increasing numbers of Joshua trees, yucca, creosote and other features of arid beauty. The outer landscape and Emma's inner mindscape were merging as she traversed the road into the desert. She loved being out here again.

Even though it was February, it was quite warm. Emma turned up the air conditioning a notch. She knew this time of year could be variable. She hoped it would be nice to go for a walk later. Deadly heat wouldn't be expected for several weeks yet. It was probably too early for reptiles to emerge. Too bad. She enjoyed seeing spiny swifts and other lizards darting around on rocks or joshuas. The odd snake would also be welcome. Emma considered them not only an essential part of the ecosystem, but beautiful, well-tailored adaptations to an unsympathetic environment.

   As she drove along the concrete ribbon through the desert landscape, Emma again found that earworm squirming out of her subconscious. Interesting how her son Anthony managed to get that one in there. He often came up with unusual statements at odd times, but they didn't usually stick. Not that she really minded that so much. He was quite bright and could be very interesting, but she occasionally found it sad. Anthony sometimes got caught up in thought resembling unresolved bugs in software code. Emma was always aware that life can be complicated, but it wasn't until Anthony was first diagnosed with schizophrenia that things went temporarily off the rails. It was a difficult time. The family had never really experienced hardship until onset began to unfold. Then for a few years it cascaded into mayhem. Fortunately, her marriage turned out to be the pillar that kept their lives from collapse.

   Emma originally met her husband while studying in Montreal for a year on an exchange program. Concordia was one of the first universities in North America to study communications when the department was created in the mid '60s. The opportunity was irresistible; the experience was transforming. When she met Jean-Marc Collier, he was enrolled in business management, a field that ultimately led to success in investment banking. At the time, she harbored some doubt that an investor could be interesting, but Emma soon found Jean-Marc alluring, intelligent and courteous in a way more likely found on movie screens back in L.A. Perhaps the French accent was a contributing factor, but admittedly, she had been swept off her feet. Jean-Marc was also entranced with someone who defied expectations, or perhaps stereotypes. Unlike the valley-girl image emerging from Los Angeles via Hollywood depictions of the '80's scene at the time, Emma was down-to-earth, pragmatic, and open-minded. She was also an ardent nature-lover, unexpected in a person raised in one of the great urban sprawls on the continent.

   During her time there, Emma fell in love with the city of Montreal. It felt lived in like home should feel, she thought. Its unique linguistic and cultural identity created a distinctive and exceptional experience. To this day, she considered it the best kept secret in North America. Visitors compared it to French cities in Europe, and particularly Paris, but Emma couldn't agree. There was a distinctive feel to Montreal that was like nowhere else. How fitting it should be on an island. It felt uniquely authentic not only when walking the cobblestone streets of Old Montreal,

14

but when sitting on a patio either in the charming French district of St Denis, or the distinctly English district of Westmount.

Money was tight when they were both students, but Emma and Jean-Marc enjoyed frugal pleasures like climbing Mont Royal to walk the beautiful park at the top of the city. The grounds were already over a century old when she arrived in Montreal. Emma remembered being surprised to learn that it had been designed by Frederick Olmstead, the same designer behind New York's Central Park. "Same designer perhaps," Jean-Marc commented, "but distinctive qualities in both parks were derived from the cities that flourished and matured around them."

The pair also enjoyed walking along the Lachine Canal from St Henri, an old working class municipality absorbed into Montreal just after the turn of the 20th century. They rented an apartment together, often strolling along the canal to the Atwater Market where they would stop for a burger and fries while others enjoyed Montreal smoked meat or poutine. Domestic partnership between the couple turned into marriage, not because of any obeisance to a crumbling institution or tradition, but as an expedient strategy to facilitate the lives they intended together in the same country.

Life at that time was idyllic for the young couple, at least while they were still students. Economic reality would change that after graduation. For many in 1980s Montreal, the city was just beginning to recover some semblance of its former stability. The Parti Quebecois' mid-70s' landslide victory had almost separated the Province of Quebec from the rest of Canada. Almost ten years later, sighs of relief were warranted. Recovery, however, would take decades. In the year after the '76 election alone, over 46,000 people left Montreal to travel the 500 kilometres along Highway 401 to relocate in Toronto. Real estate plummeted, a boon to struggling students like Emma and Jean-Marc. Fortunately, the flat they rented in Saint Henri was just $240 a month, but that one advantage would soon be upended by a cold realization. It wasn't so easy for a unilingual English-speaking American to find a communications job in a province where French was the only official language. Neither was it easy for a young career-minded investment banker to assume any ladder-climbing would go very far in a city where all major financial institutions, even the Bank of Montreal, had moved to Toronto. Although a decade behind the original exodus, Emma and Jean-Marc were soon driving a U-Haul westward along the 401 to the towering glass city on the north shore of Lake Ontario.

15

Life in Canada was good. Emma had loved Montreal, but soon discovered Toronto's charm as well. Not long after establishing themselves, she and Jean-Marc added plans for a family. Anthony was born just under three years later. After that, the years passed quickly. Canada became home, partly because Emma was happy with life in general, but also because Los Angeles didn't seem far away. As the computer age advanced in the 90s, online communication brought the rest of the world much closer together.

As Emma and Jean-Marc became successful in their respective fields, traveling back to Southern California became easily affordable. Finding time off, however, was another story. Both became engrossed in their work. Emma became an executive at the CBC, which ultimately consumed a lot of time. The work was stimulating and financially rewarding, so the trade-off seemed worth it. Jean-Marc too was busy, and often on the phone day and night. He followed global stock markets and financial news fanatically. Money was good, but time scarce. Together, Emma and Jean-Marc provided a decent lifestyle for their little family.

Anthony seemed to be a happy boy growing up. He was also bright, but his pursuits were streamlined. When he was young, his parents read to him, but when he learned to read himself, he also began collecting comics and books of his own. Even before his teens, Anthony spent a lot of time to himself. He didn't seem to need or want much company. His time was often spent alone in his room. He ventured out to the kitchen periodically, but online access, a television, stereo, a small library and even a private bathroom adjoining his room made it the place he wanted to spend his time. An unusual disruption, however, occurred not long after Anthony's eighteenth birthday.

Perhaps Emma and Jean-Marc should have seen it coming. For years they wondered whether the onset of schizophrenia could have been prevented in some way. For a long time, Emma questioned whether her own career-mindedness and Jean-Marc's increasing devotion to the religion of money were contributing factors. The so-called experts stated that several variables, including genetics, could have been contributing factors. Looking for an explanation was natural, they had been told, but psychiatrists and psychologists still know very little about the etiology and onset of schizophrenia. It is thought to have a genetic predisposition that must then be triggered by external factors for onset to occur. Emma knew that theory wasn't set in stone, but she didn't rule out family anomalies. Some family members easily popped into mind. At this point, she reasoned, does it really matter how onset came on? The fact is that her son is schizophrenic and despite many medical marvels, that was unlikely to change. Again, that lingering earworm from

16

her conversation with Anthony came to mind. "Humans need to start looking at the big picture. We get so focused on our everyday reality that we don't really see reality at all."

In retrospect, Emma had to laugh. Her rush to get out of the door back in Toronto led to frantic scurrying about and rechecking every detail. Jean-Marc was away on business for a couple days. Anthony had come over to their place to go over routines for taking care of the cat. She left him money on the counter for helping out with Tabby and the house, but in her rush, forgot to mention it. No problem, Emma thought. She had left a note with a couple of donuts in a distinctive Timmy's bag. He would find it.

Poor Anthony had been chatting away to her the whole time she scrambled to get ready. As she recalled the scene, Emma laughed again. Did Anthony realize she wasn't listening to him, or did he just not care? It seemed amusing at first, but as she considered it further, it once again emerged as a bit of a sad moment. She might inadvertently have been doing what people often do in the presence of someone a little different. People with disabilities or features highlighting difference are often dismissed, or just plain treated differently. It doesn't necessarily happen intentionally, but insensitively. Sensibilities were improving, but slowly. Emma could see how it was easy to fall into that trap, but that didn't excuse it. The thing about that kind of scenario is that it can easily be misrepresented through common stereotypes. The person who is different might very well do or say something exceptionally clever, but still be inadvertently dismissed. That's what happened there. Several minutes before Anthony's 'humans must evolve comment,' Emma had already been lost to whatever point he was trying to verbalize. At the time, she became aware of not paying attention, excused herself, and asked him if he could remind her what they were talking about. When he replied by saying, "can't," she wanted to know why not. "Kant with a K," not "can't," he corrected her. Emma was suddenly laughing out loud.

What was it with Anthony and the philosopher Immanuel Kant anyway? Some years ago he had borrowed Kant's *Critique of Pure Reason* from the library. Later, he even bought a copy for himself. He went on and on about it until one day she sat down with every intention of listening to whatever it was that intrigued him about this book. When she did, however, his weaving in and out of topics, sometimes mid-sentence, was mind-numbing. Not only was she sure that she did not get what he was saying, but she suspected he didn't fully understand what he was saying either. Maybe he wasn't explaining it well, or maybe her bad habit of not paying attention was the sole culprit here. Anthony was a bright young man, but Emma often thought the vocabulary he used in

17

his explanations were mere reiterations of what he had read, and then memorized. He often repeated concepts he was into for weeks at a time. She and Jean-Marc both loved their son dearly, but sometimes the circumstances of his illness could be tiring. Perhaps there was good reason for not paying attention sometimes.

Anyway, Emma thought, she had apologized to him for not keeping up with the conversation. Now she was hoping it was enough, but as she considered the matter still further, Emma abruptly remembered something else Anthony had said to her. She was on her way out the door after hugging and kissing him goodbye. She had just finished thanking him for helping with Tabby. When Anthony called out after her as she walked to the cab, he told her to "at least listen to the voice in the desert; sometimes there's treasure there." Anthony's tone implied it was a reminder. Then he smiled and waved goodbye without any hint he thought it unusual in the least. Maybe it just seemed like that. After all, Emma had not been paying attention earlier. Maybe he was joking. She hadn't picked up on it. Anything was possible.

That son of hers, Emma thought, smiling as she slowed the car and turned off the Pearblossom Highway onto a gravel lot. If it isn't Kant, then it's alien cover-up conspiracies. She parked beside a pump at an old desert gas station situated there. The place looked in need of paint. The sign at the corner of the road verified this was where she had to turn off the highway. Looking up the road, she could see it ribbon up toward the base of the San Gabriel range. Almost there, she thought with a tinge of excitement. I deserve this and I'm going to take advantage of it. It's nice to be here just for this purpose, renewal, redirection, relaxation.

The car was less than half a tank down, but Emma thought she would fill it up. It gave her a chance to stretch a bit after being in the car for almost two hours. Scouring the surrounding desert while she pumped gas, Emma welcomed the warm rays of the sun. The particularly warm February day here could easily double as a beautiful summer day in the land of the Leaf. She enjoyed every second of it, and certainly did not miss the high humidity typical of a hot Toronto summer day.

When humidity came to mind, even for just a fleeting moment, so did ice cream. It was a recurrent temptation. Emma decided to indulge it this time. The gas station probably had the nearest convenience store to where she would be staying. Emma topped off the gas, returned the nozzle, parked the car to the side of the station, and walked in. There was an old-fashioned sliding-glass-top chest-freezer at the back. She leaned over, spied the dozen or more choices, all of which she noted looked delicious, but ended up choosing a chocolate nut-topped waffle cone. She paid the old man at the counter, then stepped out of the store. Emma wanted to stand in the dry heat of the desert enjoying her indulgence.

The desert often looked sparse and barren, especially to stressed-out urbanites, weekend gamblers and hedonists traveling from L.A. to Vegas and back with little thought of the landscape in between. A common description of the four-to-five-hour drive is that it is "boring" or that there is "nothing" between L.A. and Sin City. Emma walked across the road from the gas station to admire a tall yucca standing there, then looked out across the desert spread wide open behind it. Such diversity, she marveled, as her gaze moved to a nearby Joshua Tree. The iconic plant was a distinctive feature of the Mohave because it is confined to an elevation corridor between 1,200 and 5,900 feet above sea level. Interesting that she still remembered some of these facts, she thought. What ever happened to her childhood dream of becoming a forest ranger like her father? Life happens, she mused again.

While enjoying her ice cream, Emma also found herself noting the abundance of creosote bushes as far as she could see. A much smaller plant than the Joshua, it often went unnoticed except as a nuisance, a desert weed of sorts. Who would suspect that the scraggly evergreen shrubs were considered the oldest living things on the planet? It was just one of many fascinating and little-known facts that her father would remind her were "hidden in plain sight." Her father, she thought. If he were here now, he would be scouring the desert appreciatively. She was sure he would be enjoying an ice cream as well. Emma finished her cone and made her way back to the car. It hadn't taken long for the vehicle to heat up inside. She should have left a window open. Emma turned up the air-con full blast and then checked her GPS. Ten minutes and she would be there.

Enjoying the view, Emma drove up the road and finally forgot about the persistent earworm inside her head. The driveway to the ranchbnb was clearly marked. She turned onto it, leaving a trail of dust behind. There were only two other vehicles in the parking lot. It was a good sign, the promise of peace and quiet.

Emma thought it might be nice to have some "afternoon tea" as her grandmother used to call it. A little shot might help her settle into relaxation mode. Just get your stuff inside first, she said to herself. As she pulled her suitcase from the back seat and closed the door, Emma was welcomed by a man wearing a cowboy hat. An aging German shepherd followed slowly behind. He had stepped out of the front door when he saw her car pulling up to park.

"Hello," he called out walking toward her. "You must be Emma Collier. We haven't spoken personally, but you're my first reservation. Actually, you are my only reservation. The place just opened for business a week ago and already I'm wondering if my ranchbnb is even going to be a go. I'm Enrique Bramandez. This is my old friend Bender and this is my place" he said, tipping his hat with one hand while extending the other. "Welcome."

"Enrique Bramandez," Emma repeated slowly. She extended her hand toward his, looking closer at the man's face. Her eyes were squinting slightly, then reopened in recognition as a hesitant smile betrayed an old memory. "I think we've met before," she said.

2

After almost 40 years, they shared a few laughs. Once Emma and Enrique got over their initial surprise, both agreed they could readily see the young people they once knew in the older versions encountered today. Karen and Roger's names came up, but since neither Emma nor Enrique had maintained a connection with either one over the years, there wasn't much to discuss.

Enrique helped carry Emma's luggage into the house and upstairs to the suite where the window facing southwest afforded the best natural light. He wanted the first guest to have the best, even if he didn't know she was going to be an old acquaintance. Emma particularly liked the small reading table situated in front of the bay window looking out onto the desert. The slopes of the San Gabriels snaked down towards the Pearblossom Highway a few miles back down the road. Smooth wind-carved rock streamlined the slope like exposed muscle. Giant boulders and clumps of rock dotted a prehistoric landscape. That little corner of the room was going to be a favourite spot, she thought, looking back at Enrique. "That must be one of the reading nooks mentioned in the write-up."

"It is, but not quite the finest. Here, follow me." Enrique stepped out into the hallway and around a corner to the right. "Too bad this wasn't situated in one of the bedrooms. I can see guests vying for a cozy spot to curl up with a book, or these days with their Kindle. I like to come and sit in here fairly often myself. It's a good place to ruminate. It can also be a good place to sit with a laptop or tablet. There are wifi boosters in every room. We're a bit far out for typical internet access here, but we're connected by satellite link. It works just fine."

Emma was duly impressed. At the end of the hallway was a round window nestled like a large porthole into what might once have been a closet or storage room. Three stairs led up to a cushioned platform with pillows scattered about. The two walls and ceiling conformed to the circular shape of the window to create a tube-like enclosure. A reader could curl-up comfortably inside and peer out. "This is both clever and unusual Enrique. Did you do the renovation to this old ranch house yourself?" Emma crawled up into the nook and nudged herself comfortably between two cushions. She glanced upward and touched the ceiling just above her head. A convenient in-laid reading light with sliding dimmer were situated within reach. "This is great Enrique. I'll have to take advantage of it if someone else doesn't claim it first."

"No one else has booked for this week, at least not yet. It's still unfamiliar and in an unusual location – in the middle of nowhere. I don't know if this is going to work and to be honest, I don't really care much one way or the other. My brother and I inherited this place from our father who bought it for almost nothing years ago. Originally, we thought we would use it as a shared retirement place together, but I bought him out recently. My brother is soon to be a proud abuelo, a grandpa, but his kids live down in Orange County. This place is too far to see the grandkids regularly, so he plans to retire closer to where they are. He and his wife still work, although that isn't likely to last much longer. He's only two years younger than me. Ultimately, I would like this to be a place where he and the grandkids can come and spend some time. We're family. We're close. I thought turning the place into an Airbnb for a few years would help pay for amenities the kids would enjoy. I'm considering a pool and a few other things. There are some ideas on the burner, so to speak. I have a lot of things I want to do out here in pursuit of my own interests. Keeping a guesthouse for a while was actually my brother's idea. He said he knows how involved I can get in my projects and thought having at least occasional guests would keep me from going stir crazy out here. He says that without family, it's just a barren wilderness. There's probably some truth in that." They both laughed. "Come on out of there Emma. Let me show you the rest of the place."

Emma followed Enrique back downstairs where Bender was waiting patiently. "This old boy still likes to follow me around much of the time, but he has difficulty going up the stairs these days." Bender slowly rose from his spot as they approached the bottom of the stairs. Enrique turned the corner, walked through a short corridor where he pointed out the availability of a fully-stocked bar, and entered the kitchen/dining room area. As soon as Emma walked into the sunlit room behind him, she had to stop and look around in wonder.

The space was wide open with ample natural light coming through to illuminate a virtual emporium of visual delights. Four unusually-shaped tables arranged with plentiful space between them immediately caught Emma's attention. Most kitchen tables she had ever seen were rectangular or round. These resembled decorative handiwork fashioned from tree trunks or stumps and often referred to as gnome furniture in tourist-oriented curiosity shops. Some of the curvature and branching replicated wooden features, but the material looked suspiciously dissimilar. Not one of the chairs was the same as another. The cupboards too displayed subtle bends and curvature that made them appear more natural than designed, but they did not appear to be made of wood.

Emma's eyes widened as she looked back and forth before finally commenting. "This is the most amazing dining area I have ever seen," she said. "What is this?"

"It almost sounds like you're impressed," Enrique replied. "Good. I was hoping this would be an eye-catcher. It's not only functional and beautiful, it's green technology."

"Green technology? Did you build all of this stuff yourself? It's extraordinary."

"It is extraordinary, and I did make it, but didn't build it exactly. It's mycelium. I grew it."

"Mycelium? What do you mean, you grew it?"

"I mean just that, I grew it. Mycelium is the vegetative part of fungus. It is actually a colony of bacteria. Most people don't know it, but mycelium is found in soil and many other surfaces. It has many vital uses in nature, some of which we have only recently been discovering. It is also very durable. I created it using 3-D-printed molds to use as framework and let the mycelium grow into the shapes you see here. It is durable furniture that was grown into being and will naturally biodegrade back out of being when it is discarded. It's clean and ecofriendly. It is also incredibly waterproof and able to support significant stress. Who knows? It has the potential to be an important material of the future. Mother nature seems to think it's a good idea. So does my brother. He thinks I should patent some of these designs. It was a fun project, but I'm not interested in committing all of my time to one main focus anymore. That's why I retired. It's time to pursue other interests."

Enrique took a little time to show Emma the rest of the house. In every room they entered, she was impressed by both décor and layout. A lot of thought had clearly been put into design, including optimum functionality. There were several little gadgets she had to ask about. Not surprisingly, Enrique and Mateo had tinkered with many of them. Some were rigged from scratch. Others were existing technologies one of the brothers had customized. He downplayed any exceptionality, saying most adaptations simply required slightly modified circuit design and code adjustments. "Matty and I are science nerds. He's still at Caltech. I was at JPL and not so sure I'm completely out of there yet. Both of our jobs required brainstorming. Sometimes it's not so easy to just shut it off after work – or retirement."

Emma had been most impressed by the kitchen during Enrique's house tour, that is, until he brought her to his sound room. This was a recent addition to the house completed only a few weeks earlier. He referred to it as the best feature of the whole place. Even before stepping into the room, Emma had no doubt it was going to be special – and it was. The space was the size of a large living room, but circular. The walls curved up into the ceiling just above the height where twelve speakers were built into it all the way around the room. The pit in the center occupied most of the floor space. A circular couch was installed around its perimeter, except nearest the entrance where access stairs stepped down into it. The space resembled a miniature concert hall. When the door was closed, acoustics were impeccable inside and soundproofed from disturbing anyone outside. "If you like to listen to music the way it should be listened to," he told her, "then you are going to love this. See these rods hanging from the ceiling? They help absorb sound and keep audio waves from bouncing around for greater clarity. I also used mycelium to create a softer, smoother surface wall and near-domed ceiling to help absorb rather than reflect sound. Modern concert halls use the same technology. The small circular table in the middle of the pit down here is the control center. A screen and keyboard are built into the table top. If you would like to watch and listen, the wall functions as a screen and yes, even multiple screens. You can't see the four small holes placed around the room in this circular wall, but projectors built in behind can project video onto wall surface either on one spot or four evenly-spaced locations around the wall. A projector from the tabletop can also project a view of our galaxy onto the domed ceiling. As you may have noticed, the couch sinks in deeper at the back to facilitate viewing. I first saw a display like this at an observatory in the late '70s featuring the music of Pink Floyd. It is a very relaxing motif to display while listening to whatever I please. It's a nice little touch and an easy feature to install. Most music you can think of can be accessed, either from a large collection my brother and I accumulated over the past almost fifty years, or from Spotify. There aren't too many other houses in the vicinity, so I can definitely say this sound system is the best one on the block. Anyway Emma, I don't want to saturate you with my technical tedium. You can check this all out later at your leisure. I am going to let you settle in. You've been traveling today."

They decided to meet and catch-up again later. Enrique suggested that if she were interested, they could go for a walk in the surrounding desert just before the late winter sun goes down. "It is much more beautiful than one might expect," he told her. "It always depends on how closely one is willing to look." For now though, the whole idea was to make herself at home. Emma agreed that a walk later would be nice, but did plan to unwind with a short nap and maybe some reading first. There were a few things Enrique wanted to do around the place that afternoon too, so the arrangement was made.

Once settled in her room, Emma laid down, shut her eyes, took slow, deep breaths, and began to relax. Images dispatched fleetingly as her stream of consciousness melted into dreamscape. Her body sank comfortably into the bed, mind drifting seamlessly from one theme into another. Emma's breathing slowed to long draughts and tire-leak expirations. She drifted off for a while, but was soon roused by a nagging urge. An effort to ignore the annoyance was valiant, but like a mythical siren, the bathroom's call was compelling.

It had already been a long day, but lying down for less than an hour still proved refreshing. Emma decided to complete the process with a quick shower. Undressing quickly, she leaned over the bath and turned the faucet. It was always trial and error to get temperature right in a strange bathroom. She wanted a revitalizing cool, but not shockingly cold dowsing. Emma really just wanted to run water over her body, having no plans to redo makeup. Spry revitalization for now; she could always run a bath later. Emma shed the relatively short but tedious flight under waterflow. Then turning it off, she wrapped herself in a towel, opened her make-up bag and performed an almost imperceptible retouch. Scarce effort went into choosing clothes as well. Emma rummaged quickly through the few things she packed for herself while entertaining a self-compliment for a rare show of discipline in this regard. Jeans and a blouse would do. A sweater would probably be necessary later. Desert temperatures in February could drop significantly.

Emma sat down at the nook by the window, placing two magazines she purchased at the airport on the table. Spectacular, she thought, scouring the view from mountain ridge to valley floor. The Pearblossom highway could be seen meandering through the desert toward Palmdale down below. There was still time to relax before meeting Enrique for their walk. She never did read an article on the plane, so she could flip through them now. Maybe she would go into town tomorrow and find a book or two.

The next couple of hours passed quickly. Emma brushed her shoulder-length hair, looking closer in the mirror for rogue grey specimens. Maybe she should have had her hair coloured before flying down. Ah, so what? I'm on vacation now, she assured herself. Deciding to go downstairs for a bite to eat, Emma grabbed one of the magazines from the nook, turned back for a last glance in the mirror, and walked out of the room.

Stepping into the kitchen, she couldn't help but admire it anew. She opened cupboards and drawers to get a general sense where everything was. Then she peered into the fridge. A plastic container of fresh spinach caught her eye immediately. Onions, tomatoes and peppers were readily

25

found in the produce drawer below. Emma found two choices for dressing. One was a typical store-bought balsamic vinaigrette. The other was in a mason jar with a hand-written label, perhaps an old family favourite. Emma was curious. She had never tried cactus pear-lemon vinaigrette. Opening the jar and venturing a whiff, Emma was pleasantly surprised. It smelled both delicious and fresh. Placing it and the salad container on the counter, Emma found a cutting board and sliced the chosen veggies. She was impressed to find some real bacon bits and cheddar. Like being at home, she thought. Wonderful. Soon Emma was sitting at one of the tables, heartily enjoying her salad while peering out the window.

At first it was quiet in the house. Enrique was probably still occupied. She enjoyed the salad and an equally revitalizing cider to compliment it. Emma looked around from where she was sitting. Sunlight streamed into the house, but it was pleasantly cool inside. Floor to ceiling glass along one wall afforded a panoramic view of the surrounding desert and mountains. Several Joshua trees and other, more common southwest flora highlighted a serene, peaceful setting. Enrique had decorated the place with various blown-up photographs of nearby terrain. He apparently appreciated not only landscapes but close-ups of some of the reptiles and other fauna to be found in the area. A photo of two small burrowing owls sparked Emma's particular interest. It had been decades since she had actually seen one herself.

Emma's focus on the photo was interrupted when she heard an unexpected door opening inside the house. Initial curiosity was quickly doused when she heard Bender sauntering toward the kitchen. Enrique must be around here somewhere. Then she heard an unusual sound coming from the same direction. Otherworldly and even hypnotic, it first reminded her of the intro theme music to the original Star Trek series, but she didn't detect scene changes or hear dialogue and decided it wasn't a TV. She walked out of the kitchen toward the sound to realize that it was coming from Enrique's sound room. Bender must have come out of there.

Emma opened the door to peer in, then quietly slipped inside. Enrique was sitting at the table in the pit facing her right. Clearly engaged in whatever he was doing, his arms were outstretched around a small gadget with an antenna. Enrique looked like a soothsayer hovering and rotating his hands around a crystal ball. The strange humming noise adjusted pitch and tone to changes in their position. Enrique did not acknowledge Emma's presence and continued mimicking mastery of an invisible musical instrument. What is this new little wonder, she thought? Soon Emma found herself closing her eyes and being carried away by the ethereal sound emanating from the speakers around the room. A few moments later, it ceased. She opened her eyes. Enrique flipped a switch on the gadget and turned toward her. "Was I disturbing you?"

"Not at all," Emma replied. "I was in the kitchen grabbing a bite. I think Bender probably detected me in there and came out to see. It wasn't until I heard a door open and saw him walking over that I heard that strange sound. What is that gadget you were hovering over like an orchestra conductor? One of your various technical modifications?"

"Not at all," Enrique said grinning from ear to ear. "It's an actual musical instrument called a theremin. It does have a pretty strange sound unlike any other instrument except maybe a synthesizer. It would be difficult to direct the flow of sound on a keyboard in the same way one could create it using free hand movements. When I play that thing, it almost feels like crafting music on a potter's wheel. There's a more pure interaction with sound than seems possible when mediated through the body of an instrument by plucking strings, or pressing keys. It is musical creation by natural movement, a pure experience. Theremins have been around for many years. Remember Led Zeppelin's Whole Lotta Love? That may be one of the first places you heard a theremin used to great effect and that was back in '69. Even if you don't play any other instrument, you would derive genuine pleasure from interacting with one of these. Do you want to try?"

"I might sometime, but the afternoon is almost over and it's still February, so the sun sets early. You mentioned a walk earlier. Are you still up for that?"

"I am. In fact, I finished the few things I had to do with time to spare. That's why I was taking a few minutes to enjoy playing in the sound room. I was probably torturing Bender though. No wonder he came out to see what you were up to. Did you find everything you needed?"

When she joked that she was surprised to find something as refreshingly different as the cactus pear-lemon vinaigrette, Enrique beamed. "It's an old recipe mi abuela handed down to the family," he said proudly. "I just made that yesterday. Glad you enjoyed some." Emma got up when she finished her plate, walked over and began rinsing it in the sink. When Enrique recommended just putting it in the dishwasher, she felt right at home already. That's what she liked about the B and B business model. It offered an interpersonal approach making it more affable, even charming.

It was actually after 5:00 already. Sunset would be in just over half an hour. Emma went back upstairs for a sweater. Enrique suggested a couple of light layers. Temperatures sometimes dropped quickly. He asked her if she was up for a bit of a climb and indicated good walking shoes were a good idea. There was a great vantage point from where they could appreciate what may

27

prove a dazzling sunset to conclude a beautiful February day. Enrique also offered to show her a small, but spectacular wind-carved cave with a natural window looking out onto the San Gabriels. Emma thought that sounded interesting. Within a few minutes, Enrique was locking the door and they set off with Bender following somewhat hesitantly behind them.

Enrique brought a small backpack with him. Ever since moving out here, it became a habit. It was always a good idea to be prepared if you planned to be out in the desert for even an hour. Extra water, a flashlight, small first aid kit and some energy snacks were the usual add-ins. Sun glasses were necessary to filter rays angled directly toward them as they climbed westward. Enrique took the lead with Emma a few paces behind. A small king snake slithered past a rock and into the brush. It was a sure sign of a warmer than usual winter day. When Emma commented on the reptile's beauty, Enrique was surprised she wasn't startled. Most people he ever met were cautious about snakes, if not outright fearful. She mentioned that she and her father spent some time outdoors at places like Vasquez, Placerita and other spots near Santa Clarita. Emma suggested with some pride that when she was young, her parents often labeled her a 'Tomboy.'

Emma wasn't sure where to take the conversation from introductory small talk. Enrique seemed like a man of fewer words than most. Or perhaps he just wasn't one for small talk. She couldn't let it descend into weather chat already. Emma faintly recalled that Enrique's father worked at Edwards Airforce base near Lancaster. The base couldn't be more than 40 or so miles from the ranch. That was probably a motivating factor in determining Enrique's own career path. He had mentioned working at JPL. Not everyone can say that. She had to ask if it was as interesting and exciting as most people might think. He fondly recounted his years at the Central Engineering Building where he worked most of his career. Originally, he had a work placement there just after its grand opening in '86 while still at university. That eventually led to a full-time hire and he remained there until retirement. Central Engineering was the first major building to open at the famed site in nearly a decade. The timing was off though. The Challenger disaster occurred that same year. It was a while after that before things got moving again. Public support waned, making funding cuts inevitable. Enrique recalled being kept busy with various projects though, because the year before he came on board, decisions were made to combine Defense and Civilian programs to reflect JPL's changing scope of operations. Realignment of the Computing and Information Services offices made Enrique's hire possible. Although still in the early days of computing, JPL boasted over 2,100 personal computers in operation at the Lab after Central Engineering's completion. Budget cuts aside, moving ideas and activities forward was essential not only for exploration purposes, but ultimately, if more covertly, for national security.

Enrique's somewhat lengthy but fond descriptions of his time at JPL were clear indications of how much he had enjoyed work. He mentioned being married once for a few years, but they drifted apart for similar reasons – both were actually married to their careers. It was a good thing they didn't have children first; his family would have been persistently opposed to a divorce. Enrique and his Ex remained friendly for years, but immersion into separate lives eventually eroded their connection. He lived on his own for a few years, but once his brother Mateo started a family, Enrique was talked into renting a room with them. "It would be good for everyone," his brother admonished. "Family is family, right? We could save money and use it to invest – make the money do some of the work, eh?" It did make sense at the time. Enrique was quite happy working extra hours and wasn't home much anyway. Meanwhile, Mateo had also started an interesting career at Caltech in Pasadena, following in his brother's steps as an aerospace engineer. Who better to commiserate similar interests and responsibilities with than one's own brother and best friend?

Enrique and Mateo's parents were now gone. Their mother passed away first, and their father followed only weeks afterward, a common occurrence amongst long-time partners. Both had lived long lives, but eventually succumbed to slow deterioration and illness. Their two boys inherited the retirement ranch their parents lived in after their father's career at Edwards ended. For a few years, the house remained somewhat empty, except on weekends. The brothers would go out there to spend time considering, and then implementing, renovations. That was when they entertained the idea to experiment with mycelium. Both thought the place was developing a unique character, but original plans for Enrique, his brother and sister-in-law to move in once Mateo's kids went off to college or university fell apart. Mateo decided to stay in Orange County, so Enrique bought him out. As far as Enrique was concerned, if his brother ever changed his mind, they would still be more than welcome to come move in with him. Un poco de dar y devolver, ¿verdad?

Despite family qualms about seclusion, Enrique maintained connections with former colleagues. Some had become good friends over the years. Casual conversation over a beer or two would occasionally drift into ongoing projects he was, or would have been associated with had he remained. He didn't mind that at all, but sometimes it did lure him back on site. Although clearance procedures were strict, even for former employees, Enrique occasionally 'volunteered,' especially when volun-requested and prearranged by former colleagues. Otherwise, he tried to stay focused on new interests and opportunities. Despite loving the work he did, he was still learning to let go.

Enrique enjoyed photography, which accounted for the many pictures of the surrounding area on ranch house walls. He briefly mentioned trying his hand at painting local landscapes. Emma hadn't noticed any paintings in the house and suspected he might not consider them suitable for display, at least not yet. Enrique had also taken an interest in geology and paleontology. He tried to get out for a morning walk on most days to study the surrounding terrain. He made observations about rock formations, determined what elements could be found in various samples of earth, documented various insects he found, counted reptiles and variant plant species found at different locations and elevations. He always took notes. Then later he would do further research, often over a coffee. It sounded rather methodical to Emma, but Enrique assured her it was both stimulating and fun. If he acquired sufficient knowledge to feel it worthwhile sharing, he might even try his hand at writing a book on the topic. He joked that if he ever followed through on that, he would consider calling the book *Mental Masturbation in the High Desert: Observations No One Else Cares to Ponder*. The two laughed while Bender attempted a half-hearted bark of inclusion.

Enrique admitted he could sometimes become engrossed in activities and neglect necessities – like human contact. By allowing just a few guests on site at a time, he wouldn't be overly preoccupied with attending to business for money he didn't need. At the same time, he could maintain the kind of socialization everyone needs. "I suppose it might really have been an effort to stave off predictable family persistence," he said. "How about you Emma? What's been going on with you these past forty years?"

The two continued walking along the path slowly. "I suppose I could just say 'life' and leave it at that," she responded, "but life seems to have a lot of twists and turns and that's probably what you're asking about." They exchanged some humourous quips about people's perceptions about life before Emma began. She recalled her time at Cal State Northridge down in the Valley just after she had originally met Enrique and Roger. She dated a couple guys once or twice, but for the most part, she really became absorbed in her studies. When the opportunity to apply for a program exchange to Montreal became apparent, she decided to go for it. Her father died unexpectedly that same year. That made things difficult for a while and impeded preparations, but she figured things out and soon decided to go ahead with plans.

Emma spent time illustrating her experiences in both Montreal and Toronto. She fondly referred to her now 35-year relationship with Jean-Marc as both ideal and enduring. They have enjoyed a comfortable, if not semi-affluent, life. She described distinct cultural differences between the cities. Situated only 300 miles apart, she suggested that if Enrique ever decided to come north, he should explore both on the same trip. Emma had much to say in favour of Toronto, where she had now lived a little over half her life. "Toronto may not be Los Angeles," she interjected as a side note, "but it does have a good music scene. That's been important in our family. We have a son, Anthony, who loves music as much as we do. For some years, we even went to concerts together with the express purpose of introducing new music to one another. That was Jean-Marc's brilliant idea. Anthony and I bought in right away and a family tradition emerged. It's turned out to be a real boon living there.

Enrique loved hearing about family activities involving music. "Those are the best activities ever," he chuckled. "It's a great way to retain and grow connections through something constantly changing." He lamented not spending more time seeking out new music. Band names he dropped included Giant Sand, Dirtmusic and the Walkabouts, favorites both he and Mateo enjoyed. "Putting that sound room together is a good way to keep my brother coming back, even though he's down in Orange now. We have always loved listening to tunes and finding good bands," he reminisced.

Enrique, Emma and Bender continued along a slow but steady climb. There were some large rocks clumped together up ahead. They were still a short distance away, but Enrique pointed it out as their first destination. As they approached the crest of the hill, the sky began to glow orange on the horizon. Emma marveled at how quickly the sun seemed to descend at this latitude. Back in Canada, sunsets seemed to occur much more slowly. It also remained light much longer. Even before summer officially arrived, she knew sunsets anywhere in Canada occurred an hour or more after the sun set in the City of Angels. She remembered once describing a Los Angeles sunset to her son Anthony when he was younger. He laughed when she characterized it with a descending whistle and told him it always dropped quickly like a cartoon sunset.

The conversation veered to talking about children. Every once in a while, Enrique referred to one or another of his brother's kids, always in favourable terms and often mentioning individual

31

strengths and characteristics. He was clearly close to all three and had enjoyed watching them grow up. Enrique was as proud an uncle as Mateo was a Papa. Both were particularly proud that the three children were now second generation college and university students.

Emma similarly described Anthony as a great kid with multiple interests and talent. Family life seemed idyllic for years. As mentioned, the three of them often enjoyed music together. Once a teen, however, he rarely wanted to spend time with them. That was normal, of course, but by the time high school started, he was in with what parents back in the day used to characterize as the 'wrong group of kids.' Anthony was once an excellent student, but began getting into trouble at school. He got into drugs. He got into some minor trouble with the law too. Then he went off the rails.

Emma and Jean-Marc weren't sure how it was all connected, or even if there was a connection. Neither of them knew much about schizophrenia before their son's diagnosis. Whenever it was characterized by actors on film and television, it was not only negative, but often threatening. Things seemed to progress quickly from concern to crisis. Looking back, they often thought that maybe they should have seen patterns emerging sooner. They should have responded differently to observations they were making at the time. Perhaps their response could have been more rapid and effective. Eventually, they decided to find counseling for themselves as well as their son.

Neither Emma nor Jean-Marc fell apart, but they had been shaken. Initially, the situation presented as catastrophic. It was important to get solid information and not react impulsively to the upheaval they were all going through. Counseling would give them access to a psychologist. They needed help navigating uncharted waters. When Anthony was eventually diagnosed, a logical response could be coordinated. "Although the waters were turbulent for a couple years," she told Enrique, "we felt that probably did help mitigate a more disastrous outcome." They were initially horrified to learn of high suicide statistics amongst schizophrenics compared to the general population, especially during onset. That was what made it so scary at first. Eventually Anthony was stabilized with medications. Support and social programs allowed him to move into an independent, supported living arrangement close by. "That stability has lasted these past few years," she concluded, raising her head toward a sudden brightness pouring over the crest of the hill.

They arrived at the cluster of rocks Emma first viewed a short way back. One huge boulder leaning against another permitted a gap through which the path crawled. The waning sun's rays shone radiantly in dazzling compliment to the approaching nocturne. Their arrival was well-timed. The fissure was both tall and wide enough to rest underneath and watch the display. Smaller rock debris surrounding the opening afforded seating. Having appreciated the walk and conversation to this point, both now sat down and refocused their attention toward the glowing orb.

For a while they sat serenely lost in their own thoughts. It was so nice to be back in this immensely beautiful space. Emma realized that in relating parts of her story to Enrique, she was also reliving it. There were no regrets of any kind, no self-pity. She had made it through. What was that saying - What doesn't kill you makes you stronger? Emma was resilient. She was confident. Everything was good. In fact it was really good. Anthony was doing as well as could be expected. She and Jean-Marc had managed to come through all adversity. Reflections on life were satisfactory, even if somehow incomplete, not quite finished. That was the future she had yet to conceive, to imagine. While gazing at the reddening sky, the sun finally set. Emma began to sense something unanticipated, something unforeseen. She was on the verge of a new life, or at least a new stage of her life. How might this unfold?

Enrique was lost in a similar train of thought. He found himself reflecting on life, the past, the present, and even the future. It was good to be out here, just far enough from the metropolis to contemplate quiet serenity. Look at this place out here, he thought. A vast expanse that many think barren. Aren't deserts metaphorically equated with nothing? Crazy. One can look out on its vastness and be lost in philosophical, contemplative reverie.

The dusk enticed bats from hidden daytime perches to stalk insects congregating above the desert floor. Enrique followed their erratic movements and marveled at the precision they achieved without sight. "Echo location," he muttered under his breath. "Another aspect of sound worth investigating." What other unusual creatures might have passed by here through the mists of time? What other living forms once lived here? What remnants have we not yet discovered? Such thoughts were breathtaking. Almost losing awareness of Emma's presence nearby, he tried to imagine everything from here to the horizon cell by cell, composition by composition, the invisibles that made the visible possible. The complexity of it all is unfathomable. So many questions, he thought. So many questions.

Stars were beginning to appear as dusk dissolved into evening. Venus could easily be spotted in the early night sky. It seemed so close, yet so very distant. Enrique scanned the heavens. In what far places might another creature be harboring similar contemplations while observing its own night sky? What beautiful landscape might surround that creature as it ponders related sentiment? In what ways might some distant desert or mountainscape be comparable to what I am viewing right here? He smiled to think about his career. How fortunate to have been involved at the forefront of exploration. Yet for all we know or have learned, he thought, it is all still so very mysterious.

Enrique's contemplations were abruptly interrupted when Emma began to speak. "You know," she said while looking up at the night sky and then pausing. "My son believes that aliens are all around us and have been among us for some time. He thinks they will intervene when we lose control and are on the brink of disaster."

3

Enrique found that oddly fascinating. He had just been thinking about extraterrestrials as well. They hadn't shared a word for a prolonged interval. He thought it unusual that a glance at the stars should invoke similar inspiration. Did the stars themselves induce questions about possibilities? Do humans always inject themselves, or something similar to themselves, into every equation? Have cultural ideas skewed the associations we make with the night sky? The answer to that, he reminded himself, is like the answer to most things, isn't it? It's about complexity. The endless intricacy we observe all around us implies many possibilities and explanations. Imagination is everything, and culture, our simmering stew of collective inventiveness, often influences our perceptions. In his own mind, Enrique never credited humanity with more than an emergent understanding of whatever the big picture might be. Especially while working in an environment like NASA, it remained clear we are still far from resolving many questions conclusively.

Emma continued chatting about Anthony's fascination with extraterrestrials. "No doubt Star Wars was his favourite when he was younger, but as he got older, he preferred Star Trek." She wasn't a huge fan of sci-fi, but admitted enjoying conversations with Anthony about 'Space.' "Anthony claims he grew out of Star Wars because it was too one-dimensional. Star Trek tended to explore possibilities," she said, enlarging her eyes to emphasize its distinct appeal. "It wasn't just good versus evil. Anthony thought that was unsophisticated. Trek plots are more intellectually satisfying, he would say." Emma didn't often follow Anthony's musings about plot details, but when conversations veered toward space documentaries, then she would engage.

Emma told Enrique that her son was a dreamer both before and after his diagnosis. She emphasized just how deeply he could get wrapped up in something, literally holding on to some things for years. She pointed out his captivation with a book by philosopher Immanuel Kant as an example. He first started reading it a few years ago, but still brought it up frequently. Emma didn't understand his captivation. Even after listening to him on several occasions, she failed to grasp concepts he tried to convey. "Anthony can literally become obsessed," she said. "Something triggers his imagination, then for the next while he exhibits a one-track mind."

Enrique listened attentively as Emma spoke, but continued scanning the night sky. Distant glimmering points of light materialized into awareness as evening darkened into night. Emma's soft voice seemed to betray a hint of sadness. She drifted from her son's interest in extraterrestrials to concerns about his condition, but then became aware of her audience. Enrique didn't know Anthony and she hadn't been in contact with Enrique for the better part of 40 years. It was probably too serious a topic for an initial conversation. Emma apologized, pivoting back to aliens and space. "Anthony often watches episodes of *Ancient Aliens* on the History Channel. He would do so over and over again, at least before he moved into his supported living arrangement." Emma admitted that show sometimes caught her attention too, but never took it as seriously.

While rarely considering any of the program's more extravagant claims, Emma never ruled out the possibility that aliens existed. Therefore, Anthony would point out, that meant she couldn't rule out the possibility that contact could, or may have already occurred. She noted that such talk arose often. Eventually she conceded another possibility too. If Extraterrestrials were smart enough to come here, they are probably smart enough to move around undetected. Only recently, a leaked sighting by U.S military personnel had gained viral infamy. If nothing else, it was food for thought. She half-heartedly, at least, leaned toward belief.

Enrique finally interjected with a chuckle and pointed out that while he worked at JPL, whether it be on the job or taking a break, almost all conversation was space talk of some kind. "All of us guys interested in space are obsessed," he said. "Maybe your son is just one of us. If there is one thing we all believe at JPL, it's what Einstein told the world long ago: Imagination is more important than knowledge." Enrique said he believed in many possibilities, but didn't think aliens were here in the capacity her son believes. Furthermore, he doubted humanity could rely on extraterrestrials saving us from ourselves. "People seem to need something to believe in though," he pointed out. "Maybe extraterrestrials will find their way into some new religion one day," he said laughing. "The way things have been changing over the past few years, who knows?"

"New ideas can lead to new movements of all kinds. Traditional world views have been crumbling since before you and I were born Emma. The world is ripe for change." Enrique spoke in earnest, but tried to keep his narrative concise. As an example, he highlighted the role religion had played in connecting people around a set of ideas for centuries. "Social progression and new technologies have rendered many of those ideas obsolete. Miracles, resurrections and promises of eternal bliss or damnation are out of sync with the knowledge we've accumulated scientifically. What could the Bible, the Koran, the Talmud, the Upanishads or Vedic texts tell us about atoms, nuclear power, robotics or the Internet? Ideas and inspiration don't need a supernatural being to qualify as a religion. Hell, money functions as a type of deity in the religion of capitalism."

"Many new religions could emerge to dominate future belief systems," he continued. "More relevant ideas and metaphors might strike a chord as technology continues changing the landscape of human experience. Scientology is probably the best known modern example. It may not even have been the first to discuss such things as a galactic confederacy, previously confined to science fiction. There are other so-called UFO religions like the Aetherius Society that believes their sacred texts come from different planets."

Enrique had to mention the Roswell, New Mexico incident of 1947. "When a nuclear test surveillance balloon crashed, people continued to believe in conspiracy theories around it. After that happened, a few UFO religions began to emerge. It shouldn't be surprising that if some people believed they saw a UFO, or that they were abducted by a UFO, that they might want to play Paul Revere and let everyone know that the aliens were coming. The interesting thing Emma, indeed the most important thing to think about is this: UFO sightings as such have only occurred since science fiction writing first emerged. People have claimed to see things in the sky throughout the centuries, but they always had an explanation that corresponded to current beliefs. For example, the ancient Greeks were aware of planets like Venus and Mars but thought, or at least referred to them as gods. The first UFO reports didn't come until the 1880s. Books by Jules Verne had already become prominent. H.G. Wells writings became immensely popular shortly afterward. One could say it was already in the air."

Emma couldn't help but interject. She remembered seeing television programs as a child that claimed there were runways in South America and other evidence of visitors to Earth dating back to ancient times.

"Erich Von Daniken was influential for a few years in the late '60s and early '70s," Enrique agreed, "but his theories were debunked until resurrected by programs like *Ancient Aliens*. New generations and new potential believers can be mined again. There is money to be made!"

For all the time Enrique spent at NASA's JPL and actually considered what the possibilities were, he still couldn't say he was sure of anything. He challenged Emma to think about it for a minute. "Space is very big. Any aliens coming to Earth would have to come from a very long way. Why would they do that and then, as Anthony and others have suggested, do nothing, or wait, until we do something stupid to make themselves known? It doesn't make sense. Our Voyager 1 spacecraft travels at 38,000 miles per hour and has only recently left the solar system. The closest star to our own is Proxima Centauri which would take us 75,000 years to reach at the speed of Voyager 1. If we believe that other life forms exist in our universe, then they must have to follow the same laws of the universe that we have to. They can't get here any faster than the speed of light and that means they would need very good reasons to even make the attempt. Furthermore," he added, "in any credible reports of UFO sightings, there are never any actual physical interactions with the witness of the event. Any claims of actual interactions are usually of abductions, which evidence strongly suggests are caused by drug-induced hallucinations, sleep deprivation or past abuse."

Enrique mentioned a friend of his who worked at the SETI Institute. "Even this guy doesn't believe extraterrestrials are likely to come here. He compares it to Columbus discovering America. Imagine Columbus coming to a new world, but deciding not to take Native land, plunder any riches or spread disease. Why would he and his men have skirted around the fringes of Native settlements, only to produce baffling sightings?" He stopped looking at the sky for a moment and turned to Emma. "Have you ever heard of the Fermi paradox?"

It didn't ring a bell. If Emma had heard of it, Anthony would likely have been the source. Enrique waved his hand across the starry landscape and asked her to scan its magnificence. A short while ago Emma, you claimed most people believe in life on other planets. That's the basis of the Fermi paradox too. Among all those stars in front of our eyes, and many we can't even see, there must be billions of them similar to our star, the Sun. Many are much older. Some are so ancient, they don't even exist anymore. Their light is only reaching us now after billions of years of travel at light speed. "Imagine that," he said slowly, pausing for just a moment. "And from that huge number, it isn't too hard to imagine that at least some of these stars might have Earth-like planets around them, right?" Emma nodded in agreement.

"Well, if Earth is typical in size and is situated at a relatively typical distance from its star, then it should follow that it might be possible for intelligent life to develop on these other, similar planets. Would you agree with that too?" Emma nodded again.

"Okay, so, since residents of Earth are now contemplating the possibilities of interstellar travel, it also follows that other intelligent life much older than humanity might have developed the capability of venturing beyond their own solar system. Even at the slow pace of travel I already specified Emma, the whole Milky Way could be crossed in just a few million years. So this is my question. Actually, it's Fermi's question. Where is everybody?"

They both smiled. "I see," said Emma. "Good question."

"It is. The Fermi paradox is really an argument between scale and probability," Enrique explained. "Since we are here actually communicating the idea that life might exist elsewhere, then it seems obvious that there could be someone else out there looking at these stars from his or her vantage point and wondering the same thing we are. Of the approximate 70 sextillion stars in the 'observable universe,'" he emphasized, "the fact that there is life here on Earth indicates that it must occur -- at least rarely. Even if intelligent life is rare, in a number that large, it would still hint at the probability of numerous civilizations existing at varying levels of complexity and capability. So why is there no real hard evidence of this on Earth or anywhere Earth probes have traveled? That's the paradox. There should be, but there isn't! It really does make you think about it all, doesn't it?" Maybe it's just like Bowie's Ziggy Stardust proclaimed: *There's a Starman waiting in the sky. He'd like to come and meet us, but he thinks he'd blow our minds.* I guess humanity will have to wait and see."

"Ah," he muttered abruptly, as though that thought triggered a memory. Enrique reached into his shirt pocket and retrieved a slightly crumpled pre-rolled joint. Emma caught the move out of the corner of her eye as he placed it between his lips, covered it from any slight breeze, and lit it. It gave off a pleasant odour. He took a slow drag, then extending his arm in her direction, offered it to Emma.

A faint smile emerged. She reached over, casually, but confidently, pulled it toward her, gently pressed her lips to paper and breathed in slowly, tilting her head upwards to look at the stars. She exhaled slowly as if it were routine. "Canada and California do have some things in common," she said.

They chatted for several minutes while sharing the spliff back and forth. Emma was quite pleased with how the day had turned out. Her plan to relax and refocus had begun along the lines she intended. The walk back in the night air, a bite to eat, and maybe a bath ought to round it up perfectly. She wished she had brought a book with her. The magazines were fine to breeze through, but she thought it might be fun to read something she could really curl up with. She would look into it tomorrow.

Enrique suggested they should start heading back to the ranch. He still wanted to show Emma the small cave first. "It's just a short detour off the path we came up," he said. "Maybe eight or ten minutes from here. I originally told you it has a little window that looks out onto the mountains. The stars will be perfectly framed by it too. Are you up for that?"

Emma nodded. "Why not? Let's go."

Enrique bent down and gave Bender a short gentle pat on the head. The old dog reluctantly got up with some effort. Emma picked up the conversation as they walked along. "So is there any resolution to the Fermi paradox?"

It really came down to a few queries as far as he could see. "Maybe intelligent life is rarer than we expect. Despite the odd characters I meet on a regular basis, I don't think any of them are aliens." Becoming a little more serious, Enrique argued that it probably had to do with the fact that we don't actually know very much. "We like to think we do, but what we know is really just the beginning of what there is to know. The bottom line," he concluded, "is that our current scientific understanding is incomplete. As soon as we think we've gained some insight, that insight tends to prove there is still more to consider."

Enrique's flashlight illuminated the way ahead. The trail was sketchy here. Each step through thickening brush and over stone had to be traversed more carefully. He kept his eyes on the ground now. His long-time familiarity with the area was advantageous. The rising moon provided some brightness, but a flashlight was still essential. He slowed his pace, pointing out each plant with sword-shaped leaves. As they walked along, he'd repeat now and again, "Watch for the yuccas."

The night air was becoming chilly. Emma put on her sweater. It was less quiet than she might have expected. Enrique knew the desert came alive at night and savoured the thought. He had been out for an evening hike at least once a week since moving to the ranch. There was something unique, even special about being out in the desert at night. An owl flew by just above. They didn't hear a sound, but its wingspan cancelled stars from view as it passed overhead. Moments later, coyotes could be heard howling in the distance; the likely victim a desert cottontail or black-tailed jackrabbit. Who ever said the desert was desolate?

At one time this was wild cat country. Bobcats and mountain lions were once plentiful in the San Gabriels. So were bears. Most of the lions had retreated further from the encroaching metropolis to the San Bernardino Mountains decades ago. Enrique had never seen one in these hills. He had to think about when he last saw a bobcat too. Must have been at least six or seven years earlier, and that was in Switzer Canyon up in the mountains, a few miles from where it comes out near JPL. He briefly glanced up at the stars again, an exquisite panorama. Even the ancients had extensive knowledge of its myriad motions. Their interpretations influenced social, religious and political configurations. Even if we don't know as much as we would like to think we do, Enrique thought, an interconnectedness between everything seems implicit. "Truly beautiful," he whispered.

Just east of the makeshift path they made through the terrain, several rock formations emerged from the ground. The peculiar up-tilted configuration of sedimentary rock rose from the canyon floor looming in upward spires like embellished towers of Pisa. Mr. Spock would feel at home here. Enrique never ceased to admire the magnificent, ancient structures, now illuminated by starlight. Formed over millions of years by the continuing action of uplift between intersecting faults far underground, they now stood tall, monuments to time. When he told her what they were, Emma recognized the name. She had heard of it, but didn't remember ever coming here. The Devil's Punchbowl was known to people in the surrounding area, but not frequented either by locals or tourists. As far as Enrique knew, it wasn't advertised except by a small, faded sign just before the turnoff from the highway. It wasn't a place easily stumbled upon.

Enrique said they were just passing by a short stretch along its boundary. They weren't far from the cave now. As he scanned the wider area down to the desert floor, he could easily imagine being back in the old west. Hell, that was barely more than a century ago, he thought. If he had lived here just a few generations earlier, he might have been one of the settlers who came through on the Southern Pacific Railway from Bakersfield to Los Angeles. Reaching the Antelope Valley by the mid 1870's, it laid the foundation for surrounding communities at the top end of L.A. County. Before that, it was just wild country. The caves in this area could easily have been used by the infamous Californio bandido Tiburcio Vásquez. He famously terrorized the area rustling horses just before the railway came in. Littlerock Creek, only fifteen or so miles away, had been his first known Southern California hideout. Enrique imagined Vasquez and his gang camping out up here. There was quite a view of the surrounding area. The nearby rocks were a natural fortress. Only a hundred years ago, he thought again. Change is one thing that always stays the same.

They continued winding along the path around the chaparral, pinyon pines, yucca, creosote and other local flora. Soon, a formation rose up in front of them, jutting eastward like a huge thumb. Enrique identified it as their destination. He remembered sitting up in the cave having a smoke just days ago. It was a great little hideaway. Coming here made Enrique feel like a kid again. At first, it looked steep, and the opening was not immediately evident. Accessible from the opposite side of the

41

formation, Enrique said they would have to climb around. Emma admitted she hadn't climbed much of anything in recent decades, but Enrique assured her it was safe. Traction on the sandstone was good. He secured his own footing, turned slightly and held a hand down toward her.

Emma reached for Enrique's arm and pulled herself up that first step. Her shoes gripped easily, reassuring her that it wasn't difficult. Within moments they clambered up and around to the edge of the cave entrance. As soon as Enrique illuminated the opening with his flashlight, he saw a pair of running shoes laid neatly just a few feet in front of him, socks tucked inside. He looked over at Emma. Then using his right foot to gain a higher foothold, he leaned forward and peaked around the corner. A grey-bearded man was lying in a sleeping bag. Enrique focused his light on the person's face. It was partly covered by long, disheveled hair. His mouth was open. The man made no movement. Only the whites of his eyes could be seen. He appeared to be breathing, if only slowly. Enrique redirected his flashlight around the cave. There was a half-empty mickey of whiskey on the floor. A small backpack leaned against the cavern wall a yard to the left of the man's head. A large plastic bottle lay next to it. Overall, the entire scene was strangely tidy.

Emma pulled herself up to see what Enrique was looking at and emitted a muffled gasp. She scanned the small cave and then looked directly at Enrique. "Do we have cell phone service out here? This man needs help right away." Just as she uttered the words, the man began to make a rattling sound. Enrique and Emma froze momentarily and stared. The rattling repeated several times. Then he exhaled slowly and seemed to stop breathing. "Oh shit Enrique. Did he just die?"

The man's hand was draped over his chest. Enrique reached over and placed two fingers around the man's wrist. He began counting. His fingers inched over once, then again in an attempt to locate a pulse. Then, suddenly, the man sat up with his eyes bulging. He breathed in heavily with a gasp, shook his body back and forth, and exhaled sluggishly. He glanced briefly at Emma, then Enrique. Dried saliva was smeared onto hair and beard. He turned and lifted his head toward the small window Enrique had described earlier, then slumped again. "Terra Cognita," the man muttered. Emma asked him if he was alright, then waited for a response. He didn't speak another word. The man gently closed his eyes and slumped back, unconscious.

4

What a crazy night this turned out to be. An interesting evening under starlight became a maelstrom of park rangers, police, medical responders, and even two journalists. Enrique and Emma were also obligated to come in to issue formal statements. They had already been questioned extensively back at the ranch. Police were in no rush. Processing was a systematic and meticulous formality. Witness statements were routine for anything from car accidents to the most serious of crimes. Anything unusual was treated as usual here. Office staff were minimal when they arrived shortly after 10:00; no one appeared to be in any hurry. Enrique and Emma were eventually called in to separate rooms to make statements and sign affidavits. It was already after midnight.

Enrique was told he could go back to the waiting room. There might be a few more questions before they could go. Aside from the extensive witness statement he had just made, he couldn't imagine what other information they might need. A little perturbed, Enrique tried to convince himself that all this was just routine. It was just processing. As he walked around the corner, he could see the waiting room down the hall. Emma appeared to be conversing with an older man. Enrique recognized the uniform, but didn't remember seeing him earlier back at the ranch. He figured these guys probably came in for this stuff routinely.

Enrique knew he was probably detained longer than Emma because he owned the ranch. To be fair, the incident did happen on his property. Probing the situation was legally justified. He might know something of interest or value. The questioning sometimes bordered on finger-pointing, or even blame-finding. They asked him about hikers traversing his property, about any recent guests to the ranch, about his own background, profession, interests, knowledge of the area, and on and on. It was arduous, but probably within guidelines.

At one point, Enrique became agitated when an officer asked what happened to the person's I.D., money and keys, insinuating 'he' might know. He hated to even think it, but sometimes suspected bigotry. It could be so subtle, so pervasive. He usually preferred to shrug it off and move forward. He lived at the edge of the desert. It was redneck country after all, par for the course. Enrique offered to let them search him, his vehicle and the ranch if they seriously thought he had taken anything. If they really suspected foul play of any sort, they wouldn't need his permission anyway. He told them Emma was the first guest to come to the ranch and had just arrived that afternoon. "Why would our first response to finding a stranger in medical distress be to rob him?

Most people have a little more empathy than that! Besides, we didn't need to check for I.D. Our first and only real concern was to get help as soon as possible. Of what immediate importance was the stranger's identity? It could be handled by you guys later. Also, the guy sat up and spoke once, even if only momentarily and somewhat inaudibly. As far as we were concerned, that could have happened again. By the time help came, he might be able to speak for himself. His stuff is his own business. Emma and I never even discussed checking for I.D." The conversation was still going round in his head. Let it go, he thought. Let it go.

As Enrique walked up to Emma and the first responder, she asked if he had been sitting in there having coffee with the brass. The remark instigated a look, then a hesitant smile. Apparently, Emma and the responder had both been interviewed almost an hour earlier.

Detecting Enrique's agitation, the responder commented that in unusual cases like this one, drawn-out questioning was commonplace. He had seen it before. "No surprise there," he told them. "Medical rescue missions, especially by helicopter, often warranted investigation. "The other medevac here with me is still talking to them. He's the lead on the ground. That's why. I'm just the pilot. My job is to let the team do their thing. I'm allowed to give support if they need it, but under the team-leader's direction." After talking for more than a few minutes about routine experiences, the man suddenly reached his hand out to Enrique and apologized. "I wasn't thinking because we've been carrying on a conversation for a while already. My name is Darnell. I'm pleased to meet you."

"I'm Enrique. Thanks. Pleased to meet you as well. I guess you would be familiar with the process around here. Still, sometimes these guys can make you look or feel guilty, even if that's as far from the truth as possible. I hope we can all go soon."

Enrique and Emma enjoyed conversing with Darnell. He didn't seem to have a propensity for chatter, but was clearly well-informed. They became fascinated when he told them there had been a few strange cases like this recently.

"In this job, you see a lot of unusual things the public is generally unaware of. That might be a good thing. I'm not sure you could say a pattern is emerging, but there have been similar occurrences within the past couple of months. I'm one of several helicopter pilots in the county system. We are usually stationed at a specific location, sometimes for years, but every once in a while they like to rotate schedules. That's why I didn't happen to be flying when the other incidents occurred. I've been working up here in the Antelope Valley for years now. I like that because I

44

live up here too. It's nice to be just above the crazy hustle bustle of the LA sprawl. Anyway, if you're interested, you might want to wait for my colleague Kevin. He's still in being questioned. As I mentioned, he was the lead on the ground. There have been at least two other incidents like this one handled by a crew from our hospital. He was on one of them. I can tell you that both of the other victims were found without I.D., just like our transport tonight. There was also some controversy about how they managed to get as far away from civilization as they did. No vehicles or traces of any were established. Even short-term carry-alongs like flasks of water were absent from their surroundings. Anyway, I just try to do my job and not get too involved. Once we deliver transports to the hospital, they become the responsibility of staff there. I rarely ever hear anything about a patient once we've completed our job. As I said a moment ago, you may want to speak with Kevin. His wheels are turning tonight, I'll tell you. He seems to think he has some idea of what this is all about. I don't share his views, but they are interesting."

All three turned their heads when the sound of footsteps became apparent. It was the other responder coming down the hallway. Darnell's face lit up with a mischievous smile. "You weren't trying to ask them about any X-files, were you Kev?"

"I might have been tempted to, but they never gave me a chance. One guy was on about the transport's missing identification and other possible personal items like money. These guys do realize we're bonded, right?" Kevin looked at Enrique and Emma. "Hello again. We didn't meet formally back at the scene. I'm Kevin."

"Well, at least I'm not the only person around here with a suspicious-looking face." Enrique recognized him as the responder who first climbed up the sandstone formation to the cave entrance. He got right on it, taking vital signs and giving instructions to the other responders. "Pleased to meet you now that the excitement is winding down. I'm Enrique. I just went through the same thing. Your colleague here tells me it's just routine," he said, turning to Darnell. "Sometimes I admit suspecting other motives, but maybe these blue shirts really are just following protocol."

"And I'm Emma. Thankfully, that didn't come up during my questioning. I've been here chatting a good while with your colleague. Maybe you two do look suspicious," she joked.

Just as Darnell repeated this was all routine, a cop came down the hallway and told them they were free to go. Emma asked if they knew anything about the stranger found in the cave. "It's too early to say," he responded curtly. "Circumstances were considered critical upon arrival. Sometimes things don't turn out well."

Darnell and Kevin had accepted a ride to the station with police. One of the officers promised a ride back with whoever was available on shift when they were done. All patrol vehicles were out of the station at the moment, but the officer at the desk told them one of them would come by soon. Enrique offered to give them a ride. "Come on. It's late. You guys probably want to get home as much as we do. It won't take us any extra time to drop you off."

It was nice to step outside. The air was fresh and had cooled noticeably. The sky was still clear. Once in the car, chatter resumed. Kevin initiated commentary about the night's incident.

"While you were waiting together back there, did Darnell mention this was the third similar case in less than two months." He continued without waiting for a response. "Neither of us were on shift for the first one, but I was there for the second. We might have been on all three of them had scheduling not been shuffled around. Darnel and I usually work together. We get along fine too. One of these days, we might even become friends," he joked.

He did mention it, but we didn't have much of a chance to get into details. I don't know about Enrique," Emma said, "but I would like to hear a little more about that."

"I'm kind of glad you brought it up Kev. I told these nice folks you had some interesting ideas about it, even if I'm not sure whether I agree with you or not."

"I have caught your interest though Darnell. If these situations continue to occur, I expect you'll consider my ideas more seriously." Kevin leaned forward to make sure the two in front could hear him clearly. "When we were called out to the desert for a possible hiking accident in the middle of nowhere some five weeks ago now, I immediately thought of the circumstances described by our colleagues on the first of these desert transports. Don't misunderstand me. We do get calls to rescue people in desert terrain periodically, but mishaps usually occur along established trails. Hikers in more rugged areas are usually well-prepared and have the gear and supplies they need. Not one of the three I am referring to even had water flasks with them. Look at the guy we transported tonight. He had some pills, a mickey of booze and a sleeping bag. I didn't see a pack or any other supplies. That cave was actually quite tidy. It wasn't possible to miss anything. I had two of my team scour the immediate area too. Nothing. One of the cops on the scene told me they had one of their own birds flying over roads in the vicinity. He confirmed no abandoned vehicles were found anywhere. Apparently, this was true of the other victims as well.

Remember, we're talking about the Mohave Desert here. It may not be as hot as it is in the summer, but it is still an extreme environment. One has to be cautious and prepared when venturing out into it. Since this guy was found near your place Enrique, it's not surprising they asked you mucho questions tonight."

Kevin said he wasn't someone who just jumps onto every viral bandwagon. He had thought about this stuff for some time now. There was good reason to think these particular cases were something out of the norm. Kevin was acutely aware that doubters frequently ridiculed UFOs, or anything alien, and often rightfully so. "Listen," he said, "I'm not your stereotypical 30-something armchair-alien-enthusiast living in his parents' basement appropriating ideas from wannabe documentaries spewing bunk out there."

"That's right," Darnell interjected with a chuckle. "He's just your 30-something armchair-alien-enthusiast appropriating ideas from online… shall we call them experts?"

Everyone laughed, including Kevin who was now donning a self-deprecating smile. "Funny Gramps." Then leaning toward the front seat again, he addressed Enrique and Emma exclusively. "Darnell is a good colleague and even a friend, but like many people, he dismisses the idea of extraterrestrials outright. He's never taken the time to ask some basic questions or seek rudimentary answers. The fact that we're here proves there is life in the universe, period. Doesn't that alone beg the question about other possible residents in this vast expanse we see above our heads each night? Aside from what's kept secret from the public for good reason, there's also a lot of bunk out there, but…" Kevin paused and looked over at Darnell. "Maybe I should just leave it there."

"Believe it or not," Emma jumped in, "We began talking about stars and aliens just before finding the stranger tonight. If nothing else, it's a topic of interest. Enrique told me earlier that he used to work at JPL before he retired." She looked over at Enrique, then back at Kevin. "No doubt you two could have an interesting conversation. Darnell and I could probably learn something from you guys 'in the know.'"

Enrique was quick to point out that he didn't believe in aliens per se, but when Kevin tried to advance the conversation, it triggered a sudden memory in Emma's mind.

"Oh my goodness," she blurted out. "You just reminded me of something really weird." Leaning downward, she put her hand up to her forehead momentarily, as if trying to remember it precisely. "Yesterday morning just before I left Toronto, my son said something bizarre to me, but

47

I just thought it was one of his ramblings. He told me to 'at least listen to the voice in the desert; sometimes there's treasure there.' Oh my goodness," she said again, trying to recall as much of Anthony's chatter as possible. She looked at Enrique. "What did he mean by that? Did he somehow know about the stranger? If I could just remember the context. I'm not sure there was a context…if it was connected to something he was talking about earlier inside… We were out in the driveway when ..." Emma's voice trailed off into a mumbling thought-spree. Her eyes widened. The other three remained quiet. Kevin looked at Darnell with renewed interest.

5

There was an awareness of lying down. It was not particularly soft but adequate. At first there was only darkness, then faded blotches of colour – reds, yellows, oranges and white, lots of white. An image emerged, first as a blinding brightness, then pure white light. Is this now? Is it a memory? There was warmth, immersive, fluent, assured. He remembered being very small, a child, closing his eyes while looking up at the sun. He saw the child from all angles, from distances near and far, but also through the child's eyes, from inside. There was a sense of permeating the entire space, experiencing it effusively, wholly, in chorus.

His eyes were closed and heavy. Breathing slowed. Becoming aware of internal processes, he sensed the flow of blood cells, plasma, nutrients, intracellular fluids and oxygen. Muscles tightened and eased. Gastrointestinal juices began to issue from liver and pancreas. Thought absorbed it all, simultaneous calculations performing functions, executing arrays. Fully cognizant, yet without desire or reason to move, or even consider movement, he lay still, in rhythm and unison with all. Every cell in his body, every neuron firing in his brain yearned for that moment in salivating anticipation: the taste of something forgotten. There was expectancy, aspiration.

His body was separated from the gaze of others by a mere curtain. He heard monitors beeping, voices nearby, distant indicators turning on and off, a low buzzing sound, steps shuffling past. Recognition emerged slowly; a faint impression of a hospital entered his thought stream. Yet all felt remote, otherworldly, ephemeral. A few square feet of privacy afforded him solitary passage, drifting in and out of innumerable memories. Faces and names. Well-defined, distinctive, yet alike. Same, same, but different, he reflected, a phrase once learned, or perhaps always known.

He was unaccompanied, yet family, friends, places, sounds, emotions and knowledge - everything he once knew or had ever felt – merged into a form of musical tapestry, conveying thought and permeating all aspect of being. He became immersed, enthralled, becoming the music and resonating wave-like in sonic aurora shimmering. All comprehension coalesced together in an elaborate harmonious interplay.

He thought of familiar music, timeless, alluring, imaginative. Music had always been there. It was the one constant in an absurd, yet incredible life. He had always been in love with it wholeheartedly, passionately. It transported him through times nothing else possibly could. Its endless inspiration, emotional expression, the offspring of pure thought, the very ether of 'what is' flowed through, and emanated from him. Music became the interpretive vehicle integrated into his very essence, and he in turn was part of its ebb and flow.

Consumed by this expression of infinite beauty, he became unaware of breathing, or any need to do so. Intervals between breaths had been growing longer, dissipating. There was no panic. There was no pain. There was no drifting into the long sleep. He began to detect a stirring. He felt an awakening. Thoughts flooded his psyche. Everything he once knew now seemed incomplete, partial, veiled. He was beginning to see anew, seeing vastness itself as familiar, understood. Instinctively, he felt a sensation akin to opening one's eyes. Perception, awareness, sensitivity and discernment were unfolding. A new expanded consciousness was emerging, transcending restraint. Once chained to life, he now comprehended openness, a freedom unlike anything ever imagined. All constraint gave way. With a burst of energy from the very core of his inner being, a great light exploded simultaneously in all directions. Transcendence at the speed of light. Suddenly, he no longer felt the limitation of locale, of place. Everything emanated from mind as though it were not only perceived, but brought into creation by thought. He sensed belonging. He was all things, and all things were him – everyone and everything woven together into the magnificent fabric of 'what is' – a fantastic crescendo in the music of the universe, the universal music. He melted into it, and fell in love with it all.

Everything seemed new and vibrant, yet familiar, pulsating with energy. The expanse of the universe was immense, yet somehow within reach, a world without - a world within, existence as state of mind. There were no walls, partitions or barriers, no further internment. Neither fatigue nor heaviness could be discerned. The emerging transformation was immense, astonishing.

Was this death? Cessation suspended? A novel new paradigm?

Through reflection, a realization emerged. If this was death, then it was unlike anything he ever considered or believed. Through great deliberation in life, there were minimal expectations. He had literally expected nothing. Dust unto dust. This transcended the expectations of any belief ever conceived. There were no pearly gates. There were no thrones, no angels, not even a yellow brick road…and fortunately, no waiting room, no limbo, no Bosch-depiction of hellish torment. St. Peter? Apparently absent… and not a single human virgin to be awarded the male faithful in the afterlife anticipated. How, he humorously contemplated, could there be relevance now to such petty corporeal concerns?

Yet, if this was death and thought occurred still, then an afterlife, a continuum is real. Was this reincarnation then? He thought of his body again, but attempted no movement. He still perceived it lying on the bed. Others were gathering - hospital staff taking pulse and checking monitors. He comprehended it all without fazing. There was no shock, no regret. There was no sadness or any emotion at all. It was simply an observation of what is, or was. The body once occupied was conduit, instrument, containment apparatus.

Everything he had experienced in material form, was now encapsulated into a unified whole. There was no sense of loss. Observation, thought, and comprehension were more encompassing. than ever before possible. The corpse on the table, the temporal instrument and conduit, was freely abandoned. He began to recognize what this was, what it has always been. There was recollection, as of a long lost memory, a renewed awareness and insight, much like one might imagine an emergence from a coma only to question: Where am I? How much time has passed?

Ah, time. Order and succession, the means by which we distinguish between events, understood to have begun with the inception of the universe, the so-called Big Bang. He found that he could now encapsulate his former life in detailed entirety, every thought, every word, every act, every connection. There was no distinction between events, no stream-like linear delineation of occurrences moving from past toward future. Now he comprehended everything, could choose a focus and retrieve it effortlessly. Comprehensive, thorough, absolute illumination. He suddenly understood time to be the construct it was – chained to the form he had once inhabited – a filter for interpretation. Now all was in the present; simultaneous, experienced, understood and accessible.

And what of the universe whose inception created time as he had once known it? What of its perceived great expanse? Great it was, yet no longer remote, unattainable, or distant. What was he becoming? He might have considered such a thought before transcendence. His memory now served to reformulate. It wasn't about what he was becoming. It was about what he had always been.

He used to feel detached, isolated, asserting we are all alone. He even wrote it down one time as if to write in stone. "No one else is in my body. No one else is in my shoes. No one else is in my psyche. No one else knows all my views." But now he perceived wisdom, a comprehensive understanding of all he could imagine. There were no windows to look in upon anything, for all

51

had merged together into a great oneness. The realization of this rose into a boundless, immense crescendo of thought and sensation transcending all. What was this?

And then suddenly, there was an experience of plummeting, rapid descension, gravitational pull. Spiral in nature, the draining into a sinkhole, colour and sound swirled into a maelstrom, the return of a genie to its lamp. The thought became pervasive. The sensation of expansiveness, of oneness, began to dissolve. The aperture was closing. The drapery fell. A perception of reverting, of revisiting something, Déjà vu, confusion; fatigue.

There was difficulty breathing. His chest caved-in. He was utterly drained. The light was gone. It no longer emanated from him; it no longer illuminated, nor made transparent.

All became quiet; all became dark.

He tried to reach out, but felt no movement. He struggled to see, but all had become obscure. Dark shadows layered in darkness of mind, darkness of memory, a heaviness, a sinking, a sensation of pressure, first smothering, then crushing, then silencing…

Then nothing.

6

"At least listen to the voice in the desert; sometimes there's treasure in a cave." The words were now resonating in her head. Emma couldn't stop thinking about what Anthony had said yesterday morning and what Kevin had just been saying over the past few minutes. She was struck by the bizarre events that suggested a connection where there couldn't possibly be one.

It wasn't just what had been said. Emma had been hearing similar stories and arguments from Anthony for as long as she could remember. This was different. The stories weren't just coming from a child, or someone with a known psychological disorder. She wasn't hearing the narrative from one of the many pseudo-documentaries trafficking loosely-linked occurrences and perspectives as established fact. She just heard a compelling set of actual occurrences and weighted viewpoints from a licensed, employed professional in the medical field. Emma understood that didn't necessarily guarantee an accurate perspective, but she expected professional discretion to influence opinion. Furthermore, Kevin relayed first-hand information in one instance, and a second-hand account in another. In her opinion, his overall credibility had also been bolstered by sensitive comments he made about schizophrenia and schizophrenics when Emma had spoken about Anthony. In Emma's mind, he had clearly thought through some of the complexities inherent in a little-understood disorder. So when Kevin's comments about aliens triggered her memory of what Anthony had said to her yesterday morning, it instantly infused credibility into Anthony's perspectives and insights too. Emma suddenly had much to think about.

Earlier that night she had spoken to Enrique about Anthony's obsession with aliens. Crazy coincidence, she thought, but then remembered a discussion at work back in Toronto some time ago. Six or seven of her colleagues had become embroiled in conversation about coincidences over lunch. One of them described an experience she had that morning. After further discussion, they agreed that coincidences were more than just random happenstance, but failed to presume how. It was an interesting conversation that included people with varying backgrounds and perceptions on life in general.

Even the skeptics in the group admitted an interest in the topic, but emphasized subjective interpretations abounded. Furthermore, what and what did not constitute a coincidence? An amazing variety of experiences might qualify, but what exactly compels us to lump varying experiences together into one elusively non-descript category? It leaves us with a sense that something has sent a disturbing ripple through the normal fabric of life.

Emma focused on the strange nature of what had occurred here. The more she thought about it, the more she realized this wasn't a typical coincidence. This wasn't just recognizing a connection with someone you meet, or running into someone unexpectedly. This wasn't just a simultaneous occurrence of events like having the same birthday, or unexpectedly choosing the winning number in a lottery. Anthony's admonishment to 'listen to the voice in the desert' and then pointing out that 'sometimes there's treasure in a cave' was a little too specific to be counted as mere coincidence. How could Anthony possibly know about the guy in the cave before she and Enrique found him there? He even mentioned it before she flew down to California. The whole idea was bat-shit crazy.

Or was she extending a bridge too far? Emma was aware of a latent tendency to jump to conclusions before considering a more balanced assessment. When she thought something through carefully, she usually arrived at more logical inferences. Sometimes I let the things on my mind bleed out into my world, she reminded herself.

When Emma shared some of her passing thoughts about coincidences, the chatter in the truck accelerated. The medevacs both shared memorable experiences. Then the discussion came back around to Emma's son and the comment he had made the day before. She became a little self-conscious and felt it necessary to explain Anthony's situation. Her tone changed slightly. The others detected a tinge of sadness in her voice.

Kevin stopped her right there. He also detected a defensive posture, an apprehension of others' views about her son's condition. Kevin told her he had an opportunity to work with several young people coping with severe mental disorders before taking his current job.

"You know, this might be important to say to everyone here because whether we talk about it much or not, most people I know are connected with somebody – a friend's child, a cousin, a sister, brother or even a parent who suffers from some form of mental illness. While complicated, the various mental disorders we deal with in society vary significantly. Furthermore, even within a particular mental disorder, there is often a wide spectrum of symptoms and other identifying features that make addressing the issues tough problems to work on. Now I know that what I'm about to say isn't strictly scientific, and I certainly cannot prove what I'm about to say to you either, but here it goes. If there is one thing I have noticed, or at least interpreted in the particular way that I have, it's that people I have met and come to know who were diagnosed with schizophrenia seem to be connected, or plugged in, if you will, to something else. There, I said it! It can also seem like they step in and out of our shared reality to experience another one equally real. A good example is the famous artist William Blake who died over two-hundred years ago now. If you aren't familiar with him, look him up. You will find his case interesting. I suspect he was schizophrenic. The term didn't exist then, but his behaviours would fall into the spectrum of behaviours we categorize as such today. There are many similar examples throughout history."

Kevin stopped short of suggesting schizophrenics may be on a higher plane of thinking. He knew better than to share too much too soon. If people are open to ideas, it is always better to give them a little taste to savour before offering a meal. The fact was, however, that Kevin had often pondered whether some schizophrenics' conditions could really be described as a disorder. A few he met seemed to operate from another plane of existence. That in itself would be alien to most people, but maybe it is a unique condition with possible advantages. Someone living on a different level of experience would naturally have a difficult time looking normal in a society where the norm is not what most people are experiencing…and so a term like disorder could easily creep into the assessment.

Kevin had been interested enough in the matter to spend time looking into it. Schizophrenics have often suffered a sad and oppressed history. There has always been great confusion about what schizophrenia is. Popular culture pegs it through a narrow lens, leaving the public at large to believe it's a fractured personality, someone unpredictable and probably dangerous. Almost all schizophrenics Kevin had ever come in contact with fit a bill that seemed quite opposite the stereotypes. Misunderstanding has probably always been the case as it is now, he acknowledged. Throughout ancient times it was seen as some sort of divine punishment or demonic possession. He couldn't help but imagine what some of those individuals had to endure in a cruel and less-lawful world. The ancient Greeks altered that only marginally. Schizophrenia may have changed designation to a disorder or a disease, but its stigma has never really subsided.

As far as Kevin was concerned, all of that was just part of the story – a very small part of many stories that may never come to light. Some schizophrenics have proven themselves capable of cohesive thought in ways non-schizophrenics rarely acknowledge. Some have made significant contributions. Van Gogh isn't the only one known to the public. The names of beat writer Jack Kerouac, Fleetwood Mac founder Peter Green, and mathematician John Nash are just a few to figure prominently. Kevin thought it interesting that schizophrenics found prominence in the arts, particularly in music, which required exceptional creativity and refined focus. The Beach Boys' Brian Wilson and Pink Floyd's Syd Barrett also came to mind.

Kevin couldn't help but realize that a very broad set of circumstances would have to come together for a schizophrenic person to achieve prominence among 'normal' peers in any field of interest. How many people like Kerouac, Green, Nash, Wilson and Barrett have existed, but are not known or remembered for their contributions? Will they still be lauded 100 years from now? Kevin hoped that was beginning to change. His little spiel to this group was a small opportunity to contribute to that change.

Emma appreciated Kevin's insight. His general description of a schizophrenic was the best and most positive she had ever heard – someone plugged into something else. It envisioned the possibility that schizophrenia was not so much a disorder, but an alternate way of perceiving, perhaps an extra sense, or insight, or…she wasn't quite sure what to think now, but she suddenly felt more positive about her son overall. For some time, she had felt deflated, fraught, even helpless. She had watched Anthony withdraw from friends and a life where he once fit in, but from which he quickly became estranged. He was once a well-rounded individual who became a square peg still trying to fit into the round hole. For whatever reasons, it no longer worked for him. His life changed. He sometimes surprised her with his insights, but if she were honest, she would have to admit that she often dismissed them. She hadn't really appreciated any relevance they might have. Anthony's inability to function as readily in the world he once functioned in superbly dimmed his prospects, both in her eyes and in Jean-Marc's. Anthony and his father were particularly close, but Jean-Marc, like Emma, was unsure of how to navigate this the best way possible. Neither of them felt like they were particularly successful in this endeavor.

Kevin's ideas and Emma's positive response had them all upping the chatter and speculation. Everyone acknowledged an unusual occurrence. A few suggestions about possibilities were bandied about. It wasn't absolutely impossible for Anthony and the person lying in hospital to have made some previous connection. All ideas seemed to produce further questions and conundrums.

It was Enrique who reminded everyone that excited, random assumption often had little or nothing to do with the truth. "This all sounds very interesting. The mysterious can certainly generate some excitement, but slow your horses for a moment. I can't help but think about the seriousness of this situation. We found a dying man out in the desert. You might eventually find out whether there is some connection between your son and this guy, but for now, that connection, if there is one, may already be disconnected. We are unaware of what has been going on over the past few hours while we were at the police station. That John Doe we found alone in the desert may very well have died since we left him – and he will likely have been just as alone on a hospital bed as he was in that cave. I hope we didn't take away any last moment of peace he may have sought." That sobering thought produced a moment of silence.

Then Emma's cell phone emitted the familiar opening guitar sequence from The Animals' version of *House of the Rising Sun*. It was Anthony. Emma immediately realized she had not called to confirm her arrival as promised. Had she thought of it, she would have realized Anthony was probably waiting for her call. Clearly she had been distracted. The freedom of driving through the high desert, the sense of being back home with its associated nostalgia, the California sunshine, and then all of the events that had happened simply made her forget. She hadn't even been here for twenty-four hours yet. Crazy. She answered her cell.

"You must be having quite a good time," was the first thing she heard. Emma proceeded to apologize to her son, but he was calm and didn't seem the least concerned. "Have you had a chance to visit much?" Emma was taken aback. She paused, took it in.

"Have I had a chance to visit much? What do you mean? I remember telling you all how much I was looking forward to some seclusion. This visit isn't about family and friends down here. It's about refocusing, spending some me time."

Everyone else in the car became absolutely silent, quiet enough to hear the discernable male's voice at the other end of the phone. Emma glanced at Enrique. He, Darnell and Kevin were all listening attentively.

"Yes, I remember. It isn't like you to forget to call, so I thought... well, never mind. I'm glad you made it and are doing what you went down there for. Solitude can be a good thing."

"I'm actually in a truck with three others at the moment. Bit of a long story."

"Ah, I knew something unusual was up. Although you might not think so, a series of unusual events can be a very good thing. I'll let you go then Mum. Everything is good up here. Enjoy the week and remember to listen to the voice in the desert. Don't forget what I told you. Sometimes there's treasure in a cave. That may be a mixed metaphor, but I think you understand what I mean. Relish all of it. It just might be what you really need. We'll talk when you get back." While Emma was still listening in disbelief, she heard the familiar Canadian refrain of "Have a great day" followed closely by "Love you lots" and a hang-up signal, then a dial tone.

First there was a short pause. Then, Emma looked at Enrique. "We need to get to that hospital."

"We're almost there. It's just a matter of parking when we get around the corner from here." Enrique pulled up to what seemed like the longest street light Emma had ever experienced. Then he turned left into the hospital parking lot. It was still very early in the morning, but the lot was already half-occupied. Darnell suggested driving around the building. The first responders unit was on the other side. He knew at least two spots would be open for another couple of hours. They were reserved for medevac staff, but no one would be checking up on it at this time of day.

Emma's mind seemed to be firing in several directions. Her thoughts jumped from Anthony's words to Kevin's, then back again. She thought of various events over the past number of years. Perhaps she and Jean-Marc didn't realize just how fortunate they have been. Everything seemed so idyllic from the time they met in Montreal to when things first fell apart with Anthony. Emma felt terrible just for thinking about it like that. For the most part, things turned out as well as could be expected. Anthony was stable, bottom line. She and Jean-Marc may not have reacted or responded perfectly, but the three of them maintained a decent relationship. They had all adjusted and things were on a good track again. Her accident was a bit of a fallback, but that was receding into the past now too. The series of events in the past 24 hours really had her head spinning. She realized it was important to keep it together. Except for the stranger, no one's life was in danger here. If she really thought about what Anthony had said, she might come to a different conclusion than the one she jumped to, but then again, maybe not. In the meantime, she would see what she could find out here at the hospital. This was a manageable situation.

There was still a lot of babble going on as Enrique parked the truck. All three men had some interesting questions or comments to make, although Emma hadn't managed to pay attention to most of them. It was all speculation anyway. Aside from knowing that the stranger was in real jeopardy and could easily die if he hadn't already done so, they knew nothing about this guy. Somehow, a possible connection between the stranger and her son Anthony had been implied. At least, that's how she understood it. Was she wrong? Had she jumped to a conclusion that could easily have been made because of the way the information was phrased? Although a possibility, her gut feeling was that her interpretation was correct. Any connection was yet to be verified, but even if there was a connection between Anthony and the stranger, did it infer any kind of threat or vulnerability to her son? Emma felt strongly about needing to find out. It was highly unlikely that the stranger was an alien as Kevin seemed to think. Given the circumstances, it crossed Emma's mind that he might be schizophrenic. If so, that could be a possible connection. She had no idea whether or not Anthony had been encouraged to join online support forums or if that was even a thing. The whole situation was likely to be something completely different from any speculation made so far. Emma only knew she had to find out more than what anyone seemed to know right now. It didn't really matter to her what any of these guys were thinking. She just hoped that the stranger was still alive. If at all possible, she was going to want to meet him under much better conditions than she had earlier that evening.

As soon as the car was parked, all four got out and moved toward the nearby staff entrance. Darnell led them through the main hall and past the small crowd of sick and injured waiting to be registered and attended to. As soon as they walked through a second set of doors, someone recognized Darnell and called him over. The man in a white coat was standing in a small group that included two police officers. Darnell intuited the situation immediately and told the other three to come with him. When the groups converged, the man in white, clearly a doctor, initiated introductions. He introduced Darnell and Kevin to another doctor, identified as a psychologist, and a medical assistant. The police introduced themselves. One of the officers recognized Enrique and Emma as the people from the ranch. He smiled and joked about how long investigative questioning often takes. Since Enrique and Emma walked in with the medevacs and one of the officers recognized them, no one questioned their right to be included in the impromptu circle.

We're just updating these officers on the status of the person you brought in earlier," said Dr. Halundi, the man who had called Darnell over. "He's another John Doe by the way. How many guys with the same name do you boys intend to find over your careers?"

Darnell chuckled and looked down at his feet. He had little to say. It was Emma who asked how the stranger was doing.

"Not well," was the prompt response. Dr. Halundi was mindful to speak softly in the corridor. "The patient appears to be in his late forties or early fifties, although his grey beard and various surgery scars indicate a few years added on. As you already heard me say, he's a John Doe. Police have provided no identification or verification of identity. These officers say there

59

have been no calls about missing persons just yet. I understand that John Doe's circumstance has now been made known to other law enforcement agencies in the event that a missing persons' report might match up." Halundi looked at the policemen. Both officers nodded.

The doctor continued by stating that the patient had ingested approximately two-hundred and sixty-seven Tylenol tablets. The bottle found in the cave had two-hundred and thirty-three of the five-hundred count labeled on the plastic bottle itself. Police and rangers on the scene stated there were only a few pills on the cave floor, and they were retrieved. "I understand that you two," pointing to Enrique and Emma, "found him and had also reported a neat and orderly surrounding." They nodded in agreement. Dr. Halundi then pointed out that the maximum dose an adult is allowed to take is 4,000 milligrams a day. "That's eight of these pills. At 500 milligrams each and having taken the amount he did, that's one hundred and thirty-three thousand, five-hundred milligrams."

"That can't be good," one of the police officers muttered. Darnell, Kevin, Enrique and Emma all displayed blank looks on their faces.

"You're right about that." Dr. Halundi sighed. "It isn't good at all. The numbers tell the story. That's somewhere between thirty and forty times the maximum amount allowable and we haven't quite reached 24 hours since the estimated time of ingestion. It takes about that amount of time for acetaminophen to take full effect. If he ingested all that within a short amount of time, his liver will be incredibly overloaded. I'm not sure how this might progress, but the outcome cannot, and will not, be positive." Everyone was looking intently at the doctor as he continued. "The statistical toxicology assays have already yielded results. We were lucky to have an indication of what medication the patient took so that we could test specifically for that. Again, one of you just stated that this can't be good and unfortunately, you're absolutely right."

Dr. Halundi glanced at everyone before continuing. "Here is the situation right now: As far as we know, the patient ingested the pills about twenty hours ago. If that's the case, then survival is virtually impossible. When blood levels show a reading of 50 mcg per milliliters after a twelve-hour period, then serious liver damage is expected. Kidneys are highly vulnerable too. We scattered two tests over the past few hours since he arrived. The news is disheartening. The second reading was higher than the first by a significant amount. His toxicology level is still rising rapidly, and indications are worse: His body has already absorbed over 640 mcg per milliliter so far. It verifies our approximation of the number of pills he took. The amount he has taken could already have killed a dozen adults. However, as I mentioned before, this is a slow acting toxin. Even though the outcome is imminent, some victims who have ingested a lethal dosage last as long as 72 hours from the time pills were taken. Here's the issue. A typical lethal ingestion of Tylenol is much lower than the dosage this man took. Given the likelihood this all occurred almost a full day ago, I highly doubt he will survive even the next few hours. The fact that he is alive now means we are in uncharted territory. It is difficult to make any predictions. It's a good thing Mr. John Doe isn't represented by any insurance company we know of. I'm already going to have problems explaining toxicity levels, but verifying ongoing services for someone who should technically be dead will be a formidable task."

"Clearly this is a serious suicide attempt then." One of the officers who had been taking notes began jotting down a few more.

"It isn't an attempt officer. It's a suicide – period." The doctor looked at both officers somewhat contemptuously. Then he turned to the medevacs and the medical assistant. "What is crazy about all of this is that despite confirmation of toxicology levels, that man has been in and out of coma. There is no explanation. He was unconscious when he came in, but awakened for a short while earlier. He looked up at staff, but didn't speak. At some point fairly soon he will drift off one last time. We can't help him, but we can at least keep him comfortable." Then Dr. Halundi looked at the psychiatrist. "Even if he was ever able to awaken Dr. Sridhar, you won't have the pleasure of speaking to him. He's a John Doe. Without insurance, he will only get essential services and that doesn't include any psych appointments. In the unlikely chance he survives, he will be released as soon as he can walk out of here on his own. It's just how it is."

Only essential services? Insurance? It's always about fucking money, isn't it? Emma instantly realized what she had to do. She quickly and silently slipped out of the gathering and began walking down the hall.

7

Once the update was over, the doctor, the psychiatrist and the medical assistant each excused themselves. It was only then that Enrique realized Emma was no longer standing with the group. He looked around, then walked over to the nearby seating area to see if she was there.

As soon as the others seemed out of earshot, Kevin turned to Darnell. "This is more interesting than either of the other incidents." He was becoming animated. "It's crazy that we are even in a position to have insight into something like this. It is the third similar incident we know of – a very unusual pattern of events that might have been impossible to discover, except that as first responders, we've been in a unique position to notice the pattern. We have three unusual suicides in the desert, the most recent still being played out here at the hospital. Now we have news, not just of a medical mystery, but according to professional opinion, a medical impossibility. That's pretty wild my friend! I think it's something worth paying attention to."

Kevin repeated the estimated dosage of drugs the stranger had ingested. "Given the time frame," he argued, "the stranger should already have been dead when they found him. Dr. Halundi basically said that given the amount ingested, the slower absorption rate was irrelevant. Even a fraction of what the stranger took would have overwhelmed his liver and kidneys. Come on Darnell. You know there are very few responders or emergency room staff who aren't aware of how little it can take to overdose. I think all of this is significant Darnell. For all the talk of coincidence earlier in the truck, I don't think that's what this is."

"Look," Kevin told Darnell in an even more subdued voice. "Insurance companies may very well have a say in determining what toxicity level represents a likely, or even certain mortality. You can bet that has to take into account some variation. That variation would have to be determined by data documenting numerous cases. Insurance companies don't like to lose money – and they usually don't lose money. Governments don't want to let insurance companies go under either, because then bailouts may become necessary. That's why payouts are skewed in favour of insurance companies in the first place. It's how things work. That's what makes this situation so unusual. That guy we medevacked last night has exceeded all expectations for survival – far beyond any expected outcome."

Darnell admitted this was probably the most unusual overdose case he ever knew, but he wasn't having any more of Kevin's speculation that morning. "Unusual isn't necessarily impossible Kevin. I'm too tired to discuss it anymore. Our shift is long over. I'm going home. Besides, tired minds can spin out of control. You should go home too. Why don't you come in a few minutes earlier before shift starts tonight. Then you can check in and see if Mr. John Doe is still with us or not. If that stranger is still alive, well, then you can rant all night long and I'll give you a listen."

Enrique came walking back toward Darnell and Kevin. "I'm not sure where Emma's gone off too. I should probably just wait here for her. I doubt she'll be long."

"Okay, well have a good evening Mr. Enrique. It was a pleasure meeting you this evening," Darnell said. "It's been quite a night, hasn't it? I'm tired now and I'm going home. Give my regards to your friend Emma for me too. You've had a rough night. I hope you both have a good day." He tipped his head toward Kevin, turned and walked down the hall.

Darnell was barely out of sight when Kevin picked up the conversation. "I don't think I could be working with a better man. Darnel is as professional a person as you could ever meet. He's a good helicopter pilot too. Whatever difficulties we may come across on the job do not include worrying about his skill maneuvering complicated terrain, or crowded urban accident scenes. He's even better at maneuvering people who can be difficult. If there's one thing I've come to see more clearly while working on this job Enrique, it's that a qualified black man in America still has to deal with a lot of bullshit. I can't tell you how many times authorities in complicated situations like we had last night assumed I was the pilot – and for no other reason than I'm white. Darnell always handles situations like that with more grace than I could muster. He's a deeply religious man, although he rarely discusses it. When he does, it's usually because I've made reference to it, and then usually in fun. That's fine with Darnell though. I've never seen him lose his cool. He's as intelligent and well-rounded an individual as you'll ever meet. When we have slow nights around here, he has to put up with my crazy ideas. He's actually a good person to bounce ideas off. He'll tell you what he thinks if you like, or he'll just listen when you need to get something off your mind. He's a good guy."

Moving on from the topic of Darnell and work, Kevin asked Enrique if he had worked the Airbnb for long. He couldn't be more pleasantly surprised to discover that Enrique had recently retired from NASA's Jet Propulsion Lab down in Pasadena. He understood that not everyone would want to listen to his alien suppositions, but couldn't resist engaging Enrique anyway. He asked him about JPL and NASA in general, but then asked him point-blank: "So what do the people at NASA really think about aliens?"

Bingo! Enrique figured that once Kevin discovered he had worked at JPL, he wouldn't be able to help himself from asking the alien question. It wasn't like he hadn't been asked before. Enrique figured that most people on the planet have looked up at the vastness of the night sky above them, just as he and Emma had done several hours before, only to wonder what is out there. When you consider that there are now almost eight billion people on the planet and as of yet, only a few space agencies scattered around the world, how often would one of those eight billion people have an opportunity to meet someone involved in a space program?

Enrique couldn't help himself either. He had to have a little fun with this.. He moved a little closer to Kevin, slowly raised an eyebrow and said as somberly as possible: "Do you really think it would be a good idea for NASA to let the world know what they really think is out there?" Enrique paused, then spoke even more softly. "Do you think that would be helpful Kevin?" Then he leaned back slowly and stood as straight as he could, all the while looking directly at Kevin in the eyes. What a great effect, he thought. He savoured it, then chuckled and let his shoulders down.

"Aw, you're just fucking with me now, aren't you?" Kevin chuckled too, but then suddenly stopped smiling, straightened himself, and looked directly back at Enrique. "Seriously, what does NASA think?"

Enrique became stone-faced. It was like someone had just pulled a gun on him. As soon as Kevin saw it, he dropped his shoulders and laughed loudly. Then they both let loose. "I guess I deserved that one," Enrique acknowledged. He softened his glance, nodded his head, and then proceeded to answer the question.

Kevin listened earnestly as Enrique told him that life could undoubtedly be found in space. This wasn't exactly a secret. He began illuminating scientific insight into the topic by bringing Kevin's attention to a creature already known on Earth since the late 1770s. Tardigrades were originally discovered by a German zoologist named Johann Goeze. Kevin acknowledged having heard the term before, but couldn't remember any details. That opened the door for Enrique to engage in one of the things he liked to do best – talk science, talk space and engage in thought-provoking, mind-expanding possibilities. Clearly this guy Kevin was interested in more than just playing video games. Why not indulge him?

"Tardigrades," he said again. "In school, they tend to refer to them colloquially as moss piglets or water bears. That's where you might have heard the name before. Tardigrades are tiny creatures about half a millimeter long. They can even be seen under less-powerful microscopes used in public schools. What makes tardigrades interesting is that they can exist almost anywhere. They have been found in extremely cold places like Antarctica, but also in extremely warm conditions, specifically in mud domes formed by active volcanoes." Enrique had never seen a documentary about them, but imagined that if one of the newer, more sensationalized documentaries now seen on the boob tube were to describe them, tardigrades would be labeled extreme organisms, stated in an ominous voice complete with heavy metal background music.

"These little creatures are pretty incredible," Enrique emphasized. "They are so resilient that not only can they be exposed to extreme temperatures, but also extreme pressures. Tardigrades can be completely dehydrated and starved. They can survive conditions without air. They can even withstand radiation. They have been around long enough to leave fossils dating back over half a billion years to the Cambrian period, a time when most animals were still single-celled organisms. That in itself is something to think about. Since then, tardigrades have evolved into well over a thousand species. It may sound completely alien having all of these qualities, but tardigrades have lived on Earth for much longer than most other creatures. That is something else to think about."

Then things became really interesting for Kevin. Enrique explained the Cambrian period from where the earliest tardigrade fossils date. During that time, there was an explosion in life forms. When Enrique was just getting into his university studies in the late 1970s, there was a raging debate about whether the sudden explosion in life forms appeared suddenly during the Cambrian, or whether they might have been there earlier, but didn't leave any fossil record. This leaves the issue wide open for those in the science community who have been arguing that life may have come to Earth via comets streaming by. Creatures like tardigrades might very well survive a journey through space. "Remember," Enrique said, "these things are resistant to radiation." He emphasized the point by telling Kevin that guys like him have only been hoping to see aliens for a little over a century. Meanwhile, they may already have been here in the form of tardigrades for over half a billion years.

Kevin became absorbed by Enrique's line of argument. He imagined these tiny creatures making their way across the void to other worlds, possibly seeding all of them with life that originated elsewhere. What a mind-fuck, he thought. A faint smile broke out on his trance-like face as he listened even more intently.

Both men lit up as the explanation progressed. "This is why it is so important to get as much information as we can about everything we can," Enrique emphasized. "Then we can cross-reference it all and make new connections, see new patterns, begin to learn how it all comes together. That's how we will be able to make sense of it all. Isn't that what we all want? To have some idea, some insight into what it's all about? Okay, well, it's one thing to speculate about whether creatures like tardigrades could have come here from somewhere else, but it is quite another to provide evidence for just such a possibility. This, my friend, is where it gets interesting."

"Oh yeah, how?" Kevin was riveted.

Enrique continued. "You had to ask me what I thought about aliens because you found out I had worked at JPL. Information from NASA could corroborate this discovery, but it isn't the only institution that can. There's another one that already has."

"What do you mean?"

"Everyone is familiar with the idea of Russians being in space. Hell, they made it there before we did. Anyway, most people don't know that Russia's version of NASA, their modernized space agency is called Roscosmos. Well, Roscosmos made an interesting announcement in June, 2017. It wasn't mentioned much in Western media, although science geeks could learn about it from a number of sources online. I'm not sure why. No doubt it would have generated a lot of interest by the public at large. Anyway, they collected samples from outside the International Space Station's windows containing specimens of these life forms. If nothing else, at least it proves that life exists outside of Earth's atmosphere. Roscosmos has speculated that the ISS might be a unique collector of comet substance. That includes these bits of biomaterial of extraterrestrial origin. Even more interesting, a British astrobiologist has said the Russian findings corroborate research by his own team who have isolated similar biomaterial from the stratosphere above the British Isles. Never mind all the science fiction movies we have ever seen – they are all fiction. This is something tangible – proof of life that did not originate here. These organisms were isolated from micrometeorites, dust found on the outside of the ISS. Think about that. It is very exciting, but it isn't what people like you hope for. It isn't some green guy, an E.T., a Vulcan or Klingon, or even Robin William's Mork, but it is life, and that in itself is an incredible thought. It really does open up all kinds of possibilities."

"So you NASA guys don't really think there's any such thing as intelligent life out there? There isn't much to hope for or worry about? Even Stephen Hawking thought we should be wary about trying to contact aliens."

"He did. I'm not saying there might not be something to that, but it is always important in science to try and stick to the evidence that you have. Future evidence can change all that, but wait until you actually have it. Science is trying to find evidence for aliens. That is why SETI, the Search for Extra Terrestrial Intelligence, exists. Actually, it isn't a single project. It is a collective term for various projects looking for signs that we are not alone. Even Mr. Hawking, who as you point out thought we should be wary, helped found the Breakthrough Initiatives back in 2015. These initiatives include several projects focusing on numerous academic interests. Right now, we are scanning and searching over a million known stars for artificial radio or laser signals for the purpose of identifying Earth-sized rocky planets. We are sending out probes to determine whether hunches about distant planets and other space objects are correct or incorrect. We have created and disseminated messages representative of humanity and Earth itself. These creatures found on the outside of the ISS, these tardigrades I was telling you about, are all mounting evidence. The truth is this Kevin. Our awareness of what might be out there has only just begun. At this point, it is safe to say that we know very little. That is the position of almost everyone at NASA, and probably any other space agency."

Kevin lowered his head, nodding. Enrique almost felt sorry for him. He may have taken the proverbial wind out of his sails, but that's okay he thought. In a world of wonder, there is much to marvel at without having to make it up.

Then both men turned their heads in simultaneous recognition of the sound of steps approaching. They spotted Emma walking toward them. Kevin tapped Enrique on the side of his arm. "Thanks man. That was really interesting. I'll let you two get going. I should be taking Darnell's advice and getting some sleep anyway. Take care." Kevin shook Enrique's hand, and nodded his head toward Emma. "Good night," he said, turned and walked away.

Enrique wished Kevin a good day, then looked back toward Emma. She was still several yards away when a voice called out. Emma stopped and turned around. It was the psychiatrist who had dispersed with the others just a short while earlier. Emma held up her index finger to Enrique, indicating she would be a minute, then waited for the psychiatrist.

Noticing just how tired he really was, Enrique decided to take a seat in the nearby waiting area. He pulled out his cell phone to check for any email or texts.

Dr. Sridhar caught up with Emma and introduced herself. "Hello. I know introductions were shared earlier, but I didn't get your name? I'm Danielle Sridhar, director of psychiatry here at the hospital."

"Hi. My name is Emma, Emma Collier," she said, probably looking a little puzzled. "What can I do for you?"

"I simply have a question for you. I saw you slip away, presumably to the bathroom, but you didn't return before we dispersed. Later, as I was walking to my office, I saw you leaving the registration window. Then, shortly afterward, I had a text from Dr. Halundi telling me that if John Doe survives, I will have access to him after all. I understand coverage has been 'arranged.' This may not be my business, but did you have anything to do with that? Do you know him? Who is he?"

"I thought you had one question for me." Emma looked impatient. "No, I don't know him."

"Well, may I ask why you are helping out a patient, a dying patient – you don't even know?" Danielle realized she was probably coming on a little strong, and may even have crossed a line. She sighed, gave Emma a look of empathy, and softened her voice. "Listen, you can call me Danielle. I would really like to help. I'm curious about this man. A suicide attempt in the manner he did is kind of unusual. I can't help but wonder what it was all about. If you know something Emma… May I call you Emma? Maybe it could help too."

Emma paused for a few moments before saying what was on her mind. "We share one idea Danielle. This person is unusual, or at least his situation is unusual. I really don't know him, but yes, I arranged to help with his medical bills. It may seem impulsive, and I suppose it is, but I had to try and help if I could. I need to know something."

"You need to know something? What is it you need to know Emma?"

"It's kind of crazy doctor, but I guess you know crazy being a psychiatrist anyway." It was an ice breaker between the two women. Emma provided some background by giving Danielle a brief overview of her son Anthony's condition, her trip down to the California desert, what Anthony had said, how she and Enrique had found the stranger in the cave, conversations with the medevac guys, and the fact that John Doe is alive after what he had done to himself. Emma explained she had to know if there was some kind of weird connection as Anthony had eluded to, or if it was all just something else, whatever that may be.

Danielle could see there was a lot of history right here in front of her. It was a history of coping, a history of wishing for different outcomes, a history of misunderstanding, a history of frustration, and a history of helplessness. They are all part of the experience of families living with schizophrenia. She told Emma that even as a professional, it is exceedingly difficult to really understand what it is that schizophrenics experience. Listening to their own attempts to explain rarely yields more insight. The psychiatrist apologized for her own field of expertise. She admitted there was still much to learn about most disorders. Danielle felt it was important to be absolutely honest about John Doe's prospects. "It is unlikely he will survive, or even come out of his coma. Overdosing is a problem frequently seen in our emergency rooms. Even patients under long-term care often succumb to impulsive acts. Sadly," she told Emma, "that is the legacy of some unsuccessfully treated conditions."

The two women conversed for some time. Finally, she offered Emma her card and suggested Emma could call back later if she liked. Danielle promised to check regularly on John Doe's condition until the expected outcome occurred. They both expressed their pleasure meeting one another. Emma promised to connect again later that day. Danielle turned to head back toward her office. Emma walked to the waiting area where Enrique was tapping away at his phone.

"Okay, I'm sorry Enrique. I had to go to the restroom, ran into someone I knew, and then got called over by the psychiatrist. Let's get back to the ranch. You must be tired. I know I am."

"What did the psych want? Did you say you knew her?"

"No, I was talking to someone else after I first slipped away. The psychiatrist, who just called me over on my way back, thought we might know the stranger. She was hoping I could give her some information about him. One thing led to another. I chatted to her a little about Anthony. She even told me I could call back later to see how the stranger was doing. Sorry to keep you waiting."

Enrique looked at Emma. "That's okay. It's been quite a night and you're right, I'm as exhausted as you are. I feel badly for the stranger though. You have to wonder what brings a person to a place where self-harm seems like the best option, or maybe the only option. I can't help but think that he might have had his reasons. They might even be good ones. We just don't know. I'm not sure there's any point in phoning to find out what happened when everyone here made it quite

69

clear the outcome is inevitable. Let it go Emma. There isn't anything you can do about it. The medevac guys seemed to be enthralled with this guy too, but I don't think there is anything more to it than what we saw. It's a tragic occurrence, but nothing new in the great scheme of things."

8

Dr. Danielle Sridhar left her office and made her way to the elevator. After a long night that ended with an unusual case, she managed to get in a few hours' sleep before returning for another round. Having arrived a few hours later than she would normally, she scolded herself for letting paperwork pile up so high. It was a bad habit not usually resolved until she had to devote several extra hours at once to catch up. Reports. Deadlines. They were a part of the job she actually despised. She had been going over files of patients registered on what she often thought of as 'her ward.' Almost all of them had been emergency admissions to be weeded out for legitimacy. Some would be released within a day or two to become the responsibility of outpatient services. Others would be transferred to a facility dealing specifically with psychological disorders, long-term patients, and those experiencing a breakdown or some other mental crisis.

It can be difficult to assess what constitutes an emergency. Psychological determinations are more difficult to establish than medical ones. Medical determinations depend on measurable levels like blood pressure, heart rate and temperature. Mental states are highly subjective, deeply personal conditions. Professional help is dependent on patient descriptions of what they are going through, and even more dependent on patient participation in therapeutic endeavors. Psychological interventions are often long-term, if not life-long. Positive advances and outcomes are usually slow.

That's why she was struck by cautious disbelief when she received the news. Dr. Halundi called to inform her that John Doe had regained consciousness and was being admitted to her ward. He may already be there. This was particularly surprising because just hours ago, the good doctor had explained how dire the situation was. She soon learned that a rising influx of patients with unusual flu-like symptoms were recently stretching emergency ward resources a little thin. At first, Danielle wondered why room would be made for apparently less-serious cases than John Doe's in an emergency ward, but accepted the explanation.

The news necessitated a change in Danielle's morning itinerary. The list of visits she had planned now had to be bumped. Given the circumstances, the patient may fall asleep again, or slip back into coma before she had a chance to see him. With toxicity levels remaining high, the patient was not out of the proverbial woods just yet. He was still an anomaly. Anyone who had ever worked in a hospital knew that conditions could change swiftly. Surprisingly, John Doe had been gesturing to staff with nods and had even mumbled a few words. Halundi had told her that nurses reported an almost Herculean effort by the patient to sit up and try to engage with them. It would seem this patient is full of surprises, she thought. It was important to see him as soon as possible.

The time dragged on waiting for the elevator. Feeling slightly impatient, Danielle pushed the button a second time. When the door finally opened, a throng of people poured out. A crowd also swarmed in. The elevator stopped at every floor before arriving at her stop on six. Excusing herself past the other sardines, she stepped out of the elevator and sighed in relief. It would have been worth climbing the stairs. Put it all behind you, she told herself. Be professional. Just get on with your day.

Dr. Sridhar greeted everyone with a hello or a good morning as she made her way to the nurse's station. Two nurses were chatting back and forth while typing at different ends of the counter. Checking the register, she realized there were two John Does – one and two. How Dr. Seuss! She was already familiar with John Doe One, a younger man slated to be transferred to the Hill Street facility downtown. John Doe Two had to be the one in room 610. When she asked about the new admittant, one of the nurses informed her that he would nod responses to questions, but refused to eat any breakfast. When she last saw him about ten minutes earlier, he looked like he might drift off again. The three exchanged brief pleasantries before the doctor excused herself and made her way to the patient's room.

As she approached, Dr. Sridhar greeted the monitor sitting on a chair just outside 610. Monitors were protocol for attempted suicides who needed to be closely watched. 'Liability' was the dirtiest word that could be uttered in the place. The monitor, an older woman, nodded a hello and smiled, then made a gesture with outstretched arm into the room that said enter. Danielle stepped inside.

The room was spacious given the fact it housed only one bed. Psychiatric wards in hospitals were finally beginning to accommodate the complex needs of patients. The room was also quite bright. Curtains were drawn open and the sun was shining in. The man in the bed lay somewhat elevated, but his eyes were closed. She wasn't sure if he was sleeping.

For a short while, Dr. Sridhar just stood and looked around the room. She thought of Emma Collier, the woman she met in the wee hours of the morning who had committed herself to helping a complete stranger. Dr. Sridhar sometimes found it difficult to express a lot of faith in humanity in general. She believed that everyone had it within themselves to reach a little higher, but was often disappointed by a culture where individualism and greed dominate social values. It took a different kind of person to put herself out for someone she didn't know, especially when it was likely that there would be no reward for doing so. When Emma arranged to take care of John Doe's medical bills, it was already established that he was not only likely to die, but that it was only a matter of time. What kind of person shows empathy so spontaneously and freely without concern of subsequent complications for themself? Such an act was unusual, but inspirational.

Dr. Sridhar turned her attention to the patient. She noticed his eyelid twitch and wondered again if he was sleeping at all. Was he trying to avoid interaction? There was a chair a little closer to the window. She walked over, quietly lifted it and brought it to the end of the bed. She would sit down for a while and wait. Perhaps not very scientific, but she recalled a childhood belief that if you stare at a person, they will sense it. Maybe it would work here. She realized it was a foolish little game she was playing with herself, but found herself eyeing the stranger inquisitively. Curiously enough, only a few minutes passed before a blink or two occurred. Then both eyes opened. Dr. Sridhar waited a moment, letting him get his bearings. When he seemed to set his eyes on her, she introduced herself.

"Good morning. It is good to see you awaken. My name is Dr. Sridhar. I'm the hospital psychiatrist. How are you feeling today?"

A response was delayed. The patient blinked a couple more times, closed his eyes and pursed his lips as he stretched his neck one way, then the other, as if testing to see if it still moved. He took a deep breath in, then exhaled quietly. He slowly opened his eyes, staring down toward the end of the bed and concentrating, as though taking inventory of internal bodily processes to ensure they were still operational. He gave no indication of recognizing the doctor's presence, but gradually pulled himself up into a full sitting position. Dr. Sridhar continued to observe patiently, waiting to see if a response would come. The man breathed in and out a few more times, then raised his head and looked directly at her.

"Sridhar is an Indian name, but you sound like you're from New York." He yielded a faint smile.

He spoke, she thought. It prompted a smile from her as well. "Long Island," she said. "The name is Indian but I'm third generation American. You have a good ear. You don't sound like a New Yorker yourself, but then, not everyone who lives in New York sounds like they come from there. Are you?"

The stranger ignored the question. "Isn't Sridhar a given name for males in India? Are you the feminine version of a Boy named Sue?"

Wow! Where did that come from, she wondered? This guy clearly isn't Indian. Did he live, maybe work in India? Even so, how well might a non-native be expected to know any of India's 22 official languages? Aside from all that, it was an unusually strange thing for someone to say, especially a suicidal individual just emerging from a coma. It was odd and outlandish, she thought. And only last week…only last week her father, a second-generation native-born American, had told her that he had discovered from her ailing grandfather that very same fact. Sridhar was usually a name given to boys in South India where their family was from. It had only become a surname since the family moved to the States in the late 1950s. He did not know why the name was changed. Danielle Sridhar's elderly grandfather did not reveal that, but her father found it amusing.

"Yes, Sridhar is a name for males in the South of India. Apparently it only became used as a surname after moving to the West. Interestingly, I only found this out recently. It's a strange coincidence that you would have knowledge of this, or mention it at all. You don't appear to be of Indian heritage yourself, so I can't help but be curious. How would you know that?" She paused for a moment. "How do you know that?"

The patient now looked amused. "I probably heard it used like that in a film," he said. "Bollywood is big now."

Bollywood? This guy has just emerged from a coma, she thought again. It was bewildering. Dr. Sridhar made an effort not to show any hint of surprise. After initially being taken aback, she realized he really was awake. He also appeared to be cognizant and coherent enough to be questioned. She could make inroads after all. It should be taken advantage of while the opportunity lasted, she thought. "Has anyone had a chance to speak to you very much yet? Do you know where you are or why you are here?"

"I haven't really spoken to anyone here yet." The man was looking directly at her, still exhibiting a faint smile. "Of course I know I am in a hospital. Just by looking out the window, I can also tell you where I am. Would you like a weather report with that?"

"You're quite an anomaly here," Dr. Sridhar said, disregarding that last comment. "I'm surprised you haven't met Dr. Halundi. I'm sure he would have explained your situation to you in detail if you were cognizant enough to listen." She paused only for a second. "Strangely enough, you do seem cognizant enough to listen."

74

"People have been talking to me on and off," he said, "but I can't say I was paying any of them much attention. I don't know who Dr. Halundi is. Maybe he did. It doesn't matter."

"Well, it does matter," Dr. Sridhar said. "It does matter. You have been in and out of a coma, your liver enzymes are critically high – although I don't know the up-to-the-minute specifics of that, and the medical team have expected you not to survive the massive drug overdose you apparently administered yourself. You were found unconscious in a cave out in the desert. We still don't even know your name. We have been using John Doe for record-keeping up to now." The two maintained eye contact after that barrage of information. Dr. Sridhar looked at him pleadingly. "What is your name?"

The stranger suddenly seemed to become fully aware, even confident. He appeared unable to sit up completely straight, but made the effort. He was now clearly smiling and almost staring at Dr. Sridhar. "You already said my name," he said softly with an air of confidentiality. "John Doe is as good a name as any, but with that pleasant New York accent of yours, you can call me Jahny" He stretched out the vowel sound creating more of a Beantown accent than one from the Big Apple. "Just like that," he said. "J-a-h-n-y, Jahny." Dr. Sridhar wasn't sure how to respond.

"Okay. Thank-you Jahny. I suppose that will do for a start, but I'm curious. Why did you feel like your action was the only option available to you a few days ago. Would you like to talk about that at all? I would like to know how to help you and where to begin. Do you think you could help me with that?"

"Hmmm, do I think I could help you with that? Do you think answering will really help either one of us? I know what I did a few days ago. You found enough drugs in me to kill half a dozen people, didn't you? I did enough of an overdose to take down an elephant on a rampage. My liver and kidneys should already have been overwhelmed enough to be rotting by now."

Dr. Sridhar looked at the man sitting up in the bed in front of her. She suddenly, acutely felt his individual rawness, his piercing ability to get right to the crux of the matter. He was right. He was an individual who had made his move, made his final play. Was he really still teetering over that precipice, she wondered. Perhaps little, or even nothing mattered, only that he was still here. "No," she admitted. "We do not know why you are still here. The last numbers that I saw indicated levels much higher than what is known to effectively stop bodily functioning."

There was a short pause before Jahny responded. Then he began slowly. "Do you want to know what I was thinking before committing this act, an act which most people think is terrible,

75

so tragic, etc., etc.? Are you curious to know that one last thing in a person's mind when they are about to die? Is it horrible? Is it as bad as one imagines? Is it filled with remorse? Doubt? Maybe tinged with regret? Is it the worst thing one can feel or think at the worst possible moment?" Jahny was almost sneering now; he paused again, perhaps for effect. "Do you really want to know what I was thinking Dr. Sridhar?" He paused yet again, for just a moment. "I was thinking…It's a good day to die. What a beautiful day it is today." Jahny's face lit up. He smiled with a sense of deep affection. His eyes appeared to well-up momentarily.

Then there was a long silence. Danielle Sridhar tried to absorb what was happening. Was he leading her on, just messing with her? What was he really thinking? What is he thinking now? Whatever this is, it is different. He's already been quite a bag of surprises. She wasn't sure how, or in what way yet, but it was different. She couldn't help thinking yet again that this guy was in a coma just a short while ago. He wouldn't speak to anyone. Yet here he was speaking with an authoritative manner and emphatic tone of voice. I came here to question this guy, she thought, but it's almost like he is luring me into his narrative.

"You seem taken aback by my response," continued Jahny. "Perhaps better described in other words: Astonished? Astounded? Amazed? Flabbergasted?" He lowered his head, tilting slightly to the left. "Stunned? Stupefied?" He looked amused. "Is it so difficult to imagine a joyful exit Dr. Sridhar?" She just looked at him quietly, giving him the opportunity to continue uninterrupted, but he chose to segue instead. "Now we're thinking. Good. Let's get on a more even plane. My name is Jahny as we have already established. May I ask your first name Dr. Sridhar? Wait! You said you were third generation? Indian families often tend to be traditional, even when the family immigrated more than a generation before. Names can be among the last things of cultural importance to diminish or fade. Look at ancient names like John or Sarah, now ubiquitous designations throughout much of the world. Many would be hard pressed to identify their origin. Yes, let me guess. Is it something like Aesha which means 'a wish?' Charu which means 'attractive?' Possibly Jyothi, 'sunlight' or Laranya, 'the graceful one?'"

"My given name is Suhanisa, which means 'enlightened,' but I go by the name Danielle, thank-you."

"Both names are beautiful," Jahny said softly, "especially your Indian name. Why you have chosen a more Western-sounding name as your colloquial designation is your own business, so I won't comment. May I call you Danielle?"

"If you prefer, that's fine." She didn't elaborate any preference, encouraging him to continue talking, which he did.

"Your given name means 'enlightened,' but you're a psychiatrist."

Jahny's words struck Danielle as a statement, but the slightly higher intonation at the end made it sound like a question. She couldn't help but wonder if he was testing her in some way, or if he had some kind of a hate-on for psych professionals. That would indicate a history involving psychologists. Step by step here, she thought. Maybe it would be better to stop playing Psych for a moment and just engage with this patient – let him direct the course of discussion. He appeared willing to talk anyway. It could improve her chances of accruing valuable information. If she chose to barrage him with questions, he may or may not answer honestly. She already saw that. It often came down to intuitive interaction. That requires not only knowledge, intuition, insight and strategy on the part of the professional, but it also involves ability, willingness and honesty on the part of the client. Both were essential to make progress. That can be a tough challenge. The doctor simply smiled and asked: "You don't think psychiatrists can be enlightened?"

"I don't know. Hard to tell." Jahny revealed a smile, but responded seriously. "Any psychiatrist or psychologist I have ever met tends to adhere to either one school of thought or another. Even a hundred years on, many continue to think of themselves as Freudian or Adlerian. Some are Jungian, Skinnerian, follow Laing, Piaget, or whomever. The thing is, they tend to be strict adherents of one vein of thought over the others. They are inclined to become tunnel-visioned. They see and interpret their observations through that particular framework. A patient's behaviours are expected to fit nicely and make sense within that framework."

Danielle was quickly becoming intrigued. "You seem to know a little about psychology and definitely have an opinion about it Jahny. Where does that come from?"

"Experience, observation, maybe a little analysis," came Jahny's rapid reply. "Where does your professional outlook come from Danielle? Textbooks at university? Participating in class discussions? Conducting psychological surveys as part of your training program perhaps? Psych students often develop and test their ideas using other psych students as sampling cases for so-called studies. Then they call it research." I wonder how many graduate school papers, even doctoral papers, have been accomplished in that way? What was your doctoral thesis about Danielle? Are you qualified enough to figure out all the people that come through here? How do you even do that by asking a question here, or making an observation there, Danielle? It must be difficult having to make professional guesses you hope turn out to be correct. That's a lot to live up to, especially when most people never even figure themselves out. Think about that Dr. Sridhar, Think about that for a while. Have you figured yourself out?" Jahny leaned back and actually looked exhausted. "I'm really tired again," he said. "I need to rest for a bit. Think about that for a while. Then come back later if you like."

9

When Danielle Sridhar stepped off the elevator into a small crowd on the main floor, she spotted a familiar face. It was the woman who had stepped-up to help John Doe 2. Although lined-up for the elevator, Emma stepped aside when Danielle greeted her and nodded to indicate she wanted to have a word with her.

"Good coincidence meeting you here right now," Danielle said smiling. "I just spoke with the stranger you found. He is taking a nap now. These elevators and corridors are always busy. Why don't you come to my office for a moment?"

Emma wasn't surprised. She already knew that the stranger had regained consciousness. After a restless attempt to sleep earlier, she gave in to curiosity and called the hospital ICU, hoping to glean some news. She was told he had been moved onto a ward up on sixth, but received no further information. At least she knew he was still hanging on. Staff at registration during the night were more congenial, she thought, but that may have been out of necessity. They wanted and needed a contact source for payment of services rendered. Emma became that source. Again, it's always about money, she thought. When told he was now on a ward, she realized there must have been surprising improvement. Otherwise, he would have remained in intensive care.

"I was expecting a call from you at some point today," Danielle said, "but here you are. You seemed very concerned. I admit it really moved me when I learned you had decided to go out on a limb to help someone you didn't know. No doubt you're here to see about him. Are you far from here?"

"No, well, yes, I'm staying at an Airbnb out near Pearblossom. Originally, I'm from SoCal, but have been living in Canada since the eighties. It's complicated. The stranger has definitely been on my mind for the reason I briefly explained earlier this morning. If he was going to be unconscious, or worse, I knew you wouldn't be very involved, so I didn't really want to bother you. I appreciated your offer, but thought that calling intensive care would yield information at the source. I apologize."

"No need," Danielle quickly responded. "That makes sense. Have you been able to find out his real name yet?"

"How would I? I haven't spoken to him. As far as I knew, the hospital still didn't know. How would I find out otherwise? If hospital staff had found out his name, wouldn't registration staff have adjusted corresponding information? You said you just spoke to him. Didn't he tell you?" Emma already guessed the answer.

"I'm not sure what to tell you about that. He said his name was Jahny, and made an attempt to pronounce it with a New York accent. I don't know if his name really is John; he said that in response to my telling him that we had been referring to him as John Doe. I didn't want to press him on it, at least not yet. I need to assess him and didn't want to expend either his energy or mine on less important information. His medical condition may have improved, but he isn't out of the woods, not even close. His data numbers are stacked against him. He was moved upstairs because we are already doing what little we can for him and his condition. This thing is going to play itself out."

Danielle stopped walking for a moment and faced Emma directly. "I will tell you this. He's intelligent, or at least sounds knowledgeable. He actually floored me. Our meeting was different than expected." The two resumed the short walk to Danielle's office. "Here we are," she said, unlocking the door. "Come on in." Danielle gestured Emma to enter, then followed her, closing the door behind them. "Take a seat. Would you like something to drink? I could make coffee. There's also some soda or bottled water if you prefer."

"I'm fine," Emma said. She was anxious to hear about the stranger. "So you've been talking to him. I know you probably can't tell me much, but what do you think? Is the situation still as bad as the doctor informed us earlier? The outlook seemed dire, yet he's already been moved to a less-intensive unit."

"Hard to say anything at this point Emma. As I mentioned, the hospital has already done what it can. We will continue to make sure he is comfortable. Dr. Halundi will likely keep me informed, especially if details continue to be a threat. As for patient/doctor confidentiality Emma, of course that's private, but the conversation I had with Jahny revealed very little I would have to be confidential about. In fact, it was quite short. I introduced myself, but from that point on, he managed to direct the conversation." Danielle recalled the exchange with a grin. "He actually disarmed me with some of his insights. I was sort of expecting a feeble individual, someone who looked as close to death's door as doctors were saying. He was definitely not that person Emma. It was actually strange. In my profession, one doesn't usually get surprised very easily."

"Yes, strange," Emma repeated slowly. "It's all very strange Danielle. Imagine finding someone out in the desert like that. Then, as I briefly told you this morning, my son said a few

80

things that indicated he knows this guy, or knows about him. The whole thing is actually surreal to me. It's what led to my impulsivity earlier. I don't regret trying to help out, but I do admit it was impulsive. Despite what you seem to think doctor, I didn't do it out of the goodness of my heart. It was decidedly more selfish than that." She paused. "I'm not sure what I'm grasping for Danielle. Maybe it's just a chance to make a difference in my son's life somehow. I don't know."

"You told me briefly that your son is schizophrenic. Looking for some solutions to difficult circumstances is hardly selfish Emma." Danielle leaned forward. "Perhaps I can help you make sense of some of this. You don't have to figure this out all on your own. Is your husband here with you today?"

"My husband?" Emma suddenly looked surprised, but then realized that Danielle meant Enrique. "Enrique is not my husband. He owns the ranch, the Airbnb where I'm staying. We found the man in the cave while going for a sunset walk in the desert. That's why we both had to come in for questioning. We ended up back at the hospital giving a ride to the medevacs caught up in all this too. No, Enrique is not my husband. When I met him at the ranch, he did turn out to be an old acquaintance from decades ago. That's why we were out walking and chatting in the first place."

Emma realized that was already too much information as soon as the words spilled out. She was generally private, and rarely gave out more information than required. Perhaps it showed some trust in Danielle, or just revealed how out of sorts she was over all this. "This has piqued Enrique's curiosity though," she said. "You might see him here with me again sometime. He's well aware of how important I think this might be."

"In what way Emma? What do you think might be the connection, if any, between Jahny and your son Anthony?" There was no definitive response. The two women just looked at one another for a moment in silence. "Maybe I can help you find what you are looking for Emma. If you have any thoughts or questions that come within my area of expertise, perhaps I could at least verify or dispel possibilities. I expect you have a lot of questions about your son's condition. We all have questions about schizophrenia. That's expected. There aren't any easy answers, but if I can help you Emma, I will."

"Thank-You Dr. Sri..., Danielle. Thank-You." Emma shrugged, drooped shoulders, and sighed, almost deactivated like a science fiction robot. She looked up at the psychiatrist again. "I know that answers for Anthony may not be out there Danielle, not yet, but if there is any chance of finding something, something that...."

81

Danielle finished the sentence. "Something that would help you worry less about him once you're not able to be there for him?"

"That might be it Danielle. I don't know. He seems happy overall these days, but there is always the knowledge that his condition could change from day to day, week to week, or month to month, at any time. I'm not getting any younger. Things happen… you know? Everything is stable for Anthony right now, but who will assure him of that once his father and I are gone? Anthony's true destiny was taken away from him when onset began. Modern medicine can't give that back to him, at least not yet, but if I could make things so that I knew he would be alright….If money could buy anything Danielle, then we would be fortunate enough to help Anthony, but things don't always work that way. Even money has its limitations. This is the situation, so if there is anything that can help me understand Anthony and his condition better…that at least should be an advantage. Anything that can shed some light on it would be helpful. It might seem like grasping at straws but maybe that's all we have at this point."

"If you're wondering if that's crazy, it isn't," Danielle said smiling. "Many of the great minds throughout history were grasping at straws when they stumbled upon their discoveries. Gunpowder, penicillin, x-rays, plastic, nuclear fission and synthetic dyes were all discovered by accident. In most cases, these great minds were working on something else. Grasping at straws might not get you exactly what you're looking for, but it may yield an important discovery nonetheless."

That sounds precariously close to being a platitude, thought Emma, but Danielle's kindness shone through. "This may sound weird and possibly stepping over the line doctor, but do you think it's possible that the stranger is schizophrenic like my son?"

Danielle formulated her thoughts carefully before responding. "It is entirely possible that our stranger suffers from a wide range of probable disorders. Schizophrenia is one of them. Bipolar disorder and unipolar depression are other possibilities, and there are others. Not all people who attempt, or even succeed at committing suicide, are suffering from a longstanding psychological disorder, but many are. It might take a little while before we can determine what it is. Who knows? He may already be diagnosed. Our John Doe seems to have something against psychologists. That could be indicative of having had some experience with them." Danielle lifted her brows as if to say she just doesn't know yet, then tried to look reassuring. "Were you asking me if your son might end up in a situation like Jahny is in because your son is schizophrenic?"

"It's crossed my mind. It may very well gnaw at every parent with a child who suffers from mental instability. From what I've heard and read, there is much reason to worry about things ending that way." Emma looked weighed down in thought, but then revealed a spark of resilience. "Do you think it is possible for schizophrenics to be tuned into a different vibe or energy of some kind? Just last night, I happened to be speaking with someone who had worked with schizophrenics before. He is convinced that they are in a class of their own. He said that he often had the impression that they were plugged into something else. I don't know exactly what he meant by that. I'm not sure he knew exactly what he meant, but what if there is something to that? It has made me wonder whether there is something else going on. Maybe it's something we haven't tapped into, or discovered any clue about yet. Is that possible Danielle?"

"If truth be told Emma, I would have to say that I honestly don't know. I keep up-to-date on research in my field of expertise. We certainly know more than what we knew twenty, thirty, forty years ago, but it isn't nearly enough. What professionals know in most areas of study is still emergent. Science, and scientific methods have only existed for a few hundred years of our very long human history. Look at the speed at which society has changed in just our lifetime, let alone the past two hundred years. We have transformed our world, raised millions out of abject poverty, advanced our technologies, increased our lifespan, and many other wonders even our recent ancestors would not have believed possible. Yet we don't know all there is to know. We are far from it. So to answer your question about whether there is something we haven't tapped into, well, I would say quite possibly." Danielle paused, but Emma said nothing. She was attentive, and looked like she was expecting a little more. Danielle continued.

"You know Emma, our friend Jahny just finished challenging me before I left him to rest. He asked me where my professional outlook came from, and also asked me some hard questions for self-reflection. Almost immediately, I wondered if this man was a teacher, or another psych. If not, maybe he should have been. I can't ever remember a lecturer, or any mentor, ever challenging me like that patient did today. And now, talking to you, some of what he said makes sense in light of what you are asking. It's imperative to evaluate and reevaluate our ideas, motivations and purpose. This is especially important in a field dealing with matters that could make a significant difference in people's lives. It's easy to leave the ivory tower of a university, become enmeshed in one's work, and fall into a routine based on the idea that one is now a professional. Interestingly enough, when I was in university, I was very interested in the ideas Carl Jung had brought forward during the first half of the twentieth century. He was a pioneer in the field and, in my opinion, much more interesting and convincing than his mentor Sigmund Freud. Some of what he elaborated at great length may be of interest to you in this matter. Jung is a towering figure both in psychology and in twentieth century culture. Are you familiar with him or his work?"

"No offense Danielle, but I've never had much interest in psychology. Everyone has heard of Freud, probably because he delved into taboo subjects like sex. I've heard of Jung too, but until you just said it, I wouldn't even have remembered his first name."

"Well Emma, you might just find Carl Jung a good introduction to psychology. His ideas were a lot different than Freud's were. There is still much interest in his work, especially since he died in the early Sixties, but few psychologists today would call themselves Jungian. Too many of his ideas and theories touch on subjects out of vogue in scientific circles, but may provide an avenue of interest to you."

"How?" Emma was curious, but a little skeptical.

"Have you ever ruminated about something that happened, maybe an unpleasant conversation with someone, and then gone over and over it in your head?" Before Emma could reply, Danielle continued. "Sometimes a phrase can instantly click in your mind with a line from a song you know. Then that song gets seared into your head. Over and over, the tune goes round the virtual turntable in your skull. You then get into your car and turn the radio on, and it is the first tune that blares out of the speakers. Or you walk into a store to shop, and that very tune is playing in the background."

"Yes, I've experienced that. Hasn't everybody?"

"That's right. Everyone has had experiences where strange little coincidences like that occur. They make enough of an impact to take note of them, maybe even share the oddity with a friend in conversation. Well, Carl Jung called such coincidences synchronicities."

Doesn't synchronicity mean the same thing as being synchronized, like a watch might be? Something that happens at the same time," asked Emma?

"That's right. A synchronicity occurs when coincidences happen and seem to be related in a meaningful way, even though there doesn't appear to be any noticeable cause for the coincidence. It happens often to people, yet we never really stop to consider what the connections might be or why they occur. We just continue on with whatever we are doing at the time, even if the coincidence registered as odd, or even significant in some way. It's a strange, but regular phenomenon. Jung delved into it more deeply than anyone. He even wrote a book on it called *Synchronicity: An Acausal Connecting Principle*. It's very interesting stuff."

"Are you suggesting that coincidences may be more than that?" Now Emma was really curious, and perhaps a little less skeptical.

"I'm not sure what I'm suggesting. Just like the rest of the professional psych community in recent decades, I haven't given it much thought. The academic/scientific community reject the idea of synchronicity extending beyond mere coincidence. I never invested too much into it. I guess I just wanted to have a meaningful career where I could make a contribution. I'm not out to prove anything, or attempt to advance or discredit psychological theory. I'm more of a pragmatist. I don't want to be consumed by something like many famous theorists have been. It has occurred to me that some of these geniuses may have truly been inspired, or perhaps ensnared in OCD tendencies. When I am finished work, I like to relax and enjoy myself with activities totally unrelated to work."

"So is Jung's idea of synchronicity not accepted in the professional community?"

"As I said, it isn't given much thought in Western professional communities. In an eastern culture like the one my family came from a few generations ago, there is little differentiation between science and spiritualism. One example would be Buddhism, which is not so much a religion as it is a worldview. Knowledge and self-improvement are more dependent on personal experience than on the guidance or authority of sacred texts. For people with a more eastern outlook, we might not be able to explain coincidences, but that doesn't mean there isn't an explanation. We simply don't know what it is, or at least, not yet. It leaves the door open to possibilities."

"So should I be trying to read Jung? I'm not sure I'm up for that. It seems like an endless task, Sisyphean in nature.

"Not necessarily reading Jung, just leaving the door open to possibilities. I wouldn't read too much into this situation Emma. Just be open to whatever might help find an answer, or even just a direction toward an answer."

"So how do I do that Danielle?"

"Why don't you start by doing what you came here for today - taking an opportunity to meet Jahny. He may awaken shortly, but he may not. Give him a little more time to rest. Then take it from there. See what happens. If it appears like a conversation might be too much for him, please let him continue resting. If you do get to speak to him, I don't expect you will find much to solidify any hunches you have at this point, but who knows? At least you will have done what you could to discover any connection. That may only be a small reassurance, but it is still a benefit."

"Okay Danielle, I will. I think I'll step out for a bit first. I saw a place across the street that might come in handy. Thanks." With that comment, Emma got up from her chair, reached out and shook Danielle's hand. She thanked her again and walked out, closing the door behind her.

Danielle hoped Emma would find what she was looking for. Solace in a cruel world is hard to find. Danielle wondered if she would ever meet Emma again.

10

Emma walked out of the hospital toward the busy intersection. The light turned green in sync with her arrival at the corner. She crossed the wide avenue, keeping pace with others moving in the same direction. The place she had spotted earlier appeared even more curious as she approached. It certainly wasn't a recognizable franchise. A couple could be seen chatting and sipping cappuccinos through one of the large, tinted porthole windows along the front. The bookstore/café's unusual name, *Down the Rabbit Hole*, suggested an experience as well as a good read. Even the front door caught her eye. Beautifully hand-carved leaves and fractal branching adorned the oak surface. Flower-shaped apertures were crafted in leaded, cathedral glass. She paused to admire it before traversing the stairs to the basement-level entrance.

Stepping into the shop was an unexpected pleasantry too. A great deal of thought and creativity had clearly gone into its elaborate interior design. The front room might well have been an adaptation of Bilbo's hobbit hole. Yet it also suggested scientific inquiry. Numerous antique instruments of navigation, copies of ancient maps, and portraits of famous writers, explorers and inventors adorned empty wall space wherever it could be found. Intricately carved wooden frames embellished windows. Carved leaf-crown mouldings where walls met ceiling gave the place a warm and natural atmosphere. Emma found it amazing. It was architectural brain candy.

A middle room featured six large round tables, encouraging both the exploration of books and the company of fellow bibliophiles. Emma noticed that the other patrons venturing into the Rabbit Hole that afternoon were rather curious themselves. Many exhibited unique appearances. One wore clothing emphasizing fashion long gone. Another had shaved one side of her head, but featured multicoloured layers of hair down the other. Yet another seated at the barista's counter sported a handlebar moustache, newly-waxed. Two others were wearing huge round spectacles while scouring magazines at a corner table. Faces were buried in books. The exceptions were the barista, the couple seated by the window drinking fancy coffees, and staff Emma identified by their green shirts or blouses. Each and every one could be characters derived from books themselves, she mused. They stand in stark contrast to the cell-phone addicted minions outside. She couldn't think of an adequate description of the place, but it inspired her to move about and explore.

What section should she delve into first? Unique titles categorized an unusual arrangement of topics in this place. *Exploration and Discovery* was the first one she noticed. It featured historical content that combined Newton and Einstein with Magellan and Cook. Historical accounts of wars, famous military leaders, or Machiavellian strategies were relegated to a section on *Human Aggression*. That was an interesting arrangement. Yet another titled *Perspective* mingled books typically found in *Philosophy*, *Psychology*, *Religion* and *Self-Help* sections in other bookstores. Emma thought it refreshing and thought-provoking. She hadn't considered how labels and categories can frame perspectives and corral interpretation. Very interesting, she thought. This place seems to generate a magic of its own. Just being in here is mind-opening.

Emma figured she would give the stranger an hour to nap. Minus the time maneuvering the boulevard in both directions, that still gave her time to explore. It's almost funny, she thought. This is not the getaway I planned, but it has become intriguing. She recounted recent coincidences and circumstances. On her way out to the ranch, she had been thinking about old acquaintances, and then encountered one when she arrived there. While walking out into the desert, often portrayed as a barren and lonely place, they come across a stranger near death, who may have a possible connection to her son thousands of kilometers away.

On her way to *Perspective*, she had to pass through an area marked *Imaginarium*, which featured books in fantasy literature and science fiction. Given the décor, this had to be the heart and soul of the place. Amazingly, it not only featured Tolkien's greatest work, *The Lord of the Rings*, but all of his many works edited and published posthumously by his son Christopher. Maps and drawings of Middle Earth were affixed to angled boards reaching from the top shelves on each side to the ceiling at the center of the aisle. Décor and special lighting gave the impression of being inside a castle corridor. Emma glanced in and out of several books in this section, then continued browsing the aisles.

When she arrived at *Perspective*, Emma scoured the shelves by alphabet until she came to the letter 'J,' and then specifically to *Jung*. The store had an extraordinary collection of the psychoanalyst's work. The titles themselves were fascinating. *Experimental Research* caught Emma's eye, but it was in volume two of the man's collected works. Too much. She was surprised by the number of titles. Many were by Jung himself, but there were also several biographies and interpretations of his work. When you explore deeply enough, individuals and specific topics can become a world unto themselves. She was fascinated. One could spend a lifetime reading about what we know, and never get through an acceptable portion of it all. Imagine what is to come! Emma realized she had not only spent most of her life working with money, but thinking in terms of money, like it was the framework that defined all things important. Yet in this odd little bookstore, there was a wealth of knowledge she could only begin to comprehend. Emma's mind set sail.

A moment later, she recalled her purpose here. She was still standing in front of a number of books that were either by Carl Gustav Jung, or about him and his work. '*Man and his Symbols,*' '*Modern Man in Search of a Soul,*' '*The Undiscovered Self: The Dilemma of the Individual in Modern Society,*' were all thought-provoking titles by the man himself. Emma picked up book after book, looked at the contents, read a few sentences in various sections, and contemplated both content and writing style. She soon determined Jung was best-known for his ideas about synchronicity, which Danielle had mentioned, archetypes, and the collective unconscious. These topics seemed to be extensively explored, both by Jung and the critics who hoped to hang on to his intellectual coattails. She had heard of the collective unconscious before, but aside from a quick impression derived from its name, she knew nothing about it.

Emma had already spent a good fifteen minutes in the same section. She was feeling a bit pressured by time. The stranger might already be awake. His room might be occupied by nurses, doctors, and karma forbid, a hospital lunch to further poison him back into unconsciousness. Okay, she was exaggerating a little. A last quick scouring of the titles left her undecided until she came across a book titled '*Jung: A Very Short Introduction*' by so and so... This would have to do for now.

Remaining in the *Perspective* section, Emma found Immanuel Kant just two shelves to the right of Jung. There were as many volumes by the philosopher and his interpreters as there were with the psychoanalyst. Various copies and translations of his most notable work, the *Critique of Pure Reason,* were printed both in hardback and soft. It was also the one Anthony quoted frequently. Who would have guessed a 240-year-old philosophy book would still be well-read?

Emma lifted a paperback copy from the shelf, fingering through the pages at various junctures. At first she found herself breezing through a paragraph, only to realize she hadn't retained a word. Okay, slow down. Emma read the same passage again. This isn't pulp fiction. It was pretty deep. Her eyes scoured the shelves for a similar overview to the one she had found on Jung. Emma pulled a few titles from the shelves, then walked over to a table and sat down.

Emma hoped to narrow her purchases by scouring the table of contents in each. She had already decided on the short introduction to Jung. It was a matter of narrowing down four Kant books to one, or maybe two. Certain chapter titles jumped out at her. Again she flipped through pages. "Genius is the ability to independently arrive at and understand concepts that would normally have to be taught by another person," she read in one. "Have the courage to use your own reason. That is the motto of enlightenment," she read on another. "Space and time are the framework within which the mind is constrained to construct its experience of reality." This was heady stuff, not to be placed on the easy reading shelf.

Emma narrowed it down to three books – two overviews and a paperback copy of Kant's *Critique of Pure Reason*. There were a couple other topics to check out. She had considered finding a fact-based book about alien speculation, but quickly realized that might take time to determine. Forget that stuff for now, she thought. Danielle Sridhar's suggestion was probably more sound than pursuing the validity of anything alien. As for more information about schizophrenia, well, she and Jean-Marc had saturated themselves with that topic. Leave it for now too.

For years, she submitted to Anthony's diagnosis which, for all intents and purposes, was a description of inability. It was also dehumanizing in ways driven by fear and lack of knowledge. Kevin's description kept repeating in Emma's mind… "people plugged into something else." What exactly is normality anyway? It was a question she had often heard, especially by people rationalizing their own 'crazy' thoughts or behaviours away. This time she stopped to think about it. What did make Anthony so different from others? What really makes anyone so different from anyone else?

A quick google defined 'normal' as 'conforming to a standard; usual, typical, or expected.' Hmmm, she reasoned. That seems less like a standard to live up to, and more like a description of herd behaviour and mentality. Anthony wasn't a conformist in any way, even before onset. He had become quite a loner once his friends couldn't relate any more. Once it became evident he thought differently than others around him, then he became the 'other.' It seemed so unfair. He was struck down by illness in the prime of his life. There she went again, thinking of it as an illness, but is it? Again, Kevin's words popped into her head.

It probably is, Emma conceded, but with lingering doubt. Yet, there is more to most people than meets the eye. A label like Anthony's can be outright damning in ways others never experience. But what is normal, Emma asked herself again? Anthony can hold a decent conversation with others. He may say something that seems out of context or unconnected sometimes. Does that mean he isn't normal? He's well-read. He can make interesting contributions to various topics of conversation. What if it just means he has a different perspective – perhaps a more informed perspective? Hell, she thought. If a guy like Einstein were at a party of 'normal' people, how well might he fit in? Others might try to engage him on a physics question, but would his explanation be grasped by these 'normal' people? Or would much of what he had to say just go over their heads? There was little question about Einstein himself. He would seem odd! Had his work not become famous, Einstein might well be ignored or avoided just like her Anthony.

Maybe there really isn't any such thing as being normal, just different. Of course, Emma had heard that many times before too, but maybe it was true. Just like the section references organized in this bookstore, she thought. It's about looking at familiar things a little differently...exploration and discovery...perspective. Emma had to laugh quietly. There really is something special about this little bookshop, she thought. I came here in desperation. Now my mind is awakening to who knows what? She checked her phone for the time. Emma got up from the table and walked to the cashier near the coffee counter at the front of the store.

"Find everything you were looking for," asked the girl in a green uniform?

"And then some," Emma replied.

11

Emma walked to the main desk across from the elevator and asked one of the nurses for directions to Room 610. The nurse was somewhat surprised that the patient without an identity should have a visitor, but politely gave Emma directions down the hall and to the right.

Well, this is it, Emma thought. I'm either going to have some idea that this was a worthwhile impulse, or I'm going to find out what an impulsive fool I've been. She walked somewhat briskly, slowing down twice to appreciate the progression of room numbers. When she determined the door to the stranger's room, she approached a little reluctantly. She had no idea what to expect. This man on the precipice had regained consciousness. What was going on in his head right now, she wondered? What was going on in his head the other day? What's been going on in his head for some time?

She turned slowly into the room. He was slightly elevated by pillows. His eyes were closed. Emma assumed he was still sleeping. She stood in the doorway staring. His long greying hair had been brushed back. It hung down well below his shoulder. She thought of Jesus. She thought of the Maharishi Mahesh Yogi. But he wasn't like her image of them. He looked haggard. No, not haggard, but tired, very tired. He may well have been Father Time himself. Baggy eyes, dark circles, creases, and emerging wrinkles added to the effect. Strangely enough, he actually seemed peaceful in repose. Exquisite irony, she mused. Chaos at rest.

There were two chairs to the left side of the bed facing the window across the room. From where she stood at the doorway, only blue sky could be seen through the large pane. The hospital was the tallest building in the area. Emma walked quietly toward the chairs and set her bag down. Jahny did not move. She watched him carefully, moving around the front of his bed. Then she approached the window and turned her glance outside. Hundreds of houses and commercial structures came into view.

Emma looked out onto the desert community. The extended hand of the great metropolis was grasping for more land to feed its sprawling expanse. She began losing herself in thought, in daydreams of times past. As crazy as L.A. could be, she still loved the place. Fortunately she could afford to return whenever she wanted, but did so less and less as time passed. Canada was home now. Her family lived there. She wouldn't have it any other way. Emma loved being untethered, feeling at home in more than one place. Home is a state of mind, not a place defined by borders. Her mind flitted from one set of memories to another.

Suddenly, a voice spoke from the bed behind her. "Good afternoon Emma. I have been looking forward to meeting you."

Emma was surprised, but not startled. It may have been because she was already expecting the unexpected. It may have been the softly-spoken voice in which the greeting was made. Emma realized she was smiling as she turned around. "Dr. Sridhar must have told you to expect me today," she stated with confidence.

There was a short pause. "Even if someone had told me, would it be normal to expect meeting the same good Samaritan twice?"

"So you were told more than just my name." Emma's smile broadened. "How are you feeling? You've had a rough few days, I'm sure."

"That's what I've been told. Much of the time has been spent in exquisite silence and darkness, almost like being in a kind of suspended animation." Jahny's face was one of bliss as he spoke the words, but then changed abruptly. "And then I awakened to this." He looked away from Emma and scoured the room as though disappointed by what he saw. "Not now, but earlier," he started again as he turned back toward her. "Your presence improves the entire scene." A faint smile emerged. "I understand you were one of two people who found me out in the desert. Having rescued me from a sure death would be considered favour enough by most," Jahny said slowly, "but you have also chosen to pay for hospital bills as well. You do realize that it is likely to be money poorly spent. I am conscious for the moment, but that could easily change a moment from now. I am told that I'm not out of the proverbial woods, and may never be. I have no money to repay you and am likely to die anyway. Besides, how do you know that I won't simply walk out of here to make the same attempt? Do yourself a favour and walk away Emma."

Emma wasn't sure how to respond. It was probably true. She recalled the amount of drugs this man had ingested and how impossibly high toxicity readings had climbed. She wondered what the numbers were now. This is a strange experience, she thought. I'm in a room speaking to a man who should be dead, but is speaking to me as though it were afternoon tea. I have sought to keep him alive, not for his own sake, but for my own reasons.

"I can't walk away, at least not yet," she said. It just came out. "I need to know something. I doubt you can help me with this Jahny – may I call you Jahny? – but I just couldn't walk away without finding out one way or another." She stopped, looked at Jahny for a moment, and then turned away. Emma felt uneasy about revealing a selfish motive. She shrugged and sighed.

Before she could sort out her thoughts, Jahny began to speak. "Emma, come sit down here please." He gestured toward the empty chair. "All is good, believe me." He motioned her to sit down again. This time Emma moved toward the chair at the other side of the bed. She sat down and looked at Jahny attentively, waiting several moments before he began. Jahny first looked directly at her, then turned to look out the window. "You have helped me, called in to check up on my progress, and have now come to see me. We have never met before, except out in the desert, which I do not recollect. Essentially, this is our first meeting. I can see no way in which I might be profitable to you. I have no idea what you do, but I can assure you that the work I did in life was never going to make me rich, let alone you. That's fine. I've never had any need or desire to become rich. This all begs the question though. What could your motivation in this situation be?

Emma found herself virtually staring at Jahny now. This man could not only speak clearly, but was actually formulating a hypothesis about her presence here. She thought about Danielle's impression of the man. She couldn't help but think the same thing. Who is this guy?

Jahny continued. "Since you were able to make a quick decision about money, I have to assume you are a woman of at least some means. Money isn't much of an issue. In the end, however, I expect you had a more humane reason for helping me. In no way am I suggesting that you have done it for any love of me. You don't know me. Therefore, someone or something else must be in the equation. You believe I may have some important information. The kind of urgency that led you to help a stranger is probably key here. I suspect a loved one is involved."

There was another short pause, but Emma did not take advantage of it to verify or negate anything he said. She wanted to hear more. Jahny continued. "I see that you have bought some books. While most readers tend to buy fiction, they usually do so one book at a time. It looks like you have at least two, and maybe three in that bag. Is it possible that at least one of the books you have there is also related to your concerns?"

This guy's like Sherlock Holmes. Emma was curious and somewhat amused. Just like the literary sleuth, his deductions sounded logical. She was encouraged. Maybe her impulsivity was going to pay off. This was her chance. She had this man to herself for however long he might be able to stay awake. He may be right. He could be gone at any time. It was now or never. Emma was just about to speak, but Jahny continued..

"The only thing I can think of that might connect us in any way is the attempted event out in the desert. Suicide freaks people out, doesn't it? It's probably something everyone has thought about at some time or another, but that's different from those consumed by an inevitability. I acted on impulse. In your mind, that elevates me to a different plane. It is both disconcerting and promising. That scares you to your core. It reinforces your fear, but also provides an opportunity to learn. Someone close to you has exhibited a similar tendency. Impulsivity can be dangerous. Seven-tenths of all suicides are male, an overwhelming majority by any standard. So if I were to guess, I would say you came here because you need some insight into the workings of a twisted mind. I happened to cross your path. Convenient. You're worried about someone close to you. You must discover what compels someone toward the ultimate self-destructive act. It is unlikely to be a spouse or partner with whom you have a long-term relationship. Dangerous impulsivities rarely produce long-lasting relationships. No offense, but you're old enough to have grown children. Is it possible you have a child who has either fallen in with the proverbial wrong crowd, or who has developed a medical disorder? At least two psychological disorders are associated with high incidences of suicide. Both tend to become evident through an onset event typically initiated in one's late teens or early twenties. Am I arriving anywhere near the truth yet Emma?"

Jahny looked calm but confident. Emma thought she might disintegrate into an emotional puddle. She maintained her composure though, raising her gaze back to Jahny. "I have a son," she said.

"He is actually an amazing young man, but I couldn't say that I understand him as much as I'd like. He's had some difficult periods in the past. His father and I have worried extensively about him. He seems to be doing much better right now, but... He is quite smart; probably smarter than either his father or me. We're successful in business, but he doesn't fit that mold. He believes there are things much more important than money. An atypical outlook I know, but that's our Anthony. He's a big ideas guy, a visionary, but that can also be interpreted as being just a dreamer."

"Interesting. Let me interject if I may. You say your son is bright, but you have been worried about him, at least in the past, if not right now. Yet you are concerned enough to impulsively reach out to me. He has a disorder that could flare up. That presents a real threat you hope to avert. The two disorders most often associated with suicidal behaviour are bipolar disorder and schizophrenia. He seems to be in a stable period right now, but there are never any guarantees that will be the case permanently. You must tell me if I am close yet."

"You are close enough," Emma said hesitantly. She was about to tell him more, but Jahny added two more questions.

"What possible connection do you think I might have with your son? Or was the possibility that we share a similar disorder the only connection you considered?"

Emma hesitated before answering. This seemed crazy, but… Fuck it, she thought, and proceeded. "Yesterday while scrambling to leave for the airport in Toronto, my son called out to me as I was getting into my cab. He said something strange although I gave it no thought at the time. He said, "at least listen to the voice in the desert; sometimes there's treasure in a cave." He said it like it was a reminder. Then given the rush out of LAX, yada, yada when I arrived, I didn't end up connecting with my son again until the early hours of this morning. Actually, he called me. I was on my way back here from the police station where I had to make a statement about finding you. I told him I was driving with a few others, but never said a single word about the series of events that had occurred. Do you know what he said to me on the phone? Let me emphasize, I said nothing to him. He said he knew something was up. He also told me that although I might not think so, a series of unusual events can be a very good thing. He told me to enjoy my week and to remember to listen to the voice in the desert. He also told me not to forget that sometimes there's treasure in a cave. That seems a little too coincidental to ignore. I don't know how it could be possible, but do you somehow know my son, Jahny?"

Jahny seemed to anticipate her question. "Perhaps," he said. "You've heard of six degrees of separation?"

"Yeah, it's a common expression. Isn't it the idea that the world is now so integrated, that a chain of random connections between only six people basically connects you with everyone else on the planet?"

"Not just people, but all living things and everything else there is too. It is an interesting concept to think about. It is related to our notion of a shrinking world coupled with an expanding knowledge base. The idea was first suggested almost a century ago by Hungarian writer Frigyes Karinthy in his 1929 short story, 'Chains.' There seems to be widespread awareness of the concept now, but it wasn't really made famous until well-known playwright John Guare penned his Pulitzer-nominated play called what else? 'Six Degrees of Separation.' That was over 30 years ago. Interestingly enough, growing knowledge of the concept itself probably contributes to its fulfillment."

"That's it?" Emma was disappointed. "Six degrees of separation? That's the explanation? That's all you've got?" She waited only a moment. "I guess I deserved that. I'm sorry Jahny. I didn't mean to put this on you. It just seems like there has to be something to this. One thing led to another… I guess I just got caught up in it all. I had no right to expect any explanation from you. I have also infringed on a difficult time for you. Again, I'm sorry."

"I wasn't chiding or taunting you," Jahny replied in a softer tone. "What I meant to get across was that we are all connected, us and everything else. There seems to be a sense of connectedness that begs to become known. Your inquisitiveness about what connection there may be is important. It's not just a frivolous pursuit. As distracted as most of us are with the business of the world we find ourselves in, I think we are all drawn toward finding and making connections. It takes different forms. You might make a discovery, something you were unaware of. It could be the simple pleasure of acquiring knowledge or gaining insight in many ways. It might be making a friend. You may develop an interest that leads to yet other interests. It could be attaining a goal. All of these things create extensions of ourselves, an ultimate understanding of the connectivity of it all. Much of my life has been wound up in this pursuit. Yet, I am only recently realizing this more fully."

Emma watched this man as he spoke. Again she wondered what brought him to the brink. Despite his medical predicament, he seems full of life today. When he stopped speaking, she looked directly at him and just blurted it out.

"Why did you do what you did the other day Jahny?"

Emma waited, not sure what to do next. Jahny was looking right back at her. He didn't seem taken aback by the question. He was even smiling, if only faintly. She wanted to ask so much more. The question reverberated in her head. Why did you do what you did the other day Jahny? Why did you do what you did the other day Jahny?

"Why did I do what I did the other day Emma?" Jahny asked, as though he had read her mind. He now looked completely content.

"I did it Emma because… it was a beautiful day. I think I wanted to just give myself to it entirely because it is, because I am, because we are, because everything is. That sounds incomplete,

I know, even crazy, but it is the best concise explanation I can give you. There is much to be said about it for sure, but that encapsulates it. Perhaps the problem is that the key to understanding it completely is to give in to it completely. But that is insanity, at least by normal conventions, isn't it?" Jahny chuckled quietly. Then he became most serious. "Let's get back to connections Emma."

"It is the connection between the 86 to 100 billion neurons in our brains that create our very perception of existence. Every organism with a nervous system operates much like modern computer circuitry utilizing the simple on/off arrangement of binary mathematics. When enough neurons are connected together, they can produce amazing complexity. We basically process the outside world through our nervous system. It creates a model of our existence, and a forum for the experiences we have. Interestingly enough, the brain is ultra-dependent on the world it processes. Even when it comes to generating a concept of self, the role of others is vital in shaping self-perception. It's all about connections. It's always about connections. The patterns of spreading electrical connections are the very language of our mental lives."

Emma wasn't sure where Jahny was going with this, but wanted to hear more. "To think that we only use about 10 percent of our brains… If we used more, who knows what might be possible?"

Jahny quickly dispelled what he referred to as 'that neuromyth.' "People still say that a lot, but it isn't correct," he said. It's been a popular falsehood for over a century. The idea has been attributed to two different men. One is American psychologist and educator William James; the other is Einstein himself. James simply stated in an essay called *The Energies of Men* that we only make use of a small part of our possible mental and physical resources. Einstein reputedly used the idea to explain his own intellect in the area of physics. The specific number of 10 percent never came up in either reference though. That makes sense to me. Our brains weigh a meagre three pounds, but these small lumps of flesh hoard 20% of the energy we use. It has to take up a fair amount. Think about it Emma. The brain is active all the time, even when we're asleep. It's responsible not only for what we think we are directing it to do, but for numerous necessary autonomic functions. Heart beats, breathing, temperature regulation, protein building – it goes on and on - they all continue without our conscious awareness, let alone any intent to direct them. It isn't the mystery of unused portions of the brain we should look to for answers. It is the autonomic functions that we are unaware of that may provide clues to connections we are unable to explain otherwise. I expect we will discover these things, or be able to refute them eventually. In other words Emma, it is possible to imagine solutions to currently unsolved enigmas, but just like everyone else, I don't have all the answers. For that, I apologize to you."

"I guess," Emma responded, somewhat deflated. "If only it were possible to find all the answers when you need them, right?"

"Well, you may be on the right track – but not by coming here to see me necessarily. The books you bought today....I have already suggested that at least some of these are not fiction. I expect that at least one, if not all of them, are directly related to your son Anthony, aren't they? At least one was written by a psychologist. Tell me, what treasures did you find in that shop?"

Emma was pleasantly bewildered. This man may claim not to have any more answers than anyone else, but he seemed intuitive, observant, or something Sherlock-ish. She reached into the bag on the chair next to her. "You're close Jahny," she said, pulling them out. "I picked up two overviews – one on Carl Jung, a psychologist as you guessed, and the other on Immanuel Kant, the philosopher. I also picked up a book by Kant."

"The *Critique of Pure Reason* no doubt," said Jahny with a wide smile on his face. "Some good choices... for a beginning."

"For a beginning?" Emma echoed the words with a raised eyebrow. "So you are familiar with these guys?"

"These guys," Jahny began, "are prominent figures in the realm of looking at things differently. If you read them with an open mind and are interested in understanding even just a little more than you do now, then you are on the right track." Jahny closed his eyes for a moment, then reopened them. "Emma, there may be an answer to your earlier question, but at this time, I am unable to say why your son Anthony told you to tell me that he knows who I am."

I don't think he is necessarily referring to me personally. You heard me say that I did what I did the other day because it was a beautiful day, because it is, because everything is. I am a seeker Emma. It is important to me to learn what I can. He may well be woven from similar cloth, so to speak. He too may be a seeker. He sounds like one, at least from the little you have shared about him. Didn't you say he was interested in things more important than money? Perhaps if I learn a little more about him and you learn a little more about me, we will figure out the connection. Remember, everything is connected. He and I may not know one another directly, but there is a recognition of type, or like-kind, that must exist, because we recognize something in ourselves that cannot be unique. It must exist elsewhere as well. We are drawn to it as though it is a missing part of ourselves."

Jahny was breathing more heavily. He leaned back into his pillows. "Emma, could we please continue this conversation later." His body seemed to relax comfortably.

The monitors made no changes Emma would notice. He must be tired. As he had pointed out, our brains take care of a lot more than we are conscious of. His body surely had a few things to work on right now. She pulled a small notebook and a pen from her purse. "Thanks for talking to me today Jahny. I have a good feeling you will still be here for some time. Rest up. I look forward to seeing you again tomorrow."

12

The ranch house was quiet when she returned from the hospital. It was still mid-to late afternoon. Emma stopped in the kitchen first. She pulled a glass from the cupboard while admiring the mycelium décor yet again. It was warmer this afternoon than the day before. She filled the glass with ice, then with some fruit and veggie juice. Bender was nowhere around to impart a pleading look. She brought her drink and bag of books upstairs.

Emma considered nestling into the wicker chair with her treasure, but the room was exceptionally bright this time of day. Another thought arose. She took her books out to the pillowed cubby hole with the circular window in the hallway around the corner. The large tree outside provided shade from the sun. It was perfect. She made herself comfortable amongst the pillows, then brought out her little treasures. Emma flipped through chapters, read a passage for a page or more, stopped to ruminate, then wandered to another. She wanted to acquire a good overview, not attain doctorate-level expertise. Hours slipped away until her head felt full. An emergent understanding began to pattern around the concepts she read. Now it was going to take some contemplation. Her way of learning had always involved focusing, ruminating, reviewing, then ruminating again. Depending on complexity, the formula could be repeated. It always seemed to work best for her. Several pages in all three books were folded-in to mark passages she wanted to revisit. For now, Kant and Jung were going to have to take a rest. She placed the books beside her.

Emma was staring out the window, but only looking through her mind's eye. She pondered the many ideas, phrases and supportive arguments churning through her thoughts. Eventually noticing the distant sound of an approaching vehicle, she adjusted her focus to the road leading up to the house. The long trail of dust behind Enrique's truck reflected the setting sun. If it wasn't already a classic desert shot in a movie scene somewhere, it should be, she thought. Her phone showed 5:34 PM. Emma hadn't seen Enrique all day. If he didn't mind listening, there was much to talk about. Thoughts continued to stir and toss inside her head. There was little chance it would all turn off anytime soon. It could be helpful to ask an opinion. Maybe Enrique wouldn't mind chatting with her about some of it.

Emma had been absorbed all afternoon. She didn't realize how hungry she actually was until just now. She could've had a bite near the hospital, but had been too absorbed by Danielle, the bookstore, Jahny, Anthony, and now Jung and Kant. She hoped Enrique hadn't eaten either. It would be nice to make some supper, then relax, take in her day and share some chat. She gathered her books, hopped down from the cubby and went back to her room. Placing Kant and Jung on the small side table next to the chair, Emma took a quick glance in the mirror, then left the room and made her way downstairs.

Enrique opened the front door and let Bender into the house first. Emma turned the corner at the bottom of the stairs just in time to greet the old dog. It made its way toward her, sluggishly wagging its tail.

"Hey Emma, good to see you. Could you please do me a favour? Actually, could you please do Bender a favour?" Barely waiting for an okay, Enrique asked if she could take Bender's clean dish off the counter and place it in front of the spigot coming out of the wall around the corner. "Bender will take it from there."

Curious, Emma peeked around the corner. Bender's empty food dish sat on a mat below a spigot emerging from the wall a foot above the floor. She reached for the dish on the counter and placed it on the mat next to the food dish under the spigot. As if on cue, Bender slowly sauntered over, tapped his nose on the left side of the spigot and waited. Water began to pour into the dish. When it stopped a neat distance from the top, the old dog began lapping it up. She didn't remember seeing that feature before.

"You were out fairly early today for someone on vacation," Enrique said. "I wouldn't have expected that of any guest." He turned and went back out, letting the screen door close loudly. Bender looked up. "Don't worry boy," Enrique called back. "I'm not going anywhere without you."

Enrique walked back into the house carrying a small box. He left it on the floor in the back room he referred to as the junk stop. "I've been meaning to take that box out of my truck for almost a week," he called out. "Job done," he said, walking back toward the kitchen. "I'm about as thirsty as Bender, but I'm going to have one of those nice cold cokes just waiting for me." He reached into the fridge and pulled out a red can, flipped the top and put it on the counter. A glass was pulled from a row of them sitting ice cold in the freezer. Enrique poured the bubbling liquid into it. He tipped his glass to Emma and Bender, then quickly began drinking before the rising coke slush poured over the side. The sight mirrored any of a million commercial scenes for the product seen by everyone over decades.

"I would have thought you would go for a nice cold beer. It isn't as hot out as it will be in another month or so, but you look like you might have had a busy day. Have you had supper yet? Emma looked down at the dog. What about you Bender?"

"Bender is going to have much the same dinner he always does. I try to make sure he gets the best. It's just part of general maintenance for the old guy. I haven't eaten anything since mid-morning though. Two guests who were supposed to come to the ranch tonight cancelled and rebooked for next week instead. Apparently, they decided to stay a little longer out in Santa Fe. They sound like a couple of retirees enjoying a long vacation where schedules and deadlines no longer matter. I kind of like that about retirement too. Anyway, I bought enough steak and shrimp for four before receiving that news. I was in Victorville picking up a few things when they called."

"Would they be charged a fee for late cancellation then?"

"Of course not. It was just a postponement anyway. I had no other bookings for next week, so no harm done. I'm not out to penny-pinch customers. I want to run a friendly place that will bring back repeat business. Since we rate each other on an app in the first place, I figure it wouldn't be long before a somewhat regular, rotating clientele develops. As we all get to know one another better, it might just work out to be somewhat of a rotating-friends-gathering – a good idea for a solitary guy. It's quiet out here. I don't need the extra income. So as far as the extra food goes today, it won't go to waste. Bender is quietly, but obviously, listening in. Look at him eyeing me now. He's imagining a share of the steak and shrimp I bet. Have you eaten yet Emma?"

"Just before I came downstairs, I realized how hungry I was. It's been a busy day with a few different phases to it. We can talk about it over supper. In the meantime, tell me about your day."

"Okay, I'll get the barbecue going on the porch and prep the steak and shrimp. If you would like to put together a salad or something, we can still chat as we work. This coke's done already. Maybe I will have a beer after all. What about you?"

"No alcohol on an empty stomach, but I may have some wine with dinner. I'll look in the fridge and see what I can put together."

'I try to keep it fairly well stocked. Be as creative as you like." Enrique stepped back out through the screen door and over to the barbecue on the front veranda. "This will take a few minutes to warm up. I'll prep the meat and clean the shrimp." Walking back into the house, Enrique put away the few groceries he brought home. He wiped down the main counter and the surface of the island before placing cutting boards on both. "I'll use this sink to clean the shrimp. You take the island. It has more surface to maneuver on."

Emma crouched down in front of the open fridge, moved items around and scoured for ingredients that would help decide what kind of salad she should make. "So how was your day?"

"My day has been perfect so far. I got up early and went walking out in the desert before it got too hot. I saw a couple of snakes again, both rattlers. It's a sure sign the hotter weather is on its way. I love seeing them. Magnificent creatures. I mentioned the other day that I was interested in the surrounding landscape and what is out there. Sure, I didn't suspect a possible alien might be out there," Enrique said laughing, "but there are a lot of very alien-like life forms that few people would recognize. By the way, I'm not saying I believe that any aliens are here, but one of the medevac guys we met the other night sure does, remember? It may look bleak out in the desert to most people, but not only is it anything but that, there is a lot of history right here under our feet."

"My Dad used to say things like that. He used to like to bring me out to the desert and up to the mountains around here you know. I can't tell you how many times we hiked a large area around Vasquez. On my way up here, I stopped for some ice cream at the old place at the bottom of Longview. I was admiring the Joshua trees and scruffy-looking creosote which is everywhere out here. People walk by them all the time without notice, but my father told me they were at least hundreds of years old."

"Yes, there is a lot of creosote out here. My land is covered in it. And yes, it is very old, older than your father speculated if he was just guessing in the hundreds of years. The oldest known creosote bushes have been dated at just under 12,000 years old. That's much older than the famed sequoia trees a couple hours north of here. It also puts them among some of the oldest living things on this planet, and they aren't the only ones. You just mentioned Joshua trees. They often grow to more than 200 years old. That's not quite creosote longevity, but it is two to three times the current life span of humans. Even the ubiquitous Galetta Grass found in many places out on the Mohave – a mere grass – lives to be about a century old. If your Dad has taught you about desert flora, you may have noticed some of the Buckhorn Cholla along the side of the path the other evening. Some can be found about half way between the ranch house and the spot where we stopped for some stargazing and a chat. It can live somewhere between 800 and 900 years too. Also, some of the Menodora, a flowering plant in the olive family, found in a small canyon at the western end of the property also lives to be about 425 years. East Mohave buckwheat lives for about 700 years. It goes on and on. If these plants could talk, so to speak…think of the human history of this area over that period of time."

"That is fascinating to think about," Emma replied, while rinsing some spinach and lettuce. "It doesn't really matter where we are though, does it? Every environment on the planet must have spectacular features and histories we are unaware of. We are all so busy with our current lives and concerns. It's easy to overlook anything that might have been here before. We even overlook everything that's here right now, often right under our noses. Do you know anyone who could name all the insects they can find in their own backyards – or even in their own house? So, I can see how someone might be interested in probing the secrets of the very place where they live. I can also see how someone might be fascinated with how others might have lived here before too. From what you've mentioned so far Enrique, you seem knowledgeable about the various flora and fauna around here. Do you keep track of what you learn about the plants and creatures on your property?

"I've been pursuing a few strategies. Cataloguing is essential for sure. I keep separate databases for plants, reptiles, mammals, geographical features and even elements found in the sand, soil and rock here. Sixty-four acres might not seem like much if you see this land as barren, at least in comparison with other regions one could own property. Or maybe it seems like a lot of nothing out here in the desert, but it is anything but barren – or a lot of nothing. If you take into account all of the information I seek, there is much to be done. I hope to develop a comprehensive understanding of this place that includes not only an idea of the flora and fauna here now, but what might have been here before. I want to know how this place fits in with the overall ecosystem of this area, both now and through different periods in the past. There may be resources here I'm unaware of too. That's a matter of lesser interest though; I don't think of this place as a source of wealth. It's not about that. It's more of a field of discovery, and a place to pursue a multitude of interests. You've already seen my little music sanctuary. That's only one aspect of my interest in sound. There is a whole world to be discovered in the soundscapes to be found just on this property. That, however, is a whole other subject, and an interesting one too, but we won't get into it now.

Getting back to the age of creosote really begins to put some things into perspective, doesn't it? Imagine this Emma! Extinct animals like the sabretooth cats or ground sloths that once lived here could easily have been the animals who stamped ancient seeds into the ground just in passing. Some of those very seeds might be the creosote plants we walk by out here without even noticing them. Thoughts focused like that show how easily one thing is connected to another, and so on. The incredible complexity of 'what is' seems to occupy more and more of my thinking as time goes on. Such thinking certainly found fertile ground while I was working at NASA. Learning about what is on my land and what it all means has added to that immensely. I love that I'm old enough to have been around for a while to learn a few things. It is even better having some free time to ponder any complexities I might choose to focus on. Maybe one day I will achieve the status of being un anciano sabio, or in English, a wise old man. The view from here is most intriguing."

"The complexity of 'what is'... Funny you should say that Enrique," Emma interjected. "That's exactly what I need – someone who tends to see connections between things that aren't readily noticeable to most of us every day."

"Most people don't care about anything that doesn't seem to pertain to their current, everyday lives, interests, immediate needs.... or often, just their entertainment," Enrique responded. "We're a shallow bunch generally...and speaking of immediate needs and shallow thinking, let me get these steaks on the bar-b. We can chat when we sit down. I'm looking forward to hearing why you need someone who sees connections. You aren't beginning to make similar connections that medevac guy thinks he's established, are you?"

Emma laughed now. "I don't think so, but yeah, let's get dinner together, then chat. It's been quite a day." She managed to put together a respectable spinach salad with the ingredients she had found, sliced, chopped and rinsed. Dishes and silverware were already set on the table by the time Enrique announced a two-minute warning that steaks were almost ready. Emma asked him if the contents of the wine rack in the dining room were available for selection. She knew some people were collectors who reserved openings for special occasions. With a resounding "of course" in response, Emma proceeded reading labels on individual bottles. Red with steak she recalled, choosing a three-year-old Hungarian bottle.

A few moments later, Enrique came through the door holding up a plate with sizzling hot steaks. Bender came drooling in tow behind him. Once everything was on the table, the two sat down. Enrique opened the bottle and poured just a dash into Emma's wine glass. She lifted the glass, waved it slowly in front of her lips, catching the delicate, fruity 'nose' of the wine. Enrique waited for the customary nod of approval before filling her glass. He lifted what remained of his beer, clicked her glass with it, and toasted the evening. "To an interesting account of your day and the possibility of solving complexities," he said.

"Complexities," Emma slowly pondered aloud in repetition. "Hmmm, the very reason I came here was to relax, to regroup so to speak," she emphasized. "It was to avoid complexities and ponder possibilities instead. That hasn't turned out to be the case so far, but I can't say that's a bad thing. I'm not sure what to think of it all. That's why it comes across as complex I guess," she said, laughing a little more nervously this time. "But let me tell you about my day."

As the two sat enjoying dinner, Emma began to recount her adventures. She thought she would backtrack a bit first. That would explain her disappearance at the hospital while the group were discussing the stranger. Emma connected her decision to help the stranger with the disconcerting, but intriguing phone call she had from her son Anthony. This piqued Enrique's interest. He recalled much of what Emma had shared about Anthony on their hike before discovering the stranger, and then afterward in the car when they were driving back to the hospital. He couldn't help but think about Kevin, the medevac guy who was so intrigued about the stranger. Enrique had just made a joking reference to Kevin believing in aliens a few minutes earlier. Now he was wondering if Emma might really be following Kevin's train of thought. He didn't comment further, but just listened.

"I couldn't help but feel that there was some kind of eerie connection between Anthony and the guy we found out in the desert," she revealed. "It was weird. It really impacted me. Maybe some of what Kevin said did influence me somewhat, but I couldn't say that I believe this guy is an alien, even if something about him is," she said. "I actually met him today Enrique. You wouldn't think he was on death's door. He was intuitive, intelligent and a lot of other things I couldn't quite put my finger on, so to speak."

Enrique remained quiet and let her continue.

"He almost seemed like someone I've known for a long time, almost like someone you know you can trust or have confidence in. I keep saying 'almost' because, like I said, you just can't put your finger on what it was. He seemed ancient, yet contemporary. There was no doubt that he was highly knowledgeable about a wide range of topics, yet he seemed simple in his ways. No, that's not quite right either. It felt, yes, that's it. It actually felt, not seemed. It felt… like he was someone or something you've never encountered before, but still knew quite well. That might be an alien quality of sorts, I don't know. He certainly didn't seem, or feel dangerous in any way. In fact, he almost seemed fatherly or grandfatherly, if that makes any sense."

There was a brief silence before Enrique spoke. He was clearly mulling over Emma's words. "That's an interesting description Emma, but give me more. What did he say to you that gave off such an awe-inspiring impression? What made him so interesting? It must have been more than just a feeling. Did you find out his name? Why did he do what he did that night out in the desert? How did he know that spot was on my land? I'm surprised he isn't dead! I thought he had ingested a fatal dose. Isn't that what we were told? I can't help but think he must have frailties that outweigh anything you are describing. Remember what he tried to do Emma." Enrique sliced a piece of the meat on his plate and held it on his fork. "I didn't think anything could interest me more than this steak for supper, but you have my attention now. Please continue." He smiled and then chewed that slice with great satisfaction, but continued listening. Bender just stared up in quiet, expectant admiration beside his chair.

Emma sipped her wine and gently placed the glass back on the table. She appreciated Enrique's light-hearted response. It encouraged her to relax and say what came to mind. Hypothesizing as you go can quickly lead to false premises. She was still formulating ideas about everything that had happened over the past day and a half. Coming out with whatever came to mind might help. "Let me start at the beginning. It seems like a lot has happened."

Emma began with the moment she slipped away from the conversation about the stranger at the hospital. Based on the doctor's dire report, she had a sudden impulse to act. She knew what she wanted to do, but not exactly why. The possibility of a connection between this guy and her son weighed heavily on her mind. Anthony's call while they were on their way back to the hospital had jolted her. Emma divulged setting up coverage for the stranger's med bills, at least temporarily. Admitting some doubt about any real connection, she conceded seeking an opportunity to understand her son a little better. She suspected that if nothing else, her son and the stranger may well share a similar diagnosis. She had no idea how her impulsive act might help, but she was already involved just by finding the stranger. Then there was Anthony's call, the doctor's predictions, the discussions with Danielle, and Jahny himself. It all added to the lingering idea that this was all somehow significant. Emma did feel strongly about one thing. It would all play out sooner than later.

Emma then told Enrique about her wonderful experience down the Rabbit Hole. It had to be one of the best-kept secrets in L.A. County. She smiled emphatically while describing her sense of the place and her multifaceted experience there. Then she became serious again. Emma shared her first thoughts about Jahny. She recalled how images of Jesus and the Maharishi Mahesh Yogi came to mind. What subliminal connections were occurring there? Emma laughed, recalling her impression. "Would you believe that when I walked into his room, he seemed to be asleep, but after I spent some time looking out the window, he suddenly spoke, softly, referring to me by name? That was unusual enough, but as he spoke, he began developing assumptions about my reason for being there. He even speculated on what books I had in the bag from the bookstore, why I had purchased them, and the connection they had with my visit. It was unsettling, but not uncomfortable, if that makes sense. The guy was Sherlock incarnate."

"So, this guy was not only conscious, but alert enough to have meaningful conversation? Asombroso! Amazing! If I ever get a serious diagnosis though, think I'll get a second opinion. Maybe even a third one. That sounds like the most unlikely outcome based on what we were told by the doctor – and that was literally only 15 hours or so ago. ¡Increíble! Unbelievable. He must have had means to learn some info about you beforehand. What about the psychiatrist you spoke to? Did she give him a heads-up?"

"Well, yes. At least she could have. I thought of that too. She said she had just seen him before I ran into her at the elevator in the hospital. She told me he's still a John Doe. The stranger refers to himself as Jahny. It's all very unusual. Even Danielle, the psychiatrist, was quite intrigued by him Enrique. She's cautious about labeling him without knowing him, but may never have a chance to do so. The doctors are apparently astounded and have no explanation for the current situation. By all accounts, it's an uncommon situation with a curious person at the center of it."

"Your food is getting cold Emma. Mine is already digesting." Looking satisfied, Enrique put down his knife and fork, a conspicuous sign to his good friend Bender that there would be no treats coming off the table. He picked up the bottle of Hungarian wine Emma had opened, but then put it back down again. The beer he finished was too good for just one. Enrique got up and reached for another cold one out of the fridge. Emma enjoyed a few bites of steak and salad before picking up the conversation again. Bender silently moved over to her side of the table.

"I came back here almost three hours ago now," Emma said, looking up at a clock on the dining room wall. "I've been glancing through those books I bought at that cool little bookstore today. Have you been in there?"

"No, I haven't, but it sounds unique, and I probably should go check it out just for the hell of it. Over the past few years, I have been buying eBooks. I've got a virtual library on my Kindle – and the whole thing is smaller and weighs less than most printed books. I carry it around with me everywhere. If I have to wait for anything anywhere, I like to have my reading material. So tell me about the books you picked up today." Enrique took a swig of his beer.

"Do you know who Immanuel Kant and Carl Jung are?"

"I know one's a famous psychologist and the other a philosopher, but don't ask me to tell you what specific ideas either of them had. Is there any connection between them?"

"I can't say I knew any more than that about them either, except my son will often talk about Kant and his *Critique of Pure Reason*. I wouldn't say Anthony's obsessed by him, but he has brought him up several times over the past couple of years. I should know more about Kant because of it, but admittedly, I wasn't paying close attention. I guess I was just indulging him as he has very few people he talks to these days. For what little it's worth, it provides an outlet for him. The Jung connection simply came up when I was talking to Danielle. She encouraged me to visit with Jahny, but asked me to wait until after he had a bit of a nap. That's why I went to the bookstore. While there, I sought some information on both of these guys. I bought Kant's book because of Anthony, but picked up a book about each of them to get an overview of their stuff. An old university trick, I guess. I want to try to make some sense of all this, not digest a semester's worth of information and analysis.

"Anything interesting?" Enrique was enjoying the beer and the conversation.

"There is, but I can't pretend I've learned everything there is to know about them and their ideas. Both can be very abstract. Over the last couple of hours, I've been scanning passages, jotting a few notes and bending page corners to remind me which ones I want to go back to. I was just mulling over what I'd read when you came driving up to the house. From what I can ascertain so far, Jung has made many contributions to analytical psychology. He was a contemporary of Freud, but his reputation and ideas have endured much more favourably. He has become best known in current modern culture for his concepts of synchronicity and the collective unconscious. Big words and vague meanings I know, but give me a minute. I think I get this part at least."

Enrique was still sipping his beer, listening intently. He couldn't remember that last time he enjoyed a good dinner and intriguing conversation. He was also impressed. Emma had apparently dug right in to the information she claimed to be only scanning. She began her explanation.

"If we were to stop and think about it, most of us would agree that reality is a series of causes and effects. One event causes other things to occur. For example, I hit a ball with a bat. The force of the bat redirects the ball to follow a new trajectory. Simple enough, right? For Jung, that exists, but might also include an acausal connection to other events we perceive around us. That is, one where we can't really determine the cause of an event or circumstance. Such acausal events that don't seem to have a cause are conspicuously manifested in the form of coincidences. Coincidences suggest some meaning is attached, but leaves one to guess what that meaning actually is. You perceive a connection, but can't quite formulate it. An example of this might be running into someone you know in an unusual place in a large city. Then the same thing happens a few days or a maybe a week later. That kind of coincidence might spark the idea that it means something, even if you can't figure out what it is."

"Yeah, so?"

"Well, it would be easy to think that this guy was a quack and possibly the reason why often enough, all psychologists are referred to as quacks, but get this Enrique: Carl Jung was a friend of Albert Einstein and had him over for dinner on several occasions. Despite what people might have thought originally, no one ever refers to Einstein as a quack. Everyone knows he came up with the well-accepted theories of general and special relativity. The guy revolutionized our scientific understanding. Well, at the time when he was still developing his first theory of relativity, Einstein and Carl Jung were discussing the topic. It occurred to Jung that there might be a psychic conditionality to the relativity of time as well as space."

"What do you mean psychic conditionality?"

"Well, don't think of psychic as a person who makes sense of things that you are not able to. Instead, think of it as a mental condition whereby you recognize a coincidence and afford it some meaning, even if you don't have evidence of that meaning other than the coincidence itself. To make a long story short, Jung believed that life is not a series of random events, but is a kind of expression of a deeper order to what reality is. When you think of it, Mister-guy-who-used-to-work-at-NASA, that isn't all that far-fetched, is it? Even kids at school learn that what we see all

111

around us is illusionary. We are actually made up of subatomic particles which we can't see with the naked eye. These subatomic particles constitute our very being and that of everything around us. That speaks loudly of an underlying structure to the reality apparent to us. There, I said it. I think that makes some sense, doesn't it?"

"Okay, so what you are saying is that nothing really is as it seems, but again, so what?"

"Well, that suggests that there are lots of things we may be unaware of, or have difficulty tapping into. For example, people think of radio as a recent technological development, and it is, but as you know, radio waves were around long before humanity or any other life form evolved."

"That's right," Enrique interjected. "Heinrich Rudolph Hertz didn't discover electromagnetic waves, which includes radio waves, until the 1880s." Several people came across the phenomenon before that, but were not quite able to formulate what it was. Throughout the 1800s, there were attempts to understand the connection between electricity and magnetism. James Clerk Maxwell put it all together in a theory of electromagnetic radiation only a decade or so before Hertz actually discovered it. Things moved fast from there. Marconi was on it by the 1890s and created the first device for transmitting waves. By Christmas Eve, 1906, a Canadian guy named Reginald Fessenden became the first person to make a public broadcast using wireless technology."

"You're a hardcore science guy all around, not just by profession, aren't you? I didn't know any of that, of course. That's just it. Everyone takes this stuff for granted these days, but until less than 150 years ago, it would have been considered magic. Humans often jump to supernatural answers for natural phenomena when they don't understand something. That's why this whole idea that there are aliens may just be a modern substitute for previous guesses about unknowns – like divine entities, gods. It's a way of explaining something that we can't explain otherwise. So getting back to Jahny…What if this guy has somehow managed to tap into a previously unknown aspect of humanity that most of us are unaware of just yet – sort of like an adult capability which children would still have to grow into to understand? Maybe this guy and others like him are advance specimens on the evolutionary road toward human possibility."

"Whoa, whoa, whoa Emma. It's one thing to think of this guy as an anomaly, something unusual, but contemplating the idea that he might be an advanced specimen, a pioneer in human possibility, is quite a stretch. It would have to be based on a lot more than what I've heard so far.

Also, if that were true, a guy like that would be unlikely to want to do himself in as he tried to do, don't you think? It doesn't make sense to me."

"I don't know Enrique. There is something about this guy that's really different, even if I can't put my finger on it. It's like intuition spilling over the brim into something else that isn't quite clarified. Maybe this comparison makes it a little clearer: It is like following a road, even though you don't know where it is taking you, but you know there has to be a destination at the end." Emma took another sip of her wine. Enrique had already drained his second beer.

Emma's cell phone dinged. She glanced at the popup text. "My son Anthony," she said. "Two seconds. Let me get this." She clicked in her pin and opened the text. She seemed frozen, even in shock. Her face paled.

"Everything okay? Emma? What does the text say?"

Emma looked at Enrique and then looked back down at the text again. "Enrique, I don't understand how this is possible. I haven't spoken or texted with Anthony since last night. What he said to me then surprised me enough, but listen to this: 'Hi Mum, sorry to bug you again so soon. I can't remember if you had told me last night that you met a caveman, or some reference like that, or if I just dreamed it. I couldn't sleep until early this morning and slept most of my day away. Anyway, if that doesn't make sense, which I expect it won't, don't bother to get back to me. I probably dreamed it. Hope you're having a good time.' Oh my goodness Enrique. This is weird. Would you consider coming to the hospital with me tomorrow? I would really like your opinion about this guy."

113

13

"Good evening there old guy, how are you doing?" Kevin turned the combination to his locker in the medevac staff room and placed a small backpack inside. It was in fact a re-purposed storeroom for the two or three people who might be in there at any given time. A small table against the back wall featured a coffee machine and a few stacks of paper cups sitting on top. An old-style television hung from a ceiling mount to the left of the door. With just three chairs, half a dozen lockers, a small sink and mirror, it was home for the medevacs on call several hours a night.

Darnell wheeled his chair around to face the table. "Evening, Kevin. Want a coffee? This pot's fresh."

"Yes please," Kevin responded promptly. "Thanks. You're a good man Darnell. Have you checked up on our alien friend tonight? Do you know if he is still alive?"

"Haven't given it any thought my man. I did say a prayer for the poor soul last night. His prognosis seemed pretty dim. It's out of our hands. Whatever happens, happens. It's in the Lord's hands now. Comes with the job. You know we have to leave work at work. Medevacs need to go from one emergency to the next. It's our professional responsibility. That kind of baggage can get heavy very quickly. You have to hand it over to the doctors when you bring them in. Then you let it go. It's a medical relay race. Eventually, it becomes second nature. You do your part. Then others do theirs. Tomorrow's another day."

Kevin was only expecting a 'yes' or 'no.' He had no intention of letting John Doe go yet. "It seemed impossible that he was alive after everything we heard. I suppose stranger things have happened. You know Darnell, last night after you left, I stayed for a bit to talk to Enrique, the guy that gave us a lift back. In the car, we were told he owned the bed and breakfast out in the desert where our evacuee was found. Well, get this. He only just recently got into that business. He used to work at JPL. I guess I kind of got a little excited about that and couldn't help myself from asking some questions."

"Haha, of course you couldn't Kevin. Did you ask him if he's seen any little green men? Does he know Captain Kirk? This ought to be better than the TV I've been watching." Darnell turned down the volume. "Let's hear it young Skywalker. What did NASA man have to say?"

"Anything he has to say must be better than anything you watch on TV Darnell. What were you watching when I walked in? The 700 Club again? Listen, this guy Enrique was pretty interesting. He brought me down to Earth a little too. Made me think a little harder about stuff I've been reading in forums or watching on TV, YouTube and so on. But 'down to Earth' doesn't mean he eradicated my belief in extraterrestrial visitors. I wouldn't expect him to believe in little green men or Star Trek scenarios without some kind of solid evidence, but he did tell me something interesting. He said there is proof of life in space. In fact Darnell, get this: There may have been aliens here on Earth for over half a billion years already."

"No surprise there my friend. Angels walk among us. You don't take my faith seriously, but scripture does reference extraterrestrials somewhere. I just can't remember the specific verses off-hand. I don't buy into a lot of the modern ideas about aliens, but that doesn't mean I don't think something unusual is possible. I'm open to ideas, but prefer to base my beliefs on something solid. The good book is it."

"Put your good book aside for a minute Darnell. Listen, Enrique kind of played a little joke on me last night, but there was something in it. When I asked him what do people at NASA really think about aliens, he leaned in toward me and spoke softly. Then he asked me if I really thought it would be a good idea for NASA to let the world know what they think. When I thought about it, I realized he had a point. He may even be right. Just imagine what it would be like everywhere on the planet if there was an announcement on television that we had made first contact. That might even bump Trump from the headlines! It would really be something. But then what? Some panic would probably set in, and to what end?"

"Well, there has been a precedent for that kind of thing. You may be a little too young to know about this – we both are actually, but on Halloween about 80 years ago or so, actor/producer Orson Welles did a radio show presenting H.G. Wells' book, *The War of the Worlds*. If you know the story, then you know it wouldn't be so easy for aliens to just come here. Unforeseen complications could arise. Orson Welles decided to tell it in the form of news broadcasts over the radio. Although the show was announced as an adaptation of the book, many listeners did not hear or pay attention to that important fact. Many panicked. It was a well-known incident among the general public for decades."

"Wells' War of the Worlds just became a new television series this past Fall," Kevin said while nodding his head. "I'm familiar with the story, and vaguely remember hearing about the Orson Welles incident. Depending on circumstances, there would be pros and cons to informing the public. If there was imminent danger, the public needs the opportunity to react accordingly to protect themselves, their families, and maybe their property. If there is some interplanetary dialogue occurring that has the potential to be mutually beneficial, then the public should be in on it. That's a whole other topic though Darnell. We can get into it another time if you like. Are you interested in hearing what Enrique said last night?"

"I'm all ears. What did NASA-Man tell you?" Darnell enjoyed the usual banter. Downtime can be lengthy some nights. They often engaged over news items on the tube. The odd time they watched and discussed documentaries. This conversation was more promising than most already.

"NASA-Man?" Kevin couldn't help but smile. He usually enjoyed the banter with Darnell as well. "Okay, NASA-Man said this. Question first though. Have you ever heard of tardigrades?"

Darnell erupted in laughter. "Tardy grades? Hell yeah, I used to get them in school all the time when I was a kid. Catholic school you know."

Kevin was laughing too. That only half-made sense. "Tardy grades. I can see why! Just listen for a minute. This stuff is interesting." Darnell was still chuckling, but Kevin continued.

"These tardigrades are microscopic creatures. They can actually be seen, even under a cheap microscope Darnell. They were discovered a few hundred years ago. Apparently, they've been studied extensively since then. They're also known as water bears. Sounds cute, but these things are super resilient to extreme temperatures and conditions. You like watching nature shows Darnell. You've probably heard of them before, but just don't remember. When I read up on them at home this morning, I learned the water bears reference is common amongst school kids. So they're no secret. It doesn't matter whether you've heard of them or not, they're real. Listen to this. They can not only live in volcanic vents at very high temperatures, but have also been found in Antarctica. They have been found in the upper reaches of the atmosphere too. The Russians have even found them on the outside of the International Space Station. These things can survive radiation! Now that's crazy shit! You don't have to believe me Darnell. Research it yourself."

"I probably will. You sure you didn't get your info on Fox? It's important to know your sources you know."

Kevin was well-seasoned by Darnell's jabs and jokes. He ignored them. "Being a hard-core Christian Darnell, I know you have doubts about how old the Earth is, but let me share this with you. Enrique says that the fossil record shows that your 'tardy-grades' have been around for half a billion years. The period is known as the Cambrian. It was a time when all of a sudden, life

116

forms appeared in the fossil record. Now that might have happened simply because we haven't found earlier fossils of these life forms yet, or…" Kevin paused to let his point sink in. "Or," he said again, "maybe life forms from somewhere else survived the journey through space. And maybe," he emphasized, "Earth is only one of many planets seeded by life forms like this."

"Well that's a good story Kevin," Darnell said, "but the sudden appearance of life in the fossil record doesn't prove your tardigrades infiltrated it."

"You're right. Enrique said as much himself. He strongly cautioned me to stick to the evidence," Kevin conceded. "It really has me thinking about all this. I wish I could have pursued studies in this field, but I'm probably just not smart enough."

"You were probably just a lazy student in grade school like I was. Weren't you an expert in 'tardy-grades' when you were a kid too?" Darnell poured himself another coffee. "You ready for a second one yet, or have you been too busy talking to drink that one?"

"Wait," Kevin interjected. "You don't need another coffee, do you? You've probably drank a pot already. "What do you say we find out what's going on with Spaceman?"

"You go ahead. If I don't have one more coffee, I will be a spaceman on the job tonight. You go find out and tell me all about it when you come back on time!"

"I think I'll do just that," retorted Kevin. "Relax, we still have almost half-an-hour. See you shortly Darnell." Kevin was out the door. It wasn't far from Emergency. Kevin knew many of the doctors, nurses and support staff on the unit. They were probably busy as usual, He would find a support staff to tell him what happened to the spaceman. He spied a long-time colleague on shift behind one of the 'Emergency Area Registration' windows. It was free. Perfect!

Dan looked up just as Kevin was approaching the window. "Hey Dude, don't tell me you actually came in before Darnell tonight."

"You kidding? He's on his second pot of coffee. How are you Danny?"

"Okay I guess. Off in half an hour. It's been busy tonight. You might wish today was your day off."

"I don't mind being busy. Makes the time go quickly. Besides, the job's interesting. The guy Darnell and I brought in last night is a good example. He's a John Doe, or was anyway. Speaking of him, do you know if he's still here?"

117

"Do you mean, is he still alive? Believe it or not, he is. Staff have been commenting. He's been awake on and off, last I heard. He's not in Emerge any more. They needed the room, so he's up on six. Even with his numbers through the roof, he's more stable than expected. Crazy, huh?"

"Yeah, crazy," Kevin repeated. Last night they said he'd be transferred from here if he survived because he's a John Doe. So, what's he doing upstairs?"

"Well get this. Someone has picked up his tab, at least for now. I heard the person doesn't even know him. Crazy times too. What makes you ask about him now? Don't you medevacs move on from one day to the next?"

"Sounds like you've been talking to Darnell. A stranger picked up his tab? Hmm, that's interesting. I can't stop thinking about the guy. I guess his case just stuck with me. Could you check where they sent him? If possible, I'd like to stop by and see how he's doing. Can you give me a room number there Buddy?"

Dan punched a few keys on his computer. "610 Kev. You better get going. Aren't you and Darnell on at ten?"

"Shift change is at ten, right? You're probably off in 20 minutes, no? Have a good night man. Thanks. See you soon." Kevin turned and walked toward the nearest elevator. "610," he muttered to himself.

14

It was quiet on the ward upstairs. Visiting hours were long over. Although recognizing his uniform, the desk nurse said nothing until Kevin introduced himself. When he stated his purpose, it prompted a smile. It was unusual, but kind of him to follow up. Her first instinct was to ask if he knew the man, but quickly remembered the patient was a John Doe. She glanced at the register, then the clock.

"Last nurse to check on him noted he was sleeping just over 20 minutes ago." She scanned notes from the last number of rounds. "He has been doing that on and off all day. Vitals are still far from stable. His situation isn't encouraging. Are you just coming on shift at ten?"

"Yeah, I don't have much time. Just wanted to check in. This guy generated some excitement last night. Things weren't looking good. I was surprised to find out downstairs that he was up on a ward."

"You don't have much time. Go ahead. He's down the hall in 610. Blood sample nurse is making her rounds. She may have awakened him for you. Good luck."

Kevin thanked her as he walked away. 610 was almost at the end of the hall. He walked in to find John Doe sitting up in bed. He seemed to be looking toward the doorway in expectation, perhaps for the blood nurse. Kevin gathered he must have heard footsteps approaching. Perhaps he had interrupted the stranger gazing out the window. The stranger spoke before Kevin even had a chance to introduce himself.

"No doubt you are a friend, or at least an acquaintance of Emma's? Your uniform suggests you are not the companion and proprietor of the bed and breakfast where she is staying. Ah, I see you are ambulance staff. You probably met me just the other day then." The stranger had a subtle smile on his face, clearly awaiting a response.

Intrigued, Kevin responded slowly. "Hello. That was unanticipated," he muttered in a slow voice. "How are you?" The stranger simply nodded. "Yes, Emma," Kevin continued. "Well, I can't really say I know her. We spoke on our way back to hospital from the police station after answering some questions about our encounter with you. It was a short ride though. Not much time to really get acquainted. Do you know Emma? She gave no indication..."

"Emma was here early this afternoon," the stranger responded promptly. "When we spoke, she told me she had some conversation with others about the situation. Given various questions she asked me, it seems reasonable to expect that your conversation with her was similar. Our visit wasn't long, but I enjoyed speaking to her. Prior to her arrival, a doctor gave me some background. That's the extent of it. I couldn't say we know one another either."

"No, I guess not. I can't say I expected to see her again," Kevin put forward. "I also wouldn't have expected her to come back here again, but now I'm curious. Did she ask you if you knew her son?"

"Introductions first. May I ask your name good sir?"

"Kevin. My name is Kevin." He walked toward the bed to shake the stranger's hand. "And you?"

The man weakly shook Kevin's hand, then motioned him to take a chair. "Everyone here knows me as Jahny," he said, extending the 'ah' to invoke a common reference to Nicholson in *The Shining*. "As a matter of fact, she did. She was hoping to find some clarity on a situation involving her son. You became familiar with that situation in just a short car ride?"

"Probably much less familiar than you are. Actually…not really," Kevin conceded. "I happened to be there when her son phoned her. She expressed some concern afterward, that's it. I can't say I know much more than that. I'm not here because of any conversation with Emma."

"Interesting. Then you are here to witness the spectacle…to see if I have attained the impossible?" Jahny raised an eyebrow.

"The impossible?" Kevin waited for clarification.

"Cheating death Kevin! It sounds like my condition is perplexing. Perhaps staff are making wagers. Are there odds? It doesn't matter. Whatever their opinions, everyone is fascinated by death, especially cheating it under impossible circumstances. It's the stuff of action movies, isn't it? The thing is, I haven't cheated death. If anything, I do believe that it has cheated me."

Kevin thought about that for a moment. A simple revelation took root. Despite all the possibilities he had considered, one had evaded him. Or perhaps he had evaded it by fitting the circumstances neatly into his own little theory. Could it really have been just that, an attempt at death? He grasped at earlier assumptions. They still had merit, he thought, but doubt set in.

"I'm feeling a little foolish now," Kevin said with a smile. "Maybe a little confused. You seem to be doing much better than your prognosis. I'm happy for you. Hopefully, you'll get through this." He raised his hands to acknowledge a miscalculation. "I apologize for my intrusion Jahny. I truly wish you all the best." Kevin got up and turned to leave.

"Why do you feel foolish? Did you come to check up on me? Or did you come because you had a question of your own? Perhaps it is quite different than Emma's. There is nothing wrong with that. Certainly no need to feel foolish. If you have a minute, please sit down. If I can answer your question, I will."

Kevin slowly stopped, turned back around and looked at Jahny. He hesitated, not sure what to do. Hell, he thought. What have I got to lose? He slowly sat down again. Here he was, face to face with the stranger. It could be an epic moment. It could be the opportunity of his lifetime. He had imagined all kinds of possibilities. He had drawn arguments from several sources he had read, watched, or listened to. Now, here he was. They were alone. There was no one else to hear his question. The stranger already stated he would answer. This could be tremendously enlightening. It could also be frustratingly disappointing. Or it might ultimately prove to be a hopelessly futile endeavor. Even if this guy just ended up laughing at him, Kevin had to find out. He wanted to know. He looked at the clock. Time was short. It was now, or possibly never. Say something!

"Well, first, is your name really Jahny? I understand you were a John Doe at admittance."

"Why should identification be important to you? Does it make any difference to the real question you came to ask?"

"Not enough for me to pursue it." Kevin looked at the stranger, then out the window. Jahny waited patiently. "Jahny, does the word 'Oumuamua' mean anything to you? Does it ring a bell? What about 21/Borisov, a more recent example?"

Kevin suddenly did feel foolish, realizing that Oumuamua and 21/Borisov were names given to space objects by earth observers. If the stranger really were an alien, these monikers would mean nothing.

"Ring a bell? A recent example of what? Is this something I should be remembering?"

"Okay," Kevin said slowly, gathering his thoughts. "A year or so ago, I read a news article referring to a paper published in the reputable science journal, Astrophysical Journal Letters. The paper was written by two Harvard scientists. One of them is well known for accomplishments in his field. In fact, this Oumuamua is apparently the first major interstellar object we have detected coming through our solar system. The astronomer who discovered it through a telescope in Hawaii

121

gave it its Hawaiian name. 'Oumuamua' means 'scout.' Anyway, these Harvard researchers," Kevin said, emphasizing Harvard, "have raised the possibility that this object could be an extraterrestrial probe. 21/Borisov is the second, and most recent, interstellar object to fly through our solar system. I like to keep up on space news. It's fascinating."

Kevin hoped to detect any clue on Jahny's face indicating interest. He gathered his courage to continue. "You aren't the only person this hospital medevac unit has been called out to evacuate from a remote location," he began. "I was on one of the other calls. Neither of you had any I.D. Furthermore, neither of you seemed to have a means of getting out to the locations where you were found – not without basic supplies. You didn't even have any water with you! Also, I checked. The third person brought in by another team from our unit said circumstances with their patient were the same."

There, Kevin had come out with it, but refrained from mentioning everything flitting through his mind now. He was unsure whether to continue, or to wait and listen. What exactly was he hoping to hear?

"So, are you asking me if I am an alien?" Jahny was smiling, almost beaming now.

"Yeah, I guess I am," Kevin stated with some determination. "Yes I am. I suppose I'm asking if you're somehow linked to specific events – like our detection of Oumuamua and 21/Borisov. There could have been others that we didn't detect too, maybe many. The three of you found in the desert were at different locations. They also happened at different times, but maybe close enough to be connected. Maybe you three were on a mission, or on separate, but related missions and had to abort. At least, it could explain the suicide attempts, two of which were successful... I suppose I should tell you that the other two are dead. They didn't survive circumstances very similar to your own. All I am saying Jahny, is that I am acutely interested in knowing. In fact, it has practically been a lifelong interest. I don't work for the government. I am no threat to you in any way. I am simply someone who wants to know."

Kevin gained some confidence and was emboldened. He might as well go for it all now. "Listen, I know... Shit, everybody knows! We're in trouble here on Earth. It isn't that difficult to see. The state of the world is crazy. I come from an average family, just like most people. Things have changed a lot over the past few generations. My grandparents grew up with a good dose of hardship before living through World War II. They emerged from all of that to work hard in a place where working hard meant you could have a decent life. From what I understand, things

122

couldn't have been better than they were in the first couple decades after the war. Then it all began to change. New technologies and new ideas emerged. Hell, that's become a daily occurrence these days. Perhaps it isn't change that's causing all the problems, just the accelerated rate of change. Even younger people like me can remember times when things were very different than they are right now. Confidence is at an all-time low. People's sense of trust, even in things they once trusted unquestioningly, has diminished significantly. Most people have come to see a system that's rigged against them. Machines and algorithms replace people in many sectors of the workforce now. Anxiety and alarm are setting in. People see a useless class emerging in modern society. That petrifies them. Many things scare them. People are at each other's throats these days. There is literally a mass shooting in this country almost every day now. Our institutions, and much of what we once collectively believed, is unraveling. People are looking for something, someone to believe in, and something, anything to make it right. People see that we have been lied to. We've been promised better over and over again – probably throughout history, but certainly since the advent of media. Many people see all of this and feel like enough is enough. It has reached the boiling point. Damn, I voted for that idiot in the White House with many of these things in mind back in '16, but it is clear that things are much worse than they were. There was plenty of talk about draining the swamp, but in just over three years, we've produced the greatest swamp monster ever seen in this country. The biggest liar we have ever elected has created and stoked a culture of total misinformation. People don't know what to believe any more. They have no idea of who, or what, to look to for some semblance of stability in this world-in-constant-flux scenario. We all know what fake news is now, but not so many people have any idea of how to distinguish what is true or real from what isn't. Furthermore, the public has been more than well-aware of how many classified documents are kept by governments and corporations alike. If it isn't false information, it's withheld information. That is why anything and everything has become possible in the minds of various segments of the population. Conspiracy theories abound. Within that context Jahny, could anything I might ask you about be all that outrageous?"

There was a prolonged silence. Then Jahny spoke calmly. "You haven't spoken about anything remotely foolish. It's good to air things out when the opportunity arises." He smiled reassuringly. "You know Kevin, if I were an alien of some kind, there might very well be much to discuss. In fact, I agree with you. If I were an alien, I could see how Earth's inhabitants might have much to worry about. This planet is coming to a crossroads. There are many possibilities, but

123

various outcomes may emerge. Numerous crises are gaining intensity. Nonetheless, these matters are no longer my concern."

"No longer your concern," Kevin asked? "You know, I spent a short stint in the armed forces before entering this career in civilian life. That sounds like you could be referring to an aborted mission Jahny. You know, we've been referring to you as the stranger – not just because you're a John Doe, but because of your very strange circumstances. I repeat, very strange circumstances. So tell me. If you are from here, why is it no longer your concern?"

"My present circumstances dictate a very short period of concern for matters of any kind. My 'mission,' as you put it, is over. Let's get back to your actual question. If you want truth Kevin, then hear it in the form of facts, particulars, realities. If you consider me alien, then realign, or 'tweak' your reference to be more accurate. That is, less like an alien, and more like an alien spaceship of sorts. Hear me out. An organism of my size and weight has about 100 trillion cells giving shape to what you see as me -- just as an organism of your size and weight has about the same number of cells giving shape to what I see as you. Yet, interestingly enough, only about 10 trillion cells – only 10 percent of 'us' – make up what you or I would consider to be ourselves. The other 90 percent consists of bacteria, fungi, viruses and other microorganisms. We are conglomerations that could easily be expressed in similar terms to an old biblical reference to demons: 'We are legion.' When we think of ourselves in these terms, we are all aliens. So my answer to you on that point then is: Of course, an unambiguous, indisputable, and very explicit yes! Take it as you will."

Jahny did not give Kevin time to respond. "Earth has always been a tumultuous place, just as any planet harbouring life would be. Life is always adapting to ongoing change. Long before Homo Sapiens even existed, numerous species of plants, fungus, protists, archaea, bacteria, insects and countless animal lifeforms came about, and existed for long periods of time. Then they exited their stage in Earth's history. Since life began, life forms either changed and adapted to mutable conditions, or they went extinct. There have even been what we refer to as other intelligent species, although it is unclear how we happen to be in any position to determine that. They made tools. They knew how to create and use fire to advantage. They developed social groupings and early cultural adaptations, but… They are no longer here to tell their tale. We must now unearth it through paleoanthropology, the study of fossil hominids. We must dig it up and dust it off with archeology, concerned with human activity through the recovery and analysis of material culture.

124

We must examine biology, in-depth research into physical structure, chemical processes, molecular interactions, physiological mechanisms, development and evolution. And of course, we must explore anthropology, the intensely interesting study of human behavior and societies, both in the past and the present. This is only the short list Kevin, but evidence continues to mount. Our knowledge continues to grow. Accumulated facts continue to change our perspective, but that's magnificent! It means that we continue to learn. We continue to clarify and perceive a larger and better picture."

Jahny saw Kevin look up at the clock. "Just give me another minute or two, please. What we do know is that most life forms experienced life in difficult terms. The lives of everyone's ancestors in prehistory were arduous as well as short. Many, if not most, would have lost their lives in some form of violence. It would have been rare to live on into your late 30s or early 40s as a hunter-gatherer. That life lasted for numerous millennia. When we finally achieved rudimentary language, a cognitive revolution began to emerge. The distinct advantage of language enabled culture and the development of strategy. The long, slow accumulation of knowledge about resources found in the environment led to manipulation of the environment. It eventually led to an agricultural revolution. Different, more specialized skills were required to accommodate advances in food and tool production. More advanced communication facilitated both coherence and specialization among larger groups. This created further opportunities for advancement. Amongst other marvels, such advancement included the ability to create stories and histories. It enabled complex organizational skills, systems and symbols. Writing and mathematics evolved to communicate ideas over long distances and even between generations. It also enabled the waging of larger and more deadly conflicts."

Kevin was captivated. This guy is on death row? He looked up at the clock a second time. Jahny was now passionately delivering an outright dissertation.

"Despite great advances in knowledge over a short geological span of time, humans know very little, especially about themselves," Jahny went on. "Until the advent of writing, which emerged less than 6,000 years ago, the ability to organize and manipulate populations on a large scale was not possible. What we refer to as religions, especially the so-called great ones, were agricultural-era inventions used to do just that – mobilize large groups to do what smaller groups could not. They advanced beyond villages to develop towns, and then cities. They organized division of labour and classes with distinct functions. They created trade routes for access to goods

125

not available locally. They developed strategic projects like irrigation systems. Large-scale food production became possible."

Jahny glanced up at the clock as well, then continued.

"I'm almost finished. As the expression goes, 'it is clear.' Rapidly-occurring changes create uncertainty. They also create imbalances. How could such recurring events on ever larger scales not lead the species into issue after issue, problem after problem, until crises reach catastrophic points? This is exactly where humanity is now. You're right Kevin. Those who think about this, and even those who spend little time doing so, are all hoping for something to save them from the very real possibility of catastrophe, whatever shape that might take. But it isn't about looking to others, or to whatever promises a quick fix. It isn't about blaming something, or blaming others, for such a perception either. It is about…"

Kevin looked at the clock a third time. This time he held up a hand and interjected. "I'm sorry Jahny. This is exceptionally fascinating. I would like nothing better than to continue this conversation with you, but time dictates otherwise." He pointed to the clock. "I have to start work downstairs. I'm already five minutes late. My partner will be waiting and wondering where the hell I am." He was already up from his chair and walking toward the door. "Thank-You very much for taking a few minutes to speak to me. I have to go, but I will be back – either in the morning after work, or later in the day, if that's okay. Again, I apologize."

Jahny was still nodding his approval when Kevin walked out of the room.

15

"We've been on the clock for almost fifteen minutes already Kevin. You know we always have to be ready yesterday for any emergency that might come up."

Darnell was pouring himself a fresh cup of coffee. "Night-Super was just in here verifying her shift crew. I told her you were here. She probably assumed you were in the restroom. No emergencies yet. That's good because I want to hear what you have to say. You were gone long enough, so I expect you have some kind of scoop for me. Now let's hope it's a quiet night, at least for a while. How's your spaceman?"

"I do have a story to tell you Darnell." Kevin was clearly animated. "You are going to find this interesting," he said, pointing directly at Darnell and donning a knowing smile. "He isn't dead, and not only is he not dead Darnell, but he seems more than alive – even though his actual condition is apparently still critical. He threw me off my game right from the start. It's very strange." he said. "You should meet this guy. I was completely amazed by his composure, by everything he said. Then I realized I was late, kind of panicked, excused myself, and left."

"This might actually be important," Kevin mumbled. This guy is not your typical person Darnell. He really blew me away. Man, I've got a million things coursing through my brain right now! This might actually be important. It could be real. It might be true. Hell, I'm not even sure where to start. What do you think of it all Darnell?"

"Whoa, whoa, whoa. Slow down my friend. Slow down. I get it. You're impressed, maybe a little over-excited. It's easy to jump to conclusions. Here, have some caffeine. Works like Ritalin on ADHD for me. Won't hurt you either. Sit down. You're moving around like a human strobe light." Darnell pulled a chair out for Kevin and motioned him to take it. "Now, to answer your question: I don't think anything about it. You haven't told me anything yet."

"First of all," Kevin continued, unable to sit down just yet, "this guy seemed to be waiting for me. I barely had a chance to speak at all. He identified me as one of the medevacs who airlifted him here…"

"He saw your uniform genius."

"Okay, he did, but how would he know – so confidently, I might add – that I was an acquaintance of the woman we met last night, or that I had a question for him, right from the get-go?"

"What woman? How did he know you wanted to question him?"

"The woman and her friend who were questioned at the cop shop last night at the same time…"

"Yeah, okay, I remember. It was just hard to follow you there for a moment. Well, if he knew the woman, why didn't he just refer to her by name?"

"As a matter of fact, he did! He actually said something to the effect that I was a friend or acquaintance of Emma's. Then he eliminated the possibility that I was her friend, the Nasa guy, Enrique – although he didn't refer to him as the NASA guy, but he did specify that I must be one of the medevacs."

"That doesn't make him a spaceman. What NASA guy? Oh yeah, that Enrique guy. It's been a while since I've seen you this excited about anything my man. I must admit, Lord strike me down, I do enjoy seeing you wound up in a frenzy like this Kev. It makes my night so much more interesting," Darnell said chuckling.

"Well, I guess he didn't actually know my name," Kevin muttered to himself. Then he looked at Darnell. "I don't think he even used my name after we introduced ourselves," he said, pulling the chair out a little further before finally sitting down.

Darnell was eager to hear it all now. "So, what did this guy talk about? Was he lucid? Did he seem ill, or at the point of death like they said? The doc made it sound like imminent death."

"He says his name is Jahny." Kevin tried to sound it out like Jahny had, but didn't quite pull it off. "I'm not sure it's his real name, and he wouldn't verify that it was. He says everything is taken care of, whatever that means; but whatever it does mean, he hasn't been transferred anywhere else yet. The insurance issue the doc mentioned must have been taken care of one way or another. The conversation moved along quickly. I wouldn't inquire about that anyway. It's not my business or concern. Besides, I was a little nervous to ask him anything at first. I even felt a little foolish."

"You?" Darnell interjected with a smile.

Kevin ignored that too. "He took me by surprise right when I walked into his room, but he did encourage me to ask whatever question I had. He assured me there was no reason to feel foolish. He seemed pretty in-tune with the situation, or with my intrusion, or… I don't know. At this point, he reminded me of school teachers who say the same thing to their students. There are no foolish questions. Just before that though Darnell, he suggested I went up there out of curiosity, that maybe I was simply inquisitive about whether he was still alive or not. How did he put it? Something like, maybe I wondered how he had cheated death. He seemed to make light of the whole thing, at least at first. He did say that he felt like death had cheated him, implying his attempt was a failure rather than seeing the outcome as fortunate, at least so far."

"He sounds like he had more than enough strength to carry on a conversation with you. Didn't he seem weak at all?"

"He certainly had enough strength to speak and formulate his thoughts logically, even methodically, like it was a planned discourse. That might be what made me think of him as the personification of Father Time. I'm not sure how to explain what I mean. He seemed confident or something, like he was aware and prepared, like there was little to worry about. In fact, when the Father Time thought first popped into my head, it made me feel like I was very much being caught up in something bigger than I had thought of before. It wasn't like he was the cause of any of this, but maybe the agent – an agent of an awakening in some way. He wasn't foreboding or threatening. He was calm, just confident, as I said. I had an idea that he might very well be involved in something bigger than I'm aware of, something that most of the rest of us haven't tuned into. He certainly had intuitive skills and analytical ones to match. He was kind of like-how you would expect any adaptation of the fictional Sherlock Holmes character to be. He wasn't pompous or intimidating like Sherlock is always portrayed, but seemed to convey things in a way that made you feel like you already knew, but may have forgotten, if that makes any sense."

"So let me ask you this then Kevin. After all you speculated before meeting him, do you still really think this character is some kind of spaceman? Did that subject come up in any way?"

"Actually, it did, but before you ask any more questions or start making fun of all this, hear me out." Kevin's face lit up. "Darnell, do you remember hearing about an object passing through the solar system a year or so ago? Astronomers said it was as large as a couple football fields. It was given a Hawaiian name, Oumuamua. I seem to remember bringing it up, but that was a while ago now."

"It sounds vaguely familiar. Anyway, go on."

"Well, two Harvard scientists suggested it could actually be a space probe. You don't often hear a Harvard guy spouting off about something his peers likely view as ridiculous, right?"

"Ah, yes I do remember. I recall having some fun with you about that for the same reason. It does seem ridiculous."

"Just listen Darnell. I mentioned it and the more recent 21/Borisov object – the other strange entity observed coming through the solar system. I also mentioned the other two strange desert evacuations that were brought to this hospital recently. I was on one of the evacs on a day when you were out for some reason, remember? Well, they're both dead, as you know. I told him so."

"Yeah, yeah, I remember. So what did he say?"

"Well, I was kind of fumbling my words and just spilled it all out. He put it together and asked me straight-up if I was asking if he was an alien. He almost seemed amused Darnell."

"Amused? Of course he was! If someone implied they thought you were an alien, wouldn't you find it amusing?"

"Yeah, there was quite a smile on his face. I had put my foot into it by then, so I came right out and said that I was… I was asking him just that."

"Now I wish I had come up there with you. That's pretty crazy. Did he think you were?"

"What, an alien or crazy?"

"Crazy! It isn't something you ask someone every day. He must have had some reaction." Darnell was captivated now.

"Well, I didn't give him a chance," Kevin continued. "Once I started to spill it all out, I kept going. Stuff kept coming to me as I told him about the other two strangers. For a moment, I let myself think this guy really did just venture out into the desert to do himself in, but then it occurred to me. These three strangers came separately. These desert suicides were spread apart, or spaced out. Maybe this guy really was trying to commit suicide, but maybe it was an aborted mission of some kind. The coincidence really is too great to dismiss a link between them. I couldn't let it go. My head was spinning. It still is. Then he started talking about how maybe I should think of him as a spaceship, and that he was made up of many organisms. He even made a biblical reference, something you might be interested in Darnell. What was it again? Oh, yeah! He said, 'We are legion,' whatever that refers to."

"We are legion?" Darnell wasn't just intrigued. Now he was absorbed. "What else? Go on."

"He started to talk about how humans know very little about themselves and so on, but then I noticed the time. I quickly excused myself, as I told you, and came back down here. It was quite an experience Darnell."

"Well, this all sounds very interesting Kev. I see why you are excited about your encounter with this guy, but I'm not sure he is what you think he is."

"What do you mean?"

Just then a message came in from dispatch. Darnell responded quickly. "Let's go," he said. "First run of the evening."

16

It was a quiet night. Darnell couldn't believe they spent the last six hours uninterrupted. Although there was an early call, it turned out to be a false alarm. Dispatch reallocated a ground vehicle closer to the scene. No air unit was needed. He and Kevin patiently waited for the next call in the small staff room. For the first time in weeks, no call ever came. The night had consisted of coffee, playing cards, and more coffee. There was some chat in between. The television was on low in the background, but ignored most of the time.

It was obvious to Darnell that Kevin couldn't get the spaceman off his mind. Periodically, he would remark on something Jahny had said. Then, more than once, he would bring it up again later when he had an alternate thought or interpretation. Darnell would always listen, but responded sporadically. The cards required his attention, although that wasn't helping much. Kevin was clearly making enough good moves to remain ahead, but Darnell could detect distraction. The proverbial wheels were turning. As those wheels progressed, the road along which Kevin's thoughts were traveling led closer to his original suspicion. This guy Jahny had to be an alien. Darnell was just as intrigued by Kevin's impression as he was of the situation itself. It was both amusing and thought-provoking.

Darnell could see how people might make inferences similar to the one Kevin had deduced. Space travel and aliens have been enduring themes in modern culture for more than a century. As an ardent film buff, he knew that Georges Méliès' 'Le Voyage dans la Lune' was released in 1902. It foresaw space travel to the moon. That was a year before the Wright brothers even achieved the first flight on Earth. It was two years before the first cars rolled off an assembly line. As a boy in the '60s, Darnell discovered Jules Verne's 'From the Earth to the Moon' in the school library. He remembered being duly impressed when the librarian smugly pointed out it was just over a century old, having been published the same year the American Civil War ended in 1865. Yet those stories were nothing compared to the sci-fi films he enjoyed as he got older. Modern special effects in the movies are spectacular, but Darnell never contemplated aliens as an established reality. The idea always endured as an unlikely possibility. Friends and acquaintances were much the same. Many ventured to guess that life on other planets was certainly possible, but that was usually the extent of anyone's commitment to the idea.

Kevin was the only diehard alien enthusiast Darnell had ever met. It was all the more interesting because Kevin was clearly intelligent. They had worked together long enough to get to know one another relatively well. Both were respectful of one another's private lives in their conversations, but there was room for chat on an infinite number of topics. The television in the background often spurred comments and jokes. Then conversations would sometimes take-off from there. Darnell noted early-on on that Kevin was well-informed, and not just by Facebook and other social media sources, which were always questionable. Kevin seemed to take an in-depth interest in things enough to pursue more than just headline information. From what Darnell could infer, Kevin had been interested in all things alien most of his life. Funny how people will reach for the stars, so to speak. Many will make sense out of something they can't prove, he mused.

Sitting at the table playing another hand, Darnell had to acknowledge that might be true of himself too. After all, he adhered to what he believed to be spot-on accurate as well. As a Christian, Darnell truly believed he had always known the Truth with a capital T. Yet two of the most important tenets of what he had always believed in, faith and hope, were the very essence of believing in something without solid evidence.

Kevin unexpectedly laid his cards down. It was another winning hand. Darnell frowned, then laughed. His partner often got the better of him when they played crib. That, he realized, was because his own mind often wandered too. Darnell dealt the next hand. He didn't do himself any favours and wasn't expecting the round to go his way.

Darnell knew he was already playing on autopilot. Cards were often just a medium for passing time anyway. He couldn't seem to help going down wormholes this shift. Across the table, Kevin appeared to be doing the same.

Darnell began to consider his own perspectives. He had been a lifelong Christian, his perspective had evolved considerably. Faith had been a part of the equation since he could remember. As a child, it was the 'truth' he grew up with. Sunday wouldn't have been Sunday if it didn't mean going to church. Mama wouldn't have had it any other way. Great-Grandad was a preacher, he was told, so having a fear of the Lord was a long, strong tradition at home.

Being raised in a relatively middle-class neighborhood in the '60s and '70s wasn't without hardship for a young urban black man, but it was clearly much easier than the lives of others he met later in the military. The one thing they did have in common was a belief in the Lord, or at least, a Lord. Most came from similarly ardent Christian families, although at that time, the

133

teachings of Mohammed were gaining influence among young men of colour. That was the first time Darnell truly realized not everyone believed in the same fundamental reality he believed in. The military attracted many young men with different ideas. Some, to Darnell's surprise and disbelief, didn't believe in a deity at all.

Darnell remained in the military for years. He relished a rare opportunity to qualify for special training to become a helicopter pilot. It became a career for over 20 years. Early on, he was involved in the U.S. operations against Grenada and Panama. They weren't faith-shaking experiences, but later, first in Iraq, then Afghanistan, things were decidedly different. As a seasoned pilot, he was involved in some operations that, as a Christian, he couldn't just shelve and ignore. He never verbalized his growing discomfort, but increasingly, it became difficult to reconcile his beliefs with his actions. It took a toll. It took much reflection. It took a change.

Darnell exited the military and found this job in civilian life. He had changed. His faith had changed too. He was no longer a regular church goer, but his faith seemed deeper, more personally spiritual now than it had ever been. With his life no longer dictated by commitments in the armed forces, Darnell made more time for personal interests. Call it a pastime, call it a hobby, or call it a quest of sorts, Darnell began studying scripture. He didn't set out to do so intentionally, but then one thing led to another. He had been going through old possessions accumulated since before his time in uniform. After wiping a layer of dust off one battered box, he found an old Thompson Chain-Reference Bible inside. He knew it well. His grandmother had given it to him after his 'Pa' died back in '75. Although he had carried it to Sunday School for a couple years, he never used it to bolster his faith. The book was only opened on Sundays to whatever passage was being discussed. After all these years, he became curious and decided to take a closer look. What he found inspired him to initiate study on his own.

The Thompson Chain-Reference was an original study Bible first published back in 1908 by Methodists in New York. Dr. Frank Charles Thompson, the reference's namesake, first developed it because he found current reference Bibles available to preachers to be poorly thought-out and organized. He also wanted a reference that could be utilized by lay people as easily as church ministers. The reference approached Bible study from a number of vantage points. It allowed the interested reader to delve into details never explored or divulged from pulpits on Sundays. Instead of tasting a weekly appetizer, a dedicated Bible researcher could indulge in a buffet. As Darnell explored the possibilities, he became inspired. The reference actually assembled verses related by a particular subject or theme throughout the Bible into a chain. The chain links were printed in the margins beside each verse exhibiting one of them. That way, researchers could look at all the references to that topic in the Bible and make associations or establish contrasts. Comparisons could be made, and patterns developed to discern the teaching more accurately. Darnell could see how that might bypass established patterns of belief. Discernment, whether by an individual, a representative of a group of believers, or a formal organization professing a particular perspective, is always subjective. The chain-reference method skirted the need for an interpretation by the local pastor. Darnell was aware that what he learned could fine-tune his faith in ways that differed from formal interpretations. While many pastors might describe that prospect as a slippery-slope, he could see that the reference was a solid aid. It looked at the historical setting of the various books of the Bible, key thoughts of the writers of each book, and provided a synoPSIs of contents. Verses within chapters were analyzed into topics that ran in regular order throughout the Bible. It included biographies of prominent characters from the Old and New Testaments, and highlighted archeological discoveries that shed light on Bible history. References and chains could be found in the margins of each page to make connections between topic references easy to follow. It opened up a whole new vista for Darnell to explore his faith. The copy he was given used the King James version, but he soon discovered more contemporary English versions on the Internet. Online links made following chains more efficient. Regardless of what church leaders might consider a slippery slope, Darnell felt confident about one thing. If the Bible is a map providing direction, then why would God discourage the faithful to use it on their spiritual journey?

Darnell was more than well-aware he had been given a study Bible at the time his grandmother gave it to him, but what had been impressed upon him at that time did not in fact impress him – until now. Things can be like that sometimes. Conditions have to be just right to appreciate them. Darnell consciously decided to take a less passive approach to understanding his own faith.

Everything had settled into routine since then. For the most part, he was content. Darnell believed the work he was engaged in was a good community service in and of itself. Therefore, he felt justified hoarding some of his personal time to study without interruption. Much of that time was spent studying scriptures, but he also took interest in current events and politics. Even though he considered himself to be open-minded, Darnell identified himself as a small 'c' conservative.

He maintained some core beliefs that government should not try and reach into every aspect of citizens' lives, that taxes should be kept at a minimum, and that good people believed in God. He enjoyed engaging others in small talk, but rarely divulged his own opinion in any detail. He considered his views to be in the middle of the normal distribution curve in society. Just by listening to others, he was confident that his views were validated by the opinions of most people in his orbit. Although church attendance had declined in his lifetime, Darnell believed most people maintained an underlying belief in God. They expressed it often enough in their daily language. A 'thank-God," "Oh my God," or even an overt use of the Lord's name as an expletive were common occurrences.

Through some of his own studies, Darnell realized that even though he maintained some core beliefs, his overall perspective of God had progressed. He didn't believe that God was as petty as often conceived. It seemed to be more of a reflection of the people who believed in him. Why would an all-powerful being capable of creating everything else then need that creation to worship him? Furthermore, why would that be a consideration requiring punishment for disobedience? It seemed to be beyond the realm of concern for one deemed omnipotent.

There was little point arguing such issues. Darnell understood that people rarely change their minds through argument. Besides, if there was a core belief he held most strongly, it was that spirituality was a deeply personal experience. It is a quest people must undertake by themselves for themselves.

Yet, as a Christian, Darnell did believe that God operated in ways that concerned and affected everyone. God certainly seemed to be moving in ways that fulfilled prophecies preachers had been talking about all his life. Overall, he perceived that even unbelievers were coming around to ideas and beliefs in line with scripture too. Increasingly, people were seeing the future in dystopic terms. That's the way it's referred to in secular circles. The threat of apocalypse was thematic in more movies, and now video games, than at any other time he could remember. People were all becoming aware of biblical prophecies whether they recognized them as such or not. Wars and rumours of wars, earthquakes, pestilence and so on, were all common events and expectations in the current zeitgeist. Darnell was a keen observer, and one to note what he observed, but in keeping with personal conviction, he kept those cards off the table.

That was probably a good thing for more than one reason. As Darnell proceeded to explore avenues of insight and belief, he also became more aware of others' convictions. If there was one

136

sad truth he seemed to recognize, it was that true believers tended to be harsh critics of one another. That observation was actually prominent among both believers and non-believers. Who has not heard the dictum that more people have died in the name of religion than for any other cause? While Christians rarely engaged in fighting and killing one another anymore, Darnell was well-aware they did engage in shunning, shaming, condemnation, and excommunication of dissenters. Personal spirituality was open to brutal criticism.

One sure area of contention was any discussion involving science, especially where it contradicted long held belief. Evolution versus creationism was probably the most contentious issue of all in modern times, but throughout history there have been others. Ask Galileo! Darnell couldn't place himself wholly on one side or the other. He believed that if something is deemed to be truth, then it should be able to stand up to any and all scrutiny. If, and Darnell believed it to be a big IF, both science and religion were avenues to that truth, then they must share some common ground, even if he wasn't privy to what that was just yet. Darnell didn't believe that God would thwart a believer in an earnest spiritual quest, so at some point, he would have to capitulate to evidence, wherever that might lead him. Darnell felt that was the best way to put trust in something much bigger than himself.

Darnell first came around to that idea about science and spirituality after discovering an interesting character who lived during the Enlightenment. Immanuel Swedenborg was a scientist, philosopher, and mystic. He was also a rare pluralistic Christian theologian, tolerant of religious diversity. Born in between two better-known Enlightenment figures, Sir Isaac Newton and Immanuel Kant, Swedenborg was influenced by one, and influenced the other. All in all, that made him a singular figure worth looking into. Darnell found many of Swedenborg's concepts fascinating, especially since some of his spiritual explorations influenced the secular advancement of ideas. There is evidence to suggest that after reading Swedenborg's *Arcana Celestia*, Kant was at last partially motivated to write his most influential book, the *Critique of Pure Reason.*

Darnell knew little to nothing about Kant, but over the past few years, had spent a sizeable portion of time looking into the works of Swedenborg. Like Sir Isaac Newton, Swedenborg's prolific career in science existed harmoniously alongside deep spiritual conviction. His life experience culminated in what he considered nothing less than a spiritual awakening. Darnell found a copy of *The Apocalypse Explained According to the Spiritual Sense: In Which the Arcana Therein Predicted But* by Emmanuel Swedenborg, a work reproduced from the original artifact, his *Arcana Celestia*. Darnell was first drawn to the book because it conveyed a broader significance of spiritual concepts. Scholars consider it a document of fundamental cultural importance. That designation lured Darnell even further. He had been fascinated ever since, especially with a particular thread of insight. Swedenborg was convinced he had been granted access to inner worlds. The concept blew Darnell's probing mind. He came to believe that Swedenborg had intuited a rare link between what Christians believed, and what some other world religions believed. Perhaps he was exploring a deeper level of spirituality, something Darnell yearned to uncover.

Thoughts of deeper levels of spirituality led Darnell down a wild wormhole of imagination. He knew Swedenborg envisaged other worlds, whimsical incarnations of eternity heretofore unimagined. Although incited by medieval typecast, Boschian depictions of angels and demons, he clearly probed spiritual matters in greater depth, and with meticulous insight. What special effects might Emmanuel have imagined, though filtered through the culture of the age in which he thrived? He was profound. He was visionary, something greater than imaginative. Darnell could imagine. He loved to daydream, but envision 'what is' by a novel approach, an innovative technique? Not so easy. He might picture a futuristic paradise, a technological utopia, but he wasn't sure he could transcend the current zeitgeist, the ideas and beliefs of our time. Darnell recognized, somewhat ironically, that any pie-in-the-sky imagery he generated could easily be compared with any intergalactic bucket of ideas his partner Kevin might consider. He had to laugh.

Like a broken spell, both men abruptly refocused, assessing their cards. "What are you chuckling about over there," Kevin asked?

Darnell looked up at the clock. "I'm chuckling at the fact that we've had a pretty good night over these last six hours or so," he said. "Play your hand and then let's call it game. Shift's just about done, and I've got nothing. You win tonight my good man; well, this morning, I guess."

"Excellent. That went by fairly quickly despite it being a slow night. We should've started cleaning up a few minutes ago though," Kevin said, suddenly looking eager to leave.

"Don't worry about it Kev. You go home and get a good day's sleep. I'll clean up the sink and put some fresh coffee on for the next shift. See you again tonight."

Kevin opened his locker and pulled out a few things. "Okay, Darnell. Thanks. See you then." Kevin nodded his head and gave Darnell a friendly salute. "Don't take too long here. You old guys need your sleep." He closed his locker, slipped the lock through, clicked it shut and walked out the door.

Darnell gave the coffee machine and the sink a quick wipe. His thoughts returned to the signs of the times he had been thinking about earlier. He thought of some of his own life experiences. Both every day occurrences and more unique events hinted at unfolding biblical prophecy. The nightly news was like the Bible coming alive for the world to see.

Just before clicking off the television, Darnell heard the president spouting off. He had a hard time listening to it day after day. The politics he used to follow enthusiastically had descended into a maelstrom. Is the whole freakin' thing a mess, he asked himself, or is all of this somehow part of the plan? Darnell clicked the damn box off. "The end times," he muttered to himself. "The end times."

There was one thing Darnell adhered to for years on that topic. Never put a date on the apocalypse, even if it appears all the signs are there. Many a devout believer had made that mistake. Every time a date comes and goes, more people will question the validity of its imminence. Miscalculations take their toll. Non-Christian predictions of an apocalypse tend to murk the waters too. Even Kevin, who quoted recently deceased Stephen Hawking on the topic, believes it's possible Earth could face an apocalypse at the hands of aliens. It was easy for Darnell to consider that possibility ridiculous, but Christian predictions could be scorned with equal effect.

It was the thought of scorn and ridicule that drew Darnell into the matter. Again, it was also about being confident in what he believed, and not just believing what he had been told without question. How long had people been expecting the end of the world? Thank God for Wikipedia and Google. He easily found lists of predictions. Darnell couldn't remember all of the specific dates that never transpired, but a few did stand out. A fairly recent prediction was for April, 2018, made by a Christian numerologist named David Meade. That slipped by unfulfilled. Then there was that Weinland guy, a pastor from the Church of God who had predicted the Messiah's return in 2011, 2012, 2013 and June, 2019. Those dates didn't pan out either.

Looking at various sources, Darnell noticed that many predictions were beginning to converge within close range of one another. He thought that might mean something, especially since different Christian factions approached their understanding of end times prophecies from different angles. They might all be inching closer to understanding how God wants to unfold this final historical event. If that's true, Darnell thought, then some of the differences between

139

denominations might be bridged as greater clarity emerged. They may find that they all hold critical pieces of the puzzle. It made sense that God would divulge clues rather than the overall strategy. What commander in chief wouldn't exploit strategic advantage to attain an intended outcome? If it wasn't done that way, many would ignore divine guidance until warnings were heeded too late. That's why events seemed to be unfolding slowly. He had heard about the end times his whole life. God was continuing to test and guide his chosen. Darnell didn't really intend to presume what God's intentions were, but he believed they were appearing more and more clear.

Others seemed to be similarly cautious about making meticulous predictions. That pastor from the large Mariners' Church down in Orange County said he believes the second coming will happen sometime between 2018 and 2028. That kind of prediction confirmed Darnell's personal belief that the time frame for imminent events were variable. After all, even the earliest Christians believed the end times were imminent, yet two-thousand years have passed since, and we're still waiting.

Non-Christians have contributed to the dialogue in ways that lent credibility to biblical predictions as well. Darnell once humorously commented that he wouldn't give any awards to most of them. He remembered reading about the famous 20th century psychic and astrologer Jeane Dixon. She predicted the biblical event of Armageddon would happen in 2020, but then, she had also predicted it would occur in 1962. No prizes for those ones either. Maybe these people, who seem to have some insight, he believed, see 'through a glass darkly,' as the King James version of the Bible says. "Only God knows for sure," he repeated to himself. "Only God knows for sure."

Despite his certainty on the matter, the Bible actually had much to say about the end of the world. Darnell had become well versed in the subject known as eschatology, the study of the end times. He believed sections of the Gospel of Matthew were central to his current understanding, because in that book, Jesus' disciples asked him about it directly. Jesus answered them by spelling it out in stages. There would be wars and rumours of wars. Nation would rise against nation and kingdom against kingdom. There would be famines, pestilences and earthquakes, yet these would only be the beginning of sorrows. The faithful were to look for a specific sign, the abomination of desolation spoken about by the old testament prophet Daniel. The prophet had interpreted a dream King Nebuchadnezzar of Babylon had about the image of a man depicting the ages of the earth. Darnell remembered an interpretation he read a few years back. The image characterized the age of empires from Babylon's golden age to Rome's age of iron. The breaking of the great Roman empire into the nations of Europe were the broken pieces of clay portrayed in the dream.

Christians have come to believe Daniel's interpretation to mean that this final age has lasted from the fall of the Roman Empire to the present. Jesus mentioned the words spoken by Daniel specifically, explaining them as only 'the beginning of sorrows' in Matthew's gospel, chapter 23, verse 15. Only 'when all of the other signs come to pass,' Jesus said, 'should we know about when the apocalypse is coming.' Darnell knew Matthew went on to talk about tribulations and people pretending to be the Messiah. Matthew says that 'when you see these things, know that it is near, even at the doors.' He paused and thought about it all. "Matthew 24, verse 33," Darnell muttered, "pretending to be the Messiah... know it is near... even at the door... hmmm."

Darnell had voted Republican in the '16 election, just as he always did, but much had happened since then. Most of it led him to actually feel confused about his decision. Either he had not been paying attention to politics as diligently as he believed, or the nature of politics had been turned on its head. The President did not follow usual protocols. Instead, many decisions seemed to be dividing points for just about everything. It wasn't just at home here either. In just the past few years, the whole world seemed to be going crazy.

The more Darnell thought about it, the more he began to see current events coinciding with the words of Daniel, the words of Jesus, and the Apostle John's book of Revelation. Now, if some global pestilence were to come about anytime soon, he would definitely believe things were near, even at the door. ...and what might be behind the door?

The incident out in the desert, and the circumstances around that man they medevacked, had the potential to line up with other observations Darnell had been making. It wasn't really until Kevin told him that the stranger referred to himself as 'legion' though, that things started to click together. "We are legion," Kevin had quoted the stranger as saying. At the time, Darnell immediately recognized that line was straight out of the New Testament.

Darnell walked out of the staff room, made his way to an exit to the parking lot, and walked toward his truck. He beeped it open, climbed into the cab, reached over to the glove box, opened it and retrieved a small Bible. Darnell was familiar with the story about Jesus casting devils out of someone. Versions could be found in both the gospels of Matthew and Mark. He flipped pages back and forth until he located one of them.

In Mark 5, verses 8 and 9, when Jesus commanded an unclean spirit to come out of a man possessed, he asked it what its name was. The unclean spirit responded with, "My name is Legion: for we are many."

Holy crap, Darnell thought. I don't know every instance and interpretation of end times scripture, but there seems to be a connection here. He sat back in his seat and contemplated the whole thing. Many divergent ideas flowed through his mind. Then one singular thought came to the fore and he focused on it like a magnet to metal. This guy Jahny was still alive three days after they retrieved him from the desert. The numbers tell the story, he remembered the doctor saying on the night they brought him in. As far as Darnell understood, that meant there wasn't any hope for Jahny. Yet here he was, still alive.

The number three struck Darnell as particularly significant. So was the fact that they had retrieved Jahny from the Mohave. Jesus was known to have fasted in the desert where he was tempted by the devil, just as he was tempted in the garden of Gethsemane before being handed over to be killed. Three days later he rose from the dead. Darnell's mind exploded with questions. Was Jahny's survival at this juncture of end times history a mockery of Christ's achievement, or even a challenge to it? Was this somehow connected to the so-called abomination of desolation? Was Jahny's declaration of being legion just as the devil cast out by Jesus in the New Testament proof of who, or what he really is? Was Jahny's sudden appearance a piece of the great puzzle coming together? Darnell paused for a moment to review the whole thing. He marveled at how that pattern of thought came together. It certainly wasn't complete, but there was an emergent thread that made sense. It definitely warranted further thought.

Darnell acknowledged this was heady stuff. There was little chance of going home and sleeping right now. He put his bible back in the glove box, pulled his keys out of the ignition where he had habitually placed them, and got out of his truck. He had to meet the stranger for himself. Never mind Kevin's idea that this guy might be an alien. He might be something much more important than that.

Darnell walked back into the building and walked down the hall. He turned to go to the elevators where he saw two people waiting. To his surprise, it was the man and woman he met the other night.

The woman noticed him immediately. "Hello, Darnell. Are you just getting off your shift now?" She smiled and reached out her hand. Then the man she was with extended his hand too.

"Funny meeting you here again," she said. "You wouldn't happen to be going upstairs, would you?"

17

Darnell smiled as he shook Enrique's hand, then Emma's. "Funny meeting you two here. I didn't expect to see you again. I hope everything is alright. It's Enrique and Emma, right? I'm Darnell." He had a sudden hunch they were on their way to the same room upstairs.

"I haven't forgotten your name yet. It's barely been a couple of days," Enrique emphasized with a huge smile. We're just on our way up to see our survivor. "You guys must be doing an amazing job."

"The stranger's name is Jahny. At least that is what he goes by," added Emma.

"So it is." Darnell acknowledged. "I haven't met him yet, but believe it or not, I was just on my way up there to see him as well. No doubt you remember my partner Kevin. He's been transfixed by this guy. He's been on and on about him enough that he's got me interested in finding out a few things for myself. He sounds like quite a character." Darnell chuckled and shook his head, implying it was unusual to be roused by another's fixation. "As for doing a great job, the only thing we did to help our stranger was already job-done the night we met. Medevacs are just the first rung on the ladder. Maybe the doctors deserve a compliment. Maybe the patient found something within himself to pull through this far. Or maybe there's a higher power responsible. Who's to say?"

"The patient is quite a character, that's for sure. If you haven't met him yet, he may prove different than anticipated," Emma said. "I met him briefly yesterday afternoon. It would be interesting to know what impressed Kevin about him. Jahny isn't easy to describe. He was much more talkative than you might expect."

The elevator indicator dinged, and the doors opened. The three waited for passengers to exit before stepping inside with a horde of others. Every button on the panel was pressed and lit. It was going to be stop and go. The doors closed. Various colognes, perfumes and other odours circulated to form unique combinations. When the panel mercifully indicated their arrival on six, stepping out into the antiseptic aroma of a hospital ward brought relief.

Enrique and Darnell followed Emma down the hall and past the nurses' station. "Let me guess, room 610?" The nurse behind the counter stopped typing to address the group. "Another visitor just came up to see him as well. One of yours," she said, glancing at Darnell in uniform.

"Speak of the devil," muttered Darnell with a smirk on his face.

"The patient is in serious condition and needs to rest as much as possible," came the follow-up comment in a clichéd, schoolmarm tone. "Having a crowd in there is probably not the best thing. We strongly encourage limiting numbers unless they are direct family... And, if by chance, any of you," she stressed, "are direct family, we need some information – starting with identity."

Emma conceded none were family, but all had been involved in the stranger's rescue. She promised to keep the visit short. If they had a chance to speak with him and learned anything, they would be sure to pass on that information. Emma thought it might help to mention that the psychiatrist had encouraged her visit, although she didn't disclose that was in reference to yesterday's meeting. The nurse was clearly disposed against it, but made no further comment.

It was no surprise to find Kevin standing at the side of Jahny's bed in 610. He turned toward them immediately. "Hello Darnell... and the two of you as well. I'm surprised to see you all here, especially together. I just arrived myself."

"Of course you did," said Darnell. "We just parted company less than ten minutes ago." He gave Kevin a look. "I thought you were going straight home. We ran into one another at the elevator downstairs and happened to be coming to the same place." Darnell leaned around Kevin to address Jahny, who was observing the interaction with some interest. "Please excuse us," he said. "My name is Darnell. Kevin and I work together." Enrique also stepped forward and introduced himself as a friend of Emma's. Both then stepped back to rejoin the others at the foot of the bed.

Jahny scanned all three before a broader smile emerged on his face. Each felt slightly uncomfortable, scrutinized, as though for an audition. Jahny's expression shouldn't have contributed to any uneasiness. He appeared composed, calm and relaxed. Their individual impulses to know more about him made them feel like children asking for something they weren't likely to get. Despite Jahny's tranquil demeanor, he was a stranger in a hospital room, in literal, mortal danger. Although his visitors were drawn by who or what he might be, they were primarily fascinated by the fact that he was still alive at all. They were the first four people to be caught up in a still-unfolding drama. Everyone but Enrique wondered if, and when, there would be others. Enrique had come without questions or expectations, but he did harbor some curiosity.

Humans have a great capacity for seeing patterns and then becoming preoccupied with interpreting their meaning. The minds of three of the four people at the foot of the bed were swirling with projection. For an extended moment, there was uneasy silence in the room. Only the sounds of beeps and distant conversation could be heard. Were it possible to hear the collective internal cranial buzz, however, cacophony would reign.

Finally, Jahny broke the silence. "What can I do for you? Or, let me specify, for each of you? Surely you haven't come for the same reasons," he said, raising an eyebrow.

Darnell abruptly cleared his throat and spoke up.

"It's probably fair to point at curiosity, but some may be looking for answers to questions. I'm not sure if I actually came here to ask any, or if I just wanted to meet you and see if I could figure out the answers for myself. I understand you have some serious medical challenges and I'm not here to complicate them in any way. The thing is," Darnell said with a pause as he looked Jahny directly in the eye, "the thing is, it doesn't seem like your medical challenges are as complicated as we were led to believe. My friend and colleague over here," he said, pointing in Kevin's general direction, "seems quite enthralled with the meeting he had with you last night. Clearly, these two are also captivated with you for some reason or other of their own. After all, they're here to visit someone they encountered only recently under highly unusual circumstances." Darnell took a deep breath. "The reason I'm here has to do with something specific that caught my attention. It was something you said last night to my partner over here."

Jahny listened attentively without interjection. He could see Darnell formulating his thoughts and waited politely. A few moments passed.

"These may not be your words exactly, but when Kevin admitted some of his ideas about who he thought you might be, you elaborated on his suggestion and referred to yourself as 'legion.' It sounded like you specifically inferred that you weren't just one, but many. What was that about?"

This time Jahny interjected swiftly. "And so, do you imagine me to be a demon from hell below come to do mischief?"

Emma and Kevin were taken aback. A faint smile appeared on Enrique's face. Darnell looked around the room. He suddenly felt self-conscious, even stunned at his own unusual impulsivity, but he was in it now. He looked directly at Jahny again. "I suppose the reference could refer to inclusion in a group of some kind, but yes, the religious reference is the one intended."

"So, were you thinking there might be a connection between the devils whom Jesus purportedly drove out in the biblical story and me," Jahny asked with a hint of condescension? His curiosity was piqued, amusement faintly evident. "Continue," he said.

146

"I suppose I could continue," Darnell replied, "but these people didn't come to hear me rambling on about my ideas. I was simply hoping you would elaborate on the legion statement and tell me why, if it was only a metaphor, did you choose a biblical one. I wouldn't expect spacemen to know much about the Bible; and I wouldn't expect one of the few desert suicides we have come across to either, at least not these days. I'm sorry if that sounded forward and lacking in empathy Mr. Jahny, but…"

"Just a moment," Jahny said, nodding approvingly, and holding up an index finger to indicate he would return to Darnell's concern. "I'm not offended. Each of the others can state their purpose here today as well. I will try to address everyone's questions or concerns."

Darnell felt somewhat slighted, but deferred to his usual model of patience.

Jahny turned to Emma. "You couldn't have finished those books you picked up. There was a lot to absorb. I wasn't expecting you back so promptly."

"Good morning Jahny," Emma responded with a smile. They were her first words to him since walking in with the others. "I had to come back as soon as I could this morning. When I saw you yesterday afternoon, you said that if you could learn a little more about my son Anthony, and if I could learn a little more about you, then maybe we could discover what the connection, if any, is between you. I had originally only suspected a connection, but now I'm almost certain there is Jahny. You did say there was a connection between everything, didn't you? Last night when Enrique and I were having dinner and chatting, my son texted me. Let me read this to you." Emma fumbled with her cellphone for a second, then brought it closer so she could see the text. She read it out loud, just as she had to Enrique at dinner the night before:

"'Hi Mum, sorry to bug you again so soon. I can't remember if you had told me last night that you met a caveman, or some reference like that, or if I just dreamed it. I couldn't sleep until early this morning and slept most of my day away. Anyway, if that doesn't make sense, which I expect it won't, don't bother to get back to me. I probably dreamed it. Hope you're having a good time.'"

Emma shuffled past Darnell, walked around the side of the bed and held out her cellphone for Jahny to see. "I do think this is highly unusual. The reference to a caveman is too much of a coincidence to just ignore. I may not understand my intuition Jahny, but I do rely on it when I have nothing else to go on. I came here today, not to talk to you about Kant or Jung, but to verify or negate my intuition. You seem very knowledgeable about things in general. I figure we just didn't

147

have enough time to get down to specifics yesterday." Emma looked at the others standing in front of the bed, then back at Jahny. She lowered her voice. "Originally, I thought we might have a little time to do that today. I brought my friend Enrique because he's more of an evidence-based kind of guy. I thought his perspective, along with some further conversation with you, might shed some light on all of this." She looked at the others again, then stepped back from the footboard.

Jahny nodded and smiled. "Okay. Thanks Emma. Another person might indeed feel like an alien at this point. Maybe we can make some sense of it though," he said. "or, maybe not." He turned to Kevin, raised his brows in anticipation and smiled. Kevin acknowledged the gesture, feeling a little more relaxed than he had been. He stepped around to the side of the bed, wanting to face everyone in the room.

"I kind of left in a hurry last night, but certainly didn't mean to be rude," he said, addressing Jahny first. "In fact, I was enthralled with what you were saying, just as my partner said a few minutes ago. I was about to be late for my shift. Then, of course, I'd have to answer to this guy here," he said, pointing directly at Darnell and making a face, hoping to garner a laugh to lighten up any tension in the room. A few chuckles ensued. "We didn't have a chance to really get into it. I don't want you or any of these people here to think that I just randomly came up with the idea that you might be an alien." Kevin was thinking specifically about his conversation with Enrique two nights earlier. "Let me tell you all something," he said, looking more serious. "I might just be a medevac responder, but I aspire to be the best damn medevac responder I can be. I love what we do out there every day and I am proud of it. I actually come from quite a medical family. Two were doctors in their day, and there are four generations of nurses on my mother's side of the family. I guess we all have a strong awareness of life's fragility."

Then Kevin looked directly at Jahny again. "So if you think that I might have some harmful intent toward you because I suspect you might be from somewhere else other than here Jahny, then think again. I am truly just curious about you, and as I said just a few seconds ago, I didn't just randomly come up with my suspicion about you. Let me share this. Let me tell you all why I just elaborated on my family's medical history. There's something you all should know about medical people. They are often there when nobody else is there. Medical people are there at times when some of their patients don't have much time left. Sometimes," Kevin said, pointing to his partner, "and you know this is true Darnell, you know that when people realize you might be the last person to listen to anything they might have to say before they go, they sometimes share deeply personal

148

information. It might be a wish; it might be a regret, it might be a message for someone, or, it might just be a sentiment of some kind, but sometimes they really need to get it out."

"So you thought," Jahny interjected, "that because I was at death's door, that somehow I might be desperate enough to tell you I was an alien?"

"I don't know what I thought exactly, but I do know this," Kevin stated emphatically. "I do know something that my great aunt told me. I had just turned 20 and was about to go into EMR training. It was something that changed my life and made me interested in the whole alien question in the first place. Listen to this story. My great aunt Margaret was a nurse at the Walter Reed Medical Center in Bethesda, Maryland near D.C. That was in the '50s and early '60s. We all know it as the place where Presidents go for both medical emergencies, and their annual checkups. Military brass including Pentagon staff go there because it's the closest military medical center in the D.C. area. My great aunt had already been a nurse for fifteen years or so. A young man in his mid-thirties suffered a heart attack and was brought in. Apparently he had a history of heart issues. She chatted with him as she did with all her patients. Anyway, he told her that he was an air force captain and that he was on a team in the 1950s that investigated UFOs. He had even written a book titled *The Report on Unidentified Flying Objects*. My great-aunt wasn't sure his story was true, but thought it fascinating. She claimed never to have found the book, but I don't think she looked too aggressively, if more than once."

Kevin smiled proudly, scanning everyone in the room like a professional speaker. "But I did. As it turned out, there was such a book. It was relatively easy to find the information I was looking for on the Web. Interestingly enough, that book was published in 1956 by a Captain Edward J. Ruppelt. Imagine my surprise and heightened interest after discovering Captain Ruppelt died of a heart attack at the age of 37! That's not all. I discovered an interesting series of systematic studies about UFOs conducted by the air force for almost 20 years from the early '50s until 1970. Those studies were called Project Blue Book. Coincidentally Emma, since you are interested in coincidences, just last year in January 2019, the History Channel started airing a television series called guess what? That's right, Project Blue Book. It is a very loose adaptation of actual events and never focuses on, or even mentions Ruppelt, but actually, he was the first director of Project Blue Book. Apparently he was the most serious about following through on the mission as well. In 1948, Ruppelt wrote about intelligence sources as cited in an earlier air force study on the subject. It concluded with, and this is an actual quote I memorized because I was so blown away:

'the flying saucers were real craft, were not made by either the Soviet Union or the United States, and were likely extraterrestrial in origin,' quote, unquote." Kevin looked around at everyone again.

Jahny interrupted. "That is very interesting. Much to talk about there for sure, but first," he said, much to Kevin's dismay, and looking at Enrique, "and did you come simply to accompany Emma? Or have you now heard enough to have some questions of your own?"

Enrique felt a bit shy being addressed without warning, but answered promptly. "I have to admit that this is all very interesting. I may have some questions in a bit, but you might say I'm still collecting evidence. It's always best not to say too much if you don't know too much. Besides Jahny, it seems like these three have some important matters they would really like your input on. Since you're still a patient here, we shouldn't be taking up much of your time. The nurse at the desk was sure to make that point. You probably do need to rest. Some porter could also show up to take you away for testing somewhere."

"Fair enough. Noted," Jahny responded, and turning back toward Darnell, said, "it does seem like some disciples came for edification."

"Again, a biblical reference," Darnell protested, having taken Jahny's bait without realizing it. "Why the use of biblical references? Are your circumstances somehow related to biblical events? Are you as unusual or different as some here consider you to be? Or Jahny, are you no different than some of the other tragic cases someone with a job like mine comes across every once in a while? I know that I might be sounding somewhat out of place, and maybe even bordering on inappropriate, especially since you are in fact a hospital patient in very serious condition. Just a quick answer, and I'll leave you alone. I guess that what I'm really asking is, are you someone we should be looking out for? Are you someone who is going to change our lives in some way? Are you someone who could do a lot of damage? Are you someone who might do some good? You see Jahny, I'm not predisposed to thinking you might be dangerous. I believe there may be many agents coming to engage in end times events. The Bible talks about both good and evil entities entering the fray. You might be a dangerous herald or a divine godsend. Things are crazy these days. Not too much would surprise me anymore."

The silence couldn't have been louder. All four of Jahny's guests found themselves slipping into thoughtful reverie. Then Jahny broke the spell. "I appreciate all of you coming here. The fact that most of you have questions and concerns adds an element of mystique to your presence. If I had concerns as pertinent as yours, I too would be seeking answers. And I commend

150

you. Many people ask impulsive questions, and then abandon them just as hastily. Others assume they have the answers mostly figured out already, and continue about their business. You have taken a step up from that. It is an easily bypassed, but important step. Your persistence reveals you are people of some substance, despite the unusual nature of your ideas about me. Whether your inquiries have to do with the possibility of extraterrestrial life, the possibility of prophecy fulfillment, or the possibility of unknown connections between strangers, they all have something in common. They are all related to questions of existence, seminal in nature, probing for clues to deep, underlying unknowns. Perhaps they are only forgotten, waiting to be remembered. While I might have much to say about such inquiries, because I have been an avid student of very similar issues myself, you should know from the outset that I do not have definitive answers. It isn't that I haven't tried to root them out, simply that it is not possible," and here Jahny paused, perhaps for effect. "It isn't possible just yet."

Everyone in the room was now fixated on Jahny. The beeps, voices down the hall, and sounds from outside continued in the background, but the four people standing around Jahny's bed heard nothing, but what he was saying. They were mesmerized.

"Whether you realize it or not, you are all thinkers,' he continued. "You are all individuals who recognize that there is more to life than what meets the eye, and you are interested enough to pursue an avenue which you believe will reveal whatever that 'more' is. In that respect, as I have alluded to already, we are alike. Perhaps our coming together like this will prove to be advantageous, even enlightening, but before we engage the curiosity that compelled you to come here, it is important to note that we should all be mindful of one very important idea. That is, the nature of 'what is,' and all the things we might be convinced of as being real, or true, may be very different than we have thought. It is easy to live in a bubble when choosing to be surrounded by others who think the same way, because then one's way of thinking is always validated. It becomes possible to believe without alteration. Let's talk about questions of existence for a moment."

Jahny looked around the room with an aura of confidence, appearing to prepare for a dissertation, sermon or lecture. "Can we find enough chairs for all of you to sit? You may as well be comfortable," he said. The irony of seeing Jahny wired with sensors connected to a monitor, an intravenous delivering essential liquids into his body, and the tube connecting a catheter to a urine waste bag as he uttered the word 'comfortable' didn't pass unnoticed by his visitors. Emma and Kevin chose to utilize the chairs immediately available around Jahny's bed. There were others to the side of a second bed, still vacant beside Jahny, but both Darnell and Enrique indicated a preference to stand. When everyone seemed settled, Jahny continued.

"Again, each of you have expressed an interest in questions of existence. Let's begin with you Darnell. Your interest in spiritual matters has given you a very definite framework of existence. Your coming here has to do with wondering how the conclusion of existence, as you believe in it, will be impacted if, as you are beginning to suspect, I am somehow related to the predictions of a book you wholeheartedly believe in. You believe that an all-powerful entity, or being, created the universe, has a plan for it as laid out in that book, and that the culmination of humanity's existence in this creation will be brought about by a devastating apocalyptic event. You also believe that this event, the very end of the world, will lead to an eternity of salvation and bliss for some, or an eternity of hellfire and damnation for others, depending on how they adhered to the creator's whims and dictums. Interestingly enough, this framework of existence you believe in is based on faith, simply a belief that it is true. You have grown up being taught that there is an all-powerful, all loving being who knows everything, is everywhere, created everything in the universe, including all of us, and that he has a plan for each of us which we can either live up to for the ultimate self-benefit just mentioned, or violate to our everlasting peril. Everything you believe somehow fits into that framework Darnell, but there is one very important question which must be asked and answered. Does the evidence support it? Can simply choosing to believe in something make it true?

"Likewise Kevin," Jahny continued without giving Darnell time to respond, "your interest in a perspective currently in vogue is based on much the same thing. To believe life must exist elsewhere in a vast universe is a logical premise, but a logical premise by itself is still not evidence. Believing in that premise does not make it true either."

Then looking at Emma, Jahny said, "Your intuition is a strong feeling that can be compelling, but a feeling, however convincing, also cannot be counted as evidence. I'm not trying to disparage any of your ideas about 'what is' my friends. The idea that there is more to our existence is a very old one, but our urges to stipulate what that might be have always fallen short. Questions of existence are complex."

"Enrique is wise to gather as much information as possible before making determinations. As he suggested, it's better not to say too much if you don't know too much. The thing is, I can't imagine ever knowing enough. There is an inherent paradox in the acquisition of knowledge. The more you know, the more you realize that you don't know. That is why it is important to use reason to evaluate the evidence we have and move forward incrementally. Assumptions tend to limit what can be learned because they occur within a framework already set in place. That's too deterministic. So Darnell, your religious view may be correct. Kevin's belief in star travelers may also have scientific merit, and Emma's emerging idea of intuition as an integral part of reality may itself prove intuitive. However, conjecture is not fact. Evidence is of paramount importance. I don't believe there is any eternal mystery to anything. Ultimately, with the acquisition of enough knowledge and evidence to verify it, shouldn't it be possible to uncover the truth about everything?"

"That's quite a discourse coming from an individual whose name we have yet to learn." The voice came from the doorway. Everyone around the bed turned to look. It was the hospital psychiatrist, Dr. Sridhar. "Well, isn't this interesting? Yesterday, I left you to have some rest. I return today and find you conducting class. Feeling better?"

18

The elevator doors opened on the first floor. Among the group of people flooding out through the main foyer were Jahny's four visitors. Kevin slowed down as soon as he cleared the crowd, then stopped and turned around. He wanted to corral the others for their opinions before scattering. "Let's step back into this hallway and get out of traffic for a minute. I would like to hear what you all thought of our short visit." Everyone paused, acknowledging Kevin's request, then followed him into the hallway to the side of the foyer and formed a small circle. "So, what did you think of that interesting display?"

"Display?" What do you mean?" Enrique was skeptical, but smiling. "Except for those wires connecting him to various devices around the bed he lay in, that man appeared to be just fine. Maybe the doctors made a mistake in determining the severity of the situation. Didn't he seem fine to each of you?" The other three glanced at one another, not quite sure how to respond. "Really?" Enrique continued calmly, but resolutely. "Maybe I really was the only one who didn't come here with a predisposed idea about the guy. It was interesting. I stood back to watch the interaction. Darnell jumped right in, but then Jahny took over and asked each of us what questions we might have for him to answer. If we weren't interrupted by the psychiatrist, it looked like Jahny was about to disprove each of your individual theories, and capably. That may have put your questions and concerns to rest. The guy is an enigma, I'll give you that, but in the end, he turned out to be different than any of us were expecting, didn't he?"

Enrique waited only a few seconds before continuing. "I know you think there might be some kind of hidden connection between this guy and your son Emma, but when you really think about it, how can that be true? Your son is a couple thousand miles away, and at least a generation younger than this guy. Unless they met up online through similar interests, what other realistic possibilities are there really? If you believe there is an online connection, you could start by asking information directly from your son. After all, he brought up the topic. He may just answer any question you have. If he only gives you general answers, you will still have leads. By pursuing a more casual line of thinking, you can relax, not jump to conclusions, and proceed to find out if there is any connection first. If there is, then you should be able to determine if the connection poses a risk of any kind. To be sure, it would be easy enough to become alarmed just by knowing he's on Facebook. I guess my point Emma, is that you don't want to be intruding unnecessarily into something that is neither dangerous, nor your concern beyond simple curiosity. Your son is an adult. He can connect with whom he pleases. If Anthony and Jahny did manage to meet online, it's likely they were discussing something of common interest anyway – like that Kant book on pure reason you were talking about last night. You did make reference to both of them being interested in that book, didn't you? That doesn't sound dangerous, or sinister."

Enrique turned to Kevin and Darnell. "I'm not trying to denigrate either of your initial ideas about this guy either, but he hardly seems like an alien, a messiah, or antichrist. He may be ill enough to hurt himself, but I doubt he's ill enough to have a messiah complex, or to believe he comes from another planet. For all it's worth, this guy is probably what he seems like on the surface – an individual who, for whatever reason, fell into a moment of despair and drastic impulsivity. Who knows what circumstances brought him to that point? Believe it or not, that isn't so far out of the ordinary. You medevac guys must know that people fall apart sometimes. He seems to be on the rebound physically, if not mentally. That's why the psych is with him now, and needs to be with him. We need to let this guy recover so he can get on with his life. I would like to say as politely as possible that maybe each of you should consider doing the same. What do you think? Doesn't that make sense to you?"

"That sounds sensible, and your logic is sound Enrique, but somehow, it just doesn't fit." The response came from Kevin. "Have you ever met any astronauts while working at JPL Enrique? They have to be the most qualified people on and off the planet to have opinions about extraterrestrials. Or were you just one of the grunts working in the background? If so, your opinion would be the same as everyone else's – just an opinion. Or, maybe you have met an astronaut or two. Maybe you're part of what NASA, the government, and other governments around the world have been up to for a very long time – a cover-up. Either way, I wouldn't expect you, or most people, to share my ideas on these things, not openly anyway, so it is unlikely we would agree about the guy upstairs. Some people are knowledgeable about these things, but most don't fall into that category. Whether you're trying to, or not Enrique, denigrating our ideas probably makes little difference. Maybe there is something you haven't considered. I can think of at least one. The three of us might have different ideas about this guy, but we've all been captivated by him in a way that most people are never captivated by anyone else. I don't think that any of us are particularly stupid, or gullible, at least not any more than the average person. Maybe that means something in itself. Maybe that's the point. This guy is different in a way that really distinguishes him from others we've met. He has instigated a curiosity and interest we can't quite pinpoint, but are equally

155

interested in finding out. It's like that early Spielberg movie, Close Encounters, when Richard Dreyfus develops an obsession with a shape he knows is significant, but doesn't understand how – until he pursues the matter and makes an incredible discovery. People don't just become captivated with others in this way. This is different. So please, don't just cast all of this to the wind like it's nothing, because there is something here. We just don't know what it is yet." Kevin took a deep breath and looked around. The others didn't say anything. He continued. "I didn't give you much chance to answer my initial question Enrique, but have you ever met any astronauts?"

Enrique looked at the other three before answering Kevin's question. Then he shrugged his shoulders. "I didn't mean to denigrate your ideas Kevin. Yes, I have met some astronauts, and I think I know where you are going with this. You are about to ask me if I have ever spoken to Edgar Mitchell, aren't you?"

A wide smile appeared on Kevin's face. "So, you are one of those NASA guys who doesn't want to admit what he knows? You're one of the guys covering up what more and more people are beginning to realize."

"Wait," interjected Emma. "Who is Edgar Mitchell? What cover-up are you referring to?"

Enrique answered. "There's no cover-up. Edgar Mitchell was an astronaut with NASA. In fact, if you were a NASA enthusiast and had a knack for remembering NASA crew names from the early seventies, you would recognize Mitchell as the lunar pilot for Apollo 14. He was also the sixth person to step on the moon where he spent nine hours working on the lunar surface." Enrique looked at Kevin while answering Emma's question, as if to seek approval of his description of Mitchell. "Although he is a towering figure in American spaceflight, he is little known by the public, certainly no Alan Shepherd, John Glen or Buzz Aldrin in our collective imagination."

"That's because," Kevin said, quickly picking up the conversation, "NASA would rather as little attention as possible be afforded former astronaut Mitchell. He spoke openly for years about things NASA repeatedly refused to. Perhaps astronauts are barred from doing so. We may never know, but Mitchell once said that he was privileged enough to be in on the fact that we've been visited on this planet. He verified that the UFO phenomenon is real. That's powerful stuff coming from a guy who was part of the space program and had been to space himself. Although NASA, and whoever pulls their strings, might prefer Mitchell be characterized as off-base, they don't put the kind of money they put into Mitchell to train him and let him pilot a spacecraft if

156

they thought he was a risk in any way, now would they? He worked in the space program for years and was also involved on the ground for many other missions."

Kevin looked at Enrique to see if he would challenge that assertion. Then he continued. "That's because he never was off-base. Mitchell put his time, money and reputation where his mind was too. He became the founding chairman of the Institute for Noetic Sciences up in Palo Alto. You might find that pretty interesting yourself Emma. It is a non-profit research institute which, for over 45 years now, has been studying parapsychological and paranormal phenomena. It might sound kooky to some, but it has even been employed by the CIA to look into suspected phenomena they are interested in. The Russians, and others, are also interested in these matters. Mitchell was always dedicated to scientific inquiry and pursuing accepted methods as the standard for approaching topics no one else has. That's because these things fall outside the current scientific paradigm and are summarily dismissed. Furthermore, he has done it without fanfare. The pursuit of funding is always a necessity in research, but he never wanted to court public interest in beliefs and superstitions of all kinds. This is about serious research into little-researched phenomena. This isn't conspiracy theory stuff. You can look it up in reputable sources. It is easy enough to learn about, and has even found its way into popular fiction. Dan Brown, writer of *The DaVinci Code*, wrote another book called *The Lost Symbol* where he mentions the institute. Like many things, it is hidden in plain sight. There is more to what we don't know. People are finally beginning to ask rational questions and strive for coherent, logical answers. We know valid answers must be out there. Internet connectivity has made it possible to pursue more avenues of discovery. Enrique probably knows all of this, having worked at NASA's JPL, but ignores or covers up what he knows under the guise of skepticism. Either that, or he just doesn't want to fuel your interest in intuition and coincidences for reasons of his own. Maybe he thinks that there are some things people shouldn't venture into, that both people and information need to be censored for the good of all, or some other bullshit like that."

"Well," Enrique retorted, but still calm, "it would seem that a call for common sense has touched a nerve. Be that as it may, it is important to stick to actual evidence if you really want to get to the truth, any truth. Falling back on intuition or any concept that can't be nailed down in some way is to default to caveman logic of sorts. To really think outside of the box, one even has to question what the box is made of, as it too might be a lattice upon which all of our knowledge and beliefs rest. Everything is suspect. Skepticism is a good idea. Without it, we can be easily led."

"Exactly my point. To what extent have you questioned or challenged notions you've had much, if not all of your life Enrique? Actually, I put that question to all of you." Kevin almost appeared defiant. "To what extent have any of you ever really changed your mind about something you strongly believed in?"

Realizing his rising intensity, Kevin took another deep breath, slowly dropped his shoulders, and smiled. He looked at his partner. "Darnell, my friend, you're a good guy. I love working with you, and you've taught me a lot. If you don't mind my saying, as a Christian, you are a good example of someone entrenched in a worldview you've always had. You grew up in a Christian household. One of your grandfathers was even a preacher, right? Well, it isn't so easy to upend something like the framework of belief you've built since you learned to speak. What if… What if you suddenly had reason to believe that the very ideas upon which you've built a spiritual foundation might be questionable? And what if it actually turned out that everything you believed in, whether it is Jesus, or Mohammed, or Buddha, or whatever… What if it ultimately turned out to be clearly untrue? That would be earth-shattering, now wouldn't it?"

"That's not going to happen. My faith is unshakeable. That's not just me either. Many people who consciously pursue living spiritually have unshakeable faith." Darnell looked at Kevin with some discomfort. He already expected the response.

"Of course it could never happen, but not because your religion or spiritual beliefs are necessarily true Darnell, but because under no circumstances would you consider giving them up." Kevin smiled to gesture he wasn't attacking his friend in any way, just making a point. "You have already made up your mind. The case is closed. Fair enough. We can all choose to do that, and for the most part, it is what we do. Faith, which is simply belief when there is no evidence, is what keeps all the faithful coming back, but a belief in something is not the same as that something being true. They are two very different things altogether. Realizing that is exactly what Enrique here was saying too, and he is right. The purpose of trying to climb out of the box is so that you can think freely for the very first time. That first step is the biggest step of all." Kevin looked as earnest as anyone possibly could. "Yes, I have been researching and thinking about these things for a long time, and yes, I've tried to connect with others seeking the same tower Richard Dreyfus was looking for in Close Encounters, so to speak. But, I have also really questioned what I believe in. I've even tried to disprove my ideas as a scientifically-minded, evidence-based person should," Kevin said, looking directly at Enrique. "I'm going to continue to do that too. I'm not, as some of you might think, just trying to find facts to fit my theory. I'm interested in seeing, no, actually, I need to know if unshakeable evidence of what seems plausible exists. And that's it. I don't mean anyone any harm, and I'm not out to evangelize the world about it either. I really just want to know. Don't we all?" For several moments, that thought drowned out the clamor in the busy foyer. "Yeah, I think if people really stopped to think for a moment, they would all want to know the answer to the biggest question we can ask: What is it all about?" Kevin looked around one last time. "I think I've said my piece. You all have a good day." Kevin didn't wait to hear the opinions he had corralled the small group together to listen to. He feigned tipping a hat in adieu, turned, and walked down the hallway until out of sight.

The other three looked at one another. Darnell spoke first. "Words to think about. If I had to be perfectly honest, I'd have to say he may be right. It's all been very interesting this morning, even mind-bending. Kevin left us with something to think about, but so have you two. Jahny was quite prolific upstairs himself. Maybe we would learn more if we took the time to consider alternate views. Maybe most of us don't take time to think about what is important. Or, if we do, it's fleeting, dealt with like looking at a familiar object, but then throwing it back in the drawer. Maybe everyone does want to know the answers to the big questions as Kevin said, but maybe, most of us don't spend too much time on them because they are just that, the big questions. They might actually be too big to answer. They may be out of our league, beyond our capability.

"I don't know Darnell," said Enrique. "I'm not sure I believe anything is impossible to know. We certainly don't know everything, or even much of anything yet, but when you look at the progress made in just the last century, you have to believe that we can do even better. Given enough time, it might be possible to understand more than we can even imagine right now. It's all about figuring out new ways to explore. It's all about finding new tools for making measurements. It's all about verifying what we think we've learned. All I'm saying is don't let your imagination get away with you. Seek out truth if you must, but make sure it is truth, and not just something you hope is truth. That's important. One more thing: It might be important to think about Jahny's condition after all. I know I said he didn't look like he was in the condition we were initially told, but they don't keep people in hospital longer than necessary. Aren't we disregarding his condition to satisfy our own interests?"

"I'm not so sure about that," Emma replied immediately. "He seemed very content having us there and addressing our interests. In fact, he was definitely enjoying the exchange. I'm not the psychiatrist, but maybe she would think that connecting with others is a good first step to recovery. One thing is clear to me anyway. Jahny is intelligent as well as knowledgeable. I understand that you think we should proceed methodically and scientifically Enrique, and I agree. Yet, I agree with Kevin as well. There is something here we have all tuned into, even if our perceptions and questions are different. You said yourself that we are far from understanding everything. If there is something to be learned from the knowledge we've gained, it's that there was much more possible than we could imagine earlier. We have learned about things well beyond our comprehension only a few generations before. We are beginning to learn about inner processes too, but medical realities show we still have much to learn, even about ourselves. Maybe people like Anthony and Jahny are different, but differences can give us a more encompassing idea of what it is to be on the human spectrum. Maybe there is something about us as a species that we don't know about, or fully understand yet. I agree with Darnell. It's important to listen to one another to move forward."

"Well, there is something to say about that," Enrique said. "History books depict military strength and prowess as the primary agent of advantage and change. Actually, the marketplace, where ideas and goods are exchanged, is where advantage and change really develop. Revolutionary ideas rarely trickle down from the seats of power. It occurs where there is opportunity to mingle. It is coffee stirred together with sugar and cream. It is where exquisite blends can be brewed from distinctions. Finding common ground creates fertile ground. We all benefit."

"A good place to conclude Enrique," chuckled Darnell. "That sounds like a whole other conversation of interest, but I have to get going. I have an appointment later this morning. Thank goodness Kevin and I have our weekend starting today. We're not back in until Friday. It would be nice to get together for another chat sometime. Do you expect to be coming back to the hospital over the next few days?"

"I may very well come," said Emma. "Enrique mentioned being busy tomorrow. He seems like a busy guy generally. I loosely planned to stay a week, but have flexibility. Toronto will still be there when I do return."

"Well, if I don't see you Emma, I hope you enjoy the rest of your time here. You take care too Enrique," Darnell said, then shaking his hand. "If I do see you two, all the better. It's been, well, an experience to say the least. Have a good day." Darnell lifted his hand in a small waving gesture as he walked down the hall in the direction Kevin had gone.

"Well, where to from here Emma? It has been quite a morning. As you said, I'm busy and have things to do at the ranch. Would you prefer to stay in town for a bit, or come back to the ranch now? I could always come back a little later."

"Let's go back to the ranch. I left my books there and may want to get some reading in. I could also get my car if I do choose to come back. That way you're free to do whatever you have to. We could always meet up later for a chat if you like, but I may just choose to have some alone time. Despite the talk about exchange of ideas, sometimes a little reflection is in order as well. Let's go."

19

Dr. Danielle Sridhar moved toward the foot of the bed and waited until Jahny's four guests departed the room. When she walked by on her way out, Emma glanced at her with a look that said their departure was fine. She had met the patient as planned. The encounter was noteworthy. Amazing what eyes can convey, Danelle thought. If that look meant what she sensed it did, then her interest was piqued. When she spoke to Emma the day before, she was going to visit the patient that afternoon. If she had done so as planned, then this would be her second visit.

Danielle wondered if all four of Jahny's guests had arrived together. She recognized them from the impromptu hallway meeting the night the patient was brought into the hospital. It wasn't extraordinary that people might exhibit concern for a stranger, but it was unusual they would all return to the hospital to inquire about him. Danielle understood Emma's interest, but why the others? Medevac responders didn't make a habit of revisiting emergency patients as far as she knew. So why this one? Other questions crossed her mind, but Dr. Sridhar had the patient to attend to here and now. She refocused on the task at hand.

"Good morning Jahny. I have to admit that I'm a little surprised visitors came to see you, especially since technically, you are still a John Doe. When I left you yesterday, we spoke very little. You said that you were tired. I agreed you needed rest. It was important for you to have intermittent naps at least. I hoped you would be taking it easy. It's important to take advantage of the time to recover. Other than this morning, have you been doing that?"

"You have a good sense of humour Danielle. I hope you don't mind if I call you by your first name. Surely, you're making light of the fact that it is nearly impossible to get some rest in a hospital. Someone is always coming in to check stats, assess intravenous status and supply, take blood pressure, draw blood for analysis or, and this is the best way a hospital can provide for a restful stay, to wake me up so that I can be given a sleeping pill. As for my visitors, two of them were already here yesterday; one in the afternoon and one last night. Perhaps I was so engaging, they had to tell friends. Humour aside, it was curiously stimulating to visit with them. Apparently, they all have an interest in meeting me, although for different reasons. Do you know what was interesting doctor? Not many people take the time to ponder the really important, big questions in life, the ones that should be asked and reflected upon naturally by all of us. All of my visitors have a genuine interest in questions and ideas about existence, so to speak. For some reason, however, their questions or ideas were stimulated unexpectedly by me in some way, or so they indicated."

"Stimulated by you in some way?" Danielle smiled, not emitting an expression of curiosity so much, but as encouragement to speak further. She had only been in Jahny's presence for a few minutes again, but her initial premise about him was already supported by his perception of being the center of interest. She again mulled over a possible diagnosis of schizotypal ideation with, at least, transient psychosis.

"Not just stimulated, but stimulated by three different interests," Jahny replied. "I know you've met Emma already, so you are aware she thinks there may be a connection between her son and I. One of the medevac responders considers me an alien, while the other considers the possibility I might be a harbinger of the apocalypse. Emma's acquaintance, Enrique, came as both support for Emma, and as a skeptic of sorts. He claimed not to have an agenda himself. Such a well-rounded group. The whole scenario would be perfect for a miniseries, don't you think?"

"It sounds complicated." Danielle was already looking forward to further assessment, but needed to focus on gathering information. "Perhaps we can get back to it shortly Jahny, but first, I need to talk to you about some basics. We really didn't get much of a chance to converse yesterday, but it's important that we do."

"If you are going to begin by asking for my name and so on, let's just move on please. Is it really important? People here already know me as Jahny. And before you start probing into my life to produce a diagnosis, which no doubt you are already engaged in formulating, did you remember to probe into your own? A nice glass of your favourite drink and some quiet time to reflect make good evening companions. I suggested yesterday that it might be of value to explore yourself before attempting to explore others. Knowing where you are helps determine where you want to go. Does it not?"

Danielle quickly realized a second time that this exchange wasn't typical. She intended to remain focused. Hopefully, she would get more information than yesterday. "There is some elegance in your technique to persuade," she said, "but isn't that a bit of a deflection Jahny? To use your own phrase, it isn't of importance. There is no urgency requiring me to probe myself today. You, on the other hand…"

She didn't wait for a response. There should be no further opportunity for deflection. Nip that pattern in the bud, she thought. "You were brought into this hospital under very serious

163

circumstances, circumstances which remain serious," she emphasized. "The fact that you can sit up in your bed and speak to me now at all is quite extraordinary. When I last checked with nursing staff less than an hour ago, your numbers were still well beyond safe levels. The fact that you are talking, and, well, even discoursing in a small group as you were doing just moments ago, defies what your doctors are telling me. I think it is important that we find out - that you find out," she stressed, "what brought you to such a point where you initiated this serious situation. It's crucial. Things could change quickly." Danielle's expression accentuated genuine concern. "You are clearly an engaging individual Jahny. Anyone meeting you right now would be surprised by your recent actions and current circumstance. So what happened?"

"Yesterday you told me that it was a beautiful day, that it was a good day to die. Is there really any good day to die Jahny? It is the cessation of being, at least in the only form that you know or can remember, depending on what you believe. You just told me that the people who came here to see you all had questions or ideas to do with existence. Maybe your actions have made them stop and think about their own existence and how fragile it is. It is fragile," she repeated with added emphasis. "It's fragile for everyone. Any of a million things could happen to bring it all to an end. Maybe your visitors' questions and concerns were ignited by crossing paths with you. Maybe it was you who recognized this because of your own deep-seated questions about it. Either way, you are right. Questions of existence are big questions. They probably should be pondered by everyone at some point in their lives. Trying to look at the big picture can help us see what our small part in it might be. It is no surprise to me that this would be of profound importance to you right now Jahny. A couple days have passed. How do you feel about it all now? Have you, to take your own advice, probed yourself to see what this is all about?"

Jahny smiled. "Perhaps you have indeed been self-reflecting Danielle," he stated with reassuring conviction. "It has a way of encouraging existential questions, whether one is brought to a moment of truth by a deliberate act, or not." Jahny lifted his eyes to look at Danielle directly, but softly. Suddenly, he appeared wretched, as someone who had been through it all, exhausted, lost in the woods. For just a few moments, he looked diminished, fragmented. Then as suddenly as that vision appeared, it dissipated again. His eyes brightened. His shoulders seem to lift as he adjusted himself upward from the reclining bed.

"Is it so difficult to believe that the day of one's death might be a beautiful one," he asked? Jahny paused, as if recalling his thoughts and emotions from that day. The expression on his face

164

revealed he was moved by the memory. Danielle sensed no deflection. He was being frank. "I came close. It was beautiful," he said, as if inspired. "There was, as someone from your background culture might call it, a samadhi experience, almost trance-like, a glimpse into oneness."

"And as some profess to see during a near-death experience, did you see a light?" Danielle surprised herself by blurting that out. Unprofessional, she thought immediately. Inadvertently leading a patient to a particular idea or conclusion could be counterproductive and non-therapeutic. She quickly attempted to correct her error. "In some accounts there is mention of seeing a light. For decades now, books, television programs and films have featured such accounts. Whatever one might believe about the possibility of an afterlife, it is interesting to hear others' perspectives. When anyone claims to have insight into a possibility most of us can only speculate about, it draws interest, even if peoples' reactions and opinions differ greatly. Some claim to remember nothing at all. There is a wide range of variance in experience."

"No Danielle, I did not see a light." Jahny was aware that her question might reflect personal beliefs or inclinations. He also detected mild cynicism, but wasn't concerned with what she believed, or didn't believe. "If anything, I felt like I was the light," he said. "It seemed like I knew and understood everything there is to know and understand, like being everywhere at once. It was all-encompassing. It would be difficult to describe it more clearly. It was, for lack of a better description, an awakening. I used the word oneness, because it's the closest description I can think of."

"Is it something you would seek again?" That was a second impulsive utterance, but as the patient's psychiatrist, Danielle had to determine whether another suicide attempt might be imminent. The response immediately raised a red flag.

"Anyone who experienced it as I have would seek it again doctor. Who would not, could not, be enticed by a sensation of ultimate ecstasy, of being?" Then Jahny's tone changed from one of exuberance almost to apathy. "Yet its memory has already faded. It was merely a glimpse. I remember it was incredible, but would increasingly struggle to explain what I experienced. Perhaps it was an illusion. As the vision effectively fades, one easily wonders why the impression left by a mere glimpse was so magnificent." Jahny paused momentarily to ponder this realization. "I have heard, or read somewhere, that when the body dies, that the brain enacts multiple functions. It emits chemicals providing feelings of bliss and freedom from pain. It may actually recall cherished memories and draw from learned beliefs to formulate a virtual expression of what you always hoped would, or could occur after death. Many expect to arrive in paradise, welcomed by a loving saviour…and so they do." Jahny looked at Danielle earnestly. "But I didn't see it that way. I haven't believed in heaven or hell for decades now. I think all religions are misguided representations and explanations of matters we have no idea about. If people questioned everything thoroughly, they would discover as I have, that all the gods ever presented to us throughout history fall far short of divinity. All have been created in our own image, not the other way around. Here toward the end of my life, perhaps the very end of it, yes, there are doubts even here. For all the things I have tried to learn in my life, I have come to realize that I know, that we all know, very little indeed. It seems to take a lifetime to learn enough just to get to the next rung on the ladder, the next level of understanding. So, if by asking me if I would seek it again, I must assume you are asking if I am still a danger to myself. My honest answer to you is that I don't know. At this point, I'm not sure it's possible to be any further danger to myself. It's out of my hands now, The question is moot."

She nodded to indicate at least some shared understanding of what Jahny was saying. "You mentioned a samadhi experience. I can't say I know too much about it really, but I believe it is a state of meditative consciousness, a way of drawing from within what is needed to attain a higher path. It is an ancient belief. I agree with you though Jahny. My own family has a long tradition of religious belief in concepts that are older than those of all other religions, dating back to the Vedic texts of India. Yet, regardless of how long such concepts have been established, they do seem lacking. We have grown up in an age of science and technology where we see new wonders appear continuously. We know how they work, or we can know if we take the time to do the research. We are finding answers for new things all the time. But this is also taking me off track. I am just trying to say that what is important must come from within you Jahny. It could be a goal or purpose. It might be a realization. Whatever it takes to move you forward is what is truly important. Sometimes, at least for interim periods, that might be just one step at a time. The here and now are all that's important. If there is some higher truth about our existence, it will still be there when we get there. In fact, I suspect that being here, or getting there, are both part of whatever that higher truth might be. We don't need to rush things along. It is difficult for the finite to imagine the infinite. That's why we must accept our existence within the parameters of our experience. The answer, as the fading memory of your glimpse beyond is revealing to you Jahny, is not knowable from where we are now. If there is some destiny in store for us, let it unfold. Only the present is important. We can no longer do anything about the past, nor the future which is beyond our ability to control. At least for now, your attempt to take your own life has failed. It proves that even well-laid plans have uncertain outcomes. It is truly difficult to engineer a specific, flawlessly-executed future. If you do survive this episode in your life Jahny, you really should stick around. Clearly, you realize there is much yet to know. Use the time you have to indulge your interest in learning. Small epiphanies, from time to time, can make life most stimulating."

Jahny appeared to be considering Danielle's words carefully. He didn't respond immediately, but one could clearly see the proverbial wheels turning. He was moved by her words. "As I began to acknowledge a few minutes ago, there is some depth to you Danielle. Your words are both stimulating and moving, but I can't agree with all you've said. I might be able to agree that the present is important. I might also agree that only the present is certain. It is, after all, where all the action takes place. The thing is Danielle, what we perceive is limited by the very senses we depend on to gather information. We only see part of the light spectrum. We only hear within a range of frequencies. Both are limited, even in comparison with other creatures. Furthermore, our very bodies are a collective symbiosis of separate microscopic organisms. Everything is connected in ways we don't readily recognize. When I really ponder it all, however, I can't help but think there have to be clues Danielle. There are clues to whatever the ultimate reality is right here in what we do know. We just have to figure out how to recognize those clues."

"You know Jahny, if that's your conviction, your way of seeing the big picture, then you should think about acting on it. Not by trying to get there prematurely, but by learning to either understand it, or by being able to disprove whatever it is you think you may have stumbled upon. The truth is, you're not a young man. This act you have committed against yourself may well have consequences, even if you do survive for now. Despite the glimpse you believe you've had, you also said its memory is fading. That's okay. I haven't even asked you any really personal questions yet, but I expect you probably have much to live for. In the short while we have been conversing, I have found you to be interesting, knowledgeable, insightful – probably more than most people I have met in quite a while. It's refreshing. What about the world you belong to in the here and now Jahny? What do you do, or what did you do? Is your family in the L.A. area? What about friends? You seem to have made some new ones," Danielle quipped, "but what about your regular friends, people you hang out with and so on? Tell me a little bit about yourself. Are you married? Do you have children? Who are you?"

20

"A plethora of questions," Jahny stated. "Okay, let's begin with the first one. You want to know what I do."

"That's a good place to start. It isn't so linear, like, beginning with the year you were born and progressing to the present. Learning about what one does can provide insight into many things about them. Many are fortunate enough to choose a career trajectory they are interested in. Others follow opportunity. These and other factors can reveal much about opportunity, privilege, character, interests, and so on." Danielle pulled a chair over to the end of the bed and sat down. "We have already had some in-depth discussion, and yet I know very little about you. Are you working right now Jahny?"

"Remember doctor, right now, the present, is where all the action takes place. Right now I am reclined in a hospital bed speaking to the psychiatrist assigned my case. She would like to gain insight into why I came to a point where I thought it necessary to end my life." Jahny gave a look indicating puzzlement. "Am I working, and what do I do, are often meant to mean the same thing. Work is only a small part of what 'I do' Danielle. What 'I do,'" he emphasized a second time, "has evolved somewhat, but has essentially been the same for as long as I can remember. No doubt," Jahny expressed cynically, "you will consider that important. Psychiatrists are always interested in their patients' pasts. They believe the past is a vast depository formed by the scars of experience, a place to mine clues and information. The clues gleaned unveil the etiology of mental conflicts that have arisen. All inference of course, and often piloted by the line of questioning from the psychiatric 'therapist.' I try not to rely on my memories as stand-alone facts. It is too easy to apply a continuously-evolving perspective to the memories themselves. It alters them. It adapts them to the current version of one's perspective, and does so shrewdly, imperceptibly. I probably think of my life experience a little differently than most people."

"Tell me about that. I would really like to hear your perspective, especially now. It has taken on an air of urgency. What is your perspective on life Jahny?" Danielle wanted to be specific, but quickly realized the scope of the question as it rolled off her tongue.

Jahny smiled, gathering his many thoughts on this poignant, intoxicating question. He had pondered it many, many times. The topic had come up in conversation before, but he had difficulty taking others' suggestions seriously. Cliché answers were the norm. Most perspectives included goals to have fun, to travel, to complete a bucket list, and so on. The purpose of life for Jahny included many things, but was more encompassing. He wanted it all. He needed it all – not as any collection of possessions, or opportunities gained, but as knowledge complimented by understanding. For Jahny, understanding was everything, the crown jewel in a vast treasure trove of knowledge. He equated understanding with perfection. Throughout his life, Jahny pursued knowledge ravenously. It was a lifeline to the future – a future. In reflection, it was indeed his raison d'etre. No one had ever seriously asked him a question that tapped into it. He never seriously considered speaking about it either. People don't typically care about what others' perspectives on life are; it can be difficult enough figuring out one's own. Yet now he found himself relishing the opportunity. Where should he start? How should he formulate what he believed?

Danielle anticipated his response patiently, giving him time to formulate his ideas. It could be critical to understanding this patient. Jahny looked directly at Danielle, as though he suddenly realized she was waiting for him. He still paused for a moment.

"We came alive in a prehistoric time," he began. "Before language. Before differentiation of self. Before memory." Jahny spoke softly, slowly. "It was for me personally, as it must be for everyone… as it must have been for all of us together as a species in distant prehistory. That's right. We first awakened, I first awakened Danielle. I awakened, and I found myself to be conscious in a matrix, to use a now-overused cliché, that we humans call 'the universe.' Although I often feel like I am looking out from behind two eyes, I am acutely aware that everything I know, and can know about this matrix, must come through my senses. I am not actually seeing out from behind my eyes, but light is coming in through them to be analyzed in my brain, an object physically-trapped inside this cranium," Jahny said, pointing to his head. "Everything that goes on, as far as any of us are aware, goes on inside our craniums – hard shells with some soft, enfolded grey matter inside." Jahny's smile widened thinking of it. "'Cogito ergo sum – I think, therefore I am' – is the fundamental truth about our existence as we know it to be. It is from this starting point that we proceed to discover what we can about 'this place' we find ourselves in. Exploration and analysis provide clues to 'what is.' So, what I do Danielle, is presumably, what everyone else does too. That is, I try to figure out everything around me. It is important to learn what my relationship, or connection is, to whatever is 'out there.' That includes other people, life forms, objects, ideas, expectations and demands in a cornucopia of concern that also includes the pursuit of basic needs, necessities we are all faced with continuously."

170

Jahny held up an index finger. "In addition to that, I attempt to make sense of it all through the filter of the culture I find myself in. So I step back, observe, and contemplate. I organize into patterns for analysis. I am compelled to analyze the small picture of my life within the context of the bigger picture. The bigger picture is everything there is to know and understand. It's a quest for full comprehension. General questions lead to more specific ones, but in the end, it all condenses into a focus on fundamental concepts formulated as questions: Who am I? What am I? What is this place where I find myself? How did it come to be here in the first place? What does it all mean? These questions are only the beginning. As you might imagine, there is much to know. How far have we come? Whatever you may think of this pursuit of knowledge and understanding, it is Danielle, to answer your question, what I do. I try to learn as much as I can in pursuit of both the big questions and the small. I'm not willing to abide by views inadequately, or unconvincingly explained."

"Why is it so important to pursue these things Jahny? The answers are unlikely to change everyday life in any fundamental way. You can still exist without knowing why or how. The rest of us animals do it all the time. Can your life not be fulfilled just by being? Now you need to remember," Danielle emphasized, "the present is everything. You have referred to this perspective, or these concerns, as questions about existence. Maybe what you are really looking for is some certainty of truth. What is the truth about our existence maybe?"

"That may be more precise, even accurate Danielle. I think truth is, to quite an extent, elusive. I was raised in a household where you were taught what to believe and expected not to question it. The luxury of learning to follow insights toward their own conclusions would have been luxurious indeed. The society we live in also has a core set of beliefs and principles that we all, either loosely or fervently, adhere to. Individual acts of rebellion against those beliefs, whether encoded in law or not, can be, and often is seen unfavourably by the community at large. We have seen it over and over again. Aberrations from what is believed to be the truth at any given time throughout history could result in ridicule, social ostracism, economic disadvantage, and in extreme cases, death. This has often been the case not only between groups of people who might see things differently, but even amongst friends and family. Truth, as it is often professed, is inherently subjective. I believed very strongly in what I was taught as I grew up, but then I did begin to ask questions. For me, those questions were begging to be asked! All I was given initially were lame answers. I was told that too many questions lead to confusion, or that I had to have faith

171

when logic didn't seem to stand up. Perhaps I misunderstood the meaning of truth. I thought it should be clear and able to stand up to any questioning. Perhaps foolishly, I believed that truth should be the only answer to a particular question that made logical sense." Jahny lowered his head, staring at the bedsheet covering his crossed legs for a moment. He took in a deep breath.

"How did that play out then Jahny?" Danielle took advantage of the brief pause. "You said you were raised in a household where you were taught what to believe. You said earlier that you haven't believed in heaven and hell for decades, and that divinities tend to be in our own image, rather than we in theirs as taught in some religions. How did the belief system you grew up with collapse when you asked the hard questions? How did that impact you? Was it a liberating, positive experience or a devastating negative one?"

While never ceding feelings on the subject as passionately as her patient, Danielle too had questioned her family's belief system when younger. Rooted as it was, in a very ancient religion and culture, she found that her perceptions and beliefs varied considerably from older family members. She never ventured into such issues as deeply as Jahny had done. She never felt the need to do so, but now found herself connecting with Jahny's passionate resolve. The search for significance was not a needless pursuit. As a psychiatrist, she knew self-esteem and efficacy depended on it. As Jahny paused to formulate his thoughts, Danielle now found herself churning ideas along similar lines. If she were honest, she had never fully established what she believed beyond pragmatic concerns. Danielle never really weighed such questions deeply. In effect, she ignored them in favour of chasing traditional goals. For her, as with extended family, life was about maintaining good health, pursuing a respectable career, developing financial independence, and so on. She considered these to be admirable aims and objectives. Yet, she had to appreciate Jahny's ambition. He sought to surpass common life-oriented objectives. He's trying to see long-distance. He's hoping to recognize truth when he sees it. He wants the security of full comprehension, but is that possible? Have the religions of the world not come closest to imagining and comprehending the 'what is' Jahny talks about?

Then, as if reading Danielle's very thoughts, Jahny spoke again. "The knowledge and understanding can be gained, but however that happens, I don't believe it is through any established religion. Religion is simply ritualized belief. It requires guidance by intermediaries like priests, ministers or imams to maintain clarity of thought within the tenets of the faith. A true

172

spiritual journey is something one undergoes alone. Enlightenment cannot be imparted to others. It must be attained on one's own."

"Are you saying that it's virtually impossible to understand 'what is,' through the various religious paths humanity has taken over the millennia?"

"What I am suggesting is that once you try to codify an idea by naming and describing it, you limit its potential. The potential has been encapsulated by the very naming and description itself. It becomes a known quantity. It becomes a truth. That's why it is difficult to change. Truth is, well, true, isn't it? The belief system becomes closed and its followers become closed-minded. There is now an impasse on the road to deeper understanding. Spirituality cannot be equated with being religious. Rituals and rites are the very antithesis to spiritual growth. Religious affirmation is a poor mirror of enlightenment."

"Loosely speaking, you have bridged some differences between eastern and western spirituality Jahny."

"I don't believe either are adequate. If we have learned anything from the Enlightenment, it is to apply reason. If spirituality, or even religion is truth, then shouldn't science be able to verify their claims? It hasn't done so. Yet, despite all the mayhem we see around us these days Danielle, I think we are moving forward toward something much greater than we perceive right now. Whatever 'this' is all about," Jahny stated with arms outstretched, "whatever this is, it is much bigger than we have heretofore imagined. We're still trying to see what's outside the box. You were curious about my near-death experience Danielle. I will say this: My experience at the very edge was mind-blowing. It was a glimpse into something more encompassing than I can effectively describe. There is little point trying to describe it. It can't be encapsulated."

Jahny didn't give Danielle time to absorb what he was saying. "I hope that answers your first question," he said, smiling. "The collapse of my belief system opened doors for me. I still don't understand it all, but ..." Then Jahny pivoted. "You also wanted to know about my family?"

"Uh, yes. I guess that was my next question." Danielle looked up at the clock out of habit. It didn't really matter what time it was. Everything else could wait. This was important. So far, conversation had been intellectually absorbing, but gathering information for a correct diagnosis was paramount. Danielle was still pondering deep-seated psychopathy, but evidence of that seemed questionable. Their conversation was informative. Jahny made it abundantly clear that he has been engaged in a major pursuit most of his life. That hinted at obsessive behaviour. If the

173

obsession was eventually identified as the instigating cause of a suicidal act, it could help determine a path for treatment. Yet, so far, Danielle recognized that Jahny's discourse had not been a collection of mad ramblings. His arguments were well-thought-out and explained. She had become just as intellectually engaged with him as the four people visiting earlier. He was compelling enough for two of the four to return. Fascinating, she thought, but back to determining a diagnosis. "Thanks for bringing us back on track," she said, prompting Jahny to continue.

"In order to answer your question about family Danielle, it may be appropriate to define how we refer to family. The traditional concept has evolved to become inaccurately confining and outdated. The established definition and understanding of family for millennia has been through blood lines. Parents, siblings and children are immediate family. Cousins, aunts, uncles, great-grandparents and great-grandchildren are extended family. Today's society offers many examples of interlocking connections that have rearranged the traditional order. That actually reflects the many diverse pieces of the puzzle it takes to complete an interlocking whole. When we think of common ancestors, it must be one that includes all of us.

That isn't only distant great, great sets of grandparents and further ancestors like Royal Houses can recount. It isn't just the bits we have found here and there that give us clues either. We are much more than Homo Sapiens, branched off from earlier humaniforms like Neanderthals, Homo Erectus/Ergaster, the Denisovans or Australopithecines. We belong to a long lineage of connected species going back to the very origin of life on this planet. Our family consists of everything that has ever been alive. Ultimately, our family emerged from the primal ingredients that gave rise to life in the first place."

"You're deflecting again Jahny. Your discourse is beautifully philosophical and perhaps scientific too, but stop for a moment please. I really would like to know a little something about you and your family. You do have traditional family?" Danielle smiled. She may have pushed the limit here, but she was confident Jahny wouldn't just shut her down.

"I do have family," Jahny replied almost immediately. "They are spread out all over the place. For the most part, we are at least connected electronically. Like most families, we have become a loosely-connected collection of people with one foot in the so-called real world, and the other in the digital world. Connections, interactions and the pursuit of most activities has shifted to the global, online platform that growing volumes of people now have access to."

"You find that your actual relationships have become online relationships? Like many others, you find you are on your phone more than you would like to be then?"

"I don't own a cell phone Danielle. If I had one, you would probably see it in my hand. I would be glancing down at it periodically. Isn't that what most people do? I'm surprised I haven't seen your cell phone in hand."

"We may still get interrupted," Danielle replied. "I admit, cell phones can be relentless." She smiled and squinted as she glanced at Jahny intently. "No cell phone? That's unusual these days. You may be the only person I know who doesn't have one. Even my parents have cell phones. I've known people who held out against them for years, but they all eventually relented. Do you not see them as a necessity these days Jahny?"

"Not really, or at least, not yet. I'm not a Luddite though. I do have a laptop and use computers regularly, but I prefer to utilize technology as tools and not have them following me around like spies, social influencers, or outright task masters. Our conversation here is much more interesting than it would be if I tweeted, texted or emailed you, but our situation here is relatively unique. Everything is changing. Families are undergoing vast changes because the species as a whole is doing so Danielle. Humanity is moving online. We are transitioning to the next tier of our evolution. Marshall McLuhan's 'global village' has become reality. Interestingly, the medium by which this is accelerating offers both new opportunities and new obstacles. The internet, which can clearly bring more of us closer together, is the same medium being used to divide us in unprecedented ways. I find myself receding into the background of this grand picture to become more of an observer than a participant. There is much to take in. Collectively, we are emerging into a super consciousness." Jahny paused. "Or perhaps…"

"Perhaps what Jahny?"

"Perhaps nothing. Not yet anyway. I feel like I'm on the verge of something, a realization maybe, but I'm not quite there yet. It's still formulating. Let's leave it at that Danielle."

Danielle wasn't sure it was a good idea to just leave it. The conversation was still progressing. Let's keep it general, she thought. It was important to keep it going. "Do you think we humans are making progress then, or not? You have signified a personal withdrawal from society, but admitted a fascination with the evolution of that society. Does that translate into acceptance or rejection of our emerging future? What do you see Jahny? Has what you see influenced you to withdraw?"

175

"You tend to release a barrage of questions at once Danielle," Jahny responded with a low-key chuckle, "but I have thought about all these things for some time. I'm not sure what I see has influenced me to withdraw, but it can be overwhelming at times. The influx of information is constant. Much of it is garbage, but still requires filtering and analysis. Most people skip the analysis, deferring to catch-line anecdotes and misleading memes. That doesn't particularly work well for important information. I would argue it doesn't work well for most information, but that's another topic altogether. As for humanity itself, I have a split outlook on its future."

"Positive and negative?" Danielle was enjoying the exchange. It was still on track. She couldn't remember an exchange with a patient as engaging as this had become. She forsook taking notes. It was important not to formalize a good conversation. She could mine it later for clues to an etiology, but for now, she just wanted to run with the opportunity that presented itself.

Jahny continued. "It depends on how you look at it. People tend to see things up close Danielle. It's where they are. It's more immediate, and therefore more relevant. It's what's going on right now, or within close proximity of the present. I'm talking about hours, days, maybe a few weeks. Most people live within this experiential time-frame. As my knowledge base has expanded with experience and some active research, so has my overall perspective. The more you know, the greater number of factors make up your world view. That makes sense, at least to me. It also seems to extend one's experiential time-frame. I won't get into too much detail. You might accuse me of deflection again, but let me give you an example: When looking at the historical event of World War II, it is generally agreed that unresolved outcomes of World War I were a direct cause. Yet when one goes a step further, also considering the causes of World War I, the whole picture becomes larger. The decay of longstanding rival empires were at least part of the cause. That's true not only of World Wars I and II, but of the entire post-war world that's been emerging right up to this day. World-changing processes often take longer than single lifetimes. That's why we often fail to see the larger picture. The more one steps back to see what's going on, the larger the picture continues to get. Knowing and understanding more is essential. It is the same for the outlook on humanity. It isn't enough to see where we are now to see where we are going. It is important to glean as much information as possible about every part of our evolution from tree-dwelling primates to a high-tech global culture. Where we have been, and how we got here, all help point to our future."

"Interesting. So give me a sense of your thoughts about that larger context."

"Easy enough. If there is something most people can agree on these days, it's that things have changed at a rapid pace now for generations. Even young people have seen massive change in their own short lives. Some would say this acceleration began in the 20th century. Others would extend its origin back to the beginning of the Industrial Revolution in the late 1700s. Yet, when we look at the evidence of our progress as a species, we have been making spectacularly rapid progress for much longer than that. Yet in the grand scheme of things, it hasn't been very long at all. Let me explain. We may have been hunters and gatherers for countless millennia, but the invention of agriculture only emerged about 12,000 years ago. That's about 600 generations of the human species. It sounds like a lot, but it isn't. Mice can produce 600 generations in only 150 years. Without getting into all the details, suffice it to say that the agricultural revolution brought about massive change…"

"…The industrial revolution brought about even more massive change Danielle, and in much less time. One can already see the acceleration. Hunting and gathering humans lasted for multiple millennia, with remnants even today. Agricultural humans have been around for twelve-thousand years. Only 250 years have passed since the Industrial Revolution, but most nations of the world are on at least some industrial footing….and now we have entered the digital age, the one where massive change happens not generationally, but continuously. When you really try to step back and look at the whole picture, it is an expanding universe in more ways than one."

Danielle noticed Jahny's eyes suddenly shift toward the door. She turned around. It was Dr. Halundi.

"Shouldn't you be resting? Good morning Dr. Sridhar. Good morning Jahny. I've come to check up on you myself," he said without much expression. When he proceeded forward, two others followed him into the room. The nurse walked directly toward the monitors. A young intern stood back to observe quietly. The doctor asked a few questions. Jahny responded, giving him little more to go on than he was 'fine.' Halundi glanced across the bed to the monitors. The nurse continued collecting stats and made note on the patient's chart.

"It is amazing that you are feeling fine. It is surprising, and without corroboration from the stats, but I'm glad to hear it. You remain an anomaly Jahny. These numbers would still be sufficient to pronounce you deceased, yet I walk in to your room to find you lecturing like a teacher to attentive students. It is imperative that you get some rest. With these numbers, you should still be in a coma. You may yet slip back into it. I cannot stress this enough. You need to rest. We are doing what we can in a situation where we shouldn't be able to do anything. If your body is trying to help us along in this endeavor, then you need to rest so that it can do its job."

Dr. Halundi made a few comments to the intern. When he finished, he looked first at Jahny, then at Danielle. "Please, follow my instructions on this matter. One more time; you must rest. As I just stated, your body is trying to address this situation. Let it. I'll come back to check on you again. In the meantime, others will be keeping me informed of your status. Have a good day. You too Dr. Sridhar." Dr. Halundi made his way to the door followed by the nurse and intern.

Danielle smiled. "I should leave you for now Jahny. It's been a pleasure talking to you today. Let's hope that what we see is stronger than what these monitors are reading. I will return when I can. Listen to what Halundi said. Get some rest."

"Yes," Jahny said. I will relax and contemplate our conversation. I hope we'll have opportunity to chat again. We have yet to touch on the next natural progression in any conversation about existence you know – that is, one about consciousness itself."

21

Darnell couldn't remember the last time he had to scramble like he did this morning. He also couldn't believe he had forgotten his appointment. Normally, he would have chided himself for being in this situation. He knew better than to be messing with his standard routine. This morning was already anything but that. His impromptu decision to go visit Jahny was the catalyst for the current rush he found himself in. Had he been the only visitor, he might have been in and out, relatively speaking. That's not how it turned out. He met the others on the way up there, then stayed for the wild discussion that ensued. Routine had been thrown out the window.

Having taken an opportunity to work straight night shifts years ago, Darnell was quite used to sleeping during the day. He very rarely made commitments that could interfere with work if possible. His job was an important and necessary service. Flying a medical chopper within the boundaries of the great metropolis required a pilot's full skill and attention. Not every night was going to be as quiet as last night.

Nonetheless, things had changed. Now there was an incentive for making an extra effort, especially for the change in routine today. What he had heard and seen this morning could very well tie in with this thing he was going to anyway. Darnell had only been to a prayer breakfast once before. He wasn't all that impressed then, so had little intention of attending any further such breakfasts. He agreed to this one inadvertently after being caught up in stimulating conversation. Foolishly, the commitment was made before discovering it was happening mid-week. Darnel knew businessmen's prayer breakfasts had been monthly Saturday events for years. Apparently, the unusual scheduling had to do with speaker availability. They must be highly sought after, he thought. That could be a good thing, but Darnell also felt it smacked of typical commercial Christianity riding the secular rails on the splashy entertainment train. Hey 700! What's-up Huntley?

Darnell tried to avoid the kind of churchy Christianity he felt paid lip service to genuine spirituality. Unlike his wife Neveah, who went to church faithfully on Sundays, Darnell rarely went at all. Unlike most believers, he didn't believe you had to go to church to please God. The Bible was pretty clear that the Church was the people of God themselves. Church was the community of believers. Church happened wherever two or more believers gathered together. The building itself was just a building; it was a place where the Church could meet. The Church wasn't meant to be separated into denominations by differences in belief. It wasn't Baptist, Pentecostal, Methodist, Catholic, or anything else.

The Church, as scripture attested, consists of believers trying to gain insight into Jesus' teachings and following them faithfully. They are not to be concerned with judging others' interpretations. That is between the 'others' and God. Whenever Darnell had gone to church, he would cringe at outward representations of moralizing and piety. They loudly rang hollow. 'Praise the Lord' and 'Thank-You Jesus' were oft-used phrases during church services. Sometimes, these terms were bantered about among fellow believers in public too, but usually maintaining social discretions. Darnell viewed such phrases as convenient passwords between members of an exclusive club.

Church in general often seemed like band-aid ritualism, retained to uphold diluted traditional belief. For Darnell, institutional Christianity could not embody spiritual essence; it could only provide a fragmented reflection. Most Sunday sermons were preached from pulpits annually. Even while still a young man, Darnell observed that sermons about tithing, the practice of giving ten percent of personal income to the church, tended to be repeated more often than other sermons. Conversely, many Bible passages were completely unknown, even among the devout. Darnell had read through the good book more than once. He estimated there were far more passages never mentioned on Sundays than ones routinely repeated. Weren't all God's words important, or at least, relevant? Most Christians seemed to believe that if you went to church regularly, paid tithes, avoided lying, stealing, or murdering anyone, that you would earn your place in eternal paradise. Wasn't that the objective?

Darnell couldn't fall in line with these ways of thinking. Pastor Dave was the only reason he was now making his way through L.A. traffic down to Anaheim. Even though Darnell rarely went to church, he met Pastor Dave at the Fall barbecue a few months earlier, an event he would never bypass. Neveah took advantage of Darnell's love of a good barbecue. She was pursuing an ongoing scheme to get her husband more engaged in the church community she loved. Pastor Dave had only come on board two months earlier to assist Reverend George at First Assembly, but had already managed to ruffle feathers. He had ideas and interpretations of scripture not routinely taught in church forums. That presented an ideal opportunity for Neveah. Her Darnell was a devout Christian, but not very traditional either. He might be interested enough in Pastor Dave's ideas to come to church more often. It could benefit both of them. When she introduced Darnell to the young new pastor, they ended up engaging in lengthy conversation. Darnell's favourable assessment of the encounter afterward was license for Neveah to plan a dinner together.

As a new pastor and member of the board, Pastor Dave had a busy schedule. That made it difficult for Neveah to arrange the planned dinner. Eventually, they were able to lock in a date, which happened to be this past Saturday. Once again, Darnell and Dave got involved in deep conversation about scripture and its interpretation. They continued to find common ground. To Neveah's dismay, the plan showed wrinkles when Pastor Dave actually told Darnell that he had no problem with Christians not attending church services regularly. He even agreed with Darnell entirely; the Church was the body of believers, not the building they attended. As far as Neveah was concerned, her scheme still had merit. It might not achieve the objective of getting Darnell to attend church more regularly, but at least it encouraged some proper Christian fellowship. It was a first step.

The pastor's position on any point could never convince Darnell to attend church regularly. Even a one-time visit to a prayer meeting to hear a highly-touted speaker would normally be out of the question. It was Pastor Dave's ideas about eschatology, an area of scripture Darnell had not formulated definite opinions about, that first piqued his interest. Then when the pastor said he planned to attend a prayer meeting he normally preferred to avoid, yes avoid, Darnell's curiosity gave way. His wife's description of the new pastor proved true. He was someone with different ideas. Many were similar ideas Darnell held. Dave's excited anticipation of the speaker booked for the prayer meeting became infectious. It wasn't until after Darnell agreed to go that he found out it was mid-week.

Neveah teasingly encouraged him not to be such an old man entrenched in routine. Besides, he might benefit from insight into scripture he hadn't delved into before. That comment was meant to entice. It hit the mark.

Darnell considered eschatology an interesting, but controversial area of Christian belief. That's why he tended not to delve into parts of the Bible where it was the primary focus. He was more interested in trying to live a good life here and now, not live it in fear of the future. Eschatology specifically focused on humanity's final destiny. For all intents and purposes, it was the great singularity that ends reality on earth and initiates reunion with the divine. In common parlance, it was the end times, the end of the world. Christians have believed the end times are upon us for centuries already. Even Jesus' disciples believed his second coming would happen in

181

their lifetime. The events of the past few years had increased Darnell's awareness of that possibility too. All of that was interesting enough, but things had changed since Pastor Dave and his wife came over for dinner. Jahny had entered the picture. Now there was a whole new reason for being interested in eschatological matters. Combined with the pastor's promotion of speakers booked for this prayer breakfast, it all promised to make for an interesting morning.

Darnell continued down the Antelope Valley Freeway, over the Newhall Pass interchange, then onto the 5 for the short distance to the San Diego Freeway. Once mired in the infamous crawling king snake traffic of the 405, his thoughts drifted.

Prayer breakfasts were wonderful places of fellowship, he once overheard Reverend George from Neveah's beloved First Assembly say at a barbecue. The Reverend referred to the breakfasts in general as important functions of The Fellowship, emphasizing 'The.' He said they were all about Christians doing the work of the Lord. They had multidimensional focus, implying spiritual omnipresence into specific economic activity. The Reverend made them sound much like Darnell knew them to be – Christian businessmen's functions primarily interested in seeking the Lord's blessings: that is, prosperity. Praying together meant doing business together, just as the Lord would want it of course. Darnell cynically coined such thinly-veiled activities as functions of the religion of money.

Intrigued by the Reverend's use of the word 'fellowship,' he pondered that for a moment. It was a common term in Christian parlance, referring to friendly association amongst believers. It was the word 'fellow' that suddenly seemed to take on added air of significance though. Darnell knew the word had been used discriminately amongst university elite for centuries, especially in Britain. A fellow was a member of an academy, a learned group of people pursuing mutual knowledge or practice. This organized group of people, some of whom did so in mysterious ways, as the Reverend put it, may well be learned and positioned enough to be real movers and shakers. After all, there was a long history of politically active Christian organizations in America. Early successes by some brought about Prohibition a century earlier. The past half century produced several more. Some are now gone, but were inevitably replaced by others. Big names included the Christian Voice, the Moral Majority, the Religious Roundtable and the National Christian Action Coalition. Darnell remembered being thankful for their demise in the late Eighties. He had reservations about Christians becoming politically active. It smacked of the kind of fanaticism he opposed while fighting with U.S. forces in Middle East conflicts.

182

Darnell was well-aware of such organizations operating today as well. Advance America, the Faith and Freedom Coalition, the Traditional Values Coalition, and Vision America were just some of the influential groups out there. He hoped none of these would be represented at today's meeting, although he acknowledged it could prove interesting to learn how such groups focused their efforts. He thought it particularly curious that prayer breakfasts had probably served as elaborate, but obscure distributers of information to activists for decades. What was he getting himself into today?

Garden Grove was a fair distance from Lancaster. In typical plodding traffic through L.A., the clock crawled through almost two hours. Once he arrived, Darnell could see the location was impressive. He had never actually seen the huge glass structure that used to be on television every Sunday morning. At one time it was known as the Crystal Cathedral, but after filing for bankruptcy, it was sold to the local Catholic diocese. The Prayer Breakfasts were evangelical in nature, but organized by various cooperating denominations, including Charismatic Catholics. That, at least, seemed more ideologically Christian to Darnell than any separation into denominations. It was a positive vibe to set the tone.

Trying to park threatened the upbeat vibe. Darnell had never imagined a church needing adjacent parking to accommodate a weekly congregation, but then, he had never been to a church that could seat three thousand people. There was a sense of it being an attraction like a theme park. That probably shouldn't be so surprising, he thought. Disneyland was less than five miles away. The main lot was already filled. Darnell decided his best bet was to find a spot at the periphery of the adjacent lot. He was happy to find a shady space at the other end. Darnell made note of the location posted nearby before getting out of the car. No sooner had he clicked the remote to lock the vehicle when he heard someone call out, "Mr. Jones!"

"Good morning Darnell." It was Pastor Dave. "I guess you didn't notice me following you into the lot and parking two spots over. I recognized you at the light back there. How are you this morning? Glad you made it."

"I'm good, thanks. Bit of a drive though. I was wondering if I was going to make it on time. How are you today?"

"Good, good. Look at this splendid glass building in front of you," Pastor Dave began as they walked across the lot. "Most people coming here today would say it just goes to show how God can bless a congregation when they're faithful to him. It may be an impressive piece of

183

architecture, but the only blessing worth paying attention to today will be the speakers. If you don't mind my using a secular term, it's likely to be mind-blowing."

"I hope so. That would be a blessing indeed. As for the building being a tangible blessing to the faithful who built it, wouldn't you expect God would have allowed them to keep it and not have to file for bankruptcy?" As soon as he said it, Darnell realized it may have been offensive, but Pastor Dave laughed.

"As I've said on many occasions Darnell, God works in mysterious ways." Pastor Dave laughed again. "Who knows what happened there? About this prayer breakfast though, we may have to wait before the speakers come on. We can mingle first. Even though I don't always come either, there will be folks I know here. Neveah has told me you come to church barbecues regularly, so you may know some people here too. Then there will be announcements, prayers, and the speakers. Afterward, there will be food downstairs and more mingling. You and I can stick together if you like, or feel free to wander and mingle on your own. Please be patient. This will be worth it.

As they entered the building, everyone was encouraged to print their name and church affiliation on a name tag. Pastor Dave ran into acquaintances almost immediately. Dave chatted while Darnell completed tags for both of them, then offered introductions.

"Darnell, I would like you to meet Jakob Nilsson. Jakob and I have known one another for a number of years now, well preceding my time at First Assembly. I don't get to see him nearly as often as I would like. Jakob, this is Darnell Jones, a newer friend of mine I first met a few months ago."

"Pleased to meet you," Jakob said, extending his hand to Darnell. "It's surprising to meet anyone with Dave at one of these prayer meetings."

Dave laughed. "I do have difficulty with these types of get-togethers, as you well know. I prefer a good conversation exploring the depths of spiritual truths. However, I learned who was booked for today and had to come. I shared my enthusiasm at dinner last week over at Darnell and his wife Neveah's place. That's why we're both here today, despite my usual reservations about these kinds of meetings."

"Well, good to see you here. We should probably get our seats right away. These meetings usually begin on time. I anticipated meeting friends and saved a few seats. You two will do I guess," Jakob said, chuckling. The short walk back was frequently interrupted by greetings from others. Both Pastor Dave and Jacob seemed to be well-connected. People were now scrambling to find places in the auditorium-sized space. There were indeed seats available where Jakob had left a few friends. One appeared relieved that Jakob had returned. Others may have been questioning about the available space beside them. Jakob shimmied into the pew to where his friend was waiting. Pastor Dave and Darnell filed in behind him. Jakob facilitated introductions to those already seated before the three of them sat down as well.

Many people were still gathered in pairs or small groups, chattering even as they shuffled around looking for seating. Jakob was already busy talking with his acquaintances. Darnell was impressed to discover that the pastor knew all of them. He sat back and listened to bits of various conversations as the shuffling continued all around. More dominant voices distracted him back and forth from one conversation to another. Darnell found it intriguing to hear the number of times he heard the phrase 'Praise the Lord' in between the tangled web of exchanges about business, economic, and social concerns, family, connections and of course, politics. He wondered if all these people really spoke like this all the time, or if they just felt empowered being with others who had similar interests, both spiritual and secular. It reminded him of a popular slogan amongst fans of a lacrosse team he followed as a young man living in the north Midwest: Come for the party; stay for the game. Darnell almost felt sacrilegious, but observed there may be a grain of truth in the idea.

A sudden loud patter came through speakers surrounding the complex walls. A man stood at the podium tapping his finger against the microphone. Calling everyone to attention, he announced the prayer breakfast was about to begin. He welcomed all of the attendees and requested that everyone find their seat as quickly as possible. There was a reminder to fill out a name tag during break if you haven't already. The man waited patiently for the crowd to find seating before going any further. To Darnell's surprise, the entire auditorium quickly organized itself around this objective and fell into silence. Those not punctual enough to enter the auditorium and find seats were arranging themselves outside the various entrances, respectfully acknowledging commencement. All eyes in the auditorium where now on the man standing at the microphone. Thanking everyone at first, he then proceeded to mention various individuals and groups who helped organize the occasion. He also pointed out people and special interest groups it was his privilege to welcome. Some would be speaking as the day progressed. Others would be leading

185

focus groups in the afternoon. It was at this point that Darnell realized this prayer breakfast was going to be an all-day event. His first reaction was to consider an excuse to leave by noon if possible. That was still an hour and a half away, but longer than he originally hoped he would be here.

The speaker at the podium introduced one of the priests who served the home congregation of this magnificent building. Father Sean introduced himself as an enthusiastic Charismatic Catholic, a designation distinguishing this fringe segment from traditional Roman Catholicism. Charismatic Catholics worshipped similarly to their protestant counterparts, the Pentecostals. Both groups strongly believed that spiritual gifts written about in the biblical books of Acts and Corinthians still applied to the faithful today. These so-called 'sign gifts' included prophecy, healing, more often referred to as the laying on of hands, speaking in tongues with subsequent interpretation, and other spiritual aptitudes. Most notably, the charismatics did not rely on rote prayers, but prayed from their hearts as Father Sean declared he was about to do now.

"Dear Father in Heaven," he began. Pausing for just a moment, one could hear a proverbial pin drop in the auditorium, a roaring silence accentuating a meditative moment. "Dear Father," he repeated. "Thank-you for bringing together your faithful children today and assembling them together to seek out your will and do your work oh Lord. Thank-you for opening our hearts to the truth and the light. You have blessed us and continue to do so. May we be worthy of following your word faithfully. Thank-you Lord and your son, Jesus Christ, our Savior for enabling us to recognize the power and the glory that is your majesty. Thank-you Lord for the beautiful and righteous country you have blessed us with. Thank-you for making us a nation that is the envy of the world. May the world come to know the same blessings you have bestowed on us as your will unfolds to fulfill the scriptures written of old. Thank-you for the president of our great republic, and all of our leaders in Congress, the Senate, and Judiciary. Thank-you for all those who serve in government, who believe in you, and who know that our country's greatness depends on its willingness to follow your word oh Lord. We pray that you will guide our leaders, even though they may exhibit the weakness inherited through original sin. We pray that they will be used as vessels for your glory, even if we don't understand the mysterious ways in which you unfold your majesty oh Lord. May you bless this day and this gathering. We praise you Lord. Amen."

Throughout the prayer, Darnell heard numerous individuals calling out "Praise the Lord" or "Amen" in response to everything the priest had given thanks for. At the end of his supplication, the whole auditorium seemed to respond as a unified chorus in repeating his final 'Amen.' Many stood with hand over heart during the prayer before sitting down again. The priest bowed his head humbly, then handed the microphone back to the man who had introduced him.

"Now I know some of you are beginning to feel a little hungry already," said the man to audience chuckles and laughter, "but before we enjoy the bounty the Lord has given us this morning, we who are even more hungry for his word will feed satisfyingly on those to be shared momentarily by our first speaker. Many of you know him from his many guest appearances on various Christian programs, both online and on television. Others are familiar with his books on many subjects of Christian interest. His newest publication entitled *The End of Times: Things Seen and Unseen* is a most interesting work. I encourage you to pick up a copy in the foyer afterward where his works, and those of others in the service of the Lord, will be made available. Please give him a warm welcome, Reverend Hal Findley!" A thunderous applause broke out for a man Darnell had never heard of.

A short man walked up to the microphone and shook hands with the host who introduced him. He wore a blue suit and long red tie that reminded Darnell of how the President was often seen on television. Oddly enough, the man's hair style and colour also resembled him. He smiled and waved to the audience repeating the phrase 'Praise the Lord' several times. Many stood up enthusiastically. The clapping of hands continued until he finally motioned them to be seated.

"Thank-You very much. Thank-You very much everyone. Praise the Lord." He stood there looking at the audience patiently. Finally, the place receded into silence once more. There was a sense of expectation, an air of suspense. Reverend Hal brushed his hair back with his hand and took the mike from the stand in front of him. He looked down at the floor for a moment, as if in deep thought. Then he raised his head and glanced back and forth across the auditorium. Everyone in the audience felt he had caught their eye individually. All were mesmerized.

"Praise the Lord," he said again. Thunderous applause spattered with repetitive shouts of 'Praise the Lord' or 'Amen' rang throughout the auditorium. Mr. Findlay looked around to what he must have recognized as an adoring crowd. Echoes of the three words he had just spoken slowly filtered out. The crowd finally quietened themselves, attentively awaiting his next word.

"Welcome all," he declared. "I will be conscientious about time. I know many volunteers from various participating denominations are downstairs preparing a wonderful breakfast for our attendees today. Hot food isn't so easy to keep warm for the multitudes. However, I must say that if something were to go wrong here, it wouldn't be surprising if the good Lord pulled a few loaves and fishes from his sleeve if need be." More shouts of 'Praise the Lord' and 'Amen' could be heard around the auditorium. "Thank-you very much to our volunteers." Further applause ensued.

"You know ladies and gentlemen, I have now been a servant of the Lord for 43 years. Early on, I knew I wanted to devote my life to God and serve him. That purpose in life has led to an immense blessing throughout my years. Like everyone else, I have had my trials and tribulations, but with the help of my God and savior Jesus Christ, I have come through it all. I have lived long enough to see these very interesting days we are now living in. We are blessed to be living in the very end times anticipated by all the saints that have ever lived. We are witnesses to events that have been predicted, prophesied, foreseen and awaited since Jesus Christ was taken up into heaven almost two-thousand years ago. Now I know you are expecting me to discuss my new book called The End of Time." He paused for the inevitable chuckles from the audience. "I suppose just a little bit of that might come up," he continued with perfect timing to elicit outright bursts of laughter. "But seriously folks, we have much to be thankful for. We do live in exciting times. I will speak about the many important things going on these days. Furthermore, I will support the insights the Lord has given me with scripture, but first, I want to make mention of some very special agents among us today. Special," Reverend Hal repeated. "The faithful have been waiting for the second coming of Jesus Christ, but even today, many are unaware of the work of the Lord that's being accomplished. This is true even in high places. It is true in the halls of power. Those who conduct God's work, those committed to unfolding God's plan, are actually angels on assignment. You've heard of them before!" The crowd erupted again, this time in recognition of various best-selling book titles using the expression. It had become a well-known buzz-phrase among the faithful.

"We often don't hear good reports on the news, but angels on assignment exist. They are every much as real as the agents of the devil whom we recognize so much more readily. God's children have long been aware of the signs of the times described in the Bible. Remember the words found in Matthew's gospel, chapter 24: 'Ye shall hear of wars and rumours of wars: see that ye be not troubled: for all these things must come to pass, but the end is not yet. For nation shall rise against nation, and kingdom against kingdom: and there shall be famines, and pestilences, and earthquakes in diverse places.' Ladies and gentlemen, all ye faithful of the Lord, you have heard these words before, and you have heard other preachers expound their meaning and relevance to events today. Many have prayed for these times to come quickly. The faithful long to receive their reward in heaven." Now at this point, Reverend Hal stopped and looked around at his audience once again. It was an effective pause inciting expectations of what he was going to say next. "But," he said before pausing for effect one more time, "but, you have probably never heard anyone emphasize the words stated ever so clearly in verse 6 of Matthew 24 where Jesus says – and I want you to listen to this very clearly my brothers and sisters, where Jesus says, 'see that ye be not troubled." Then, first in a lower voice, then in a much louder voice, he repeated the phrase, 'See that ye be not troubled. See that ye be not troubled.'"

"This is a very important point and one the faithful may have overlooked to some extent," Reverend Hal continued. "You know we have often preached from many a pulpit that the Lord works in mysterious ways my friends. You have all heard that said on many, many occasions, but we have rarely, if ever, dared to ponder what that may actually mean. When we say that the Lord works in mysterious ways, that may include ways that seem mysterious to us, the faithful. Now, what if these mysterious ways actually were to seem like an affront to us and our moral sensitivities?"

Reverend Hal paused yet again. The effect was predictable. The crowd fell utterly silent in anticipation. Darnell was mesmerized by the speaker's technique. The man was a master of sermon delivery and audience direction. An actor or comedian performing with such prowess might refer to it as working the crowd. Reverend Hal continued.

"During the life and times of Jesus, Samaritans were not seen as being faithful to the strict religious teachings and observances of mainstream Judaism. There may have been other reasons why Samaritans were shunned. Yet, it was a Samaritan, an outsider, who performed a deed of undisputed kindness when others would not. The incident is made known to us through a parable told by Jesus himself. With that in mind, I would very much like to thank Father Sean, who opened this breakfast in prayer just minutes ago. He took time this morning to pray for our leader, the President of the United States himself, who as we are all aware, is a lightning rod for controversy." More than a few chuckles erupted around the auditorium.

Reverend Hal did not acknowledge the laughter. "There is no need to go into some of his many actual controversies. We are all aware of what they are. The media makes sure of that. But I would like to bring something to your attention brothers and sisters." He paused again for absolute quiet. Then he began to nod his head up and down, first slowly, then a little more rapidly as he continued to speak. "We have some good works come from this man whom so many refer to as vile. So far, we have seen more conservative judges appointed to court system, even the Supreme Court. We have seen changes sweeping the land that portend the eventual removing of Roe v. Wade. We see an actual eye on the good works of the Lord," he emphasized strongly. "That's right. We see the good works of the Lord! While the president may say and do things we've been taught to see as worldly, we must also remember that it is not our place to judge. Remember the scriptures state that we should 'judge not, lest ye be judged.' Furthermore, the Lord may choose whomever he pleases to perform his good works. We may not know the details of the plan, but God does. I do not for a moment think that God would allow anyone to occupy an office as important as that of the President of the United States if that man were not part of God's eternal plan. The Bible gives us various examples of leaders who could not be considered among the faithful, but who clearly were agents of the Lord's work. Remember that Nebuchadnezzar of ancient Babylon and Pharaoh Ramses of Egypt both played important roles in God's plan for his chosen people. Brothers and sisters, let me tell you that God is still enacting his plan as it has always been." More applause along with refrains of 'Praise the Lord' and 'Amen' erupted.

"Reverend Hal looked around at his audience with one arm outstretched in front of him as he walked from one side of the stage to the other and back again. "Enough about the President of the United States. God bless him! I just want to leave you with a very important thought one more time before we move on though. That thought is this: We see God in his works. We see God's plan unfolding. The scriptures are coming to life before our very eyes." Still more applause and refrains of 'Praise the Lord' and 'Amen.'

Darnell found himself scanning the auditorium again. He watched and listened intently. The awe with which the audience were drawn to the speaker and his message was impressive. The man had full command of the room. Everyone's eyes were on this guy. The entire spectacle was fascinating.

Reverend Hal became more animated as his sermon fired up. He continued to pace back and forth across the stage, addressing each section of the auditorium. When the preacher's gaze fell in his direction, Darnell had the sensation of being spoken to directly. Looking around the auditorium again, he was convinced that most people were similarly captivated. Reverend Hal's presence was riveting. His voice continued to rise and fall dramatically as he spoke about angels on assignment. Darnell abruptly stopped glancing at the audience. Reverend Hal suddenly had his complete attention. The man's next words were unexpected, but their portent struck Darnell forcefully.

"And while we're speaking of angels on assignment," Reverend Hal continued, "we need to stop for a moment. We need to thank the many men and women here today who are absolutely nothing less than that: angels on assignment. We have often spoke about the cherubim in heaven who watch over us. Some are personal guardian angels. Others go about doing the work of the Lord. I want to bring your attention to these angels on assignment. I want to thank the many people who work at the highest levels of our government. These people understand that if America is to remain the greatest nation on Earth, it has to remain a nation devoted to God. You know, back in 2017, not long after the President took office, I heard the most joyous bit of news I think I have ever heard. I was listening to an interview with the Vice President on the Christian Broadcasting Network when he declared for all to hear: 'There's prayer on a regular basis in this White House.' Think about that folks. There's prayer on a regular basis in this White House!"

Shouts of 'Praise the Lord' and 'Amen' erupted around the auditorium once again. Darnell glanced around the large open space. It was simply amazing. There were hundreds upon hundreds of people sharply focused on every word this man uttered. He could sense the collective excitement growing in the room. It was gathering strength. Darnell's scan of the crowd was drawn back to the speaker on stage. Reverend Hal Findley's eyes were closed. He stood at the center of the platform with head bowed, his arms hanging limp. The lighting in the place seemed to make him glow. He appeared to be a humble, devoted servant in prayerful communion with the Heavenly Father. It evoked a powerful image and implied full legitimacy. Its significance was not lost on Darnell. As the din lowered and the praise subdued, Reverend Hal reopened his eyes. When the room was quiet again, he slowly stepped back in front of the microphone. His expression was pensive.

"Many of you may not be aware of this, but prayer in the White House has been a regular feature for decades. Billy Graham became known as pastor to the presidents in the years after Eisenhower first asked him for advice back in 1953. That's right, advice. In fact, Eisenhower found the Lord while serving in the White House. He's the only President to ever be baptized while in office. I believe that was no mistake. We were well into the Cold War by that time. Nuclear destruction was hanging over our heads like the Sword of Damocles. You know folks, if you stop to think about that for a moment, isn't it evident that God has a plan?" Then raising his voice, Findley asked the question again. "Isn't it evident that God has a plan?"

Another round of praise and thanks erupted from the audience. "Praise the Lord! Thank-You Jesus!"

Then in an even louder voice, Findley shouted: "Yes! God does have a plan and he is executing it whether we recognize it or not! Thank-You Jesus!" The place exploded. It only took seconds after the first person stood up for the rest of the congregation to stand on their feet. Arms were outstretched with hands in the air. When someone broke out in song, arms began swaying back and forth in unison. Hundreds of voices joined the rising chorus of 'Amazing Grace.' Darnell was up on his feet as well, but only to see above the other heads. He could feel the excitement. There was an infusion of energy in the room. It was infectious, transformative. This went on for several minutes before the Reverend held out his arms to encourage quiet once again. The din subdued. Then in a more hushed tone, he began again slowly.

"I have a long-time friend who happens to be one of these angels on assignment. He would probably prefer not to be named as he does not seek recognition for the work he performs so faithfully. His mission began back in the 1990s when Mr. Clinton was President. The White House Prayer Initiative started in Washington, DC in 1998. It was established for the good of our government and the nation. The angel on assignment who created the initiative has stated that prayer is inextricably linked to the advancement of the Kingdom of God on earth. This isn't just speculation. It isn't just something we want to pray for and hope it happens. It is happening! It is just one of the many aspects of God's plan that is unfolding right now."

The audience began shouting more words of praise and thankfulness, but Reverend Hal continued speaking above them. "It isn't just the President of the United States who is ultimately influenced to enact God's plan. It isn't just senators and congressman. It's not only ambassadors and consuls, or even just people here in the United States. I want to thank people in the foreign service. I want to thank the non-partisan patriots who work in many levels of government. They do the work of our country, but more importantly, they are doing the work of the Lord. They are facilitating the spread of God's word and good works wherever they can. They support, admonish, give advice and promote policies, laws and ordinances that give glory to God and his son Jesus Christ. You know ladies and gentlemen, brothers and sisters, all ye who love the Lord, it is good to know that not only those angels whom we can't see, but those whom we can see are at work for good in the world. It serves the purposes of the Lord and helps to fulfil his word, especially in these end times we are living in today…"

After that, it was all blah, blah, blah to Darnell. His mind was racing. He had heard some of the most incredible things he had ever heard in his life. His head was spinning. He thought about what Reverend Hal was saying. He also remembered ideas Pastor Dave had shared with him at dinner last Saturday. He thought about Kevin and Jahny, and Bible passages, and things he had been taught while growing up. It was overwhelming. Suddenly, Darnell felt as though he were awakening. Things might not be what he thought at first. He may have jumped to conclusions too quickly. Jahny may not be at all like the devilish 'legion' out of scripture. He could even be significant in ways neither he nor Kevin imagined. Jahny might be an agent for good, one of the angels on assignment Reverend Hal was talking about. Jahny was already important for one thing. His appearance in the desert set off a chain of events leading to Darnell's unusual experience at the prayer breakfast.

Darnell thought about that for a moment. There were a lot of 'ifs' embedded in all of this: If he hadn't come across Jahny's case; if he didn't work with someone like Kevin who took an unusual interest in the situation; if he didn't decide to meet Jahny for himself; if he didn't see how important Jahny was to people other than Kevin; if he didn't know Jahny had referred to himself as 'legion;' and if Darnell hadn't come to the prayer breakfast this morning, he would not have heard what he did today. It was crazy! It was incredible! Darnell realized he was almost hyperventilating. He had to get up. He had to go outside.

Then Darnell realized Pastor Dave had noticed his agitation. He asked Darnell if he was alright. Darnell nodded and whispered something to the effect that he had to get some air, but would be fine. He looked around the audience one last time, then at Reverend Hal. The circus was still ramping up. Darnell slowly, but anxiously got up, walked out to the foyer, and headed for the building exit. Once outside, he stopped, took in a deep breath and thought again about what he had just heard and experienced. He felt like going for a drive. His day here was done. Darnell walked back to his car.

193

22

"Well Bender, looks like we'll make it on time after all. We're even a few minutes early." Enrique's old dog didn't even bother opening its eyes. It was comfortably curled-up on the passenger seat of the truck. They were travelling along the 210 to Pasadena and were almost there. It had been a busy morning. First, he and Emma drove in to the hospital to visit Jahny. That turned out to be a conference with the medevac boys as well, and an unusual one at that. Caught up in conversation afterward as well, they didn't leave until one of them remembered he had an appointment to go to. That broke up the last segment of the hospital conference, but morning was already slipping by.

Emma had driven into town with Enrique, so he was obliged to drive her back to the ranch afterward. She'd already had quite a day and was hoping to get in some quiet reading. Perfect. Enrique basically dropped her off, stopping just long enough to run in and grab a few things out of the house. He decided to bring Bender too. The dog could wait in the travel doghouse Enrique rigged for him while he had lunch in Pas. Bender could continue his snooze in plush carpet, air conditioning, and water on demand in the back of the truck. Enrique had other plans for the rest of the day. His old friend would want to come.

Pulling into the grounds of the California Institute of Technology, Enrique drove toward the South Wilson parking structure. People usually avoided the top level because it was out in the sun. That wasn't going to matter to Bender, given his hook-up. Free spaces were more likely up there. It was also closer to Enrique's lunch destination. With minutes to spare, he could walk the grounds leisurely toward his destination.

Enrique realized he hadn't been here in a while. The whole retirement idea still felt new, but several months had slipped by already. Of the three main restaurants at Caltech, the Chandler was his favourite. Nothing had changed yet. Although he primarily worked at JPL before retirement, he often found himself traversing the six miles or so here and back. Some projects were conducted from both sites; Caltech manages and operates JPL.

Enrique's return to his own stomping grounds was prompted by a text from his brother Mateo. Matty had been here for years too. The premise for the invitation was a simple 'Hey Miho, haven't seen you for a while.' Enrique connected with his brother fairly often, so he figured Matty had something on his mind. He knew his brother. The careers they had chosen were much more than work. The brothers considered aerospace engineering a visionary vocation. They loved picking one another's brains. They valued challenges and exhilarated in finding solutions, even when hard-won. Sibling rivalry was positive. They realized early on that whenever either of them scored, both improved their game. As their careers progressed, both recognized the value of bringing fresh minds to a problem. Working at locations that were connected, but separate, Enrique and Mateo rarely worked on the same project. That allowed them to bring fresh ideas to each other's work. They had an advantage that couldn't be realized by other individuals navigating typical office rivalries, politics and funding acquisitions. Their expertise became well-respected and sought after.

Teams that are focused on complex projects sometimes reach an impasse. Then it makes sense to stop, step back, and try to gain a perspective from a different angle. As teams usually came to realize, it often made sense to bring someone in with a fresh outlook. If that's all that was going on here, Enrique figured he might not mind. He had no intention of returning to work in any capacity, but he could contribute ideas. If anyone could coax a straightforward assessment out of him, it was Mateo. It had been almost a year since the brothers brainstormed anything serious together.

Enrique ordered a soft drink while waiting for his brother. He checked to see if his favourite item was still on the menu, but the waiter informed him that he had missed it by a day. Next time he agreed to meet Matty here, Enrique thought, he was going to make sure he came on chicken curry with fresh lime and cilantro day. There wasn't much of a complaint to be made anyway. Enrique could easily choose something he hadn't tried before. He was hungry. Everything looked good. He had just decided on a consolation item when Mateo walked up to the table.

"Hey Bro, it's been a while," Mateo said with a wide smile and patting Enrique on the shoulder. "How are you doing today man?" He pulled out the chair at the other end of the table and sat down.

"Hey Matty. Good to see you. I already ordered a drink, but made sure not to tempt you with a beer. You're working Miho." Both men laughed. "Yeah, I'm good," Enrique continued. "Life's treating me well. I love being out at the ranch. Some people prefer being out by the ocean. I love it out in the desert. It's like nowhere else a person could be. You should come out more often and listen to a few tunes. You haven't seen the music studio since I finished it, have you?"

"No Bro. Sounds great, but I'm not retired like you." Mateo adjusted his glasses and sat forward. "There's work to be done Enrique. You know how it is. This Mars mission set of projects is interesting as hell, but it's taking it out of me these past couple of months. Much of the work is being done by Caltech and JPL, but some is being coordinated with private enterprise as well. You know it's been going in that direction for years. It's good to have funded expertise from different sources sprouting up now that guys like Musk, Branson, Bezos and others have jumped into various space ventures. The whole industry has been energized in a way it hasn't been since the '60s and early '70s."

"I hope you're not overworking. Life's short Matty. There are other things to explore. I've really been enjoying the overall change. You know, getting into cosas para las que tenía poco tiempo antes, as Papa used to say – things I didn't have time for before. Aren't you planning to retire soon yourself?"

Before Mateo could respond, the waiter came to the table. He greeted them warmly, mentioning he hadn't seen Enrique in a while. After reciting the specials, the waiter asked if they were ready to order. Lighthearted joking ensued when he teased Mateo, who quickly picked up the menu to take a look. A daily regular, he always ordered the same meal. All three laughed a little harder when he confirmed he was going to have his wood-fired personal pizza with anchovies and bacon today too. "Just make sure to leave a jug of water on the table, please." The waiter smiled, then took Enrique's order as well. He thanked them both, walked to the kitchen window to put the order in, and moved on to the next table.

Mateo picked up the conversation where they left off. "Enrique, you know that I always work myself hard. This has to be one of the most exciting jobs in the world. I have thought about retiring, but I think I'll stick around until the early stages of this mission are well under way. This isn't just a job Enrique, you know that. It's an historical initiative. I love being part of it. You know exactly what I mean. Look at you. You may be retired, but you've had an amazing career working at JPL – and here at C.T. Come on. You miss it a little bit, don't you?"

"It was an incredible line of work to get into for sure. I'll give you that Mateo, but as I already said, there are a lot of other things to explore and enjoy. We only have one life. As you must be aware by now, it's a lot shorter than it looked when you were still young. Neither of us falls into that category anymore." Enrique was smiling wryly now.

"Life is shorter than it looks. I know that," Matty replied. "I have to tell you Bro, your enthusiasm and inquisitive nature inspired me to push myself harder too. You delved into the great work you've done over the years, but also built an incredible knowledge base studying other subjects. Dammit Enrique, you are one of the few people I would consider an autodidact. You're self-taught in so many areas. You're a Renaissance man!" Mateo smiled and sat back in his chair. The brothers looked at one another. "That has made me want to do the same Miho. It has made me want to reach for the very stars. We've done that Enrique, but it's not my time to retire just yet. Your achievements are numerous man. You've had a storied career. You were on a team that advised motion picture and television industries on scientific accuracy. You mentored interns on aerospace technologies and engineering, even robotics. Your engineering expertise is legendary around here, and it's only one of the things you're known for. You may be an engineer, but you're almost as knowledgeable about physics as any physicist, especially in the so-called 'spooky' area of quantum physics. You can afford to branch out into other interests now Bro. When these initiatives are established and well on their way, I will let go and branch out too."

Enrique looked down at his glass. "Thanks Matty. You're a good brother. Good enough to qualify as a friend." They both laughed. "I'm not convinced about the accolades though. A Renaissance man? You and I are cut from the same cloth. We're just fucking curious man. Making a breakthrough to some new, higher level understanding can really be exciting, maybe addictive too. Even better than beer Mateo." They laughed again. "And that's why you're really hesitating to leave all this. As for your reference to Einstein's 'spooky' comment, had he lived any longer, he might never have lived that one down."

Enrique was unexpectedly distracted. "Recognize someone," Mateo asked?

"Maybe. Yes, but no…speaking of physicists, is that the theoretical physicist and podcaster Sean Carroll sitting over there?"

Mateo turned in the direction Enrique was looking. "It is. He works over at the Burke building around the corner. You know C.T. always tries to bring in the best, at least for a year or two. He may be permanent, I don't know. I haven't had a chance to speak to him one-on-one. Don't keep trying to change the subject Enrique. I haven't seen you for a bit. I was giving you a compliment."

"Complimenting me, or buttering me up? What's the real reason for lunch here today Mateo?" Enrique was still smiling, but now waited expectantly with a raised eyebrow.

"Hell, I knew you'd figure it out, but that's okay. You know I meant everything I said. I just wanted to rekindle that aura of exhilaration you used to feel when involved in this stuff. This is the thing Enrique. One of the projects I'm supervising is presenting issues and anomalies in an area you are probably more familiar with than anyone, harmonics. You were involved in the development of satellites that required solving harmonic distortion. We have some good guys on it, but they don't have your experience. Look, I won't beat around the bush. I've got an okay from upper management to try and recruit you into just a part-time consultant's position here at Caltech. It wouldn't take much of your time, but you could take a look and maybe make some suggestions. Well, maybe we would like to have you stick around for a while. It's going to take a bit to see these projects well on their way, but as I said, just part-time. For the most part, you can work from the ranch in your much-loved peace and quiet. Admin was willing, albeit reluctantly at first, to be flexible on this."

The two men looked at one another. This time Mateo raised his eyebrow, hoping it would serve as a humorous nudge in the right direction. Enrique was hesitant, so Mateo took advantage of the moment. "Listen Enrique, I understand you probably want to think about it for a little bit. I probably surprised you by pouncing on you with that one, but you know how these projects can be. There is all kinds of pressure for updates on progress, covering every possible base, making sure no unexpected errors occur… You know Enrique, everything has to be perfect. When NASA makes an error, it reverberates for years, affects funding, and sometimes the unthinkable, projects are put on hold or dismissed entirely."

"Yes, I do know, but that's what retirement is Mateo: Leaving all of that behind – because it's time! Besides, it may be cliché, but you know everyone can be replaced. I'm no exception. Those younger men and women working for you will figure it out. Give them a chance. They may come up with novel solutions. It's called progress Bro. Things have come a long way since we started in the industry. They will go a long way too. As you just said about Carroll, Caltech brings in the best. Combined with JPL's staff, these men and women are as top of the line as you're going to find. Give them a little rope Mateo. They won't use it to shimmy down to some resting place. They'll use it to climb up to the next level."

Mateo became hesitant. He wasn't sure what to do. He could continue trying to press Enrique for an answer, even a tentative one. He could let his brother think about it, or he could just drop it and tell admin it's a no go. It was true that his people were bright. A little time might show just how bright they were. Often, the stress was created by deadlines for updates. Administrative concerns often weren't aligned with frontline challenges. As far As Mateo could remember, it's always been that way. Administrators would be invited to come and see the progress for themselves. When that happened, they would often mouth appreciation for the work being done, but there were always further expectations. Administrators had their higher-ups too – people in Congress and the Senate. When it came right down to it, Mateo realized, thoughts about legacy kept him going, but retirement was the goal. It was probably what prompted him to get Enrique involved one last time – get these projects well under way, then head out into the sunset with complete satisfaction.

"Okay Enrique, I'll let it go," Mateo finally said. "I would like you think about it seriously, but if you're really decided against it, then I respect that, pure and simple. Let's change the subject. How are you really doing up there on the old ranch? You were set to open when we last chatted. Have you booked many guests?"

"No, I don't think I'm going to accept guests all the time Matty. It isn't really a business venture. I don't need to care about additional income and I don't want to be tied to routine. As we discussed when I first bought you out, it can be quiet out here. It's a good idea to have people come by once in a while. Casual conversation is a good way to distract from deep thinking and problem-solving. You know I keep myself busy. I may be out in the desert Mateo, but the landscape, the flora and fauna of the area are all so very interesting. Sometimes I enjoy spending my day out on the land seeing what I can see, and finding what I can find. You mentioned me being an amateur physicist. Well, right now I'm acquiring knowledge about geology and biology too. The more you know, the larger the big picture becomes Mateo. That desert out there has as much of a story to tell as any other environment on this planet. I'm discovering part of that story in my own backyard."

Mateo was listening intently, but couldn't see himself spending retirement quite the same way. It was way too hot out there much of the year, at least without a pool and a drink. "What could be so interesting in such a hostile environment? I agree. We do live on a magnificent planet, but you've chosen to settle down in one of its most inhospitable areas. Other than snakeskins, coyote skulls and scorpions, what are you expecting to find in that barren expanse?"

Conversation was interrupted. The waiter arrived with their lunch and asked if there was anything else he could bring them. The brothers indicated they were fine and thanked him. "These both look pretty good," Enrique said, placing the linen napkin on his lap. "Let me answer your question Matty. You wouldn't believe the unusual things one could find in a desert. I could go into the details of the plant life out there. That alone would fascinate you. We could talk about the abundance of desert insects, reptiles and other fauna. We could chat about their interactions. There is also much to disclose about how the elements change the very landscape itself. The landscape is home to many things, and much more activity than people assume. Human activity is itself a factor. Let me skip to a story that just might catch your attention. You want to know what can be found in that barren expanse? Let me tell you."

"Okay, you have my attention Enrique. What exactly can you find out in that barren expanse where you live? You aren't one to stir up drama for its own sake. This should be interesting."

"This isn't only about what I found out in the desert Mateo. It's about how people see things. You know I tend to be reserved about a new idea, at least until I'm sure it's on sound footing. The truth is, just like the quantum physics you referred to before, sometimes what you see may be completely different than what you expected. Maybe Einstein was right when he referred to some aspects of it as spooky."

"What exactly are we talking about here Enrique?"

"It's a bit of a story, but listen carefully." Enrique paused for a moment. "You know Mateo, maybe, just maybe, I agreed to come to see you today because I also have a hidden agenda. I would like your opinion on something."

"I'm all ears. This wood-fire pizza is better than usual today. Want some?"

"No thanks. This is quite good too." Enrique wanted to keep it concise. Being back at an old work environment made him conscious about time. Matty had mentioned pressing deadlines earlier. They were only meeting for lunch. Enrique checked his phone. "You don't have much time Matty. I'll be quick."

"We have a bit of time. Tell me what's going on."

"This probably needs a little context. Okay, a few weeks ago I remember telling you that I was set to open and had planned the date. That was this past Monday, February 17th. I did open. The website had already gone up before that, but I've only had a couple of bookings so far. Maybe you're right. People might not want to come out to the middle of the desert to stay at a bnb. One of the bookings, a couple coming out from New Mexico, have already called to postpone and reschedule for a few days later. Who knows? They may or may not come at all. The other booking was a woman traveling down from Canada. She actually did arrive as scheduled on the 17th, the first day. As it turned out, she's an old acquaintance from the 70s."

"Whoa. Really? That's crazy Miho. Do I know her?"

"I don't know, or can't remember. Do you remember that guy Roger from England who came to stay with our neighbours, the Coopers way back when? The Coops were relatives. He came to go to school in Northridge. He dropped out though because he was a budding musician. Then his family discontinued funding his stay here. He took off. We never saw him again."

"The story sounds familiar, but I don't remember him. If you guys hung out, I wasn't too aware of it. I was probably hanging with the ladies anyway."

"Yeah, right, so you probably don't know Emma either then. They went out until Roger left. After that, the small group that hung out together kind of went their own ways. It happens. I don't remember thinking all that much about it at the time. Anyway, I probably wouldn't have recognized her at all, but she recognized me shortly after arriving. That was crazy enough, but it was just the beginning."

"This is getting interesting," Mateo interjected. "Keep going."

"Not long after you and I agreed to terms settling the property, I began to scope it out in more detail. There are a lot of rocks on one of the ridges, so there are a lot of crevices and openings. It's an ideal habitat for reptiles. Just down from one of the ridges, there is a rocky mound – one of many that rise up from the desert floor. The wind has carved out a small cave at the top. It must have taken centuries. You have to climb a bit to get to it. It's a great little spot. Definitely a good place to get out of the sun on a hot day. It's an even better spot to have a toke and ruminate. There's even a small window carved into one of the walls looking up at the mountains. The whole time Papá owned the place, he never mentioned it. I can't imagine he didn't know about it. We've been by there before. We even had a toke in there before. Maybe you don't remember."

"Anyway," Enrique continued, "after Emma settled in, we had something to eat and caught up on the last forty-plus years. She grew up in Santa Clarita, but went off to Montreal to go to university way back when. She met someone there, had a family and stayed in Canada. Apparently, she's had some recent challenges. That made her want to rethink her future. That's why she wanted

201

to come back down here. A place in the desert was perfect for the getaway she wanted and needed right now. We got talking about the place, then I suggested going for a walk. We ended up having a toke below the first ridge. Then I thought of the cave. The stars were visible and it wasn't far. I figured she would love to peek through the window up to the moonlit mountains. We walked the short distance only to find something completely unexpected Matty."

Mateo laughed. "Not that unexpected Bro. "There was a snake in there, wasn't there? Or worse, a snake den? You know the desert comes alive at night."

"I've seen a couple snakes during the day already, but it's still too cool at night for snakes in February."

"Oh, right. So what was in there, a coyote with pups? What?"

"An unconscious man Mateo. If we hadn't found him, he would surely have died. It was an attempted suicide."

"Say what Bro? That's fucking crazy! So how did he get there? Where was his car? That's a long road up to your place. Was he there for a while? Do you think he was he trying to squat on your land or something like that? Maybe he's a fugitive man! Holy shit!"

"No, I don't think it's like that, but I don't know for sure. I don't think anyone knows so far. He's a John Doe too…and if you think your imagination is going wild about this, you should hear what some other people are thinking. That's why I said this story is also about how people see things."

"Oh man. Do people think he's a serial killer Dude?"

"Settle down Matty. Just listen. There was an empty mickey of booze and a large plastic bottle of pills. The seal had been opened there. It was at least half empty. I checked." Enrique's original concern resurfaced as he relived the incident. "Anyway, that played out. We found out later that he did ingest all of those pills."

"You called 9-1-1 obviously, but how long did it take for help to come out there? You must have worried about him dying, no? Or did you already think he was dead? Imagine that man! If you had found a dead body on your property, it could lead to all kinds of problems. It could go on for a long time too. That's actually a nightmarish scenario Enrique. Shit, I'm rambling again. So what happened?"

Enrique nodded his head. "Geez. Until you just verbalized it, I didn't really stop to think about how this whole thing might have unfolded, but you're right. It really could have created problems that had nothing to do with me in the first place. So far though, everything is fine, at least as far as I'm concerned. Let me tell you what happened."

"Yes, for sure," Mateo said quickly. "Go ahead. I'm listening."

Enrique recounted how police arrived first, but that the man was not airlifted out for some time. Pinpointing the location where the cave was on the property was not so easy. Then, after all the excitement was over at the ranch, he and Emma were required to drive into Lancaster for questioning. Two other responders also ended up there. Enrique skipped the details of his questioning at the station, except to comment that it was more of an interrogation. He spoke about the ride to the hospital with the responders instead. One of them didn't have much to say about the incident, but the other guy already had some crazy ideas. Enrique told Matty about Kevin's alien theory. Then he described the phone call on the way back to the hospital, and the wild suspicion of a possible connection between Emma's schizophrenic son and the guy in the cave. "Before you ask any more questions, let me tell you this Matty. It was like being under the Big Top. The whole night, well into the early hours of the morning, turned into more of a circus than I'm used to."

Enrique noted how extraordinary the whole thing was in retrospect. "When we arrived at the hospital with the medevacs, Emma and I were inadvertently included in an impromptu gathering between them and some doctors. They were discussing the situation in the hallway. According to the doctor in charge at the ER, the patient was at death's door." Enrique's disposition became even more serious when he recapped Emma's impulsive act to help the stranger. He admitted thinking about it disapprovingly, even though it wasn't his business. Nonetheless, Emma involved herself. That prompted subsequent visits. Enrique made a point of telling Mateo that staff were actually confounded by this guy's ability to hang on.

"Now Mateo, if you think this story is out there so far, then just hold on." Mateo kept his silence this time. He just nodded. Enrique continued. "They still haven't figured out who this guy is yet. Or at least they didn't know this morning. He goes by the name of Johnny which he emphasizes in a pseudo New York drawl - Jahny. The guy must have a sense of humour anyway."

"Wow, that's wild Enrique. The guy's near death, but he's talking and joking around?"

"Maybe not joking exactly, but he is talking all right. I'll tell you more about that in a second. Let me continue. When the doctors dispersed, one of the medevac guys also left. That's when I first noticed Emma wasn't standing there with the rest of us anymore. I figured she may have slipped off to the restroom or something. The other medevac, a younger guy, stuck around to talk to me while I waited for her. He seemed like a half-intelligent guy as per his conversation in the car, but he's an enthusiastic believer in aliens. He buys into theories that governments know aliens are among us, but are covering it up. I know those guys are out there, but never met a serious one before. It was an eye-opener."

"Let me guess. He thinks the guy in the cave is an alien. Enrique, man, this is good. I'm loving it. Oh, hey! If the guy is Martian and he gets better, maybe he would like to help us with the Mars projects here. What do you think Bro?" They both laughed.

"Terrible idea. If he's an alien, chances are he's illegal too." More laughter. "Listen, the medevac guy was serious. He strongly suspects Jahny might be an actual alien."

"Really? Why?"

"You asked about where he parked his car earlier. Other than the pills and the mickey he almost finished, the guy only had a sleeping bag, but no other supplies. According to police we spoke to afterward, there were no reports of abandoned vehicles anywhere in the vicinity. As you know, it's out there. That would have been a long walk from any of the so-called nearby communities. He didn't have any water with him. It's a desert in February. Not impossible maybe, but almost. This medevac guy, Kevin, said there had been other incidents of lone strangers being found in the desert. He was on one of those other airlifts personally, and spoke to colleagues directly involved in another. Apparently they were John Does too, but were already dead or died shortly after discovery. Neither of them were near my property, but there's a lot of desert out there."

"So you said this all happened this past Monday? He was at death's door then, but you know he was still alive this morning?"

"As far as I know, but listen. As I said, Emma is convinced there may be a connection between this guy and her son. That phone call she got on our way to the hospital Monday night – Tuesday morning really – wasn't the only one. To make a long story short, her son made references that led Emma to believe he and this Jahny guy are somehow acquainted. It freaked her out. How could he know about someone she was about to find in a cave out in the desert? Anyway, I don't want to explain all of that now. The point is that she's become quite caught up in all this. She has spoken to the psych assigned to Jahny's case. Apparently she, the psych that is, was also taken by this guy. She thinks he's an anomaly as well. If it sounds complicated, it is, and became that way quickly."

"Wow, so where is this situation now? Have you met this guy since finding him on your property?"

"I have, and I'll tell you Mateo, the guy is unusual, even interesting. He certainly isn't what you might expect."

"I'm still listening."

"Everyone who has had access to this guy is intrigued by him. That includes Emma, the two medevac guys, the psych, and doctors. What's more interesting is that they all have different reasons for being intrigued. Just this morning, we all converged in Jahny's hospital room before being dispersed by the psychiatrist. That was quite a session, I'll tell you. While we were there, this guy was like a guru. He engaged everyone individually about their thoughts and ideas. It was surrealistic. If you were a fly on the wall Matty, you would almost be able to see the wheels turning in everyone's heads. You could practically measure the flood of thoughts each were experiencing when conversing with this guy. He appeared solemn, but often smiled when engaging someone directly. He seemed to comprehend where each was coming from and responded directly to their interests. I'm not sure it's an accurate observation, but everyone gave me the impression they felt he understood them implicitly. There was something about this guy that made these people think he had answers to their concerns. They were all compelled to go there and see him this morning."

"Wow, and all this from a guy who's at death's door," Mateo interjected. "Sorry Bro. This is a pretty wild story."

"Well yes, that's just it," Enrique agreed. "This guy was supposed to be dead, period. Every instrument and measurement hospital staff have to determine his condition points to a medical impossibility. Yet there he was looking and acting like a teacher interacting with motivated students. Actually, they gave me the impression of being more like disciples. So there, I've narrowed down my impression. He's either Socrates or Jesus. It was bizarre."

Okay Enrique, where does all this stand now? What has Emma said about all this? And my most pressing question would be, what do you think about all this – besides that it's all strange?"

"Good questions. Are you still good for time?"

'Yeah, yeah, my staff is proving their worth, remember? They can continue without me. If need be, I'll make up the time later. Go on."

"Even before she met Jahny personally, she had spoken to the psych. Do you remember that I told you she slipped away during an impromptu hallway conversation? Well, she ran into the psych on her way back. Apparently, they engaged in conversation not only about Emma's financial intervention, but about her son. That led to another encounter with the psych who encouraged her to visit with Jahny. Don't you think that's a little unusual too? Anyway, the psych suggested Emma give Jahny a chance to rest first, so she went to a bookstore across the street. She ended up buying a few books. A couple were about Carl Jung's works. Another was a book by a philosopher…" Enrique paused momentarily to recall the name. "Kant, Immanuel Kant. I've never been too big on philosophy, but I know the guy is important."

"Hmmm, that's interesting. Jung and Kant, eh? Also interesting that philosophy is an area you haven't explored yet Enrique. You're slacking off. Perhaps you're not quite the Renaissance man I perceived," Mateo said teasingly. "So again, what do you think?"

Enrique sighed. "I'm not sure what to think yet Mateo. That's why I'm bouncing this stuff off you. Things can be difficult to explain. It's important not to jump to conclusions until having as much evidence as possible. It's just as important not to become enamored by coincidence or circumstantial evidence. I can see why people who don't read science, or prefer science fiction, might have broader imaginations about what is possible. After all, imagination is everything."

"That's right Bro. Even Einstein said it was more important than knowledge. As a species, we follow our dreams to create and recreate a world in progress. Imagination may be everything, but it doesn't necessarily unfold right away." Mateo leaned forward and lowered his voice. "Sometimes, it's two steps forward, one step back. We've seen this a lot lately, even in the halls of academia. I know this is obvious, but people tend to build mental frameworks about reality. These frameworks even determine what they are open to believing or not. Many, many people who see facts that don't fit their mental framework tend to adapt the facts, not question the framework. In other words, people tend to see something very close to what they're looking for. Politics is a particularly potent example these days my good man."

"That's why I try not to pay too much attention to it. It's so easy to get into a way of thinking and believing there's nothing more to add to it, no matter what it is. People who believe they have the truth tend to think another perspective is not just off the mark, but generally outrageous just for being an alternative. Once sides are drawn, participants see only one truth. All others are deluded. That's why it can be dangerous to believe in something too strongly before having the facts. People tend to find factoids that fit the belief. The real facts become blurred, or even irrelevant. You really should've been a fly on the wall this morning Matty. As I said earlier, you could see the wheels turning. All of their minds were racing."

"I wish I was."

"Really Mateo. They all left the hospital energized by their individual mental machinations. Emma's back at the ranch right now. She isn't relaxing and focusing on the reason she came down here. She's doing research, visiting with, and attempting to help a stranger we discovered dying in the desert. The others are energized too. The psych has a more interesting case than she might normally have; it's a complicated set of anomalies. Both of the medevac guys are highly interested in who this guy might really be. One thinks he's an alien; the other thinks he may bring on the apocalypse. Even the doctors are perplexed. You know Matty, despite not having any vested interest in this situation like the others, it's amazing how I've been caught up in it all. It has captured my attention."

Enrique looked down at the table, then directly at his brother with a piercing glare. "What do I think about it you ask? Well brother, I have to say that I really don't know. There's a lot that none of us know. That's why it's important to keep an open mind. Our knowledge is emergent. It's still unfolding. And you know Mateo, lately I just can't help but recognize the whole damn universe as emergent, still unfolding and taking us all on a wild ride."

"Beautiful man," Mateo said. "I like how you convey your ideas, even when they are uncertain. But I think you do have some idea of this strange set of circumstances. You're probably working it all out in your head. You haven't completed your assessment. You just haven't worked it all out to your own satisfaction - yet. That's good Enrique. That's fine. I know you. You don't really need me to help figure it out. You just need someone to bounce your ideas off of. I wish I had more time to watch this whole process unfold too. I have seen it before. A few classic examples immediately come to mind. One of my favourites was a side project you were interested in some years ago. You know what I'm talking about, that research into quantum cohesion. How did that go again? Something about…"

Enrique busted a huge smile. "That was smooth buddy. You're trying to bring me back to your project now, aren't you? You pay more attention than I give you credit for."

"Similar backgrounds Bro. You shouldn't be surprised. Whenever we've chatted over the years, especially over a beer, or when we've had a chance for some tokes and tunes, I've listened to what you've had to say. Our conversations have meandered all over the place, but they've always been memorable. Hmmm, come to think of it, I'm not sure how that link popped into my head. Must be subliminal. All good Bro. No pressure about helping us here – sort of. Anyway, since that's come up now, update me. That was an interesting side venture you pursued diligently. Tell me again Enrique, what was that quantum cohesion idea all about?"

"Do you still have some time? This place has almost emptied out. Lunch must be over."

"I'm busy, but I'm the lead on this project. There's a little leeway. I'll head back shortly. We don't actually get to see one another as much I would like these days."

"Okay then. I'm not pressed for time like you are, but I should probably head out soon too. Bender's in the truck, albeit more than comfortable, but I have things to do before heading back to the ranch later as well. Quantum cohesion, eh? I haven't thought about it too seriously since working it all out back then. It wasn't an obsession. My interest was generated by others who were exceptionally enthusiastic about their work in the field. We really don't have time for me to explain it in detail here. You would have to be well versed in the terminology. To cut it short, we'll bypass some of the definitions. If you're really interested Mateo, there's a lot of accessible scientific literature on quantum theory. Here it is in something slightly larger than a nutshell."

"Cool man. I'm still all ears."

"You know enough about QT to know that it deals with physics at a very small level – the level of atoms, electrons, protons, quarks and qubits."

"Qubits?"

"The very small. Anyway, we spoke about Einstein's idea of spooky action earlier, so you do understand, at least generally, that there is something called nonlocal entanglement. That's where particles entangled together can share information instantaneously, no matter how far apart they may travel. This has been proven in controlled studies over and over again for decades now. Einstein called it spooky because in his theories of relativity, nothing can go faster than the speed of light. Yet, in all these studies, we see that somehow, information is being transmitted between entangled particles over immense distances. It happens instantaneously, without taking even a miniscule amount of time like it would traveling at the speed of light. It's more complicated than how I'm describing it, but basically, the reason is that everything is occurring within a unified field. Literally everything is part of this field. It's like the universe is one single thing, but with various extended aspects to it. Information already exists throughout the universe because it's all one thing. What's interesting about this Mateo, is that they thought these quantum effects could only be manifest in the realm of the very small. Yet, back in the '70s, cylindrical structures were unexpectedly discovered in brain neurons that were just nanometer-sized. As you know Mateo, that's super small. It wasn't until the mid-90s that an anesthesiologist at the University of Arizona suggested that these microtubules, as they are called, might be a possible site for quantum effects in the brain. It took a guy who suspends consciousness by putting people out before surgeries to realize that there was a connection between these previously overlooked microtubules and consciousness itself."

"Hold on," Mateo said. "Are you telling me that this is relevant to your friend Emma's concern about her son? Are you saying that the connection between her son and this Jahny guy might somehow be possible scientifically in quantum terms?"

"I'm not sure about anything I'm saying yet, but the unusual situation between Emma's son and Jahny keeps bringing me back to this idea. You know I'm a skeptic at heart Mateo, but maybe, just maybe, there is a scientific basis for communication by thought alone - telepathy. There may be an explanation for mysteries we haven't been able to explain before. Is it possible people inadvertently interact with one another in this manner without realizing it consciously? After all, we are well-aware that communication is accomplished by more than just verbalization alone. This could just be an added feature of that process.

23

Lunchtime had slipped into mid-afternoon before Enrique left Caltech. His old dog had been sleeping in the back of the truck the whole time he was chatting with Mateo. Bender fared well in the digital comfort of his improvised mobile, temperature-controlled doghouse. Not only did it provide shade in the warmer weather, but also intermittent water vapour emissions. The setup was sensor controlled and powered by a solar panel with battery storage. Not your typical doghouse, but it worked well for the man and his best friend.

Enrique was looking forward to the next part of his day. He had already begun scheming for quiet time while at the hospital earlier this morning. That was best done either out in the desert, or in the forest up in the San Gabriels. No more appointments or responsibilities had to be taken care of that day. That's what retirement is all about, he gloated. He could make a good day happen. Enrique relished having the time to do what he wanted when he wanted. It takes almost a lifetime to get here, so it has to be honoured for the privilege it is. He acknowledged some responsibility to consider Mateo's request, but he had already made up his mind. The proverbial baton had been passed to the next set of minds. They can pick up the future from where I left off, he mused.

Enrique recollected other points and ideas he and Mateo discussed at lunch. His brother remembered his interest in harmonics, but clearly didn't realize Enrique was still advancing his understanding of its complexities. Mateo brought it up because it was related to current issues with the Mars projects. Had he been aware of Enrique's ongoing pursuits, he would have pressed the opportunity to join the projects. He knew his brother. Mateo definitely would have emphasized the benefit of getting paid. The money didn't concern Enrique. When he and Mateo both had time, he would be glad to offer ideas and insight, but he was finished with formal employment. Deadlines, memos, meetings, phone and video calls were now completely off the table.

Enrique and his brother had also discussed Emma's son Anthony. Mateo enjoyed hearing all about that. Enrique knew the back-and-forth might generate ideas to help Emma solve her mystery. Well, it may or may not, he thought, and smiled at the impulsivity he displayed during their conversation by throwing the word 'telepathy' out there. In retrospect, his brother might easily have laughed at the suggestion, but he didn't. That's the good thing about bantering ideas about with other scientific minds. Anything can go on the table until proven it shouldn't be there. It's about considering all the possibilities, then moving forward through checks and balances. The telepathy comment came at the end of a string of topics. One thing always leads to another. This lunch exchange had meandered from Mateo's projects at work to the crisis at the ranch on Monday night. Then it progressed to Jahny's situation, Anthony's phone calls, everyone's varying perspectives on it all, and finally, on harmonics, quantum physics and entanglement. Wow! That was quite a conversation, especially toward the end. Enrique loved how science blew his mind on a regular basis. That would continue too. There were so many intellectual triggers he would like to pull, detonating brain neurons into paradise. That's why it truly was time for retirement – not so much to relax, but to explore other wormholes.

Turning on the truck's ignition, Enrique backed out of his parking spot, and meandered his way back down through the parking garage. Earlier, on his way to Pasadena that morning, he intended to head right back after lunch. He thought about retreating to one of his spots in the surrounding desert. Maybe he would return to the cave with the aperture.

Emma was likely to be at the ranch. She had wanted to spend some time reading, but might be inclined to chat by now. No doubt she's been gathering more ideas, either from her books, or by contemplating everything that's happened. That was fine, but could wait until later. Besides, if Enrique wanted to help Emma advance her ideas or leads, he needed something solid to offer. That took some thought, some deep thought. Enrique knew he may very well have contributions to make, but just heading back and chatting might not be the best way to roll it out.

The day was still young, even if daylight hours were short. It only took seconds to decide. He needed time to ruminate. He also wanted to pursue another interest. Today he could indulge both pursuits.

Being close to his old stomping grounds anyway, Enrique considered a favourite haunt. The Gabrielino Trail began its climb up into the mountains from Millard Canyon behind JPL's massive parking structure. When he still worked there, Enrique would often slip into the woods behind the complex at lunch. Sometimes he just wanted to bathe in the natural soundscape. It unchained his mind from the mundane regularities of interaction with others. He was free to wrestle with novel possibilities instead. The natural environment behind JPL became an idea factory fueling creativity. As he approached the Oak Grove Dr. exit in La Cañada to access the canyon, however, Enrique suddenly had an even better idea. He checked the rear-view mirror, then signaled back into the center lane.

The Millard Canyon access to the trail had increasingly become more popular over the past two decades. Enrique didn't feel like having to hike a distance just to get away from the hikers or day-walkers who might disturb his train of thought. If he was going to go for a hike, then he was going to make it well worth the effort. Just up the highway a few minutes, he could exit the Angeles Crest Highway, and head up into the San Gabriels. The other end of the trail was less accessible and much less traveled.

"Feel like going up to Switzer Canyon there Bender?" The shepherd looked up at him anxiously. The tone suggested a walk. Although nestled comfortably on the passenger seat, Bender would never hesitate to get his old body out for a romp outdoors. The dog wouldn't recognize the name Switzer, but he looked at Enrique with anticipation. That dog practically had a smile on his face. He understood.

Enrique was smiling too. This was a great idea. The Foothill Boulevard exit at La Cañada was the next one off the highway. He signaled a right at the top of the ramp, then turned onto the Angeles Crest Highway. It was a regularly-used paved road up into the San Gabriels, but it could hardly be called a highway. With only a single lane in each direction, it ribboned along switchbacks for 66 miles up into the mountains. The view was incredible, but the drive was not for the faint-hearted. Enrique only needed to drive ten or twelve miles. Winding along the route heightened Bender's expectations. He sat up on the passenger seat and looked out the window.

Enrique hadn't spent much time on the project the last few weeks. Getting the ranch ready for bed and breakfast status proved to be a distraction. The larger renovations had already been completed beforehand, but several small finishing touches were necessary. Had no guests booked for opening day as Emma did, he would have been back at this project again on Monday. It was only Wednesday, so no harm, no foul, as the basketball cliché went. He expected interruptions once the ranch opened up anyway. Even a part-time bed and breakfast was going to be an additional ball to juggle. All good, he thought. As long as it remains interesting. Enrique acknowledged it was already proving to be just that.

As for this project, being up in the mountains was going to afford him a great opportunity to advance previous progress. Enrique had spent a lot of time on this at various locations around the ranch before. Now he was going to take a few hours to study a different econiche. The early winter darkness would be advantageous. Fortunately, Enrique realized appreciatively, the equipment he needed was still in his shoulder pack on the floor behind the seat. The pack was

212

essential. He was going to have to take the equipment for a hike first. It probably wasn't a great idea leaving it all in the truck for more than a few days. Things were less than normal this week though, so he excused the oversight.

Enrique became lost in thought as the truck meandered frequent switchbacks. He calculated time, distance and elevation-climb for the trek ahead. He knew the area well and had hiked Switzer many times, but the afternoon was ticking by. Enrique figured he could easily make the intended grove by nightfall if he were on his own, but Bender was with him. He better check the battery charge in the big flashlight when he got to the trailhead. Enrique already planned on bringing a lantern, but the flashlight would provide good backup.

A minor tinge of guilt crept in, but was quickly addressed. Enrique had considered texting Emma, but was already out of cell range. She can enjoy her books quietly, he thought. If she's still up when I return, we'll have plenty to talk about. She isn't stuck there anyway. She has her rental car.

Enrique loved the mountains. Viewing them from the property wasn't always sufficient. Before inheriting the ranch, the San Gabriels were his most accessible escape to the natural world. Since moving out to the desert, his property had become not only a refuge, but his extended lab. That brought his mind back to some of his projects. It's kind of funny, he thought. When Matty and I were chatting this afternoon, he asked me about living out on the ranch. I told him that I was interested in the flora, fauna and other aspects of an unexpectedly rich environment like a desert. He didn't think to ask me about harmonics then, did he? Yet he knows about my interest in sub-branches of that field. If Mateo had more time on his hands, he would surely have been interested in this project too. Enrique chuckled out loud. Bender looked over with an expression that said, 'just drive.'

As he drove up along the Crest towards Switzer, Enrique figured Bender was going to need nourishment. If he was going to drag his old buddy along rough terrain, he would need the energy to do it. Good thing he also kept dry food in the truck for unplanned intervals out and about. As for his own nourishment, he had enjoyed enough food at the Chandler to keep him until he got home later. If he burned more calories than expected until then, well, he could afford a pound or two anyway. He had lots of water. That was always most important.

One had to pay attention for fallen rock on this drive, especially when cornering switchbacks. Changing views of the desert canyons below were distracting. At the top of the Crest,

213

the main road split. A left turn meandered its way down to the Mohave and home. He would take it later once he finished up here. Enrique pulled into a drive on the right instead. He had to stop at the Clear Creek Info Center for a parking pass. Signs at all trailheads up in the mountains threatened to tow away vehicles whose owners hadn't secured one. It was midweek. The winter afternoon sun was already waning. Enrique doubted any ranger would bother with a citation now. Would they really strand hikers or bring a tow truck up here at night for a thirty-dollar violation? Then he thought of past bureaucracies he had experience with; it was probably a good idea to just get the pass.

Once back in the truck, he only had to drive a hundred yards or so before turning right onto a dirt road. The steeply-descending grade must have been tricky to implement from this access point. Enrique had always considered it treacherous. Although unlikely, a heavy rainstorm could probably eliminate sections irreparably. He inched his vehicle down slowly. Another truck had strategically stopped at the first of two narrow switchbacks below. Having clearly spotted Enrique first, the driver waited along the slightly-widened curve. Enrique nodded in appreciation as he crawled by. The turn was tight with scant room for error.

When Enrique reached the bottom of the canyon and turned into the parking area, he noticed there were no other vehicles. The truck on the switchback was the last to leave for the day. Makes sense, Enrique thought. It's mid to late afternoon on a winter's day. Light in the deeper canyons would already be fading. Anyone still up here would want to head back down before dark. Nowone would be up here for the same reason he had come today. What other reasons would there be? The Sierra Club sometimes organized night hikes in the mountains, but they were usually weekend outings. He didn't expect to see anyone else now. Perhaps that truck had been the only other vehicle here all day. Enrique turned the key off.

"Well boy. We're here. Time for a walk."

Bender was given some of his dry food while Enrique made his way to the only man-made bathroom around. It was habit to look out for snakes in and around outhouses, even if finding one now was unlikely. It was always a little cooler in the parking lot. The oak grove here at the trailhead kept it in shade all day, and it was still too early in the year for reptiles at this altitude.

While Bender licked his bowl clean, Enrique organized the few things he needed to take along the trail. It started to cool off quickly as the afternoon waned, so he made sure to bring his jacket and even some gloves. A small bag of dry food for Bender was also placed in his pack along

214

with the equipment. His old friend would need it later before the trek back. Enrique locked up the truck and they set off.

There were quite a few birds chirping in the grove where the trail began. Avian activity always seemed to heighten perceptibly as evening approached. Bender looked around longingly, but knew to reign in distraction and keep pace. Not far from where the truck was parked, there was a small waterfall. The stream that flowed from it would follow the trail for some time. The Arroyo Seco was one of the few streams that managed to run all year long in this arid climate. It afforded lush greenery through the fourteen-mile-long canyon down to the Jet Propulsion Lab. The much-needed water also serviced a variety of creatures along the canyon bottom.

Enrique and Bender walked quietly along the path. As the trail progressed, the stream went over another falls into the first of a series of deep pools of water. The water was cold, even in summer, but Enrique had seen young people swimming in the first one on more than one occasion. Whenever he hiked by this section of the trail, it always reminded him of a scene in the old Disney movie *Swiss Family Robinson*. Stranded on a desert island, the kids found a pool to slide into like this one. Enrique used to wonder if this was the location of that shoot. He actually looked it up online years ago, but discovered most locations were in Trinidad and Tobago. Nonetheless, the pool continued to remind him of that scene.

Enrique paid attention to the changing sound of the biome as the trail gained elevation. He and Bender climbed from under the trees to above the canopy. Birds dominated all other sounds. The din was increasing. Among some treetops, there was even an outright ruckus.

Once they climbed the ridge, Switzer waterfalls came into view on the opposite wall of the canyon. It isn't Niagara. Someone unfamiliar with the area could easily miss the thin stream falling a hundred or more feet to join the Arroyo Seco below. It's seasonal flow often discontinued during warmer months. Unless walking along from the other direction, the falls were unlikely to be noticed by random hikers at all.

Bender was a little slower than Enrique had expected and was lagging behind. The slope was steeper than anything his dog had to undertake in a while. When they reached the highest point on the trail just below the summit, Enrique put his pack down to give Bender some more water. The old shepherd was panting heavily for some minutes. Enrique waited, but not too long. Bender could have more water from the Arroyo when they reached the bottom again. "It's all downhill from here on good buddy," he muttered. "We don't have too far to go. Then you can rest." Bender got up when Enrique spoke. He followed slowly, but faithfully.

Once they reached the canyon floor again, the stream came close to the path. The trail turned a few degrees to follow it, motivated by centuries of erosion. The cliff they had been walking alongside continued to turn further than the trail itself and cut off to Enrique's right. He stopped and scanned the section of forest in that direction. This was the place he was looking for. He had been here before and determined to return just for this purpose. Due to the curve in the canyon wall and the distracting recurrence of the stream running alongside the trail, it was easy to walk by the grove. There was no path in, so it was unenticing. A shallow stream flowed from inside the heavily-wooded thicket to join the Arroyo Seco. The copious undergrowth all around it would hide one's feet, activating latent fears of unseen creatures crawling and slithering. Hikers wouldn't think twice about passing by.

"This is where we leave the trail Bender. You're going to like it in here and you can have a long cool drink. You can relax for a long while too. We won't be heading back for at least a few hours."

Enrique walked through the brush making sure not to trample anything he could avoid. He stopped to examine a fallen tree. It wouldn't take much to determine its approximate age. Some decay had occurred, but he could ascertain the approximate time that had passed since it toppled to its resting place. He wanted to pick at it with his knife, but chose not to retrieve it from his pack. If there is time after setting up, he thought, I can come back. Light is fading fast.

A few moments later, he stopped again. "Why don't you lie down here boy." He bent down, petted Bender, and ran his hand along the dog's back. "Lie down old boy. I'm going to set up. We need to be quiet. We want to disturb the area as little as possible. It's a good time for you to take a snooze." Bender slowly crouched down to the ground and nestled into a comfortable spot. Enrique continued to pet him quietly until the dog was relaxed and knew they were staying.

Enrique looked around to make note of the dominant vegetation in the surrounding area. He was only interested in a section of it, maybe a 40 to 50 foot radius. The spot where they had stopped was ideal, he thought. With the cliff behind, and the stream winding around this sandy bar stretched out from the rock wall, there shouldn't be any unwelcome surprises. Enrique wasn't worried about venomous reptiles. It was too cool at this elevation and time of year. Although rare, mountain lions and bears roamed the San Gabriel mountains. The large predators were unlikely to

216

be a problem either. There were too few of them. Enrique's friend at the State Fish and Game Commission told him recently not to be surprised if endangered species status was extended to the big cats later this year. Urban expansion all around left the mountains as their only remaining territory, driving numbers down. Bears had the same problem and were rarely seen anywhere in Southern California.

Enrique opened the front section of his pack and pulled out a tarp. He unfolded a small section and laid it on the ground close to the rock wall. Except for the small areas he and Bender would occupy, he wanted to make sure the area was untouched. Carefully taking out each piece of equipment from their containers, he laid them out on the tarp.

The light was now waning quickly, but there was still enough time to complete the set up. Enrique leaned back to where Bender was laying and gently ran his hand down the dog's back. "You know the routine boy. I'm going to do a quick survey of the immediate surroundings, set up the equipment and take a leak. You can stay here and sleep." Bender opened his eyes momentarily, but did not move. Enrique's tone was soothing. The dog was content.

Enrique scanned the vegetation and noted various species. He recognized many, but took photos of several others for later identification. Recognizing differences from species along the main path, he understood that some plants flourishing in the grove were not as resilient to heavier traffic. Enrique could see no prints, even in the soft sand along the edge of the quiet stream. Larger animal traffic in the grove must also be rare. Smaller, more fragile species of creatures could thrive in a relatively safe enclave below the cliff. It spawned a tiny sub-ecosystem within the larger environment. Enrique felt relaxed and peaceful in here, yet excited. Maybe it wasn't exactly excitement, but senses were heightened.

Enrique wondered about the biome in the grove, refocusing on distinctions from plant clusters out along the path. In a complex topography like the San Gabriels, vegetation could change drastically from one area to the next. Several factors influenced vegetation patterns. Direction modified temperature, precipitation, and even radiation from the sun. Elevation affected them as well. Available moisture was at least partially determined by faulting and fractures in the surrounding base rock too. All of these factors affect eco-possibilities. That's why Enrique needed to study varying econiches. In science, the importance of data comparisons couldn't be overstated. It's all so wonderfully intricate, he thought. It's endlessly fascinating.

Enrique soon finished scoping out details within the target radius. Determining the geology and biology of an area was important, but not the actual focus of the session. He picked up three small metal dishes from the tarp where his equipment was laid out. One was to be placed at each of three boundary points. All of them had to face back toward the spot below the cliff where he had set up a microphone. The rising rock wall would help amplify sounds being collected. After re-measuring distances between dishes and the microphone, Enrique made adjustments. Using other instruments, he was able to determine exact elevation, wind direction and moisture. A few soil samples revealed granular anorthosite and granite with lesser amounts of crystalline shist.

Once all the equipment was in place, Enrique pulled out his palmtop and ran the accompanying app to establish a field grid. Setting recording specifications and determining quality of playback was essential before starting the session. All other gadgets, including Enrique's cell phone, were turned off. The last piece of necessary equipment was a folding three-legged stool a friend had recommended for just such occasions.

One last review of the setup had to be conducted. Darkness was setting in. Enrique walked past grid boundaries to relieve himself. After stooping down to rinse his hands in the stream, he leaned over Bender to give him one last pat on the shoulder. He unfolded the tarp a little wider, then placed the stool on top. Finally, he pulled out a notepad and a pencil. That was quieter than fiddling with tech and emitted no light. He could jot down notes by sense and interpret the scribble later. The environs had to be as natural as possible. His presence had to be virtually invisible, totally non-intrusive. Enrique placed the flashlight within reach. Using it would disrupt the session, but knowing where it was made him feel secure. It made sense to be pragmatic. Enrique wasn't afraid of being out in the mountains alone at night. Under the circumstances, it was going to be exhilarating.

Enrique turned on the equipment. Everything was set. He sat comfortably, but very still. It would take some time for the quiet to dissipate, but soon the biome would begin to express its presence. He settled in and waited patiently.

24

Sitting as quietly as possible was not something that came easy to Enrique. He sat on his stool adjusting to the waning light. It was much darker in the canyon grove than on the ridge above the canopy, but it was still possible to see the outlines of surrounding vegetation. Bender was barely visible on the ground two yards away. That good old dog was both well aware of, and secure about, Enrique's proximity.

Bender was unlikely to be roused by the natural biophony of the location unless a larger intruder came to disturb it. His ears took in a greater sample of the relevant soundscape than Enrique's could, so Enrique knew that if his dog didn't stir, then he could focus on the task at hand. This wasn't just about collecting information. It was about capturing the essence of a place, a unique biological setting. Once he mastered sitting still, he needed to concentrate on listening, just listening. He wanted to reach an almost meditative state. It was about letting himself melt into the surroundings.

Several minutes passed. Enrique's breathing relaxed into a slower meditative rhythm. He began to notice an increase in the distinct sounds that could be heard in the focus area. Other sounds emanated from outside those parameters, but consisted mostly of louder calls or screeches. Birds were settling onto roosts before night fell. Slowly, the more localized din rose to subjugate the rich, extended diversity of sound. Nothing outside his immediate surroundings could now be seen clearly, except for the window-like openings through the tree tops far above. He did not look up toward the stars that were now emerging, but instead closed his eyes to completely focus on his auditory environs.

Enrique wanted to completely immerse himself in the experience. One particular goal was to attain the best recording possible. It was critical that all possible sounds from the biome itself be distinguished from any interfering noise. Aircraft were likely culprits for disturbing samples, probably the only ones this far from any road. Enrique knew no day hikers would traverse this far down the trail at dark. The rising natural din in the surrounding forest provided evidence. Most creatures tended to discontinue contributions to the chorus when detecting interruption. It usually took time for various species to settle in and feel secure enough to risk betraying location. Frogs and toads were an interesting exception. They tended to vocalize together, providing acoustic camouflage for numerous contributing individuals in discrete whereabouts. Enrique could detect croaking within the focus area, but knew that included reverberations from the forest at large.

The sensation of being in the woods alone at night was distinctive. This wasn't the first time Enrique had undertaken such a venture, but it was always something he had to ease into. He didn't feel particularly afraid. There was little chance of real danger. It just took a little time to accustom himself to the true serenity of this place. Urban aptitudes and acumen needed to dissolve into the contextual ambience of the natural world. Just keeping track of time was a subtle extension of civilization necessary to dissolve. For Enrique, it involved process. It was a matter of reducing awareness right down to the rhythm of his own breathing. Slow deep breath in; slow deep breath out, repeat. It was about letting go of any thought or sensation from the world outside this place. It was about being here and now. It was about paring thought distractions right down to the subtle nuances of the existing soundscape. It was about relaxing, allowing his ears to collect resonant data. It was about creating a mental impression of this place.

This was something very different from Enrique's everyday experience. It wasn't the hustle and bustle of the city. It wasn't casual conversation with others throughout the day. It wasn't the collective mindset of an industrious and technological world. It was blending rain into pond water, alikeness become oneness. The sounds of the surrounding forest became internal sensations. He could feel the forest. It was the place itself. Enrique mingled into an emergent awareness of his environs. He became its reflection. It was the trees. It was the undergrowth too. It was insect. It was amphibian. It was the gentlest of breezes on his face. It was even the rocks behind him and the ground beneath. It was the relative, subtle vibrations of surrounding entities. It was essence. Theirs. His.

To comprehend this place was to be very much in the present. It is now. It extends seamlessly toward the outer reaches of an expanding universe. Here within himself, his eyes still closed, was The Universe. As Enrique breathed, it breathed. As his heart beat, it pulsed. There was unison, not just of space, but time. Spacetime. Shifting. Intuitively meandering, channeling infinity. Chimera. Gradually, unhurriedly, gently, the sounds around him transformed into voices, intonations, cadences, accentuations of otherness. It was the combined modulations and sentience of the universe in the moment.

The voices, the otherness, the emergent song of all that was this place filled Enrique's mind. It was ever-present. I am here along with everything that has ever been here, he thought. It is a flow of information, a river of transformation. It is the continually-emergent nature of what is.

Enrique tried to imagine how he might describe the subtle differences in the sounds now bathing his ears. What acoustic textures could be distinguished and given words to describe them? This is where language becomes insufficient, he lamented. Words couldn't begin to describe the rich diversity of sounds blending into the overall soundscape. The experience was sensual, phenomenal, completely subjective. It was immersion into the essence and being of the place.

Enrique remembered trying to describe such experiences to Mateo. It was when he first began recording soundscapes around the ranch. Immersing oneself into a soundscape was not like viewing a photograph. An amazing photograph can be awe-inspiring and emote complex responses, but it could never replicate primal sensitivities like immersion into a soundscape can. "Imagine watching a film without the sound," he remembered telling his brother. "It would leave much to be desired. But, if you could close-off all other sounds and were to listen to a recording of a protracted silence followed by a soft, low growl in the immediate vicinity, you would feel the goosebumps rising on your arms in response. You would feel the pit of fear in your stomach."

There was nothing in the surrounding biophony to arouse Enrique's defences. Except for an instance of flapping wings above the trees moments earlier, all bird sounds had ceased. The chorus of toads and frogs now dominated the overall din. Enrique tried to ascertain distinct voices within the focus area, but his thoughts soon began drifting. Resonances of the croaking and humming activity mutated in Enrique's imagination, hinting at playful twitter and children's laughter. He began to imagine others here. He envisaged an ancient camp in these mountains long before Europeans found North American shores. How different that must have been.

Even more intriguing was the thought of more ancient sentients, small pre-historic groups who may or may not have yet harnessed fire. What might their experience of life been like in the forests they occupied? Even uncontacted tribes of the Brazilian forest have been observed using fire. Those who came before are entities of the deep past. To retrieve what we once were, we must reimagine it. That requires places like this one, Enrique thought. Only immersion into the essence of a place can nurture such recollection.

Enrique recognized an emerging pattern from previous soundscape sessions. His ability to remain as still as possible was key to clarifying his experience of a place. It was meditative, a type of magic, consenting to merge into the landscape and channel its very lifeblood. If one were to appropriate a metaphor from modern imagination, it was a mind-meld with nature.

Long ago, sitting quietly wasn't an unusual activity conducted in the midst of an estranged technological world. Enrique could imagine living in such a time, perhaps way back in distant prehistory. People who lived in or near the forest would have been thoroughly attuned to their environment. It shaped who they were because it shaped what they could be. They thought differently. They had to be aware of their environment much more acutely than Enrique could envisage. That reciprocity with place facilitated survival. Basic instincts provided basic sustenance. Remaining in the food chain could be challenging enough. Moving up the food chain required something extra.

Enrique thought about this. The species needed something that provided an advantage. It necessitated an advantage different than just superior speed or strength. It had to supersede them, subordinate all other advantages. He realized that in hindsight, one could see that was what had to happen only because that's what did happen. Earlier forms made contributions. Australopithecines, Homo Erectus, Homo Neanderthalensis and others survived for millennia. Only Homo Sapiens prevailed. Now we transform the planet. Now we transform ourselves. Heady stuff, Enrique thought. He marveled at all he imagined, even as he consciously receded into the confines of the surrounding grove.

Enrique continued absorbing the sounds of the forest. It was intoxicating, encouraging further dreamworlds from a distant past. He strove to imagine how ideas evolved, slowly, ever so slowly over millennia. Curiosity may have killed the cat, but surely it empowered humanity. Curiosity incited learning. Learning increased and differentiated knowledge. Symbolism emerged. Language arose. Specialization was born. Hence, the birth of the shaman – an intermediary with, and interpreter of both nature and the supernatural.

Enrique tried to envisage the role of the shaman. Anthropology often characterized them as early medicine men, individuals utilizing the unknown as hocus pocus. The very term shaman implied primitivism, perhaps in condescension. Enrique knew such ways of thinking were changing now, but still didn't portray the important role the shaman actually performed. Sitting here in the dark and listening to the chorus surrounding him, he visualized the shaman as intermediary. The shaman was the connection, the relation, the link between the human community and the larger environment they were part of. The shaman immersed himself into the web of relations between all he could observe. By learning the intricacies of cycles and patterns, the shaman sought to ensure a current of nourishment from landscape to community and back again, reciprocal, interchangeable, balanced.

Enrique could feel this place now. He slowly breathed it in, then out again. He envisaged its response to his presence. There was an emergent aliveness that transcended the sum of life contained therein. It was all-encompassing, intriguing. The soundscape amplified his conscious focus. It grew to encompass all he could imagine. Enrique could feel the earth beneath his feet. Its nuanced unevenness manifested itself ever so delicately on the soles of his feet. He quietly leaned forward and pressed his fingers to the ground. He felt himself extending into the landscape, merging together. He was becoming shaman, participant in a secret world of varying intelligences, interpreter of language without words. The shaman enters coitus with the forest, the breeze, the scents, the sounds, the minute vibrations unveiling animate and inanimate. The natural world around him is no longer mere scenery. It was not the world Enrique inhabited earlier that day. Therein is the difference, he thought. We see nature as an 'it,' an 'other' in relation to ourselves, but we are nature. It is us.

Enrique glimpsed deeper meaning. He indulged this beautiful sensation. Showered in sound, he bathed in the intricate arrangement. The vibrations, subtle, yet pervasive, intertwined to create a synesthetic experience, a blending of sensations. The sounds became images, the images tactile. The pattern, the interplay, the melodies were interwoven into a fabric of comprehension, its language derived from primal essence.

The external din of the surrounding forest continued to influence Enrique's internal, hypnotic dreamscape. His eyes were still closed. His body remained motionless, but his mind opened to encompass all sensual input. In the spirit of an authentic shaman, Enrique realized the quintessence of shamanic magic. It was not mythical, spiritually obscure, fraught with meaningless charms and enchantment. It was a vital indulgence in the essential interplay between all that is.

These ears are truly magical receptors, Enrique mused. Imagine if I retained the capacity I did as a younger man. That's where recording equipment comes in handy, he reasoned. It allows me to extend natural capabilities for technically enhanced ones. Still, the most important thing is actually being present for the recording. As considered earlier, if I wasn't here to experience the recording as it was happening, it could never invoke the manifestation of place in the same way it is at this moment. Or could it?

As Enrique sat quietly in the canyon grove, the surrounding biophony enticed him further. Individual vocalizations could be distinguished, alternating emphasis in natural symphony. It moves me emotionally, he thought. It elevates me. It inspires me, but also, Enrique marveled, it can sadden me, or increase a defensive posture. Its continual change alters focus, initiating mood variation, and evoking memories, deliberations, actions. The acoustic structure of place is not only influenced by my presence. It's a dance. We reciprocate.

These thoughts continued to play in his mind. Striving to imagine the shamanic mindset from a distant past, Enrique considered early human progress. It took extensive observance, comparison and analysis spanning millennia. It required awareness, emergent insight and comprehension. Yet, these higher-level skills arose from primal prerequisites addressing sight and sound. It compelled observation, but necessitated attention to sound. Familiarity with environment was crucial.

Observation was best-achieved from a position of advantage – seeing without being seen. By remaining perfectly still, as Enrique was attempting to do here, one could procure such advantage. One could become invisible. Numerous species do this well, even though each approaches visual perception by varying means. Interpreting the surrounding environment may occur by daytime, night-time and twilight visual specializations. Ranges exist as well. Humans, giraffes and hawks may all have photopic daytime vision, but specialization occurs along scale. Some have better than others.

Sound, as Enrique loved to think about it, is more pervasive, a field of activity. It entices one to listen, not just to hear. It is an arrangement emerging from primal vibrations. To know them enables one to utilize them. This would have been a mind-blowing discovery and realization in the distant past. Conveying sound for purposeful objectives may have been one of the earliest strategies developed to counter advantages possessed by other species.

Enrique tried to imagine early mimicry of natural sounds. Developing skills to mimic animals could have numerous applications. Various species could be lured or scared into various successful hunting schemes. Bird calls could be used for communication purposes. To do this expertly, one would have to be aware of a location's acoustic composition. One would have to be mindful and attentive of both distinctive and subtle sound intrusions. One would need to discern nearly imperceptible swishes, splashes, clicks, taps, echoes and resonances at varying ranges. One would have to create symmetry from chaos.

Enrique understood the chaotic din emanating from an econiche was anything but chaotic. Later, it would be possible to distinguish every creature's vocalizations using the sensitive recording made here. The overall biophony included vocalizations relative to one another in frequency, pitch and other possible measurements. Sounds could be separated and analyzed separately, or recognized as individual instruments in any bio-symphonic locale.

When Enrique first experienced this himself, he remembered being inspired beyond any expectation. At this primal level of affective, sensuous experience, he was immersed and participant in an animated, communicative landscape. They became familiar. It was how Enrique recognized a natural likelihood. The language and music that humans developed over time probably emanated from the soundscapes of the natural world around them. No wonder I often feel renewed being alone out in nature. I'm not really alone, Enrique thought. In a sense, it's a recognition of, and a return to, a concept of Eden we've drifted away from. Eden is humanity in sync with nature. It is a condition, not a place.

Enrique almost laughed out loud, but caught himself before interfering with the session. Perhaps emergence from that Eden-like experience necessitated formal religion. Harmony within the vibration of all things, the original music, would have been the original source of spirituality, the original religion of humanity. As we gained advantage over the surroundings we emerged from, there was need for ideas reflecting the achievements we made. Of necessity, these ideas had to reflect us, and so we created the gods. Hmmm, he thought. All very interesting, but back to the task at hand.

Aside from the natural biophony emanating from the forest around him, Enrique also became more aware of a very low, buzzing sound in the air. He had noticed this often enough in the city, or even out on the ranch. It occurred whether indoors or out, but he tended to notice it more when other sounds became subdued. Enrique noted this phenomenon more often these days and realized age-related hearing loss may be playing a role. That realization became concern, so he decided to do some research.

Enrique learned that a very small current actually flows through the atmosphere, even away from thunderstorm activity. Natural resonances of Earth's vibrations can be found in the electromagnetic field spectrum of the Earth's ionosphere. Known as Schumann resonances, They are peaks in the extremely low-frequency portion. These resonances are sustained in the ionosphere at all times by stability from lightning strikes. An average of fifty lightning events per

225

second around the planet at any given time maintains that stability. This places everyone within an electrostatic sphere that explains some of the audible buzzing.

Unexpectedly, Enrique had a thought that suddenly made sense. When he first read about an electrical current flowing through the atmosphere we all live in, he also come across another interesting study. Two Russian researchers linked Schumann resonances to human brain waves by discovering a discernible resonance to the slowest delta frequency in the human brain.

"That's it," Enrique blurted out loud. Bender stood up quickly and turned his head toward him. "Well boy," Enrique said in a much lower voice, "I guess that's it for the recording." He flipped the switch and turned the recorder off. "Excellent session though. I've realized a few things tonight." He looked upward through the canopy of tall trees to see a starry sky. Hesitant to move at first, he stretched his arms and let out a deep yawn. He reached over and turned on the lantern.

Enrique gave himself a little time to emerge from the dreamscape he had been enjoying. After a few more stretches, he got up and started collecting his equipment. Now he was focused on that one thought. Delta waves, he recalled, are high amplitude neural oscillations. They only occur between 0.5 and 4 hertz. If we humans have this occurring in our brains and we are living in a fishbowl where resonances are occurring at the same frequencies, wouldn't it follow that information from outside our heads is flowing through our heads as well?

Enrique smiled and swung his pack around onto his back. With his flashlight beaming from his left hand, he bent over and patted Bender on the head.

"Maybe I do have some information that could help Emma. C'mon boy. We have a bit of a walk ahead of us."

25

Emma was never one to sleep in. It was almost 6 AM. Coffee was already brewing. It could be a three-cup morning. She planned to relax and ease into her day. A small choice of liqueurs were found in the makeshift liquor cabinet between the kitchen and dining rooms. Two of the three were unopened. One was an Irish cream Emma could not pass by. Enrique had told her to make herself at home. That's exactly what she was doing. She poured a little into a mug, then waited for the coffee to steep in the French press. She looked out the window into the darkness. The stars were just as bright as they were when she went to bed. It would still be several weeks before summer light would shine this early. Since she arrived, the weather inspired an illusion of summer days. It was freezing up in Toronto. A quick glance at her phone showed they were expecting snow. Emma wasn't missing it at all.

With coffee in hand, Emma returned to her room. She opened the blind, then sat in the chair by the window. It was already a favourite spot. She glanced out at the stars sipping her brew. "Daydream into your day," she whispered softly. Or, she quickly thought, pick up from the reverie you left off before bed.

Emma had spent time reading Kant and Jung much of the day after returning from the hospital yesterday morning. The meeting with Jahny and the others was an eye-opener and an intriguing way to start her day. Before Enrique dropped her off back at the ranch, he said he was going to visit his brother in Pasadena. He never returned until late last night. Emma was still so engrossed in reading, she didn't bother to go down and chat. She figured he probably had a busy day and might not be up for chatting first thing anyway.

Delving into her books, Emma was completely intrigued by what she had been learning. Kant was the more complicated read. It was important to go over statements and concepts a couple of times before inching further. There was depth and progression to the arguments, so contemplating their meaning was stimulating. Grasping and reflecting on various concepts proved gratifying. Emma actually felt like she had crammed in a course or two in less than a couple hours. She began to think she had been missing something valuable. Philosophy didn't seem like a topic of genuine modern interest. She remembered wondering why Anthony was drawn to it, and to Kant specifically, but never enough to look into it before now. It certainly wasn't a quick read like a novel, but Emma was beginning to realize it was more intoxicating than most novels she could remember.

Soon after picking up Kant's *Critique of Pure Reason*, she found herself scribbling notes, underlining statements, drawing parentheses around entire paragraphs, and adding concise comments. They were meant as trigger-reminders for later review. Her reading entertainment and casual inquiry began reflecting ingrained university study habits. She even condensed, underlined and memorized one line:

'That all our knowledge begins with experience there can be no doubt, Kant had stated, but...it by no means follows that all (knowledge) arises out of experience.'

At first Emma considered it eloquent, but vague. Kant didn't intend it that way, but she needed time to ponder it. Kant's insight began to make sense through subsequent points. She went over them again and again. Eventually, they clicked.

Emma recast the statement in modern parlance. She wanted to keep it simple. Human reason, she theorized, is the ability to think about, and then provide, an explanation. Kant believed that humanity couldn't turn away from questions it is able to ask. She interpreted his point to mean that humanity's natural ability to ask the question in the first place is the basis for thinking it is possible to find an answer. Yet what he is saying explicitly, is that the human mind is unable to even fathom the answer. It is outside the scope of our species' abilities.

This is about ultimate knowledge, Emma reasoned. It's a way of looking at humans in a similar context to how we might look at 'lesser' life forms - something like worms, for example. A worm can't fathom the complexities of modern human life. It has no experience of the human form. Neither does it have the intricate brain connections and functioning required to process and analyze complex sensory information – period. When Kant says, 'presented by its own nature,' he means that an organism's physical makeup determines its abilities. Both physical and mental abilities are encapsulated in the form itself. All of that makes sense, she reasoned.

Kant reinforces the idea that all human knowledge begins with experience, but then he also emphasizes it doesn't mean that all knowledge arises out of that unique individual experience.

Emma went over that in her head. She looked at her notes, then out the window and back again. Well then, where does that knowledge come from? She didn't consider it an imponderability, but it was enough of one to remind her why she was reading this stuff in the first place.

Emma continued reading and making notes. She also went back to review notes made on Jung's work the night before. She recognized some convergence between Kant and Jung's ideas, but found Jung's more accessible. Clearly, he was influenced by Kant, who died some 70 years before Jung was born. The author of the overview was convinced that some of Jung's concept definitions were overwhelmingly Kantian. Emma wasn't concerned with that. She was looking for information relevant to her quest. That's why she became preoccupied with the word 'intuition' as both Kant and Jung bantered it about. Kant believed some categories of reality are not perceived through the senses, but through intuition. He stated that space itself, the area in which everything exists, is 'no general conception of the relations of things, but a pure intuition, a concept of mind.' Emma thought Jung made it clearer. He said that "intuition is not a 'guess' or a perception of general patterns, it is a mode of perception by other means than sensory data." Contemplating that mode of perception eventually led Jung to develop his concept of 'archetypes.'

Archetypes, as Emma interpreted Jung's explanation, were universal, underlying patterns and images that come from a collective unconscious, an unconscious we all share. Archetypes are a kind of psychic counterpart to instinct. Emma had heard of the concept of the collective unconscious before, but couldn't recall what it meant. Reading Jung now was insightful, inspiring.

Emma had never considered connections between humanity other than biological. Now she imagined an electric-like force enabling a flow of conceivable information. It can be accessed and utilized, it can be disregarded, or go unnoticed by individuals. It is part of an underlying structure to what we are collectively. It was an innovative concept.

Emma grasped its possible significance. She understood archetypes were clues to the connection between us all. They may not be easily recognized as we pursue our busy lives, but can be conjured by associations encountered while processing sensory information. That wasn't far-fetched. Any high school science student knows that the true structure of everything around us is composed of elements we do not see. They form the underlying structure to everything we know. Why would this only be true for physical structure?

It could explain why coincidences spill into everyday experience. It might explain why some faces we see in passing remind us of others. It may illuminate why we sometimes feel like we've been somewhere before when it is unlikely we have been, and so on. It's all about recognizing associations, connections, and patterns. It's like a woven tapestry. Several unique elements create a complete narrative, but it takes a participant viewer to comprehend it. Emma was impressed. She felt Jung was on to something, and began to feel like she was too. It was important to grasp this, to solidify the concept. She wanted to compare the idea with something more familiar. She wanted to set this concept in stone. She thought of her cell phone and all of the incredible tools and functions available using its simple interface. Yet under the surface of that interface is the electrical flow and connectivity that makes all the magic happen. That is a current, feasible, relevant comparison, she realized triumphantly.

So, what about these archetypes Jung talks about? If they are underlying links between us, how do they work? How could that explain a connection between Anthony and Jahny?

Reading further, Emma visualized archetypes and archetypal templates as a type of framework. That framework is continuously customized by humanity through life experience, culture, and individual perspectives, but all rooted in an underlying commonality. That underlying commonality is the collective unconscious. It provides cohesion we are not typically aware of, but associations exist. Different cultures may have varying religious beliefs, but differences are insignificant when one sees the big picture. What is significant is that religious ideas arose in the first place, even if different. It suggests an inclination to do so. Inclination is predisposition. It's a necessary component of the underlying framework, a type of instinct. That's why it's considered unconscious. It is 'underneath', beneath conscious view, or interpretation. It is elementary, primordial in essence. The framework is the guide. It is how bees instinctively shape hexagons to produce the mathematical perfection of the beehive. The archetypal templates are a framework, but also function as algorithms for possibilities.

Such thoughts jarred Emma's memory. Years earlier when she and Jean-Marc were still in Montreal, she remembered them watching a documentary. It really inspired Jean-Marc. She recalled it as a series of interviews conducted by Bill Moyers, a well-known PBS broadcaster at the time. In the series, he interviewed Joseph Campbell, a renowned professor of literature known for his work on comparative mythology. Jean-Marc had enthusiastically read his work before, so coming across a television interview with the author was exciting. As Emma recalled, Jean-Marc discussed Campbell's work frequently afterward. She may have heard reference to Jung and the collective unconscious there.

Jean-Marc chose a career path that followed the money, but his heart was in the arts. He exhibited a wide appreciation of literature not limited to fiction. He enjoyed biographies, science, mythology, and other curiosities. He had a wandering mind. Interestingly enough, Emma was realizing, Jean-Marc may also have been attracted to reading philosophy. It would not have been unusual. Taking one step further, it wasn't difficult to see how their son Anthony might fit into a similar mould. Connections, Emma thought again, connections…

…Good time to check her own connections. She unplugged the charged cell phone, tapped in her password, and opened Google. She typed-in Joseph Campbell. A list of references appeared. Wikipedia, Britannica, the Joseph Campbell Foundation, even reference to the interviews on Moyers' own site all came up immediately. Emma began scouring the information. There were several images of the man. She remembered his face now. It looked weathered by knowledge and insight. "Hmm," she muttered. He had already died when the interviews with Moyer aired. That was in the late 80's. His most well-known book was *The Hero with a Thousand Faces*. That sounded familiar. Perhaps it was one of the books Jean-Marc had read.

Deciding to go down that wormhole, she clicked the link. In …*a Thousand Faces*, he discusses his theory of the journey of the archetypal hero. It's a narrative shared by the world's various mythologies. Campbell saw all mythic narratives as variations on one great story, a template as it were. Although he had been writing and lecturing since the 1940s, Joseph Campbell didn't gain widespread recognition until Star Wars' filmmaker George Lucas famously credited him with influencing his space saga. Isn't that interesting, Emma thought. Even more so, she read that Campbell 'made heavy use of Carl Jung's theories on the structure of the human psyche.' Another connection, she thought. It was also a clear example of the template idea. Emma was delighted she had remembered bantering these ideas with Jean-Marc all those years ago. Amazing random memory recall, she thought. Coincidence, or another example of interconnectedness?

Emma considered George Lucas' interest in Campbell's work and how it influenced him. She had to wonder if Star Wars incredible success couldn't be attributed to the natural affinity we all have with archetypal concepts. Was the connection so natural that its relevance was transparent? The best kept secrets are often hidden in plain sight. A dominant concept that emerged from Star Wars was 'the Force.' It was a kind of non-denominational, impersonal religious concept. It was godlike without being a god. It was a type of energy… and clearly derived from the archetypal template. A stimulating idea, Emma realized.

Streaks of light were beginning to break up the night. Only the brightest stars could still be seen. Emma suddenly remembered her coffee. It had to be cold by now. She smiled, basking in the rare feeling of awakening to, or realizing a newly expanding comprehension. It was emergent, in the act of becoming, part of the reinvention of self. She realized things rarely unfold as expected. Maybe she was accomplishing what she came for after all.

This newly expanding comprehension came from multiple sources. She came here seeking solitude, and it remained available, but listening to others had provided valuable input. In the past few days, she was not only reunited with an old acquaintance, but found new ones. Each contributed something different. Emma mulled over the varying perspectives. Whether they were religious, scientific, medical, or speculative, Darnell, Enrique, Danielle, and Kevin's views all suggested references to a framework of belief, a guiding set of ideas. Jahny's perspectives were prodigiously philosophical, permeating inclusively through linked topics of conversation. Perhaps that linkage, that interconnection was what drew everyone together.

The books she'd been reading were advancing interconnected elements to an even higher plane. Whether it was Kant's arguments on knowledge and experience, Campbell's mythic narratives as variations on one great story, or Jung's archetypes, all seemed to be coming together into a unified whole. It was all about connections.

All contributions expand comprehension, but in the end, it was about the sense Emma could make of it all. So, was the knowledge she sensed she was gaining come from experience, or from a mode of perception by other means?

Emma got up from her spot at the window. She felt inspired, even energetic. It couldn't have been the coffee. She barely touched it. Tinkering sounds she had noticed coming from downstairs a short while ago now moved outside. The screen door closed and footsteps could be heard on the front porch. Enrique was clearly up and at it already. Daylight had arrived. Sunrise couldn't be far off. By the time Emma walked into the kitchen to warm her coffee, Enrique had already backed the truck and was pulling away from the house. For a guy settling into retirement, he sure kept busy. That's okay, she thought. Emma was feeling energetic enough and decided not to finish her coffee. She would go out for a short hike instead.

Bender must have shadowed Enrique. He usually did. If the dog was in the house, he would be on his spot in the livingroom, a small section of carpet where he could keep an eye on much of the main floor. Emma went back up to her room to get a jacket. Even though it was February, it could warm quickly. Wearing layers was practical. She remembered to bring water as well. It was an essential not to be forgotten. "Walk light, but do it right," her dad used to quip.

The dust from Enrique's truck could still be seen settling in the distance when Emma stepped outside. She glanced over the desert landscape. A hawk patrolled high above the chaparral. There was no other detectable movement. Emma decided to walk the same path they strolled the other night.

Walking along the trail was much different at sunrise than sunset. Numerous shades of brown, tan and sage were both distinctive and complimentary. The sun already felt warm. Her jacket wouldn't be needed for long. Emma continued to stir Kant, Jung, and Campbell's words about while appreciating the surrounding view. She recalled other unrelated images, memories, thoughts and words both recent and long gone. All immersed into one another.

Then Emma recalled something else. Kevin had mentioned a place she might be interested in checking out. He said it was founded by an astronaut. It took a few moments, but she finally remembered it was called the Institute of Noetic Sciences, an odd name. What did noetic mean?

Emma stopped for a moment and took out her cell phone. "No connection here. Too far from the ranch," she muttered out loud, "later." She remembered the astronaut's name at least – Edgar Mitchell. Kevin said he wrote a book, but couldn't remember if he mentioned the title. It didn't matter. Mitchell was the author. If he has written more than one book, then she would have a choice. All good. Originally Emma had planned to stick around the ranch today. Now it seemed a good idea to go back down the Rabbit Hole, meaning the bookstore back in town. She wanted to continue searching for answers. She could pick up a copy of Mitchell's book. She could look up info about the Institute of Noetic Science. She could…

Wait, take it easy, she thought. Look where you are. If this isn't an ideal place to contemplate quietly for a while… She looked around. It's still early, she reasoned, quite early. I can have my proverbial cake and eat it too.

Lunch was still hours away. Emma could go to town afterward. That would give her time to have a bite to eat. If Enrique returned before she left, she could ask him what he knows about Mitchell and his work. Maybe he would come to the book shop with her. Whatever happened, the day was shaping up to be a good one. She planned to take it in stride, but for now, she would enjoy walking the trail a while longer.

26

Emma continued walking up the trail. One's overall perception of the desert landscape was intricately deepened by its early morning beauty. It was an apt compliment to experiencing it at dusk, as she had a few nights ago. A day in the desert can be a metaphor for life, she thought. It looks bright and inviting in the morning. As the day progresses, traversing it can become arduous and demanding. Dusk initiates the darkness, realm of dreams, a gesture of reprieve from the long journey. It is a time of reflection, a restoration of balance.

It felt like that the other evening when she first traversed this path with Enrique. It was still dusk. The sky, illuminated in oranges and crimson, were wonderfully relaxing, she recalled, a prelude to the colourful sequence of events about to unfold. Emma believed she needed solitude and rest. Her goal was to plot a new direction, to start anew. The accident she had suffered demanded it, necessitated it. There were times when she understood Jahny's dark resolve. When perspective is lost or unclear, life and death have equal value.

Sometimes going forward means starting again. When you can't see too far ahead, take one step at a time. Emma was doing that. Maybe Jahny was too. And what of the others? Enrique recently retired, sort of. Both Darnell and Kevin have questions of their own, indications of flux. Emma had questions too. She was in flux. She was moving. It's always forward, isn't it? The arrow of time goes only one direction she reminded herself.

Finding direction is the only true goal. Opening the door to possibilities is a way to find one's path, she mused, even as it seems to find you. There is interactivity there, reciprocity. It can be captivating, hypnotic – consuming to a point where even time is altered, or one's sense of it.

It was like that now. Finding Jahny seemed a distant occurrence. That was less than three days ago. Emma should have anticipated the unusual. Reconnecting with an old acquaintance altered plans for desert solitude from the get-go. It didn't alter plans for change. It became transition. The past has a way of traveling through the present toward the future. It's that arrow of time thing again. This is about more than a restart, Emma noted. It's about more than figuring out coincidences like running into Enrique, or figuring out what connection there may be between Anthony and Jahny. It's a focus on something larger, more comprehensive. It's more of a seminal occurrence, a fundamental reorganization of perspective.

The perception of time can be peculiar. It often shifts throughout the day. Work tends to go slowly while fun passes quickly; at least, that's the general consensus. The more Emma contemplated it, the more amazing it seemed that anyone had a normal experience of time at all. One would expect change itself to be the norm. Significant events notoriously influence the sensation of time, as she knew, but there are numerous other factors too.

The experience of time is influenced in subtle ways. Emma believed women were slightly more aware of bodily time-keeping mechanisms. A while had passed since the dominating rhythm in her own life had discontinued. It was notable evidence of the aging process itself. Other rhythms are less noticeable. Throughout life, the circadian rhythm regulating sleep-wake patterns governs activity at its most fundamental level. It is only one of thousands of rhythms regulating numerous functions like adrenaline production and cell-division. It inevitably occurred to Emma that out of necessity, both the conscious and the subconscious were contributing factors in human experience. That must be why guys like Kant and Jung excavated and explored it. Both subtle and hidden factors are essential components of the bio-infrastructure that makes sentience and experience even possible.

The material Emma had been reading emphasized that point. She was beginning to understand Anthony's attraction to Kant's ideas. Although challenging at first, persistence helped turn the light on. Then it became easier to see the road. Passages here and there reminded her of points Anthony had gone on about back home. Now that she paid attention to the source and actually focused, they made more sense.

That poor boy, Emma lamented. He never really had anyone to rant to about his interests. She felt remorse for not showing greater interest herself. Anthony had little possibility of finding peers with whom to discuss concerns or curiosity. They were too different from mainstream preoccupations. He's a nerdy philosopher type, Emma thought. He's more introspective than most young people.

Excessive introspection can deter social interactivity, but it didn't deter personal growth. Emma recognized her son's immense capability as well as his distinctive exceptionality. Unfortunately, she knew capability may not eclipse exceptionality. She realized society could, and probably would, constrain potential. We haven't got past that yet, she lamented.

Emma was still getting past it herself. She was just beginning to realize where Anthony was at. He's a genius in a bottle, she punned. He's got more going for him than I've been able to recognize. Perhaps much more. He's well immersed in ideas that I'm only coming across now. He's already explored concepts challenging our perception of what is. He probably understands the possibilities better than most.

Does any of this relate to Anthony's connection with Jahny? Could it, Emma wondered? Was there a connection at all? That remained a primary question. It was important not to stuff philosophical assumptions into a thesis. Emma was aware of that risk. Progressive logic supported by facts must prevail. These things take time. Revelation isn't impulsive. Preparation advances in stages. Yeast takes time to rise. She was on a trail of discovery, but not there yet.

Emma arrived at the rock where she and Enrique had smoked a joint and chatted the other evening. She stopped there again, recollecting the beautiful moment when the night sky opened a window to the universe. The thought amusingly begged the obvious: Was it the evening sky, or was it the joint that made the moment so beautiful? Emma chuckled. So cliché. Had she expressed it to others, it would have provoked a predictable laugh. The known effects of cannabis are an easy punchline, but in this case, side-tracks one's attention from an important point. The answer, she knew, was neither the evening sky, nor the joint. All incoming sensory information is indirect. It's analysis and interpretation is generated in one's mind. Beauty is conceived, not merely appreciated.

Conscious comprehension involves inference, clarification, questioning and organization of knowledge. Emma remembered that according to Kant, knowledge exists inherently in the mind, independent of experience. Does it also suggest that knowledge exists prior to experience? If so, Emma reasoned, perhaps knowledge exists in the archetypes Jung talks about in his work. Maybe Kant and Jung were talking about the same thing. Jung simply took it a step further. Kant's generalized knowledge may have become Jung's collective unconscious. Archetypes are original patterns expressed in varying ways, much like eye colour may be expressed differently. The possibilities emerge from the original, but may articulate divergence. Kant and Jung may have been alluding to the same insight. Humanity is more than we have realized all along. Wow, Emma thought. Maybe a little puff would have been nice now too.

Emma glanced over the valley floor on her right, then to the rising mountain range on the left. The sun already felt much warmer on her back than when she left the ranch. That was less than half an hour ago. She had water with her, but hadn't planned to be out in the desert heat too long. Intending to go a little further before heading back, Emma headed down the side path that led to the cave where they found Jahny. She remembered it didn't take long to get there from here the other night. Now that it had warmed up, she kept her eyes on the ground. Words her father often repeated when she was young came to mind. 'Be aware of where you're walking in the woods and in the desert. Surprises can be averted.' Emma wasn't afraid of desert creatures, not even rattlers, but she did respect them and the territory they inhabited. It was just good sense.

The upward slope to the cave Enrique had climbed soon appeared after turning a bend on the trail. Emma wasn't sure why she was returning to this spot. She stopped for a moment in hesitation, but with renewed resolve climbed up to the entrance. Slowly, she peered inside.

There was no evidence anyone had been here at all. The wind-carved rock was smooth, featuring rounded walls and floor space. The wind is housemaid through here, Emma mused. There was very little eroded rock, or sand to be found. The surface was too hard and dry to leave animal prints either, even if one may have ventured inside. The space was cleaner than most homes. She remembered Enrique finding the partially-filled pill container, and a few other small items. The medevacs must have collected them along with Jahny.

That was quite a night, Emma recalled. The emergency blurred everything. She couldn't remember Enrique calling 9-1-1. He must have tried to regain cell range by backtracking. It seemed to take a long time before help arrived. Emergency vehicle lights could eventually be seen racing across the desert along Pearblossom highway in the distance. The ranch was at least half an hour from the city. Once they found their way to the ranch, they soon realized the victim was not accessible with the equipment they had. The helicopter wasn't called in until then, losing more valuable time. The whole thing became confusing. Emma began to think she must have been in shock at the time. She couldn't remember all the details. Jahny eventually made it to hospital, thank goodness.

Emma looked around the cave, then focused on the aperture on the south wall facing the mountains. It was a small, bent cigar-shaped window, clearly fashioned by wind erosion. It was a curious little aberration. Wind erosion was a common effect at desert locations. The Vasquez Rocks area just down the 14 was well-known to many. Apertures through cave walls, however, were rare. Emma didn't remember seeing one before. How long does it take to wear rock down in this way, she wondered? Years? Centuries? Millennia? The more she looked at it, and looked through it, the more mesmerizing it seemed. She couldn't help but wonder how many people had ever crawled into this space before. How many have sat here looking out the window, maybe asking the same questions I am now, she thought. How long has it been carved-out like this?

The cave was too small to stand upright, but one could recline against the curved walls comfortably. Emma shuffled over to the back wall, positioning herself to look through the aperture. It afforded her an oblong, almost eye-shaped view of the San Gabriel mountains. She could see why Enrique enjoyed this place. She could even envision why Jahny might have felt comforted, as well as comfortable here. It was an exceptional, even intriguing little space. She imagined the inside of an egg. If it weren't for the aperture and crawl-sized opening to climb inside, Emma could imagine it as a secret safe-place. She imagined the discovery of ancient texts like the Dead Sea Scrolls in the Qumran caves of the Judean desert. She imagined their hidden location to be just as compact and arid. In truth, she realized, it wouldn't be out of place historically as a small burial enclosure. Archeology has long proven the practice existed well into prehistory.

As her mind wandered, Emma began to wonder about Jahny. She couldn't buy Kevin's idea that he might be an alien on a mission, or an aborted one. No doubt an unusual story lurked behind the incident inside here, but that interpretation didn't gel. So what was Jahny's story then, she wondered? The cave was a small, secure space where one might choose to sleep a night. It wasn't large or accommodating enough to consider setting up camp. If anything, Emma thought, it was more like a cubby-hole hideaway for an avid reader.

Was it possible Jahny was familiar with this area and had been here before? He was in the same age group as she and Enrique were. If he lived somewhere in the vicinity, he may have known about the cave even longer than Enrique has. It was possible. If the place was known to him, he may have considered the cave a personal inner sanctum. Perhaps his final plan was intended, coordinated and arranged. People often assume that suicides are desperate, unhappy and inconsolable for whatever reason. Maybe that's not always true. Jahny certainly didn't come across that way to her.

Emma sat thinking about Jahny's motive. Why? The answer could provide clues to his frame of mind at the time, maybe his frame of mind now too. What was it like to be him in that moment when he acted on his decision? Again, the picture was unclear. Something didn't quite fit. Was there some significance to this place itself, it's size, shape, seclusion? Emma noted how peaceful it was here. Why did small animals not seem to make use of it? Was the short climb to the entrance a deterrent? She saw no evidence of feces, even small droppings in the place. It really did seem cleaner than many people keep their homes. Had Jahny swept it in preparation beforehand? That would be an odd activity for someone presumed to have lost hope or purpose.

Emma knew there had to be an explanation. Any indications she harboured, however, were speculation at best. Almost everything about Jahny was assumption or conjecture so far. It was fascinating that he had generated so much interest and curiosity. It was even more fascinating that people had such differing ideas about him. If Anthony's phone call hadn't occurred in the truck on the way to the hospital, she wouldn't have had to explain to others what he had said. If that had not happened, ideas about Jahny wouldn't have diverged the way they did. As she recalled, Kevin was quick to speculate. He would have believed what he did about Jahny had Anthony called or not. He was already talking about the unusual nature of the incident and its similarity to previous incidents. Anthony's call just elevated Kevin's interest level. It probably fed Emma's curiosity too, if she were honest. She was surprised by something she couldn't explain. So when someone else suggested a possible explanation, it automatically became part of the speculation.

Anthony seemed to make a specific reference to Jahny by asking what Emma thought of the caveman. It was too unusual a reference to ignore. Not clarifying it since then has likely exaggerated its significance, she conceded, but what was the connection? She had now spent a couple days following clues. She had immersed herself further.

Given the immediate circumstances at the time, Emma had decided to prevent Jahny from being transferred elsewhere. She secured medical coverage for him, at least until his identity could be discovered anyway. She managed to actually meet him. They even got into deep discussion. New vistas of perception and understanding began to emerge as a result. She also seemed to be caught up in something bigger – something that involved the others she had met this week – Enrique, Danielle, Kevin and Darnell. Perhaps they formed a crowd compared to the solitude she thought she needed this week, but they were also a clear example of the interconnected nature of things, a theme that sprang up often as the week had progressed. She also enjoyed relevant reading material to supplement it all. Emma couldn't visualize the complete picture just yet, but she felt she was right on the verge. Sitting in this egg-like compartment, this introspective space, this little cave with the unusual aperture, she believed she could incubate further insight.

Emma scoured the cave walls, experiencing the inner beauty of this very personal little cubicle. How strange that it should be hidden in the middle of a desert expanse. She marveled at the seamless curvature of the walls, ceiling and floor. Being inside a wind-carved skull suggested being the consciousness inside. There was a perceptive awareness to looking out through the crudely oval-shaped aperture, its eye to the universe. Momentarily, psychologically, one might do a double-take, recognizing the similarity between looking through the aperture and through one's own eyes. It was recognition of scale, a nested-doll, matryoshka-like perception conveying the infinite nature of what is.

The thought was mind-blowing. Unexpectedly, Emma felt a deep reverence for this place. There was a sacredness to being inside here. It wasn't so much about the space itself. It was more about an inner realization the place induced. Again, there was a sense of being connected, associated, linked, but the association was still forming, still taking shape. It prompted a recall of Einstein's famous dictum: 'the most beautiful thing we can experience is the mysterious.'

Perhaps this was the perfect spot to contemplate what she had been reading recently. Peculiarly, Emma sensed that returning here was not just an impulse, but an essential step toward understanding Kant and Jung's explorations. It was important for her own exploration. She began to recognize that real comprehension can't be taught. It didn't matter how clearly books might explain intricacies and detail. Ideas provide springboards toward comprehension, but ultimately, one must come to a realization of one's own.

Emma believed Jahny must have had a similar reverence for being here. As an alcove in the desert rock, it was little more than an oubliette, a perfect place to quietly return to the earth, for one's individuality to be forgotten. As Emma considered previously, it was common back into prehistory. Maybe Jahny's exploit wasn't so much out of place as it was out of time…and maybe then, it wasn't so desperate an act as modern humanity assumes. Whatever Jahny may have thought about this place, it wasn't an actual oubliette, forgotten, a spot for quiet resignation. At least one other was aware of its special attributes as well. Enrique had deliberately sought to share that with her the other night.

Emma considered that for a while. Enrique already had a quiet place out in the middle of the desert, yet he came here recurrently. No doubt he often brought a puff with him for further introspection – or connection. It was contemplative, a ritualized act for escape. Enrique had spoken about his research of the area around the ranch – its flora and fauna. It too was about exploration, about discovery. That's thought-provoking, she noted. Emma again looked round the walls and ceiling before returning her focus on the aperture. Despite being small, it was the central feature. Staring outward from where she sat, Emma could only see the swelling ground and rocks near the mountain's base. She inched forward to follow its rise toward the sky. From where Jahny lay losing consciousness, he may well have positioned himself to see up through the aperture as well. Through the eye of a needle, he gave himself up to the universe. He didn't come from out there, as Kevin speculates, but he was, he is part of there. We all are. He was returning home.

Emma was mesmerized. She also continued gazing through the aperture. She revisited the idea of being the consciousness inside this cranium-like headspace. It was like looking from the inside out. That sparked another thought, a flashback to something she learned long ago. She had completely forgotten it, a classroom discussion way back when. Now it returned to memory, clearly, as though it were recent. It was practically a lifetime ago. Emma was still in high school then. She remembered it was a discussion about the brain, and how we perceive the world. That teacher blew everyone's minds when he argued that everything out there is really all in here. He pointed to his head amusingly, making a face suggesting he'd gone mad.

Emma remembered it being an unusual class. Virtually everyone became embroiled in the conversation. The teacher's name slipped her mind, but that was inconsequential. The important thing was that she still remembered the idea he presented so effectively. He argued that even though we interact with the world, and have very definite ideas about what it is like 'out there,' everything is actually happening inside our brains - always. Of course, he just had to bring up the old 'if a tree falls in the forest and there is no one there to hear it, does it make a sound' question. Surprisingly, there were several advocates for both possible answers.

One student had apparently not been presented with the question before. "Why would a tree not make a sound just because no one was there to hear it," he asked? That prompted frantic hand-raising as other students jockeyed to provide the answer.

Emma remembered the teacher selecting a girl no one expected to ever raise her hand, or speak at all. Yet she confidently, and eloquently, proceeded to explain that the tree falling does not produce sound per se. It displaces air and matter that creates vibration as it topples to the forest floor. The impact could affect other organisms in the immediate vicinity, but can only be heard by organisms that have the biological machinery to interpret the vibrations as sound. To everyone's surprise, that girl went on to explain that snakes can feel vibration, but they cannot hear. They have no ears. Even human ears are only capable of 'hearing' within a range of frequencies, so the sounds we do hear are only part of the symphony that's out there.

"That's right," the teacher continued, going on to say that almost everyone believes there is a world "out there" that's being viewed from behind our eyes. The teacher went on to make several points. Nothing is ever perceived by anyone except the perceptions themselves. The outside world you are looking at is located in your brain – and actually, the back of your brain. Your senses provide information, but it is your mind that makes sense of that information. The sound you hear when a tree is falling in the forest is a unique experience made possible by the architecture of the organism experiencing the vibration.

Emma marveled recalling the event at all, but now realized that teacher had to have read Kant. His statement that 'we only perceive our perceptions' is a direct reference to Kant's *Critique of Pure Reason*. She remembered the teacher had produced further examples, but didn't remember them. Emma understood the main point. We are convinced that the world is exactly as we perceive it, but scientific evidence proves that it isn't.

This may be where people get caught up with religious interpretations, Emma believed. She had never seriously had to grapple with religious idealism throughout her life. Her father was a staunch atheist. "We are humanity. We're an emergent organism in a quiet corner of the galaxy," he would say. "We've become knowledgeable enough to know that the universe that spawned us will also die someday." It was a sobering thought, but one that inspired him all the more. He believed in pushing limits, improving what we can while we're here. "We don't live up to higher principles because any god threatens to punish us if we don't," he would declare. "We choose to live up to higher principles because they are our ideals."

There were similarities between Emma's father and her son Anthony. This wasn't the first time she'd recognized that. It was fascinating to observe cross-generational resemblances between two people who had never even met one another. Physical resemblance between her father and son were minimal. Emma recognized their similarity in character. They both struggled with mundane daily activity, for one thing. Their minds were aloft, existing elsewhere, ever discovering new topics to explore and analyze. Emma's father may have been more of a scientific mind, but they shared philosophical inclinations. Emma was sure they would have found one another most interesting.

They are both interesting. They may not have known one another, but I have known them. It's my knowledge and experience of them individually that recognizes the connection between them. Invisible associations have meaning. Conduits, channels, mediums endure and operate beneath the obvious, as undercurrent submerged below the evident in our daily lives.

Emma considered that one step further. She stopped to focus on the connection between Anthony and Jahny. It was implied specifically because of Anthony's caveman comment. Was it possible she misheard the comment? The word caveman is often used metaphorically in everyday conversation. Did she mistakenly understand it literally, and then make the connection between Anthony and Jahny herself? Was she the conduit, the channel here?

Emma abruptly wondered how long she'd been sitting here deep in thought. The scenarios she'd been traversing melded down into a quiet moment of recognition. She was still in the cave. She's been staring through the aperture. Exploration and contemplation, she mused, the consciousness inside. The window to the outside was the window to the inside. The invisible became just a little clearer.

It was still early. Emma planned to make the best of her day. She could digest all this a little more in the car when she drove into town. She intended to keep her date with the Rabbit Hole. She would get what she was looking for, then head back to the ranch. There was a lot to think about, but she had something more important to attend to as well. If Enrique was still out, it would be quiet back at the ranch. It might be a good idea to give Anthony a call.

27

Emma checked her cell phone and decided to get going. That last bit of cappuccino was still sitting in front of her. It was the second time she let a drink get cold that day.

Looking around the bookstore, she realized that part of the magic of the Rabbit Hole was its clientele. Emma actually recognized two people who were sitting there earlier in the week. Bookworms, she intuited, secretly-learned people who blend in at work, indeed in all their daily activities, but live to find another spot to consume more pages. Perhaps she could soon enjoy the luxury of becoming one herself. Emma placed the book she'd been skimming through on the table. Cold or not, she wasn't going to waste the cappuccino. Earlier this morning while back at the cave, she intended to call Anthony when she returned to the ranch. She changed her mind, remembering that he often kept to a daily routine. They could connect when she got back from the bookstore. There was no rush. She continued glancing round the bookshop.

Emma had come for the book by Edgar Mitchell, the astronaut Kevin had mentioned. She hoped to find a copy to take back to the ranch. Being lured by the smell of good brew, she decided to look up the title rather than spend time scouring shelves. Surprisingly, the shop had two copies. That seemed like a rare treat, especially from a small independent book store. Emma thought she would extend the pleasure by sitting down to explore its pages with a nice hot cappuccino. A coffee would have been sufficient, but she was anticipating something special. She was supposed to be enjoying somewhat of a retreat anyway. The barista invited her to find a spot anywhere she pleased. He would bring her drink momentarily. Emma found a small table in a corner within sight of the counter.

Looking first at the cover, it struck her that *The Way of the Explorer: An Apollo Astronaut's Journey Through the Material and Mystical Worlds* was somewhat of a curious title. Everyone finds space-related topics mystical, but she detected that wasn't the implication here. The title specified two aspects of the astronaut's journey. Emma found it particularly interesting that the words 'material' and 'mystical' were chosen. It provided fertile ground for questions. Excellent advertising technique too, she observed. Clever marketing is one thing, Emma noted, but I'm not looking for an autobiographical account of a space journey, or potentially kooky mystical notions. I'm looking for answers. Still glancing at the cover, she wondered whether this might just be fodder for wannabe believers in the unusual. Kevin was a believer in aliens. Who knows what he considers credible, or how much stock he puts into other areas of speculation? He was the one who mentioned the book in the first place. Intending to enjoy her cappuccino, Emma thought she would take her time glancing through this title. If it didn't strike a chord, she had enough to read back at the ranch anyway.

Flipping through the book, Emma's interest was unexpectedly aroused. She soon noticed a recurrent commitment to science and scientific methodology. It immediately reminded her of various people who would laud its importance for doing so. That included Jean-Marc and Anthony of course, but also Enrique, and probably Jahny too. Her own conviction of its importance was reassured by Mitchell's endeavors to establish that demonstrably. That was one point for the book. It diminished her suspicions about populist mysticism luring and enticing less scrupulous readers.

From Emma's perspective, a second point for the book emerged when the astronaut described the universe as being in some way 'conscious.' Emma quickly assumed that was a reference to God, or some new age interpretation thereof. Yet again however, she was pleasantly surprised to have an assumption burst. Mitchell macheted the idea at its root. He acknowledged that many were hasty to attribute religious interpretations to that description, but adamant that his perception was different. Emma was already confident there would be an adequate explanation to support his assertion.

Convinced the book was worth buying, Emma decided to head out. She could mull over what she'd read so far in the car. Letting things simmer in her brain for a while was a good way to digest information. Some of her best insights were gained while driving alone and listening to music. It was often engaging and productive.

Emma walked up to the register to pay. This was going to be a good afternoon. Anthony was likely to be busy until after supper. She was a few hours behind Toronto, and could call him later this afternoon. In the meantime, she could get into the mystical and material of Mitchell's book.

Emma relished the desert drive back to the ranch. Her head was already embroiled in concepts from the book. She was fascinated by a point the astronaut had made. He didn't understand how intellect, emotion, and intuition were interrelated until he was older. Emma remembered many times being fascinated by coincidence, intuition and similar topics, but never took them seriously. She had never heard or read any scientific explanations attempting to account for them. It never even occurred to her that these might be topics studied seriously. Many believe in such things casually. Emma's impression was that most people assume them to be fringe topics.

'Fringe topics' was an expression Jean-Marc often employed. It usually referred to things people tended to place in a limbo of sorts, often between science and religion. These were things Jean-Marc believed couldn't really be explained definitively by either. He would say that's why people often express their opinions one way or another, but rarely back them with anything solid. Conclusive evidence may not exist. For some things, there are only theories. And for some things in religious circles, there can only be faith. Emma remembered all too clearly that for people like Jean-Marc and Anthony, and no doubt for Enrique, the definition of faith was just the belief in something for which there is no evidence. It provides little confidence or value to any earnest investigation.

In Emma's mind, a third point in favour of the book emerged when she read Mitchell's account of his return from the moon. He was able to see more clearly how modern-day experience might be difficult to explain using traditional modes of interpretation. It's an interesting observation, she thought, especially since religious belief remains a subject of controversy. Religion, more so in the States than back in Canada, she believed, is still highly-valued. This was true in her own family. Emma recalled her father's fervent atheism was a break from strict family tradition. It became a wedge between family members. He used to bitterly refer to religion as a superstitious remnant of our distant past.

So what is the answer, Emma wondered? A lot of people still retain religious beliefs. Whether she was influenced by her father, her husband and son, or by her own beliefs and inclinations, Emma did feel strongly about one thing. Religions tend to be static. People who adhere to them believe they have definitive answers to everything. All is set in stone, determined by a divine entity. It is the last word, even if interpretation of important statutes do eventually splinter and vary over time.

To be fair, Emma conceded, others put their faith in science just as strongly. It isn't the same though. The approach is different. The immovable nature of religious belief is such that the answers are already established, therefore new information must be discredited. Scientific perspectives are readjusted whenever new information comes to light. That has to be the way to go, she reasoned. It's pragmatic. One can only make more accurate judgements when one has the most information, the best information possible. As that changes, so might perspective.

If there is an ultimate answer to everything, maybe it stands apart from anything we can know. There were hints of that in the other books back at the ranch. Emma realized she was almost there. Longview Road was just ahead. Well, she remembered, Mitchell had stated something about human beings being part of a continuously evolving process. At the time she read that assertion, Emma was immediately aware that he didn't say humans were continually evolving, he said humans were part of an evolving process. That was worth pondering. It opened up a whole field of possibility.

Emma became so embroiled in thought that she was abruptly surprised to find herself driving up to the ranch house. Thank-you autopilot, she thought, but winced at the notion of not remembering the last stretch she drove. The truck wasn't here, so Enrique was still out and about today. He may have been here and left again. No problem, Emma thought. I'll have time to digest some of this before calling Anthony. It was still early in the day. She could put together a bite to eat and head back to the small cave with the aperture. It could get warm outside, but would likely remain cool in there. Emma was delighted by the idea. She quickly found some bottled water in the fridge, then scurried out the door toward the path into the desert.

This was only Emma's fourth day back in the Southland. Much had already happened. She hoped Enrique wasn't feeling besieged by the unusual intrusion into his otherwise tranquil existence. She wanted to probe his scientific insight with science-related questions of her own. Reading more of Mitchell's book was likely to add to that.

Emma recalled Enrique saying that he wanted to regulate the flow of guests to the ranch. He didn't need the business. Bringing in guests to a bed and breakfast setting provided opportunities to retain regular socialization in a relatively remote location. Emma figured people in science-related fields probably chatted science with non-professionals only occasionally. She imagined it wasn't so easy, since non-professionals wouldn't be familiar with terms related to specific fields. Conversations could begin to sound condescending if frequent explanations have to be given. When people start feeling stupid, simply because they are unfamiliar with something, a disconnect happens. Conversation can end unsatisfactorily for all involved. So if she was going to ask questions, or engage Enrique in any scientific conversation, it should be focused. That way he would see she has some knowledge of the topic, even if only acquired recently. In that case, Enrique might relish a question or two.

248

Hell, Emma thought, her son Anthony might appreciate a question or two as well. She had let him rant on many times, but as Emma recognized earlier, she barely paid attention. There was little retention of details, and only nominal curiosity to feign a passing interest in what he was talking about. In retrospect, he probably noticed, but expressed ideas he was digesting for his own purposes. Emma chuckled. Classic OCD strategy, she recognized. It's part of his methodology for retaining information. He knows how to efficiently catalogue ideas of interest, or of particular importance. Anthony really did need to socialize.

Hmmm, that was pretentious and condescending, Emma admitted to herself. Despite any issues, or what others considered issues, he deserves not to be condescended to, not to be treated like a child. Yet it suddenly seemed painfully obvious that she had been doing so. Inadvertently or not, it had to stop. As she recalled several instances, she felt remorse. Emma vowed to discontinue. She was determined to be more considerate. No, that wasn't quite what she meant. The word wasn't formulating, but she knew what she wanted to express. Perhaps she needed to find the word, if for nothing else, but to follow the same strategy Anthony used for cementing ideas into his head. She wanted to be more mindful and attentive – engaged really. Wrangling through these issues, and then contemplating relationship-building endeavors, Emma found herself gliding into, then navigating conversational scenarios with her son.

Various occasions reeled through Emma's memory as she recalled excerpts from chats and exchanges over the years. She never really gave Anthony credit for his endeavors. She often saw them more as distractions, even odd diversions from the trajectory his life might have taken. Worrying about the path of his schizophrenic onset and whatever might follow in its wake had changed Emma. It had twisted and fashioned how she perceived her son. She fell into the trap of seeing him primarily as the victim of a tragic event. Emma could see now that became a focus on disability rather than ability. She had lost her image of Anthony as the complex individual that he still was, and continues to be. How had she not realized this before? Or had she detected hints of it, but evaded the issue? Neither she, nor Jean-Marc really knew what to do. It all seemed so overwhelming. They eventually lost their way. Somehow Anthony became something apart from what he once was. Crazy how you can be close to someone and still be so distant.

Emma was feeling guilty, but also inspired. She had recognized something that could be changed, could be made right. That doesn't always happen. People often don't recognize what's important. They don't see opportunities, connections, or other positive avenues that can improve situations. Sometimes these things are right in front of you, but inexplicably obscured, just not there.

That realization jolted her. Emma abruptly became aware she was still operating on autopilot. She had completely bypassed grabbing something to eat at the ranch house and barely remembered pulling a bottled water out of the fridge. She was well along the trail, almost half-way up to where the cave was located.

The sun was quite warm now. Emma spied a spiny swift lizard sunning itself on a rock. It spied her too, but was unafraid. She was far enough not to cast shade on its sandstone throne. The reptile provided momentary distraction from the continually-unfolding bits of chatter in her head. She continued walking along the trail, but reimagined herself back at home in Toronto. Anthony was discussing his observations on Kant's *Critique* with her, repeating arguments Emma had heard more than once before. In this rendition of conversation, she imagined herself more attentive to the points her son was making. She was also engaged, injecting points of her own. The banter was lively and went back and forth fluently. She made clever observations and laid them out intelligently. Anthony would comment and build on her points, or adapt the conversation's direction toward points directly from Kant. He even remarked on how much he enjoyed their 'frequent' exchanges of ideas. He made a joke about their mutual love of verbal jousting. Imagined, fabricated, fashioned into something hoped for, it was all good. Emma still felt consoled. She sensed a rebirth, the possibility of a renewed relationship. There was still a connection.

Emma sought to extend their association, broaden lines of communication. She imagined asking her son why he loved reading philosophy as much as he did. The anticipated smile that would likely appear on his face was reminiscent of an expression on Jahny's face when asked a similar question recently. Emma found that intriguing. Did that suggest a link, or was it Emma's perception of similar reactions from them that suggested a link? Likewise, when she imagined Anthony's response to a statement or argument to be the same as a response his father might make, did that suggest a link between them? Or did the perceived link emerge from her own thoughts and perceptions?

Emma maintained belief that there were actual links. She may not be sure about connections between Anthony and Jahny, but links between Anthony and Jean-Marc were unmistakable. Both conceded an interest in religious and scientific ideas, but doubted the two sets of views were even remotely compatible. How many times had she heard one or the other making

250

similar claims, complaints and objections, especially about religion? Emma and Jean-Marc rarely ever had conversations about such things anymore, but Anthony had, if nothing else, picked up that torch and has run with it ever since. He often pointed out grey areas where neither science nor religion had sufficient explanations. One of Anthony's favourite grey areas to highlight was the obvious, but overlooked explanations for how and why we are here. "How did it all begin," he would ask in a tone of disbelief? "Ultimately, religion depends on an all-powerful being who has always existed, even though there is no explanation for such a possibility. Science is little better on the origin question by claiming the big bang was the beginning of everything." Anthony would quickly remind anyone listening that science makes it very clear that something cannot come out of nothing. The big bang might be as far back as we can see or determine, but it can't be the actual beginning of what is. "We, quite simply, do not know. Or at least," Anthony often emphasized, "neither of those explanations is satisfactory. They are inconclusive, and therefore, wholly unsatisfactory."

Emma continued imagining Anthony's rant on the topic. "Philosophy explores logic," he declared. "It tries to eliminate what can't be true in order to find out what might be true. It makes predictions to be worked out until proven or disproven. Philosophy builds on the past, but is forward thinking. It seeks higher terrain. It scaffolds previous accomplishments toward greater understanding. It expands the human mind – where everything is in the first place, isn't it?"

Anthony's discourse continued unabated. "Humanity is an important part, perhaps one of the most important parts, of an evolving process. We are definitely missing something when we try to see the big picture. Puzzle pieces are missing, or obscured. I feel like I'm on the verge of a breakthrough," she heard him say. That sounded familiar too. Emma imagined Anthony arriving closer toward revelation. "I believe I'm... I'm close to discovering what the grand explanation of explanations is," he continued, "but haven't quite made it there yet. It's both exhilarating and frustrating, almost painfully frustrating, yet... I do believe this venture will ultimately be successful. Others have likely been successful, although maybe few and far between. Maybe one day, everyone will. Maybe we are all destined to learn what the meaning of life is, one way or another. The information must be out there, or perhaps in here," Anthony stated, pointing to his head. "I sense it. I know it. I think that maybe it's always been there. Information is an essential component of everything that exists in the first place."

For an instant, Emma anticipated Anthony staring quietly into space with a dreamy, satisfied expression. It was a moment caught in slow motion. She emerged from the momentary image, to be drawn back into the ongoing conversation. "You know Mum," Anthony continued, "it's good to be able to express these ideas with you, but surely you believe these are the peculiar ravings of a lunatic. That may be correct as well, I suppose. You perceive my excitement and hear what I'm saying, but you probably don't have a clue what I'm going on about, do you?" Anthony laughed. "That doesn't make my rambling insanity though. It's just miscommunication. You might say we're not connecting on the same frequency. Wouldn't that be the best way to characterize it?"

Emma's thought-stream was abruptly interrupted by a realization. She had arrived back at the little cave with the aperture. She took a sip from the bottled water she brought with her, then made the short climb up into the opening. Still consumed by her thoughts, Emma sat back against the curvature of the cave wall, and let the mental reel continue rolling.

Anthony's discourse resumed. So did Emma's evaluation of what she heard him saying. Somehow, sitting in this place diverted her attention from one focus to a second one. She wasn't just re-evaluating her thoughts about Anthony, but about herself as well. That was probably a good thing. Even in this mental reconstruction of conversation with her son, she found herself reverting to pervasive assumptions about him. At least she was catching them as they arose. Assumptions are often roadblocks, sometimes requiring extensive detours to one's destination. Openness, Emma perceived, was the key to change, to transformation.

The thought-stream continued. Emma sat back in the cave feeling both comfortable and secure. The space she occupied inside the encircling curvature of rock walls was like the interior of an egg, or an urn. Again, she was the consciousness in this hollowed-out little space. She was the genie in the lamp. Her mind was spinning with converging insights, ideas and considerations. Excerpts of conversation resounded like a film depiction of an acid flashback, coming to the fore, then receding, or dissolving into a continuum of sensation. Being in this space and embroiled in space of mind momentarily, then intermittently, it all fused together into what Emma interpreted as an experience of oneness. There was a sense of being both inside and outside simultaneously. It came on like a sequence from a thaumatrope. Still pictures flipped-through rapidly to create the illusion of motion. She was still there with Anthony embroiled in conversation, discourse. It was almost telepathic, nearly pure communication.

252

Images, phrases and emotion intermingled as thought-stream, superseding conversation. What had been an exclusive exchange with Anthony only moments ago was now the coalescence of all interactions Emma could recall. Memories flooded into consciousness from a vast reservoir, far-exceeding what she thought she knew, or had ever known before. Archetypal images transcending culture suggested multiple affiliations. The warmth and comfort she drew from them were as familiar remembrances of lifetimes. The Imaginarium expanded. Sounds, scents and tactile sensations merged together as a gathering multiplicity of thought imagery.

Emma could no longer describe them as being in her head, but in a mind transcending personal boundaries. Yet the entire experience was indeed personal. There remained distinction, yet unity, oneness transcending any possible linguistic portrayal. She heard Anthony's words but it was more akin to sensing thought patterns. His thought was her thought. The flow of information transcended physical means. Emma imagined radio waves, television signals, remote controls and Bluetooth, all technologies accessed through specific frequencies. The same concept seemed to emerge here. Many things came to mind as Emma realized she could expand or contract her scope as easily as directing body movement by thought. This is incredible, she realized, an expansion of consciousness. The inconceivable became conceivable, emanating naturally.

The conversation with Anthony gradually receded into background static, still existing as potential, but not at the fore of thought and focus. Emma scanned images, sounds, feelings and thought, focusing in rapid succession through infinite diversity. As soon as each image or sensation came to the fore, it receded again into an electrostatic stream, not learned as though new, but remembered in entirety as always-known. Thoughts of Anthony flitted in between, resounding like a dial inaccurately pinpointing a specific frequency, coming in and out as it were. There was not only Anthony, his ideas, his words, his state of mind, or his feelings as he stated them, but also his associations, his extended experience and influences, his likes, dislikes and the context in which these all operated. Emma was imagining what it was like to be Anthony.

Was all of this reciprocal, Emma wondered? Was Anthony experiencing the same thing? Was this a two-way thoroughfare? But before she could focus on that idea, both Jahny and Kevin merged into mind. Was this free association or specific association with Anthony? The question was immediate, as was the response. It could actually be both. They exist as potential. Emma's intent had been to see if there was any association between her son and Jahny in the first place. Had she subliminally refocused on that objective? Or was there an actual association with Jahny through an enlarged field of perception, now within range of focus? Was there also an association between Kevin and Anthony then? Were these Anthony's thoughts she was gathering, or her own? Were they shared?

The wormhole of thought Emma descended into suddenly began to dissipate. She refocused on the cave's encircling walls, recalling much of what she had just undergone, but sensing it fade in intensity. She marveled at the experience, scrambling to remember everything as it had unfolded. Much was still flowing through her mind, but now Emma found herself in the quiet seclusion of the little cave with the aperture. She reflected on these last few minutes, or were they hours? Checking her phone, she could see that it was barely afternoon. Her sense of time was warped. She hadn't been here long. Just sit back and relax, she thought. There's no hurry. Think. Reflect. Retain as much as you can.

Emma closed her eyes. Words and images continued to scroll. She soon realized that words, phrases and concepts from the books she'd been exploring were firing in imagination. Excerpts of phrases that had caught her attention when first reading them reconstituted into present focus: The unconscious transcends mere subjectivity; consciousness is a fundamental characteristic of the universe itself; knowledge begins with experience, but not all knowledge arises from it. Emma recognized the back and forth between Kant and Jung, concepts she had clearly absorbed. She had connected with their words – the machinery representing lifetimes of thought and study. Emma had internalized them, giving birth to threads of an answer to her query.

Suddenly, Emma realized she didn't need to call Anthony. She would leave that for now, go back to the ranch house and finally make some lunch. She would relax. If Enrique came back soon, maybe they could chat. But tomorrow…tomorrow she would go back to the hospital and see Jahny one more time.

28

Danielle Sridhar glanced at the clock. Technically, her day was almost over, but as was often the case, it wasn't going to be over until she was done. There were still a few loose ends to tie up before going home. A glass of wine would certainly be in order when she got there, but that was likely still hours away. She still hadn't managed to see her most intriguing patient since yesterday morning when she found him conversing with a small crowd. It was already Thursday afternoon now.

Although she attempted a visit before leaving last night, she was met with a surprise. Jahny's bed was empty when she walked into the room. A quick inquiry with the desk nurse for the ward fueled Danielle's fears. Ongoing concerns about possible organ shutdown were heightened by typical indicators. She reported that Dr. Halundi came up to the ward a second time the same day to evaluate Jahny's condition. Repeated testing and alternate strategies to address evolving circumstances were employed. Danielle had patiently listened to the nurse prattle on about these signs: labored breathing, changes in urination, swelling of feet, and so on. Liver toxicity numbers were still impossibly high too. The nurse may have detected the psychiatrist's impatience. After listing all details, she blurted out the obvious. "Everyone is doing what they can, given the situation." She went on to tell Danielle that the patient was expected back on the ward sometime later in the evening, but there was no telling when. There was often a line-up for various tests and procedures well into the night. Multiple requests for up-to-date, highly specialized information was incessant. The psychiatrist acknowledged the difficulties and commended everyone's efforts, then told the nurse she would come by and try again the next day.

That gave Danielle some time to assess how she was going to approach the situation with Jahny. She desperately needed to gain insight for a possible diagnosis. She acknowledged it wasn't going to be easy, certainly not as straightforward as it was in many cases. All psychiatrists knew by experience that some sharper and more knowledgeable individuals could present significant difficulties for developing a correct diagnosis. That might be the case here. When she went over notes from her last conversation with Jahny, Danielle realized that it might help to use his strengths to her own advantage. Before she left him the other day, Jahny had suggested that they had not yet touched on the next natural progression in any conversation about existence – a discussion of consciousness itself. That could be challenging, but yield results. Many of her past patients had expressed difficulty with racing thoughts. Anxiety and depression often went hand-in-hand. Some regularly expressed being overwhelmed and just tired of it all. Over the years, a few had even articulated a desperate need to just shut it all off. Danielle didn't expect Jahny to come out and say such a thing, but suspected racing thoughts may be a problem for him too. It was something to explore, a possible lead. A former patient once told her that his mind felt like a prison furnished with an effective self-torture apparatus. It was more than he could deal with much longer. She lost that patient a few weeks later.

The afternoon had been creeping along. Paperwork always seemed to make the time go by slowly. Danielle knew that Dr. Halundi's usual rounds should be long over by now. If testing results from the day before were satisfactory, he was unlikely to return to the ward a second time again today. Hopefully no more testing was ordered. Then she could meet with the patient successfully before going home. Danielle understood that medical necessity often trumped psychological concerns, but a determined patient could easily sabotage all efforts to achieve recovery. Hopefully, that wouldn't happen this time. She was already convinced there was more to this patient than met the eye, but didn't know much about him yet. He may have the potential to fully recover, or he might turn out to be nearly impossible to really help. If truth be told, such patients existed.

On her way up to the ward, Danielle decided she would circumvent potential surprises. She wanted to avoid walking into an empty room, but also one that included Dr. Halundi, or a range of possible outside guests. She just hoped to connect with Jahny without interruption. She stopped at the nurses station, where the same RN from the night before was working at the desk. Recognizing Danielle immediately, she strained a smile, but told her the patient in 610 was there tonight and had no visitors. She reported that everything seemed to be stable at the moment, but things could still change. She gave Danielle the details before veering off into personal opinion.

"He's a little different than the other patients. Doesn't seem to like TV at all," she went on. "That sets him apart, doesn't it? He never watches it. Seems to prefer ruminating about whatever's going through his mind. He looks out the window a lot."

Danielle thought it to be an unusual remark, but found it interesting. She thanked the nurse for the information, and began walking toward Jahny's room. As interested and curious as she was to see this peculiar patient again, she almost felt nervous. This guy had a way of catching people off guard. His words were often challenging in ways that went well beyond comments about the weather.

256

When she stepped into 610, Danielle found him just as anticipated. Jahny was sitting up looking as though he was expecting her. She figured he probably heard her walking down the hallway. It was unlikely he was expecting anyone specific, especially if Halundi had already come by to assess the situation.

"Good afternoon Jahny." Danielle noticed that the dark rings he had under his eyes the other day seemed even darker. She didn't have Halundi's expertise, but assumed it wasn't a particularly good sign. No doubt he needed rest, but would he get it if she decided to leave him alone today? A racing mind never seems to rest. Many of her patients have difficulty sleeping. Although no one is exempt from an ongoing stream of thought, some, as she had already been contemplating, found it overwhelming. Yet, despite appearing unwell, Jahny was clearly relaxed. That was somewhat of a contradiction with her running thesis. She smiled encouragingly, but was already unsure of her approach. "How are you doing today? I understand you've been moved around to get some testing done."

"I probably feel better than I should be," Jahny responded. "How are you doing Dr. Sridhar? It's kind of late in the afternoon for making rounds, isn't it? Shouldn't you be on your way home?"

"I should, but as you know, salaried employees often have more work than they can fit into a typical eight-hour day. Besides, I really wanted to catch up with you. Yesterday's opportunity to do so was scuttled by your testing. I'm glad you're still with us and even looking, may I suggest, a little better?" That was at best a grey lie, but Danielle thought it had greater potential benefit than harm. "I have enjoyed our conversations so far Jahny, but as you are well aware, I still can't say I know that much about you. It is important to have something to show for my visits with you. My notes so far are rather scant. I know you need rest, so I'll try not to take up too much of your time, but it is good to see that we have an opportunity to talk. I'd like to take advantage of that please."

Jahny smiled, gestured her to sit down, but said nothing. Danielle pulled one of the chairs around to the back of the bed and sat down, facing him directly. She wasn't going to over-think her approach. She was just going to dive in.

"You've told me that your family are spread out and that most of your communications tend to be online," she continued. "When I tried to find out what you do for a living, you were very abstract and managed to evade the question. Much of this could be seen as outright distraction. We still don't know who you actually are." Danielle's smile faded. She became more serious. "You've

257

been fortunate to have a benefactor. That allows you to stay here for the time being, but in all honesty Jahny, as I just stated a moment ago, I've not made much progress with you. Given the fact that you're still here, Dr. Halundi may have been a little more successful. You are still here," she emphasized, "as we have been marveling, but all of that could change. These monitors you're attached to are constant reminders; so are the regular updates from doctors and nurses. I would really like to be able to help you," she emphasized. "We all would, but without your buy-in Jahny, everything we do here will all be for nothing. You are still very much in danger."

Jahny was still smiling. "I can't say that I feel very much in danger Danielle. As you have just acknowledged yourself, I feel very much relaxed…and am not worried about dying. Like anyone else, I have normal concerns about having an easy passage when it happens, but the outcome itself is of no concern."

"Well, it should be Jahny," Danielle retorted. "Don't you think? Even just a little?"

"No, I don't think so. Please listen to me Danielle. You are a doctor, a psychiatrist. Your raison d'être is to try and unravel psychological difficulties that prevent patients from living the best lives they could live. Does that sound like a fair assessment in a nutshell?"

"Yes, the goal is for everyone to live a meaningful, self-directed life – at least as much as possible."

"Well, let me tell you Danielle, I have lived a meaningful, self-directed life. Even now, we are having meaningful conversation where I am as much engaged as you are. I even admit enjoying the banter back and forth. As we've established, I'm relaxed as well. How can I help you understand that everything that's happened over the past few days is not distressing? It is simply what it is. Where I go from here is now somewhat out of my hands, but that in itself could frame a challenge worth taking on, couldn't it? Life and death are flip sides of the same coin: Both are clearly defined by comparison with the other; both are equally mysterious. Didn't Einstein once say that 'The most beautiful thing we can experience is the mysterious? It is the source of all true art and science. He to whom the emotion is a stranger, who can no longer pause to wonder and stand wrapped in awe, is as good as dead; his eyes are closed.' I think you misunderstand me on a fundamental level doctor. Are you expecting me to try and jump out of a window at my first opportunity? Despite being held here both for medical and psychiatric reasons, I could easily walk whatever walk you are expecting of me for a few days, get myself released according to protocol, walk to the nearest gun shop, and buy myself a suicide weapon. Hell, this is the States, job done. Do I seem like someone bent on doing that?"

"Well, I really can't answer that. Maybe you are just walking the walk as you say, although I might add, it could be a little while before you're released." Danielle looked at him directly, but retained her calm as well. "What brought you here then Jahny? Did you not just commit such an act by taking an impossibly large overdose of drugs? That act should have caused your death. It may still lead to your demise. Do you think it's unreasonable for hospital staff to be addressing concerns about your well-being? Do you think that we should assume you are calm because you are able to speak calmly? Does your demeanor automatically mean you are no longer a danger to yourself? Somehow, you don't seem that fickle Jahny. A serious and very dangerous self-inflicted act has occurred. That is significant, even if you are not recognizing it as such. What you just calmly stated about not being concerned about death is in fact very concerning. This is a serious situation and it is being taken seriously."

Jahny appeared unmoved. He was still smiling. "In all honesty Danielle, or maybe I should address you as Dr. Sridhar. That way, I might garner your attention more completely. Just how are you going to help me? What do you really think you can do for me? What can you do for any of the psychiatric patients you deal with routinely? Seriously, what can you do? Will you hold me for an extra 72-hours if, and when, Dr. Halundi clears me for medical release? Will you determine my diagnosis, then send me off with the latest drugs used to address that diagnosis? Will you continue to apply the recommended medication and dosage for a fully-expected recovery maybe? Will you set me up with both individual and group therapy perhaps? What professional bag of tricks can be implemented so that you can go home every night to revel in the success of having saved yet another despondent patient?"

"There's more to it than that Jahny." Danielle raised her voice slightly, but remained both calm and professional. "I understand your cynicism. Mistrust and scorn are actually normal responses to psychological distress. They are recognition that psychological distress can be complex. That translates into difficulties, or at least perceived difficulties. But what about the ever present possibilities for change? Life is always in flux. What about that Jahny?"

"Look Dr. Sridhar," her patient responded sincerely. "I didn't mean any disrespect to you personally. You are absolutely right. There is more to it all, but that's exactly why cynicism is appropriate, not just in this case, but in most cases. Psychiatry is the practice of diagnosing and treating mental disorders, but the truth of the matter is that psychiatry still has far to go towards understanding what it's actually dealing with. You don't have to answer this next question doctor, but how many people have you successfully diagnosed and cured? Really, how many? You don't have to answer that question because we already know the answer. There's a reason why we know the answer too Dr. Sridhar. The answer is that psychiatry is dealing with conscious, complex beings and the basic problem here is that we know very little, almost nothing at all, about what consciousness is. That's right. Even though we experience it every day, we can't explain much about it at all."

Danielle was taken aback, but fascinated. It was true, but beside the point as far as she was concerned at the moment. Despite a tentative plan of action before coming to see this patient, he managed to surprise her again. Yet, overall, the plan was going well. He had steered their conversation back to consciousness, a topic of importance to him. It's where they left off the other day and where she had hoped to return. Well, now they were there. This was her chance to recapture the initiative and learn more. Danielle decided to usurp the conversation before Jahny could continue, not to interrupt him, but hopefully, to steer it along somewhat.

"Actually Jahny, we can explain much more now than we could twenty, even just ten years ago. Some recent estimates are that modern humans have more than 80 billion neurons transmitting information by electrochemical signaling. That's still far in advance of any computer humans have devised so far. Clearly, we may still have much to learn about brain functioning, but we have at least a general understanding of what is going on, even if the full picture isn't complete just yet."

Jahny laughed. "Do you really believe we have a good idea of brain functioning doctor? Are you able to explain how firing of all these billions of neurons, for all their complexity, can produce the remarkable experience of consciousness? The experience can't be explained by simply stating a large number of neurons interact in a complex manner. That isn't an explanation, just an assumption. It dismisses the true magic that is occurring. Modern physics can't explain how a group of material molecules in our brains actually creates the conscious experience. Think about this doctor! It is one thing to explain how our eyes filters light, sends electronic messages to the brain to let us know what is out there, and gives us the opportunity to 'see' a sunset, but how does one explain the experience of the beauty of that sunset? What variables describe that accurately? How is the recognition of the sensation of beauty generated at all from raw information? Consider experiencing the taste of a particular food you like. Science can explain the composition of whatever it is, but how does science describe the unique sensation one experiences when tasting it? There's more to it than stating that different receptors identify and distinguish saltiness or sweetness. What is it that we are actually experiencing in the manner described? It isn't so easy to answer, is it? In fact, science can't answer it because that taste is a property of mind, not matter. I agree that we have increased our knowledge of physical processes, including those of the brain as you have pointed out, but are brain and mind the same thing doctor? It's an important question, don't you think?"

Danielle Sridhar did not respond. She was listening and waiting. She could almost see Jahny formulating his next thoughts. Here it comes, she thought. He is about to become a fountain of information She hoped it would be useful. She hoped no one would come into the room and interrupt them right now.

Jahny continued. "This is something I have really thought about for some time Dr. Sridhar, but now I'm going to call you Danielle again. I want to appeal to your own personal inner experience of consciousness. When you think about who or what is inside your head, you have a sense of self, don't you? That sense is almost like looking from the inside out, so to speak. You know what I mean?"

"Yes, that's right, I have a sense of self. It probably is best described as a sense of looking out from inside my head – which as we would both agree, we are in fact doing, would we not?"

"Of course. That's why I described it as such, assuming you and everyone else feels the same way. Maybe a more accurate description of this is that we all feel like we inhabit our bodies. One can begin to see how religious ideas of a soul developed to describe the experience. Yet, I personally think that's not quite right. I'm not sure I can explain my ideas accurately, or even if my ideas are solid on this just yet. As I've thought many, many times Danielle, I feel like I'm on to something, but haven't quite identified what it is yet. I also believe it has something to do with what I am – what we all are – and with the fact that we have this marvelous experience of consciousness."

Jahny stopped to laugh again. "It's a little ironic that you're concerned about me snuffing out my own consciousness Danielle, especially when I'm addressing your concerns with high praise of the state of consciousness itself." He laughed again. "This is fascinating stuff! Maybe I could explain it sufficiently enough to give you a glimpse of what I'm seeing," he said. "Please be mindful that I'm venturing an explanation doctor, not claiming an established theory."

261

Jahny only paused for a moment as he gathered his thoughts. "I'm not really sure about this sense of self we were just talking about. Despite my 'self' feeling like a single entity inhabiting this body, I realize there are several processes contributing information to that experience. We are most aware of information coming through apparent senses – sight, sound, touch – but sometimes I feel aware of more than that. Where do all the thoughts that just seem to pop into my head come from? They are wide-ranging in scope and often unique constructions, not just rearranged bits of information already known. They seem to come from nowhere, or maybe everywhere. They may be intuition. They may be subtle clues from the environment. I don't know Danielle. Developmental psychologists would venture so far as to say that our sense of self comes from a brain surprisingly dependent on the world it processes through its senses. Therefore, the generation of that sense of self must be shaped by the role of others in the world being processed. I think there's more to it than that too though. It's almost like I feel plugged into a macro consciousness that somehow includes everything, but the micro consciousness contained in this body gives me my sense of self, my distinction from everything else. That concept now seems less and less likely. It's like having a view from the inside looking out, but also a view from the outside looking in – simultaneously. If one can seem to be in more than one place, where are the borders? Where is the separation?"

"Anyway Danielle, as I've already stated emphatically, be mindful that I'm venturing an explanation. I'm not claiming to have one fully formulated. So don't be jumping to conclusions about multiple personality syndrome or schizophrenia too readily. Don't just grab for straws that are easy to reach. Schizophrenia, multiple personality syndrome, bipolar disorder, etc., may come quickly to mind given your training, but think about this doctor: Think about what I'm saying, what I'm talking about here. Don't just spend your time trying to connect my words to a possible diagnosis for your update on my progress. Furthermore, don't let whatever parameters currently define those disorders box in your analysis of what I'm talking about here. There's more to it than that."

Hmmm, that was a lot to take in, Danielle thought, but clearly, he had more to say. You're surfing a wave now, she told herself. Hold the course. "Okay Jahny," she said. "I will try and keep an open mind. Please continue."

"Earlier I criticized the field of psychology for being inadequate. I admit that's not entirely fair. By hoping to probe the depths of human consciousness, psychology aspires toward lofty aims.

As a serious psychiatrist interested in any deep study of such issues Danielle, you must have come to an important realization: Absolutely everything you have ever perceived, analyzed or studied, everything that you have ever dreamed, imagined, or thought about all happens in this milieu, this field of operation, or this matrix, if you prefer, we call consciousness. Therefore consciousness itself must be a component of the big picture, part of what reality is in some way. Even science will attest to the fact that space and time are tools of the mind. They are a way to frame and organize what we experience within that matrix of mind."

Jahny paused for a moment. Danielle waited patiently. This is good, she thought. He's getting it all out, even exploring these ideas as he shares them with me. She wasn't sure where he was going with all of this, or what it all meant in terms of a possible diagnosis. She would work it out later. Maybe part of what this was all about was processing – having a place to let it all out. Or maybe, it was about having a person who cared enough to listen, to take his ideas seriously. Sometimes just verbalizing issues, problems, conundrums, and so on, can give them a kind of materiality to work with, to iron them out, so to speak. On a more primal level, it might simply be about making a human connection about something very human indeed – the ability to think, to reason. Danielle didn't have to wait long before Jahny continued once more.

"When I think of my own perception of what is 'out there', so to speak Danielle, I'm not sure if what I conceive of is actually astronomically big, or infinitesimally small. When I try to imagine the universe, somehow I think of it as a giant thing floating around in space with parameters that somehow end somewhere. After all, what is it that's expanding if there are no edges to define parameters? What exactly does the universe expand into anyway – more space? If the universe is supposed to contain everything, then what is outside of that – the area it is increasing into? We tend to believe many things that cannot be proven with any certainty. Many of our explanations don't make a lot of sense, or are incomplete. It is easy to criticize the religious idea that some kind of god created the universe, but is the current scientific paradigm that features the big bang as our ultimate point of origin any better? It seems incomplete. How does a densely compacted universe expand from virtual nothingness into something? Science does not support the idea that something can come from nothing. Sometimes I think it's all in our heads, or perhaps only in mine. I have no way of verifying that anything else outside of what I am thinking about actually exists apart from my thinking about it. It is Descartes' idea that 'I think, therefore I am, but what about everything outside of what I am thinking? Perhaps, everything, I mean everything,

263

exists inside my mind. So which is it Danielle? Is reality an infinitely large universe that is too big for me to comprehend? Or is it infinitely small and contained inside my mind? Analyze and diagnose that doctor!"

29

Danielle Sridhar was still hoping to make some headway with this patient. By now, it should have been apparent Jahny may not cooperate in any anticipated manner. She wasn't disappointed though. It was challenging, but the session was moving forward. They were developing a rapport with one another. She was confident further progress could be made. There was going to have to be some give and take. She wanted answers, but was going to have to engage by answering his questions as well. Fair enough. That's how good rapports are developed – a little give and take.

Jahny had challenged her with compelling ideas. He had also posed tough questions. She acknowledged she was dealing with a reader, someone interested in more than mainstream magazines. It was clear he wasn't simply reciting points from a recently discovered pop-sci article or two. He seemed able to focus on, and pursue ideas toward either a logical conclusion or a dead end. Most people never delved into philosophical musing. It demanded too much time and energy on matters often considered to have little practical application. The doctor had an inclination to suspect OCD, obsessive-compulsive disorder, but remembered Jahny's admonition. Just moments ago, he advised her not to box him into officially-described parameters, narrowing him down to a specific disorder. She noted his caution. It could pre-frame, and therefore limit, her ability to learn what she claimed she wanted to learn. Jahny was actually correct on that point, she conceded. Descriptions of disorders often lagged behind current, updated insight. Locking into an official description could be a step backward rather than one forward. Maintain an open mind, she reminded herself. Proceed carefully. This stuff is clearly important, at least to him, so it's important for understanding what's going on here as well.

Neither philosophy, nor theoretical science have ever been my forte, Danielle thought, but this is it. I need to engage if I want the flow of information to continue. Her mind was picking up speed now. It sought to branch off into numerous directions. Jahny had actually triggered several compelling notions into motion. She found herself recalling past techniques to remain focused on the task at hand. She had to address his challenge. This was on the spot. This was key. If she failed to engage, the situation could diffuse. She remembered something Jahny said earlier: 'What professional bag of tricks can be implemented so that you can go home every night to revel in the success of having saved yet another despondent patient?' There was some truism in that sentiment too, but not to be focused on now. The truth is, Danielle realized, she had never really considered weighty issues like those Jahny rendered. At first, she thought that a position of disadvantage, but then realized not necessarily so. Jahny was looking for honesty in this exchange. If she were to spew some professional bullshit, as he might see it, she could lose him. He was probably right. Put aside Doctor Sridhar. Just be Danielle. Suddenly, her thoughts were interrupted.

"I appreciate you considering this carefully," Jahny said after an extended silence. He had been watching quietly. Danielle realized how quickly and deeply she had receded into her own thoughts. She smiled.

"Your observations impress me," she said. "Not because I'm surprised you've thought about such things so extensively, but because they actually move me." Danielle was particularly focused on Jahny's point concerning Descartes' "I think therefore I am" statement. She could hardly fault him for asking the same kinds of questions that many of history's most fertile minds have sought to answer as well. Jahny's words echoed in her mind: "So which is it Danielle? Is reality an infinitely large universe that is too big for me to comprehend? Or is it infinitely small and contained inside my mind?" The challenge was daunting.

"As you know," she began, "it would be simpler – and as any doctor might say – more 'professional' to fall back on basic training. That means providing treatment in the traditional doctor-patient manner prescribed by professional standards. You have challenged me to provide a personal perspective to your inquiries. Personal input, rather than strictly professional input, is generally frowned upon. However, standards in such professional practice are offered as ethics guidelines; they are not intended to establish rule of law. Somehow Jahny, I just don't believe that strict adherence to guidelines is going to do the trick here. I'm going to be completely honest with you - again. Put simply, I can't analyze what you're asking of me – straight-up."

Danielle stood up, sauntered slowly toward the window and looked outward. "You know Jahny, every day I wake up, and the first thing I do is look out the window – just like this. I contemplate the day ahead. As I get ready for work, I go through a to-do list in my head. Some are already recorded on my daily scheduler; others are just thoughts about less formal responsibilities. It's all about rolling out my day in an efficient manner. Often, when I get home, I'm still going through a mental checklist of the day's responsibilities. Several considerations have to be taken into account, not just about patients, but about administrative duties, meetings, conferences, email and telephone responses. It's about staying on top of things. Also, I have had, and continue to have personal goals and aspirations over and above daily considerations. As for most people, these are down to earth, even typical objectives: Getting an education; establishing a career; advancing opportunities; having a nice home; etc. There is nothing wrong with any of these things of course. They are practical, well-thought-out, purposeful aims. Yet, when I listen to you speak Jahny – whether it's in a one-on-one session like today, or in a group setting like the other day – when you speak, I recognize how incredible it is that we can ask such questions, and explore such ideas in the first place."

Danielle turned from the window and looked directly at Jahny. "You said earlier that you felt like you were on the verge of discovering what you've been searching for. You implied it was within reach. I'm inclined to agree. In general, humanity has developed a collective expectation that we can find answers to our questions. This has probably emerged from The Enlightenment, also known as The Age of Reason. It all makes me wonder though Jahny. With all the time and amazing resources we have to learn about whatever we can imagine, why are most people merely gratified by entertainment? Why don't more people spend time at least wondering about what you wonder about? The questions you've posed may not seem to address everyday concerns about living in the here and now, but is that true? Focusing on ideas and concerns about who and what we are in the context of where we are could very well be crucial. As I believe you've already inferred, understanding the bigger picture is essential to understanding the smaller ones contained within. It's kind of crazy how our immediate, specific, localized concerns loom large, while larger contextual concerns are barely recognized. It really is like being in the box and not caring about what's outside. Immediate needs are being met in the box, so it doesn't matter how it all got there. Despite paying lip service to various philosophical or religious explanations, this is the attitude most of us have."

"Exactly Danielle. So why do some of us bother to care? Why do so few feel the need to know? Why do some dare to ask hard questions while others plod on in apparent satisfaction with simple explanations? Religion does come to mind immediately, but science can be slow to address even pressing questions too. Thomas Kuhn's *Structure of Scientific Revolutions* clearly demolished the idea that science followed an objective progression toward truth. It's where we got the term 'paradigm shift.' He exposed patterns of peaceful ideological interludes in scientific circles that became periodically disrupted by fiercely complex conceptual revolutions. It's always about achieving a new threshold of understanding, only to find anomalies that require an even higher threshold of understanding to incorporate. When people like Galileo, Newton, or Einstein

267

take the time to ponder and come to a verifiable conclusion, many are moved and even amazed. Yet it leads to problems. The introduction of new ideas always invites pushback. But, we are digressing here. My question about the universe still goes unanswered doctor."

The doctor felt it was time to move on. "I don't think I have an answer for you Jahny. I'm not sure that when it comes to existential matters like this, that anyone can tell anyone else what to think. There is a high degree of subjectivity involved. However, there are some observations I would like to make concerning existential matters, specifically, the matter at hand. Let's pivot slightly. Let's go over the details, at least as I see them. You may object at any time Jahny. This is a discussion, not a lecture. Then we will attempt a return to your question. Is that acceptable?"

"Of course doctor," Jahny replied politely. He smiled, pulling himself up from a slouched-back position to one sitting up. "I am holding a mental bookmark at my question, but paying full attention. Temporary digression only please."

"The details are as follows," Danielle continued. "You were brought into the hospital by medevac helicopter at the beginning of this week. To be specific, that was just three days ago. As more information emerged, it became evident you had made a very serious suicide attempt. It may yet prove successful. Your situation remains tenuous. We actually know very little about you. Even your name remains anonymous as you have not confirmed your real identity. The circumstances around how you arrived at the location where you were found is still a mystery as well. Although monitors indicated intermittent discontinuity of vital life signs during your first night here, you have managed to hang on in surprisingly good form. Well enough, in fact, to hold conversations with doctors, nurses and a round of guests to boot. Clearly, you are an intelligent individual, but it is also clear that you are not functioning adequately. You have demonstrated both willingness and ability to cause yourself serious harm. We may not share the same perspective on such an act Jahny, but as a professional on such matters, I can tell you that is not wellness-functioning. There is something very wrong about a situation where someone with obvious potential wants to simply discard it. Am I to understand that it is all for a question, perhaps a series of questions, or ideas? It could be construed that there are similarities with the type of phenomenon that led that group near San Diego back in the '90s to…"

Jahny interjected mid-sentence. "…The Heaven's Gate cult?" He knew exactly what Danielle was alluding to. He snickered with derision. "No, this is nothing like that. They were a religious group that thought they could catch a ride with a spaceship they believed was following the Hale-Bopp comet. Despite what the medevac guy who was in here with the others thinks, I am no spaceman. Neither am I a wannabe. You may have details doctor, but not all the facts. You made the assumption that my ideas and questions are at the root of the behaviour you're focusing on. Again, don't be so prepared to box me in."

"Well then Jahny, maybe you should just tell me. Maybe it's time for you to be straightforward. Why keep me running around in circles? You're right. I don't have all the facts. Yet you criticize me for making assumptions. When one doesn't have all the facts, then making assumptions, and determining whether they have merit or not, is the way to move closer toward the facts. Trial and error are ways of chipping away at raw material to create an accurate image. If you don't want me making assumptions, then show me the picture. I'm only a psychiatrist, not a mind reader."

There was a long silence afterward, or so it felt. Danielle realized that impact might make a difference here. Let those words sink in. The point has been made.

It was Jahny who broke the silence. "I'm not trying to be an asshole. I'm not trying to make your life difficult doctor. Maybe there is something I'm trying to say, but I'm not sure there is anything of substance to reveal to you. It isn't fully formulated yet. It's as though I'm a woman in labour, but have no idea what the child is yet. As far as you are concerned, however, there is indeed merit in asking you not to make assumptions. I have no doubt you're a good doctor. You're probably very good at what you do, but sometimes that is the problem. Professionals become entrenched in their expertise. They go through the motions, or the process of what they do routinely. All the while, they keep in mind specific outcomes they might expect from patients. It should be no surprise they usually find what they are looking for. They are boxed-in by professional routine. They cannot see wider meaning in what is there." Jahny looked directly at the doctor. "If I really am living through the final hours of my life, maybe that's not good enough. Maybe an elective c-section of the process is not what's needed here. A full and natural labour must proceed to bring this birth to healthy fruition."

Yet another silence ensued. Perhaps Jahny was employing the same technique to make a counter impression. "I apologize Jahny," Danielle said. "Again, you have a point. Things don't always progress as anticipated. I also agree that professionalism, or overconfidence in one's professionalism, can cloud pathways to new discoveries. If you're only looking in the ditch, you might miss something on the road. Maybe that is what's going on here. Let's backtrack a bit. When

269

you said you weren't sure if the universe was astronomically big or infinitesimally small Jahny, where were you going with that?"

Jahny's eyes widened and a smile resurfaced. Then he sighed. It appeared to Danielle like he had suddenly glimpsed and recognized a recurrent dream, only to lose it again.

"When I drift into thinking about things more intensely," Jahny began, "when I explore as many possibilities as I can gather together in one sitting, I almost believe it's possible to achieve a holistic understanding of what is. Many people have a deeply-held sense that is possible only after death – when there is some kind of afterlife. They believe in a heaven – whatever that might be. There's a scripture in the Bible that talks about only seeing through a glass darkly. There is an inherent promise of being able to see more clearly later. Many religious tenets are vague, even for true believers. Yet it might reflect an inherent human expectation of progression, which would require further knowledge. If it's possible to acquire more knowledge, as we are often able to do, then it may be possible to get it all." This time, Jahny turned to look out the window.

"For most of my life Danielle, I have not believed in an afterlife – and certainly not in heaven. Yet somehow, I do believe that there is the possibility for an epiphany to occur, perhaps at a final point – maybe at the very moment one reaches the end. Maybe then, for just the briefest of moments, there is some consummate comprehension and understanding of everything. Maybe, because I am close to that point, I have an inherent expectation of finally discovering the answer to it all." Jahny raised his eyebrows and smiled at the doctor. "Or perhaps, that is insanity."

There was no pause for effect. Jahny continued without interruption. "You know Danielle, when I go down wormholes of thought, they often begin with a very specific idea or question and progress from there. The more deeply I think about every aspect and contributing factor to the topic at hand, it grows to encompass more and more, eventually grasping at everything that comes to mind. It may begin with a memory, perhaps an image from personal history, or some other recollection simply triggered by an occurrence in the present. As a stream of pure thought, it has a feel, or gives a sense that it is, a living field – a field of energy, electric in nature – like an interference pattern of sorts."

"What do you mean Jahny?"

"It's not so easy to describe. It's as if ideas or questions begin in my head, but then spread out to include information from regions I imagine to be outside – I use the term outside because I don't recall knowing that information before. It seems to have just popped into my mind somehow.

It's like my brainwaves aren't only contained in my head, but spread out everywhere. When I begin drifting into thoughts about who I am, or what I am, maybe what we all are, I often see, or feel myself, to be in the middle of deep space, perhaps in the very center of the universe. And not only that Danielle, but from there I envision its expansion, and comprehend its expanse as though it were always within reach. It's like the acquisition of new knowledge itself triggers a sense of familiarity that predates my memory of the knowledge being acquired. It's like my consciousness is reminding itself that it was already aware. It gives me a sense that I've always been here, that I am aware of it all, but am just remembering it now."

"There is more doctor." Jahny appeared comfortable as well as confident. He was letting it out, letting his thoughts flow. There was still a faint smile on his face as he sought to find the right words to explain them. "During those rare moments when I feel like I can reach the summit, grasp the enormity of it all, it becomes much more than knowledge. It becomes synesthetic. Images, sounds and smells converge to provide a holistic, multi-sensory experience. There's an out of body sensation where I feel as though I am everywhere at once, yet contained by a sense of selfness. In plain language Danielle, it is an all for one, and one for all actuality, a seamless web of what is. There is no cacophony; there is no chaos. There is an availability of all there is for any particular focus that may be intended." Jahny began to laugh softly. "I don't know if you are familiar with Tolkien, Danielle, but all this reminds me of his famous adage in The Lord of the Rings: Not all who wander are lost."

"I have a question Jahny," Danielle interjected. "Is this feeling of oneness a type of soliPSIsm where one believes the external world only exists in the mind – or that everything is only an extension of the mind, of one's consciousness?"

"My knowledge of soliPSIsm is minimal doctor. I am only trying to describe what I feel, what I think about when exploring these thoughts and ideas. If I follow what you're asking me, then you want to know if I see myself as an isolated individual whose mind is generating everything. That would mean that no one else - that nothing else – is anything more than a figment of my imagination. That's not it doctor. If that's what soliPSIsm is, then it isn't what I'm attempting to describe here."

Jahny was still looking out the window. "Yet," he continued, "there is an exchange that occurs between others and myself, whether we are in one another's actual presence or not. This exchange is more than the sum of physical descriptions, or personality characterizations, that might

271

be used to comprehend these 'others.' For example, when considering someone I have never met, perhaps a lesser-known historical figure like playwright Christopher Marlowe, or even a fictional figure like Voltaire's Candide, I almost instantly develop a perspective. I 'create' a rudimentary image of them. I say rudimentary, because if asked to describe specifics, even just about their appearance, it would be difficult to generate more than a guess. While I could imagine a face, a haircut style, colour of hair, some specific article of clothing, or another so-called obvious aspect about them, the description would still be vague. Descriptions of people I couldn't have met, or of fictional characters, might very well come from a book. In that case, the description is coming from the author. The description would include things the author thought were important to convey – and may or may not include things I would try to convey if I were describing the character. My point is that when not provided every detail, my mind will 'fill-in' the specifics itself. Whether I consciously realize it or not, it does that to maintain continuity in the overall image being generated. Both the author and I contribute to the creation of the character, but also any action in the book. There is an exchange occurring through generation of the perceived reality."

"Furthermore Danielle, once characters and actions have been generated, I gain a sense of familiarity with them. Let's say I pick up a biography about Cicero, the famous Roman orator and lawyer. When I read details about that person's life and imagine them in my head, I can imagine being confronted with his life circumstances – challenges, problems, triumphs, whatever. As I get into all such detail, I don't feel like I've been introduced to someone I knew nothing about earlier. It feels like I'm being reacquainted with someone I already know. There is an association. Maybe that association is there because of existing familiarities – we all have challenges, problems and triumphs. If one memory triggers another memory, then the link clarifies both a little further. In a way, it's like triangulating an area mathematically to gain a specific insight, such as the angle of a curve. That's the same strategy used to develop the calculation of pi – the ratio of circumference to diameter. It's never exact or complete, but every number added to its definition with further calculation brings it ever closer to perfection."

"And that's how you see your quest to understand everything too Jahny?"

Jahny turned away from the window and looked at the doctor. He smiled as though it were a mixed blessing. "Maybe, maybe it is possible, but I'm not sure. The ongoing advance toward a more perfect understanding of everything may very well be the same as pi. It always gets closer, but never quite arrives at the ultimate goal. Perhaps the persistent pursuit of perfection is both an eternal quest and final destination. Maybe reality is like a circle – no beginning, no ending."

Danielle took in a deep breath and sighed. "Well Jahny, there is a lot to think about there." She felt the need to interject before conversation became too esoteric. The doctor wanted to return to the practical concerns she needed to address. "Clearly, you've thought about all this extensively. As I've already indicated, you've managed to captivate my imagination. I haven't delved into such matters in the same way you have, but can see why they are important. Despite your circumstances, you present your ideas lucidly too Jahny. From my perspective, that gives me some insight, but I have to fill in details in the same way you just explained. I'm like the proverbial reader who participates in the creation of a book's characters and actions by adding filler. You've already warned me about making assumptions. Wouldn't that be filler? That wouldn't be necessary if you provided more details. You've been vivid in your description of ideas. How about describing details I've been asking for specifically? Having listened to what you've had to say so far, one point stands out. You see a clear connection between everything in the universe – everything that is. Therefore, your focus must include discovering your place in all of it. I get the impression that your pursuit of all knowledge is a way of coming to terms with yourself in a world, or a universe, that is mysterious to us all. Fair enough. You're trying to find your bearings, but it begs the question: How do you see the circumstances of your own life in this grand context? You've spoken about not knowing whether the universe is infinitely large or infinitely small. I would like you to adjust the question. Never mind its scale. How do you think you fit into the picture? Maybe you could give me some specifics."

"Is this your clever way of getting me to tell you about my background, the antecedents to my crisis Dr. Sridhar? I must admit it was skillful, especially given the twists and turns our conversation has taken. Although there is a goldmine to excavate from what's been said so far, I suppose it is only fair to indulge your request. After all, it isn't the first time you've made the request, and you've been listening to my ramblings patiently. If you have a little more time Danielle, why don't you pull up that chair again. Take a seat, relax. I'm sure you agree we're getting somewhere today. Let me take you a little further then."

30

"Of course I have a little more time. I will make a little more time," Dr. Sridhar assured Jahny. She decided to follow his suggestion, pulled the chair round to the side of the bed nearest the window, and sat down. She was satisfied with progress so far. Unless there was an emergency, everything else could wait.

"I haven't spent this time in discussion with you only to abandon that endeavor now. This has been enlightening so far – and I admit, most interesting. As I said a few moments ago, you've spoken with a high degree of clarity about your ideas and the questions you retain. That's all fine and good, but I want and need basic background information. Don't worry about trying to give me what you think I'm looking for Jahny. I'm more interested in what you think is significant. Aside from the challenge I just posed about placing your life circumstances in context, I'm more interested in the basics first. Maybe you could tell me what you think were formative events. That would provide context from your perspective. It would be from your vantage point. Could you please share something tangible? We still don't know your real name."

The proverbial doctor/patient relationship softened into an exchange between engaged conversationalists, almost like old friends. Jahny felt no need to be defensive, or secretive. Danielle felt no further need to push the issue. She was confident this would proceed as she had hoped, perhaps better. She slipped her note pad back into her bag. Informality was essential at this juncture. She not only appeared to relax, but did so. She wanted to signal he do the same. It was a portal to openness. He appeared to respond as anticipated.

"Well doctor," Jahny began with a less enthusiastic tone in his voice than she had noticed up to now. "I seem to remember telling you that my relationship with family tends to be much like everyone else's these days. It is usually online if, and when, it does occur. To be completely honest, contact with family has been inconsistent since I was old enough to leave. As for my name, I will say for the last time that it isn't important. Should I die sometime in the next few hours or days, I will very quickly become a non-entity anyway. Surely, you're aware of how this all works doctor. All records of my existence will be purged from banks, insurance agreements, debts, subscriptions, and any other attachment I may have had. In a very short time, it will be as if I never existed at all. Whether your notes refer to me as Jahny or some other name will not matter. They will still end up in a closed file until they can be legally discarded entirely. It is possible other concerns come to mind. Let all concern go doctor. If you are disturbed about that wonderful woman Emma, who has taken it upon herself to cover my costs here, do not be. It has nothing to do with you. She entered into the situation of her own volition, and as it turns out, without personal cost. I have arranged to leave information that covers any expenditure incurred here. There will be no complications. Emma will be exonerated from any responsibility in the matter. So it is of no consequence whether or not you learn my real name. It is my particular case that you are interested in unravelling. Perhaps it could enlighten your insight into other cases."

Determined to stay on point, Danielle disregarded that last comment. "You know Jahny, I can't help but think that for a person who wants to know and understand everything, it is strange you don't even want to make sense of what happened this past week. Why is that?" Danielle realized she was sounding a little impatient. She attempted to rein it in a little by smiling. "Give me something here Jahny. Throw me a bone, will you? This is more important for you than it is for me. I would like to get to the bottom of all this professionally, but you need to get to the bottom of all this personally. At least that's the case if you have any intention, or will, to move forward from here."

A few moments passed before the silence was broken again. "This isn't the first time I have been on the edge doctor. To some extent, being on the edge has been the story of my life. When I said you were on the wrong track by thinking that a tragedy or disappointment led to my actions, that was mostly true. The truth is always more complicated. Perhaps in your professional experience, tragedy and disappointment are often catalysts. Nonetheless, I'm sure that in the end, you will realize my case doesn't meet your expectations. You don't think that I've tried to make sense of what you see as a senseless act, but I have. You see doctor, I have been thinking about these things for a very long time indeed. No doubt you are aware that suicidal ideation is often pervasive. It is an underlying current flowing constantly."

"Constantly? For how long, might I ask? Are you talking about weeks, months, or years Jahny?"

"Decades doctor," Jahny replied promptly. "Decades, but before you begin salivating at the thought of a rich narrative to adorn your documentation, remember this: I have benefitted from difficult circumstances even more than from circumstances people generally prefer and welcome. The thesis I might present, if this were a formal discourse, follows Nietzsche's well known dictum: 'That which does not kill us makes us stronger.' Perhaps your note pad will come in handy after all doctor. Don't hesitate to pull it back out of your bag, and keep it open. You might need it to catch the bone being thrown in your direction."

"One thing is abundantly clear in every historical narrative I have ever come across," Jahny continued as though there were no interruption. "No one has ever lived a life devoid of difficulty. Historically speaking, the idea that happiness can be achieved at all is a fairly new one. Even the American Constitution mentions only the 'pursuit of happiness.' That is the high-bar objective. The world has a long trail of misery that leads right up to the present. When and how do psychologists think most people will rise above coping skills, especially in a world in constant flux? Your family comes from a culture that is as old as any on earth Danielle. You know that misery has been a well-established feature of life there since memory began. As for the modern world, the illusion of previously unimagined material wealth is just that, an illusion. Is it not true that more people take prescription drugs for psychological ailments here in the U.S. than any other place on Earth? Yet, this is the richest, most prosperous country in the history of the world. That paradox cannot go unnoticed. You can go almost anywhere here in L.A. to see the stark disparity between rich and poor."

"You know doctor, I have an uncommon habit which I often indulge. Usually reading will instigate it, but other triggers can also set me down similar pathways. I love to imagine what it was like to live in a previous time period, or a different part of the world. Unfamiliarity and curiosity blend into enticement. I have to explore further, and when I do, the experience can become eidetic. Vividness and detail are exquisite, the sense of familiarity hallucinatory. I am there, or perhaps, it is here."

"Have you ever noticed that most books, especially fiction, generally provide great detail, except for our most common experiences? Being common experiences makes them less enticing to write about, but over time, subtle changes to what were once common experiences are lost to memory. Try not to laugh at this example doctor, but consider the point I want to make. If I try to imagine what it was like to relieve myself during any particular time in history, it isn't so easy. I can't think of any novel that describes, or even mentions, any aspect of the all too common bathroom experience. Yet, stopping to imagine the bathroom experience in an unfamiliar time or place can greatly aid one to imagine the phenomenal experience of actually being alive there. I think that's because it is so down to earth, it's so basic, so fundamental in essence. Going to the bathroom is the one intermittent time-out, however short, common to all human experience throughout history. It provides a brief respite from activities that are exciting or boring, dangerous or enjoyable, exhilarating or tiring, to produce moments of reflection, placing into context one's overall phenomenal experience. Perhaps the process of relief is meant not only for relieving physical waste, but psychological waste as well."

"Even so, the 'common experience' just described was not always common – not for people throughout different periods in history, and not for people arranged in different classes of privilege. When I was young Danielle, a great-uncle of mine was still alive and lived on a farm he had owned since the 1930s. He died when I was in my mid-teens in the '70s, but there was still an outhouse on his property, testament to the rapid changes that had taken place during his time there. Consequently, when I first thought about going to the bathroom before modern times, I imagined the outhouse as the standard for millennia. Yet outhouses, although indescribably old, weren't the norm for several reasons – nomadic lifestyles, poverty, lack of resources, and so on. For the most part, people relied on the great outdoors. They might dig a small hole, like people camping in the backcountry will do nowadays. They often used water sources like streams and rivers. Even today, the poor in many parts of the world use designated areas, often wooded, but otherwise unsheltered for such purposes. In early modern times, chamber pots were used. One would relieve themself into it, perhaps privately in a closet, and then without any thought, empty it out the window and onto the street below. When one considers the fact that streets were not paved until fairly recent times, it is possible to imagine walking through tainted mud on virtually every street in every city, every town, and every village in the world."

"The miserable lives people have lived throughout history are reflected even more accurately by other conditions. Brutality and lawlessness continue to be common occurrences. Even slavery still exists. Many continue to live in abject poverty. Here in the richest country in the world, we still grapple to identify and address disparity and injustice. Just in my lifetime, movements have emerged, but still battle to achieve legitimate goals. Gender equality, women's rights, gay rights, fighting racism and economic disparity, etc., etc., are all still necessary pursuits. There is much misery to go around. There always has been. Thank goodness we are beginning to look at these things now, but much has to be done. My point is that human evolution is still an emergent enterprise. We are forged toward perfection through a fiery process. It isn't easy. It can't be easy."

"All very interesting Jahny, but you are still speaking in generalities. I think we could all agree that life has been difficult throughout most of history. Please give me some personal specifics about your life."

"This information is all contextual doctor. My life experience is not any different from common life experience throughout history. Settings and circumstances may differ, but difficulties, challenges, obstacles and deterrents are part of life. They can lead to the negative outcomes psychologists tend to look for, but also positive outcomes achieved through resilience, determination, and actual effort. I agree with a field of study that seeks to guide toward positive outcomes, but disagree with general approaches that amount to one-size-fits-all frameworks. Prepare to hear two points you might consider professional sacrilege doctor. First, not everyone needs a psychologist. Second, psychologists must realize current textbook definitions and guidelines are incomplete. A field of study that seeks to understand all psychological complications experienced by humanity cannot yet claim to do so. That field of study is still young. It is still emergent. The fact that I am still here lends credibility to the idea that my life couldn't have been all that bad. I'm not a young man anymore. I've been around for a while. Should it end now, would it really be so tragic? Nonetheless doctor, if you insist on content for your notes, I will summarize my existence for you and make sure to highlight important junctures."

Jahny reached for a cup of juice the food service attendant had left on his side table earlier. He sipped it slowly, then placed the cup down again. He folded his arms on his lap, and looked up at Danielle. "Okay, here it goes doctor. Do you have your note pad ready?"

"I do. Thank-you Jahny. Please proceed."

"I was born in the 1950s in a small town up north and back east. My parents were European, both young people who came over after World War II. They weren't from the same country and met on this side of the pond. They spoke different languages, communicating to one another through heavily accented, broken English. Their marriage lasted over sixty years, but was tumultuous throughout. Like many, it wasn't the model home portrayed during the early days of television."

"Within a few weeks of my birth, I began to exhibit breathing difficulties and other ailments leading to my first hospitalization. Complications progressed. By the age of nine, chronic acute asthma necessitated stays at the Children's Hospital in a nearby city. For years afterward, my parents fearfully recounted the night they were called to the hospital because I wasn't expected to survive the night. Needless to say, I did survive, and for many years, continued to exhibit severe asthma. For several months after being released from hospital, I had to live in an oxygen tent at home. A local chapter of Kiwanis International, a well-known service organization that seeks to strengthen communities and particularly children, helped with expenses. It wasn't just the oxygen tent, but an ongoing need for various medications and a makeshift respirator. I say makeshift, because single-use respirators for use outside hospitals hadn't been developed yet. The respirator I used for almost a decade was converted from a small, standard 1950s and '60s-style paint-sprayer. My family just referred to it as 'the machine.' As you can imagine, chronic breathing issues restricted activities. Circumstances certainly impacted me, but did not kill me. So don't think about causes of mental illness here doctor. Remember Nietzsche's dictum. That which does not kill me..."

"It was during this time that I became introspective and reclusive. I spent a lot of time alone in my room. Numerous allergies that could trigger asthma attacks, and an overprotective parent, made that an inevitability. Interestingly, a silver lining emerged at the same time. Two pastimes I had already established -- reading books and listening to music – became much more engaging and important to me. Books and music enabled me to venture outside my room. They could carry me anywhere. I became an avid reader and music lover. In fact, these two interests became ardent pursuits. Eventually, both collections amassed into a personal library."

Jahny paused in contemplation. "I might add, for your particular interest doctor, that books and music have been two necessary staples in my life. They have constrained me through good times, and sustained me through difficult ones. I feel exceptionally fortunate to have had the opportunity to indulge my interest in books. When one chooses to read, one chooses to discover, one chooses to learn, one chooses to transcend."

Jahny chuckled momentarily. "And music doctor, music! Is anything comparable? Music can comfort when in the depths of despair. It can lift to orgasmic heights. It's a vehicle for exploration, consideration and discovery. When one travels the musical ocean, one may voyage far, far away."

"Did you have access to a lot of books and music at home Jahny?"

"My parents listened to radio, They didn't have many records. Most of the dozen or so albums at our house by the time I left home had been there since I was very young. My parents were never fussy about their records like I later became with mine, so they indulged my interest.

279

They taught me how to use the record player in their early '60s-style entertainment cabinet when I was four years old. They regretted that quickly enough when they realized I could tolerate listening to the same ones over and over again. I don't really remember hearing the radio in the house so much, but always in the car. Radio became a regular feature at home later, at least during the day. My mother preferred to listen to country at home, but once requests began, they would tolerate listening to a top 30 station in the car. I believe that started when I first began learning about popular music from other kids at school. Two of my very good friends had older siblings who were into music. Another friend's father was into collecting music. I still remember what an impact it had on me to be invited to their house after school one day to listen to his Dad's new Beatles album, Hard Day's Night. 1964 is almost 60 years ago now."

"As for access to books, until the early '70s, the only one available at our house was the TV Guide. That posed no problem. Growing up in a small town, the library was in proximity to most residents. The library in our town also just happened to be located next to my doctor's office. For years, I had to go there every Tuesday after school for a shot because of my asthma, so I also stopped in at the library. I would borrow the maximum three books allowed each week, then finish them off before returning the following Tuesday."

Once hospital stays tapered off, and I was able to return to school full-time, we were learning about explorers in social studies. My interest had been triggered. I became immersed, and began hoarding biographies of explorers from the library each week. That led to an interest in acquiring books too. I had already been collecting comic books since the mid '60s, but I didn't start amassing proper books and music until I was eleven. By then, the '60s were almost over."

"That sounds like you found positive avenues for development despite your circumstances Jahny. However, if such a case was presented to me now, I would be very concerned about a child who spent too much time alone, especially isolated by illness. I appreciate your willingness to look for a silver lining, but I don't think you could say that circumstances were altogether positive, would you?"

"Maybe not, but as the maxim goes, it is what it is, or was what it was. Perhaps you would be concerned because my escape routes were essentially psychological and could be enacted from my room. Please don't tell me you were conjuring the premise for a possible personality, or even multiple personality disorder diagnosis, doctor. Don't engage your professional acumen into a wild goose chase strategy. It goes nowhere, and wouldn't be worth a page from your notepad. Besides, you have nothing to worry about. I was able to devise another loophole to escape what had become a very restrictive existence. It allowed me an alternative to my room."

"An escape? An alternative to your room?" Danielle scribbled a quick note, but kept looking at Jahny. She knew he was aware…but was he providing a narrative, or crafting one?

"Yes! The great outdoors," he continued. "The year before I spent so much time in hospital, we moved to a new subdivision where the woods began just behind our backyard. Only a small field of long grass, the forgotten remains of an old farm, lay in between. My mother was adamant I don't go there, reminding me constantly of my allergies. She soon discovered it wasn't so easy to prevent. I sought to enter the woods daily after school, when access was less likely to be detected. I knew she would never consider coming to its edge to call after me. Tall grass harbored garter snakes. She was mortally afraid of them. Many unwanted little creatures found their way into our yard periodically, so she was always on guard."

"As for my allergies, they became only a minor trade-off. They were frequently triggered, but I always carried one of the early asthma inhaler sprays with me. At the time, I imagined myself to be like Jacques Cousteau, but instead of exploring the oceans with a breathing apparatus, I was exploring the forest behind our house. My inhalers were a lifeline in more ways than one."

"Did you find having a chronic illness unyieldingly difficult Jahny? It can be debilitating. Kids like to be out playing with their friends. They want to engage in sports, games, and so on. I imagine the physical restrictions were frustrating."

"There were times when it really was restrictive. There were times it was frustrating too. During the late '60s, I was often prevented from doing things I wanted to do, but much of the time, I couldn't do them anyway. Once I was able to keep an inhaler with me at all times, I was willing to take more and more risks. I accepted the trade-off. Boys will be boys, right?"

Danielle just smiled and nodded, keeping notes to a minimum.

"Getting out to the woods and other wilderness places remains important. That foray out to the desert was not my first. Likewise, books continue to guide me through many exploratory ventures… but music, Danielle, music… of my main personal interests, music is with me always, and frequently in my conscious focus. Sometimes, it almost seems like a higher frame of reference, a means of alternate perception. It's a telescopic lens, with a mirror reflection. It can express anything imaginable, becoming fine-tuned within. It is a phenomenal link with all else."

"Once I began collecting, music became an obsession Danielle. I was familiar with all the disc jockeys on my go-to radio station, and even had favourites. The station followed a top 30 format, and did a chart countdown every Saturday. Every week, they distributed the updated chart in brochure form to record stores in the metropolitan area. If you couldn't get to a record store, they also published the charts in the newspaper. For the first couple of years collecting music, that was my guide, a virtual Bible. I used to enjoy calculating the top 100 songs of the year by assigning a value to each of the 30 positions on the chart. When a song had finished its run, I added the total number of points it had accumulated by landing on one position or another each week. The system wasn't perfect, but did afford a fairly high degree of accuracy. At junior high, I was already a go-to music guy. A friend and I used to write parody lyrics to popular tunes just to entertain classmates and draw ire from teachers. That's right Yankovic, well before your time."

Without pausing, Jahny pivoted to a more serious topic. "My parents' marriage really deteriorated in the early '70s. It soon became unbearable. I couldn't say I remember, or even know how my siblings dealt with it, but I hibernated in my room and blasted music. By the time I was 15, I was well into drugs. I actually ran away from home when I was fifteen and managed to get over 2500 miles away before being caught by the cops. I spent a little time in youth detention for that. When I got back home, there were only a few months to wait before I could legally emancipate myself. During that time, I made plans. On my sixteenth birthday, I handed in my books at high school and left permanently. I had already managed to start working full-time after school and on weekends as part of my strategy to avoid going home. Being on my own meant couch-surfing for a while. Shortly afterward, I would rent rooms, or share apartments with friends."

"Achieving a huge objective like that was a confidence-booster and helped to shape a course of self-determination. At the same time, I was also pretty high continuously, and delving into more reckless behaviour. I was already using syringes before leaving home. Difficulty with access meant using several of them over and over. I knew it was risky, but didn't care."

"That's a bit of a surprise Jahny," Danielle interjected. "Despite what happened earlier this week, I wouldn't have suspected you to be involved at that level of drug abuse. You're very fortunate to have survived a stretch of heedless self-harm like that. How long did that go on for? How did you manage to get off that fast track to disaster?"

"Things came to a head and deteriorated when I was 17. A close friend overdosed and died. He was only 19. I became more reclusive and self-destructive in the months afterward. One thing led to another. I ended up at a drug rehab for six weeks or so. Eventually, I was kicked out after pleading for a day pass, then returning with drugs and overdosing in my room. I was in hospital for days. When safe enough to be released, they told me I was a bad influence on the other patients. I had to go, but had nowhere to go. I wandered for days – in a daze. Stepping out aimlessly onto a street, I was almost run over by a car."

"It sounds like you were completely lost at that point Jahny. How did you ever get back on track?"

"Well doctor, what happened next could never have been predicted. At age 17, I already felt like an old man. That good friend who died wasn't the only overdose victim I knew, and other friends and acquaintances had been killed either by car or motorcycle accidents. I had indulged in reckless behaviour for years, and had no intention of changing course. Many around me considered my descent into hard drugs a train wreck in the making. I truly believed death was imminent as well. For many, it might have been. This was obviously a low point, but very quickly, things changed completely. It began when that car almost hit me while wandering the streets."

"Did you receive a settlement because of the accident?"

"There was no accident doctor. I said the car almost hit me."

"Well, now I'm intrigued Jahny. What happened?"

"The older woman who was driving the car that almost struck me was an acquaintance from the job I held before going to rehab. Despite my long hair and a penchant for sticking to myself, she was always as friendly to me as she was to everyone else. When she recognized who she almost hit, she insisted I come to her house for supper with her family. Now this is a story that I haven't recalled in some time Danielle." Jahny looked contemplative, but a faint smile could be detected. "I still can't believe I ever accepted her invitation, but that move was the first step in a long series of steps that have brought me here."

"How so?" Danielle asked while scribbling a quick note.

"As I have already mentioned, I grew up in a strict Catholic family, and wholeheartedly believed the claim that it was the original, and therefore, true Christian faith. It would have been a cardinal sin not to. At this point in my life, I accepted that I was a sinner, as taught. Full-indoctrination meant knowing instinctively that I was hell bound. It had already been some time since I had attended church, so cardinal sins were being committed. At the time, none of this motivated me to consider changing my ways. I had resigned myself to the inevitability that I would be dead soon, and probably deserved hell anyway. Keep all this in mind as you hear the following narrative unfold doctor."

"I hadn't been invited anywhere for supper in some time. Despite sitting with a strange family, the experience was unexpectedly relaxed, even comfortable. That made the family itself seem strange. The woman's husband came home unaware of any invited guests, but welcomed me warmly nonetheless. Her two children, both older than me, were in their twenties, still living at home, and present for supper. Everyone got along well. Laughter erupted often during the meal. Parents and children alike were aware of one another's agenda and asked how this or that went that day. Needless to say, this dazed and confused, long-haired freak had to wonder: Was this part of an all-encompassing hallucination?"

"As conversation progressed, it became apparent her daughter had plans for the evening. She was excited about an event friends were planning to attend as well. Whether any further details were mentioned, I can't remember, but I was invited to go along. I had no plans. Why not spend a few hours with her daughter and friends? I agreed." Jahny noticed an abrupt smile on Danielle's face. "What is it," he asked?

"I have an idea where this is going," Danielle replied, "but continue. I apologize for distracting you."

"Ah, you assume I developed a relationship with that woman's daughter, who then saved me from imminent self-destruction, right?"

"Relationships can do that. You're a music guy. Think Johnny Cash. He repeatedly acknowledged that his relationship with June Carter saved him. It's an oft-repeated story."

"Well, that's not what happened here doctor. Again, avoid relaPSIng into assumption. I made one that evening, expecting an event with free live music and a crowd. It was an event with live music, and quite a crowd too, but I could never have foreseen what it was all about. We parked in a field like we were going to a fair, then walked toward a huge structure that was clearly the center of activity. There were hundreds of young people in their teens and twenties engaging with one another enthusiastically. An air of excitement and good times created a hive of activity. Many people appeared to be more than casual acquaintances. Greetings were being exchanged continuously. I had never seen anything quite like it. Then something happened that I could never have anticipated. I caught someone in the crowd do a double-take in my direction. We recognized one another simultaneously. Suddenly, I felt completely out of place Danielle. Had I been aware of the concept of alternate universes then, I might have believed I had awakened in one. That person began walking toward me. He was a good friend. We hadn't spoken since our friend's funeral a few months earlier. Having sunken into a reclusive, stoned-out spiral since then, I imagined he must have done the same. We both had good reason to believe the other might be dead by now too."

"As it turned out, my friend – and everyone else who had come to this event – were Christians, there to celebrate an annual event that included much gathering for social activities and music. It seemed much livelier than any Christian event I had ever known. Except for attending church and celebrating Christmas and Easter, I was unaware of Christian events in general. Having grown up Catholic, I believed myself to be a life-long Christian since baptism, so all this was out of place. By the end of the evening, it became apparent these people had made personal commitments to live a Christian life according to biblical principles. This wasn't just a group of people who gathered on Sundays for an hour to fulfill an obligation. This was a community of people connected with one another in ways I was completely unfamiliar with."

"In my endeavor to keep this long story short Danielle, from that point on, I became a more consciously-dedicated Christian than I had been, or already thought I was before. A distinction had been made. It was a fork in the road, so to speak. I chose to walk in a different direction. Everything changed. I quickly and effortlessly became more social. I moved into a large house being shared by a number of people, about eight to ten at any given time. I also quit doing drugs, without really thinking much about it. Most importantly, I soon became good friends with an ex-minister of an evangelical church. He introduced me to some revolutionary concepts that set me on an exceptional course of discovery."

"The plot thickens further Jahny. You continue to surprise. The details, please."

"The key to real discovery comes from a very simple idea doctor. Question everything! Of course, as a young early '70s freak immersed in the rebellious idealism of the period, questioning everything was routine – except for one thing. My strict Catholic upbringing provided a framework that did not allow for certain kinds of questions. Therefore, questioning God was unimaginable. Although of slightly lesser importance, questioning other tenets of Christianity was just as unlikely. So when a former minister of a church introduced ideas that broke this mold and enlarged my personal frame of reference, it completely blew my mind. It also motivated me, and shaped my direction."

"Tell me about that Jahny."

"The first revolutionary idea I had ever personally considered up to that point was mentioned casually by my new friend. He said that anyone could study the Bible for themselves. They didn't need someone else to interpret it for them. God could speak to them directly. One did not need a priest or any other intermediary for that. The second revolutionary idea was that church buildings were not the focal point of Christian duty. Any community of believers who gathered together were the Church. Third, a person could practice the faith without having to belong to a particular denomination. No organization had a monopoly on the Christian faith. These were truly revolutionary ideas to me at the time doctor."

"What I find interesting Jahny, is that you were able to change your situation profoundly. You weren't being passively resilient, but made distinct changes in your life. Choosing less seclusion was important. Whether you saw it that way at the time, or not, it was a good move, a smart move. Also, you were open to new ideas. That may have been because you were at a low point in your life, but that's how it works sometimes. When one's world comes crashing down, they can either be crushed by it, or clean up and start anew. You seem to have chosen the latter readily. I just wanted to make those points. Thanks for letting me interject Jahny. Please continue."

"These were completely different concepts than I had been taught Danielle. They helped open the door to a search for real truth. That's been important to me since then. Being a bookworm anyway, it opened a very large door. A whole new universe became available for discovery. Not only did I read and collect a wide range of books on Christian theology, apologetics, and systematic argumentative discourse, but I even took an interest in studying the elements of Hebrew and Classical Greek, the languages in which the Bible was written."

"My interest and diligence were noticed. Within months, I was asked to teach a youth group on Sunday mornings. It was at a church belonging to a specific denomination, but I did not recognize the restriction. Venturing out to meet groups from other denominations, I was soon invited to speak to congregations with varying interpretations of Christianity."

"Not surprisingly, issues arose. The idea that youth from different denominations could and should meet in interdenominational get-togethers did not sit well with pastors and parents from any of the groups. Baptists, Methodists, Pentecostals and Charismatic Catholics couldn't allow their youth to adopt such radical ideas. It was outright sacrilege. I soon realized that organized Christianity, with all of its denominations and ideological variations, was probably as far from the Christian ideal expressed in the gospels and epistles of the New Testament as they could possibly be. I became disillusioned. I also left any Christian affiliations I had maintained up to that point, and sought to find answers to some very fundamental questions."

"And was it then that you walked away from believing in anything spiritual Jahny?"

"It was then that I walked away from anything officially religious. A few years had passed. I had learned much, but it still never occurred to me to question the existence of God. I never considered exploring other modes of belief. I did, however, decide to delve into philosophy and other fields of study. One thing led to another."

"I can't say I've ever met anyone interested in reading philosophy. Sometimes reading the philosophical basis for a chosen field can be tedious enough."

"It wasn't actually too much of a jump. Delving into Christian apologetics meant reading the works of Christian philosophers. Pierre Teilhard de Chardin comes to mind immediately. He was not only a Jesuit priest, but a scientist, paleontologist, teacher and philosopher. His outlook tended to be Darwinian – not a list of qualities many would expect from a Christian philosopher. C.S. Lewis, author of the children's books, *The Chronicles of Narnia*, was also a Christian intellectual and philosopher. His book *Mere Christianity* was a thought-provoking read. Virtually all philosophers throughout history have had much to say about God. The existence of God, or of deities, is part of the philosophy of religion. A branch of philosophy called epistemology deals with the nature and origins of what we know. It's all related. Needless to say Danielle, there were many interesting perspectives to explore. And then, I found the *Twilight of the Idols*."

"The Twilight of the Idols," Danielle repeated questioningly? "Sounds familiar. Sounds philosophical, but I couldn't tell you who wrote it. It is a book, right?"

"It is a book. A very important book along with others made famous by the same philosopher. Perhaps you are more familiar with other titles: Beyond Good and Evil? Human, All Too Human, maybe? Also Sprach Zarathustra – Thus spoke Zarathustra in English perhaps? There are others as well."

"If I were on Jeopardy right now, I would venture to say Nietzsche, but I'm not sure I could tell you his full name. Wasn't Zarathustra the book where he scandalously declared in the late 1800s that God was dead? You also mentioned Nietzsche earlier."

"Ah, you do know something about philosophy then. Excellent. I can appreciate your mind all the more knowing that you cast a wide net in your own pursuit of knowledge doctor. I can't express how important I think it is for people to learn as much as they can about as wide a range of topics as possible. I tell my…" Jahny stopped short of finishing his sentence momentarily, then restarted. "I tell my friends all the time."

"I believe I just detected a near slip of the tongue there Jahny. You weren't going to say friends at first, were you? Were you going to say your students?" This time Danielle paused momentarily. "Are you an educator Jahny? That would explain much."

Now we are making some progress, Danielle thought. She waited for Jahny to respond, figuring he was gauging his response. The silence in the room suddenly became pronounced. Monitors beside the bed, distant chatter and footsteps out in the hallway began to pervade the room. She hoped no one would walk in to interrupt this important moment. Seconds went by, maybe a minute or two. Finally, Jahny spoke.

"I did almost say students doctor, but you are jumping ahead. Let me tell my story. It is what you wanted, is it not?"

"It is, and I guess I am. Please continue Jahny. My apologies."

"I was expressing appreciation that you knew who Nietzsche was at all. Even those who have knowledge of his work probably heard it in a negative context. One doesn't upend millennia of belief in gods and other supernatural beings by declaring them dead – not without significant backlash. I was drawn into Nietzsche's passionate language, deep questions, and detailed logical responses to the difficult concepts he sought to address. It was insightful. It was transformative. Some two years after walking away from formal religion, I realized I was taking a first step out of the box. I was peaking over the edge. Unforeseeably, I became an atheist. Despite this personal paradigm shift in perspective, I didn't believe I had 'arrived' at anything. Instead, I saw it as a new beginning. I knew I was embarking on an adventure – a long and winding road."

"Both thought-provoking and noteworthy Jahny. Several questions come to mind. How many years had passed since you left formal education? As commendable as your studies were,

288

they were informal. Didn't any route toward a career in education seem daunting at that point in your life?"

"You're getting ahead of me again doctor. Quite frankly, it never occurred to me then. There have been a number of interesting chapters in my life Danielle, but what happened shortly after the remarkable revelation that God was dead is almost unbelievable. Almost a decade had passed since I quit high school, but as you have just heard, that doesn't mean I was forfeiting an education. It's true they weren't formal studies, but as you will see, they did have value."

"In addition to my vigorous pursuit of reading over the years Danielle, I also moved around a lot and worked in many different fields of work. I gained varying experience picking fruit, painting, working as a night auditor, learning how to cook haute cuisine, serving tables, doing odd jobs, and apprenticing in a stained glass studio. I have lived in small towns, cities of varying size, and even in a remote fly-in-only community. That unbelievable event I just mentioned, happened while working as a waiter in a big city." Some of the staff at the restaurant where I worked attended universities. One waiter, whom I conversed with regularly, asked me an interesting, but provocative question one day. He wanted to know why someone interested in learning wouldn't pursue higher education. 'After all,' he said, 'what are you going to do with your life? Be a waiter?'"

"That must have been truly thought-provoking for you Jahny. You were clearly someone preoccupied with academic interests. Working in minimum-wage positions, often menial, must have seemed daunting, especially to someone with chronic illness."

"That is true," Jahny confirmed. "I haven't mentioned that asthma was only one of two chronic illnesses. The other didn't begin to develop until I was in my teens – kypho-scoliosis, a degenerating deformation of the spine. I don't need to get into all that here, but it spoke loudly to the point made by my fellow waiter. Perhaps you have not noticed the crooked nature of my back because you only see me lying in this bed. Metal rods were inserted to support my spine over forty years ago. Otherwise, my life would have been spent in a wheelchair. There were definite challenges, but challenges can be excellent motivators."

"Getting back to that waiter's point, he went on to suggest that I apply to a prestigious university in the city. Of course, I scoffed at the idea. A high school dropout with no intention of returning to make up lost classes had little chance of acceptance. As far as I was concerned, that proverbial train had left the station. However, Danielle, there is something to be said about persistence. The next time we were on shift together, he brought an application and encouraged me to apply as a mature student. I appreciated the gesture, but continued to scoff at the possibility. So we made a deal. I would follow through and apply, but when I was summarily dismissed, as I resolutely believed I would be, he would have to stop badgering me about my education and let the matter drop."

"So how did this proceed Jahny? You said you had no intention of making up lost studies. Prestigious universities don't typically recruit high school dropouts."

"Exactly. That's why I was profoundly surprised to be invited to an interview in the first place. After getting over the initial shock, I fully realized that if the possibility were real, I would have to make up lost studies. If universities were going to give outliers a chance, they would want to make sure that chance could succeed. Success or failure could be seen as a reflection on the university. Although committed to going to the interview, I didn't expect much of anything."

"I expect that's how the process goes Jahny. People are expected to take make-up courses to bring them up to par in English, math, science and social studies. It improves their odds. Otherwise, they might become overwhelmed and fail to follow through. So what happened in the interview?"

"I was feeling nervous, somewhat embarrassed, and definitely out of place. By going to the interview, I was just following through on the deal with my fellow waiter. Nothing would materialize out of this, except the badgering would stop. To believe otherwise was foolish. The logistical chances of succeeding in my circumstances was virtually nil. Nonetheless, the interviewer was polite. We sat in his office, surrounded by shelves of books. A window looked out on the grounds and older buildings of the university. It was formal, and a little intimidating. I figured he wasn't too impressed by a long-haired, blue-jeaned waiter who had dropped out of high school almost a decade earlier. He probably considered this a waste of time too, but as mentioned, he was polite, and asked me what my interests were."

"I hope you didn't just mention your interest in reading Jahny, but conveyed your deep interest in learning. Stereotypes are everywhere. Interviewers at prestigious schools probably meet several people who just aren't going to make the cut for whatever reason. Every applicant likely mentions an interest in reading. The interviewer might easily have assumed you to be a pulp fiction buff, like most of the others."

"I told him music and reading were foremost among my interests. When he asked me what I was reading lately, I told him Hermann Hesse and Friedrich Nietzsche. He was visibly surprised. We engaged in conversation for some time. I actually became relaxed, enjoying the exchange. He may have detected some potential, or just had a hunch, I don't know. As I was leaving his office, he said to me: 'I'll make sure you have an acceptance letter in the mail within a couple weeks; you make sure to keep up your GPA.' Needless to say Danielle, I walked out of that office wondering if what had just happened had really happened, but I took that ball and ran with it. Within five years, I earned an undergraduate degree in English, then a graduate degree in education psychology."

"That is an unusual story Jahny. One doesn't hear of too many high school dropouts who go on to achieve university degrees, or a career in education. You must have felt like you found your niche. Given your description of prior events, the future must have looked quite bright from this new vantage point. You had shown yourself to be a resilient, motivated, and diligent individual. So, I'm a little confused. How does someone exhibiting such qualities arrive at a point where you were this past week?"

"Ah, but you should have some idea about that doctor. I'm sure you've heard similar stories from many patients over the years. It doesn't matter how successful or how happy others think you should be because of fortunate circumstances. History is full of examples of successful people who committed suicide. Ernest Hemingway, Sylvia Plath, Hunter S. Thompson, Robin Williams, Chris Cornell, Kurt Cobain and Keith Emerson quickly come to mind, but there are numerous others. All were profoundly successful at what they did. The question has been asked before, but needs to be asked again. Who can say that the decision each of these people made wasn't an appropriate one at that juncture in their lives? Who among us truly knows better what is right or most appropriate for someone else? Of course I understand that your profession would never even consider acknowledging such a question. It could open the door to unnecessary and poorly-thought-out suicides. I must ask you a question doctor, a question plain and simple: Is life always better than death?"

Danielle noticed throughout their conversation that Jahny referred to her as Danielle and doctor interchangeably. Was that an act invoking familiarity, or distinction? Was it intentional? She was reluctant to answer. He could be asking for an honest opinion as a fellow sentient being;

he could be setting bait for an expected, typical professional response. To her surprise, Jahny didn't wait for the response.

"You know Danielle, music lyrics, like poetry, can pierce you with a truth so evident, one marvels at the simplicity with which it is brought forth in verse. The recurring lyric of one such song that comes to mind is this: 'Everything is beautiful because everything is dying.' That may actually be the crux of it all. As you know, everything exists in flux. Everything changes continuously, traveling along the directional arrow of time toward entropy. If one accepts the inexplicable beauty of the universe, perhaps it is most natural to drift into this eventual disorder along with it. Departing this existential experience in a hospital may provide a level of comfort, but it's a distraction. Indeed, I was just fine where they found me."

"Somehow this all seems too neat and tidy Jahny. It's idealistic, but it doesn't make much sense to me. You say that your action did not necessarily come from a place of despair. You talk about the beauty of 'what is.' Wouldn't recognition of that beauty seek to indulge in it, not be separated from it?"

"A recognition of that beauty does seek to indulge in it – everything that it is, including eventual cessation. Things are not always what they seem, and can seem more complicated than they are. It may be much simpler than we imagine. I have had unusual experiences, and sought illumination. Any answers I may have are those I've formulated. I have insight no more definitive than anyone else. Any ideas I can formulate must be through the indirect lens of my senses. I must make out what is out there from in here," Jahny said pointing to his head. "We all do."

"That's justification for your recent action Jahny? A few minutes ago, you also stated it was not uncommon for successful individuals to turn to suicide. I would argue that it is far more common for people to fight for their lives. There are countless stories of people fighting for a better existence despite difficult, if not impossible odds. I can't help but think that there is something we aren't discussing here, a missing piece to all of this."

"There isn't much to say doctor," Jahny said, now sounding more formal. "I could regale you with self-indulgent stories portraying personal and professional satisfaction. Any comparison between my early and later lives would acknowledge an upward trajectory. Yet, we've come to an impasse Danielle. We are not making a connection. I'm not sure I can provide you with what you're looking for. We may simply be on parallel tracks, moving alongside one another without any possibility of intersection."

"I'm not so sure Jahny. I admit there is a poor connection on this issue, but we've made some progress. I appreciate our exchange today.

"I appreciate our conversations too doctor, even if we are on non-intersecting tracks. I have also enjoyed each of the others who came by to speak with me as well. That may not have reached a conclusion yet either. We shall see. As much as this has been a pleasure Danielle, I admit I'm fatigued now. Perhaps we could pick up this conversation again soon."

"You should get some much needed rest. You have a recovery to achieve Jahny. Thank-you for sharing with me today. You may feel like we are on parallel tracks, but I believe we're moving forward. If nothing else, we managed to converse without interruptions. That in itself is an impressive feat in a hospital setting. I hope you can rest without interruption as well. I think I will go home and have a glass of wine now. Let's chat again soon Jahny. Thanks again."

Jahny had already closed his eyes, but softly thanked her in return. Danielle walked quietly out of the room. Only the sound of monitors and the muffled traffic outside could be heard as Jahny slipped off to sleep.

31

It was absolutely mind-blowing. Darnell could not remember a time when he had been so studious and engrossed in something that truly inspired him. It quite simply had not happened before. Responding to his wife Neveah's second call for supper, he reluctantly closed the lid of his laptop, stood up and stretched. He had spent much of the last two days in his man cave following leads, reading lengthy passages, and analyzing information. All this was the result of going to that prayer meeting yesterday morning.

Darnell stepped into the bathroom to wash his hands before sitting down to supper. When he walked into the dining room, Neveah greeted him with a "hello stranger." Darnell sat down in his usual spot and looked at the clock. It was almost an hour later than their usual time for supper.

"I guess I've been pretty absorbed in my office the last couple of days," he commented.

"And I guess there's good reason why I refer to your 'office' as a man cave. You've been holed up in there like an old bear in winter. Don't get me wrong. I'm pleased you found something to bring you round to some Christian fellowship with Pastor Dave, but now I'm curious. You've been holed up by yourself in that cave of yours working more diligently than ever. What is it that has you so excited and worked up? You stayed up long after you normally would. You were up even earlier than I was this morning – on your day off! Now that's something. Well, let's break that spell for a moment Darnell. I made you one of your favourite meals, complete with a freshly-baked pumpkin pie. We can sit down and enjoy it while you share some of the excitement you picked up at that prayer meeting yesterday. Or is it all something secret you want to keep to yourself?"

"I'm not sure I could keep it all to myself Neveah, not if I knew what it was really all about, but I feel like I'm just seeing the tip of the iceberg now. You know me. I shy away from organized religion because it's like listening to commercial music on the radio. It's just meant to keep the attention of the most passive listeners long enough to entice them for more time, which also translates into more 'support.' Knowing the pop hits makes the listeners feel like music enthusiasts. They keep coming back. Everyone's kept happy, even if none the wiser. You know I choose not to play that game, but you also know me to be an ardent believer. I may study privately in my office, or man cave as you like to tease me, but at least I'm serious about it. I'm actually hungry for the truth Neveah. This has been a crazy week, I'll tell you. When most people say that, they tend to mean it was rough in some way. It was unusual, I admit that, but it has turned out to be – is turning out to be amazing. The best thing about this week is that I discovered there are others out there hungry for truth too. That's exciting." Darnell's eyes widened in expression, drawing a coy smile from Neveah.

"So you and Pastor Dave made a spiritual connection then?"

"Well, I know you would like to think that Neveah. You just love that organized religion so much," Darnell said chuckling, "but there's more to this story Sweetie. Don't get me wrong. Pastor Dave is, at least in a small way, one piece of it all, but the part he's played, at least so far, only became relevant because of something that happened at work earlier this week."

Neveah sat down with a plate for herself and quickly said grace. "Okay you big bear, let's eat. If you don't mind, I'd like to hear about what happened at work this week."

"Okay, but a preliminary note first," Darnell uttered with his mouth full. "You've outdone yourself this time Neveah. Either that, or I'm hungrier than a bear come out of his cave. Everything on this plate is dee-licious, mmm, mmm. Thank-you very much."

"You're very welcome you old bear. Now back to what happened this week please."

"Well, I'm going to have to backtrack a bit. Can't remember the date, but that doesn't matter – maybe. I know you still haven't met my young partner Kevin at work, but you've heard me talk about him numerous times. He's a good guy, and a smart guy too. He's a reader, but likes to get into much different material than I do. No doubt he would say the same thing about me, but he has some unusual ideas about things. He believes more strongly than most in matters that have not been proven conclusively. That spilled over into work after an unusual event happened at work – well, maybe more than one."

"What do you mean by 'unusual' event, or events?"

"When I say unusual, I don't mean crazy, just different from what might be considered the norm. Christians fall into that category too Neveah. After all, most of us believe in things others see no proof for. Miracles are a good example. Even belief in God falls into that category for many. Anyway, as I said, Kevin is a reader. It wouldn't be incorrect to say he was studious. He's definitely not crazy, but some of his ideas are out there. He believes in aliens."

"Lots of people believe in aliens Darnell. I might think that's misguided, but I wouldn't say it was crazy. Who knows if there are aliens, or not? Maybe God doesn't think it's necessary to inform us about his creation elsewhere, but that wouldn't make it impossible."

"I'm surprised to hear you say that Neveah. Most Christians are reserved, or closed-minded enough, to say that if the Bible doesn't mention it, it isn't important. Many would even say it couldn't even be true. Until this week, I too might have argued that if Martians fell from the sky, what would that do to God? If there is no mention in the Bible, and suddenly something unexpected proved true, wouldn't that plant doubt about the Word itself?"

"That might be many Christians' approach, but think about this Darnell: The Bible uses numerous metaphors, leaving true believers to seek guidance about their meaning. I agree with one thing you've often said about church. Parishioners tend to hear about some passages often, while hearing little to nothing about many others. Is it possible there are Bible passages that relate to the topic of aliens?"

"Well my dear, I'm glad you asked! But first, let me tell you all about this from the beginning." Darnell enjoyed more of his supper while gathering his thoughts. Neveah waited patiently, saying nothing while enjoying her meal as well. Darnell got up for seconds. While scooping healthy portions of pork roast, mashed potatoes and root veggies onto his plate, he finally began.

"As I said, Kevin believes in aliens. Sometimes, if it isn't busy at work, we have time to chat. After you work with someone for a while, you get into various conversations. You get to know people as much by what they talk about as what they do. Well, there have been a few times when Kevin would talk about aliens. Interestingly enough, he doesn't just watch the plethora of so-called documentaries on the boob tube to get these ideas. He actually reads a lot, as I've already mentioned. Some of the stuff he's talked about has made some sense – not that I put a lot of stock into it all, because I haven't cared very much about the topic in the first place, but he's come up with some logical arguments over the time we've worked together. I came to doubt that somewhat one night when he came in to work and started telling me about something that happened."

"What happened Darnell?"

"Well, some weeks ago, one of the medevacs on another shift was out sick. We were short, and so Kevin did an extra shift to help out. It was what happened while working that shift. An airlift was called out to the desert that night. Kevin was involved in a rescue that turned out to be a retrieval. I forget everything Kevin had to say about it when he spoke to me, but he was animated and had some hunches. I remember making a few jokes and teasing him about it, then forgetting about it – until this past Monday night, just three days ago."

"What happened Darnell," Neveah repeated?

Darnell sat back in his chair and put down his fork. "Our crew was called out to the desert on Monday night. I haven't mentioned it to you, but it's been on my mind since it happened. One thing has led to another. It even spilled over into my experience at the prayer meeting yesterday morning too – or maybe what I learned at the prayer meeting has spilled over into what happened at work. My time in the office has been spent trying to sort it all out. That's still emerging, but I think I'm on to something."

"Perhaps by talking about it, you can formulate your thoughts a little clearer," Neveah coaxed. "Papa used to say that sometimes the best way to learn something is to try and teach it to someone else."

"Okay. I'll tell it to you the way I remember it. Let's hope I can remember everything the way it happened and then condense it enough to keep your interest."

"Oh, you've already captured my interest Darnell. I haven't seen you budge much from your usual stable, predictable self for a long time – and maybe never. As motivated as you've been these past couple days, there has to be enough excitement spilling over to maintain mine. Now go ahead. Let's hear this story."

Darnell finished the last bite of food on his plate. He wiped his face with his napkin, then placed it on the table, thanking Neveah again. Then he began.

"We kind of expected Monday night to be slow. The weekend was over, People don't go out as much the day after a weekend. They tend to go home and ease into the new week. With less people out and about, there's less chance of accidents and mishaps, right?. Kevin and I often play cards, chat, and watch TV on shifts like that. This Monday night was different. We had barely clocked in at ten, when we were called out. Dispatch reported a desert destination off the beaten path, so to speak. We were instructed to follow the Pearblossom Highway out to Pearblossom, then veer south along the rise toward the mountains. There was a small contingent of police vehicles already there with lights blinking wildly near the destination site. There were also house lights where they were parked. It was easy to find in an otherwise dark area. It's out in the middle of desert brush, rock and sand. It was easy enough to see the display from a few miles away. I veered the chopper toward it. We arrived shortly afterward."

"Was there a car accident on an off-road then?"

"It wasn't a car accident at all. Police were called to a ranch on an old road up off Longview going up toward the mountains. Apparently, the owner found someone unconscious in a cave on his property. It wouldn't be easy to try and explain the location of the cave, so that's why police stationed themselves at the house until we arrived. The rancher and some police were positioned by the cave. They were waiting for a signal to flash lights from the nearest location a copter could land nearby. As soon as we were briefed at the ranch, the operation proceeded. We flew the mile or so, following the flashing lights to the designated spot. I'm the pilot, so I remained in position as per protocol. Kevin led the crew on the ground. From what I could see, it didn't look easy. The entrance to the cave wasn't very big. Kevin told me later that the cave itself was quite small. They followed every procedure. Shortly thereafter, we had the patient in transit to hospital. Kevin didn't say much while the whole operation was being undertaken, but he certainly did afterward. No sooner had we delivered the patient to emergency at the hospital and completed our report, when police requested Kevin and I to come down to the station for further questioning."

"Is that something you are often asked to do after unusual operations like that Darnell?"

"No, usually reports cover whatever details law enforcement might want, or need. This was highly unusual, but it sure had Kevin going. He was actually excited. That's when he began making connections between this incident and the incident he was involved in the night he covered that other shift. He also connected it to a third incident other medevac staff have discussed with him. It wasn't long before he had an entire scenario worked out Neveah. He was already sharing it not only with me, but the other people brought in to make statements."

"Other people were brought in to make statements about the rescue your team made?"

"It was the rancher who owned the property where the stranger was found. He wasn't there to make a statement about our rescue effort. He was there to make a statement about what happened in the first place. Apparently, he runs a bed and breakfast. A guest staying at the ranch had to come make a statement as well. She turned out to be quite an addition to the story as well."

"Was she somehow involved in what happened then?"

298

"No, no. I can see you're getting excited about this now Neveah, but let me tell the story. No, she wasn't involved in any way, but she did have a story of her own. It seemed to be entwined with what happened at the ranch somehow, but it was – is a mystery, as far as I still know anyway."

"And you thought I wouldn't be interested Darnell. Keep going."

"It actually becomes somewhat mysterious Neveah. Now, since I'm introducing new characters into the story, I should tell you their names. The rancher is Enrique. His guest's name is Emma. After we were finished at the police station, they offered Kevin and I a ride back to the hospital. The police took us to the station with them, as we were already answering questions they had. We should have thought about being stuck without a ride in the first place. Anyway, we were driving back to the hospital with them and chatting about this and that. Then Emma got a call from her son up in Toronto. She was visibly startled by it. Her son is a young man in his twenties who, despite being diagnosed with schizophrenia, lives a somewhat normal life in an apartment of his own nearby. He made a reference to this guy she and the rancher found on his property. That may not sound strange at first notice, but her son had no way to know she and the rancher had found anyone anywhere in the first place. The reference he made was apparently quite specific, referring to the stranger as the 'cave man.' Anyway, once she and Kevin got going, the whole thing blew up into a mystery that didn't stop when we got back to the hospital."

"What do you mean?"

"No sooner did we step back into the place, when we were corralled by emergency staff on shift. The doctor in charge told us how dire the situation was. The stranger was still alive, but had indeed ingested more drugs than needed to kill himself. They weren't exactly sure of the time frame, but tests showed there was no saving him. They determined to keep him comfortable during his demise, despite the fact they were flabbergasted he was still hanging on. He was still alive when I left work early yesterday morning before I went off to the prayer meeting."

"That does sound unusual, especially if his condition was as dire as reported, but how is all of this connected with the prayer meeting Darnell?"

"I'm getting there. Hold on. On Tuesday night, Kevin and I were working the last shift of the week as usual. We got in early and he was on about the stranger and the circumstances out in the desert. To make a long story short, he decided to go up and see how the stranger was doing before our shift started. As it turned out, he actually got to meet him. The man was conscious Neveah! Go figure. So believe it or not, Kevin had a chance to chat with the man. Apparently, this guy was surprisingly coherent. Kevin was taken aback by his impression of him. It also further fueled Kevin's working theory about the guy. When he got back to our little office, Kevin was going on about what happened. That's when he caught my attention, and I become interested. Forget all the details up to this one point. The important thing is that Kevin told me the guy referred to himself as 'legion.' Do you remember the passage in the Gospel of Mark where Jesus casts a demon out of a man?"

"Jesus casts demons out of various people in the Bible. Explain further."

"It's probably the most famous example of casting out demons in all of God's word. It's in the opening verses of Mark 5. A man comes out of the tombs and begins shouting at Jesus. When Jesus asks him who he is, he says that his name is Legion, 'because we are many.' Then Jesus casts the devils out. They enter a herd of pigs who then drown themselves. It's a well-known passage."

"Yes, yes, I know it. So this guy found out in the desert referred to himself as legion as well?"

"Yes, exactly. The way Kevin told me the story, it sounded exactly like the response the man in the Bible had. It immediately struck a chord. The more I thought about it, the more important this whole thing became. I checked out the verse in the Bible I keep in my truck, just to double-check. Then I decided to go up and see this stranger myself. Well, you wouldn't believe what happened next Neveah."

"What happened next Darnell? Oh my God, just continue!"

"I wasn't the only one who felt compelled to go see this guy. His name is Johnny by the way, pronounced like some movie gangster might say it – Jahny. Anyway, who did I run into at the elevator? Not just Kevin, my co-worker, but also Enrique and Emma, the rancher and his guest. We had all felt compelled to go there at the same time. It was kind of a strange coincidence, but not the strangest thing about it. When we got up to Jahny's room, he seemed to be expecting us."

"What do you mean? Did he say anything to you? What was he like?"

"He not only spoke to me, but to all of us in turn. I was so hyped up about what I was thinking about, that I just blurted it out shortly after entering his room. Considering his condition, I tried to be respectful, but I confronted him with the line he told Kevin about being legion. He came right back at me, making an immediate connection with the biblical reference. He was a little condescending, and indicated some amusement, but told me to continue. That took me by surprise, and I felt self-conscious. I came back more boldly, and perhaps somewhat irreverently, told him the others weren't there to hear me rambling. I apologized for being forward, but told him I just wanted to know if he made that statement to Kevin with reference to the Bible passage, or not. I was just hoping for a simple answer – hopefully something practical to ease my…" Darnell paused for just a moment. "Let's just call them uncertainties. Then Jahny took me by surprise again. He said he wasn't offended and told everyone that he wanted to hear why each of us had come to see him. Everyone but Enrique had an agenda of sorts; he seemed more observant than conversational. Jahny did listen to what everyone had to say, and then addressed all points afterward. He presented as being quite human, but didn't look to be as close to death's door as medical staff portrayed him to be. He was different in some way though. I think most of us there had a sense of that, but wouldn't have been able to nail it down exactly. Jahny was very knowledgeable and able to address concerns each of us had. It might sound strange to say that he seemed fatherly, but someone in the group made reference to that afterward. To sum up the experience I had – what I think everyone who was there had, it felt like being caught up in something much bigger than any of us, including Jahny himself. One could say he was the focal point in the room, but not necessarily the center of it all, if that makes any sense. I'm not sure I've quite processed it all yet, or quite how to explain it. It was an interesting experience though, but let me move on Neveah. I didn't get to the prayer meeting yet."

"Oh my goodness Darnell. Just imagining being in that room with you all made me forget. That's what I originally wanted to hear about. What happened at the prayer meeting? We can have dessert afterward."

"I don't know about that Neveah. If I can talk through supper, I can talk through dessert. It won't take near as much time to finish up. Let me serve it up. Would you like some coffee with that pumpkin pie?"

It's too late for coffee. It will interfere with my sleep later. You go ahead. Just a small piece of pie for me please. A little bit of whipped cream is okay."

"Have you been down to Orange County to the Crystal Cathedral before," Darnell asked? "It's the largest church building I've ever been in."

"No, I haven't been in there and don't particularly care to. I may like my organized religion Darnell, but I don't believe it's a good idea to be spending money so lavishly when there are much

301

more important things that could be done with it. I've seen it on TV before, although not for some years now. It's money spent on appearance, not substance. Now as far as it being a public building, it is beautiful, but not as nice as that hotel down on Figueroa with multiple blue glass towers. You know the one I'm talking about. Other buildings downtown are nicer too. So you were down there for the prayer meeting with Pastor Dave? Do tell me how that went Darnell. Was that building as lavish inside as it is out?"

"It was. I feel the same way as you about that Neveah, but let me tell you what happened. I ran into Dave out in the parking lot, so we walked in together. We did talk about the building and how its extravagance didn't pay off. Did you know that original congregation went bankrupt some years ago over it? The building was bought by the Catholic Church."

"Well, guess that speaks to my point about substance. Why would you and Pastor Dave consider a prayer meeting at a Catholic Church?"

"Now Neveah, don't be getting your denominational hackles up. That ain't no more important than appearance. If you want to hear about substance, let me finish telling you about what happened there. For one thing, the Catholic priest who opened the meeting was a Charismatic Catholic. Their beliefs are similar to various evangelical groups. I actually thought that aspect of it was outstanding. There were people there from various denominations. It kind of made the glass building we were inside a symbol for seeing through all our differences. That was the first good thing. It seemed, well, Christian, in a truer spirit than denominations usually distinguish themselves."

Neveah smiled, acknowledging he was probably quite right on that point. Darnell continued.

"It isn't that I didn't sit back and observe with some judgement. I admit it, I did. There was a lot of the usual uttering of "praise the lord" and "thank-you Jesus" in response to points any Christian would approve of anyway. I find that token gesture often gets under my skin, but soon enough, I began to get caught up in what the speaker was talking about. It just clicked. My mind began spinning. I started making connections between this and that in my head. Pretty soon, I just had to get out of there Neveah. I just had to head home and delve into it. The rest has been unfolding in my office these past two days."

"Okay, but that can't be the whole story Darnell. What did that speaker say to get you so excited? What's the connection between what happened at work this week with what happened at the prayer meeting?"

"Oh, right," Darnell countered immediately. "Sorry. I was sitting in the pew listening to the opening comments and prayers, just sort of observing it all. Then the priest introduced the first speaker. Many of the people who were there were quite familiar with who he was. His name was Hal Findlay, an apparent writer of Christian literature on the subject of the end times. I've never heard of him, but admittedly, I can't say I've spent much time even thinking about the end times. It's makes more sense to focus on day to day concerns. The future will come soon enough. No point worrying about it ahead of time. Anyway, except for the usual verses in the Gospel of Matthew, which most notably talk about natural disasters like earthquakes and pestilence, most Christians know precious little of what the Bible has to say about the end times. I've been seeing that much more clearly these past two days in my office. To be sure, Findlay quoted them too, but he went further. He spoke a lot about angels on assignment and made reference to real people making a difference as we approach the events the Bible foretold. These people, many of whom are even in government, hidden in plain sight, so to speak, are people doing the work of the Lord. He made a point of emphasizing that many times God's children don't recognize people doing good. Think of the parable of the Good Samaritan. People we might see as being less than good Christians may be doing the work of the Lord in ways we don't see, or tend to recognize. I know you and I have often wondered how God could approve of our current president being elected with all the controversy he generates, but that's just it Neveah. We don't always understand how God unfolds his plan. As Findley continued, excitement in that place grew and grew. It was truly inspirational. Listening to his words, and then thinking about Bible passages I knew as well, made just sitting there too much to handle. I felt compelled to take the ball I had been handed by the Lord in that place, and run with it. I was exploding with inspiration. It was like fireworks Neveah. You touched on some of those fireworks a few minutes ago, remember?"

"You been talking all this time Darnell. What did I touch on a few minutes ago?"

"After telling you Kevin believes in aliens, I asked what would happen to God if Martians fell from the sky; then you told me to think about the fact that the Bible uses numerous metaphors, leaving true believers to seek guidance about their meaning. I was already aware of that, and thought about it extensively on my way home yesterday. In fact, when I really thought about it, that's the main reason I never wanted to spend much time studying the last book in the Bible, the book of Revelation. It's riddled with metaphors. I used to think it could be interpreted any way people could stretch it. I have since come to think differently. The thing is, I've had a Thompson Chain Reference Bible for years. I can follow links between words and concepts that occur in the Bible more than once. It was only a starting point, but I knew it was going to consume me. That's why I've been holed up in my office like I have."

"Well my sweet man, have you come down from the mountain like Moses with God's word now clear to you? What have you learned? Or should I ask, what has God revealed to you?"

"It isn't conclusive yet my dear, but I have been learning enough to change my perspective on life, or what is, or something like that. Maybe my perspective hasn't really changed, but expanded. As I said, I've never really spent much time looking at Revelation. I was going to have to reflect on it verse by verse. Admittedly, the only thing I could remember prior to these past couple of days were its references to the four horsemen and the great desolation. When I was younger, that kind of imagery prompted fear. Thinking about how to interpret it all, when even preachers tended to shy away from doing so, seemed daunting."

"The point that this book is cloaked in metaphor was reinforced by the very first verse Neveah. It identifies the book's contents as – and I quote – '*The Revelation of Jesus Christ, which God gave unto him, to shew unto his servants things which must shortly come to pass; and he sent and signified it by his angel unto his servant John.*' This is the same John who was one of Jesus' apostles in the gospels. I'm sure you already know that. The book has been around for almost two-thousand years Neveah. Clearly, it was not a literal interpretation of things which must 'shortly' come to pass. Also, the angel mentioned was probably not meant to literally reference a winged-being in the same way as angels are portrayed in Renaissance art. Otherwise, the angel would have been named just like the angels Michael and Gabriel are elsewhere in scripture. I suspect it's a reference to the actual inspiration which John experienced."

"You know Neveah, if John was writing about visions he saw of the future, he would have been describing many strange things he had never seen before. So how accurately and clearly could he describe them to his audience? Since the book is supposed to be a message from God to show servants things which must come to pass, isn't it possible that it would only make sense to those servants who will be alive when these things come to pass? That may very well be the people who are alive now – that's us Neveah!"

304

"Yes, I'm sure that's true Darnell. Preachers have been saying that our whole lives."

"To be sure Neveah, preachers have been saying that for centuries – probably ever since the New Testament was written. That's why people tend to believe in it, but only consider its relevance to their own time period with a grain of salt. That must have already been happening way back when. If you read the Gospel of Matthew, chapter 24, Jesus' disciples asked him about future events, and he discusses specific things that will happen. Then right after he portrays a grim period before the second coming, he tells them, as reported at the beginning of chapter 25, the parable of the wise and foolish virgins. Ten of them went to meet the bridegroom and took their lamps with them for the wait. As you know, the bridegroom whom they were waiting for is Christ. Five were wise and brought extra oil with them, not knowing how long the wait would be. The others did not, and weren't prepared for a later arrival. That's the condition many of us Christians are in these days, including myself. This was one of the realizations I had at the prayer meeting. I tried to make up for lost time and dove right in to Revelation when I got home. To make a long story short, after following numerous links between references in Revelation and other books in the Bible, I realized that as interesting as it all was, I needed some assistance."

"Have you called Pastor Dave back to speak to him about all this? Couldn't he help you out Darnell?"

"No, I haven't called him. I kind of got the impression he was excited about the speaker coming to this prayer meeting because he had recently been turned on to all this too. I would love to discuss it all with him at some point soon, but I really wanted to get a more complete picture before doing so. I thought I would use the resources at my fingertips."

"What resources Darnell?"

"Well, I could have gone to Shiloh Shop, the Christian bookstore I like to slip into once in a while, and will probably still do that sometime sooner than later – but for right now, there's the internet. I figured Christian writers and scholars probably had as much of an online presence as anyone else – and I was right. There is a treasure trove of information available."

"So what did you come up with Darnell? What have you been learning in that cave of yours?"

"Hmmm, where should I start?" Darnell was tempted to grab some of the notes he's been jotting down from his office, but decided to wing it. As Neveah pointed out earlier, explaining an idea can help internalize it more firmly.

"Okay," Darnell began. "Needless to say, there were numerous sources of information to read through. Many were interesting. Reading one article after another, it became apparent to me that a more scholarly approach was to take a historicist interpretation of biblical prophecies. This meant tracking the interpretation of end-times prophecies as it has evolved throughout the ages. I wasn't aware of the term before, but eschatology is the study of end-times prophecies. As I delved into the subject, I became more and more fascinated. Prophecies about the second coming of Christ are a major feature of eschatological studies. It had already been pondered by early Roman writers such as Josephus, Irenaeus and Tertullian. Yet the main developments didn't emerge until the early days of the Reformation when people began to rebel against the Catholic Church. Interestingly enough, some of those early church reformers like John Wycliffe, Martin Luther, John Calvin, John Knox and John Wesley began to believe that the early church had gone astray. These people became the protesters, or protestants, who saw the papacy itself as a satanic institution. They saw the Pope as the embodiment of the Antichrist himself. Wow! This was a lot to take in Neveah."

"I can see that," she responded. "Most protestant churches still consider Catholics to be idolaters. Keep going."

"True. Anyway, I read and absorbed more, discovering that the book of Revelation and related links were beginning to make more sense. It was beginning to click Neveah. I felt like I was being transformed, and hungered for more. It wasn't about trying to figure out where others were wrong. It was, and is, only about discovering the truth. I was quickly gaining confidence, further fueling my hunger for more."

"So are you satisfied now my good man?" Neveah could feel Darnell's excitement as he spoke.

"On the contrary Sweetheart. I feel like my hunger is growing. I'm not even close to knowing everything about this. There may be several others who know much more about it than I do, but I doubt anyone knows the full scope of God's unfolding plan. Whatever we're being caught up in, I believe it is going to be a ride, but let me tell you what I have been learning Neveah."

"Please do. Can I get you a second piece of that pie Darnell?"

"Let's wait until after this. I am pleasantly worked up over it all over again. Let me tell you while it seems fresh in my mind. If there's one thing I have learned these past two days, it's that I've neglected reading the Old Testament. Many of the Bible stories people are most familiar with come from Genesis and Exodus, the first two books of the Old Testament. There are thirty-nine books in the Old Testament," Darnell emphasized. "I'll bet most Christians couldn't even name them. If I asked you what the book of Daniel was about, what would your response be Neveah?"

"I know my Bible Darnell. That's all about when Daniel was thrown in the lion's den for his faith. The lions knew better than to harm him. God was protecting him."

"Yeah, nice little story, and one that inspires parishioners every time, but that's only a small part of the book of Daniel. There is much to connect it with descriptions of events in Revelation, the last book of the New Testament. It's a treasure trove of prophecy, and a significant starting point for end times prophecy. Let me give you a bit of background. I'll try to keep it short."

"Take all the time you need Darnell. We aren't going anywhere. It's Thursday evening... and that pie ain't got legs. It'll wait for us."

"That's not my concern. We can put off a second piece of pie for the moment. I haven't forgotten about it. I can give you the gist of what I've been learning first. If you're interested enough, I'd be glad to open up my man cave anytime for you too Neveah. We could get into studying this stuff together. It's far more interesting that TV, even on Thursday night. Now let me tell you about it before I lose some of it. I'm starting to hear that pie calling," he pointed out with raised eyebrow.

"For us Christians, the book of Daniel is grouped in the Old Testament alongside other books by those known as the major prophets. Originally, I discovered, it was part of the Ketuvim, or Hagiographa as it is also known in the Hebrew Bible. The English translation simply means 'writings.' Although it dates back to the second century B.C.E., the events Daniel portrays occurred over three hundred years earlier. At the time, many Jews were captives in Babylon and were not released until the Persians defeated the Babylonians in 539 B.C.E. Daniel was a captive of noble Jewish heritage in Babylon at that time. According to the book, he gained prominence after interpreting dreams that disturbed Nebuchadnezzar, the powerful Babylonian king. That's where the lion's den story is embedded. The book records not only Daniel's dream interpretations, but ongoing visions he experienced afterward. I didn't realize that before, and became intrigued."

"It was shorter than Revelation and for the most part, told a story linked to the exhortations and random imagery I encountered in John's apocalypse. It was more readable and accessible than Revelation. I thought Daniel's stories seemed more cohesive than the somewhat random depictions of wild imagery described by John. When I looked for non-biblical sources confirming the events of Daniel, there were few, but at least the evidence substantiated the claim that Jews had in fact been Babylonian captives for several years."

"Of particular interest in the book of Daniel were chapters seven through twelve. The imagery was mostly cast in metaphor, just as I expected. There were vivid references to dreadful and terrible beasts with multiple horns and thrones being cast down. These beasts refer to future kingdoms associated with great destruction. Ultimately, this leads to an event called the abomination of desolation. As I progressed through the book, I noted several points I want to research further. Before long Neveah, I found myself in the proverbial chamber of 32 doors. There is much to explore."

"Anyway, I found myself scribbling notes and separating them into groups for the different leads I wanted to pursue. As the hours went by, I began to comprehend a framework I had never even considered before. It was invigorating Neveah. Not only were there connections between Daniel and Revelation, but also between other Old Testament books like that of the prophet Ezra. I remembered to note New Testament references from Paul the Apostle's letter to the Thessalonians referring to the 'man of lawlessness,' or 'man of sin.' Christians are familiar with that reference. This man of sin is the beast in Daniel and the antichrist in Revelation."

"You really have been busy in that cave of yours."

" I have Neveah, but it's been good – very good. It isn't like trying to plough through homework when we were in school. It's invigorating. The imagery is fascinating, the metaphors alluring; the implications for humanity are condemning, but also hopeful, at least for some. These are the so-called faithful, and hopefully, includes us. It's all becoming clearer Neveah, but it's a tsunami of information."

"Is there still more to tell then?"

"Oh yes, there is. I still have to connect all this information with what happened at work, remember? I'm just getting to that now."

"One of the things I really began to wonder about was the Apostle John's exhortations to the seven specific churches at the beginning of Revelation. What did they have to do with the dominant theme of end times prophecies throughout the book? I didn't come up with everything I'm about to tell you myself Neveah. I'm relying on various scholars I've discovered online these past two days. As it turns out, each church, or community of Christians that John spoke to specifically, represented different periods of future church history. His message to Ephesus, the first church, was representative of the Apostolic age from which he was speaking himself. God was pleased with the work the early Christians had done spreading news of the Messiah, but John tells them they were forgetting 'their first love,' implying they had differing ideas about how to properly express their new faith."

John's message to Smyrna, the second church mentioned in Revelation, was an acknowledgment of early examples of the persecution of Christians. That message was representative of a period of almost 300 years. Such persecutions occurred intermittently, depending on the whims of the current emperor. That lasted until Constantine legalized Christianity and made it the preferred religion of the Roman Empire.

John's messages to the third and fourth churches of Pergamos and Thyatira represent the periods in overall church history when Christianity was still consolidating. Christian and pagan beliefs and practices intermingled through to the rise of the Catholic Papacy. As you know Neveah, Popes ruled Christendom until the Protestant Reformation, a period of over a thousand years. John's messages to the remaining three of the seven churches he was admonishing have to do with the period since the Reformation. They refer to these past few hundred years, a period of global evangelism achieved because travel and communication advanced. In short, the messages to all seven of the churches mentioned in Revelation are considered to be messages to Christians living during the different periods of Christianity from the time of Jesus to the present. I must point out that is quite an impressive extrapolation of prophecy from specific, localized messages to ones believed to extend to all Christians since the time of the prophecies, but it absolutely has to be Neveah! If the Bible is a guideline for all of us, then all prophecies have to be extrapolated to include all of us, don't they?" Darnell was nodding a strong yes as he spoke.

"If there is one thing I've noticed over the years Neveah, it's that God makes things clear to us in very specific ways – and he does that through his word. When God gives you an insight into something, the words from the Bible he used to reveal that to you become personal, written especially for you at that moment. As I absorbed the information I was scouring these past two days, I realized something Neveah. Seven important messages to the people in those Christian communities represent two-thousand years of Christian faith, experience and resilience, all of which were still in the future. The specific messages were all guidelines, or pathways, toward the final events that would affect all believers. The events couldn't be described in ways familiar to his audience alive at the time. They have been cloudy and unfamiliar all these two-thousand years for the same reasons. The thing is, none of the people alive from the time John delivered these messages until now could have known what it all meant. It could only become clear to the faithful who are alive at the time when the events begin to unfold. It makes sense! It's unbelievably exciting because that time may very well be now Neveah. I know preachers have been saying that forever, but I don't think many of them understood much beyond the most overt clues given in the Bible. It had to come within our range of vision."

"What are you saying Darnell? Do you feel like all of this is somehow just coming into our range of vision now?"

"Maybe. Please let me finish what I'm trying to tell you before it slips out of my head. Those messages John sent to the churches throughout the ages were an important prelude to the visions he described, but the number itself also has significance. The number seven is persistent throughout the book of Revelation. I just told you about messages to seven churches. As I ventured further into the book, I discovered that the number seven is associated with multiple things. There are seven seals and seven trumpets. There is a passage describing a slain lamb that had seven horns and seven eyes. Scripture explained these explicitly as the 'seven Spirits of God sent forth into all the earth.' As I went over the passage a second and then a third time, I recognized the lamb was Jesus. The lamb was resurrected and had taken the book with the seven seals before sitting on a throne. It was the Messiah coming to claim his throne. It is a description of the long-awaited Second Coming of Christ – the very event all Christendom has awaited for two-thousand years."

"The connection between the number seven and all of this had me wondering Neveah. I don't know much, if anything about numerology, and casually thought it was wound up with superstition, astrology, and so on. I quickly learned, however, that numbers had great significance in ancient times. This is particularly true of the Bible as well, although I was very surprised to learn it. Perhaps I haven't been as studious as I thought Neveah."

"Well, I can't say that I've ever heard any preacher talk about the significance of numbers in the Bible Darnell."

"Me neither, but once I started looking into it, there were several references to the importance of numbers in scripture online. Apparently, many numbers – including all of the first twelve cardinal numbers – are important. The numbers three, seven and twelve are particularly significant. They all have connotations of perfection and completion. Of these three, the number seven has the greatest number of incidences denoting these qualities. I've already mentioned the seven churches, trumpets, seals, and spirits to you Neveah. There are also seven stars, seven dooms, seven personages, and even a candlestick with seven branches denoting completeness in the light of God. The number seven even occurs right at the beginning of the Bible in Genesis. As you, me and every other Christian, Muslim and Jew knows, it took seven days for God to complete his perfect creation. There are other hints at perfection embedded in nature. One very good example – perhaps the most important of all Neveah – is music."

"Music?"

"Yes, music Neveah. There are seven notes in music; Do, Re, Mi, Fa Sol, La, Ti – that's seven, then it starts again at Do - Do, Re, Mi, Fa Sol, La, Ti, Do. Taking it one note higher or lower than that scale takes you into a higher or lower octave, another dimension. It is the perfection of music. Music is also embedded in every culture known throughout history. The Bible itself provides ample proof of the connection between humanity and the divine. The book of Psalms is the longest book in the Bible, making up seven percent of the Old Testament. They are all songs, or hymns, if you prefer, and not the only ones. Other books of poetry and song include Ecclesiastes and the Song of Solomon. A connection between the mortal and immortal isn't only enacted in the New Testament as well, but encouraged wholeheartedly. Jesus and his disciples sang together after the last supper. In the Bible Neveah, music is shown to be the medium by which things happen. In chapter 16 of the book of Acts, the Apostle Paul and his friend Silas are thrown in prison. They begin to sing. An earthquake happens, then the doors were opened and their hands freed. If you think about it, that isn't so far-fetched. Both music and earthquakes are phenomena arising from vibration. Maybe God's methods aren't so mysterious after all. I've thought about this a little. If music is the medium that can initiate events, is it possible it was – is – the medium of creation itself? Now there's something to think about too, but let's not get side-tracked Neveah; the point is that the number seven is important and pervasive. It may occur much more often than we notice.

311

I think I may have noticed one of those times, and it pertains to what has been going on this week. This is going to sound like a possible stretch, and it may even sound a little crazy, but something occurred to me not long before I came up for supper. That number seven – after all I've learned these past couple of days – may be God's way of letting me know he's giving me some insight into his unfolding plan. There may be even more to all this; I just don't know what it is yet."

"What makes you think the number seven is some kind of clue telling you all that Darnell? How does the number seven apply to you?"

"God has filled me with a sense of certainty that the number seven would make itself evident to every individual faithfully awaiting the Second Coming of Christ. I already showed you the pervasive nature of that number throughout the book of Revelation. I can't ignore everything that's happened this week Neveah. That guy Jahny we pulled out of the desert is the central figure to a group of us who happen to be seven in number too. The doctor, the psychologist, the NASA guy Enrique, his friend Emma, her son Anthony, my co-worker Kevin and I are like the seven branches of the candlestick being illuminated. All seven of us were awakened to something very unusual. We're all interested in getting to the bottom of it, even if we're all pursuing different angles. I have no idea how many people may be awakening to something special like this right now Neveah, but I do know this. I was shaken awake at that prayer meeting yesterday morning. The others I've mentioned were stirred as well. I don't know to what extent, or what it all means, but I feel it coming within my range of vision. I feel like I'm beginning to look through a window, through an aperture focusing in on something."

"I can feel your enthusiasm Darnell. I sense your anticipation, but also a strong sense of feeling unsure about what it is you're anticipating.

"You know Neveah, originally I felt like this Jahny guy might be a threat. That arose from the comment that Kevin told me he said about being legion. That just didn't fit once I met him myself. Then after going to that surprising prayer meeting and delving into scripture and eschatological studies and so on, Jahny no longer seemed like a threat. Instead of imagining some kind of demon coming to play a role in the coming apocalypse, it began to seem possible that he is a messenger of some kind. If you heard him speak like we all did the other day, he would probably have the same effect on you that he did on us. He was good at explaining each of our positions. He could make people rest at ease about concerns they came to him with. As I think of it, it reminds me of John the Baptist in the gospels. He came to pave the way for the first coming

312

of Jesus. What if this guy is here to pave the way for the second coming? There are several places in the Bible where believers who have ears are admonished to listen. Maybe Jahny really is an angel on assignment, just like those mentioned by that speaker at the prayer breakfast."

"If you have ears Darnell, then maybe it's time for you to hear. It's still early in the evening. Why don't you give Pastor Dave a call now? Tell him what you've been telling me. You said he seemed pretty enthusiastic about the people who spoke at the prayer meeting yesterday. If he stayed longer than you, then he probably heard more than you did. Maybe you two could compare notes and see what you come up with. It wouldn't hurt, would it?"

"I guess not. Maybe I will call him now."

"Good idea Darnell. You do that, and if you like, I can give you that second piece of pumpkin pie you've been holding out for. You've earned it my good man."

Neveah didn't wait for a response. Darnell always liked another piece of pie. While he was on the phone, she also indulged in a second piece. She couldn't follow the conversation from the other room, and was surprised when it seemed to be cut short.

"What's going on," she asked when Darnell walked back into the dining room.

"Dave is meeting with some friends. I met one of them yesterday at the prayer meeting. Apparently, this Jakob guy and his wife are meeting with Dave in his office at the church right now. I started to brief him about my past two days, but he suggested I come down and join them. They're going to be there for a while still. He also said I was going to want to hear what they've been discussing. If you don't mind Neveah, the pie can wait. I think I'm going to head on down there right away."

32

Kevin click-locked his car and began walking up the driveway. Before reaching the ranch house, he turned aside along the cobbled path toward a one-time stand-alone mother-in-law suite. It was a beautiful night full of stars, one of the benefits of living in a rural community like Agua Dulce. The silhouette of the mountains stood out against the faint glow of light reaching up from the sprawl of the San Gabriel valley to the south. Kevin was fortunate to have rented the suite from some friends of friends. It afforded him much-valued quiet and privacy. It was a haven from city life, whether that was Palmdale and Lancaster just up the road, or down the road through Santa Clarita into L.A. Kevin considered privacy, and even solitude much-appreciated amenities. It was even more so right now. The couple living in the ranch house were back east visiting relatives.

Fumbling for keys, Kevin opened the front door only to be met by a meowing cat. It was clearly scolding him for being away past feeding time. Kevin uttered an apology to Sam, realizing he better attend to him right away. It was early Thursday evening, just half-way through his weekend. Remaining leisure time was still plentiful, but there would be little to none if the cat wasn't happy. The situation was easily solved by a half-filled dish of milk. "Here you go Sam," Kevin said, mimicking a meow afterward. Sam responded in kind, then quickly slurped the dish clean. Purr.

The suite itself was comfortable, functional, and nicely laid-out, as Kevin usually described it. It was even roomy. He enjoyed spending time listening to music, or watching a documentary in the livingroom, but particularly enjoyed the side den. It functioned as an office, a mini library, and mask room. Four bookshelves took up the length of the wall opposite where his desk and computer were situated. The shorter wall separating them was covered with masks from top to bottom. Many had been purchased in various places, but some he had carved himself. It was a pastime enjoyed mostly in times past, but occasionally revisited.

A valued possession stood proudly in front of the masked wall. He had purchased that telescope almost ten years ago already. He liked to take it onto the sundeck on evenings just like this one. Kevin loved to scan the night sky, losing himself in thought. It always came down to one question. What is really out there anyway?

There would be time to bring out the telescope later if he felt like it. Kevin picked up the rolling tray from his desk, walked back out to the livingroom and sat down. He placed the tray on the small side table to his right. The humidor was where he left it on the floor underneath. Reaching down and around, he lifted it up onto his lap. Kevin always enjoyed this part of his day. There were a few things he wanted to enjoy mulling over, so he planned to expand the field of observation. Having a toke was part of the strategy; listening to music was the other. He chose a dense little red-haired bud of Martian Atmosphere from a small open bag in the humidor, then ground the sativa for rolling through gentle fingers. The flower was dense, sticky and pungent. Twisted carefully to make sure it wasn't too tight, he added a filter. It was ready to go. Just one last step to complete preparation. A quick Bluetooth connection between phone and stereo, a speed-scroll through his digital listing, and click. As the most recent Nik Turner album began to play, he fired up the spliff. Kevin inhaled slowly as the music faded in. He slid the volume up a notch.

Overall, his mid-week 'weekend' was going well. Even though he and Darnell got off work on a Wednesday morning, it wasn't too difficult to meet up with others. He ended up staying out late down in Santa Monica. Expecting to have a few drinks in more than a few establishments, Kevin was smart to get a hotel room first. Spending a little extra to stay in the city seemed smarter than risking a D.U.I. later.

Despite being out late, Kevin awoke early. He had never found a good way to adjust sleep patterns on days off. It often made the first night back to work on Fridays a little harder, but c'est la vie. That was still more than twenty-four hours away. Kevin recalled the relaxing day he had enjoyed. He left the hotel after breakfast, but parked his car only a short distance away. He wanted to walk along Venice Beach close by. A few months had passed since he last took an opportunity to do that. Every time he did come down for a stroll here, he also made a point of following a ritual he developed some years prior. Kevin enjoyed taking time out to sit cross-legged on the beach, facing not out to the ocean, but toward the boardwalk. The ritual was only complete if he could fire one up out there without interruption, and that was almost always. Today was particularly exceptional. He enjoyed watching the many unusual characters strolling along the gentrified beachfront walkway. He ended up staying well into the afternoon. Now with this joint here at home, he was just picking up where he had left off. He might consider firing up the barbecue out on the deck later too. Life was good.

Kevin turned the stereo up another notch. This was the best part of living in a stand-alone suite on a rural property. He didn't have to worry about disturbing fellow tenants across the hall or up a floor. He wasn't blasting the music, but wanted to be comfortably immersed by it. He had discovered Turner years ago, and particularly loved the artist's years as the experimental free jazz saxophonist in British Space Rock pioneers Hawkwind. Of course Kevin was too young to have listened to the band in their '70s heyday. An uncle, whom he affectionately referred to as Uncle Music, turned him on to them when he found out Kevin had taken an interest in space science. Kevin loved the band ever since.

While listening to the album, Kevin's thoughts eventually meandered to Jahny back at the hospital. He also thought of the others. What were their impressions of that unusual meeting in Jahny's room yesterday morning? He was surprised at how Darnell blurted out his concern almost as soon as he met Jahny. Clearly, his partner had taken that whole legion thing to heart the night before. It must have really been eating away at him. Fascinating, Kevin thought. It is possible to work closely with someone five days a week for a decent length of time, and still not know that person very much. Maybe that's just the way it is with most people in a working environment. People make friends at work and sometimes even develop committed relationships there, but generally, there's an unregistered distance between most colleagues. It occurred to Kevin that Darnell probably didn't have a comprehensive idea of what he was all about either. Darnell never really probed him with questions, so he could only have as clear a picture as Kevin may have portrayed. Sure, Darnell knew he lived in Agua Dulce. He also knew Kevin didn't have a significant other, but never inquired about stuff like that further. Darnell was certainly aware of Kevin's interest in aliens, but that perception was undoubtedly overblown, skewed.

Kevin looked around the livingroom and into the den. Would Darnell be surprised he had a small personal library of books that were anything but alien-related? Darnell knew Kevin was a reader, but one serious enough to amass a collection of books was something different altogether. It suggested dedication and long-term focus. Darnell did know about the music collection though. That wasn't quite the same thing, but also suggested an intellectual depth rather than simple passive awareness. Although just a little over 500 in number so far, Kevin's vinyl collection was significant. He spoke about it often, but only because most people liked music – even if many of them didn't appreciate it quite as obsessively. Kevin was still too young to be a respectable audiophile, but he was well-informed about music he liked. Darnell was a music fan too. Although not a collector himself, he was usually up for conversation on the topic. He had enough knowledge and insight to offer perspectives on varying artists, techniques and style. It contributed to interesting banter back and forth. Other than work itself, music was the main topic of conversation between them – but that was music. Kevin didn't imagine his book collection would generate Darnell's interest much.

He took another puff off his joint. It was burning evenly. Ash accumulated slowly. Kevin watched smoke disperse throughout the room as he slowly exhaled. He tapped the end on the edge of an old glass ashtray, the ash falling intact. Taking another leisurely drag, Kevin wondered whether Emma or Enrique would find any of his books interesting either. Enrique was a science guy, so there were several titles on the shelves that might catch his attention. To be honest, Kevin thought, after that first conversation with Enrique about aliens, it wouldn't be surprising if that's what he thought I was all about, just as Darnell does. That was fair enough, Kevin supposed. After music, alien-related topics probably did come up most often between he and his partner. He could definitely understand why Darnell considered him an alien-fanatic. As for Emma, she might be open to new ideas. Established ones didn't seem to be of any help with questions she verbalized the other day. Who knows, he thought? People's ideas are all over the place these days. How many people really take the time to research questions of interest? A knee-jerk Google here and there tends to suffice most of the time.

Kevin considered his own reading interests and practices. They tended to focus on subjects or fields of study over extended periods. A close examination would reveal a progression of interests and learning. It occurred to him that gathering a collection of physical books was unusual these days. He could much more easily amass a digital collection that he could carry around with him. They're cheaper, weigh nothing, and hundreds or more titles can be stored on the same five by seven inch gadget. Yet, there was something magic about accumulating a varied collection of real books. He knew their physicality provided at least one real advantage: Several studies confirmed improved reading comprehension. Just holding a book and turning its pages can maintain local focus, discouraging scanning, scrolling, following links, and in the case of reading some eBooks, being distracted by advertisements. Such side pursuits detract from retention. If any single reason could be identified for Kevin's voracious reading habit, that reason would be retention. He purposefully made an effort to achieve that objective. It was common for him to mark up the margins of most books he opened. The books weren't there to be admired. He believed their purpose was to increase knowledge and understanding of whatever interested him. By the time he dies some day in the unforeseen future, Kevin hoped to be nothing less than a living library.

He couldn't possibly know everything there is to know, but he wanted to have at least a passing knowledge of as much as possible. It was an open-ended, but meaningful objective.

Kevin collected numerous history books that not only explored the conflicts that changed the balance of power over the centuries, but surveyed and investigated social movements, the development of currency and commerce, scientific discoveries, and new ideas. There were books on linguistics, evolution, physics, and even quantum theory. The only official post-high school study he had ever formally completed was the two-year program to become a medical responder. Everything else had been learned by reading books on his own. He felt fortunate to possess such a drive. It required persistence. It also necessitated a half-decent memory, or a self-developed means of retention adapted to his own learning style. Kevin felt he had a little of both – enough to energize the thirst for more anyway. Ah, the pursuit of knowledge and understanding…

…The music continued playing. Kevin finished his toke. He jumped up from the La-Z-Boy, walked over to the den, and stood in front of the second bookcase. He glanced down at the lower section. There were at least a few books he thought Emma might find interesting. He hadn't thought of it the night he met her, but was unlikely to mention it anyway. Darnell already thought he might be out there. If avoidable, Kevin wasn't keen to draw skepticism, let alone criticism, on more fronts than necessary. These books on PSI fall into the same category as books on aliens. It is an area of study not formally recognized by science. People find the topic interesting, but tended to fall into line with the current perspective that designated PSI to the realm of pseudoscience entertainment. Kevin was aware of sounding like a kook if he were to verbalize interest in more than one fringe belief, but he found good reason to maintain interest in this one too.

PSI is the unknown factor in extrasensory perception. It refers to experiences not known by physical or biological mechanisms of any kind. That's what puts it into fringe territory. That's also what made Kevin think Emma would be interested in this part of his library. That phone call from her son created a mysterious dilemma she couldn't explain. The details were interesting and connected to that guy Jahny back at the hospital. She didn't understand how there could be any association. Kevin considered it odd enough to be a PSI-like experience.

Actually, it seemed strange to Kevin that the people involved in this week's events were all drawn to Jahny for different reasons. Were all of the reasons as unusual as Emma's? His own reason for being interested could certainly be considered unusual. As far as he understood, the others were all drawn to Jahny for unusual reasons as well. Darnell's attraction was of a religious

318

nature – something considered by many, even the faithful, to be mysterious. Mystery is at the very center of the PSI experience, or the PSI phenomenon. Whatever it is, we're all fascinated by Jahny in some way, Kevin reminded himself. Maybe the fascination and allure of the mysterious is the link between us, even if different interests or concerns are the attraction.

As the music coursed through him, Kevin continued mulling over details. As usual, there was much to dissect. It all seemed so intricate. What was it Uncle Music used to say to him again? 'Big picture, little picture. It's all about perspective – and particularly different perspectives.' Kevin's uncle often used to be on about looking at things in different ways – trying to perceive them from different angles, different points of view. It's probably how he got into alternative music too.

That sounds like a trip, but this whole thing with Jahny is a trip, Kevin mused, dismissing any effect the herb might confer. There's something here for sure. As far as I know, herb isn't a factor in the others' suppositions about the guy. I'm not sure what it is, he thought. Darnell's not sure what it is. Emma and Enrique aren't sure what it is. I don't even think that shrink has any idea what it is…but we're all fascinated, captivated, lured by something we can't quite place, or pinpoint. It might not even be Jahny himself. Maybe it's something he inadvertently inspires us to think about, or explore about ourselves. I don't know what it is, Kevin thought to himself. I just don't know, but not knowing is an excellent reason to continue learning.

Kevin was open-minded enough to at least weigh arguments about what was considered science or pseudoscience. Given how science and scientific studies are determined, it is well-known that funding is difficult to obtain if the object of study doesn't fit within the current paradigm of scientific thinking. Whatever does not fall within the parameters of our formal collective understanding, is usually considered irrelevant until a new discovery forces reassessment. No matter how much one might try to explain what is outside of the box, until a way can be found to peek over the edge, so to speak, it is difficult, probably impossible, to truly comprehend what is beyond.

Kevin imagined himself trying to explain his position on the topic to Emma, or anyone else for that matter. PSI, he might begin a serious argument with, is a collection of phenomena that does not fall within the current paradigm of scientific understanding. Popular interest continues, however, because most people have experienced things they couldn't explain. Currently, there is no definitive scientific explanation for these occurrences, but so-called supernatural events or

319

experiences do occur in all cultures. A good example would be ghost sightings. Many people believe in ghosts and have done so for millennia, but prevailing views in science continue to relegate them to the realm of superstition. Kevin tended to believe that was probably correct. He also believed that ultimately, there is an explanation for such phenomena. We simply haven't discovered what it is yet. It is also unlikely to happen any time soon. Most funding for science research comes from government sources. It's almost impossible to obtain funding for fringe subjects. After all, trying to explain ghosts is not going to advance the capabilities of the military-industrial complex, is it? Privately, however, through diligent study complimented by a healthy dose of skepticism, Kevin was confident that what he eventually endorses intellectually is scientifically sound.

While still in his teens, Kevin read a book that profoundly influenced him in this regard. Carl Sagan's *The Demon-Haunted World: Science as a Candle in the Dark* was a mid-'90s publication where the author endeavored to explain the scientific method to the average person. He emphatically encouraged everyone to learn critical and skeptical thinking. As a young idealistic individual, Kevin took that to heart, but also remembered some interesting points the scientist had conceded. There were a few claims made in the field of ESP which deserved serious study. Some of Sagan's concessions really stood out. Kevin was particularly intrigued by the claim that some people under mild sensory deprivation could receive thought images from others. Another assertion was that young children sometimes described details of a previous life. Some claims were investigated and found to be accurate, even though there was no other way the children could have known about the things they described. As interesting and helpful to our daily lives as science is, and has been, many things remain a mystery. We simply don't have all the answers yet, Kevin concluded. It's as simple as that, but that's exactly what makes life interesting and purposeful.

This was the kind of stuff Kevin loved to ponder, especially when he had the leisure to smoke one and let his thoughts drift. It was more than that though. Back in his school days, teachers used to bandy terms like 'free association' and 'brainstorming.' He and a couple good friends at the time made up a different description: being instonative. It was a fucked-up, amusing way of saying you were enjoying an intellectual high. Kevin laughed out loud just thinking about it. He never considered himself a stereotypical nerd, but never fit into the common perception of a stoner either. Kevin never read Sagan's book until after he'd discovered herb. He believed the book would still have influenced him had that not been the case, but was also convinced he wouldn't have pondered its contents quite as thoroughly.

Kevin appreciated the prospect of having an entire evening still ahead of him. What should he immerse himself into? Perhaps he would simply continue what he was doing right now. No complaint there. A little more music, a little more herb; perhaps he would read for a while. Hmmm... Letting things incubate worked well for Kevin. When he was a kid, Uncle Music also used to encourage him to memorize his homework, then sleep on it. "Let it all sink into your mind," he would say. "It will help recall when you need it. Our minds have ways of putting it all together. Us humans are good at recognizing patterns. Recognition of similarities and differences between those patterns can spark new ideas. It can even form a chain reaction – an explosion of ideas. Just give those ideas a chance to ignite boy," he would emphasize. Good old Uncle Music. Too bad he would never have considered my method, thought Kevin, or would he have? It too has to be ignited. Well, not sure about him, Kevin thought, chuckling again, but other older relatives would have considered this my ruination. For me at least, it's not ruination; it's ruminating, and that's following Uncle's good advice.

Kevin spent more time doing just that, ruminating. Let those neurons in his brain fire away in free association. Let connections and patterns distinguish themselves from the clutter collected throughout the day. Focusing solely on research might also be narrowing the scope. Leave the aperture open, he mused. Collect the light streaming in. Remember Einstein's dictum: imagination is more important than knowledge. Ah yes, he thought. Patterns emerge to form order from chaos. It's a microcosm of how the universe itself emerged. It's a consortium of particles firing and interacting to eventually create stars, galaxies, solar systems, planets, and all other phenomena. That's it, Kevin realized. It's the universe inside my head. It was godlike in nature, infinite in scope, carried through the ether of music flowing through him. It was breathtakingly beautiful. It was divine.

Then it was over. The last track on the album faded into silence. Kevin looked around the room. The expanse of thought he enjoyed and appreciated began to coalesce, then condense around the conversation he had with Enrique, the former NASA guy. He knew he had pressed Enrique a little hard about what NASA knows while he had a chance, but wasn't really satisfied by the response. Enrique was right when he asked if I thought it was a good idea that NASA let everyone know what it knows, Kevin conceded. I suppose it isn't, but what do they know? He would love a chance to speak to more of those guys. Perhaps it was possible to run into Enrique up in Jahny's room again. That was probably too much of a coincidence to expect though. Besides, NASA employees are undoubtedly bound by commitments to secrecy. Such security agreements likely continue being valid after leaving employment too. Kevin figured Enrique had already told him everything he was ever likely to tell him.

Then Kevin abruptly thought about someone else he hadn't spoken to for a while, or rather, conversed with online. He didn't actually know much about the guy, or girl for that matter, other than his or her username: alienclone2492. It had been a while since Kevin logged on to one of those chat boards where enthusiasts discuss research and news about alien activity. Some boards were better than others. There were also varying levels of enthusiasm, both serious and less so. The quality of documentation available on various sites was a determining factor for Kevin. His finicky approach to verify authenticity often meant spending blocks of time engrossed in the process. Explanations, comparisons with other documents, and logical argumentation were highly important factors for retaining an interest in any of them. Again, ruminating was beneficial by helping sort and determine authenticity.

Kevin considered it might be a good idea to see what alienclone2492 has to say about his current ruminations. He remembered mentioning information to his acquaintance about the previous finds out in the desert. He or she seemed interested in that at the time. In earlier conversations, alienclone2492 always provided interesting and detailed information, but was careful not to divulge actual sources. Kevin might be able to learn more by chatting with AC tonight.

Yeah, Kevin thought. I might try to connect with this person again, but first…

Kevin got up from his chair, opened the sliding glass door in the kitchen and stepped out onto the sundeck. He glanced up at the night sky, looked around and marveled at its expanse. Again he wondered the same thing he did earlier. What is really out there? Sam strolled out onto the deck, began rubbing up against Kevin's leg, and purred. Kevin looked down at him. "You've already been fed Sammy boy. It's my turn now." He walked over to the barbecue and flipped it on. "But if you're lucky, I might just share a little with you. After that, you'll have to leave me alone for a bit. I'm hoping to be even further inspired tonight."

33

Kevin swallowed the last bite, and placed his napkin on the table. The steak and veggies he grilled on the barbecue were as good as he had ever made them. He was not only satisfied by the meal he just enjoyed, but how satisfyingly slow this Thursday evening was coasting. He treasured times when that happened, because weekends rarely seemed to stretch out. They were often gone in a flash.

After cleaning up the dishes, Kevin rolled himself a second joint for the evening and stepped back out onto the sundeck. The night sky prompted him to consider its similarity to a fireworks display captured on photograph. Each and every viewing of the cosmos captures a distinct moment in time. All of the light we see is what has come into view so far, he mused, never failing to marvel at its breathtaking beauty. Earlier he had enjoyed some tunes inside while relaxing to that first spliff. Now he wanted to spend a little time outside glaring up at, and feeling one with, the cosmos in view.

As he leisurely progressed through his smoke, Kevin considered leaving the glass doors open and putting on another album; maybe something ambient. Brian Eno came to mind. Feeling too comfortable on a cushioned lawn chair, he let that idea drift slowly away. There was no need for any added ambience. The desert at night exerted a musical ambience of its own. The brighter stars even shimmered dance-like against the darker nocturnal backdrop. The moon hadn't appeared yet. It would be a waning crescent this evening anyway. Kevin knew one could typically see about two-thousand celestial bodies on a clear evening. He also imagined the millions behind them. Although too distant to see with the naked eye, he viewed the night sky as a window to infinity.

Exhaling slowly, Kevin imagined the flow of the trillions of neutrinos that pass through our bodies every second, a momentary realization of the integrated complexities of the universe, and its inescapable association with mind and body. That perceived unity coincided closely with information about the universe derived from books he treasured deeply. There was communion not only because of the knowledge itself, but with the conveyors of that knowledge: discoverers, explorers, and researchers. He experienced it not just as sensation, but as something shared, archetypal knowledge, the deep structure of collective being. He envisaged not just a vast universe, but life at its furthest reaches, similar oases of perception that looked both outward and within. The stars may illuminate the cosmos, Kevin thought, but living ecosystems like Earth are the neurons of universal consciousness. They are the emergent evolution of perception and exploration in process. He visualized life forms far away who achieved intelligence equal to, and likely surpassing, he mused wryly, that which exists on this planet.

Contemplating possibilities led to mulling over the circumstances around Jahny yet again. When Kevin really thought about it, he was utterly amazed to find himself in a situation he could only have dreamed about throughout most of his life. He had been an alien-contact enthusiast even before he became a teenager. His now burgeoning book collection began humbly around the time he turned twelve. Those first books were already titles directly related to interest in alien life and possible contact with Earth. How many hours had he spent reading such comics, long before advancing into more serious books? How many television programs and computer podcasts had he tuned into over the years? How many other enthusiasts had he connected with online? Kevin realized that for all the years he'd been interested in aliens, he never expected a real encounter with one. The evidence was still circumstantial, but that could change. Less than a week had passed since this drama began, but everything seemed to fit. Kevin was gut sure that Jahny was different enough, and his circumstances were unusual enough, for him to actually be what he now strongly suspected.

Kevin continued contemplating these things while scouring the night sky from his lawn chair. Earlier, he considered connecting with an acquaintance online. He had put it off while having that second smoke and gazing upward, but it was probably an opportune time to do so now. A number of acquaintances tended to be most accessible at night through to the early hours. No doubt that reflected globally-situated contributors, but also indicated clusters at predictable distances, notably Europe and the Americas. Where might be the best place to locate alienclone2492 this evening? Where was AC physically located, Kevin wondered?

Kevin often found conversations with alienclone2492 enlightening, even if he didn't know AC, as he referred to him, well enough even to determine his or her gender. Regardless of acquaintance, there was a guarded approach between serious enthusiasts online. Discretion was considered paramount. That was particularly true on the more sophisticated sites, often accessible only through 4chan, or other even less accessible portals and alternative discussion boards.

Alienclone2492's gender didn't really matter to Kevin, even though he admitted being curious. Chat rooms often featured avatar representation, but gender-specific images were not necessarily indicative of actual user gender. These kinds of sites tended to draw real enthusiasts and nerds, so they didn't typically function as a hook-up place anyway. Entering into a conversation with another user could yield some clues about gender, age, preferences, opinions, level of knowledge, or more importantly, whether someone was a bullshit artist of course, but most of that didn't concern Kevin. There were always the curious and the annoying to sift through, unless you were looking for dedsurfs known to you.

Dedsurfs were dedicated surfers of pertinent information to site objectives. Many were loyal to sites that focused on study preferences, but a distinct few were pan-specialists actively participant on several platforms. Most were diligent about finding relevant, supportable evidence of alien activity in our solar system. Fact-checking one another's findings was an indispensable, but controversial activity on the most reputable sites.

Some dedsurfs became well-known across platforms, either by founding reputable sites responsible for advancing the cause, or establishing credible information for doing so. Aside from dedsurfs whose work he was well-acquainted with, or direct acquaintances of course, Kevin didn't pay attention to enthusiasts trying to establish credentials. He knew of earthwatch616 and solarsurveyor621, but only because they were well-known as co-webhosts and ardent researchers of Solsys3rdand1. Kevin had no idea how many people were associated with, or regularly surfed Solsys, as everyone commonly referred to it, but he figured it had to be a high number. No doubt thousands of random surfers around the world found their way to the site one way or another, but curiosity-seekers tended to surf a few pages and then exit. It might be interesting, but a little too out there for many. Dedsurfs tended to register and log in, even if some of them were irregular users of the site. Like in all areas of interest with public exposure, serious adherents like to be recognized for their contributions to that interest. Recognition, as everyone knows, is a form of payment. Many were dedicated enthusiasts. Maybe legion.

Solsys was a particularly impressive site. Kevin was familiar with others dedicated to similar interests and objectives, but this was the one he returned to most often. Even its name appealed to him. It was a simple euphemism for the location and focus of interest: Earth and its solar system. Solsys3rdand1 meant solar system, the official name of our planetary configuration according to the International Astronomical Union, or IAU. The rest of it refers to the 3rd planet with one moon. The site featured the latest news and information advances of what is believed to be going on. It was also the site most sought out by enthusiasts for in-depth articles written by prominent dedsurfs. 'Becoming Aware of Alien Interference,' 'Discerning Disinformation About

Alien Involvement,' and a 'SynoPSIs of Alien Objectives and Motivation' were just a few of the many detailed reads available, even to random surfers. Many were accompanied by study guides, film supplements and links to related material. The cumulative site had virtual tentacles into a wonderfully complex internal universe of subsidiary specializations, each of which complimented the site's overall objectives and focus. These however, required a period of consistent dedication and established connections to access. Information considered most relevant and detailed was also considered privileged, and therefore regulated.

Casual surfers randomly finding their way onto the site could view several interesting articles and visual presentations, but access to higher levels of interaction and information-sharing were carefully guarded. Kevin considered its membership reflective of ancient secret fraternal organizations like the Freemasons. Access to levels was labyrinthine and required initial access through sponsorship from an existing member with established credentials. 3-D portals and key codes in hidden virtual creations on site were standard features of access.

Kevin's original sponsor was alienclone2492. That was probably close to three years ago already. 'They' had been instrumental in Kevin's progression and advancement into higher echelons of admission. Still, achieving recognition and trust from a sponsor didn't equate with being anything much more than mutual acquaintances. For all the chats he had enjoyed with alienclone2492 since they first connected, he was never even able to figure out 'their' gender. Alienclone2492 was particularly guarded, and expertly so. Kevin rarely detected clues. Being guarded was fair enough though. There were many reasons to be wary, especially these days, and especially online.

How long had it been since he and alienclone2492 connected? They used to do so frequently, but when he pondered this, Kevin realized it might be longer than he thought. That wasn't likely to pose a problem. They managed to locate one another when they thought the other could be useful. There were times when both even exhibited reserved excitement about leads the other had contributed. That furthered the main objective of learning and verifying sought-after information. It never advanced personal acquaintance.

Kevin was careful not to jeopardize his standing amongst the dedsurf community. Avoiding personal information sharing was expected protocol. Eventually, when the whole alien question is unveiled to the public, the evidence would have to be featured exclusively. No star-quality was to be extended to anyone as a distraction from the truth that would finally be exposed. Furthermore, maintaining a focus on the evidence was best achieved by minimizing scrutiny of individuals involved in the unveiling. Fault can always be found with individuals, but that should never be allowed to taint perception of valuable information and supporting evidence. So even when an acquaintance discussed areas of personal interest and pursuit within the broader objectives of the community, one didn't press them with inquiries that could also reveal personal information. Conversation was to remain focused on pertinent, objective-based material.

AC, as Kevin preferred to refer to his sponsor, did sometimes discuss personal interests and projects. Not too long ago, AC claimed to be working on exhaustive documentation of all pertinent incidents with convincing evidence documented and uncovered so far. Interestingly, that didn't necessarily refer to, or include, famous incidents. AC had stated more than once that alien enthusiasts should forget about Roswell, New Mexico. There were many more credible occurrences that the general public are completely unaware of. AC was often dismissive of what the public did or didn't know anyway. AC believed that people in general are fickle and tend to follow the flow of media news, also buying into friends' shallow opinions. Resilient stereotypes are enough to keep the public going round in the same speculative circles for decades more yet. AC referred to it as disappointing, self-perpetuating phenomena.

Kevin appreciated learning AC's opinions. Clearly, 'they' have been a serious enthusiast for some time. That's not really a fair description though, Kevin considered. An enthusiast might choose to accept information not thoroughly supported by evidence. AC didn't fit that bill. 'They' were adamant about accepted scientific methodology. "It's the only way to counter accusations of pseudoscience, of being more than just bullshit," he would say.

Kevin suspected 'they' may be even more seriously involved than earthwatch616 or solarsurveyor621 themselves. It was amazing how many connections alienclone2492 seemed to have, Kevin thought. 'They' never divulged a fellow dedsurf's handle unless permission was secured first, and then only if that third party could contribute to a lead 'they' and Kevin were researching together. Nonetheless, over the years Kevin was involved in some interesting work. He also became further acquainted with a few other dedsurfs independently, even after completing targeted objectives alongside AC. To quite an extent, Kevin knew his acceptance in the serious Solsys community had come about through AC's analysis and acceptance of him. That was why he was careful to retain good standing with his acquaintance. Alienclone2492 had been decisively instrumental in Kevin's inclusion to an exclusive community.

This was a good time for a renewed visit. Kevin finally rose from his lawn chair, went back into the house and retrieved his laptop. He figured he might also need a light hoodie. It was still February, albeit a warm one. It wasn't too cool yet, but he might get into an intriguing session and wouldn't want to interrupt it. Kevin sat back down on the cushioned lawn chair at the corner of the sundeck and placed the machine on his lap. He turned it on, waited for start processes to complete engagement. That always included VPN activation and making sure antivirus definitions were up to date.

Kevin thought he would comb a few sites for trending information first. It was always insightful to note familiar dedsurf logins on various platforms. It gave him an idea of what trending threads of information were being taken more seriously by others already surveying the topical landscape. He skimmed various sites and read preferred chat boards, but only signed in to one or two. These were the more serious-minded sites within the genre and the places where he was most likely to run into acquaintances. Logged in as ETfrnd314, Kevin was messaged by a few other dedsurfs who saw the login notice scroll at the bottom of their screens. A couple of them messaged comments about his absence, even though Kevin didn't think it was that long. Maybe it was. In these virtual communities where obsessed, even fanatic enthusiasts were relentlessly persistent, even a few days absence could provoke insinuations of creeping disinterest. Kevin didn't quite count as one of those. He was indeed an enthusiast of longstanding interest now, but he never believed his life should revolve around any single pursuit. It's why he didn't consider himself one of these ultimate nerds. His fascination with PSI and the many other subjects his books touched on were evidence of that.

One of the dedsurfs indicated that he had connected with alienclone2492 just under an hour earlier. Skyeye1598 told Kevin that AC was in Solsys setting up a new video doc stream. It wouldn't take AC too long to set that up, Kevin thought, so he decided to cut short the chit-chat with Skyeye and go log onto Solsys. Once inside, he entered a search for alienclone2492. If AC, or any other user, designated specific others as 'privileged' in setup preferences, those others could actually contact them if both were logged in. Otherwise, requests had to be initiated and may or may not be responded to. Kevin's search returned an active designation indicating AC was logged in. "Perfect," Kevin said to himself. He opened private messaging, and typed a quick 'hello.' It didn't take long for a response.

alienclone2492: Etfrnd314, good to see you on site. It's been a little while. You'll be happy to learn I have finally completed creating my new 'office' yesterday. It's accessible from a private portal in the virtual goth bar we visited before Xmas, or by code access. I'll send you a temp-access code now if you like. You can be the first to join me in my exquisite personal 3-D space. Then we can speak casually. Typing can drag a conversation sometimes. You may only enter by choosing one of the designated avatars I programmed for this portal. It keeps direct meetings from being too distracting. All the avatars are well-known characters from various Star Trek series. I only licensed five of them for use. I've retained the Kirk avatar for myself. You'll have to choose one of the other four.

Etfrnd314: Sounds great. I hope one of the avatars represents one of my favourite characters. Send me the code. We'll chat.

A few seconds later, the code came through. 'They' sure are concerned with security, Kevin noted. The code had 15 characters, capital and lower-case letters, numbers, and three symbols. He punched them in carefully, double-checked the sequence, and pressed enter. The laptop screen went dark purple for a split second. Then it panned open like the sliding doors of an elevator. Inside were four large glass cylinders with suspended avatar images of the four Star Trek characters AC had alluded to. For some reason, Kevin was expecting all the characters to be from the original series. Lieutenant Uhura was the only one. The other licensed avatars included Captain Janeway from the Voyager series, Data, the android from the Next Generation series, and Captain Sisko from Deep Space Nine. What? No Spock? No Picard even? Kevin chose Data.

With the Data avatar interface engaged, another sliding door opened into AC's futuristic office. The first thing Kevin noticed was the large table in the center of a room resembling the bridge on the Enterprise. Captain Kirk sat waiting at the far end. There was also a screen behind the captain displaying space as it used to be portrayed on the various iconic series. It gave the impression of traveling through space, not as a conference facility hidden in a virtual bar. It was exquisite. When Kevin greeted AC as Kirk, he was surprised to hear himself sound like the character Data. "Excellent interface detail," he commented.

"Thank-You," responded AC in Kirk's voice. "Keeping occupied? Enjoying any new discoveries or insights?"

ETfrnd314: "Glad you're active tonight. I was actually hoping to find you as we haven't chatted in a while. Yeah, I've been keeping occupied. As for discoveries and insights, well, they

329

are regular occurrences in life now, aren't they? I usually enjoy everything, including work. Living the dream, as they say. I hope you have been keeping well too AC. Not overworking yourself, are you? Obsessions are slave masters you know."

alienclone2492: "Obsessions, my friend, are closely-connected chains of ideas. With a little persistence, they can lead to breakthroughs."

ETfrnd314: "They can still be slave masters."

alienclone2492: "Obsessions are indeed slave masters, but if you find the right one… If I'm to be considered a slave, I would like to think of myself as one of those educated slaves who belonged to high-ranking officials in the ancient world – a scribe or accountant for example. I would be engaged in important and interesting enough work to escape drudgery. Furthermore, I would be well taken care of, yet unimportant enough to become entangled in messy business or political concerns and rivalries. So, most importantly, a position that brings little attention to oneself. That's always an important factor, don't you think? Ok, quick pivot Etf: Do you remember some time ago now, maybe two years or so, that I showed you that leaked navy video of real UFO's, or as described in that case, UAP's?"

ETfrnd314: "Sounds familiar, but run it by me again."

alienclone2492: "It's video footage of what they are now calling Unidentified Aerial Phenomena, hence the UAP. The footage was taken in 2004. There were leaks of the video in '07 and '17, but I only have the 2017 copy. It first circulated here on the dark web, but has found its way onto more easily accessible platforms. You may have seen it elsewhere since I first showed it to you. Anyway, the Department of Defense is officially releasing it because it has been out there for a while. Just thought you would find that interesting."

ETfrnd314: "Is that the one with pilot voice-overs commenting on what they were seeing?"

alienclone2492: "That's right. One of them thought they were possibly looking at drones. He mentioned seeing several, although the video only shows the one targeted by their sensors. I can put it up on the screen behind me if you like."

ETfrnd314: "That's right. I remember. He was blown away when he managed to lock on to it for a trace."

alienclone2492: "Two secs. Let's watch it again. It's short anyway."

AC utilized a pen-like gadget with the same ease as using a cell phone. Then Kevin remembered that was just part of the visual interface. Who knows what kinds of gadgets AC may actually have access to. There's always technology that hasn't filtered down to the public yet, usually because it has to go through testing protocols and data-gathering first. Kevin didn't think twice about it. It wouldn't surprise him in the least if AC was some big tech guy in the real world. The clip quickly appeared on the large screen behind AC's Kirk avatar.

alienclone2492: "Yes, check it out! You can see the object of their interest take off quickly. Wow! Hear that? It's not easy to make out if you're paying too much attention to the visuals. One of the pilots commented on how amazing that was because headwinds were blowing at 120mph. Imagine that ETF!"

ETfrnd314: "Holy shit! Wow! You said the D.O.D. just released this?"

alienclone2492: "Going to release it in April. I don't know why the delay though. That's still five or six weeks away."

ETfrnd314: "April? How would you know that?"

alienclone2492: "Unnecessary question ETF. I have connections. Leave it at that."

ETfrnd314: "Apologies. Sometimes I forget protocol, or whatever we call it. You've mentioned contacts before AC, and you seem to gain knowledge about a lot of things that do pan out. Perhaps I'm just a little more curious than necessary. Your contacts have access to classified information?"

alienclone2492: "This is classified information! Until April anyway. Having the video doesn't prove shit, but knowing when it's going to be released officially does suggest higher level sources. It doesn't matter ETF. As long as we're useful to one another in the common cause, the objectives move forward. You admitted that my knowledge seems to pan out. That's a pattern, isn't it? Again, leave it at that. As far as the navy video goes though, just wait the five or six weeks. That will pan out too. Then see what you think."

ETfrnd314: "Relax AC. No need to become defensive. I'm not insinuating anything, or trying to pry too much. It is interesting that we've been useful to one another in the common cause. Over time, that's naturally kind of built some trust between us – at least on my part. So it seems strange that despite our mutual cooperation for years now, we don't actually know one another.

Hell, I can't even guess your gender. You may be a solid connection for a common purpose AC, but you're a guarded individual."

alienclone2492: "Always a good idea ETF. Always a good idea. I could say the same about you – and should be able to say the same thing about you. Your handle, Etfrnd314, is an obvious reference to a decades-old movie, but reveals nothing about who you are either. That's a good handle. Being a little more guarded is even better. Listen. We've been free to pursue our interest in alien encounters and possible objectives here on 3rd and 1, but once activity becomes impossible to deny, government and corporate sources may want to know what they think we might know. Then it will be good that you or I know very little about one another – period. The upcoming official D.O.D. release of that video shows that they are aware of high-interest groups operating to uncover classified info. We need to be guarded. The only reason I ever caught on that you're located somewhere near the California desert was because of that story you told me about a couple months ago. I thought that was unnecessarily careless of you at the time and probably should have said so. Yeah, that's right. It was when we last connected. It wasn't on Solsys either. That's why I thought it was particularly imprudent."

ETfrnd314: "Oh… Remind me. What story was I telling you?"

alienclone2492: "You said you had direct knowledge from acquaintances at work about two very suspicious medical retrievals made in the nearby desert. Neither of them had I.D., or supplies, but were found dead far from access to water or other amenities. You weren't clear about whether they succumbed to desert conditions or hastened their own demise in some way. If truth be told ETF, you've given me other clues to make speculation about you easier than it should be. You don't have to confirm it, but I've suspected since then that you are probably a medevac in the greater Los Angeles area yourself. Specifically, you are either closer to the north or east of the city and therefore have close access. I've narrowed it down to a few most likely communities. Don't worry. Your information is fairly safe with me."

ETfrnd314: "I guess that could be considered careless, but as I've stated, we've cooperated for some time successfully AC. Trust kind of creeps in under positive conditions. As for that story, it was both suspicious and interesting, but I didn't find out more, until perhaps, recently."

alienclone2492: "Hmmm, I guess I'm not the only one with well-placed contacts."

ETfrnd314: "My information was direct from the source. I spoke to one of the helicopter medevacs. He was directly involved in one of the retrievals – originally expected to be a rescue.

He also told me of a similar case where another medevac team he works with were involved in an almost identical situation. It was strange, but highly interesting. What about it? What made you think of that now?"

alienclone2492: "I found it fascinating when you told me originally. You and I haven't connected since then, but I decided to look into it further. It is a good idea to note that records of all kinds of official activities can be found in digital documentation required by institutions, corporations, and governments everywhere."

ETfrnd314: "So do tell. Did you find anything?"

alienclone2492: "Not much at first, but a little digging confirmed your report. Don't forget ETF, we're always trying to corroborate all information to make sure it's legit. I have also learned that at least a third and fourth such situations have occurred within the last week. You just said you didn't find out more until perhaps recently. So what have you got?"

Kevin was slightly shocked, but also fascinated. If this was just a coincidence, then it was a crazy one. Crazy timing too. His decision to connect with AC was prompted by thoughts about Jahny. Just a few minutes chat and then this comes up. Fascinating, Kevin thought to himself a second time. He wanted to find out what AC knows first.

ETfrnd314: "You say there's been a third and fourth incident?"

alienclone2492: "Yes. One of them was out in the Mohave somewhere east of Palmdale, but not as far as the interstate running north and south, the I-15, I believe."

ETfrnd314: "And the other?"

alienclone2492: "There was another one not far from Edwards Air Force Base, also in the Mohave. As a point of interest, that's the same general area. It's a little over 20 miles from Lancaster, near to Palmdale, and also near to where those you first informed me about occurred."

ETfrnd314: "You were able to find digital records of two events that both happened recently?"

alienclone2492: "Not a pertinent question ETF. I have information. One was still alive when he arrived at hospital. Very interesting, don't you think? A report on the second confirmed him dead at the scene."

ETfrnd314: "When did these two occur?"

alienclone2492: "The first one, the one out on the rancher's property happened close to a week ago. The alien was found in a cave. The second one just happened late last night or early this morning. That one's dead."

ETfrnd314: "Wait a second. You said the alien was found in a cave. No report would have actually stated anything about an alien."

alienclone2492: "Of course not. No one wanting to keep their job would report such a thing. That's my input to you. I'm referring to the retrieved individual as an alien. This wasn't all that difficult to put together. Let's stop beating around the bush here. You aren't my only contact. A few minutes ago, you made it clear I'm not your only contact either. That's a good thing all around. The name of the game is identifying information and then being able to verify it with evidence. That's what I was doing. I hope you operate similarly – very important. We want to progress, not go 'round in circles."

ETfrnd314: "So do you have evidence that identifies the guy found in the cave as an alien?"

alienclone2492: "I've been working on it. Let's look at the facts as we've accumulated them so far: 1) Between us, we have information about four individuals who were found in various locations in the Mohave desert. Although the incidents were miles apart, the Mohave is the largest desert in North America. When I compared the locations where the individuals were found, they were all within 120 square miles proximity of one another. That may sound like a lot, but it's within an area of desert spanning 25,000 square miles. That's probably significant. 2) Accumulated information indicates that all four apparently made suicide attempts. Three of them are dead – so far. 3) Documentation allegedly shows that except for the clothes on their backs, two had sleeping bags, and two also left evidence of drugs used to make their attempts, but there were no other supplies, keys, or identification with them. Without vehicles, it wouldn't have been easy to access the locations where they were found. 4) A number of questions need to be asked here: Why did all four of them choose to access remote locations to do something most would-be suicides often do at home, or close-by? Have they been here for a while, or did they simply abort an operation in progress? They all had access to products procured here – clothing and drugs. Does that mean there are others in relatively close proximity operating freely, but covertly? Why were their circumstances similar? To what extent is that significant? All these questions deserve answers ETF. When you begin to look at the facts and circumstances, don't patterns emerge, even jump out to suggest a bigger picture?"

334

Kevin agreed that patterns had jumped out at him from the beginning, but that question wasn't what he was suddenly focused on. A more interesting question was pressing. How deeply embedded was alienclone2492 in the overall established intelligence on these matters? Was he a dedicated dedsurf, or something even more involved than that? Was it possible he was a government or military operative of some kind? Was his presence on Solsys and other platforms an infiltration of the kind he suggested the Feds might want to penetrate earlier? Kevin quickly became reluctant to divulge his own thoughts and suspicions about Jahny. He couldn't put his finger on it, but this meeting with AC was turning out to be much more than anticipated, or hoped for. Should he share information about Jahny hanging on to life beyond reasonable hope? Might that information have an effect on the possible outcomes of the situation? Could sharing this information with AC help or hurt? When in doubt, think it out, Kevin reasoned. If he shared what he knew, he would also have to divulge information about the other people involved in this drama. Might sharing that information be problematic for them in any way? This stuff couldn't be dismissed nonchalantly. Kevin suddenly realized this whole thing was much bigger than he had considered. So was his own involvement – just by being associated with AC2492. This may actually be dangerous in ways he never anticipated. After thinking about it for a moment, Kevin thought the best plan at this moment would be to pivot the conversation. It was probably important to be wary, even of long-time acquaintances.

ETfrnd314: "So how were you able to verify my information AC? Did you hack into hospital files? Are you connected to operatives with direct access to your information?"

There wasn't an immediate response. It occurred to Kevin that alienclone2492 might also be evaluating what information to share with him now as well.

alienclone2492: "One of my contacts is further connected with others – others in conveniently advantageous positions. I was wary of believing the intel at first myself, but after a little follow-up, was able to verify that was probably reliable. I happen to know for a fact that the three dead retrievals had no I.D. Notably interesting is the fact that no relatives or significant others ever came forward to inquire about any of their whereabouts or state of health. That made it easy for the Feds to retrieve their bodies for further analysis. All three of those dead are now located at an undisclosed army base. That's all you need to know right now."

ETfrnd314: "That's all I need to know or that's all you're going to tell me right now?"

alienclone2492: It's the same thing. I have to go. Perhaps we can chat again soon ETF."

335

Immediately, AC's avatar began to dissolve in a visual replicating Captain Kirk being beamed out of the room. Nice effect, Kevin conceded, then logged himself out of Solsys. He was alone on the back porch again. He closed his laptop, got up from his lawn chair, and went inside.

Stunning! Kevin wasn't sure if alienclone2492's sudden exit was because the conversation had intensified. Maybe AC felt like he had shared a little too much this time, or maybe he detected my aroused suspicions. Something shifted there.

Kevin began to generate numerous questions himself. Just how prominent were some of AC's contacts? Who were those other three retrievals, and why did they die when Jahny seemed to defy death so spectacularly? How did the Feds first become aware of these unusual finds in the desert? To what extent are they involved? Had another medevac involved in one of the retrievals decided to inform them about suspicions, or actual knowledge about Jahny? Was it possible that his partner Darnell made a call? After all, he seemed fairly upset when they all first met in Jahny's room.

Hmmm, he thought. There's a lot to think about here – and it's still Thursday. It was now clear this was going to be a three-joint evening.

34

That was a good move connecting with AC tonight, Kevin thought. Sometimes you just sense a subtle inclination to do something, and it turns out to be important – like it was meant to be. "PSI again," he mumbled to himself, "anomalous outcomes, things that can't be clearly accounted for..." He began contemplating the fun he could have thinking about this for a while. I can stay up and think about this to my heart's content. It's still nice out here on the deck. Sleeping in tomorrow is an option, so no interference with responsibilities. That was an underlying personal guideline: no interference with responsibilities. Feel free to indulge in personal pleasures and activities – like getting high – as long as they don't interfere with obligations to self or others.

Kevin was already experiencing a cerebral big bang. His mind was exploding with the info he had just gleaned online. It was time to slow it down and cruise through it all. With that in mind, he decided to roll the third joint of the evening. Often when he became stimulated to the point of overload, he would catch himself jumping from one thing to the next in rapid succession. He had suspected a possible attention deficit disorder for years, but it was never diagnosed. He didn't really categorize it as debilitating anyway. He had learned to use it to his advantage when he began to drift. He would surf it. Whenever Kevin recognized himself going down a wormhole of rapid-fire information, he would text quick little notes to himself. A word or short phrase jotted down here and there helped out, oddly enough. Then when he had more time, he could go back and see what was worth pursuing, and what wasn't. At that stage of the process, smoking a joint almost always helped slow him down enough to focus. Whether research corroborated that benefit as one of weed's capabilities or not, it was Kevin's sincere belief that he personally profited from it in that way. He could think of numerous times when that was clearly the case. Use all the tools you have, he reasoned.

Kevin wasn't planning to get back on the computer. He believed this was the time to let it all flow freely. What was that psych term again? Ah, free association, he quickly remembered. That's right. He got up from the lawn chair and took the laptop back inside. No need to take notes. He could use the playback feature of his session with alienclone if he needed a recall later. It would still be available to him for a few more hours. After that it was permanently deleted as per site security measures.

Kevin gathered his supplies again, but before returning outside to roll one, he decided it was time to put on some ambient tunes after all. He had considered Eno earlier, but now decided to listen to Jon Hassel instead. A little *Dream Theory in Malaya* would go well right now, he thought. The mystical effect of Hassel's trumpet playing almost always seduced Kevin into a waking daydream mode. The instrument was mixed, looped and stretched so that it never really sounded like an actual trumpet. It was likely that Eno effect by Brian, who worked on the album with Hassel and Lanois back in '81. Had Uncle Music never introduced him to that album, would he ever have discovered it on his own? There were several other gems still waiting to be discovered. He still hadn't fully explored the boxes of records Uncle Music had left him when he died. The old man simply left a note saying, "Some of my favourites."

Kevin lowered the needle to the vinyl and watched it spin round, waiting for the first notes to begin. The piece was tranquil, emerging from the relative silence of the rotating disc into a trance-like groove of flowing sound. A perfect choice, Kevin thought. He stepped back outside leaving the sliding glass door open, repositioned himself on the lawn chair, and began rolling that third spliff.

Thoughts about the session with AC were dancing in his head, but Kevin reserved sufficient focus to roll another perfect doob. The rolling process was relaxing, but engaging. It was an artisan skill, made uniquely individual by the nuances in each person's methodology. Kevin kissed the finished product, then held it high in a toast to the cosmos above. It was going to be the perfect top off to what felt like a long, but excellent day. Leaving Venice Beach to return home this afternoon seemed like ages ago already. Yet it was less than five hours since he returned to his unrestrainedly faux-starving, melodramatic cat. Since then, he had enjoyed a couple of spliffs, made a fabulous supper on the barbecue, and reconnected with AC2492. His mind funneled back to segments of their conversation. The whole thing was quite enlightening. It wasn't only what AC had said, but what they didn't say.

Perhaps the most intriguing detail for Kevin was that AC verified Jahny's condition through another contact. Was it possible they knew about it even before Kevin's original report? Kevin was in a good position to have first-hand knowledge, but who else would have even better access to info about the strangers retrieved from the desert? Alienclone would have to be extraordinarily well-connected to have two people in advantageous positions able to verify the same incidents and circumstances. Kevin assumed it would be unusual for anyone to have that kind of access without knowing operatives much better than protocol allowed. It would hinder the ability to verify their reports otherwise, wouldn't it? Who knows? Maybe AC2492 actually is a step above the rest. Now that Kevin began to think about it, that was rather obvious.

Kevin couldn't remember ever telling them about his profession, or where he worked. AC2492 often made reference to the importance of personal discretion, thereby clearly encouraging adherence. Various sites' policies routinely encouraged the use of avatars and pseudonyms. Secrecy was built into the system. Kevin couldn't think of any online contacts about whom he knew much of anything at all, but it served their collective purpose. Despite that, Kevin, or ETfrnd314, had learned a considerable amount through info sharing with other dedsurfs. If he were to rank them, AC2492 was his best contact, hands-down. Whenever Kevin had followed up with further research, he always discovered that AC had been at least one step ahead of any other source. That was why he thought about AC first and foremost this evening. They didn't disappoint, and often raised new possibilities.

Clearly, AC had been mulling over the whole situation for some time. Kevin began to suspect that 2492 knew about each and every case even before any mention of the earlier incidents. They happened before Kevin even met Jahny. The more Kevin mulled over facts gleaned from his conversation this evening, the more intriguing the whole thing became. They must all point to a clearer picture of what's going on, he reasoned, but for now, more questions arise than answers.

Aside from the fact that there must be a connection between Jahny and the other three – their circumstances are just too similar to be coincidental – why did three of them die and Jahny didn't, or at least not yet? A miscalculation? An unforeseen error? Considering the details further, Kevin realized there was much he hadn't considered. How long was Jahny out in the desert, both before he arrived at the location where he was found, and afterward? How long were the other retrieved individuals out there before they died? How did they actually get there? These were questions alienclone must have considered too. That's what gave him his edge, Kevin thought. AC was always on top of things. It was almost like the guy never rested; he was an information-gleaning machine, a kind of Spock-like character, an automaton. They could be counted-on to view things from a different angle. They could be counted-on to perceive connections and patterns before anyone else.

Kevin began thinking about his overall experience as an alien enthusiast. He had spent a good part of his life pursuing information about alien possibilities. First it was establishing a belief that aliens might really exist out there somewhere, even if they were as unable to reach us as we are them. There was scant evidence that other habitable worlds were out there when he was young. That changed considerably as Kevin grew into his teen years. By then, some of the problems with the Hubble Space Telescope had been corrected and numerous discoveries of exoplanets began to unfold. Science fiction books and movies tended to provide speculative possibilities to fill in the gaps that science could not. Although many were only loosely based on actual scientific theories, especially quantum physics, good creative writing could stretch credibility – and it did. Once the Internet opened up to the public, advancements in alien interest exploded. At first, alien conspiracy theories and complaints of government secrecy about UFOs were all the rage. Then slowly, but surely, more serious sites began to appear. Research and standards began to take hold. Eventually, sites like Solsys with dedicated, serious-minded enthusiasts were established. By that time, Kevin was already an ardent believer.

Up until now, that ardent belief was little more than a pipedream. He hoped one day the existence of aliens would be confirmed. Now, he wondered if he wasn't in a situation where that might actually happen. There was definitely more here than met the eye. The events of the past few days already established that. His conversation with AC2492 bolstered suspicions. There was more than just PSI anomalies in this mix. Kevin's sense about it all continued to strengthen. It was an assurance just begging to be uncovered. He could feel it in every fiber of his being. It was like having something on the tip of your tongue that can't be remembered momentarily, but you know it's coming. Kevin laid back on the lawn chair, still enjoying his toke. The first side of Hassell's *Dream Theory* was still playing, flowing through him as intended.

Kevin set aside thoughts of his conversation with AC momentarily to focus on the desert retrievals. As he had already determined, there had to be a connection between the four of them. If in fact they were aliens on a mission, then the circumstances of arrival could provide clues to its nature. This is where things get complicated, Kevin realized. There were numerous questions that needed answers. He caught himself muttering the first one under his breath. "Why out in the Mohave?" Then questions emerged in rapid succession. Why did the events happen separately instead of at the same time? Why did they occur within 120 square miles of one another, but not at the same site? Perhaps most importantly, how significant an event, or series of events, are these occurrences?

Despite finishing the last puff of his joint, Kevin's mind was still racing. There was a lot to digest. He got up and sauntered into the apartment to nab a notepad he kept on his desk. Perfect timing. The last track on that side of the album was over. He lifted the needle, but didn't bother flipping it over. He was already jotting down questions before returning to the lawn chair.

When Kevin was satisfied he had as many questions as he could think of, he began brainstorming responses. First, why the Mohave? That didn't take too much thought. There were obvious advantages. The Mohave is the largest desert expanse in North America. If one wanted to mitigate the possibility of surveillance or interference, then its relative remoteness was a distinct benefit. Hell, he noted, you hear about the authorities busting illegal dog or cock fighting rings out there once in a while. They can go undetected for years. The same is true for meth labs. If something like an accidental explosion didn't occur, or if a disgruntled acquaintance didn't squeal on the perpetrator, labs could evade detection easily. Yet, even though the Mohave could be remote and secretive, it also had close proximity to large population centers, most notably, Los Angeles. Sensitive facilities like Edwards Air Force Base, the Jet Propulsion Lab, Caltech, and others were also accessible. The desert is a good place to retain secrecy, even abort a mission. Not too many things that die in the desert leave a trace for very long. It was a credible possibility. Kevin did note that despite the Mohave's expanse, it may not be as secretive as some might want. His chat with AC2492 this evening proved that.

Kevin thought it particularly noteworthy that the other three bodies were now located at an undisclosed military base. Should that be disquieting, or reassuring that the Feds were actively involved? As he already believed, alien activity was being enacted to prevent humans from destroying themselves. That had to mean governments around the world were in compliance with the same objectives, either voluntarily, or compelled to do so. Enthusiasts like himself were dedicated, but at a disadvantage. They didn't have officially-recognized expertise that gave them access to well-connected intelligence. Neither did they have access to deep- pocket funding to pursue far-reaching objectives. If anyone had these capabilities, it had to be the Feds. Another very interesting observation was that AC2492 had the capability to verify deeply-sensitive information. Perhaps not surprising, but certainly intriguing, Kevin concluded. So, would the government consider these four alien agents hostile, he wondered? Or was recovery of their remains routine coverup to prevent non-approved doctors and coroners from learning too much? If any of this were true, then Kevin had to consider the possibility that probing eyes were fixed on Jahny's situation. "Holy shit," Kevin mumbled out loud.

He suddenly realized that he may have free-associated himself into something significant here. He also recognized that despite his long-standing belief that world governments and alien races were probably working together toward common goals, he didn't fully fathom what that meant. Such cooperation required vast, detailed infrastructure. Without it, numerous difficulties coordinating activities would continually arise. Objectives were of paramount importance; even the agents used to achieve them were expendable if such objectives became liabilities. If an objective or mission had to be aborted, or met mishap, there had to be a mechanism for maintaining the overall cover-up until everything is eventually revealed to the public.

What kind of infrastructure would that involve? Aside from technology, especially secret communications, there had to be a large number of personnel involved. Not all of that could be provided by military resources. Civilian professionals would also have to be embedded and participant. That meant approved personnel would have to occupy positions advantageous toward maintaining secrecy. What would we be talking about here, Kevin wondered? Just doctors and coroners? Or would a more complex network have to be set up – at least in places where interaction or intervention could be expected?

What did all this mean? If Jahny was being surveillanced by the Feds, and possibly foreign operatives as well, what could Kevin really do about it? Even if he could, should he do anything about it? And what? After all, he didn't know all the facts. He could inadvertently end up doing something counterproductive. This wasn't a scripted movie plot. He didn't have it all figured out. At best, he reasoned, he was a minor player – possibly even an accidental participant. This was much bigger and more complex than he could impact in any way. So what should he do now? Realizing where things might stand at the moment, anything he did to intervene could jeopardize the situation. He had no way to know.

Kevin knew he couldn't go to the hospital before returning to work for his shift tomorrow night. Trying to visit Jahny on a day off would seem unusual, if not outright suspicious. A supervising desk nurse was always on duty. What if she was now required to monitor visitors by taking names? If Jahny was being closely-watched, then whoever's watching was aware he had already been up to see him more than once this week. In that case, they would have run a check on him, or already known about his activities for some time. It would follow that they might be interested in what he knew, especially if they were aware of his dedsurf activities and connections. Not surprisingly, Kevin was beginning to feel slightly paranoid. Weed never affected him that way. Maybe he really did have something to worry about.

Kevin took a deep breath in, then exhaled slowly, repeating the process a number of times. Still lying on the lawn chair, he again stared up at the night sky. He slowly followed the glimmering light downward to where the silhouette of mountain ridges interrupted his view of the cosmos. He imagined himself alone on this tiny rock lost in that vastness. Then he imagined being a distant traveler on that same rock.

Kevin tried to imagine being stranded on a desolate landscape of a foreign world. Matt Damon's character in *The Martian* came to mind, but it only partially replicated any predicament alien visitors like Jahny might have on this planet. Unlike the desolate expanse on Mars, Earth is bustling with life. No doubt, aliens on a mission would be rigorously well-trained, just as our explorers and military personnel are. They wouldn't just be on foreign territory though, but on an alien planet where life evolved differently. Imagine what that must be like, Kevin thought. Even the 12 astronauts who stepped on the moon in the late '60s and early '70s would have difficulty imagining a scenario like that.

Kevin tried to imagine what being an alien would be like. Where exactly might they come from? The Milky Way galaxy we reside in is so large that just its radius is almost 53,000 light years across. That presented the first glaring problem: distance. Assuming extraterrestrials were also carbon-based organisms, their very make-up would present the same challenges for travel that humans have. Most destinations are too far. They would take numerous lifetimes to reach. Sagan believed the Milky Way probably contained a million different societies, Kevin recalled. That number seemed reasonable enough given it has several hundred billion stars. One might begin to visualize the need for galactic traffic lights given such statistics, but of course, there are often subsequent studies to temper discoveries or calculations. Kevin remembered reading a more recent paper in the Astrophysical Journal which turned such numbers on their heads. The University of Nottingham paper published in the journal suggested a shockingly deflated assessment compared to Sagan's – only between 36 and 1,000 possible societies throughout the Milky Way. Ah, but I'm digressing, Kevin realized. As soon as he readjusted his focus back to the alien retrievals, an important question arose. What could the Fed's actual role be here?

Kevin thought of the Roswell incident that alienclone liked to downplay. It happened within decades after the public's interest in alien visitors first emerged. Most accounts linked the interest to the new literary field of science fiction first pioneered by the likes of Jules Verne and H.G. Wells. Kevin wondered which actually came first: The development of science fiction, or the age of reported UFO sightings? Did reports of sightings spawn the genre, or did the genre spawn sightings? The Roswell incident happened just two years after the development of nuclear weapons. If alien intelligence was monitoring the situation, as dedsurfs believe, intervention strategies would have likely been initiated in response. Roswell almost blew the lid off the whole thing. That realization blew Kevin's mind, but the evidence persists: The public at large is still aware of the event almost 75 years later. It remains a prominent conspiracy theory. There was a lot of media attention on it at the time, but the government gained the upper hand – sort of. A lid was put on coverage and the boil reduced to a simmer, but those serious about learning the truth have continued investigating ever since. Once the internet emerged, enthusiasts were finally able to develop closer communications. The rise of dedsurfs made it difficult to keep secrets like Roswell. AC2492's information this evening about that military video soon to be released proved that to be both true and untrue. There were still plenty of secrets most dedsurfs were unaware of, like that of Jahny and the other retrievals. Yet there were special individuals like AC who were able to root them out.

Kevin couldn't imagine how governments around the world were able to keep a lid on whistleblowers. Never mind trying to retain secrecy among essential individuals like doctors and coroners. How many government professionals and bureaucrats would have to be involved as well? The overall operation would also require a specialized framework for engaging with participant foreign dignitaries. Keeping it all together would be a gargantuan task. The concept was fascinating. Kevin couldn't imagine actually being on the inside in the know. That's the difference, he suddenly realized. A guy like me who knows a little can enjoy chatting casually with others willing to engage. It's considered harmless, loosely falling under the umbrella of generalized bullshit. But if I were actually someone directly involved in official high-level actions, he reasoned, I would not only be sworn to secrecy, but could quickly become a liability in personal danger. That wouldn't necessarily depend on whether I had personally screwed up either; it could be the result of a change in plans – like an aborted mission.

Kevin's childhood fascination with aliens had now emerged as an adult pursuit that was actually fraught with risk. He stepped back from these unsettling insights momentarily to reminisce about his path trajectory. When one becomes dedicated enough, he realized early on, a kid's curiosity can evolve into an adult's passion. When he was young, Kevin imagined opportunities to interact with real aliens. He remembered wishing for years that he could be Richard Dreyfuss's blue collar character Roy Neary in the film *Close Encounters of the Third Kind*. He had long believed that if the opportunity arose, he would absolutely agree to join a crew of volunteers for exchange with alien counterparts. It would be the most exciting exploratory opportunity ever. It held the mind-blowing promise of transforming humanity's future in ways previously unimagined. For Kevin, it would be the ultimate experience. Never mind the greatest feats of explorers and adventurers throughout Earth's history; any cooperative endeavor with life forms from another world held much greater significance. Kevin remembered when he first learned that scientists were considering the possibility that the necessary ingredients for life may have originated from dust emitted by passing comets and atmosphere-penetrating meteors. It led to the idea that Earth may have been seeded from other worlds deliberately. In that scenario, extraterrestrials may not be aliens at all. An encounter between us may actually be a reunion. Humanity may be a diaspora separated from a long-forgotten ancient home. Now that was a thought to ponder.

When it came to this topic, Kevin believed there was always much to ponder. It's what gave the subject its enduring allure. Wherever it might eventually take him, becoming a dedsurf was something he would never regret. If nothing else, it had been an avenue and means towards learning the truth. Dedicated learners who embark from any path, he firmly believed, will eventually be redirected toward truth. All roads lead to Rome. Up to now, being an alien enthusiast provided its own rewards, but Kevin acknowledged they were limited to finding small answers to big questions. He often referred to this ceaseless pursuit as ponderlust. That may have a frivolous ring to it, he mused, but things seem to have changed. These past few days were helping to sharpen focus.

For years, Kevin imagined being part of the most momentous period in history – the one where humanity makes first contact. Just believing in that possibility was stimulating enough; expecting an imminent event, however, was outright exhilarating. He wasn't sure how all of it would eventually unfold, but he almost felt anxious about it all. He had a heightened sense of excitement and expectation. Maybe it was just the result of having a particularly unusual

345

conversation with AC2492. Wouldn't that be cool if AC regretted imparting less information than he should have and decided to contact him again this evening? Wishful thinking, he realized. AC didn't seem like someone who second-guessed their own actions afterward. Nonetheless, there were networks of dedsurfs out there trying to work in concert toward the same objectives. It wasn't impossible that AC might decide their conversation this evening was impetus for further action. In that case, other dedsurfs would be recruited as go-betweens to enact such action. Wheels were turning. Things were moving.

There had indeed been numerous rumblings in dedsurf circles about the imminence of a first contact announcement, but there was also skepticism. Murmuring died down over the past year or so, but Kevin knew dedsurfs generally believed that the time is rapidly approaching. Murmuring can be the result of leaks. Seeking recognition within certain circles can provide a motive for leaking information. That's why it's important to pay attention to such things. Gossip can sometimes reflect, or foreshadow actuality.

The revelation of first contact to the public may have already been in motion. A postponement may also have occurred for whatever reason. The operation Jahny and the other retrievals were part of could have been an important stage in the plan. These were all possibilities. Kevin wondered if AC might be on the same track. Who knows, he wondered? Maybe AC was closely monitoring the situation all along. Was it possible they might be an agent of the government itself? Earlier this evening that thought would have seemed fantastical, but now Kevin ventured down that wormhole. The further he ventured, the clearer his view. The kind of knowledge alienclone always seemed to have access to couldn't be the work of a single agent with vague acquaintances in supposedly strategic places. It simply wouldn't be reliable. There would have to be a vast intelligence network. Maybe he really had no idea who AC2492 was at all!

"This is truly fucking incredible," Kevin blurted out loud. He suddenly felt the full weight of this realization. He may have been unwittingly feeding a government agent with information for years. He may have been more of a pawn than a dedsurf. There was another possibility too. He might never connect with AC again. His usefulness may be past – even before he realized it. Furthermore, his actions may contribute to a favourable outcome, or possibly a detrimental one. He was no longer a driver on a trip of discovery, but a mere cog in the machinery of the vehicle being driven.

This whole thing was certainly out of his control, but it was important to rein-in that imagination. Don't latch on to assumptions too readily. Kevin had to stop and rethink this. Most governments display spectacular failures and gross ineptness. Many officials often find themselves in shoes they cannot fill, and performing actions not up to task. So again, Kevin had to question how government manages to keep a lid on all of this? And how was it being coordinated to monitor events closely? How was alienclone so involved even before Kevin gave him the information about the first retrievals? The Feds couldn't possibly be relying only on infiltration of interest groups like Solsys. No, Kevin thought, there had to be a lot more to it than that. If anything, the government was probably aware of sites like Solsys all along. Why rely only on their own intelligence when they could surveillance others' efforts? That didn't suffice by itself, but what else was possible?

For a while, Kevin just stared up at the beautiful night sky. He could daydream here for hours, but his mind kept reverting back to alienclone's involvement. He recalled much of their back and forth conversation and began analyzing it thoroughly. Maybe an intelligence network was indeed coordinating activities. That made sense. If any revelation were imminent, coordination between officials from all parties was necessary. Perhaps coordination toward that inevitability demanded ongoing cooperation. In fact, it would probably have to be highly integrated. That suggested an amalgamated effort that would have to include both extraterrestrial and human representatives – an intergalactic staff of agents and coordinators. That also suggested aliens may have been assimilated into human society for a very long time. Just how long, he wondered?

Past references came to mind. First and foremost was Von Daniken, a major proponent of the ancient astronaut hypothesis and author of *Chariots of the Gods* back in the late '60s. He became famous for suggesting ancient structures like the pyramids required higher technical knowledge than humans possessed at the time they were produced. He also claimed that ancient artwork like pictographs depicted astronauts and advanced alien technologies. He even offered reinterpretations of religious texts including passages of the Bible's Old Testament. That reminded Kevin of someone AC had introduced him to months ago. Starcherub12 was another dedsurf operating through Solsys. They had chatted a few times. Interestingly, she was less discreet about hiding personal details. Not that Kevin learned much about her, but the fact that she used the same female avatar suggested a preferred identification bias. That wasn't the reason Kevin remembered her though. She had piqued his curiosity by discussing her specialty at Solsys: delving into ancient

347

references to encounters with extraterrestrials. She had a particular interest in biblical references. Although he knew who Daniken was and what he was known for, Kevin knew that the man's claims were at least partially debunked by the 1980s. It didn't occur to him that others might still be reviewing the evidence. Apparently, Starcherub12 was a leading investigator.

A thought suddenly occurred to Kevin. Never mind looking into evidence about ancient astronauts and extraterrestrial encounters. Never mind wondering whether Jahny was an alien or not. What about AC2492? Maybe he wasn't just an enthusiast. Maybe he wasn't a dedsurf at all. Kevin suddenly recognized what may have been hidden in plain view the whole time. AC's name may not be an a.k.a. at all. Perhaps it was a designation. Alienclone may in fact be an alien clone, at least metaphorically. AC might be an extraterrestrial entity. Incredible as that seemed, Kevin reasoned, it wasn't an impossibility. In fact, it illuminated a few things. For one, it explained how AC knew so much about the retrievals. It also clarified how AC always had timely access to secretive information.

What a mind-blowing possibility, Kevin thought! The probability gained credence as he reconsidered previous conversations with alienclone. Kevin may very well have been associated with a real-life extra-terrestrial for years without knowing it. That's just it, he mused. Despite having a secretive nature, AC fits seamlessly into human interactive society. It goes to show how similar we are. It also shows it's possible to embrace the kind of society envisioned by people like Gene Roddenberry.

Just a couple hours had passed since he enjoyed his barbecue. Kevin was considering a bowl of cereal, but felt too lazy to get up from the lawn chair just yet. He was still enjoying the night sky and his many musings about AC. He also thought about his interactions with Jahny, the conversation with that former NASA guy, Enrique, his friend Emma, and the strange call from her son up in Canada. There were a lot of threads to the week's events. Did it all fit into the emerging picture here, he wondered?

A few minutes ticked by. His thoughts were suddenly interrupted by a beep from his phone. A quick glance revealed an incoming message from someone at Solsys. It was probably AC, Kevin surmised enthusiastically. He knew it! That strong feeling he had earlier might be pure PSI, but he knew the night wasn't over just yet. Kevin plugged in his password, and went straight to unread messages. There was only one, but it wasn't AC. It was Starcherub12.

348

35

As Darnell pulled into the church parking lot, he realized he had probably never been inside a church on a Thursday before. Although his wife Neveah came here regularly, Darnell had rarely even come for special occasions. It was ironic that he should be nervously excited to be coming this evening, but he hoped to glean further insight into his own investigations. After spending the better part of two days pursuing leads, following links between biblical passages, reading multiple articles online, and piecing together an emerging perspective on end times prophecy, Darnell wasn't able to establish any possible correlation with the events he became aware of this week. Did Jahny really fit into any of this, and if so, how exactly? Darnell felt sure that if his perception of end times events was more complete, he would also have a better idea about where Jahny might fit into it all.

Pastor Dave introduced him to Jakob yesterday morning at the prayer meeting, but he never spoke with the man at any length. Although Darnell considered that may have been a mistake, he thought it fortunate he had another chance at doing so. Good thing Neveah suggested calling Dave this evening. That probably wouldn't have happened if he didn't share his recent obsession with her at supper. It was also fortunate that Jakob and his wife happened to be with Dave again today. It seemed coincidental, but opportune that it should fit into place just now. Darnell was optimistic, believing it foreshadowed possibilities for further insight. Hopefully, he didn't miss anything too important to his own inquiries.

Darnell locked his car, then walked toward a door at the back of the building where Neveah told him he could access administrative offices. Everything was dark except one room illuminated up on the second floor. That had to be Dave's office. Thankfully, the back door was unlocked when he checked. Stairs were at the opposite end of the small foyer entrance. Easy enough, he thought, making sure the door clicked shut behind him. At the top of the stairs, light streamed out of an open doorway to Darnell's right. As he walked down the hall toward it, he could hear voices.

"As we were discussing after the prayer breakfast," uttered one voice, "this stuff has been spelled out in scripture for millennia. It's actually been there right before our eyes for two-thousand years. Christine has been diligent rooting out leads and references, and then making connections with…" The voice stopped as Darnell approached the doorway. After knocking lightly on the door frame and stepping into the office, he was greeted by three faces looking directly at him.

"Good evening Pastor Dave. Thanks for inviting me to join you here. That was a nice surprise. My wife Neveah and I were just talking about some things I've learned since we went to the prayer meeting yesterday. When I excitedly told her I felt on the edge of discovery, she suggested I call you. It's good to see you again Jakob," Darnell said, reaching to shake his hand. "I didn't meet your wife yesterday, so hello, I'm Darnell," he said, also reaching forward to shake her hand. "Pleased to meet you." Then turning to Dave, he thanked him again. "When you told me over the phone you were discussing matters that might pertain to what I shared with you, and that you were still engaged in discussion here tonight, I was eager to take you up on the invitation. I probably owe you at least some explanation for leaving the prayer meeting abruptly. I daresay it has invoked an awakening. As I began to digest what I was hearing there, thoughts and ideas began bubbling out of my head like a fountain. I was compelled to go home and delve into it all. I've spent the rest of these past two days in my office at home studying end times prophecy."

"Well, you've come to the right place Darnell," said Jakob. "Come join us; take a seat. It is interesting that you mention end times prophecy. Perhaps you were meant to come here just now."

Then Dave chimed in. "We didn't have time for much conversation before the program began yesterday Darnell, so introductions were scant. Jakob and Christine are missionaries who have just returned from Nigeria. Jakob and I have known one another for years. Christine and I actually grew up in the same church back in Nebraska, so we're all old friends."

"That's cool. It's good to be able to catch up with old friends. I hope my accepting your offer isn't too much of an intrusion. I can always come back another time Pastor."

"Not at all Darnell. Actually," Pastor Dave was keen to add, "aside from being dedicated to their work and being co-founders of a girls' school over there, Jakob and Christine are also well-known and respected eschatologists, at least in circles where too many feathers aren't being ruffled. Christine was just beginning to discuss an interesting insight. As suggested a moment ago, maybe you were meant to come here Darnell. Your insight may well contribute to our understanding too. I am getting quite excited about this now. I think you will too. You were going to share your ideas Christine."

"I was just about to get started on a few points," said Christine. "You haven't really missed anything yet. Jakob was still introducing the context when you walked in, but that's all good. What I have to say can wait a little longer. I can see that Darnell is brimming with excitement, despite attempting to retain a calm demeanor. I would like to hear about what he has learned studying scripture and end-times eschatology. A fresh mind applied to the subject could reveal insight overlooked by us so-called experts."

Jakob also encouraged Darnell to divulge any new insight as well, citing a general excitement being created by the current unfolding of events. "It's difficult to keep track of everything going on," he said. "If we can find others waiting and watching diligently too, then perhaps collectively, we can see much more. Please share with us what you have learned."

"Maybe I really was meant to come," Darnell conceded, chuckling softly. He felt calmer and more confident, assured he had not intruded. "The tone of your conversation sounded enthusiastic as I approached the door. I have to admit though, this weekend has excited an intellectual and studious curiosity – which I might add," Darnell said with a huge smile, "doesn't happen all that often." Now the other three laughed. "This may sound a little sacrilegious, but end-times preaching over the years has hashed and rehashed much of the same information our whole lives. You know, the rapture, tribulation, earthquakes and famine, etc., etc., but some of what I heard at the breakfast yesterday really got me thinking. I began to realize that although I've been a Christian my whole life, I've never truly awakened to some of the most exciting truths to be learned."

"Well, you're right about that Darnell. If we were all honest, we would have to admit the very same thing." Jakob had been listening and smiling enthusiastically as he observed Darnell's new-found inspiration in the Lord. "It almost sounds as though you have been newly reborn my friend – like our beloved Apostle Paul, who as an unbeliever, suddenly saw a bright light and recognized it for what it was: The Lord calling him to his ministry – and what a ministry it was! Maybe the Lord has similar ideas for you my friend. So go ahead and tell us. What have you awakened to brother?"

"To say the least, these last few days have been one surprise after another, but what have I awakened to?" Darnell smiled as he reflected on his newfound enthusiasm. "Well, I've been reading quite a bit. At first when I sat down yesterday morning to get into all this, I wasn't sure where to start. I have a chain reference Bible at home that I enjoy. It seemed like a good place to begin – at the source, so I turned to the Book of Revelation. I've enjoyed studying the Word for many years, but Revelation is the one of the few books I've kind of avoided. It has so much imagery in it, but preachers tend to depict only a general understanding of it all. I knew it was going to be tough, so I turned to online sources for help. Some echoed the same few verses preachers like to churn periodically. Others were more scholarly, avoided the usual rants, and provided detailed explanations. It was refreshing. It was more than just interesting, it fed my growing enthusiasm. Actually, I found it - still find it mind-blowing."

"Well, that it is," Pastor Dave confirmed emphatically. "In fact Darnell, I think you will become even more enthusiastic once you hear what we've been discussing. It may extend your new-found knowledge a step or two further. Listening to what Christine and Jakob have had to say has certainly extended mine."

"Okay, but what are these things? Darnell paused for just a moment. "How can we know what the meaning of the scriptures are if interpretations of them differ? Sometimes interpretations can even be opposing and highly contentious. How can they be so easily muddled, even by ministers of the Lord?"

"Remember Darnell, there will be signs and rumours of signs. That is something we have all heard many times from the pulpit. That could very well include sources online, and even come from so-called ministers of the Lord. It's important to try and be as discerning as one can be. Listen Darnell," Pastor Dave said earnestly. "No one is trying to discredit anyone for speculation, but when specific predictions are made – like when the rapture will occur, for example – and then proves incorrect, then it is wise to take further information from that source with a grain of salt. Maybe God inspired some of these writers, but some of them may have simply inspired themselves. Some may even have motives that are self-serving, rather than light-seeking. The truth of the matter is Darnell, and I'm saying this to you as a pastor of a church, that much of the food we feed to the faithful is like pablum. It is what they are able to digest. Just like you before your awakening, you listened, you studied the Word, you tried to live your life as you believed it should be, but that seed of excitement never exploded into a growth phenomenon until recently. You might say it remained in an immature, infantile state. Once that life buds forth, however, there is no turning back. You've become energized. You crave learning, and want to understand more. That requires more than just pablum. It can't just be baby food anymore Darnell. It requires the meat and vegetables needed to develop into maturity, doesn't it? Even as a pastor, it wasn't until I really began discussing such matters with people like Jakob and Christine – and others like those at the prayer breakfast yesterday – that I too became turned on to the deeper meanings of our faith. What was really surprising to me was that once you see it, you realize the evidence was there all

352

along. It is exciting, isn't it Darnell? Anyway, it is clear to me that the Lord led you here to join us for a purpose. Listen to what Christine and Jacob have come to share with me today. I think you will find it just as interesting and inspirational as I do. I've been looking forward to this since Jakob and I had a brief opportunity to reconnect yesterday. Now that Christine is with us as well, it will be all the more interesting. Jakob would be quick to acknowledge that she's the real expert on these matters."

"Okay, thanks pastor," Darnell said. "I'm definitely looking forward to hearing what you have to say Christine, but first I just want to add something to what Jakob said a minute ago."

Darnell turned to Jakob. "You mentioned the Apostle Paul's conversion and subsequent ministry. Maybe I was experiencing a profoundly moving revelation like Paul experienced – just as you suggested – although I didn't make that comparison at the time. My excitement and enthusiasm was bubbling over, as I've already mentioned, but progression sometimes inched forward inconsistently. The discrepancies between what leading scholars were saying and much of what we've been told in churches all our lives were both discouraging and enlightening. They were discouraging because they planted doubt about what I have known and believed for years, but enlightening because I really felt like I was emerging from a type of darkness. Even the rapture, something evangelicals have believed in for generations, seems to be flimsily based on only a verse or two – verses that could easily have been misinterpreted by overly-enthusiastic inference. That may border on the sacrilegious for many, but maybe we've only been seeing 'through a glass darkly' as scripture says."

"You're absolutely right Darnell," Jakob began. "Oooh, I can feel the intensity of your excitement, and it inspires me. It's important to adhere to what Dave said. A lot of what's preached in church is pablum. It's baby food. You just testified that you've spent much of your Christian life virtually in a sleep state from which you were awakened as recently as these past few days. Most church goers pass their entire lives like that. They go to church for many reasons, but often, it is because they were taught to do so from the time they were children, and have never strayed from that. They still believe what they always believed simply because they have never questioned it. Believing themselves to be good Christians, they continue to attend church faithfully, even if they aren't enthusiastic ones. The institutions of Christ keep plodding forward, but the essence of what they believe as a living ideal has often been lost. This can change, and may change spectacularly as the second coming unfolds before our very eyes. Many are awakening to this truth.

Now that you are awakening Darnell, you too will gain further insight. Your coming here this evening is only one step toward a full awakening. God may work in mysterious ways, but these so-called mysterious ways often prove to be very pragmatic when one sees the bigger picture emerge."

Christine picked up the conversation like a relay runner handed a baton. "I'm very excited by your recent awakening too Darnell. Like Jakob, I'm inspired by your enthusiasm, your thirst. It's electrifying, but Dave and Jacob are right. There are many deeper meanings that rarely reach the average congregation at church. Pastors realize they must keep their sermons within the parameters of what people are willing to hear. The messages should always be uplifting, except when a little fear of damnation might be important to keep some from straying too far. The thing is, everyone's daily lives are what are most important to parishioners. They like to feel they are good people and doing what most good people do, but few ever want to venture into a greater enthusiasm of their faith. It can appear like, and cross over into fanaticism. Consequently, most believers are set in their ways. They tend to participate along traditional, if not furrowed ways. It keeps the faith going – and the churches as well," Christine said solemnly. Then, in a quick burst of fervor, she stated, "but there is so much more Darnell. There is," she said slowly and emphatically, "so much more."

"So let me proceed with what Jakob and I were beginning to share with Pastor Dave," Christine continued. "The Fellowship prayer breakfast is a physical meeting place for some of the enthusiastically faithful, you might say. It really is only a fractional depiction of the many – like you – who are beginning to come out of the proverbial woodwork. Many are connected and working together quite intricately toward 'the common goal.' This is occurring because end times events are ramping up. More are beginning to recognize it too. It is all coming about according to the Lord's plan, but also, interestingly, because the faithful are helping to bring it about. It is the manifestation of the unity of God and his children. The modern world has helped to accelerate God's plan in ways that could never have been imagined before. Modern media, as a good example, has helped evangelism reach new heights. Billy Graham was the first huge televangelist to emerge on screen. He and a subsequent cohort of others have brought the gospel to millions. These millions have been praying, and their prayers have been heard. The long-awaited second coming has begun. All the pieces are falling into place as that unfolding accelerates. Once most of the puzzle can be visualized, the remaining pieces and the places they fit into become easier to recognize. This is where we're at right now."

"Are there stages to this great unfolding then? Darnell could barely contain himself. "Will the whole world see and understand this is what is happening?"

"The truth is Darnell, we don't exactly know how this will unfold, but many signs have become evident, so the short answer to your first question is yes, there are stages to its progression. There are always stages being enacted to move a process from initiation to completion. It could be only weeks or months, but it may still take longer than that." Christine wanted to make sure not to stray off track. "We don't know, but what is very exciting is that the faithful are part of what is making it unfold. You mentioned some of the signs you read about online. Those signs are all part of it, but there's more. There's a lot more. There are the particulars, small and large, that make it all happen. Often what is mentioned in scripture is the final visual representation of something that required many unmentioned details. Those specifics are not necessary for everyone's personal comprehension of the big picture, so they weren't provided in the text. What we are seeing right here in the United States these days is all part of the detailed unfolding of scriptural content. Even the President, who, as we have already pointed out, is a controversial figure, but even he is helping to bring about the fulfillment of scripture, whether he realizes it personally or not. We have come to see that even those who might not actively choose to be part of God's plan fall into place and perform it anyway. That's because they are caught up in something much bigger than they are. We all are! We are also beginning to realize that what the faithful have expected for centuries has been ingeniously developing right under our very eyes. It is all being revealed bit by bit by bit. It is easy to recognize something once completed and established. It is less easy to recognize the components coming together before they actually take shape. Imagine if you were shown the individual parts of a vehicle laid out for you on a flat surface. Without being shown a diagram, a picture, or even given a description of what the pieces were manufactured for, would you be able to imagine how they all come together to form a fully-loaded, high performance sports car? Not so easy, is it?"

Christine literally needed to pause for a moment. Her exuberance was infectious. The other three sat mesmerized, not daring to interrupt. She took a quick sip of her coffee, caught her breath and then continued. "Some have stated they think the President is the Antichrist himself, the one who will appear before the second coming. Yet many good things are happening because of this president's actions. Those most appalled by his behaviour are those unbelievers who can't see the

355

good that's being done. Abortion laws in this country may crumble because of his supreme court nominations. Jerusalem has become recognized as the capital of Israel by our country, the most powerful country on the planet, the leader of the free world! All eyes are on the Middle East more intently than ever. We may see Armageddon develop sooner than expected. How ironic that the faithful should wait for 2,000 years, but still be surprised when what was expected suddenly draws near," Christine mused. All three men laughed heartily.

Darnell was now mesmerized by Christine's words. She continued talking while he made mental notes of points he wanted to research later. She spoke of the armies of Christ amassing in a type of warfare that is already taking on the forces of darkness. She elaborated on the idea of angels on assignment where people placed in high places could influence events contributing to the fulfillment of scripture. She pointed out that regardless of what most people thought of the president, he had surrounded himself with numerous men and women of God, beginning with the vice president. Each have roles to play in this grand and elaborate unveiling of what Christians have believed for millennia. Christine continued to expound on this theme. Both Jakob and Pastor Dave inserted sentences here and there as she spoke.

Darnell just listened intently. The day to day news he absorbed daily suddenly became much more newsworthy. This growing new insight allowed him to see reported events much differently. Christine had given him virtual glasses. He was beginning to see what was previously unseen. As she spoke of the many different missions undertaken by angels on assignment, Darnell thought of Jahny again. Waiting until Christine finished a point she was making, he found an opportunity to interject.

"Excuse me for just a moment Christine. Excuse me everyone, please," Darnell said, looking around the group. "I can't help but listen to what you are saying. It keeps bringing me back to something I need to share now – at this juncture in the discussion. I can't help but think there is a connection between all of this and a strange set of circumstances that occurred at work this week. Coming back to what you said earlier Jakob, I think you're right. Maybe my coming here tonight and meeting you is where this whole week has been leading me. Perhaps in the same way Paul the Apostle's awakening happened on the road to Damascus, mine is happening here – well, not just here. No, not just the prayer meeting, not just my weekend of inspiration and spiritual discovery, and not just what I'm learning here tonight. I think this may all be part of something I was meant to be connected to. It's crazy, and I can't explain it, but somehow, I feel like whatever this is, it is falling into place."

Darnell turned from Jakob back to Christine. "You mentioned many entering into the service of the Lord Christine. I probably can't replicate what you said exactly, but the point was that even though Satan and his minions often impersonate the righteous, so might angels work to infiltrate the forces of darkness. That's powerful on several levels, but it makes me think of someone specific, someone I met only this past week. Originally I thought he might be an acolyte of Satan, but after what you've said, I am wondering if he might just be the exact opposite of that."

"I would very much like to know what you might think of the crazy experience I had this week. It may pertain to all of this." Darnell glanced at Pastor Dave, and apologized for having already shared a shortened version of his encounter with Jahny. Then he proceeded to mention every detail he could remember. Darnell wondered momentarily if he should mention some specifics – particularly Kevin's ideas about Jahny being an alien. It quickly made sense not to leave anything out. If he wanted their honest opinion, he should tell them everything.

So Darnell not only mentioned that Kevin believed Jahny was an alien, but tried to provide a more accurate portrayal of Kevin's views. Darnell wanted to make it clear that although he was skeptical of those views, he wasn't portraying Kevin as a kook. He was careful to point out that Kevin wasn't one to embrace conspiracy theories in general. He was indeed an ardent enthusiast, but also careful to try and pursue solid lines of evidence. At the very least, Kevin was conscientious; he wouldn't want to be embarrassed by failing to complete an argument. He was one to pursue strong, defensible points. As an example, Darnell mentioned a recent conversation where Kevin had told him NASA was planning to announce a study of UFOs, despite the risk to its professional reputation. He also pointed out an interview where former President Bill Clinton asked for an investigation into the rumours about Area 51 when he first took office. Kevin often points to the fact that we have very little idea of what is out there. We know almost nothing about more than 95 percent of the universe. How could we possibly determine that aliens exist or don't exist definitively? Kevin is simply enthusiastic about pursing an answer in as logical a manner as he knows how.

As Darnell spoke, he began to notice that the other three in the room were looking at him intently. He wasn't sure whether they were politely indulging him, or not. Both Jakob and Christine looked like they were waiting for an opportunity to interject. Soon, Jakob appeared to be chomping

357

at the bit. Darnell stopped. "Okay, is this all sounding just too ridiculous? Was that just a sidestep a little too far?"

"No," Jakob said slowly. Christine looked like she wanted desperately to interject, but she let Jakob continue. "No," Jakob repeated, "I think we have all just realized that you were in fact destined to stop by here this evening my friend. You have just touched upon the very subject Christine and I came to share with Pastor Dave more fully this evening. I had a chance to touch on it with him after the prayer breakfast yesterday. He became so inspired that we decided to indulge him in further discussion. Dave thought his church office was the best place to do that. It is nice and quiet, don't you agree? Ah, but let me stay on topic here. I think you may be in for a surprise or two this evening." Jakob clasped his hands and stood up. "This is all very exciting," he said, looking at each of the others in turn. "Let me reiterate, Darnell. I believe, and I'm sure we all believe it now. You were definitely meant to be here tonight."

Jakob sat down again, and continued. "Scripture, of course, has all the answers to anything we might need to know, but it's not always explicit. Even when it is, there may be connections not easily recognized. That makes the big picture longer to put together."

Jakob glanced at Christine and smiled. "About a year ago, Christine began to realize, or should I say, the Lord revealed to her that angels on assignment may very well appear as aliens to us. Perhaps in modern times it is the only way humanity can conceive of angels on assignment – as aliens from another world. It's widespread in popular imagination, as we are all aware. Anyway, I'm talking too much. Let me just say one more thing. Thank-you Darnell for being brave enough to bring up such a topic this evening. What you've told us may very well be a sign we've been looking for, but I will now let Christine continue without interruption. Listen to this."

This time, Christine stood up for a moment. "This is all very exciting. It's difficult to sit still," she said, smiling. She sipped the last of her coffee, sat down again, and placed the empty cup on the floor next to her chair. "Actually, it is astonishing that you should bring up that very topic here this evening Darnell. I literally have goosebumps since it happened. Jakob is right. You belong here, but may be in for some surprises this evening. You mentioned not having much prior interest in studying scripture related to end times prophecies. You also implied a preference reading books in the New Testament rather than the Old Testament. We, in turn, suggested that most church-going people don't study scripture much on their own, and that pastors often just feed pablum to their parishioners because that's all they can, or are willing to absorb. Yet, if you were to open the Bible and read it from beginning to end Darnell, you would discover a treasure trove. In fact, you wouldn't have to wait long. The Bible tells us things, but sometimes we aren't paying attention. You mentioned your colleague's belief in the possible existence of aliens. You might want to consider that a little more seriously too Darnell. If you were to open your Bible and simply go to Genesis 6 – yes, the very first chapter in the whole Bible, you would find these words: "*The sons of God saw that the daughters of humans were beautiful, and they married any of them they chose… Giants were on the earth in those days—and also afterward—when the sons of God went to the daughters of humans and had children by them. They were the heroes of old, men of renown.*"

"That's a scripture in the Bible," Darnell asked? "It seems to be saying that these sons of god, possibly angels, slash, aliens came down and bred with human women, but I've never heard anything of the sort preached from a pulpit."

"No, that's right. You haven't Darnell, and you are unlikely to in the future either, at least, not until the apocalypse has become evident to all. Ministers of the Lord may well have to scramble to help their flocks understand what is unfolding," said Jakob.

"And not many ministers of the Lord will be able to explain what is going on either," Pastor Dave chimed in. "That I can tell you from personal experience. Most ministers wouldn't touch that passage. The speculation associated with it could dig up one worm too many, so to speak. No one wants to be accused of heresy, you know. Only a couple years ago, I would have been lost in that regard too. I was still consuming spiritual pablum myself before then. What was once best left alone, however, is now a source of great inspiration."

"To answer your immediate question Darnell," continued Christine, "yes, that is really a scripture from the Bible, mentioned just before God goes on about how he wants to eliminate all humans from the earth except for Noah and his family. It is not the only passage in the Bible that points to alien visitors either. Indeed, there are many. "*Who are these that fly along like clouds, like doves to their nests?*" It is a question asked by the great prophet Isaiah in chapter 60, verse 8 of his Old Testament book. That book is very old Darnell. It dates to about the 8th century B.C.E., meaning that according to this account, aliens may have visited here almost three thousand years ago. The account in Genesis 6 would even be much older than that. Also, notice that in the older account, the aliens are spoken of as the 'sons of God.' It's all very fascinating. The prophet Isaiah speaks of aliens in more than just this one place too. In chapter 13, verse 5, he seems to declare the answer to whom he thinks fly along like clouds: "*They come from faraway lands, from the ends of the heavens— the LORD and the weapons of his wrath— to destroy the whole country*. This last part is a link to passages in the book of Revelation."

"This is where Christine's special interest in this area has become valuable," said Jakob. "A little over a year ago when she discovered these verses, she began to realize that not only were there interesting descriptions of alien visitors, but the imagery used to describe them began to illuminate passages in the Book of Revelation as well. We are beginning to realize that the unfolding of the apocalypse and subsequent second coming of Christ may be accompanied by what we suspect are aliens from other worlds. It may very well be the next stage of end times prophecies to unfold. The big picture is, of course, unravelling. It is like a huge wave crashing on the shore before you can see the next one taking shape behind it. This is why we introduced Christine as an eschatologist of rising importance. She discovered these connections, or as we prefer to say, God revealed them to her in his infinite grace. Christine has been developing this eschatological premise into a formal presentation. She is scheduled to introduce it to the faithful at the next Fellowship prayer meeting a month from now. What we are telling you is a preview, so I suggest you come and stay next time Darnell. In the meantime, I also suggest you indulge your inspiration through further study. Look into some of these things for yourself," Jakob emphasized. "Don't just believe what we tell you. Read it with your own eyes. Let God open your mind my new friend."

"Don't sound like you're dismissing him just yet Jakob." Christine looked directly at Darnell. "There's no need to start your study from scratch. If you aren't in too much of a rush, listen to a little more." Then turning to the pastor, she asked, "Dave, do you have some paper and a pen for Darnell here?"

"Right here," Pastor Dave replied, gathering a pen and pad of paper off his desk and handing them to Darnell. "There you go brother. Just turn the page for a clean sheet. I keep quite a number of notes myself. Some may resemble grocery list items, but most are notes about scripture," he said chuckling.

"Thanks Dave," Christine said, still looking directly at Darnell. "Something I've been looking at recently in the New Testament comes to mind now. It does so particularly strongly because of the story you told us tonight Darnell. You mentioned that there have been others like your stranger found in the desert fairly recently, but that at least two others had died. That was part of the discussion you and your partner at work had with the couple who found the stranger. You also mentioned the stranger was in critical condition when he was transported to hospital and his prognosis is still unstable. In fact, it has surprised doctors that he is still alive. The verses I'm thinking about come from the Apostle Paul's letter to the Hebrews in chapter 11, verses 12 and 13: '*Therefore sprang there even of one, and him as good as dead, so many as the stars of the sky in multitude, and as the sand which is by the seashore innumerable. These all died in faith, not having received the promises, but having seen them afar off, and were persuaded of them, and embraced them, and confessed that they were strangers and pilgrims on the earth.*' I have been going over this section over and over, and subsequently memorized these two verses specifically. It's kind of crazy, but it kind of fits the situation you described Darnell. Maybe other aliens have been coming to Earth for some time – and all in preparation for the great event, one that has been emerging since Christ was first taken up almost two-thousand years ago. Your friend may think of them as aliens from another world, but we understand them to be angels on assignment. They are the same thing. '*Do not forget to show hospitality to strangers, for by so doing some people have shown hospitality to angels without knowing it,*' Hebrews chapter 13, verse 2," Christine said.

"I'm not sure what to say about all of this. It's incredible!" Darnell found himself looking at three smiling individuals who clearly understood his sentiment.

Christine didn't stop there. "The first chapter in the book of Ezekiel is also very interesting. It talks about a whirlwind coming out of the north, a fire unfolding itself, and a brightness out of which four living creatures having the likeness of a man emerge. It talks about wheels being lifted up, and the spirit of the living creatures being in the wheels. It also talks about these things having two wings on each side, how they do not move, and how they can go straight without turning. It is incredible Darnell," Christine emphasized. "There are many other verses supporting these ideas. Once you check some of this stuff out for yourself, you will see that the Book of Revelation makes a little more sense to you."

Suddenly, Darnell became distracted. He turned his head toward the door. The noise came from downstairs. The back door clicked shut as it did for him when he had entered. He could hear footsteps starting to climb the stairs. "Are you expecting someone besides me? It sounds like someone's here."

"We are expecting someone," Christine affirmed, smiling again. "Before you called Dave earlier, I asked if I could invite someone to join us. Dave has not met him yet, but Jakob knows about my correspondence with him. This person is not a Christian per se, but his work and insight came to my attention inadvertently. It's a long story. Anyway, I am increasingly excited about his arrival after hearing what you've had to say Darnell. I have a rising suspicion that this may be a surprise for us all."

The footsteps approached the office, then stopped at the entrance. A figure stood there smiling directly at Darnell.

Darnell's jaw nearly dropped. "Kevin? What the..."

36

"I don't think Bender appreciated being left at the ranch just now, but it's a lot better than waiting for us while we're at the hospital. He has that high tech doghouse in the back of the truck, but he had to wait for me in there the other day when I had lunch with my brother. Just goes to show, it doesn't matter what kind of possessions one has, it's connections that count – even for dogs. He was ready for a nap anyway – enjoys several of them every day. Bender's fine." Enrique smiled. "He's a good dog, but he's getting old. I'm going to miss him when he goes."

"Bender is probably sleeping already Enrique, or will be when the sound of the truck fades into the distance. He enjoyed some scraps from our brunch as well as his own food. You also gave the old boy an extravagant rubdown before we left. He practically melted into unconscious ecstasy," Emma said. "He is a good dog. I hope he's around in good health for a while longer."

Emma enjoyed the view descending down to the desert floor where the Pearblossom highway met Longview Road, but the air con hadn't cooled the cabin down yet. That made it tempting to ask Enrique to stop at the gas station on the corner. It was just four days ago that she enjoyed an ice cream there. By the time they came to the stop sign and Enrique was looking to turn left, cooler air began to filter through. Emma decided she would rather enjoy an ice cream later in the day.

"Thanks for coming with me this afternoon Enrique. I really appreciate it," Emma said sincerely. "I fought an urge to go see Jahny after an unusual day yesterday, but thought a little rumination was in order. I sprinkled some more mental provender into the mix by exploring my books further as well. With you out and about yesterday, this place was especially quiet. I fell asleep reading in my room. It made for a great day. I have already told you Enrique, this is a great place you have here. Yesterday reinforced that. I love walking over the slope behind the house and viewing the area far and wide. People often think of deserts as barren, but my Dad taught me long ago that they have an allure of their own."

"The small cave with the aperture is quite something in and of itself," she continued. "I had to return there. It's where this adventurous week really began. The place did not disappoint. In fact, it's left a definite impression on me. I hope you decide to keep this place going for a while Enrique. I would definitely return, and may do so sooner than later if possible. The whole place is

363

marvelous, but the cave possesses a special magic of its own. That may not be a very scientific description, but it is an apt one. Would you be able to describe its allure in precise terms?"

"It is an exceptional little spot, isn't it? I've known about it for years. My father owned the property since I was in my twenties. I thought it was pretty cool when I first discovered it, but only came back to it a few times. My brother Manny and I have stopped by it, but for the most part, it's a place I prefer to go to myself. It's similar to the reading spot in the window upstairs, the one you enjoyed the other day Emma. It's a place for losing yourself in thought. It's a portal, not for anything outside its egg-like interior, but for internal exploration. I'm not asking you to tell me about the impression it left on you yesterday. I'm just describing the general feeling I get by being in there. Sometimes it leads to hours of rumination. That may not sound particularly scientific either, but if you've had any kind of mind-expanding experience in there, I'm sure you understand what I mean."

"I readily admit having a mind-expanding experience there Enrique, but as an adjunct, this whole week has been mind-expanding – practically from the moment I arrived. If truth be told, it's been dreamlike. My purpose for coming to a place of solitude near where I grew up was two-fold: First, it allowed me to come full-circle, so to speak, to see my life as a whole – where it began to where it is now. Second, coming to a place of solitude was meant to curb everyday distractions and allow me to objectify my life. That way I could attempt to assess it separately from the experience of it. Is there a better way to re-evaluate one's direction from any given point? My purpose was to do just that: re-evaluate, then determine what direction to go in. No doubt I would have found my way to a bookstore anyway, but I would probably have chosen only light reads to relax and settle into complacency, a place of complete rest. It was a tabula rasa approach that never happened. Instead, things took on a life of their own. Circumstances were influencing direction, even if I'm still not sure exactly where. What I am sure of Enrique, or at least feel confident about, is that this is leading somewhere. A lot has happened, but it doesn't seem chaotic; I sense a linearity to it. There is direction, but it goes further than any of us can see. I'm no longer sure this is about finding out what the connection between Anthony and Jahny is, if there even is one. Somehow, the inclusion of those two medevacs and their ideas about Jahny have added to the mix. There's something bigger, more important about this whole thing. It all seems wonderfully surreal, but not in any threatening way. It feels like something big is in the works, something bigger than just me, or Anthony, or Jahny, or any of us. I have no sense of what it is exactly – an event, or a realization, or something else altogether. It just feels like whatever it is, it is about to unfold, or be revealed. So if you thought your response to my question wasn't particularly scientific Enrique, then I've confirmed I understood your meaning with an even less-scientific retort."

They both laughed.

"I still don't feel like I have all the answers," Emma continued, "but perhaps that's not necessary. Nonetheless, I did want to see Jahny one last time before returning home. Whatever might happen there, I get the impression it will be conclusive. Maybe it's just an intuition as I might have thought before, but maybe it's connected to what Jung refers to as the collective unconscious. Whatever I get out of this, thanks for coming with me Enrique. Your steady observation and reluctant immersion into the combined excitement generated by the medevacs and I is much-admired and respected. It provides a counterbalance to wild speculation – always a good thing! That brings up another observation though. I do find meeting you again after so many years an amazing coincidence, especially after randomly reminiscing about the time when we were acquaintances while driving to your ranch. Was that really just coincidence, or counterbalance in action? As I've already stated, there's a bigger picture here than I'm seeing."

"That's undoubtedly true Emma. My steady observation, as you described it, is part and parcel of the scientific method, but science doesn't have all the answers. If truth be told, we are still just beginning our journey of discovery. We have barely started to realize what is out there, what is in here," Enrique emphasized pointing to his head, "and how it's all connected. That big picture you're talking about has yet to come into view. We're either too far, or too close to see it clearly. Anyway Emma, what is clear is where we are right now. We've arrived at the hospital. Are you ready?"

"I am. What time is it?"

"Just after 1:00 PM" Enrique couldn't take advantage of the parking spot the medevacs gave him access to the other night. He drove into the public garage but didn't find a space until they reached the top level. "Busy day at the infirmary today," he said. "I hope Jahny still has his spot."

*

"We ended up here a little earlier than scheduled, but such are the ways of staffing complications," Darnell mumbled. "We're going to need some fresh coffee this afternoon my friend."

"Yeah, these things happen once in a while. I wasn't expecting to be called in to cover an earlier shift today, especially after spending the last part of my weekend with, of all people, my partner from work." Kevin laughed. "We were out quite late too, but it was exceptional. I will never forget the look on your face the moment I walked in there last night Darnell." He laughed even louder. "Mind you, I didn't see my own expression at that moment. No doubt, it was also a beauty to behold, but I was just as surprised as you were! I had no idea we were going to run into each other there – or that you, of all people, would be sitting around conversing with someone like Starcherub12. That was the only time I ever met her in person. I wasn't even sure that she was a she."

"Well I certainly never thought I would run into you in a church Kev. For God's sake, I'm a Christian, and I don't go to church regularly," Darnell retorted. Now they were both laughing hard. It took a moment or two to wind down.

Darnell finished setting up the coffee. "Give it a few minutes there Kev," he said, wiping tears of laughter from his face. "No doubt you came in earlier than we needed to for the same reason I did. We can have a coffee, and still pop up to see Mr. Jahny before starting our shift. After all that talk and speculation last night, I hope he's still up there."

"S12…I mean, Christine, is probably right," Kevin said. Whatever happens, happens. If he is gone, it's beyond our ability to do anything about it. Even if he's there, he may or may not tell us what we're hoping to hear. Who are we to him? Furthermore, we still don't know for sure who he is, or what he is. Neither did Christine or Jakob."

"One thing that's been made obvious to me," Darnell added, "is that there is more interconnectivity here than any of us suspected. If that woman Emma we met would have been at that meeting last night, her exhilaration could have set off bells and whistles. Her ideas about coincidences would have been reignited. I know a few of my own bells and whistles have been going off since we left here on Wednesday morning. Last night was the proverbial icing on the cake though Kevin. You and I have worked together for some time now. We get along, we talk while we do our work, we're good work acquaintances, but…" Darnell paused for a moment… "but neither of us would ever have suspected that our perspectives on life – individual perspectives both you and I have cultivated over several years – could merge into the perspective that became evident last night… but dammit Kevin, it really makes sense, doesn't it?"

"It was strange, and yes it does. It's like I've heard you say before Darnell: We see through a glass darkly. I'm not sure that's the case anymore. The view is becoming clearer."

"Well, maybe we do see through this a little less darkly today Kevin, but I wouldn't say things are clear just yet. I do feel like things have changed and won't ever be the same again, but that doesn't provide any clear indication of what's ahead. I feel like almost everything I ever thought could potentially happen in the future, is about to happen soon. I wouldn't necessarily call it scary or threatening, but there's high anticipation. That's the only way I can describe it at the moment. I'm feeling high anticipation, like we're on the brink…"

Kevin poured the coffee. They sat down. Both were immersed in their own thoughts. Both contemplated the events of the night before. Both endeavored to reconcile prior perspectives with what they had learned. Darnell recalled the words of the prophets Christine and Jakob had revealed from scripture. Kevin remembered the claims made by the likes of Von Daniken. Were they not saying the same thing? Were they not keenly observant to what was obvious all along? Darnell and Kevin realized and appreciated the same fundamental insight: If you open your eyes, you can see!

Darnell put his coffee down on the table. "I can't finish this now. I'm too wound up. It's just after 1:00. We've got less than an hour. Let's go upstairs my friend."

"Agreed," Kevin responded, placing his cup on the table as well. "Let's go."

*

"Okay then," Danielle said with a sigh. "Thank-you for the update." Halundi's message was succinct, and given without emotion. The numbers continued to be impossibly high. She checked her watch and realized lunch had slipped by without notice. It was just after 1:00 o'clock. If Halundi was in the patient's room recently, then perhaps the patient was still awake. Then again, if the situation continues to be dire, perhaps not. Danielle didn't want to deprive Jahny of comfort or rest, but felt a distinct urge to see him nonetheless. Her conversation with him the day before went well. If he is feeling at all well, or even if he isn't, he might very well be waiting for her

367

return. He did seem to relish their discussion and she did commit to continue. Lunch could wait. She wrote a few scrambled notes on the pad at her desk, pulled her keys from the drawer, and proceeded out of her office.

Danielle had other patients to consider today as well, but Jahny's condition placed him at the top of her to do list. Regardless, she was most strongly motivated to focus on his case for reasons she couldn't quite pinpoint. There were several professional reasons why this case was particularly engaging, but something else was at play here. Therapeutic intervention was critically important given the situation, but the usual procedures and protocols didn't readily apply. Like trying to fit a square peg into a round hole, she was unable to fit a diagnosis to the behaviour that brought Jahny to her attention in the first place. It wasn't for lack of engagement. She'd had significant opportunity to converse with him despite his situation. He wasn't expected to be conscious at all. Instead, he'd even managed to draw her into his orbit of discussion and focus much more adeptly than she had managed to do. Who was the professional here? That wasn't the point, she told herself. If truth be told, the few chats they shared had succeeded in getting her to think about things too. If any therapeutic intervention was taking place, it could be described as reciprocal. They were both being influenced by the exchange. Furthermore, Jahny clearly had a similar effect on others. That woman Emma, who came to the financial rescue of a stranger, was a good example. Two other examples were the medevacs who uncharacteristically took more than a passing interest in a stranger they came across on the job. It was more than curious, she thought. In fact, it wouldn't be all that surprising if she were to run into one of them upstairs.

"Dr. Sridhar... Danielle," she heard someone call out behind her.

Danielle stopped and turned around. Well, speak of the devil, she thought to herself. It's Emma and her friend. "Good afternoon. Let me guess. You're here to see Jahny."

Emma suddenly appeared concerned. "It is still possible to see him, I hope. I didn't make it here yesterday. The last time I saw him was on Wednesday morning when we were all in his room. I didn't make it here until this afternoon because I wanted my friend Enrique to accompany me. Jahny is still upstairs, isn't he?"

"As far as I know. I just spoke to Dr. Halundi. There hasn't been any improvement. The case continues to elude explanation. That's why I'm on my way up there right now. I would say it's a coincidence meeting you at this moment Emma, but I'm not sure coincidence is the right word. Interestingly enough, it just occurred to me that I might run into you upstairs. That is a little strange I suppose, but maybe not. After all, you're aware of his condition too. That does lend a sense of urgency to the situation, doesn't it? If Jahny is awake and is comfortable with having visitors, it may be quite good for him. Let's catch the elevator and go see."

As soon as they began walking, two uniformed men crossed their paths from the adjacent hallway. All five people noticed one another simultaneously and stopped. "This isn't coincidence," Emma blurted out, "but perhaps it's fate, fortune, or even destiny. This is pretty strange Danielle."

"Well hello," Kevin said. "If it isn't Ms. Emma and the man from JPL. Hello again to you too Dr. Sridhar. I would ask what brings you three here, but I think we already know the answer to that. You're going upstairs, aren't you? So are we. Do you know if this is a good time?"

"I'm not sure about that," replied Danielle, "but good or bad, time is probably short. Come along then."

The nurse up on the unit just smiled and nodded when the group led by Danielle walked by the desk. They continued down the hall to room 610. When they arrived and walked in, Jahny was sitting up as though he was expecting them once again. Each of them noted the occurrence, but none were surprised. Jahny smiled and raised his eyebrows, but said nothing as each one shuffled in and congregated at the foot of his bed.

Dr. Sridhar was the first to speak. "Good afternoon Jahny. I ran into this curious group downstairs. Just like me, they were on their way up for a visit. They can tell you why they've returned in just a moment. How are you Jahny? Is this little intrusion appropriate, or would you rather we reconvene separately, or at another time?"

Jahny politely raised his right hand to indicate he was pleased to see them, but still didn't say a word. After a brief awkward moment, Emma spoke up first.

"Hello again Jahny," she began. "Thank-you for seeing us. I admit, I have some mixed feelings about intruding on you again this afternoon, but in my heart, I just felt like it would be okay. You look better than when I saw you last. I hope that means you are feeling better too. Maybe it's just the persona you exhibit. You tend to seem calm when I see you. In the short time since we met, you seem to exude a kind of confidence that most people rarely express. That's reassuring, even impressive, given your situation. It gives you a credibility that extends itself to any exchange between you and others in your company. Even though I don't have the answers I sought originally, I still feel reassured. Originally, I was concerned about a possible connection between you and my son. I don't feel the need to press you on this so much. I feel confident that everything will work itself out and come to light in its own time. Now I'm not sure I believe you do have any connection with him in any normally recognizable way. There's something else. I'm not sure what. Maybe that's the reason I came this one last time."

Enrique, who was standing beside Emma, made the next gesture. "Hello Jahny. Good to see you again. I don't have any pressing questions or comments. I just accompanied Emma here this afternoon. I hope your condition is improving and you're feeling better."

Kevin spoke next. "Hello Jahny. I agree with Enrique here. It's good to see you looking well. I came to speak with you if you're up for it. You already know I suspected you may be a special visitor, so to speak. I still feel that's a distinct possibility, especially after talking to some friends last night. Whether it turns out to be true, or not, please, please, please, don't think of me as a threat in any way, shape or form Jahny. It may be way off the mark, but whoever, or whatever you are, I do believe you're a key to something special. I'm hoping you are what I think you are. My partner here also happened to be visiting with the same friends last night. Despite any differences we may have presented when we spoke to you on Wednesday morning, our ideas may not differ all that much now. That's why we decided to come back together to see you."

Jahny's smile broadened as he turned toward Darnell, but he still remained quiet. Darnell recognized his cue and returned a smile, albeit a slightly nervous one. "First of all Jahny, I think I owe you an apology. For lack of a better explanation, you probably saw that I left here on Wednesday in a confused state of mind. Well, I'm feeling more inspired now. As Kevin indicated, our perspectives have shown more cohesion than we originally appreciated. That's helped to lessen my confusion, but we still wanted to come see you. We think you may still be able to clarify things further. It may seem like we all planned to come here together this afternoon, but Kevin and I just ran into the others downstairs. We just happened to be heading up here at the same time. It almost feels like we've been summoned. You do seem to have a magnetic quality to you Jahny. Just like the others, I had to come back to see you. Emma mentioned coincidences when we were here on Wednesday. I don't believe any coincidences are occurring. Something is definitely afoot. Whatever it is, you seem to be a key, as my colleague here just stated."

Danielle finally spoke again as well. "If I have gleaned anything about you so far Jahny, it's that you must be exceptionally pleased to hear all of this. During our last conversation, you were happy to have an opportunity to explore your own ideas, just as these people have come here

370

to explore theirs. It's probably a good idea to try and keep it fairly brief, but I think this little gathering might be of benefit to everyone. What do you think Jahny?"

37

Emma glanced at Jahny. He seemed to be in no rush to answer Danielle's question. Whatever he was thinking, he was clearly pleased. Was it that we came to speak to him again in the first place, or that we all came together, she wondered? He knows each of us now, and he's had two days to digest what everyone had to say last time we met. Again, he seemed to be expecting us just as much as we wanted to return. Jahny's been the focal point here, but each of the others are curious participants in this unusual drama too. Strange how they all became entangled in the circumstances of my return just days ago, yet they're all strangely familiar to me now. We all have divergent interests, but have come in expectation of having them fulfilled here, now, together. That too seems strange, because secretly I hoped, I wanted us all to come together at the same time. It validates the importance I've attached to everything that's happened this week. Their validation validates mine. It's all connected, Emma speculated, but what will Jahny tell us here?

"Thank-you for coming," Jahny said slowly, in a voice barely audible. He cleared his throat, then reached for a cup of water resting on a side table.

Emma glanced at Jahny, then briefly round to the others. She could feel their collective anticipation. This is it, she thought. Let the magic begin.

"One or more of you mentioned coming here separately, but as you can see, we aren't separated. We are anything, but detached," he emphasized. "We have come back together in anticipation of mutual benefit, just as Danielle suggested. That anticipation is what brought us back together, like a magnetic force, or even deeper, gravitational. So, to answer your question doctor, yes, I do agree. Coming together will benefit us all."

Jahny looked around at everyone. His smile appeared feeble, tired, even weak, but he was clearly determined, inspired, and motivated to say a few words. He shuffled himself up to a higher sitting position, adjusted one of the pillows behind him, then looked around again as if to say, 'I'm almost ready.' He cleared his throat again, and took another sip of water. Then his eyes seemed to widen, relishing the moment, absorbing the anticipation he must have sensed.

Finally, he began.

"It may seem like this is just another coincidence to some, but I can assure you that is not the case. The more I pay attention to things less noticeable – to those things that tend to escape a readily-packaged explanation – the more I realize there is no such thing as coincidence.

Coincidences, and other unexplained phenomena, are nothing less than ubiquitous clues that the fabric of the universe is entwined tightly together. Having dabbled in PSI studies Kevin, I'm sure you're aware of this, even if you might not come right out and state it in the same way. Isn't the possibility of a connection between everything the basis of your belief in an association with others from afar?" Kevin was smiling from ear to ear, but remained speechless. Jahny turned back to the others.

"That you should all have found different reasons for returning here this afternoon is particularly marvelous. Spacetime was Einstein's mathematical model for combining the three dimensions of space – width, length, and height – with the dimension of time into a four-dimensional manifold. This was a feature of his theory of relativity. One begins to understand the concept of relativity, or relatedness, between things that were formerly believed to be separate. That was just the beginning, of course. Since then, discoveries suggest even a creative ingenuity enfolded into the very fabric of the universe. It can be expressed through every extension of its overall being. Our coming together here today is a subtle example of its expression. You may all have marveled at recent events, however they unfolded from your perspective. You may all have had realizations that eluded you until these events occurred. Yet, you may all have lingering questions about one or more aspects enmeshed in these occurrences. That may seem disconnected, or incomplete, but there is more. There is always more. Know this: we are in tune with what is."

"Since you have put so much thought into this on your own, and have all returned to seek input from me, I feel like I owe you what little wisdom I may actually have. It may turn out to be significantly less than what you were hoping for, but who knows? Perhaps this is a moment where the universe itself has opportunity to advance self-realization – a process we are all part of whether we recognize it or not. You've come this far. You have begun to recognize it. That's why I say you are in tune with what is. Even with mortality tapping my shoulder, I feel in tune. It's okay to have questions. One should always have them. My friends, I feel weak and well-spent, yet energized by the exciting prospect of being a small extension of the universe, a neuron of sorts, in the great universal mind. I see you perking up Darnell, but don't be prematurely energized. Don't assume that by mentioning the great universal mind, that I'm making reference to any deity. Although it may be godlike, that does not infer an entity in the manner so many envision. I will explain that momentarily, but let me gather my thoughts. This is a crucial and meaningful moment."

"You have all come here because you have been moved by an idea, or a feeling. You have come to believe that I might be the key to unlocking any mystery surrounding it. You want to understand more clearly. It may have begun that way at least, but now you have returned because you realize that whatever it is you're yearning for, it's something you have wanted to know, to understand, your entire lives. It is something alluded to periodically, sometimes by random questioning, at other times through deep, ruminating thoughtfulness, and sometimes by mere coincidence, but it has been welling up in you over time. Sometimes you recognized it, sometimes not so much. That's probably quite normal. Even though most people are too busy pursuing their everyday lives, living their lives in this familiar matrix, as it were, the fundamental nature of our existence calls out to us like the mythical Greek sirens of old. Perhaps a more current metaphor can be found in a film already mentioned in conversation this week. This time I advise you not to be prematurely energized Kevin, but for those here who've seen 'Close Encounters of the Third Kind,' you will recall that the main character was drawn to an image, a shape that had relevance he didn't grasp at first. It turned out to be a location, a meeting place where a realization unfolded. That's what this is here right now. This is where it all comes together."

Jahny looked around at each person individually before continuing. "We all want to know very deeply who we are, where we came from, and where we are going… if anywhere. Perhaps an understanding of life's meaning is linked to its fulfillment, a definition in progress. It is the self-actualization in Abraham Maslow's hierarchy of needs: realizing one's full potential. Throughout my life I've spent much time aspiring toward potential. Maybe I was drawn toward finding meaning in life earlier than others tend to do. Or perhaps," Jahny said looking directly at Danielle, "such a pursuit is an enduring symptom of mental illness. It distracts from everyday life. It creates a sense of purpose and direction divorced from the activities and pursuits of people's everyday lives. Emma has come to realize through her son that much more goes on than normally appears to be the case. That's something we all need to realize if we hope to resolve questions of significance. There is a lot more going on in every aspect of our lives than we routinely consider. The answers we are all looking for are embedded with clues for us to discover them by…but we do have to recognize the clues, don't we?"

"So what are we looking for Jahny? You talk about the meaning of life, but that isn't something tangible. It can't simply be dug up like buried treasure," Emma objected.

"You're absolutely correct," Jahny replied. "It isn't tangible, but it is real. It is even scientific. That's important. It can't just be something we wish for because it sounds comforting, or seems to make sense. Anything we believe in as truth must be based on bedrock information, something really solid. Science has its imperfections, but it is the most reliable method of investigation we have. It seeks proofs. It seeks evidence. It seeks to present the best and most accurate knowledge we can glean. Before anyone can profess to believe in anything, they must recognize how they, how we, know anything. French mathematician Rene Descartes became famous for a simple insight: 'I think, therefore I am.' It established the self as the starting point of all knowledge, and it is, much more than we have realized, but we will arrive at that momentarily."

"First, I want to spend a little time going over information each of you shared with one another and with me moments ago. This is particularly important because the path that led each of you here was unique. These paths need to be considered and explored. You may need to determine whether your path can go on still further. You do not have to be told that the ideas you harbour are curtailed, incomplete. Your fundamental understanding of that is what brought you back here. I will attempt to impart whatever wisdom I can muster for you, but remember: It is likely to be just one of the puzzle pieces needed to complete the interlocking, colourful image you've been painting in your own minds."

Everyone around the room was smiling, Emma noted, even Enrique. It must have been the emphasis Jahny placed on science and evidence. Perhaps that was an intentional enticement specifically crafted for Enrique's benefit. Jahny also enticed the rest of us with references to our particular interests, she observed. He mentioned my son. He mentioned Kevin's PSI studies. He referred to Darnell's religious convictions. He also acknowledged Danielle's original question, and validated her comment about this gathering having mutual benefit. That also validated her expertise, her professionalism. How inclusive, Emma mused. It's a strategy an educator might employ.

Not one of Jahny's guests considered speaking. All waited in quiet anticipation, holding their collective breath. He scanned the room from face to face, engaging everyone directly. "I would like to ask you all a question," he said. "I'm not asking for any responses. Just think about it, consider it, casually scrutinize and dissect it." He paused for a moment to make sure everyone was ready. "I would like you to consider what made you decide to come back here at the specific time you did. By now it is apparent that you all have different reasons, but what brought you here at this moment?" Jahny's smile broadened. Everyone's eyes were on him, He could sense the mental machinery whirring. Knowing better than to interrupt right away, he gave them a few moments to probe their thoughts.

Emma understood why Jahny wanted this to come from them. They needed to own their perspectives. They all needed to clarify, to solidify their own ideas before proceeding. It was simple really. If you don't know where you are, how can you know where you're going? She imagined Jahny as sculptor, studiously determining fractures and faults on the surface, chipping away meticulously, sure and masterly, as though from some very ancient, deep experience, allowing the material to disclose a hidden perfection within. She thought of her own perceptions, inclinations and beliefs, realizing she had probably never thought more about such things than she had this week. Yet she couldn't claim to have clarified them yet – that is in fact what she was here for.

Jahny cleared his throat again, this time to garner everyone's attention. He was ready to continue.

"Each of you can trace back and think of the perceptions you had, the ideas you came up with, and the choices made that brought you from where you were earlier this week to where you are right now. Isn't that right? Perhaps it was an unusual occurrence, a comment, a contradiction, or a source of novel new information that jarred your generally routinized existence, angling perceptions, stimulating fresh viewpoints. Surfing philosophical novelties, you created and fashioned scenarios that extended your perception to include new and exciting possibilities. For some of you, it broadened perceptions you were already leaning toward. For others, it blew the lid right off the existential space – let's call it the 'box' you were occupying previously. Are we all still looking through the same window on this week's events?"

No one objected. Everyone remained in quiet anticipation, speculating how Jahny would proceed. Whenever he spoke, his guests observed every expression and gesture. When he paused, Emma discreetly assessed the others' thoughts and reactions as well. Jahny then spoke again, addressing Enrique directly.

"I get the impression that you're usually a level-headed, reserved, but somewhat skeptical fellow Enrique. The fact that we haven't spoken together directly in the same way I've had a chance to speak with the others probably indicates you are still assessing the whole situation. Marvelous. So for now, I will only mention that your point of entry into the situation was the surprising and unusual find on your property. I admit it must have been an unusual disruption. While unaware that it was on land considered anyone's property, I became fully aware of the quiet, private reconnection with nature that can be achieved there. Since you came there at an even quieter, more contemplative part of the day – twilight – and had to meander across at least a small expanse of desert to do so, I can easily conclude that it is indeed a place you come to for relaxation, and probably contemplation. That makes you someone who appreciates the value of consideration, reflection, meditation, and deliberation. Also marvelous. All are tools for progression. You mentioned only being here to accompany Emma, and I believe you. You are already on the right track and need little, if any, help from me. Please stay, as we are all going to need you here shortly. Thank-you for coming." Jahny turned to Kevin.

"Your point of entry into all this Kevin preceded Enrique's. You've been on the same track for some time. Scenarios you've imagined were complimented, or adjusted by bits of new information acquired here and there. More recently, you became aware of occurrences that began advancing expectations and anticipation. Your unplanned-for proximity to a pattern of events you would not have known about were it not for the profession you are in, fortuitously complimented the very interest you've been nurturing for years. That was first bolstered by the incident involving me on Enrique's land, but not as much as the unusual occurrence you experienced last night. That too is marvelous."

"Which brings me to you Darnell. You have also followed a set of beliefs for a very long time, indeed most of your life, but it too has been complimented by new information. You walked out of here Wednesday morning clearly perturbed. You have returned nearly elated, but that's because of what unfolded later that day. A light was first turned on there. Using your 'weekend' to pursue further enlightenment, you delved into what you already believed was truth, only to find a little more, and that's why you've returned. Perhaps both you and Kevin, now on more closely aligned paths, have merely come here for confirmation of last night's 'revelations.' Be diligent, be patient. You will attain what you're looking for. Marvelous, marvelous. Thank-you for returning Darnell." Jahny glanced at Emma, who had been focused on his words and facial expressions while he addressed the others.

"You have a central role in all this Emma. Although the others may have been jarred by my discovery in a desert cave compounded by details of severity, it was you who aroused and heightened their curiosity. When you presented your disbelief and concern about a possible connection between your son in Canada and the stranger found in the desert, everyone's attention was garnered. That's not to say that the same proverbial light was turned on in everyone's minds, but the light you switched on illuminated, or triggered ideas each of the others pursued independently. We've already spoken about an interconnection between all things. Having gone down the rabbit hole Emma, you've progressed in mere days from wondering about coincidences to considering archetypes derived from Jung's collective unconscious. Since it was you who piqued, and then triggered the others' heightened interest, I would like to make a suggestion. Consider this: If it is possible for one phenomenon to result from an earlier phenomenon, wouldn't we have to concede that the first phenomenon had the potential to produce the second one? I think we could argue, as Aristotle did in one of his discourses on physics, that the potential to produce a particular outcome is an innate property of the thing that produced it. Try to perceive your place in all this. If it doesn't come to you now, then persist until you hear the rest of our discussion here this afternoon. Let's move on then."

"You, Dr. Sridhar, didn't learn about Emma's perceived connection between me and her son until hours later when you met with Emma in your office. Yet you too were aroused, if not by her story, then by her inclination to help a complete stranger on a whim. You are the one person in this room actually commissioned to crack the enigma that I apparently am to these people. That gave you an advantage over the others. You've had a chance to try and figure out what I'm all about, but that hasn't been easy, has it? Despite having had some lengthy discussions with me in comparison to the others, you are just as challenged as they are. You haven't quite figured it all out yet either. Let me say yet again, marvelous!"

This is marvelous, Emma thought in agreement. Whatever happens next, it is going to come from each of us. Jahny is like the chef who adjusts the heat, and stirs the ingredients. Everyone has brought distinctive flavours to the proverbial table. We are about to partake.

Jahny slowly looked around the room again. Emma wondered if that was to ensure everyone was paying attention, or to influence an air of expectation. It worked either way. Everyone seemed as riveted as Emma herself. Jahny continued once more.

"We all like to believe that we have the freedom to mostly do as we please. By freedom in this context, we tend to mean that we have control over what we want to do, more or less. We make choices. We make decisions. They carry us toward achievement of short and long term objectives. According to this belief, freedom and control are exercised by the self. We have self-determination. We have self-control." Jahny paused. "Do we? Each of you believe that you came here of your own free will this afternoon, right? You ended up here this afternoon by following choices you made beginning on Monday evening and then throughout this week, but is that what happened?"

"After you arrived at the prayer breakfast Wednesday morning Darnell, you had an epiphany of sorts. It gathered and grew, bringing together various ideas into a psychological swirl, gathering insight that seemed to just pop right into your head, didn't it?" Emma noticed Darnell's eyes becoming larger as he listened in disbelief. It clearly revealed a pressing question on his mind. How does Jahny know details of what I did on Wednesday morning? Emma had to wonder too. How would Jahny know?

Jahny pressed forward. "And you Kevin…when you sat out on your deck last night looking up at the stars, enjoying a satisfyingly contemplative smoke, you had an epiphany of sorts as well. You didn't feel as though you had conjured it. It came racing into your head, almost materializing out of thin air, didn't it? You were a cosmic observer experiencing mental traffic, a biological chyron, news ticker, streamer of information."

Kevin shuffled slightly with anxious excitement, eyes also widened. Emma was absorbing it all. She no longer thought Jahny appeared weak, or tired. As he spoke, he became more animated. He appeared to be slightly larger than he was, as though he had straightened up, or even grown. Indeed, the entire scene was acquiring a sense of surrealism. Her attempt to absorb Jahny's words and expressions, the other's reactions, however subtle, amid her own expectations and thoughts was prodigious. Yet for all her attention to details in the room, she was momentarily surprised when Jahny redirected his gaze toward her.

"I've already alluded to your central role here this week Emma. Despite being instrumental as a catalyst for the others' progressions, you haven't quite figured out everything for yourself yet. You were originally trying to figure out the connection between me and your son – correction – you originally sought out a secluded locale to figure out your own direction in life. Then this external interruption distracted you, or did it? In the process, you have discovered much more. By returning to that wonderful, incredible little space with the aperture in the desert, you found a window to something much bigger. Yet, you also returned, looking for a final piece to fit the puzzle. Be patient just a little longer Emma." An almost satisfied smile appeared on her face.

Jahny's eyes moved slightly to Emma's left. "Dr. Sridhar, no doubt your professional intuition is to continue taking note of my mental health as you have throughout. I hope I've proven enough of an anomaly to make you explore much more than that," he added in a faux denigrating tone. "Think big."

"Then think bigger – all of you. Your perspective is important, but it must be pervasive. It must encompass your perception of everything. I asked you all to think about the moment you decided to return here. Each of you have ramped up efforts to satisfy curiosity, to find illumination about an unknown, or discover that elusive missing piece. For some, it is a matter of self-searching, self-discovery. In a sense, it's the holy grail. As mentioned before, most people tend not to emerge from the realities of everyday occurrence and routine. This week's events created a crucible whereby this realization could occur. Since you've placed me at the center of these events, you all had to return. You may think this is where it is located, and that may be, but if so, we are more likely to find it together. Any words I am able to contribute may be of help, but ultimately any discovery, or realization, will come from you. And so, here you are – here we are! I admitted something to the good doctor the other day that I believe is true for all of you as well: We all feel like we are on the verge of something. We all have a sense that despite any difficulty associated with it, it is a birth process.

Jahny turned his gaze to Enrique. "I would like to come back to you now Enrique. As I already said, you are the only person in this room with whom I have not had a one-on-one conversation. I realize it's been an unusual week," he said, smiling. There was some brief laughter. Enrique glanced at Jahny momentarily, but then lowered his gaze. Jahny continued. "There is much we could have discussed. Sitting in a mountain canyon immersed in its biophony must be distinctively different than one experienced in the desert. I can't imagine a more pure way of melding with a place. Its essence can be felt. Could one not describe the experience as a reinvention of the sacred?"

Enrique looked up again, but didn't say a word. He may have been surprised by Jahny's insight, just as Darnell, Kevin and Emma were, but he maintained an inscrutable demeanor, and waited. The silence in the room became deafening. Jahny quickly glanced around before speaking to Enrique again. "Perhaps you could help me with something."

All eyes were on Enrique now. "How can I be of help to you Jahny? Clearly, you have insight that eludes me at the moment."

"You are a man of many interests Enrique. Soundscapes and all they can evoke are just one aspect of your many fascinations, curiosities and attractions. Although recently retired, I have no doubt you are still being hounded for intellectual contributions. Isn't it true that colleagues, friends, and even family regularly clamour for crumbs and snippets? That is as it should be, given that you are a person rooted in scientific pursuit, seeking to learn what you can. I too clamour for snippets wherever I can find them. It's important to seek reputable sources. You may be able to help not just me Enrique, but everyone gathered here. You are someone dedicated to establishing knowledge that can be tested for verification. You believe in trying to discover, or uncover, truth. That makes you valuable as an anchor. We can utilize your expertise to measure the validity of our own ideas. Isn't that why Emma brought you with her today? I've established a fairly decent foundation upon which I've built my beliefs, but I admit it is still incomplete, and therefore emergent. More to the point, I'm not sure if I can adequately explain what I've come to understand so far. After all, understanding is one thing; explaining it often proves more difficult. My hope Enrique, is that you will have some insight into what I'm going to attempt to discuss. That way, you will be able to steer it a little straighter along the road. If not, then you can decisively dismantle my thought process and expose it for the idiocy it may present."

There was scattered laughter. To the ever observant Emma, everyone in the room appeared to be wondering where this was going. She wondered the same thing, but continued harbouring high hopes.

Enrique looked up at Jahny, avoiding everyone else's gaze. "Again, you seem to have some insight I don't have Jahny, but if I can be of some help, I will."

"Okay, thank-you. Before I ask Enrique to clarify a scientific concept for all of us, I want to emphasize what you've heard me suggest already. It's important to scrutinize ideas. There can be no validation of truth through faith alone. Truth must be verifiable to prove its own claim. As Einstein once said, 'science has the sole purpose of determining what is.' I don't know how many of you are interested in science. You may or may not have enjoyed it in school. My personal opinion is that many formal school settings tend to suck the life out of most subject matter, but that's another topic. Fortunately, there are other ways to absorb our ever advancing knowledge. Science documentaries and podcasts, when conducted diligently and imaginatively, can summarize important ideas for the public to digest. My scientific interest and knowledge has increased with age, but I always find it important to read multiple accounts of established concepts.

By offering, or emphasizing varying insights and explanations, they help reinforce ideas I'm attempting to grasp and retain. We want to stay on track as we proceed."

"Having said all of that, I would like to turn your attention to something that has long captured my imagination. In fact, as already shared with Dr. Sridhar, I first became interested in this decades ago. Since then, I've read enough books and articles to warrant a college degree, but you will likely get a better explanation from this man. Enrique, could you please explain to all of us what an interference pattern is?"

"An interference pattern," Enrique repeated? That's a common topic in physics these days. After that intro, I was expecting you to ask me something I had no idea about Jahny, so thanks for not embarrassing me. I think I can give this a decent shot."

Enrique was a little surprised by the question, and wondered where Jahny was going with this. He knew many popular magazine articles, and even books over the decades, have invoked consistent observations of quantum interference to imply a list of possibilities. Keeping this audience in mind, Enrique decided to provide the most basic explanation he could.

"Interference," he began, "is the crisscrossing pattern that happens when two or more waves ripple through each other. One of the most obvious examples of this would be dropping a small stone in a pond of still water. The disturbance causes a series of concentric waves to move outward and expand from that point. Dropping a second stone – producing a second set of these circular waves moving outward and expanding – would result in two sets of waves that pass through one another. The arrangement of wave crests and troughs that develop look complicated, and so are known as an interference pattern." Enrique looked up at Jahny again. "Is that what you were looking for?"

"It is," Jahny replied. "Thank-you. It provides a distinct image we can all relate to. I already mentioned a film from the 1970s a moment ago. Now I'm going to invoke a scene from another film to remind you of something familiar. I don't think I really need to ask if everyone here knows who the character Princess Leia Organa is, do I?" Jahny looked around the room once again, stopping at Kevin. "No doubt, our resident alien specialist here could tell us how she was introduced to Star Wars audiences the very first time. Please remind us Kevin."

Kevin responded enthusiastically. "The robot R2D2 began displaying Princess Leia's holographic image while Luke Skywalker was trying to fix its replay feature."

Jahny didn't skip a beat. "Back in 1977, that was a pretty spectacular special effect. The public had very limited experience with holograms at that time. Holograms require lasers to produce them. The laser was only invented in 1960, seventeen years earlier. Anything we might have seen before Star Wars was either a display at a science museum or the two-dimensional postcards that displayed holographic 3-D images when you angled them correctly. A few of us here are old enough to remember that they were somewhat successful commercial oddities in the '60s. The postcards couldn't use lasers. The 3-D images were made possible by a visual trick known as lenticular printing."

Turning again to Enrique, Jahny asked, "Can you please tell us what the connection between an interference pattern and a hologram is? ...And please note," Jahny said, looking around the room. "Whether the object being displayed is the Princess, a cup, an orange, or any object whatsoever, doesn't matter. I wanted to bring up the Princess Leia hologram because it is embedded in pop culture. So Enrique, tell us about interference patterns and holograms."

Enrique plunged right in. "A minute ago I mentioned the crisscrossing pattern that happens when two or more waves ripple through each other in water. Well, that crisscrossing interference pattern can happen when any kind of waves pass through one another. This includes not only waves produced in liquids like water, but also light waves, radio waves -- waves of all kinds and at all frequencies. Holograms need a focused light to create the 3-D effect visually, but holographic information is actually recorded as an interference pattern on a plate of film. If you were to look at that plate the way it is, you wouldn't see much. The holographic information represented in that interference pattern produces a hologram when a laser is used. The light beam from the laser is split into two. The first of the two beams bounces off the object to be photographed. In the case Jahny just presented, that would be Carrie Fisher as Princess Leia. The second of the two beams is then allowed to collide with the first beam via a mirror. The interference pattern that is created when they crisscross is then recorded on film. Interestingly, the pattern on the actual film appears like circles in the same way concentric waves form in water when you drop a stone into it. When a really bright light, especially another laser, is shone through the film, the original object that was filmed reappears as a 3-D image. Now, if Jahny is going where I think he might be going with this, then the fact that a 3-D image can be recorded, stored, and retrieved from a 2-D object like the plate of film is not the point. There is something else remarkable about holograms and how they are recorded as interference patterns."

Jahny sat up further in his bed. He was smiling from ear to ear now. "Brilliant," he muttered. Everyone else in the room found themselves splitting their gaze between Enrique and Jahny.

Enrique continued. "For me, one thing is particularly interesting about the holographic phenomenon. It isn't just that three-dimensionality can be derived from a two-dimensional plate with an interference pattern inscribed on it. This is what I find especially noteworthy: If that plate were to be broken and left in shards, you could still illuminate any of those broken pieces with a laser. The entire image recorded in the interference pattern will still appear as the whole image. Please let me emphasize that point one more time. No matter how many times the photographic plate containing the image of Princess Leia might be broken, each piece will still contain her whole image. There is an interesting explanation for that, but probably too detailed to get into here. The point is that the information is distributed throughout the whole, not relegated to a specific location. I have a feeling Jahny is chomping at the bit and would like to pick it up from here. Back to you Jahny."

"Absolutely brilliant Enrique," Jahny stated emphatically. "Thank-you so much for providing us all with a concise, but clear explanation. I might have rambled on for a bit on that one." Then turning to the others, Jahny prompted them to keep the interference pattern idea in the back of their minds as he proceeded. "Not too long ago during a discussion with Dr. Sridhar here, one thing led to another, and we began discussing something that is often on my mind. Perhaps it's possible that some of you have stumbled on this in some way too." Everyone's attention turned to Jahny.

"We were talking about consciousness," he said. "It's a deeply personal sensation in that, we all have a sense of self. These hands, feet, and so on are part of 'me,' so to speak. The sensations, or feelings we all have also are part of the self, generated from within. They are reactions to external stimuli, perhaps, but it's the mind's interpretation of the stimuli generating our conscious sensations, or feelings. Despite that sense of self we all have, I can't help but wonder where all of the ideas that just seem to pop inside my head come from. Hence the question I asked each of you a few minutes ago about just that point. That may sound like we're veering off into outback territory so to speak – I'm well-aware of that, but clearly, some of us acknowledge that 'extracurricular activity,' if you will, is going on. Otherwise, Emma wouldn't be wondering what the connection is between her son and me. Let me state to you right now that I have never met

Emma's son. If he claims to know me, then he should be the one to reveal how that is the case. Or perhaps," and here Jahny paused momentarily. "Perhaps he has discovered something I haven't yet." This time Emma's eyes widened.

Jahny continued. "It isn't that I disbelieve there is a mechanism for making that possible; it's just that I haven't figured out how to access or utilize it intentionally. I realize that may not explain what I'm trying to say clearly. Let me try again. Science will tell you that the neural activity in human brains operates at low frequencies. That neural activity is electrical in nature and must, like the series of concentric circles overlapping in a pond, intermingle with all the other waves going through one another. What I am saying is that I don't believe all thought that pops into mind has emerged only from within. I think there may be something to the idea that humans, and perhaps other species as well, have varying abilities to tap into information that didn't originate from the activity occurring in our own mental mechanisms. I hope I haven't lost you yet," Jahny said before pausing yet again.

The others in the room were becoming accustomed to his manner. While they waited for Jahny to resume, Emma attempted deciphering facial expressions around the room. While the rest were almost assuredly focused on Jahny's words, she was becoming interested in how everyone was processing all of this. What crumbs and snippets were racing through their minds just now? Were they off on tangents, or inextricably bound to everything being said, salivating for the next morsel?

When he was satisfied that no one had any questions, Jahny resumed. "I believe this interference pattern includes all of the waves permeating the entire universe." Then looking at Enrique directly again, Jahny continued. "That's why it's possible to derive unique experiences by exploring natural biophonies. And before you say anything, if you are planning to Enrique, I want to say this: You and I have never spoken together about that subject. In fact, as already mentioned, we have never spoken together before now. I'm not sure of the process, meaning how I know about that experience, but being in your presence somehow allows me to detect it, just as you gleaned new insight from your experience immersed in a unique biophony. There is transference. As I began to imagine your experience, it became as real to me as it was to you. Didn't you feel like you were enriched by a knowledge, or understanding, that you never had before Enrique? And didn't it seem to come to you from the very place you were in?"

All eyes returned to Enrique. Emma felt a collective excitement rising in the room, even though everyone remained as still and silent as statues. It was a fascinating moment. The back-and-forth between Jahny and Enrique was like watching professional tennis partners sparring to improve their team advantage. She was drawn into the experience by being in their presence, by conveyance transcending words.

Enrique eyed Jahny confidently. "I have indeed had such a recent experience. I also have to admit that I've been skeptical about your insight, but you do present thought-provoking observations. I also think you are earnest in your quest to fathom 'what is.' Furthermore, I think you're absolutely right. Everyone, at some point, has a need, or desire, to ask fundamental questions about who and what we are, where we came from, and where we're going. These are the reasons why institutions like those where I spent my career exist, especially JPL. To use a well-known fictional narrative, 'to boldly go where no one has gone before' is to me as inspiring a phrase as any in the English language."

"We were talking about holography and interference patterns a few minutes ago. It brings to mind an interesting individual most people have never heard of, but whom I had the great privilege of meeting at Caltech over 30 years ago. In fact, I'm pretty sure Bohm died almost that long ago now. I forget what the circumstances of his being there were exactly, but I heard much of what he had to say during his visit. Several colleagues and I had an opportunity to engage with him directly. Afterward, I researched his achievements more extensively. It's a little surprising his work isn't better known by the public."

"So, you may or may not have heard of David Bohm, but he was considered an important mid-20th century physicist. Among other places, he worked at Princeton alongside an older colleague you may have heard of: Albert Einstein. Bohm is known for his landmark work on plasmas and the collective movement of electrons. That sounds complicated, and it is I guess, but it gives you some idea of his stature in the field of physics. Bohm and Einstein had several intense conversations about quantum physics over a six-month period while discussing a textbook that Bohm had written. The book, *Quantum Theory*, is a classic that was published in the early 1950s. It was an important university text for some time, also a testament to Bohm's significance in the field. During these conversations, it became apparent that they both admired quantum theory's ability to predict phenomena, but they both had reservations with some of its foundational interpretation. We'll skip some details because they can distract from points I hope to make clear. If at any point you need to ask for clarification, just interrupt me."

Just like Jahny, Enrique effortlessly took on the persona of an effective educator. Both had an apparent ability to inspire others, to stimulate interest. Both provided glimpses into open secrets not widely-known.

Jahny sat back with an enduring smile still prominent. Emma waited for Enrique to resume along with the others. No one ventured a question or comment just yet. She found herself glancing back and forth between speakers and listeners, absorbing all interaction. This get together was everything she could have imagined. Jahny was clearly enjoying the interaction. The others appeared invariably fascinated as well. Enrique continued.

"I know everyone has heard of quantum mechanics, quantum theory, or quantum physics before, but most people have very little idea what they are. They are, in fact, the same thing, but the varying designations are just representative of the progress of quantum's evolution throughout the 20th century. There are two things to say about quantum theory. They are important to establish before we delve into Bohm any further."

"The first is that when scientists use the word 'theory,' they don't just mean it's an idea in the vicinity of a good guess. In fact, there has to be a fair amount of testable, provable evidence to support the basic concepts before it can even be elevated to the level of a working theory. By the time a set of ideas become a theory, there are already numerous facts to support the premise. Even at that level of confidence, further predictable and then confirmed evidence is required to overturn a currently accepted paradigm. We know our theories are much more than just a set of guesses because we have developed practical applications that could not have become reality otherwise. Without comprehension of the properties and processes of quantum physics, there would be no such things in our modern world as semiconductors, transistors, microprocessors, lasers, or holography, as well as many other things we take for granted in our everyday world."

"The second is that there are important and enigmatic features of quantum physics that need at least some explanation. The terms sound complicated, but I will keep it simple. It's important that you grasp the concepts. If you find yourself intrigued about anything discussed here, there are numerous books at various levels of explanation that you can find in any reputable bookstore. The Rabbit Hole, which you have visited Emma, is a good place to find such material. Mind you, going down the rabbit hole is always a good idea proverbially, as well as literally, at least in my opinion," he joked. Jahny was amused, nodding in agreement. Emma also smiled, having recently benefitted from both.

Enrique was aware that distraction could erode the moment, and continued. "A little background is needed here. Quantum physics arose early in the 20th century to explain scientific observations that just didn't gel with the physics established by Isaac Newton over 300 years ago. Solutions to these problems emerged from developments made by Max Planck in 1900, and then Einstein in 1905. That paved the road for quantum physics, which provides our basic understanding of how everything works at the very small scale of subatomic particles. The supporting evidence has been peer-reviewed and tested hundreds of times around the world since original conclusions were drawn. The same results occur over and over again. It's solid."

"There were two things Einstein established that even high school students are taught and tend to remember. The first is that nothing goes faster than the speed of light. Nothing can go faster than 299,792 kilometers per second, or if you live in either Myanmar or here in the United States and prefer the old imperial measurement, 186,282 miles per second. There is a good explanation for the specific numbers, but that's not relevant here. The second is that time and space are not separate, but facets of the same thing. That's why we now call it spacetime. There is also a good explanation for that, but again, not necessary for our purpose here."

"The work of Einstein, Planck and others, gave us solutions to well-known problems in Newtonian physics, but it also uncovered new ones. Our understanding of how the universe works at the subatomic level of reality was revealed to be inadequate. An important indication of this was a phenomenon called Quantum entanglement. All it means is that when subatomic particles are generated together, their individual states can no longer be described separately. They are now intertwined, or entangled. A weird example of this would be if one particle's spin was clockwise, then the other's would automatically be counterclockwise. Even if they traveled millions of miles apart from one another, that would stay the same. You might consider it a yin and yang quality. Another weird feature of both particles is that they exist in a sort-of blurry, undetermined state until they are actually observed. Think about that! It's like they don't really exist until the moment they are 'seen.' That is a particularly odd condition, but important to remember. I really want to emphasize how odd it is. As soon as the spin direction, or other feature, of one particle is determined by observation, peek-a-boo, then the other instantly assumes the opposite features. Both separate particles are said to be entangled because they 'know' what the other is doing all the time, no matter how far apart they are. It is not only as fast as the speed of light, it is actually instant. It happens right now. That is highly significant. If you haven't quite grasped why this is important, it's because the contradiction forces the conclusion. If the speed of light has been proven to be the fastest speed possible, and if there is instant 'communication' between separate entities over distances requiring the fastest speed possible for a measurable amount of time, however small, then distance means nothing. If something can be detected across the expanse of the universe at the moment it happens, then for all intents and purposes, there is no distance. It proves an underlying unity, or oneness, in the fabric of the universe. It's one of the spectacular feats the Hadron Collider under France and Switzerland can prove accurately over measurable distances in real time."

"This is much more profound than our earlier understanding of the universe. Physicists and lay science enthusiasts may be well-aware of this revision in our understanding, but the public has yet to catch up. The general perception is that the universe is indescribably large, consists mostly of vast, open space, littered periodically by objects both familiar and strange. It also harbors unexpected, extraordinary, even bizarre phenomena that we have already documented, or still hope to discover. In short, we have believed until recently that many separate things make up the whole – that the universe is the sum of its parts. We are coming to see more conclusively that the universe is more of a whole – totally interconnected at the subatomic level. It isn't just a great expanse where separate objects, systems, and phenomena are varying distances from one another."

"We are getting closer toward full comprehension, but haven't arrived yet. That's why the so-called 'theory of everything,' bandied about in scientific circles for decades already, continues to be elusive. It's also why the general public lags behind the actual advances made. Without a clear, easily explainable model for them to grasp, they will hold on to what they already know."

Enrique then looked directly at Emma. "This is a good place to interject a point you may already have grasped. This could possibly help explain what you've been trying to find out. An underlying, subatomic interconnection between all things could help bridge the gap, solve your puzzle. The possibility of a connection between Jahny and your son Anthony now looks more feasible Emma. That popped into mind for obvious reasons, so I had to mention it, but let me proceed with what we're discussing here."

"Earlier, when we began talking about interference patterns," Enrique resumed, "we focused on waves. I need to make some important points that are at the very heart of what quantum physics is all about. Okay, here goes. First point: At any given time, literally everything exists either in wave form, or as a particle. Again, the details and proofs can be researched further by anyone interested. Second point: Everything actually remains in wave form in a universal field of waves until aspects of it are actually observed. This is mind-blowing stuff! I've known this for most of my life now, but I have to admit, it's exciting sharing it with all of you. Let me repeat this: Everything actually remains in wave form in a universal field of waves until aspects of it are actually observed. In other words, when a 'conscious' individual seeks to determine where an individual particle is, or is going, it has to be determined either by direct sight, or by using advanced instrumentation to help the observer make the observation. The particle the observer is looking for, and expecting to detect, exists in wave form until the very moment it is detected, and therefore observed. It is at that very moment that the wave form collapses into particle form. Only then is its position determined in actual spacetime. Einstein referred to such quantum observation as spooky action, but it simply reveals an underlying reality that eludes us at the level of reality we inhabit every day."

Low murmuring in the room indicated heightened interest. Kevin and Darnell exchanged a few words. Jahny was quiet, but still smiling exuberantly. Danielle quietly supervised. Emma continued absorbing it all. Enrique was smiling too. He recalled select bits of conversation he had actually shared with Bohm all those years ago.

"David Bohm," he resumed, "came to see and believe that the universe has both an implicate and explicate order to its makeup. Let me simplify. The implicate order is the underlying aspect of the universe that exists in wave form. You might think of it as the hidden reality of what the universe is. It's the part behind the curtain. It is evidenced by our detection of its fundamental properties like electromagnetism, gravity and energy. The reality we are familiar with – the universe we experience – is what we observe in particle form. It's solid, it's material, it's what we consider 'real.' It's the present, existential matrix we inhabit and see through. It's how we interpret reality, but it is not reality itself."

"Now, after what you've heard so far, imagine this: The entire universe is a very large interference pattern that can be described as – I hope you've already guessed it – a hologram. That's right! A hologram. So as we've already established, our current understanding in physics is that space, as far out there as you can imagine – to the ends of the universe – is packed with various fields of waves, waves of all kinds, varying lengths, and forming a vast interference pattern throughout."

"It's incredible, there's no doubt about that," Enrique emphasized, "but there's even more to all this. If you're interested, there are so many reliable sources, so many books that would be worth your while to explore. It may not be what most people consider casual reading, but it certainly has its own rewards."

Enrique looked at Jahny directly. "I hope I'm not overextending this, but there's one more important thing to point out. It will help clarify the validity of an underlying order to reality." He turned back to the group as a whole. "Even before Bohm had an opportunity to learn anything about holography, before he understood how interference patterns could reproduce three-dimensional images, he once saw a device on a BBC television program that fascinated him. I remember this clearly, because when he was explaining it to us, I had a very distinct image and understanding of what he was describing. He said the device was a glass jar with a rotating cylinder inside. There was a clear liquid in it with a drop of ink floating at the top. When the cylinder was rotated, and the liquid slowly began to swirl, the ink drop slowly spread throughout the liquid until it disappeared. It predictably dissolved into it, a familiar image. Everyone here can imagine one liquid blending into another like that until it disappears. Normally, one would think that was the end of the story. However, when the cylinder was slowly turned in the opposite direction, Bohm could see the ink reconstituting itself back into a droplet. He was still excited about it when recalling the experience to us. It must have been a real 'aha' moment, a lightbulb turning on in his mind. It immediately struck him as being highly relevant to any question about order. The way he explained it, the ink must have maintained an 'organization,' or 'hidden order' that was only revealed as it reconstituted. He went on to explain that was how he first envisioned the idea of enfolded orders in the universe. It led to his ideas about wholeness. It depicts the universe as a type of holomovement. Later, after holography was first invented, or should we say, discovered, and he learned about holograms, that provided the consummate description, a perfect metaphor."

Jahny clapped approvingly. "Well said Enrique. Thank-you so, so much. I've never seen it written, or heard it laid out so straightforwardly. You have not disappointed," he stated most emphatically. "Being a man of science yourself, you lend credibility to clarity as well. These people may have come to hear a few of my words Enrique, but have likely gained a revelation from yours."

Jahny was still smiling from ear to ear as he turned to address the group. "Your timed, collective incursion into my room has proven most beneficial. What was expected to be a discourse from one, is emerging as a discussion between many. I think of it as an outward, or explicate example of interference patterning. We are blending the mixture, aren't we? As we contribute ingredients and observe transformation, our individual brains recognize emerging differences from our personal worldviews. New insight, of course, requires validation by evidence, which generates mind-blowing excitement. The facts, combined with the reaction they evoke, are tattooed onto memory, attaching significance, mapping it onto our minds. There's a name for it, but it eludes me at the moment. All of this reminds me of something else I spoke about recently with Dr. Sridhar. I expressed an intuition, or belief, that consciousness itself must be part of the big picture. It exists in reality, and must therefore be part of what reality is in some way. Einstein theorized that time and space are relative, not absolute, because both space and time can be perceived differently by thinking beings. That's because an object's movement, and how any 'thinking' creature experiences time, is always going to be relative to other things around it. My point remains the same: Consciousness itself must be part of the big picture."

Danielle stepped forward.

38

"Since this is emerging as a discussion," Danielle began, "I would like to interject with a couple of things. First, I want to make a point about something you just brought up Jahny. You were explaining how discussion can help map new information onto our brains, but you couldn't remember the term for it. There is a label being bandied about in neuropsychology circles called infotropism. Basically, infotropism is the brain's tendency to maximize incoming information. It does this by looking for dissimilarities, or variations, to focus on. It prefers to ignore static, relatively unchanging information, which is more like repetitive gossip than useful instruction. It's a description of an energy-saving strategy our brains tend to employ. That's a good thing too, since modern human brains tend to hog about twenty percent of the body's overall energy resources. If what has been said in this room over the last while is true, and interference patterning occurs between all existing waves, then maybe we don't generally hear the additional internal chatter. Perhaps it's infotropism at work in our naturally-occurring interference pattern environment. That brings me to the second thing I would like to add my two cents to, interference patterns."

Now everyone's eyes were turned toward Danielle. "As we were coming up here, I planned only to observe this impromptu gathering. It's important to make sure that our patient is benefitting from the experience, not being worn out to his detriment. If anything, you seem more energized by all of this than could possibly be expected Jahny. That's good, I think, but we should still be mindful of your need to rest. I'll keep my statement brief, so we can move on." Then, addressing the others, Danielle continued. "Okay, so when the conversation turned to holography and interference patterns, it triggered a recall of some interesting psychological research conducted decades ago. That research has helped to formulate our current understanding of how human brains work. There is, of course, much more to learn, but some of what we do know applies to our conversation here."

"Every once in a while, science news filters down through media coverage, classroom discussions, television documentaries, and even late-night talk shows. Eventually it becomes widespread public domain knowledge. You may have heard the name of Wilder Penfield, even if you don't know who he is, or what he was known for. Penfield was an early Canadian neurosurgeon at McGill University's Royal Victoria Hospital in Montreal during the 1920s. His research there became his best-known work. To summarize that research, I will simply say that he offered convincing evidence that specific memories had definite locations in the physical brain.

Researchers already suspected that various parts of the brain were responsible for different functions. I think it's fair to say that most people believe the brain functions that way. Even today, most models are diagrammed with sections and designations that include the visual cortex, the prefrontal cortex, temporal lobe, parietal lobe, and so on."

"However, in the mid-1940s, a resident neurosurgeon named Karl Pribram became involved in a Florida project involving thirty-plus years of research. It revealed something quite different and extraordinary. Even when parts of a physical brain had been damaged, memories were not damaged, or lost along with them. It was even difficult to intentionally eradicate them. In specific studies where areas of rats' brains containing memories of learned abilities were amputated, their memories persisted. That was only the beginning. Throughout his own career afterward, Pribram gathered further evidence that memories don't have specific locations, but are actually distributed throughout the brain."

"Karl Pribram lived well into his nineties. Not long after publishing a summary of his work called *The Form Within*, he died in 2015. I've known about him since my university days, but after seeing that publication, decided to refresh my original interest. That's the same text I went back to last night. I'm glad I did. Once I found it, I immediately went to the index to look up holography. Very interesting."

There was a sense of excitement rising in the room. Jahny interjected. "We just spoke yesterday Dr. Sridhar. You didn't mention anything about holograms. Neither did you mention anything when the topic of holograms came up in earlier conversation amongst the group."

Danielle was smiling now. "That's because I've learned it isn't a good idea to introduce something in your presence that I'm not prepared to explain at length Jahny. Our conversation did trigger a thought about Pribram's work, but I considered it prudent to refresh my memory first."

Jahny was satisfied and said nothing further, but nodded approval and encouragement to resume.

Danielle continued. "In the late 1950s, just a couple years before lasers and holography were invented, Pribram and others had a proverbial 'aha' moment too. They realized that electrical activity in the fine fibers of brain cells had to be regarded as forming a wave front. Pribram recognized that all of these wave fronts reaching synapses from different directions would form interference patterns. It wasn't until he read an article in a science magazine about the first construction of a hologram in the early '60s, that he realized he had a more accurate metaphor for his neuroscientific findings."

"Pribram revealed that the brain can be seen to function holographically. So as we can see, there is an important connection between what Enrique just told us about David Bohm's studies and what I've shared about Karl Pribram's work. The universe and our brains both function like holograms. I suppose that shouldn't be surprising. Logically, if the universe is a hologram, then everything about it, within it, and derived from it would also have to be holographic. Further logic would dictate that if the underlying structure of a hologram is an interference pattern, then there can be little doubt of an interconnection between all facets of the universal interference pattern. We may have found a portal for understanding many, if not all questions we could possibly ask."

For a moment, there was silence. Everyone glanced away from Danielle to scan one another's faces. No one had a question. No one made comment. Emma was particularly aware of a heightened sense of excitement. Was it just her, or did she feel it emanating from the others? Everyone was smiling with anticipation, or was it nervous anxiety? Emma caught Danielle's eye the moment she resumed.

"I also looked into later studies conducted by Karl Lashley, the researcher Pribram worked with when he was still a neurosurgical resident in Florida. As it turns out, Lashley also discovered that so-called visual centers of the brain exhibited similar features. Even after removing 90 percent of a rat's visual cortex, where the brain receives and interprets what the eye sees, the rat could still perform various tasks requiring complex visual skills afterward. The memory of how to perform them was retained. This was also proven true when further studies were conducted later on cats and monkeys. Pribram found that up to 98 percent of a cat's optic nerves can be severed without seriously impairing any memory of its visual abilities. It cemented Pribram's ideas. The brain creates internal holograms for perceiving and storing information. Vision is holographic too."

"Well, that is mind-blowing," Enrique interjected. "It explains something I've always considered baffling. I once read that the famous physicist and mathematician John Von Neumann calculated that over a typical human lifetime, the brain stores approximately 3×10^{20} bits of information. That is 300 sextillion bits of information. Most people can't fathom numbers any higher than a trillion. I've always wondered how that was possible in a piece of grey matter that only weighs three pounds and fits inside these thick skulls of ours. Well, if brains work like holograms, then one can imagine how all those folds in the brain could facilitate strategic storage

395

abilities. The angles at which all possible interference patterns intersect can be infinite, just like slicing a pie into an infinite number of thinner pieces. A brain functions like a holographic pie! It could be imagined as being defined by the function pi. That is something. Wow!"

"Even that may not be all." This time it was Kevin, who had been standing in the room quietly listening to the others the entire time. "You're right Enrique," he declared, looking straight at him with eyes wide with excitement. "This is mind-blowing! Everything that's been said so far has got me spinning. This week when I learned you worked for NASA, I just had to pick your brain. I had to engage with you to see what you know, to try and get you to reveal some of what you know. I have to admit Enrique, it was exciting to have such an opportunity. I had solid reasons for suspecting Jahny might be extraterrestrial, so when I realized that a former NASA guy owned the property where this possible alien was found, well, that seemed a little too coincidental for me to ignore. Now, after last night's revelations and hearing everything that's been shared this afternoon, I'm less curious about your connection to Jahny. The information that seems to be coming together here makes sense to me. I'm beginning to see things a little differently than I have been too. Still, there are a few thoughts I would like to share that might contribute to this discussion."

"Last night, I was sitting on my back sundeck watching the stars, just as Jahny described earlier. It was an evening made wondrous not only by staring at the vast, beautiful array of lights in the firmament above, but by that peaceful smoke I enjoyed along with it. If we really do live in the midst of a grand interference pattern as has been suggested here, then that peaceful smoke acts something like the infotropism the good doctor here described minutes ago. It helps me disregard any additional internal chatter."

There were a few chuckles, but everyone appeared eager to hear whatever was coming next. Kevin picked up on that and felt encouraged. While thinking about this group on the deck last night, he remembered wondering what they would think about his book collection. He had some doubts. After hearing what Jahny, Enrique and Danielle had to say so far today, he felt more self-assured.

"I've had an interest in the possibility that aliens exist for two reasons: The first is that if life can exist here, then why not somewhere else in this vast universe too? The second follows similar logic mentioned already: Just because we don't know all the answers, that doesn't mean that answers don't exist. I don't know about you, but when something interests me enough to raise

396

my curiosity, I absolutely need to know more. Only two things can happen as you dig deeper: Either you come to a dead end; or you learn enough to take you one step further. As long as you can continue a step further, why stop? Everyone loves a good mystery, right? I do. That's why I have books that attempt to explain so many different topics at home. On the surface, I might come across as someone susceptible to conspiracy theories, or other tales of fantasy, but listen: People like me, people like you, anybody can be drawn to something because elements of how it's presented make sense, there's some logic attached to it. That's fair enough, but only to a point. It's up to each of us to determine whether it's worth buying into further. It's up to us to figure out if supporting arguments are valid. That takes real discretion, not wishful thinking, or blind bias. I love a good story as much as anyone; I like to believe in things that seem promising, that offer hope, or can make good in some way, but – and it's a big but: it's very important that it also be verifiable. It's important to me that it's true, that it's real. Sometimes that takes a while to verify. Exploration is not only the fun part, it's the most important. What's that old saying again? Happiness is in the journey."

Kevin proceeded confidently. "Being an alien enthusiast is only one of my interests. I don't usually share my curiosity about every topic, especially those generally disregarded by the science club in the current zeitgeist. Current paradigms tend to be exclusionary, and slow to consider possibilities outside their own established observations. They are often condescending and dismissive. I would rather be challenged on evidence I present than dismissed for the topics I research. Then truths can prevail, everyone wins. I don't usually present any evidence to passing acquaintances. It's better to suggest possibilities as open questions. Let others give their opinions. If something new is learned, pursue it. If not, no harm done. Continue research. That's what I do. There are a few things I want to present here. I'm not claiming them as evidence, but as items to consider while reflecting on what's already been shared.

Except for the faint sound of traffic outside, and the intermittent beeps emitted by monitors around Jahny's bed, it was quiet. Emma took in every detail, even anticipating many. Kevin continued.

"Somewhat surprisingly, Jahny earlier referred to my dabbling in PSI, even though we've never discussed it. For those unfamiliar with the term, it basically refers to psychic phenomena. It doesn't matter what I do or don't believe about various documented incidents. A pertinent fact to point out, however, is that official tax-funded organizations and agencies utilize psychic expertise to help solve practical problems in society. Although I realize there are charlatans among them, some psychics have proven useful enough to be exploited for official purposes like solving crimes. Just last year, I read an article in Forbes magazine about a medium famous for helping law enforcement. As we're all aware, it isn't necessary to understand how something works in order to utilize it. Until fairly recently fire was a complete enigma to humans, even though early ancestors of ours learned to utilize it over a million years ago. I've never read about a psychic who claims to know how their intuitions work, just that they defy statistical probabilities for accuracy. These statistical probabilities haven't been adequately explained yet, and so they aren't incorporated into existing scientific paradigms."

Hmmm, thought Emma. Isn't that interesting. All of this began with coincidence and intuition this week. We've discussed much science since then, but here we are, not coming full-circle necessarily, but looping around to reveal grey areas between what is known and what isn't. Kevin had paused. A few in the group exchanged brief comments before waiting for him to resume. Emma barely heard the commentary. Her own thoughts intermingled with the underlying background noise of medical machinery.

Kevin appeared bolder and even more animated. "Never mind focusing on famous psychics. This holographic explanation you guys have presented is actually appropriate for other things I can think of too." Kevin looked first at Enrique, then Emma. "Remember when we were in the truck going back to the hospital, and your son surprised you with that phone call Emma? At the time, I mentioned having had experience with schizophrenics, and said that sometimes I felt like they were connected, or plugged in to something bigger than we are. There are other instances of this as well. Think about savants. What do we know about them? Not a hell of a lot, but they can often perform amazing feats the rest of us cannot. They seem able to tap into a resource not accessed by others. They are often mistaken as socially, and even mentally disabled. Many people would dismiss them as odd, but there are numerous examples of exemplary accomplishments in mathematics and music. Interestingly, mathematics and music are closely related, occasionally referred to as languages of physics, the lingua franca of the universe. I've seen savants on documentaries find cube roots of numbers with multiple digits almost instantaneously! Such calculations cannot be done that quickly by following methodical conscious processes. Medical researchers believe it arises from somewhere deep in the recesses of the subconscious. I've thought about that assessment a lot. It must be a primal, underlying property of our potential."

Emma noticed Enrique looked less reserved, almost visibly excited. He seemed to be chomping at the bit to interject, but retained his composure, letting Kevin continue.

"When you think about it," Kevin said, "other creatures have similar abilities. Most people have watched bees in action as they collect pollen from flowering plants. Bees even have a particular dance believed to be important for navigation from one plant to another. Bees haven't devised instrumentation for measuring distance or direction. It's also doubtful they perform calculations on the fly. They have managed to devise a successful evolutionary methodology for navigation; bees have been pollinating plants for much longer than humans have existed. Whatever mechanism is responsible for their abilities, there is an awareness of the need to store and share information with other bees. Call it instinct, call it environmental information-gathering, call it whatever you want, that knowledge is being derived from an underlying layer of reality not readily recognizable, or describable at our macro level of conscious experience."

"Exactly," interjected Enrique, unable to stand by quietly any further. "That's why David Bohm developed the ideas of implicate and explicate orders of reality. Again, to make this both concise and clear, the implicate order is like an interference pattern. It is the underlying hidden structure that is only made evident in the hologram derived from it. The hologram, as experienced by the viewer, is the explicate order. Here's another example easy to visualize: Computer programs and apps are written in code. That code is made up of text and various other symbols not seen by the users of those programs and apps. That code is the implicate order because it is what makes the programs and apps work, even though it is not seen by the users. The program that's executed and experienced by the user is the evident, explicate order."

Enrique, smiling from ear to ear, looked at everyone in the room individually. "This is exciting. Everything that's been said so far fits together nicely. This last part is crucial. I know we've been here for a while now, but just to be clear, let me present one more example: One really common sight that can explain this implicate-explicate order thing is that of a typical fountain you might see in a park. Often enough, fountains are elaborate ornamental displays in front of big city office buildings too. Unless you're in Vegas, or the Vatican, the basin of most fountains hold a small body of water. Anyone looking at it would consider the water in the basin as a single body of water. But if you focus on the spray that's ejected from that body of water in the fountain, you can see individual droplets emerging as separate entities, existing momentarily until gravity reabsorbs them into the single pool. The water in the basin of the fountain is the implicate order

399

from which the spraying display emerges. That brief display the viewer experiences is the explicate order. It returns to its source."

"Most interesting Enrique." It was Jahny again. "I have used that metaphor as well, and may even have used it recently in discussion with you doctor. One has to wonder if Carl Jung would have included fountain imagery as an archetype emerging from the collective unconscious."

Coincidences abound, Emma noted. Enrique and Jahny were both tuned into the fountain metaphor. There's also a connection with Jahny's mention of Jung's archetypes, something I've been reading about this week. It's kind of strange how things keep coming back to me, she mused. Emma turned her gaze from Jahny back to Enrique. "There must be a deeper explanation for how that happens. I mean, how does the hidden implicate order manifest itself into the explicate order we experience? Enrique, what were you talking about earlier when you mentioned something about waves collaPSIng into particles? Either you skipped giving us an explanation of that, or I've forgotten it already. Might that be relevant to what we're talking about here?"

"Good point Emma. In fact, it may be most relevant. Give me a few seconds. I want to get this right." Everyone in the room could sense the proverbial wheels turning in Enrique's head as he paused to gather his thoughts. They waited without a sound, but it didn't take long before he was ready to proceed. "There are a few things to clarify first. Okay, here it goes," he said.

"A few hundred years ago when scientists – then referred to as natural philosophers – were trying to figure out what light was, Isaac Newton was convinced it was made of particles. Over the years, other investigators found reason to doubt this. Then about a century later, another British scientist devised a simple, but clever way to prove that light consists of waves. He did this by focusing light on a flat sheet of paper that had variably-spaced holes punched into it. Another flat surface was placed behind the paper. The result was completely unexpected. When the light shone through the holes onto the flat surface behind, the image displayed an unusual series of bands. The scientist realized that the pattern was consistent with any alternating series of enforcing interferences with subtracting interferences. I realize that sounds complicated, but the point is that only waves can produce a result like that. Let me explain why. When encountering the peak of one wave, the trough of another wave causes both to disappear. They effectively cancel each other out. Particles can't do that!"

Enrique had to laugh. "That's not the whole story of course, so don't feel like you're missing something. Stick with me, please. For almost another century, light was then believed to consist of waves, not particles as Newton had first declared. Then Albert Einstein came along. In his famous 1905 paper, which won him the Nobel prize in physics, Einstein was able to explain a curious observation made almost twenty years earlier. It was known as the photoelectric effect. Under slightly different conditions, light presented as a series of massless points, or bullets. Einstein's explanation of light as a wave/particle dichotomy became one of the main arguments that launched the study and development of quantum physics. The first modern double-slit experiment, as it has come to be called, was conducted not long after Einstein's paper. It operated essentially the same way as the experiment conducted by the scientist who proved light consisted of waves, but instead of holes, there were slits in the paper. As discovered much earlier, the light, made up of photons, and therefore considered particle-like in nature, was expected to shine through the slits and produce detectable particle-like marks directly behind each opening. Instead, an interference pattern emerged, clearly displaying a pattern of interacting waves. That first modern experiment confirmed the original observation. Over the past century, the experiment has been replicated hundreds of times. Many universities replicate the experiment as a fundamental demonstration for physics students, so it's probably been conducted thousands of times."

Enrique paused yet again. He could see that everyone was tuned in, but wasn't sure everyone was on board. For an instant, Jahny looked like he wanted to say something. Enrique decided to bypass it. "Hold on. Almost there," he said. Stay with me just a few moments longer. If I don't stick with my train of thought, I may lose it. The most interesting thing about all this happened in subsequent studies. When solid physical structures like electrons were used instead of photons of light, the exact same result occurred over and over and over again. The realization was profound: All particles, including solid ones, have an underlying wave structure too. In the end, it became apparent. Now the interpretation of the data is accepted universally. There is no further question about it."

Enrique trudged on. "Keep in mind that in the double-slit experiment performed so many times over, there were only two slits where photons or electrons could pass through before marking the surface directly behind. Also keep in mind that these photons or electrons don't actually exist as real objects in real locations until they are actually observed. They are not even observed until they make their marks on the surface behind the paper with the slits. This is precisely what Einstein was talking about when he referred to a feature of quantum physics as spooky action. What goes through the holes aren't actual entities, even if they exhibit physical properties like electrons.

Perhaps the best way to characterize them is to describe them as ghostly probabilities of themselves. These ghostly probabilities are the photons or electrons – matter – in wave form as they approach the slits and pass through them simultaneously. By going through both holes at the same time, they interfere with themselves. When enough of these have gone through the slits to create a visual, we see the pattern emerge as it impacts the surface behind the holes. We can then actually see them as the wave they were when they passed through the slits."

"To make this absolutely clear to you. It's as if the photons or electrons don't really exist – or they exist as all possibilities of existence simultaneously – until they are observed. It is at that precise moment when they are observed that they solidify, for lack of a better term, into an actual thing we can see, or determine by instrumentation. That's when they emerge from the implicate order into the explicate order. That's when we see them in particle form. It is only at that moment that their exact location can be determined. Scientists know and understand that's how reality actually works, even though it hasn't filtered down into common knowledge, or what Dr. Sridhar referred to earlier as the public domain. Of course, that's the simplest explanation I can muster. If I was at all successful, then your minds have just been blown like mine was when I first grasped this. Again, I can't emphasize this enough. If you're interested, there are numerous books out there on the topic. It can take a while before it all sinks in, but it's well-worth pursuing."

"Again, thank-you so much Enrique," Jahny said, clasping his hands together to restrain excitement. "Absolutely wonderful, but there is one more idea to tie-in here, and that's the concept of entanglement spoken about earlier. We know that when we make an observation of one particle that is entangled with another, that we can determine the state of the other by what we observe in its entangled partner. When that wave collapses for one, it does so instantly for both, no matter how far apart they are. It's evidence of that strange oneness of a universe bifurcated into implicate and explicate realities. The collaPSIng waves identify the intersection of space and time from the observer's perspective, initiating the instantaneous emergence of the particle reality we find ourselves in. It could be stated that we create the reality we experience as we experience it. To put it this way, the reason it is so difficult to peer over the box, or framework, we exist within, has to do with the fact that we're creating the box as we try to observe what's outside of it. As per relativity and its quantum properties, shape and dimensionality change as our perceptions change. It isn't so easy to peer over an edge that is continually in flux."

Then, the sound of silence, interrupted only by intermittent hums and beeps for several moments. Everyone seemed to be letting these last words sink in. Finally, the clearing of a throat followed by a muffled, baritone apology. Darnell stepped forward. Emma raised a brow. She had been wondering when he would break his silence. He'd been standing by observing everyone else's interaction ever since the group walked in. Whenever Emma had glanced in his direction, she noted the serious visage he maintained throughout. She could see he was engaged, even if he didn't say a word until now. Darnell's voice was deep, but he spoke softly.

"This has all been most informative. Everyone's had something valuable to contribute to an incredible discussion," Darnell said slowly. "You too Kevin, but after these past couple days, after our encounter in Dave's office mere hours ago – which blew our minds well before we arrived here this afternoon – I have one question: How do we reconcile what we learned last night with what we've learned today?"

39

The question resonated. It was momentarily silent once again. "How do we reconcile what we learned last night with what we've learned today?" The sentiment behind the question was genuine. Darnell stood tall, eyes wide open with an expression of optimism. He appeared authentic, unpretentious, and sincere. There was no hint of being perturbed, defensive, or offended in any way. A smile slowly emerged on his face, edging ever wider until it spread from ear to ear. One by one, he turned his gaze to each and every person in the room. They in turn began to smile too, waiting patiently for him to speak.

"I'm not sure where to begin. I've never been much of a speaker, and I usually keep my ideas to myself. My deepest beliefs are just that: deeply personal. Given a few words here and there over the past few days, you may have gathered that I'm a person of faith. I have been since I was a child. I was raised that way, although I practice it differently than most folks do. I can't say I believe in religion, but I do believe in spirituality. Despite most people wanting to define their faith by following established rituals, customs and practices, I believe spirituality is a very individual experience. That's why I read and study the good book on my own. I've always wondered why the average person needs an interpreter to explain what God is telling us directly. It's the same for people of other faiths too. There's always a priest, a minister, an imam, rabbi or shaman of some kind to guide you through however they interpret God's word, God's intent, God's mind. I don't believe God needs any of us to be his interpreter. While I've generally followed this line of thinking for most of my adult Christian life, I have to admit, there are probably several things I still believe verbatim because I was indoctrinated into believing them. Should there ever be questions, or analysis of any specific one though, I'd like to think I would be open-minded. Having said that, however, I realize now that I wasn't too open-minded the other day when I left here 'perturbed,' as you described it Jahny. I guess I was though, being caught up in a biblical reference to evil itself. Let me just say a few words about these past few days."

"My colleague Kevin and I have worked together for a while now. If someone were to ask either of us what the other is like, we might both have similar responses. We're both reliable, we're dedicated professionals, we work well as a team, whatever. If such a discussion persisted, I would have to point out an interesting observation. People tend to get along with, and gravitate toward others with similar interests, or cultural commonalities. Kevin and I don't really have either of those, yet we often carry on conversations, laugh, and even poke fun at one another – usually about our divergent interests. You see, we're both readers, but tend to read very different kinds of material. I suppose it gives us both something different to consider besides our own interests. I think we both recognize that as an advantage. It also allows us to regurgitate information we're still trying to digest ourselves. Hearing another person's responses, both serious and comical, can be a great analytical tool. Bouncing ideas back and forth is always a good thing. It certainly doesn't have to be contentious, but it can make for some comical target shooting, so to speak. Kevin likes to rib me about my faith, and I often pick on him for his interest in aliens. It's all good fun; neither of us takes the ribbing too seriously. We do manage to get into some interesting discussions while waiting for calls at work some nights. Such banter – both serious and humorous – helps bond people socially and professionally. It's good all around. However, a funny thing happened on my way to a forum..."

"...We've already heard about Kevin's puffs of inspiration over our mid-week weekend. Mine was largely spent in my home office studying. Although my efforts led me from one revelation to another, it wasn't until I went to a very unusual meeting last night that the greatest revelations of all unfolded. Even more intriguing was the fact that Kevin showed up to the same forum. Neither of us were aware that the other would be there. However divergent our general perspectives have been throughout the time we've known one another, and however different our individual revelations may have been over the past few days, that all melted away last night. We saw how one another's ideas could actually be connected. There was a lot of discussion between us and the others we were meeting with. Many, many possibilities were discussed. To use the expression bandied about here a few times already, I think everyone's minds were blown. Interestingly enough, I think I've gained a little insight into something that may prove more important than everything else. It really is about perception, but it's also really about being open-minded. There can be no such thing as closed-truths, only doors to other levels, or aspects of the truth. Just like the universe itself, my comprehension continues expanding. I can see now that faith isn't about holding onto something you think encapsulates the whole truth. That isn't possible, and shouldn't be desirable. It's far too restricting in scope. It lacks vision. It may be that the heaven we people of faith envision isn't a place of eternal peace and contentment at all. It's one of continual exploration and revelation – in essence, comprehending what God is... and most incredibly, my friends, that brings me to a stark realization I must confess."

"I feel like I have to say this, not so much for anyone else's benefit, but for my own liberation. I've come to see that maybe, just maybe, God isn't at all as I've imagined. I'm realizing that God isn't something that can be fully imagined. I would have to be God to comprehend God. That has to mean that any depiction that I've ever imagined has been incomplete, unfinished, fragmentary. It occurs to me that the word 'deity' may not even be an accurate description. Deity implies a separate, greater other, but even the good book describes the relationship between God and humanity as one between parent and children – the one being an extension of the other. In the first epistle of John, chapter three, the good book says, 'now are we the sons of God, and it doth not yet appear what we shall be.' That implies continuation, that suggests unity – perhaps not very different than the universal oneness spoken of here this afternoon. Different individualized perceptions, but perhaps all viewing the same thing. To reference only a small part of our conversation last night, what Kevin might refer to as aliens, I might refer to as angels. Maybe they're both just explicate expressions of implicate archetypes. I can't help but think they are keys, or perhaps doors: By having an open-minded approach, by suspending entrenched religious beliefs, and also by pushing the boundaries of incomplete scientific paradigms, we transcend differences only to find similarities, linkage, connection."

"You've hit the nail on the head," interjected Jahny. "I don't think you're confused or perturbed in any way now Darnell. In fact, what you've just said may be the most significant insight brought out into the open today. You may have stepped into the taboo forum of suggesting there are constraints to both religion and science, but I agree. This is about open-mindedness, but not just open-mindedness about other ideas or things, known or unknown; that's only part of the equation. Somehow this is about process. It isn't just about trying to understand what reality is, but how we can know and understand it at all. When it comes right down to it, this is about consciousness itself. This is about understanding what consciousness is. What if the ultimate answer isn't to be found in physics, but in biology?"

"You mentioned keys, or perhaps doors Darnell, but this could explain, quite possibly, everything. Since the universe is expanding, however, the quest extends indefinitely, perhaps infinitely. At any point along the way, should one ever think full comprehension has been achieved, it becomes lost by fragmentation, discontinuing linkage from the continually-emerging whole. Be clear about this; the important actions that determine outcomes of everything first emerge from thought processes, from consciousness itself. Remember what I just said: At any point along the way, should one ever think full comprehension has been achieved, it becomes lost by fragmentation. We haven't yet achieved any final answer. There isn't one and can't be one. It's like the example you used Darnell: We have to be God to comprehend God. We have to be the universe to comprehend the universe. That can't be done by observation of the explicate order; it is experienced consciously through the implicate order."

"My friends, we came together here with different perspectives on life. Whatever they may have been, they're changing now. Yet, no one here has changed anyone else's perspectives. We've all been contributing to an emerging understanding of what is. We haven't arrived yet, even as we inch ever closer, because we can never arrive. It's akin to the calculation of pi; it's a property of the calculation of pi. It is continually defined ever more specifically, but full comprehension is an infectiously teasing, infinite quest. It defines the path of eternity."

'Infinite quest,' 'full comprehension,' 'emerging understanding,' 'implicate order,' 'comprehend the universe,' 'biology,' 'consciousness.' These words and phrases echoed repeatedly, permeating Emma's thoughts. She had to step away from where she was standing, instinctively grasping the bed rail, steadying herself. She could hear voices chattering. They seemed distant, then near, then distant again, blending into a single vocalization. Everyone's words and interwoven contributions began to sink in. Her thoughts meandered. Images from the past week passed through her mind. She retraced the days and hours since she first drove out into the desert. This whole cast of now-familiar characters she was surrounded by had all become part of her life, her reality, since then. One event led to the next. It may as well have unfolded like a dream, or watching a suspenseful movie. Even the remote backdrop of Joshua Trees in a harsh desert landscape was straight out of many opening film scenes, she thought. Had I made this story up, I might have placed it in a similar setting.

Emma even found herself retracing the thoughts that were going through her head as she drove through the desert that first day. It's all kind of crazy, she thought. The nostalgia of my surroundings first made me think of my past, and my acquaintance with Enrique. How strange that I should meet up with him again little more than an hour later, especially after all these years – and that was just the first in a string of coincidences and very odd circumstances.

Emma also remembered conversations about coincidences back in Toronto before that. It was almost as though one occurrence instigated the next. That got Emma thinking about the books she had been reading, the conversations she had been part of, and all of the events from one to the next and the next and so on. How very strange this all was, she thought again.

The background chatter, or vocalization, continued. Emma happened to look over at Jahny, who was not engaged with anyone. His eyes were closed. The smile he exhibited while listening to Enrique's earlier explanations had returned. Although worn and tired, he looked content. There almost appeared to be an angelic glow about him. Emma stepped forward a little closer to get a better look. She hoped to get a clearer picture. Instead, images of everything in the room were blurred, distant. Her gaze became fixed as she tried to focus on Jahny. Now only his smile was prominent. His colour had faded. Emma made a short, almost whispered gasp, leaning forward to look still closer. Jahny did not appear to be breathing.

Emma wasn't sure if her slight gasp had alerted the others to Jahny's sedentary posture, or if it was a collective realization. Chatter subsided. All vocalization stopped. She felt a collective staring forward, but all movement around her ceased. There was the longest pause, the loudest silence, the most consciously suspended moment Emma ever experienced…

…And then it unfolded.

Emma tried to look up at the others. She tried to focus her gaze. Everything remained blurry. She couldn't make out details. Visages and other features were no longer apparent. Danielle, Enrique, Kevin and Darnell were now completely quiet. They all began to fade like waves in a fog, then dissipate into ethereal oblivion. All contextual detail had vanished. The place was quiet. The place was void. Emma realized she was holding her breath. Beeps, whirs, and low humming continued for what seemed like a very long time.

How long had she been here? Where exactly is here? It suddenly seemed to be quite bright, a momentarily blinding light, but then, dissipating like mist over a warming lake, it gradually sifted away, disappearing altogether. Emma felt fine. Surely she was at the hospital and not back at the ranch sleeping. This couldn't be a dream. It wasn't a dream. But what was this? Emma suddenly remembered her experience back at the little cave with the aperture. That too was an otherworldly experience, but one she knew she had traversed in her own mind. This was not the same. Emma opened her eyes again, but Jahny and the others were gone. She couldn't move. Dumb-struck by all that just happened, she slowed to near suspension, approaching a frozen moment, a photographic snapshot, or a photomosaic of recent images and sensations.

Emma retraveled the desert, revisited the ranch, rehashed the conversation with the medevacs in the truck. She reassessed her initial encounter with Danielle, and reexamined the shelves down the Rabbit Hole… Again and again she came back to the books she'd been reading, the many ideas that stimulated her imagination, and of course, the walk with Enrique that catapulted her whole week into the realm of the unreal. She remembered the strange and unusual calls from Anthony, words that had provoked so many questions. Anthony, yes Anthony, she thought…

Emma suddenly realized she was in complete darkness and attempted to open her eyes, but her eyes were already open. It was still dark. The others had long dissipated. Out of sight, out of mind, or, out of mind, out of sight? Emma was alone. She sensed no longer standing in the spot where she'd been. In fact, she realized, she was no longer standing at all, but was lying in what felt like a bed. She knew there was only one bed in the room. Jahny had been lying in it until he dissipated into memory. Jahny and the others were quickly becoming a distant past. This was no dream. Everything happens in the present. This was now. Emma became aware of subtle background noises again. Now they were emerging to the forefront of awareness. Beeps, hums, and occasional whirring noises were playing their rhythms, creating music for her, generated by her. It was constant.

One, two, three, four. Emma found herself counting the intervals between sounds. The accompanying humming was becoming drone-like, interrupted only by the faint approach of footsteps becoming louder. Emma did not move. She was unable to move. The footsteps stopped.

She did not feel any alarm, but smelled fresh coffee. She detected the resonance of something being placed on a nearby surface. Everything remained dark. She heard a minor shuffle. The person who had entered the room sat down very close to where she was. It did not feel threatening. She was not alarmed. A smooth but firm hand was placed on her hand. It was familiar. It was reassuring.

"Mother," said a calm voice.

40

The voice was vaguely skewed. That is, it sounded slightly distorted, even distant, although Emma sensed it came from her immediate vicinity. There was at least tentative recognition, and an attempt to rearrange her hand to make the connection. Her hand did not move.

Anthony did not recognize any attempt; he made no reaction. His hand was already resting on hers. Whenever he came into the room, he compulsively felt for a pulse, even though a monitor continuously displayed readings. He began the habit before realizing the ever-present convenience, but continued it as a cue that she had a visitor. He thought if she was able to recognize anything, resting a hand on hers momentarily might distinguish between staff and family.

Then Emma tried to speak, but lips did not move, sound did not utter. Shuffling could be heard as Anthony arranged himself comfortably in the chair beside the bed. She could hear the sound of a cardboard container being opened, then the shuffling of paper wrap. The escaping aroma quickly revealed a bacon cheeseburger and fries. She heard him enjoying his meal over several minutes, then wrap shuffle, cardboard crunching. He dropped all remaining evidence in the small trash bag hanging from the side of the bed table. Anthony took a sip of his barely hot coffee, placed it on the table, then laid his hand back on hers again. It felt colder. He wondered if she felt chill, but saw no indication of tell-tale goose-bumps.

Emma could not see her son, but imagined him. She attended to every sensual clue she detected, mostly sounds, and rendered them into a visual narrative. It was a familiar narrative, appreciative, but frustrating. She sensed being in a medical facility, but only faintly remembering circumstances why. She rarely felt this lucid, often inhabiting a dreamworld melded by sensual input and mind drift.

"I know I said I was just going to the restroom," Anthony began saying, "but trudging through un-shoveled sidewalks earlier made me hungry. Quite a storm is predicted. It looks quieter out there now, but it's supposed to pick up again and last into tomorrow. Anyway, my timing was perfect going downstairs. I ran into my medevac friend on the way down to the cafeteria. I think I mentioned to you the other day that I hadn't seen him in a while. Now I've run into him two days in a row. Crazy coincidences do occur."

Anthony looked over at the monitors. He was fascinated by indicators keeping track of functions he knew little about. How many times over these past months had he sat here watching lights turn on and off, listening to blips, beeps, and various other nameless sounds while daydreaming endlessly? He often imagined being small enough to see what these instruments were measuring. As a kid, he enjoyed Isaac Asimov's *Fantastic Voyage* so much, that he read it a second time immediately afterward. Anthony remembered that every time Asimov's name came up. He also recalled the book's thought-provoking concept. The fantasy of entering one's eye in a microscopic submarine was an adventure like no other. Once inside, the body's complexity was mindboggling, labyrinthine, overwhelmingly impressive. The sheer number of DNA sequences that compile such complexity is particularly captivating, he thought, even if we didn't understand that when Voyage was written. Even more fascinating is the fact that we are now compiling blueprints of organisms. No skyscraper could be as complex. Anthony was amazed by the mind-bending number of processes enacted by amino acids, proteins and other subatomic elements that not only build, but maintain each distinct living organism. It was astonishingly wonderful. So many things could go wrong, but so many things do go right. The many variables interact, process, reformulate, and influence, ever moving forward, Anthony reasoned, in accordance with the arrow of time – universe evolving. Even when catastrophes arise within the arrangement, the continuous stream, the very nature of 'what is' persists unabated, absorbing and recycling even cataclysm into erudition and understanding, benefitting the whole, resiliently advancing. It is pervasive growth and progression. We should remember that when cataclysm has befallen, he thought.

Anthony looked at his Mother's face. "I do feel badly, and can't imagine what being fed through a tube must be like. I hope you're not able to absorb fine smells in silent frustration Mother. I did enjoy my lunch, even though it came from a hospital cafeteria."

There was no reply of course. Anthony could detect slight movement as she inhaled and exhaled softly. Her lips looked dry, and her hair disheveled, retaining only traces of the vibrant image she once was. It was Anthony's retention of that impression that lured him back. It wasn't so easy to let go. Nurses came in regularly enough, but most basic care was attended to in the morning, usually long before he arrived. Every once in a while, Anthony was present when attendants came by to change her position. It was an attempt to avoid bedsores and dry skin. Hopefully, it was also being attended to regularly when family wasn't there. He could see that her skin was particularly dry today. His Mother's hands showed signs of cracking, especially on knuckles and around finger nails. What was it like to lay for months in complete inactivity?

411

Despite reflecting on such matters, this was a state of consciousness Anthony could not fathom. He had spent much time pondering consciousness through philosophers like Kant and Descartes, and psychologies presented by Jung and other insightful minds, but it wasn't until his Mother's accident that he first contemplated this state of being/not-being. Anthony had long been acutely aware of his own restless mind. The brain hogs energy, an indicator of relentless activity. How could there be such a thing as prolonged unconsciousness? While his Mother could not be awakened, failed to respond to sound or light, and did not initiate voluntary actions, how could there be nothing while her body registered life? Unconsciousness is the opposite of consciousness, but to what extent is physical activity an indicator of either? Consciousness is an internal phenomenon, regardless of external expression, isn't it?

An exploration of the brain and mental processes had taken Anthony down many paths. Whenever reconsidering them, he often drifted inadvertently back to Metzinger, philosopher and co-founder of the Association for the Scientific Study of Consciousness. His mesmerizing book 'Being No One' fueled Anthony's pursuit of the matter. The conscious concept of self we all experience is an illusion. It is the amalgamation of multiple processes that form the whole, so to speak. The model is a kind of two-way aperture allowing an organism's processes to form the concept of a whole, constituted self. Dealing with both internal and external stimuli is more efficient that way. It has to be one of Mother Nature's best inventions yet.

As Anthony observed his Mother's face, he had to wonder what sense of self still registered inside her motionless form. To what extent was she 'in there?' He sometimes noticed twitches, the tightening and loosening of intrinsic muscles in her hands, or movement variations in facial musculature. Was this just process, or was it self? Anthony accepted consolation from recent studies suggesting the brain is still working, even when there's an inability to interact. Although activity varies between patients, their brains still react when their bodies do not. Electroencephalographs have revealed that one in seven patients in non-responsive conditions exhibit brain activity similar to healthy individuals. There has to be a punchline in there somewhere, Anthony noted.

"So, what is going on in there Mother? Have you absorbed anything I've spoken to you about these past months," he asked aloud?

No response, no movement, and no longer any surprise. His Mother's accident wasn't the first catastrophe in his life, but it was just as impactful. From shock to anger through despair, and

412

finally acceptance, Anthony had managed this reality. That wasn't always easy, for he was often sorting through many. Sometimes he recognized when his mind would spin off into who knows where; other times he did not. With time and experience, he had learned to detect nuances in his thought processes. He had learned to notice when things were tweaked a little differently. He had ascertained how to adapt, how to adjust into the new, bigger picture. Or was it a game? In a sense, it had to be. The rules of his existence had changed. Again, he had to figure out the new parameters. Anthony looked at his Mother's face again. She was here, but no longer there. If there was any transference, any communication now, it was a one way street. His words might just be sound waves passing through.

Since his own psychological reset, she had been an anchor for him. She could be trusted to tell him when his conversation was difficult to follow. She could be trusted to verify whether something bothering him was real, or just in his head. She was able to be all that without denigrating his feelings, his perceptions, or fueling his lowest moments, even inadvertently. Now she didn't speak at all. There was no indication she detected his presence when he visited, but he came often, three or four times a week.

That habit was the continuation of an already routinized existence. Anthony recalled moving into his own apartment. The place was made possible by a support program initiative seeking to empower individuals with disabilities to be more independent. When still living at his parents' place, he spent most of his time in his room, either reading, listening to music, or surfing online. Having his own place afforded him privacy and solitude. He wasn't one for watching too much television or listening to radio, so those ad-laden annoyances were absent from his hallowed space. Anthony appreciated the proximity to his parents' place. A branch of the Toronto library system could be accessed just blocks away too. It was uniquely appropriate, allowing him independence with readily-available support if needed. He could pursue his intellectual interests and curiosities without disruption, but more importantly, he could regulate communication with others according to need. He often craved self-imposed solitary confinement, sometimes for extended periods. As time passed, he ventured out more regularly. He would walk to his parents' place a few times a week, even before the accident. Sometimes he needed company, but only to a point. He would just be there, saying little to nothing, but appreciating another's presence. His parents recognized those times and respected his space.

Emma and Jean-Marc learned to adjust to increasingly familiar, but harmless eccentricities. As supports and services for their son were discovered and utilized, accommodations were strategized, then put into place. The process, as expected, took a few years. Fortunately, a beleaguering situation turned out better than anticipated. Between medication adjustments, appropriate accommodations, and other individualized supports in place, they came to recognize that their son could live a meaningful existence. Although thankful for what they considered a considerable relief, both Emma and Jean-Marc harboured feelings of remorse. Unwarranted perhaps, but parents often feel responsibility, even for things over which they lack influence. They wonder what else could have been done. As it turned out, it was much less tragic than originally perceived. Their son had stabilized, was engaged in meaningful activities, and was progressing in a way they couldn't have anticipated right after diagnosis. He even came by a few times a week, maintaining contact with others. As Anthony's life changed, he fell away from old friends. Emma became his main outlet for expressing ideas, sharing his thoughts. He claimed there were others, however few, but they were always online.

After the accident, Jean-Marc expected his son's stability to be significantly disrupted, but Anthony adapted in a way his Dad couldn't have foreseen. He showed greater fortitude than many others might in similar circumstances. Jean-Marc came to realize there was more to his son than he dared to acknowledge. He tried to fill Emma's role of providing an outlet for Anthony, but soon recognized that online acquaintances mentioned by his son had probably filled those shoes first. In a way, that was good. He hoped his son would branch out, knowing he would be exclusive about whom he chose to engage with. Unlike fears other parents might have about a child's online engagement, Jean-Marc recognized the internet might be the best place for Anthony to seek out others with like-minded interests. Parents hope to see children exhibit resilience in the face of adversity. Making new connections when old ones fail can be challenging, but important.

In the months that had passed since Emma's accident, Jean-Marc began to marvel at his son's adjustment. He visited his Mother in hospital as often as he had come to see her at the house beforehand. Anthony hadn't fallen into an endless pit of despair as his Dad believed could happen. Instead, his son even acquired the maturity of a caregiver. He didn't stop by the hospital to fuel despair; but to provide companionship for one now unable to connect. Anthony had understandably expressed anxiety when she first fell into this state, believing his Mother was mercilessly trapped. As he educated himself about her condition, however, he adjusted his views,

414

and sought to support her calmly, simply by speaking to her as he might have before. One could even believe he adjusted comfortably.

Anthony stared at his Mother's face for a while. He was always aware of her imprisonment by an unresponsive body, but believed he was conveying comfort and reassurance to a receptive, mindful audience.

"What was I gabbing on about before I went off for a bite again Mother?" Anthony emitted a quiet laugh. "It's still good to be with you, even though conversation is one-sided now. Sometimes I felt that way even before the accident. Not only with you of course, but with anyone I interacted with after becoming a 21st century schizoid man. It isn't all that bad though. Things may be much different for me now than they were before, but that's okay. Being somewhat of a recluse, at least in the eyes of others, suits me just fine. I take great comfort by quietly contemplating the cornucopia of curiosities and wonders all around. The chatter one picks up almost everywhere is often inconsequential. It's a clear reflection of the shallow cultural milieu we all navigate. It is often better to disembark one's imagination into a well-written book, where dialogue has been parsed, analyzed and construed, often into satisfyingly debatable trains of thought. Books inspire, they illuminate and explore progressive ideation. Downloaded into one's head, they can blend with all other resident information, then continue to grow into new species of ideas, transforming the reader into a co-narrator, co-creator as well."

"Despite such lofty inclinations, there may be a morbid aspect to this way of thinking," Anthony continued. "I have wondered what it might be like to be in a state such as you. I'm sure many would be fearful of being trapped, just as I've feared you might be feeling, Mother. Now I'm not so sure I see it that way anymore. With physical needs being attended to, that leaves one's mind free to travel where it will, to imagine without constraint. Or is it not really like that? I wish I knew."

"I know I've said this before, but I want you to know that everything's fine. You and Dad have done well in life by material standards, but that never came across as the most important thing. You both inspired me to value intellectual currency: the desire to explore; to discover; to understand. I didn't realize how important that was until everything else in my life was stripped down, leaving just me – but a seed was able to germinate and grow. After moving into my own place, I reflected on everything that happened up to that point. I even wrote some verse about it once, years ago already. I've never mentioned it to you before, but the first line went like this:

415

'When these fortress walls finally came down, I found myself standing amongst the rubble of years.' I was in complete despair like that for a long time Mother, but out of the depths, I was able to foresee an ability to rise again – like a phoenix from the ashes. It could only be described in mythical terms really, and in the latter part of that verse, it was expressed just like that: 'Consigned to a labyrinth difficult to flee, but like Jason, who fought the Minotaur and made his escape, I will battle mine and win a freedom long sought from its lair – to sail for years like Odysseus of old, challenging experience and establishing restoration.' I have been able to do that. It's what gave me the strength to come by here and try to infuse it back into you as well. Coming here and talking to you gives me hope. Maybe you're absorbing my words. Maybe you're churning them together into some semblance of comfort, some semblance of peace in your heart, in your mind, wherever."

Anthony laughed lightly. "Let's pivot here Mother. I just remembered what I wanted to get into before going down to the cafeteria." He leaned over, reached into his backpack and pulled out a book. "Since I was telling you about my preference for reading books over engaging in discussion a few minutes ago, maybe you'd like to get back to this one. I read a few excerpts from it to you last week, but I have now finished it. Good stuff."

"I know you were always too polite to show your boredom with some of my ramblings in the past. I hope reading Kant and Jung to you over these past months hasn't been too dreadful. I got through this book fairly quickly. I had just started it when I read a few excerpts to you last week. Although I've always been into aliens and space stuff, it never occurred to me to read about astronauts' experiences in space until Chris Hadfield, but Mitchell really got me thinking. Hadfield, of course, was an inspiration while growing up. My friends and I – as well as many other Canadian kids, no doubt – came to realize we didn't have to be American or Russian to get into space. It made the whole idea of a possible space encounter real to me. I came across Mitchell's book at my neighbourhood rabbit hole, the library branch down the street. It didn't take long to see this guy's commitment to science was solid. That's why I was able to stick with the book when he began discussing more esoteric ideas. I wouldn't mind getting into it with you more than I have so far, because I'm impressed. When I first introduced it, I was almost convinced you were too. There have been a few times when I've noticed your monitors indicating aberrations from the norms your vital signs tend to exhibit. I don't know what they mean Mother, but I like to think they're an indication you're responding. It might just be a response to sound, and not any reaction to what's actually being said, but who knows? I noticed monitor readings fluctuating while reading

416

Mitchell last time. Monitor readings today are kind of flat in comparison. Maybe we'll just leave it for now after all."

"I did have a chance to get into it with my psych this week anyway. He's turned out to be just as good as Dr. Wrickay, the older psych I had for a few years. I know you remember him. You thought it was cool that his family came from the same area where you grew up. Whether you're aware of it or not, I know I told you that he retired and moved back to the States right around the time of your accident. I remember telling you that because I was anxious about the new psych at first. When I received an email verification of my first appointment with him, I was kind of turned off just by his name. It sounded so formal. I expected him to be a stiff, someone about as approachable as any alien I could imagine. Anyway, Dr. Daniel Jonathan Shrader turned out to be different than I expected. He wasn't formal at all, and even took me by surprise when he said he didn't like being referred to by any title. He prefers being informal, and called by his middle name. That's why I always call him Johnny whenever I mention my sessions. I don't remember if I told you this, but I thought he was American at first, just like the other psych. His accent was definitely east coast, not unlike drawls expressed by characters in gangster movies I like to watch sometimes." Anthony laughed. "As it turns out, he's from Halifax, not New York or Jersey."

"He may be a psychiatrist, but he's clearly well-read. Our conversation about Mitchell's ideas was nothing short of inspirational. He even said he'd look into the astronaut's work himself, so we could get into it further next time. I realized afterward just how positive that really was. It probably helped me better than any other session I'd had up to then. Wrickay was decent too, but psychs tend to keep asking how you feel about this, or think about that. Johnny engages me like a peer. He doesn't condescend, even unintentionally. Anyway, that session was particularly good. It generated new questions, new insights. I love that. This psych Johnny is different, not at all what you'd expect."

Anthony took another sip of his now warm coffee, and placed Mitchell's book on the table. He peered out the window. "We've had a lot of snow this winter Mother, and it's starting to snow heavily again. I love watching Mother Nature flex her muscle. We may actually get quite a pile this time. You know, when it snows like this, I often feel like I'm being enclosed in a cocoon. It's a comfortable place where I feel safe, free to contemplate. With others scrambling about to get things done, or make their way home, it becomes possible to have a sense of being an observer, perhaps the lone observer in a sea of activity. In a strange way, it feels very private, or personal.

Although that sea of activity could involve everyone and everything else there is, it remains a solitary experience. I don't know if other people feel like that, or if I really am an alien in comparison to everyone else. Maybe that's why I've always been interested in space, and particularly aliens to the extent I have." He laughed again.

"You may not share my belief that aliens are in contact with governments here on Earth. You may not even believe that aliens exist somewhere out there at all, but you have to admit, it inspires the imagination. Consider the possibilities! We all know prominent scientists like Stephen Hawking have issued warnings about pursuing contact with whoever might be out there. We know from history that more powerful cultures have subdued and dominated lesser ones. That is a possible threat, but I don't think things are like that. Call me crazy Mother – pun intended for your entertainment, of course – but I don't believe it would be like that. If alien intelligence anywhere in the universe is able to overcome the numerous obstacles of surviving long enough, to advance far enough, to travel light years from wherever they're from, then they've likely moved past the petty differences humanity still gets hung up on. They're probably the adults in the theatre."

"If the existence of aliens were to be made evident, think of the changes that would instigate. Humanity, or substantial portions of it, would be confronted with some stark realizations. For one thing, religious dogma would be exposed as incomplete at best. Some might finally recognize the elementary nature of religious belief. They might come to see it as an important stepping stone in the past, but ultimately a childish concept to retain as creed. Then again, despite proofs for alternate explanations of 'what is,' religions and religious ideas have managed to endure. There would undoubtedly be a scramble to reconcile the new reality with long-held beliefs. The convenient solution would be the same one that's been used over and over again. Simply place an emphasis on scriptures that more-closely align to the new reality. I remember Dad offering an interesting example of that. He once explained that when industrial capitalism was firmly established in the West, Christian evangelicals adapted corresponding ideals that also took hold. For centuries it was common to hear words from Matthew's Gospel declaring 'blessed are the poor,' or 'Better is the little of the righteous than the abundance of many wicked' found in Psalm 37. Now preachers prefer to quote other verses, like another one from Psalm 37: 'Delight yourself in the Lord, and he will give you the desires of your heart.' You can now hear, watch, and donate to sources of this mantra on radio, television, via podcasts, or on websites." Anthony chuckled under his breath. "Okay, I'm being a little facetious now, but I thought a familiar quote like that from Dad would crack you up. I hope you are amused in there."

"You know Mother, I have to tell you something. It might make you feel a little better about what happened with me over these past number of years. I wish I could have formulated this in my head before your accident, but it has taken me time to make sense of it all myself. Of course, one would think that being schizophrenic would make it more difficult to make any sense of it – that's both the medical and cultural perception anyway. Yes, I am fully cognizant of the fact that I think differently than anyone who is considered normal, but I'm not convinced that my thought process is necessarily abnormal. It can be described as being on the periphery of any graph depicting normal distribution, but it's still within the range of that distribution. Is that abnormal, or just a less-crowded position on a spectrum? It hasn't been all that long since autism was recognized as a spectrum disorder. Maybe schizophrenia will be recognized as a range of alternate configurations and outcomes in the future too. Maybe it would sound less absurd if it were described as occurring along a span of frequencies. People can visualize that description. They might accept it differently than they do now. Same, same, but different, as the expression goes."

"I know you and Dad have worried about whether I was moving forward, or even able to move forward. That concern was centered around the fact that I like to spend a lot of time alone. People often think, and say out loud, that being alone too much is not good. Authorities in many places even utilize punishments like solitary confinement. It's considered harsher treatment, even a human rights abuse. Yet we know that being alone confers benefit too. Meditation, with or without fasting, takes advantage of being alone and is considered therapeutic. Various religions tout the benefit and importance of spending time alone. Moses, John the Baptist, and Jesus all spent time praying and fasting in the desert. Muslims spend Ramadan fasting, praying and contemplating matters of spiritual benefit. Buddhist and Christian monks have been known to spend much time alone and in silence. Some even became hermits. Just going for a walk alone in the forest can be emotionally and spiritually uplifting. Alone can be okay. I know I need that time, maybe more often than others, but it's important."

"You may not believe what I'm about to tell you Mother, but in a way, the onset of schizophrenia was a kind of catharsis for me. If you can hear me, then you heard that right. It was a kind of release, or a type of liberation. Oh yeah, it was difficult at first, because I didn't know what was happening to me. The world I had known, the people I was familiar with, the norms I

419

took for granted, all these things just kind of dissolved. I guess I did jump over the proverbial edge at the time, didn't I? In a sense though, everyone's reaction around me was to jump right over that edge with me. It was a crisis that didn't really have to be so intense."

"Everything is okay though," Anthony said confidently. "There is no need to worry, no need to stress. It was a turning point. Once all the dust settled, a new me began to emerge. It has been, and continues to be, a metamorphosis. Look at some of the things I've been into over the past few years. How many other people, especially my age, choose to get into reading the likes of Kant and Jung? I admit, sometimes it's two steps forward, one step back, but don't most things tend to move forward that way? Millions upon millions of people just spend their spare time streaming media or playing video games. That can be useful for rest and relaxation when needed, but it's a passive use of one's mind. One is merely following a preordained track, whether that's through the written and acted narrative of a movie or television program, or contained within the established rules and parameters of popular gaming code and algorithms. It's mere entertainment."

"Entertainment is a diversion from the mundane. It may provide temporary relief, which also confers transient benefit, but goes little further. I try to realize current limitations, and then explore, improve, push boundaries. I attempt to be a better version of myself today than I was yesterday. I'm not sure if that's choice or compulsion, but such pursuits fuel a strong drive to learn. They are the well-spring of emergence and transformation. Even the smallest or least consequential thing can be a matter of great interest. That's because nothing is as it appears to be. Everything is wonderfully complex."

"Consider the situation in this room right now Mother. We're in a familiar setting: A patient quietly lies sedentary on a hospital bed, while an attending visitor stays to provide comfort he may or may not be successfully conferring. While the exact goings-on inside your bodily constitution may be known or unknown, they can easily be characterized as a highly interwoven set of circumstances, processes, complications, and other factors, even though there is little to no outward indication of inner operations. These monitors, thankfully, are clear indicators of your inner complexity and functioning."

"In contrast, as the obvious visitor in this setting, any outside observer might assume all kinds of complexities about me, even if they don't actually observe me moving at all. They might wonder about my relationship to the patient, the circumstances that allow me to come at this time of day instead of the busier early evening hours. They might wonder about my profession, marital status, personal character, or my interests. My point in all this is as I stated: Nothing, absolutely nothing is as it appears. Furthermore, it can be made into something entirely different, simply by exercising imagination. It's crazy, it's insane, but it's also true. Think about it! Consider this setting again. Even though I've been coming here fairly regularly for months, not much ever happens. I try to keep you company by reading to you, or just by talking to you like I am today. Sometimes I just sit here quietly, reading, ruminating, or daydreaming to myself. Yet, if an imaginary observer such as I mentioned a moment ago were to look in, even fleetingly, and then retain the image of what they saw, they could fashion that image into a story, a narrative, a type of reality conjured from their own mind. Everything is kind of like that Mother." Anthony laughed a little louder. "Imagine developing a solitary, almost motionless scene like this into a book narrative."

"Anyway Mother, my metamorphosis is ongoing. So is my deep exploration of what it all means. That may unveil realizations and prospects that are promising and/or sobering, but overall, it's better to know than not to know. Being aware of the situation doesn't mean stressing over every aspect of it. For me, it means figuring out where I can make improvements, and then doing so. It also means understanding my ability and inability to make changes, and to focus on those things where I can actually make a difference. The exciting part of all that is contemplating possibilities. It's exciting because exploring possibilities is the process by which we try to peer over the top of the box we currently occupy. Clues about possibilities we didn't realize before can only arise from new learning. That's why it is so important to actively build on whatever knowledge you currently possess. No matter how much anyone does know, still more is better. Learning something new can trigger an idea, even about something completely unrelated. Darwin's observations about Galapagos Finches led to a whole new comprehension of human history."

"…And speaking of finches, birds themselves are remarkable. If we knew enough about other species, we would undoubtedly learn about previously unknown wonders. Did you know that many creatures including birds, bees and whales can perceive magnetic fields and use them to orient themselves? We're still not sure how they do this. One explanation is that birds visualize magnetic fields with some kind of special molecules in their retinas. These molecules are activated by very specific wavelengths of light. The direction of the magnetic field could affect chemical reactions in these molecules, firing signals to the bird's visual cortex, and thereby making it aware of the field's direction. Of course, this all happens at the subatomic level involving electron spin and so on. The magic is really happening at quantum levels. Another theory is that some kind of magnetic sensor exists in birds' bodies that can utilize tiny crystals of iron oxide. Iron is already used by our bodies in numerous metabolic pathways anyway. We've long been aware that iron deficiency can affect cognitive impairment. Perhaps higher levels can affect cognitive functioning to include an extra sense like magnetic positioning. We've all seen how iron can attract a magnet, right? It doesn't seem like a bridge too far. Pretty crazy! Observations and suggestions have led to more than one possible explanation as you would expect, but studies continue. Even without knowing exactly how the ability works, it is possible to imagine what it might be like to have an ability we don't have. In recent years, the film industry has become adept at doing so. They present multiple possibilities in the form of superheroes. I don't have a cartoon-like depiction of what I often feel like, but I do have a sense of being plugged-in, or connected to something that hasn't been scientifically recognized yet. That sense of being plugged-in has generally been really positive."

Anthony peered into his empty styrofoam cup, crumpled it, and tossed it into the small trash bin next to the side table. A nurse walked into the room to check Emma's monitors. She greeted Anthony and asked how he was doing. After all these months, he was familiar with most of the staff on the ward. He responded with the usual "pretty good," and asked the same question he asked during every visit. Small talk proceeded around his Mother's condition over the past day. The nurse informed Anthony that she had been downstairs for routine testing that morning, but doubted the doctor had been informed of results yet. She suggested it was likely to be similar to previous testing the week before. She hadn't noticed any changes. After checking all the monitor readings and examining the I-V insertion site, the nurse commented on slight bruising as well as dry and cracking skin. She promised to return momentarily with some lotion. Anthony told her it would be a good time for him to slip out and get himself a hot chocolate. It was snowing outside, and he didn't feel like navigating it just yet. He would return shortly.

Anthony had to take the elevator down to the basement cafeteria. It was busier than expected. While waiting, he became distracted by news headlines on a mounted television screen. After paying the cashier, he stood off to the side to follow the story to conclusion. There seemed to be a lot of hype about a possible pandemic that first erupted in China weeks earlier. Cases have been spreading in Europe and expected to reach North America soon. Anthony wasn't sure what to think. There had been an uproar about other pandemic possibilities in recent years. The Zika and Ebola viruses didn't turn out to be the imminent cataclysmic disasters media made them out to be. Anthony knew that international organizations like WHO existed to keep an eye on such things. The biggest scare in memory had occurred right here in Toronto when the SARS epidemic threatened to explode back in '03. He was still quite young then, and didn't have any personal recollection of the crisis. It was discussed at school on more than one occasion, but rarely came up in casual conversation anywhere else. He never really thought much about SARS, and wasn't giving this new pandemic threat much thought either.

When Anthony returned to his Mother's room upstairs, the nurse had just finished lathering Emma's dry arms and hands with lotion. "If I don't see you anymore this afternoon, you have a nice day," she said to him as she walked toward the door. Anthony thanked her and wished her the same. He placed his cup on the side table and sat down again.

"I'm back Mother. Since the nurse just left, I see no need to check your pulse. It was Gail today. I hope she took care of everything you needed. She's always pleasant. All of the staff here seem pretty good. They have tough jobs. They attend to the sick and dying, but are easily taken for granted. I doubt any of us appreciate them as much as we probably should. It might take a crisis to garner real appreciation for people who work in the medical system. Maybe one of those possible pandemics the media keeps hyping up will actually materialize one of these days."

Anthony stared out the window, quietly watching the snow come down. He felt warmly detached inside a room six floors above the street below. He couldn't see far, but it was evidently wreaking havoc. It wasn't rush hour yet, but vehicles were already backed up in all directions. Anthony could imagine drivers impatiently waiting for traffic to move faster while calculating alternative routes. He knew Toronto well enough to know that in weather like this, there are none.

"You should be glad you're here quietly waiting out this storm Mother. It looks like there is going to be some accumulation. It's already becoming congested down there, and rush hour is still an hour away. If it keeps coming down as hard as it is now, getting home today will be an adventure."

"I'll keep you company for a while longer. Maybe there will be a lull in the storm. I planned to walk both ways today, but if this doesn't let up at all, it will have to be a bus. I planned to spend some time online tonight. I don't remember how up-to-date I've kept you. Not that you would buy into it all anyway." Anthony started to laugh. "That's too bad though. Things are getting interesting. Sometimes when I tell you some of the stuff I'm into these days Mother, I imagine you trying to pay attention like you used to. When something suddenly clicked-in, and you realized what I was saying, you would express concerns like you were formulating a response all along." Anthony laughed again, patting his Mother's shoulder lightly. "If only that could happen one of these days. The funny thing is, I would know better than to talk to you about this stuff if you were conscious and functioning like you were. Not that my activities are disreputable, or anything. It's just research."

"I want to reconnect with some other dedsurfs and determine if recent updates on issues I'm interested in are worth further study. Recently, there's been a flurry of activity with lots of accompanying buzz. For the most part, I prefer to let others babble. It's better to pay attention and gain an overview. I hope to catch up with my buddy ETfrnd314. He's really serious about searching out new leads. I've told you about some of my conversations with him. Sometimes, I like stringing him along. He seems to believe I have an inside track on things. That makes it fun. I give him reasons to keep on thinking that, mostly by keeping my cards close to my chest. We've exchanged a lot of information, so he's curious about my identity and what I do. That's discouraged on Solsys as I've told you, so even after all this time, he only knows me as AC2492. I wouldn't be surprised if he suspects that I'm an alien." He chuckled insolently.

The snow began falling much heavier over the past few minutes. Anthony stopped talking and gazed outside. There was something invigorating about watching Mother Nature unleash her power over a city of millions. It was a stark reminder of who's who and what's what. Billions of snowflakes descended in a stunning display. A blizzard was forecast, but winds were just picking up and yet to wreak full havoc. The calm before the storm is now over, he thought, but we've been through storms before. Enjoy the display while you can.

Then, unexpectedly, he noticed his Mother's body make a sudden, subtle twitch. He might not have noticed it had he not been sitting right next to the bed. "I'm sorry Mother. I guess I got caught up in the snow falling outside. It's really coming down now." Anthony laughed. "Maybe you can hear me. Maybe you did process that dedsurfs reference after all. Or maybe you would just like me to stop daydreaming out the window and continue."

Anthony did continue glaring out the window at the scene below. Finally, he spoke. "Actually, it is a good idea to keep this conversation going. Earlier, I wanted to reassure you that everything is good. I live a meaningful life. Sharing more about my involvement in Solsys is one good way of doing that. As I've discussed with you before, dedsurfs post and peer review their accumulated information there. It's different than other, more hyped up sites one can also find more readily. Believe it or not, many scholarly articles can actually be found on a relevant range of topics on Solsys. I spent a lot of time on the site in complete anonymity for months at first. I read, followed references cited, and cross-referenced claims and other detailed information with external reliable sources. I was impressed. If there is one thing that has been ingrained into me by you and Dad, it's to always verify sources. A few teachers at school emphasized that too, but probably not enough for most students. Anyway, my involvement has become more sophisticated over time. Learning continually makes me better at new endeavors I hope to achieve. Working on interesting projects is a good way to maintain focus. Also, I plan to follow my interest as far as possible. I may end up having different conclusions than anticipated, but that's okay. My ultimate goal is not to prove what I think I know, but to discover the facts, whatever they turn out to be."

"Schizophrenia can make determination of facts challenging at times, but I continue to adapt. I keep notepads and maintain journals. I cross-reference those notes and make sure they coincide with information from multiple reputable sources. I often leave things for a while, and then get back to them. Perspective can change when considering new information. Sometimes it takes a while to digest. Slowly, but surely, I've been figuring out how to navigate this new experience of life. Now I've emerged as one of the prominent dedsurf contributors on Solsys. Schizophrenia may have deterred me from participating in normal culture and daily activities per se, but I have found avenues for personal growth that are meaningful and rewarding. Could you hope for a better future for anyone?"

"I may never acquire a university degree like you, or Dad, but if you were to read one of my articles, I'm convinced you would be satisfied with its quality, if not its content. At universities, collaboration is encouraged. I work best alone and inconspicuously. Qualifying for disability support certainly has negative connotations for many people, but it's afforded me the opportunity to figure out a path forward. Even if I did acquire a degree, it probably wouldn't help me get a job. Although strides have been made, mental illness is still stigmatized. Despite my quiet engagement and intellectual pursuits, others learning of my diagnosis are more likely to suspect I'm planning a mass murder. People are even less informed about schizophrenia than most other psychological anomalies. That makes them wary and fearful about people like me. That's too bad, because as I've indicated, I'm not sure that schizophrenia is a disability – or has to be anyway. It may eventually prove to be completely different than our current understanding. Recognizing new senses or abilities might be a bridge too far in everyone else's normal reality."

"Lately, I've had good conversations with a couple other dedsurfs. I mentioned ETfrnd314 before, but there are others, including an interesting guy I always refer to as the caveman. Remember I told you about my dream that you met him? It's crazy what can pop into your head, or be transformed through a dream sequence. He hasn't been around for a while though. I have reason to believe something has happened to him. It wouldn't really surprise me. He may be more out there than I am, but he's a thinker. He'll likely reemerge with some blockbuster info. You see Mother? Good practices, good acquaintances, good prospects. Everything's fine. It's all good."

Emma's body suddenly twitched again. It was more of a shudder this time, Anthony thought. He watched her closely. Minute by minute, he noticed increasingly intermittent tremors. She was beginning to shake. Sudden movements became more pronounced. This was unexpected. Anthony had witnessed a lesser version of this a few months ago, but stabilization since then conferred peace of mind. At the time, doctors stated she'd had minor seizures. That wasn't uncommon after accidents where head trauma had occurred. Intense shaking from convulsions would have been more dangerous, he was told then.

His Mother's breathing was becoming increasingly laboured. Her body seemed to be mounting a revolt. Twitching, shaking, and more forceful sudden movements accelerated. The monitors emitted sequences of faster, more erratic beeps. Anthony turned to see, but wasn't sure what he was looking for. Something was happening. Anthony jumped up from his chair, went for the door and called for help. He saw two staff rush around a corner halfway down the hall, hurrying toward 610. Anthony hastened back to his Mother's bed. Then he noticed a straight line appear on one of the monitors. Beeps became uninterrupted drones. How many times had he seen that indication on TV medical dramas? A staff brushed past Anthony to the opposite side of the bed. Another excused herself, prompting Anthony to quickly move aside. One took Emma's pulse while the other checked monitors, adjusted controls and issued directives to others rushing in. A few moments later, Doctor Halundi arrived. They took complimentary positions, one already administering CPR. Coordinated efforts were clearly well-practiced. Anthony almost felt confident, and watched their every move. Minutes into the activity, Anthony detected mounting frustration. Efforts became increasingly frantic, then slowed, and eventually ceased. Heads and shoulders drooped. Staff turned to focus on Anthony, who was standing helplessly aside. He understood what had just taken place.

"She's passed. I'm very sorry," the doctor muttered slowly. Anthony felt a hand rest on his shoulder for a few seconds, then dropping off slowly. Halundi walked out of the room. One of the nurses who regularly worked shifts when Anthony visited, also placed a hand on his shoulder, and asked if he was okay. He nodded affirmatively, but without word. He sat down and put his hand on his Mother's again. "I'm okay," he said to her. "Just give me a few minutes please." The nurse told him to take whatever time he needed. She removed the IV from Emma's arm, then disconnected other wiring, sticky electrode attachments, and bandaging. She secured wiring around the I-V bar and walked the equipment toward the door. The nurse turned to Anthony, repeated sentiment about the loss of his Mother, and left the room. Most of the other staff had already slipped quietly away.

Anthony was alone with his Mother's remains. It was now an empty shell, a mere remnant of who and what she once was. When this all unfolded, he was first alarmed by the sudden change that had precipitated. He had been sitting here peacefully watching the snow fall outside, speaking to his Mother as he often did while visiting. For months, he knew this day, this hour, this moment would come. He anticipated profound sadness, even a mindful reset that could plunge him back into profound depths of depression. Activity in the room dwindled. Sounds from monitors no longer emitted distinct technical rhythms. When the staff had fallen silent in failure, there was a momentary silence louder than any Anthony could remember. He became as contemplative an individual as he had ever been. Now, he quietly sat next to his Mother for what seemed like an eternity. Everything was profoundly still. Even the distant din of noises outside the room seemed muffled, almost nonexistent.

Anthony looked outside the window again. The snow continued falling furiously. He walked closer, placing his face close to the glass, staring into the swirl of white chaos, then back at the sedentary figure lying on the bed. Although he hadn't noticed it earlier, there was a faint smile on her face. He couldn't help but smile too. Everything really is okay, he thought. Anthony never felt in the present more fully than he did at that very moment. It was mood changing, uplifting, strength-infusing, even inspirational. Thoughts of his Mother through the years flitted in and out, but for the most part, his mind drifted expansively. All sorrow dissipated; he felt anything but sadness now. At first Anthony thought he was becoming anxious, but then realized it was

427

exhilaration. He felt a genuine celebration of life welling up in him – not just for his Mother, but for himself, other loved ones, old friends, indeed, all who have ever lived and died. What an incredible thing it is to have existed at all.

He looked at the face lying so peacefully, so tranquil and oblivious to the concerns and activity of the world at large. Anthony suddenly thought of his Dad. It was crucial that he know what happened. Anthony quickly realized that the hospital was probably following protocol for such matters already. He also grasped the inevitability that his Dad would call him as soon as he learned what happened. Jean-Marc wouldn't have known whether Anthony had come by today or not.

The snow was now coming down harder than ever. The wind produced sudden gusts, but then subsided intermittently. Anthony squeezed his Mother's hand, then kissed it. "Perhaps this isn't the end, only an end," he said. Anthony kissed her forehead, then slowly, reluctantly, he let her hand go, gathered his things and put on his coat, scarf and gloves. He turned off his phone before burying it into a pocket. "This would be a perfect time to go for a walk. The snow calls me. Goodbye Mother."

*

Anthony made it down to the front door of the hospital. His mind was racing, his body on autopilot. He pulled his toque down over his ears and tugged at a reluctant coat zipper until it reached his neck. He began walking. It was snowing heavily, but the temperature was bearable. The wind gusts he had witnessed through the window upstairs didn't seem as bad as they had looked. Trudging through the accumulation was slower-going. One also had to be mindful of ice hidden under the snow.

Despite the weather, Anthony had no intention of going home now. His mind was fixed on a place he enjoyed retreating to when opportune. There was a convenient natural haven, a beautiful park with many trees and large shrubbery between here and home. After visits with his Mother, he often liked to sit on a bench in a quiet corner away from the main walks, a refuge in plain sight. There would be no foliage to provide any imagined ceiling for weeks yet, but the falling snow would veil him from the sight of passersby. In a storm like this, he could easily sit in seclusion right out in the open.

The wet snow was accumulating quickly. Several centimeters lay on the ground already. Pedestrians trampled sidewalk snow into heavy slush along the streets, but walks through the park were already blanketed, rendered invisible. No one would be stopping through here now, he thought. Anthony knew the area well, and made his way toward the spot he considered his own. When he arrived, he quickly brushed the snow off half the bench, but left accumulation untouched on the other side. He placed his khaki pack on the seat. The books inside provided extra insulation from the cold bench seat. He was well prepared. All the usual amenities, including toque, scarf, gloves and a winter vest under his coat assured protection from a strengthening blizzard, at least for now. Anthony settled into the spot on the bench, feeling both comfortable and concealed.

As anticipated, there was no one else around. Snow continued falling heavily. Visual range was decreased, so he could barely see the bustle along the park's periphery. Vehicles were moving slowly on all sides. In descending darkness, buses emitted a wider glow. Lighting silhouetted passengers inside moving windows. Cars wedged past yellow traffic lights, inching along sloppy streets. Anthony observed it vaguely through the blur, while his thoughts meandered. Dancing snowflakes fell like winter petals into frost-patterned carpet, dreamily emerging into a natural crystal cathedral all around him.

The afternoon was waning, but it felt much later with the storm's shroud-like advance. The luminous glow through the snow was like an electric beehive buzzing with activity. He felt more alert, senses aroused. Similar bustling pulsated inside Anthony's head. Any distinction between what is 'out there' and what is 'in here' began to conflate, to merge together. Anthony's perception widened like an angled lens. When one's world suddenly changes, perception changes with it. This is where an aperture can open, he mused. This is where one may catch a glimpse, where realizations trigger. Dams may burst, paradigms fall.

Anthony lost all track of time. Comfortable inside insulated clothing, he relished his veiled niche, a virtual igloo, surrounded, yet nurtured by winter. He was beginning to look like a snowman himself. The mental inversion between inside and out enabled correlation with a preferred natural setting.

Settled comfortably in place, Anthony's thoughts returned to his Mother. Just minutes ago, he had left the 6th floor hospital room she had occupied for months. She was there no longer. He sat alone outside, yet inside this remnant of woods. Time itself had frozen. It was the proverbial quantum wave collaPSIng into particle form right now, specificity emerging from a field of virtual possibility.

429

I'm inside here. Everything out there is in here too, existentially lingering in mind, existentially contingent on mind. We are, so to speak, by myself. In my solitude, I am the narrator of the story in the room.

I have occasionally anticipated, even expected this moment, but never quite envisaged, or perhaps, remembered how it unfolded. Despite loss, I'm not bereaved. A more tranquil moment could not have been foreseen. I can see her now, not in hospital as she's been for months, but as alive as she's ever been. Familiar expressions, gestures, and inclinations accompany my memories of her activities, her stories, her achievements and times falling short, her hopes and disappointments. All are recalled, visualized now. I remember conversations, biases and perceptions, phrases repeated periodically, and at times predictably. I retain shared experiences of kindness, understanding, and misunderstandings too. I hear guidance, instruction, opinion and counsel, all recognizable by inspiration, or portent. This is the Mother I know, the one I visualize, the embodiment of multidimensional complexity, an all-inclusive biography in mind.

But what of the Mother I didn't know directly? What about that person apart from others, that person with private thoughts and unshared memories, that person she perceived herself to be? How inclusive can my perception of anyone actually be? Can the mental biography I've conjured possibly comprise the whole from an aspect of that whole? Can it too function holographically, containing its wholeness within each fragment?

It does seem complete, crafted perfectly, just as I need it to be. Everything relevant is carefully painted into the picture. No, it's more fluid than that, emerging as well-crafted music, familiar vibrations in alternate contexts. I extrapolate my familiarity with her routine behaviours and attitudes. Surely they permeate into her activities outside those I've been privy to, present for, or know about. Behaviours, attitudes, indeed her well-established character is recognizable, and therefore predictable from one set of circumstances to another. There are links. There are connections, though subtle, even ubiquitous.

Mother's remains will soon be cremated. All records of her existence will be purged from public records, private accounts, and consigned to final legal documentation. All hints of her presence may remain in material triggers like photos, but they are merely frozen memories, subject to fading. All that truly remains are the mental constructs formulated in the minds of those who knew, or have knowledge of her.

These could be extensive, all-permeating. Along with my own memories are those of others who knew her by varying degrees of acquaintance. Then there are my Mother's own recollections and knowledge of others she knew or had engaged with in life, however briefly - those who came before, during, or even after I ever emerged into her life-song. It stands to reason that everyone and everything throughout time are distinguished by only a few degrees of separation. I perceive a scaffolding of memories, not from there to here and only now arriving in the present, but from the present reaching deep into the past. Everything, even memories of the past and predictions for the future, exists right here, right now.

Can the memories of everyone that ever existed be enfolded into my memory of her? It's an alluring thought, perhaps even an archetypal mechanism, both derived and emerging from a collective unconscious. It's a tantalizing glimpse at infinity, a reliquary of collective conscious experience, shared information. I begin to recognize connections, visualize clarifications. An awareness is emerging, surfacing.

Ah, these short gusts of wind on my face interrupt the cerebral reverie, but are so wonderfully refreshing. Snowflakes cling to my eyebrows, but melt on my face. I sense these proceedings simultaneously, until their permeations fade into uniformity and focus gives way to other incurring phenomena. I sit here quietly, playing audience to a great symphony, conducted by quantum interaction, where consciousness and physics play together. There is no loss here, absorbed into the bigger picture, there is only elation, euphoria, true rapture. A short while ago, all was partial, incomplete, yet to achieve emergence. I now possess a more complete picture of Mother than was ever possible before. How does one lament a life well-lived? One's passing is the final stroke of the brush on the portrait of a life. Everything that I have ever known of her – or of anyone I have known, is encapsulated in mind. They are brought forth whenever I care to reminisce, to re-engage, to reanimate them. These memories, this associated knowledge, along with all those enfolded within, are part of who I am, who all of us are, what all life has ever been. We are the collective, the stardust reflecting light, the perception that completes the equation, conceiving of, and experiencing the universe. It's an exhilarating, grand realization, cogito ergo sum fully realized. All dissolves into pervasive diffusion, universal permeation, a natural, ontological inevitability. It is the reintegration of proverbial water spray back into the fountain.

This place, this representation of physical being at this moment, both as resident within this body and observer of material existence surrounding me, gives way to omnipresent awareness, expansive, all-encompassing. My consciousness is part of a boundless, eminent, pervasive cognizance, the emergent, expanding universe, the great 'what is.' I acknowledge and embrace it, a living universal heritage. All that I know, all that I remember, all that I experience, is enfolded with the knowledge, experience and memories of others. All who ever were, or will be, are a measure thereof, existing as perpetual energy in a vast interference pattern of singular potential. There can be no distinctions unless focused upon for the very purpose of establishing distinctions, for all are one, all is one. The entity I knew as my Mother, and known to others as Emma, continues to be Mother, continues to be Emma, but is also Enrique, Danielle, Jahny, Kevin and Darnell, and everyone she ever knew or imagined, including my alter ego, a mysterious, distant other.

So here we are. I, AC2492, the narrator of this story and a fictional character embedded in this tale, is now completely bound by the imagination of the reader, absorbed into the reader's own visualization of all that has occurred. It may be my story, Emma's story, Enrique's and so on, but as is now evident, it is also the reader's story isn't it? You and I now share an experience that belongs to both of us; we create all this together, right now. The observer and the observed complete the connection.

Even a rainbow is only there when someone is present to see it. If I face away from the sun so that my own shadow is directly in front of me, sunlit water drops that surround that spot at an angle of 42 degrees will produce a rainbow. The thing is, my eyes have to be located at the very spot where the refracted light from the sunlit water droplets converge to complete the necessary geometry. If they don't, there's no rainbow. And if anyone were standing nearby, their location would complete the geometry required to see a different set of sunlit water droplets. In essence, standing right next to me, another individual would be seeing a different rainbow, even though it looks similar to the one I see. The same phenomena would happen if I walked by a lawn sprinkler on a sunny day. That's the point. An observer has to be present.

Consider now the characters you've encountered here. Having read a few hundred pages, you've become familiar with them. You're familiar with their thoughts, their aspirations, their questions. You have a comprehensive idea about who they are, even an image of each of them in your mind. They've become an extension of you. They are your characters now. If you were to leaf back through these pages, taking the time to look again, you would discover something most interesting. Only rare descriptions were provided for any of the characters in this book. Any image you have of them was created by you. Was Emma's hair blonde, brown, grey or white, for

432

example? All are correct, for you the reader have filled in what I chose to leave out, but that's just it, isn't it? It is precisely what the words on the page do not reveal, or clarify, that bids your imagination to cooperate, interact, and contribute. Any description of Emma you formulated will differ from the descriptions others have done. The Emma you became familiar with was the one you created.

This is true of anyone we meet, or know, throughout our lives. We are all partakers and accomplices in the stories we listen to, read and tell; the information we receive and transmit; the interactions we conduct; the knowledge we contribute; and the emotion we share. We intermingle with all that comes into focus at any given time. We are accessories to the emergent creation and evolution of the universe we are deeply integrated with.

And so, if I, AC2492, were now to assume the persona of you, the reader, and acknowledge that I have participated in the creation of this story, I would have to stop and consider the entire scenario and ask the question: What is going on here?

Is this really something new? Perhaps it's something I've not been altogether aware of? Or is it something I've always known and momentarily forgotten? All of these could easily relate to a similar experience familiar to all. During the rapid eye movement phase of our sleep lives, we are affected by various physiological changes. We enter dreamworlds where the imaginary becomes as real as any aspect of our waking lives. Even with only a basic comprehension of the microscopic world of atoms and molecules, we understand our lives occur within a natural metaverse, a virtual environment that appears much differently than its actual composition. Navigating this in our waking lives is as much a product of mental imagery as what goes on during sleep. So do our dreamworlds seem as real as our waking lives, or do our waking lives appear as dreamily as our dreamworlds? Dreamtime, as far as my brain is concerned, is indeed all the time. All that we perceive are our perceptions, as Kant says; my brain must make sense of it all from inside here. So is it something new, something I've not been altogether aware of, or something I've always known and momentarily forgotten?

As I think back, I recall remnants from the deepest alcoves of memory. A realization emerges. All enfolded memory and knowledge resides within a universal, cosmic awareness, empowered by the very electromagnetic field that surrounds and courses through all atomic matter. It is the fountain from which the spray emerges, the well from which temporal perspectives are individualized. When I draw from this well of plenty, to appraise all I've ever sensed, ever learned,

433

or ever even imagined – then I must also realize that what I know is as I've imagined, perhaps always known. It's omnipresent, held in mind, even if not focused upon continuously…

…But what is this awareness, this omnipresence, this consciousness I experience?

Ah, deep breath in, deep breath out. I have to smile thinking about this again. How many times has this question been asked? I almost feel like I've been sitting here for all time. I may as well have been. This is a seminal moment, solitary, yet all-encompassing. The grand desire to comprehend everything is just a logical extension of being able to understand anything at all, isn't it? Consciousness is the essential, primary phenomenon of our entire life experience. I think of it as the 'magic' of being alive, since magic is how we refer to things we know precious little about. Science can't explain it yet. Even physics, the most basic and exact scientific discipline, has never been able to illuminate how a group of molecules firing off electrical signals between themselves inside a lump of grey matter creates the phenomenon of consciousness. How do multiple processes in concert create the illusion of a unified self?

We all know there's still much unexplained. Science tells us that you can never get something out of nothing, but claims the entire universe exploded out of virtually nothing 13.7 billion years ago in an event we've coined as the Big Bang. Isn't that similar to religious ideas where gods create everything magically? It's always important to remind myself that there is one important difference. Science continues to probe further. Religion claims to already have the answers. The Faithful consider their faith a legitimate alternative to explanation. Facts and explanation are indispensable, but comprehension of it all may not necessarily come from somewhere out there.

Mitchell's book comes to mind again. That's right! He wrote that passage that caught my imagination so poignantly. Let me recall how that went. Ah, memory don't fail me now. That's right, it was, it was something like, "I perceived the universe as in some way conscious…But even in the midst of epiphany I did not attach mystical or otherworldly origin to the phenomenon. Rather, I thought it curious and exciting that the brain could spontaneously reorganize information to produce such a fantastically strange experience."

Hmmm, the brain again. There's something to that. Mitchell perceived the universe as in some way conscious, but didn't attach any mystical origin to it. That's a fascinating distinction. I need to take a step back here a little bit. I need to look at this again. I need to refocus the lens to get an even clearer picture.

So, how have I…or more accurately, how have we all been looking at this so far? Several approaches have been addressed already. Darnell, of course, represents the oldest strategy for tackling existential questions. Religion has been with us for thousands of years. In contrast, Enrique spent his life pursuing solid evidence, but would be the first to admit his views aren't conclusive. Kevin embraces theories closer to the fringes of science. They may one day lead to a more comprehensive understanding, but for lack of evidence are even less conclusive. Danielle operates confidently within a profession built on theories of mind, but such confidence was also challenged by Jahny's ideas.

There is an interesting commonality shared by all these varying perceptions. They all look forward. They all exist with an inherent expectation that enlightenment is a future event to be figured out, unveiled, or discovered. That's logical. The arrow of time moves in the same direction. Cause leads to effect. The story of humanity is a narrative of progress. We amass enough knowledge to advance. In turn, advancement leads to further knowledge. The more we know, the more opportunity we have to comprehend.

Well, we may not know everything, but we've come to recognize a difficult riddle: Why do we exist in a Goldilocks universe? How can so many conditions be just right for life to exist? Improbabilities arise from the very beginning of this place we find ourselves in. If the Big Bang had been just a little more powerful than it actually was, even by the order of only one part in a million, it would have expanded too quickly. Galaxies, and everything in them, including all life, could not have emerged. If the nuclear force holding atoms together were decreased by only two percent, nuclei wouldn't even be able to hold together. Hydrogen would have been the only kind of atom in the universe, a singularly plain flavour with only one proton and electron. Who could live in a vanillaverse on a diet? If the gravitational force was any less powerful than it actually is, then our Sun and all other stars would not have been able to ignite at all. It would have been a very dark and cold vanillaverse too. These are just a few of the pertinent facts. There are several. I recall there being well over two hundred parameters that have to be exactly as they are in order for us to exist as we are. Some are sociocultural parameters, like the unusual ability to harness fire. These are unique to our species, at least on this planet.

It's becoming transparent to me now though. Our ancestors certainly had no viable means for explaining the world they experienced. Humanity interacted with the environment similarly to our fellow animals for millennia. Only the intricate interaction of these two hundred plus

435

parameters afforded unique advantages and opportunities. The slow emergence and tweaking of perceptive specialization randomly attained complex socialization, a relatively rare adaptation amongst the millions of life forms that have inhabited this planet. Eventually, and even more rarely, curiosity was aroused, an ability to question and theorize emerged, and we became able to imagine possibilities. Finding answers to questions is not so easy when beginning from scratch. There are no guides. Becoming smart enough to ask questions is not enough to answer them as well. Explaining complexities like our own existence from our primeval ancestors' observations and experience would have been impossible. So early humanity had to extrapolate from their observations and experiences. Other creatures, plants, phenomena like the wind, and even inanimate objects were considered alternate beings interacting within a shared setting. We simply personified them, fashioned them after ourselves. Those with superior natural abilities became templates for conceptualizing supernatural entities. Once supernatural beings could be conceptualized, it became easier to imagine even more extended abilities. So out of both convenience and necessity, supernatural extensions of ourselves were imagined to be infinite, all-knowing, and all-powerful. The idea, first of multiple gods, then a single all-powerful God was born. Gods couldn't create us until we created them. The rest is history. The story, in its numerous incarnations, settled in for millennia.

There is, however, a central point in all this I can't ignore. By invoking a deity, we brought a super being, a super consciousness to the table. This was a necessary, important step. I begin to see a connection. A summarized quantum explanation of the universe, with many aspects that have been peer-reviewed and confirmed numerous times over more than a century, comes to mind. The universe exists as an interconnected electromagnetic interference pattern of wave forms. No distinct entity from within that pattern can be distinguished until its activity is actually observed, completing an equation. The equation requires an observer, just like a rainbow. At the precise moment the equation is completed, the precise location of the observed is made. Wave form instantaneously becomes particle form, producing the reality we perceive. What we perceive as reality is a phenomenon that necessitates consciousness.

Consciousness, ah yes, consciousness. Interestingly enough, there is a kernel of truth to the faithful's fundamental belief that a consciousness we refer to as God could simply will everything into being. Even more interestingly, the very idea that God could do such a thing came from us, creatures with the ability to conjure both the real and unreal in our own minds. So, if we can invoke the idea that a God has such abilities, wouldn't both the concept of such a possibility and its subsequent potential have to primarily reside within the agency conjuring that possibility in the first place? That's us. That's us and all other conscious organisms. Furthermore, that's us, as enfolded into my thought stream right now. Everything about the past and present that I know, including all projections made about the future that I've ever been aware of, exists, right here, right now.

Until we began to consider and analyze our psyche just over a century ago, we had no theories about, or research into, consciousness at all. Before that, our observations and experiences were interpreted through millennia-long spiritual constructs. Our linguistic and cultural abilities elevating us to superior status above fellow organisms in our own minds simply provided chimera to explain our existence in the surroundings we found ourselves in. All this time we have been just as blind to our true nature and place in the universe as our fellow organisms, even as we collectively continue to participate in its ongoing evolution. So what is the nature of this thing we call the universe? What is this phenomenon we call reality? Come on think! I'm on the verge. Does this have to be like giving birth?

Okay, take a long deep breath. Hold it. Breathe out slowly. Ah, the air feels pleasant. Repeat, get a nice, slow rhythm going. Breathe in…out…in…out. I breathe in my very surroundings; I breathe them out. I am a functioning participant with my surroundings. I disengage from distant sounds emanating through falling snow. I hear only the wind. I sense the fresh air. I feel it on my face where snowflakes dissolve on contact. My shoulders ease, my body relaxes. I meld with my surroundings. I'm in complete contemplation of them, near and far.

I think of everything around me. I imagine the cosmos from where this all emerged. Could a chance collection of objects and phenomena produce a two-hundred-plus parameter Goldilocks environment coincidently? How does consciousness fit into the equation? I consider this question recurrently because science still can't explain how consciousness arose from physical matter. There's been no clarification of how neurons exchanging electrical impulses produce the unique experiences we have perceiving beauty, tasting infinite varieties of flavours, smelling aromas both fragrant and foul, and so on. The physical existence we all experience can't be disconnected from those bodily structures coordinating our sensory perceptions of such experiences. Remember, the only things we perceive are our perceptions. These come from our physical senses. They are the essence of our sensual experience. This 'real world' I find myself in – that we all find ourselves in

– isn't so much an object, or collection of objects. It isn't just the sum data collected by our scientific endeavors. It is more accurately visualized as a shared field of experience, an entangled matrix of impressions, awareness and ongoing assessments, all experienced from slightly different angles and circumstances.

We all know from experience that events, situations and reaction can present just as real in the imagination as they can in actuality. This was true of Emma while by herself in the cave with the aperture. It was true of Jahny engaging himself and others philosophically as he lay in a hospital bed. It was true for Enrique immersed in the soundscape of a canyon floor at night…and it is also true of everything I'm thinking about right now, right here where I am.

It is entirely possible to conjure something mentally that affects us as powerfully as if it were real. Many of us have done this religiously throughout history. We also experience this recurrently, both in our dreaming, and daydreaming lives. If I were to suddenly summon an image of a horrible accident affecting a child or close loved-one, it would hit me forcefully. I might physically recoil, even shudder. It would invoke a deep emotional sensation, even physical harm – at least until I could recollect myself and withdraw from the illusion. We prefer to actively banish such imagery as quickly as possible because it is anathema. It is unthinkable. It is too real…

…and then as we have all become aware, of course, things routinely seem real that we know are not. When we watch television, we become completely immersed in an audiovisual display produced and received as an electronic signal. Existing in wave form, it emerges in particle form as pixels on my television screen only when turned on. We view it. We adopt the story and characters, interacting with the narrative in a way that has an actual affect, even as the characters portrayed may be as alive or dead as Schrodinger's proverbial cat. We visualize them in full animation, enacting a scene linked to a random viewing event that may or may not occur. So when I inscribe others into my experience, and also if and when others inscribe me into theirs, the interweaving of our phenomenal fields acts like an interference pattern. It is in effect a single, ever-shifting fabric. It becomes a single phenomenal world. It becomes reality, a collective dimension of our entwined lives. We organically experience life in all its flexible mysterious multiplicity, even before we conceptualize it in any culturally recognizable form.

Never mind movie or television magic. Similarities occur in more primal terms. When I flick my lighter or light a candle, I observe a flame that instantly illuminates everything in its immediate surroundings. I quickly remind myself that a flame is just hot gas. Every source of light

438

emits photons of electromagnetic energy. Interestingly enough, neither electricity nor magnetism have any visual properties. I can't see them, but as these electromagnetic waves radiate outward from their source, they arrive at the retinas in my eyes… Asimov, take me down that fantastic voyage again. Ah, the biology behind our sensations and perception are fascinating. Sight is particularly fantastic. If I could voyage down to an incredibly small scale, I would access a thin little layer of tissue lining the back of my eyes, located right near the optic nerve. Its function and purpose is to receive that invisible electromagnetic energy, convert it into neural signals and then send it to my brain. I am particularly impressed that the cone-shaped cells in my retinas collecting the electromagnetic waves have to be just the right size and shape to even be able to do so. Those incoming waves happen to measure between just 400 and 700 nanometers in length from wavecrest to wavecrest. Every one of some eight million cone-shaped cells in each of my retinas sends impulses to neighbouring neurons. These impulses travel along pathways at 400 kilometres per hour until they arrive at the occipital lobe at the back of my head, assembling reality micro moments later. This is how I visualize the universe 'out there.' The imagery is uniquely assembled by my very own bodily architecture. It is reformulated, it is analyzed, and it is reconstructed to be uniquely experienced by me. All incoming visual information is processed and analyzed efficiently and realistically. I am routinely and ubiquitously convinced that what I see is a direct image of what is out there. I've learned this along the way a few times before, but now it really registers. I perceive it as it is. To put a spin on Lennon, this is life as it happens, even as I focus on other things.

These eyes aren't the only agents of transformative experience. All of my sensory inputs participate in the process. It is easy to believe that a tree falling in the forest makes a sound even when I'm not there to hear it, but as we've all learned in school, it doesn't. Only if there is an organism with the physical apparatus to detect the sudden force of displaced air and matter that occurs when a tree hits the ground, can any interpretation of that displacement by the shape of the apparatus detecting it – our ears – become what we call sound.

I'm sure many of us remember when this concept was first presented. While the explanation made sense, the novelty associated with it was rooted in the fact that we had never considered that before. The quantum connection came later. That was never discussed in high school, but it's become an underlying realization to me now. People living their everyday lives aren't aware of the ongoing transformative process making their experience so permeating, ubiquitous, and omnipresent. Revelations about the transformative processes involving vision and hearing are remarkable enough. They are like learning the tricks that made the magic believable. I comprehend the illusion.

So here I am, a complex cooperative of numerous processes, apparently residing inside the brain of this physical structure, reflecting on these sensations, imagining them to be a singular entity inside looking out – me. I maintain the dictum that all I perceive are the perceptions collected by the physical architecture of my senses. My brain, and the consciousness continuously regenerating in the present, are the source of the reality I experience. The logical premise for this arises, of course, as I am thinking about it, while I consider it. The brain, having evolved to develop, perseverate and advance consciousness evolved in calibration with, and fulfillment of, the laws of physics, the very infrastructure of the universe in which everything exists. The connection is evident, existing like a net, a mesh, a networked, intricately intertwined web.

This is where I have to try and reach for the top of the box. I need to look over the edge, to view what is beyond this enclosure, to comprehend the big picture. I can't help but think back to one who emerged from amongst us, who first stepped forward, who first saw that life is fundamentally a creative force. A true visionary, Zeno of Elea in Ancient Greece showed us how our minds put together a narrative from distinct events. It was Zeno who first showed us that our minds create the story.

Any motion we detect 'out there' is a persuasive suggestion that the universe happens 'out there,' that our senses collect information directly from 'out there.' But if I reevaluate my assumptions as Zeno did, remembering that they can be deceiving, my comprehension changes. So let me think about motion for a moment. It is movement itself that convinces us an occurrence is happening 'out there.' We are looking at it and can follow the movement. We can sense what direction a sound is coming from. We sense that while it is at one location at this moment, it will be at a different location the next, and another one the moment after until, and only if, something causes it to slow down or stop altogether. Many modern objects could demonstrate this: A ball, a train, a fast animal, a relay runner, or even a streak of lightening across the sky, but our old friend Zeno used a common object from his own time period – an arrow.

As I imagine this now, his example was simple, yet it wouldn't have been easy to present back then. He had to create an enduring thought solution. He was clearly successful, as it has existed long enough to come to my attention 2500 years later. Zeno's point was to show that

440

nothing can be in two places at the same time. Even though it is too quick for my sight to pinpoint, a traveling arrow can only be in one specific place at any given moment during the trajectory of its flight through the air, no matter how short a moment that might be. By understanding this point, I also have to comprehend that what is happening isn't really motion at all, is it? Instead, there's a series of separate events. In each successive moment, the arrow occupies a different space. Today I could demonstrate this with movie film to Zeno's appreciative delight, because the series of separate frames per second being presented in succession creates the illusion of movement and life. The film doesn't create the illusion, my mind does, just as it does with the rest of reality. Since it is my mind tying things together, the arrow's movement, or the train's movement, or a runner's movement is the embodiment of something within all of our minds as we link events together. As Einstein had already alluded to over a century ago, time itself is not an absolute reality. It's a feature of our minds. And if we also remind ourselves of the enfolded nature of this reality, we must remember Edgar Allen Poe's eloquent observation that "All that we see or seem is but a dream within a dream."

I jump over the edge and out of the box because I now can. Isn't it already evident that we all live in a universe we create? Even though we have shared experiences, it is rarely evident that we come away from them with the exact same observations or conclusions. Our perceptions must be different because there are so many variables that come together to form them. How could any of us living in a world of experience have the exact same set of experiences as another? That's the beauty of the big picture. It is clearly evident that there is advantage to variation. It allows for greater specification. It encourages greater and greater detail, making all life forms uniquely distinct points of observation, experience and reference in an emergent universe. There can be no single point of reference that is all knowing or all powerful. The emergent entity is a collective and it is expanding. By incarnation, it is pointillist in nature. Like the technique in neo-impressionist painting, tiny dots expressed in pure unique colours become blended in the eye of the viewer. Is it a photomosaic collective producing a singular image, or a singular image defined by degrees, by gradations, by subtle nuance?

It is the aforementioned water spray that emerges from, and returns to, the fountain. It is the origin and the outcome, the inception and the completion, the wellspring and the outgrowth. It is Alpha and Omega. It is the Musica Universalis, the music of the spheres... exactly how our ancestors in this emergent universe understood reality too – as rhythm and harmony.

The earliest religious ideas known to us are the Ancient Indian Vedas whose core concepts have permeated all of the major faiths and creeds of the world. The Vedic scriptures are most explicit and unambiguous in their vision of the cosmos as a form of music. The Rig Veda, 'what is heard," is the oldest of these, a collection of hymns, wisdom transmitted by song. The first resonating vibration within each individual, the Om, is also the embodiment of the universe as a whole. It is the primary syllable in Shabda, speech sound, or utterance. It is also known to humanity as the Audible Life Stream, the Greek Logos, the Tao in the Tao te Ching, the Kalima in the Qur'an, and the Word in John 1:1 of the New Testament. Stone temples, pyramids and older Christian churches were conceived as resonance chambers, designed using harmonic principles understood from ancient times. Blueprints display acoustical resonance in architecture, telling the eternal story of birth, life and death based on harmony, resonance and rhythmic cycles. Sound induces vision.

As we emerged from the soundscape of primal origin, we began to observe the movement of stars and planets. Reflection on the cycles and patterns observed gave rise to the astro-musical idea that the cosmos was a kind-of frozen music in light – the celebration of balance and perfection. Ah, how marvelous it is to think of such things! Those primary inklings were oh so pure. Unlike the diluted forms of modern spirituality reduced to mere faith, it was understood long ago that both mathematics and music were expressions of harmony in nature...

...And although many among us have lost sight of this, we too are expressions of mathematical and musical harmony in nature. Of course there is a constant reminder. Everyone, albeit to varying degrees, loves music. At one time or another, we've all been moved by it immensely. We get carried away by it, even though most of us never consider how that happens or what it means. Our very bodies are attuned to receiving and making sense of subtle vibrations. Sound waves encroach upon and impact not only our eardrums, but also the fleshy parts of our ears. The rejoinder is a chain of neurochemical and mechanical events that ultimately produces internal mental imagery we call pitch. Like the tree falling in the forest, the frequencies of the vibration cannot truly be considered pitch unless they are heard. It is a byproduct of consciousness.

As many among us know, poking and playing with sound can be captivating. From tapping on tables to tinkling utensils on glass, I've often indulged in creating music. I have to laugh, as not everyone would agree. However, I reach out to interact with my environment, and by doing so, I create the conditions necessary to both produce and detect sound. It becomes music to my ears. The equation's solution is singularly transcendent.

Musical instruments are devices of transcendence. We humans have invented many to represent the myriad nuances possible. I brandish them all through the one I best play proficiently, my stereo, and it moves me. Music always moves me. Instrumentation explores minute distinctions. Alphabets and numbers can't symbolize thought as seamlessly as music. Vibration is part of the equation. Vibration is communication. Vibration attracts focus. Vibration is life, sonic imagery. Pitch is an organism's mental representation of sonic frequency. It is a psychological phenomenon related to the frequency of vibrating molecules. It's in my brain; it isn't 'out there.' Molecules don't have pitch. Motion and oscillations can be measured, but a consciousness maps them to an internal quality we call pitch. We are part of the instrumentation and the music.

Indications abound, but go unnoticed. We live our lives in the matrixes we perceive. The very languages by which we share information have musical form. The prosodic clues we use to insinuate meaning are often tonal. Doesn't vocal intonation rise at the end of a question? Communication is songlike, derived from music where pitch evokes mood, all part of the continuum of molecular vibration. Frequencies are infinite in number, stretching out wavelike into the expanding universe.

So let us go forth in recognition of the great music we are all an essential part of. Realize the parts we play bringing unique perspectives to the universal song that is 'the Great What Is,' the expression of existence in consciousness, always in focus, always in the present. What we remember, what we project – everything is right here, right now – an entirety encapsulated, infinity permeating all potential. So gather your thoughts, harvest your memories, process your interactions with others and know that all of these things both emanate from, and are absorbed into, the song we partake in creating. Comprehend the aperture through which you have already peered. Glimpse more. Take your perceptions from the cave in the desert, from the canyon floor, from the various experiences as you perceived them, making them your own. The array of perceptions gleaned from the minds of Danielle, Jahny, Kevin, Darnell, Emma and Enrique are now my own. I begin to see that there may be purpose to the human journey after all. We may all begin to realize that any deepening sense of selfhood is directly related to an extension of empathy to broader, more inclusive domains. It is the very expansion of consciousness, the transcendent process of discovering new realms of meaning and comprehension. It is an exploration of the mystery of existence...

...And it is the enfolded nature of existence to bring along everything you have ever known and with it everything that everyone has ever known – and not just the facts, not just what we can verify, but what we can imagine – all the fiction, every what-if, each and every passing thought. Everything imagined that could be has already entered 'what is' by way of imagination. All thought creates.

Even when the lights go out, there will always be vibration. The music will always be there, limited by imagination only. So imagine, create. Proceed calmly if preferred, or at a brisk, frank pace. It's all happening right now. Follow to the ends of your universe...

Influences and Other Thoughts about Writing Aperture

My initial goal was to write a different kind of novel that would be both introspective and outward looking, introduce current and established scientific ideas, and to prompt the reader to ask new questions of their own. Hopefully, good entertainment does not require persistently violent action, adrenalin-producing car chases, or predominant themes of personality conflicts in order to maintain interest. Some of the most fundamental questions we can ask, and have ever asked, can be the most interesting to explore. Aperture challenges the reader to re-imagine 'what is.' Readers are compelled to reconsider their own perspectives on this very broad, yet personal matter. By doing so, they may all emerge from reading Aperture with varying perceptions, yet have a sense that this is in fact their story too.

This is why the author's pseudonym is the name of a fictional character from the book itself. It provides a bridge between what the writer and the reader co-create. The 'what is' the reader comes to perceive will indeed be the reader's own.

It isn't possible to list all of the numerous articles, papers, magazines and other intellectual portals whereby wonderful ideas, fact and fiction all melded together in the Imaginarium inside this head. Indeed, Aperture is an outcome of many ideas by numerous minds, not just over these past decades, but over millennia. On the following pages is a small list of the more prominent books that influenced the mental maelstrom from which this novel emerged.

AC2492, January 13th, 2023

Some of the many wonderful reads over decades that undoubtedly helped percolate the ideas that emerged into Aperture

In Alphabetical Order by Title:

The Age of Resilience by Jeremy Rifkin

Being No One by Thomas Metzinger

The Big Picture by Sean Carroll

Biocentrism by Robert Lanza and Bob Berman

Beyond Biocentrism by Robert Lanza and Bob Berman

Caveman Logic: The Persistence of Primitive Thinking by Hank Davis

The Conscious Mind (Philosophy of Mind) by David J. Chalmers

The Conscious Universe by Dean I. Radin

The Critique of Pure Reason by Immanuel Kant

The Demon-Haunted World: Science as a Candle in the Dark by Carl Sagan

The Dreams That Stuff is Made Of, edited by Stephen Hawking

The Empathic Civilization by Jeremy Rifkin

The Form Within by Karl H. Pribram

Galileo's Finger by Peter Atkins

The Genius of Birds by Jennifer Ackerman

The Grand Biocentric Design by Robert Lanza, Bob Berman and Matej Pavsic

To Have or To Be by Erich Fromm

Homo Deus by Yuval Noah Harari

Infinite Powers: How Calculus Reveals the Secrets of the Universe by Steven Strogatz

Knowledge in a Nutshell: Carl Jung by Gary Bobroff

The Little Book of Consciousness by Shelli Joye

The Matter Myth by Paul Davies and John Gribbin

Phenomenology of Perception by Maurice Merleau-Ponty

Physics and Music: The Science of Musical Sound by Harvey E. White and Donald H. White

The Power of Myth by Joseph Campbell

Quantum Enigma: Physics Encounters Consciousness by Bruce Rosenblum and Fred Kuttner

The Reality Bubble by Ziya Tong

Reinventing the Sacred by Stuart A. Kaufman

Sapiens by Yuval Noah Harari

Scale: The Universal Laws of Life, Growth and Death in Organisms, Cities and Companies by Geoffrey West

Simulacra and Simulation by Jean Baudrillard

The Social Conquest of Earth by E. O. Wilson

Something Deeply Hidden by Sean Carroll

The Spell of the Sensuous by David Abram

The Square and the Tower by Niall Ferguson

Symbiotic Planet by Lynn Margulis

Think: Why You Should Question Everything by Guy P. Harrison

This is Your Brain on Music by Daniel J. Levitin

The Time Before History by Colin Tudge

The Venus Blueprint by Richard Merrick

Void: The Strange Physics of Nothing by James Owen Weatherall

The Way of the Explorer by Edgar Mitchell

Wild Soundscapes: Discovering the Voice of the Natural World by Bernie Krause

Wholeness and the Implicate Order by David Bohm

The World As I See It by Albert Einstein

I strongly suggest exploring at least one of these books or authors.
It will further enhance your perspective.

FTP

Manufactured by Amazon.ca
Acheson, AB

13809257R00247